GODS & MONSTERS

Also by Shelby Mahurin

Serpent & Dove

Blood & Honey

GODS & MONSTERS

SHELBY MAHURIN

An Imprint of HarperCollinsPublishers

HarperTeen is an imprint of HarperCollins Publishers.

Gods & Monsters
Copyright © 2021 by Shelby Mahurin
Map art by Leo Hartas © 2021 by HarperCollins Publishers
All rights reserved. Printed in the United States of America. No part of this
book may be used or reproduced in any manner whatsoever without written
permission except in the case of brief quotations embodied in critical articles
and reviews. For information address HarperCollins Children's Books,
a division of HarperCollins Publishers, 195 Broadway, New York, NY 10007.
www.epicreads.com
Library of Congress Control Number: 2021937258
ISBN 978-0-06-303893-6 — ISBN 978-0-06-311312-1 (special edition)
ISBN 978-0-06-309436-9 (intl edition)
Typography by Sarah Nichole Kaufman
21 22 23 24 25   PC/LSCH   10 9 8 7 6 5 4 3 2 1

First Edition

To Jordan, *who is less a friend and more a sister*

PART I

Quand le chat n'est pas là, les souris dansent.
When the cat is away, the mice will play.
—French proverb

A NEST OF MICE

Nicholina

Bayberry, eyebright, belladonna
Fang of an adder, eye of an owl
Sprinkle of flora, spray of fauna
For purpose fair or possession foul.

Ichor of friend and ichor of foe
A soul stained black as starless night
For in the dark dost spirits flow
One to another in seamless flight.

The spell is familiar, oh yes, familiar indeed. Our favorite. She lets us read it often. The grimoire. The page. The spell. Our fingers trace each pen stroke, each faded letter, and they tingle with promise. They promise we'll never be alone, and we believe them. We believe *her.* Because we aren't alone—we're never alone—and mice live in nests with dozens of other mice, with *scores* of them. They burrow together to raise their pups, their children, and they find warm, dry nooks with plenty of food and magic. They find crannies without sickness, without death.

Our fingers curl on the parchment, gouging fresh tracks.

Death. Death, death, *death*, our friend and foe, as sure as breath, comes for us all.

But not me.

The dead should not remember. Beware the night they dream.

We tear at the paper now, shredding it to pieces. To angry bits. It scatters like ash in the snow. Like memory.

Mice burrow together, yes—they keep each other safe and warm—but when a pup in the litter sickens, the mice will eat it. Oh yes. They gobble it down, down, down to nourish the mother, the nest. The newest born is always sick. Always small. We shall devour the sick little mouse, and she shall nourish us.

She shall nourish us.

We shall prey on her friends, her *friends*—a snarl tears from my throat at the word, at the empty promise—and we shall feed them until they are fat with grief and guilt, with frustration and fear. Where we go, they will follow. Then we shall devour them too. And when we deliver the sick little mouse to her mother at Chateau le Blanc—when her body withers, when it *bleeds*—her soul shall stay with us forever.

She shall nourish us.

We will never be alone.

L'ENCHANTERESSE

Reid

Mist crept over the cemetery. The headstones—ancient, crumbling, their names long lost to the elements—pierced the sky from where we stood atop the cliff's edge. Even the sea below fell silent. In this eerie light before dawn, I finally understood the expression *silent as the grave.*

Coco brushed a hand across tired eyes before gesturing to the church beyond the mist. Small. Wooden. Part of the roof had caved in. No light flickered through the rectory windows. "It looks abandoned."

"What if it isn't?" Beau snorted, shaking his head, but stopped short with a yawn. He spoke around it. "It's a *church*, and our faces are plastered all over Belterra. Even a country priest will recognize us."

"Fine." Her tired voice held less bite than she probably intended. "Sleep outside with the dog."

As one, we turned to look at the spectral white dog that followed us. He'd shown up outside Cesarine, just before we'd agreed to travel the coast instead of the road. We'd all seen enough of La Fôret des Yeux to last a lifetime. For days, he'd trailed behind us, never coming near enough to touch. Wary, confused, the matagots had vanished shortly after his appearance. They hadn't returned. Perhaps the dog was a restless spirit himself—a new type of matagot. Perhaps he was merely an ill omen. Perhaps that was why Lou hadn't yet named him.

The creature watched us now, his eyes a phantom touch on my face. I gripped Lou's hand tighter. "We've been walking all night. No one will look for us inside a church. It's as good a place as any to hide. If it *isn't* abandoned"—I spoke over Beau, who started to interrupt—"we'll leave before anyone sees us. Agreed?"

Lou grinned at Beau, her mouth wide. So wide I could nearly count all her teeth. "Are you *afraid?*"

He shot her a dubious look. "After the tunnels, you should be too."

Her grin vanished, and Coco visibly stiffened, looking away. Tension straightened my own spine. Lou said nothing more, however, instead dropping my hand to stalk toward the door. She twisted the handle. "Unlocked."

Without a word, Coco and I followed her over the threshold. Beau joined us in the vestibule a moment later, eyeing the darkened room with unconcealed suspicion. A thick layer of dust coated the candelabra. Wax had dripped to the wooden floor, hardening among the dead leaves and debris. A draft swept through from the sanctuary beyond. It tasted of brine. Of decay.

"This place is haunted as shit," Beau whispered.

"Language." Scowling at him, I stepped into the sanctuary. My chest tightened at the dilapidated pews. At the loose hymnal pages collecting in the corner to rot. "This was once a holy place."

"It isn't haunted." Lou's voice echoed in the silence. She stilled behind me to stare up at a stained-glass window. The smooth face of Saint Magdaleine gazed back at her. The youngest saint in Belterra, Magdaleine had been venerated by the Church for gifting a man a blessed ring. With it, his negligent wife had fallen back in love with him, refusing to leave his side—even after he'd embarked on a perilous journey at sea. She'd followed him into the waves and drowned. Only Magdaleine's tears had revived her. "Spirits can't inhabit consecrated ground."

Beau's brows dipped. "How do you know that?"

"How do you *not*?" Lou countered.

"We should rest." I wrapped an arm around Lou's shoulders, leading her to a nearby pew. She looked paler than usual with dark shadows beneath her eyes, her hair wild and windswept from days of hard travel. More than once—when she didn't think I was looking—I'd seen her entire body convulse as if fighting sickness. It wouldn't surprise me. She'd been through a lot. We all had. "The villagers will wake soon. They'll investigate any noise."

Coco settled on a pew, closed her eyes, and pulled up the hood of her cloak. Shielding herself from us. "Someone should keep watch."

Though I opened my mouth to volunteer, Lou interrupted. "I'll do it."

"No." I shook my head, unable to recall the last time Lou had slept. Her skin felt cold, clammy, against mine. If she *was* fighting sickness, she needed the rest. "You sleep. I'll watch."

A sound reverberated from deep in her throat as she placed a hand on my cheek. Her thumb brushed my lips, lingering there. As did her eyes. "I'd much prefer to watch you. What will I see in your dreams, Chass? What will I hear in your—"

"I'll check the scullery for food," Beau muttered, shoving past us. He cast Lou a disgusted glance over his shoulder. My stomach rumbled as I watched him go. Swallowing hard, I ignored the ache of hunger. The sudden, unwelcome pressure in my chest. Gently, I removed her hand from my cheek and shrugged out of my coat. I handed it to her.

"Go to sleep, Lou. I'll wake you at sunset, and we can"—the words burned up my throat—"we can continue."

To the Chateau.

To Morgane.

To certain death.

I didn't voice my concerns again.

Lou had made it clear she'd journey to Chateau le Blanc whether or not we joined her. Despite my protests—despite reminding her *why* we'd sought allies in the first place, why we *needed* them—Lou maintained she could handle Morgane alone. *You heard Claud.* Maintained she wouldn't hesitate this time. *She can no longer touch me.* Maintained she would burn her ancestral home to the ground, along with all of her kin. *We'll build new.*

New what? I'd asked warily.

New everything.

I'd never seen her act with such single-minded intensity. No. Obsession. Most days, a ferocious glint lit her eyes—a feral sort of hunger—and others, no light touched them at all. Those days were infinitely worse. She'd watch the world with a deadened expression, refusing to acknowledge me or my weak attempts to comfort her.

Only one person could do that.

And he was gone.

She pulled me down beside her now, stroking my throat almost absently. At her cold touch, a shiver skittered down my spine, and a sudden desire to shift away seized me. I ignored it. Silence blanketed the room, thick and heavy, except for the growls of my stomach. Hunger was a constant companion now. I couldn't remember the last time I'd eaten my fill. With Troupe de Fortune? In the Hollow? The Tower? Across the aisle, Coco's breathing gradually evened. I focused on the sound, on the beams of the ceiling, rather than Lou's frigid skin or the ache in my chest.

A moment later, however, shouts exploded from the scullery, and the sanctuary door burst open. Beau shot forward, hotfooting it past the pulpit. "Bumfuzzle!" He gestured wildly toward the exit as I vaulted to my feet. "Time to go! Right now, right *now*, let's *go*—"

"Stop!" A gnarled man in the vestments of a priest charged into the sanctuary, wielding a wooden spoon. Yellowish stew dripped from it. As if Beau had interrupted his morning meal. The flecks of vegetable in his beard—grizzled, unkempt, concealing most of his face—confirmed my suspicions. "I said get *back* here—"

He stopped abruptly, skidding to a halt when he saw the rest of us. Instinctively, I turned to hide my face in the shadows. Lou flung her hood over her white hair, and Coco stood, tensing to run. But it was too late. Recognition sparked in his dark eyes.

"Reid Diggory." His dark gaze swept from my head to my toes before shifting behind me. "Louise le Blanc." Unable to help himself, Beau cleared his throat from the foyer, and the priest considered him briefly before scoffing and shaking his head. "Yes, I know who you are too, boy. *And* you," he added to Coco, whose hood still cloaked her face in darkness. True to his word, Jean Luc had added her wanted poster beside ours. The priest's eyes narrowed on the blade she'd drawn. "Put that away before you hurt yourself."

"We're sorry for trespassing." I lifted my hands in supplication, glaring at Coco in warning. Slowly, I slid into the aisle, inched toward the exit. At my back, Lou matched my steps. "We didn't mean any harm."

The priest snorted but lowered his spoon. "You broke into my home."

"It's a church." Apathy dulled Coco's voice, and her hand dropped as if it suddenly couldn't bear the dagger's weight. "Not a private residence. And the door was unlocked."

"Perhaps to lure us in," Lou suggested with unexpected relish. Head tilted, she stared at the priest in fascination. "Like a spider to its web."

The priest's brows dipped at the abrupt shift in conversation, as did mine. Beau's voice reflected our confusion. "What?"

"In the darkest parts of the forest," she explained, arching a brow, "there lives a spider who hunts other spiders. L'Enchanteresse, we call her. The Enchantress. Isn't that right, Coco?" When Coco didn't respond, she continued undeterred. "L'Enchanteresse creeps into her enemies' webs, plucking their silk strands, tricking them into believing they've ensnared their prey. When the spiders arrive to feast, she attacks, poisoning them slowly with her unique venom. She savors them for days. Indeed, she's one of the few creatures in the animal kingdom who enjoy inflicting pain."

We all stared at her. Even Coco. "That's disturbing," Beau finally said.

"It's *clever.*"

"No." He grimaced, face twisting. "It's *cannibalism.*"

"We needed shelter," I interjected a touch too loudly. Too desperately. The priest, who'd been watching them bicker with a disconcerted frown, returned his attention to me. "We didn't realize the church was occupied. We'll leave now."

He continued to assess us in silence, his lip curling slightly. Gold swelled before me in response. Seeking. Probing. Protecting. I ignored its silent question. I wouldn't need magic here. The priest wielded only a spoon. Even if he'd brandished a sword, the lines on his face marked him elderly. Wizened. Despite his tall frame, time seemed to have withered his musculature, leaving a spindly old man in its wake. We could outrun him. I seized Lou's hand in preparation, cutting a glance to Coco and Beau. They both nodded once in understanding.

Scowling, the priest lifted his spoon as if to stop us, but at that moment, a fresh wave of hunger wracked my stomach. Its growl rumbled through the room like an earthquake. Impossible to ignore. Eyes tightening, the priest tore his gaze from me to glare at Saint Magdaleine in the silence that followed. After another beat, he grudgingly muttered, "When did you last eat?"

I didn't answer. Heat pricked my cheeks. "We'll leave now," I repeated.

His eyes met mine. "That's not what I asked."

"It's been . . . a few days."

"How many days?"

Beau answered for me. "Four."

Another rumble of my stomach rocked the silence. The priest shook his head. Looking as though he'd rather swallow the spoon whole, he asked, "And . . . when did you last sleep?"

Again, Beau couldn't seem to stop himself. "We dozed in some fishermen's boats two nights ago, but one of them caught us before sunrise. He tried to snare us in his net, the half-wit."

The priest's eyes flicked to the sanctuary doors. "Could he have followed you here?"

"I just said he was a half-wit. Reid snared him in the net instead."

Those eyes found mine again. "You didn't hurt him." It wasn't a question. I didn't answer it. Instead I tightened my grip on Lou's hand and prepared to run. This man—this *holy* man—would soon sound the alarm. We needed to put miles between us before Jean Luc arrived.

Lou didn't seem to share my concern.

"What's your name, cleric?" she asked curiously.

"Achille." His scowl returned. "Achille Altier."

Though the name sounded familiar, I couldn't place it. Perhaps he'd once journeyed to Cathédral Saint-Cécile d'Cesarine. Perhaps I'd met him while under oath as a Chasseur. I eyed him with suspicion. "Why haven't you summoned the huntsmen, Father Achille?"

He looked deeply uncomfortable. Shoulders radiating tension, he stared down at his spoon. "You should eat," he said gruffly. "There's stew in the back. Should be enough for everyone."

Beau didn't hesitate. "What kind?" When I shot a glare over my shoulder, he shrugged. "He could've woken the town the moment he recognized us—"

"He still could," I reminded him, voice hard.

"—and my stomach is about to eat itself," he finished. "Yours too, by the sound of it. We need food." He sniffed and asked Father Achille, "Are there potatoes in your stew? I'm not partial to them. It's a textural thing."

The priest's eyes narrowed, and he jabbed the spoon toward the scullery. "Get out of my sight, boy, before I change my mind."

Beau inclined his head in defeat before scooting past us. Lou, Coco, and I didn't move, however. We exchanged wary looks. After a long moment, Father Achille heaved a sigh. "You can sleep here too. Just for the day," he added irritably, "so long as you don't bother me."

"It's Sunday morning." At last, Coco lowered her hood. Her lips were cracked, her face wan. "Shouldn't villagers be attending service soon?"

He scoffed. "I haven't held a service in years."

A reclusive priest. Of course. The disrepair of the chapel made sense now. Once, I would've scorned this man for his failure as a religious leader. For his failure as a man. I would've reprimanded him for turning his back on his vocation. On God.

How times had changed.

Beau reappeared with an earthen bowl and leaned casually against the doorway. Steam from the stew curled around his face. When my stomach rumbled again, he smirked. I spoke through gritted teeth. "Why would you help us, Father?"

Reluctantly, the priest's gaze trailed over my pale face, Lou's grisly scar, Coco's numb expression. The deep hollows beneath our eyes and the gaunt cut of our cheeks. Then he looked away, staring hard at the empty air above my shoulder. "What does it matter? You need food. I have food. You need a place to sleep. I have empty pews."

"Most in the Church wouldn't welcome us."

"Most in the Church wouldn't welcome their own mother if she was a sinner."

"No. But they'd burn her if she was a witch."

He arched a sardonic brow. "Is that what you're after, boy? The stake? You want me to mete out your divine punishment?"

"I believe," Beau drawled from the doorway, "he's simply pointing out that *you* are among the Church—unless you're actually the sinner of this story? Are you unwelcome amongst your peers, Father Achille?" He glanced pointedly at our dilapidated surroundings. "Though I abhor jumping to conclusions, our beloved patriarchs surely would've sent someone to repair this hovel otherwise."

Achille's eyes darkened. "Watch your tone."

I interrupted before Beau could provoke him further, spreading my arms wide. In disbelief. In frustration. In . . . everything. Pressure built in my throat at this man's unexpected kindness. It didn't make sense. It couldn't be real. As horrible a picture as Lou painted, a cannibal spider luring us into its web seemed likelier than a priest offering us sanctuary. "You know who we are. You know what we've done. You know what will happen if you're caught sheltering us."

He studied me for a long moment, expression inscrutable. "Let's not get caught, then." With a mighty *harrumph*, he stomped toward the scullery door. At the threshold, however, he paused, eyeing Beau's bowl. He seized it in the next second, ignoring Beau's protests and thrusting it at me. "You're just kids," he muttered, not meeting my eyes. When my fingers wrapped around the bowl—my stomach contracting painfully—he let go. Straightened his robes. Rubbed his neck. Nodded to the stew. "Won't be worth eating cold."

Then he turned and stormed from the room.

DARKNESS MINE

Lou

Darkness.

It shrouds everything. It envelops me, constricts me, pressing against my chest, my throat, my tongue until it *is* me. Trapped within its eye, drowning in its depths, I fold in on myself until I no longer exist at all. I am the darkness. This darkness, mine.

It *hurts.*

I should not feel pain. I should not feel anything. I am unformed and unmade, a speck in all of Creation. Without shape. Without life or lung or limb to control. I cannot see, cannot breathe, yet the darkness—it blinds. The pressure chokes, smothers, building with each passing second until it rends me apart. But I cannot scream. I cannot think. I can only listen—no, *sense*—a voice unfurling within the shadows. A beautiful, terrible voice. It snakes around me, *through* me, and whispers sweetly, promising oblivion. Promising respite.

Surrender, it croons, *and forget. Feel no pain.*

For a moment or a thousand moments, I hesitate, considering.

To surrender and forget appeals more than to resist and remember. I am weak, and I do not like pain. The voice is so beautiful, so tempting, so strong, that I nearly let it consume me. And yet . . . I cannot. If I let go, I will lose something important. *Someone* important. I cannot remember who it is.

I cannot remember who *I* am.

You are the darkness. The shadows press closer, and I fold myself tighter. A grain of sand below infinite black waves. *This darkness is yours.*

Still I hold on.

COCO'S FLAME

Reid

Coco leaned against the headstone beside me. A weatherworn statue of Saint Magdaleine towered over us, her bronze face shadowed in the gray twilight. Though she had long closed her eyes, Coco didn't sleep. She didn't speak either. She merely rubbed a scar on her palm with her opposite thumb, over and over until the skin chafed. I doubted she noticed it. I doubted she noticed anything.

She'd followed me into the cemetery after Lou had ransacked the scullery for red meat, unsatisfied with the fish Father Achille had prepared for supper. There'd been nothing inherently wrong with the way Lou had attacked the beef, even if the cut hadn't been fully cooked. We'd been famished for days. Our breakfast of stew and lunch of hard bread and cheese hadn't assuaged our hunger. And yet...

My stomach contracted without explanation.

"Is she pregnant?" Coco asked after a long moment. Her eyes flicked open, and she rolled her head to face me. Voice flat. "Tell me you've been careful. Tell me we don't have another problem."

"She bled two weeks ago, and since then, we haven't—" I cleared my throat.

Coco nodded and tipped her chin skyward once more, closing her eyes on a heavy exhale. "Good."

I stared at her. Though she hadn't cried since La Mascarade des Crânes, her lids remained swollen. Traces of kohl still flecked her cheeks. Tear tracks. "Are you . . ." The words caught in my throat. Coughing to clear it, I tried again. "I saw a tub inside if you need to bathe."

Her fingers clamped around her thumb in response, as if she could still feel Ansel's blood on her hands. She'd scrubbed them raw in the Doleur that night. Burned her garments in Léviathan, the inn where so much had gone wrong. "I'm too tired," she finally murmured.

The familiar ache of grief burned up my throat. Too familiar. "If you need to talk about it . . ."

She didn't open her eyes. "We aren't friends."

"Yes, we are."

When she didn't answer, I turned away, fighting a scowl. Fine. She didn't want to have this conversation. I wanted to have it even less. Crossing my arms against the chill, I'd just settled in for a long night of silence when Ansel's fierce expression rose behind my lids. His fierce conviction. *Lou is my friend*, he'd once told me. He'd been willing to follow her to Chateau le Blanc before I had. He'd kept her secrets. Shouldered her burdens.

Guilt tore through me. Jagged and sharp.

Like it or not, Coco and I *were* friends.

Feeling stupid, I forced myself to speak. "All I'm saying is that after the Archbishop passed, it helped me to talk about it. About *him*. So . . ." I shrugged stiffly, neck hot. Eyes burning. "If you need to . . . to talk about it . . . you can talk to me."

Now she did open her eyes. "The Archbishop was a sick fuck, Reid. Comparing him to Ansel is despicable."

"Yeah, well"—I stared at her pointedly—"you can't help who you love."

She dropped her gaze swiftly. To my shame, her lip quivered. "I know that."

"Do you?"

"Of course I do," she said with a hint of her old bite. Fire lit her features. "I know it's not my fault. Ansel loved me, and—and just because I didn't love him the same *way* doesn't mean I loved him any less. I certainly loved him more than *you*." Despite her heated assurance, her voice cracked on the last. "So you can take your advice and your condescension and your *pity*, and you can shove them up your ass." I kept my face impassive, refusing to rise. She could lash out. I could take it. Lurching to her feet, she pointed a finger at me. "And I won't sit here and let you *judge* me for—for—" Her chest heaved on a ragged breath, and a single tear tracked down her cheek. When it fell between us, sizzling against the snow, her entire body slumped. "For something I couldn't help," she finished, so soft I almost didn't hear.

Slowly, awkwardly, I rose to stand beside her. "I'm not judging you, Coco. I don't pity you either." When she scoffed, I shook my head. "I don't. Ansel was my friend too. His death wasn't your fault."

"Ansel isn't the only one who died that night."

Together, we looked to the thin plume rising from her teardrop.

Then we looked to the sky.

Smoke obscured the setting sun, dark and ominous above us. Heavy. It should've been impossible. We'd been traveling for days. The skies here, miles and miles from Cesarine—where smoke still billowed from tunnel entrances, from the cathedral, the catacombs, the castle, from cemeteries and inns and alleyways—should've been clear. But the flame beneath the capital wasn't simple fire. It was black fire, unnatural and unending, as if birthed from the bowels of Hell itself.

It was Coco's fire.

A fire with smoke to envelop an entire kingdom.

It burned hotter than regular flame, ravaging both the tunnels and the poor souls trapped within them. Worse, according to the fisherman who'd accosted us—a fisherman whose *brother* happened to be an initiate of the Chasseurs—no one could extinguish the blaze. King Auguste contained it only by posting a huntsman at each entrance. Their Balisardas prevented the blight from spreading.

It seemed La Voisin had spoken truth. When I'd pulled her aside in Léviathan, before she'd fled to the forest with her surviving Dames Rouges, her warning had been clear: *The fire rages with her grief. It will not stop until she does.*

Toulouse, Thierry, Liana, and Terrance were trapped in those tunnels.

"It still isn't your fault, Coco."

Her face twisted as she stared at the statue of Saint Magdaleine. "My tears started the fire." Sitting heavily, she folded her knees to her chest. Wrapped her arms around her shins. "They're all dead because of me."

"They aren't all dead." Immediately, my mind snapped to Madame Labelle. To her hemlock chains, her damp prison cell. To the king's hard fingers on her chin. Her lips. Rage kindled my blood. Though it made me despicable, relief flickered as well. Because of Coco's fire, King Auguste—my *father*—had more important things to deal with than my mother.

As if reading my thoughts, Coco said, "For now."

Fuck.

"We have to go back," I said gravely, the wind picking up around us. I imagined the scent of charred bodies in the smoke, of Ansel's blood on the earth. Even armed with the Dames Rouges and loup garou—even armed with the *Woodwose*—we'd still lost. Once again, I was struck by the utter foolishness of our plan. Morgane would slaughter us if we marched alone on the Chateau. "Lou won't listen to me, but maybe she'll listen to *you*. Deveraux and Blaise stayed behind to search for the others. We can help them, and afterward, we can—"

"They aren't going to find them, Reid. I told you. Anyone left in those tunnels is dead."

"The tunnels shifted before," I repeated for the dozenth time, wracking my thoughts for something—anything—I could've missed in our previous arguments. If I persuaded Coco, she could persuade Lou. I was sure of it. "Maybe they shifted again. Maybe Toulouse and Thierry are trapped in a secure passage, safe and whole."

"And maybe Liana and Terrance turn into house cats on the full moon." She didn't bother lifting her head, her voice dangerously apathetic once more. "Forget it, Reid. Lou is right. This has to end. Her way is as good as any—better, even. At least we're moving forward."

"What was the *point* of gathering allies, then?" I fought to keep the frustration from my voice. "We can't kill Morgane on our own."

"We clearly can't kill her with allies either."

"So we find new ones! We return to Cesarine, and we strategize with Deveraux—"

"What *exactly* are you expecting him to do? Who are these mysterious allies you hope to find? Shall Claud just . . . grow them on trees?" Her eyes hardened. "He couldn't save Ansel in La Mascarade des Crânes. He couldn't even save his *own* family, which means he can't help us either. He can't kill Morgane. Face it, Reid. This is our path forward. We can't search Cesarine for ghosts."

I unclenched my jaw. Heat worked up my throat. I didn't know what to do. "My mother isn't a ghost."

"Your mother can take care of herself."

"Her *life*—"

"—depends entirely on how adeptly she can lie." Beau strolled toward us casually from the church's kitchen, pointing a lazy finger at the smoke-filled sky. "Our father will be desperate to end this fire, even if he must enlist a witch to do it. As long as the clouds quite literally hang above our heads, your mother is safe. Apologies for eavesdropping, by the way," he added. "I wanted to know if either of you had noticed my new beard." He paused. "Also, Lou hasn't blinked in half an hour."

I frowned. "What?"

"She hasn't blinked," he repeated, dropping to the ground beside Coco and lifting a hand to her nape. His fingers kneaded gently. "Not once. She's spent the last thirty minutes staring at the stained glass in silence. It's unsavory. She even managed to frighten the priest away."

Unease pricked my stomach. "You timed her blinks?"

"You haven't?" Beau arched a brow in disbelief. "She's *your* wife—or lady friend, paramour, whatever label you've settled on. Something is clearly wrong with her, brother."

The wind built around us. At the edge of the church, the white dog reappeared. Pale and spectral. Silent. Watching. I forced myself to ignore it, to focus on my brother and his asinine observations. "And you don't have a beard," I said irritably, gesturing to his bare chin, "if we're voicing the obvious." I glanced at Coco, who still hid her face on her knees. "Everyone grieves differently."

"I'm telling you this goes beyond *different*."

"Do you have a point?" I glared at him. "We all know she's undergone recent . . . changes. But she's still Lou." Unbidden, I glanced back to the dog. He stared at me with preternatural stillness. Even the wind didn't ripple his fur. Standing, I lifted my hand and whistled low. "Here, boy." I stepped closer. Closer still. He didn't move. To Beau and Coco, I muttered, "Has she named him yet?"

"No," Beau said pointedly. "Or acknowledged him at all, for that matter."

"You're fixating."

"You're deflecting."

"You still don't have a beard."

His hand shot to his whisker-less chin. "And *you* still don't have—"

But he stopped short when several things happened at once. The wind picked up suddenly as the dog turned and disappeared into the trees. An alarmed *"Look out!"* rent the air—the voice familiar, *too* familiar, and sickeningly out of place amidst the smoke and shadows—followed by the earsplitting screech of metal tearing. As one, we looked up in horror. Too late.

The statue of Saint Magdaleine splintered at the waist, bust careening in the wind toward Beau and Coco. She seized him with a shriek, attempting to drag him out of the way, but their legs—

I launched forward, tackling the fallen statue midair, landing hard as Coco and Beau snatched their feet away. Time stood still for a brief second. Beau checked Coco for injury, and she closed her eyes, shuddered on a sob. Wincing at the pain in my side, I struggled to catch my breath, to sit up—to—

No.

Pain forgotten, I whirled, scrambling to my feet to face the newcomer.

"Hello, Reid," Célie whispered.

White-faced and trembling, she clutched a leather bag to her chest. Shallow cuts and scrapes marred her porcelain skin, and the hem of her gown hung in tatters around her feet. Black silk. I recognized it from Filippa's funeral.

"Célie." I stared at her for a beat, unable to believe my eyes. She couldn't be here. She couldn't have traversed the wilderness alone in only silk and slippers. But how else could I explain her presence? She hadn't just *happened* upon this exact spot at this exact moment. She'd ... she must've followed us. *Célie.* The reality of the situation crashed over my head, and I gripped her shoulders, resisting the urge to shake her, hug her, scold her. My pulse pounded in my ears. "What the *hell* are you doing here?" When she drew back, nose wrinkling, I dropped my hands and staggered backward. "I'm sorry. I didn't mean to—"

"You didn't hurt me." Her eyes—wide, panicked—dropped to my shirt. Belatedly, I noticed the dark liquid there. Metallic. Viscous. The fabric beneath clung to my skin. I frowned. "It's just that you—well, you're covered in blood."

Bewildered, I half turned, lifting my shirt to examine my ribs. The dull ache in my side felt more like a bruise than a wound.

"Reid," Beau said sharply.

Something in his voice halted my movements. Slowly, I followed his finger to where Saint Magdaleine lay in the snow.

To where tears of blood dripped down her cheeks.

LA PETITE LARME

Reid

After a moment of harried, whispered conversation—as if the statue could hear us—we retreated to the safety of the sanctuary. "It was that wretched dog," Beau said, throwing himself into the pew beside Coco. Near the pulpit, Lou rose. Candlelight illuminated half of her face, bathing the rest in shadow. A chill swept down my spine at the chthonic image, as if she were cut in two. Part Lou and part . . . something else. Something dark.

She frowned, eyes flicking between Célie and me. "What is this?"

"*This*," I said, rougher than intended, turning to scowl at Célie, "is nothing. She's going home in the morning."

Célie lifted her chin. Tightened her hands on the strap of her leather bag. They trembled slightly. "I am not."

"Célie." Exasperated, I led her to the pew beside Lou, who made no move to greet her. Odd. I'd thought the two had formed a tentative bond after what they'd endured in La Mascarade des Crânes. "You just saw how dangerous it is here. Everyone in the kingdom wants us dead."

"*I* don't want us dead." Beau crossed his ankles on the pew in front of him, slinging an arm over Coco's shoulders. When his gaze flicked to Célie, she flushed crimson. "Thank you for the warning, by the way, Mademoiselle Tremblay. It seems everyone else has forgotten their manners. Appalling, really. That statue would have crushed us if not for you."

"Statue?" Lou asked.

"The statue in the cemetery . . . fell," I murmured. I didn't mention the tears.

Ignoring both of us, cheeks still pink under Beau's perusal, Célie sank into a deep curtsy. "Y-Your Highness. They alone have not forgotten their manners. Please forgive me."

He arched a brow, smirking at me over her bowed head. "I like her."

Coco lifted her hood to hide her face. Though she didn't settle into Beau's arm, she didn't lean away, either. "She shouldn't be here."

"It's that dog," Beau repeated emphatically. "Wherever he goes, catastrophe follows. He was there when the fisherman tried to drown us too."

Célie frowned. "But the fisherman didn't—" At our stares, she stopped abruptly, blush deepening. She lifted a delicate shoulder. "The boat capsized on a swell. Do you not remember?"

"Have you been *following* us?" Lou asked.

Célie refused to look at anyone.

I sat heavily, resting my forearms on my knees. "What are you doing here, Célie?"

"I—" Her expression open, painfully vulnerable, she glanced between Lou, Beau, and Coco before settling on me. "I would like to help."

"Help," Lou echoed. Mocking.

Célie's brows furrowed at her tone. "I believe I—I believe I have resources that could benefit the group in its pursuit of M-M—" She broke off again, hoisting her leather bag higher and squaring her shoulders. "In its pursuit of La Dame des Sorcières."

"You can't even say her name," I muttered, rubbing my temples.

"I do not need to say her name to kill her."

Kill her.

Good Lord.

An unexpected cackle sounded from Lou, who grinned wide and lifted her hands to clap once. Twice. Three times. The odd glint had returned to her eyes. "Well, well, it seems the kitten has finally found her claws. I'm impressed." Her laughter burrowed under my skin, clawed at my stomach. "But my mother is not a mouse. How do you plan to kill her? Will you curtsy? Invite her to tea?"

Yes, I'd clearly misinterpreted their relationship.

By the flex of Beau's jaw, he'd done the same. "Leave her alone, Lou."

Célie flashed him an appreciative look. Bolstered, she continued in a stronger voice, "I don't know *how* to kill her—not precisely, not *yet*—but I do have information in my possession. You were correct before, Your Highness." From her leather bag, she withdrew a crisp linen envelope. I recognized Jean Luc's handwriting on the front. "King Auguste has postponed your mother's execution indefinitely. He plans to utilize her magic to eradicate the fire."

Beau nodded to me. "I told you so."

When she extended the envelope, I skimmed its contents before handing it back. "Thank you for this, Célie. Truly. But I can't let you stay. What if something happened to you? I wouldn't be able to live with myself." I paused, frowning anew. Come to think of it— "What did your parents say about this?"

She sniffed reprovingly. "Nothing at all."

My frown deepened.

"They don't know you're here, do they?" Beau smirked, arching a brow. "Clever little minx. I suppose it's better to ask forgiveness than permission."

Groaning at the implication, I buried my face in my hands. "*Célie.*"

"*What?*" Her tenuous composure snapped in an instant, and I straightened. Startled. In all the years I'd known her, Célie didn't *snap*. "You needn't worry about them sending the kingdom after me, Reid. When I last disappeared, it took *quite* some time before help arrived, if you care to remember. Heaven forbid anyone know my father cannot control his own household."

I blinked to hide my shock. Though I'd known Monsieur Tremblay had failed as a father, apparently, I'd underestimated how much. "Jean Luc will come after you. He'll bring the whole of the Chasseurs with him."

She shook the envelope in my face. "Jean Luc knows I am here. He *watched* me steal my father's carriage, for God's sake, and scolded me through the whole ordeal." I stared at her. I'd never known her to thieve, either. Or take the Lord's name in vain. She exhaled hard through her nose, stuffing the envelope into her cloak. "Regardless, I'd have thought *you* would appreciate my intervention. If I travel with your band of notorious witches and fugitives—pardon, Your Highness—Jean cannot arrest any of you without also arresting me. That will not happen. He will pursue you no further."

"Oh, to have seen the look on his face." Beau's own face twisted as if pained. "Further proof that there is a God, and He hates me."

"It doesn't matter." I shoved myself to my feet, eager to end this argument. To find Father Achille and alert him of the situation, to request an additional blanket for the night. "You can't come with us."

Seething, she watched me pass in silent fury, her shoulders square and her spine ramrod straight. Her fingers white around her leather bag. "What I *cannot do*," she finally said through clenched teeth, "is look my parents in the eye. They want to pretend nothing happened. They want to return to life as it was before. But they cannot make me." Her voice dipped dangerously low. "*You* cannot make me. The thought of s-sitting at home—curtsying to noblemen, sipping *tea*—while Morgane remains at large physically sickens me." When I didn't pause my stride, she continued desperately, "She trapped me in that coffin with Filippa for weeks, Reid. *Weeks.* She—she t-tortured me, and she mutilated those children. What I *cannot do* is nothing."

I froze at the pulpit. Surely I'd misheard her. Surely this sudden dread in my chest—it was misplaced. I didn't turn. "She what?"

A sniff in response. "Do not make me repeat it," she said.

"Célie—" When I finally moved toward her, nausea churning, she stopped my advance with the swipe of her hand. Tears fell freely down her cheeks. She didn't hide them. Didn't brush them away. That hand swung her leather bag from her shoulder, dumped its contents on the rotten floor: jewelry, *couronnes*, gemstones, even a chalice. The others stared at the small treasure trove, agog, but I couldn't see past Célie's words. Couldn't stop . . . picturing them.

Filippa had been older than us by a few years. Unlike Célie, she'd acted as my sister. A prim, disapproving sort of sister, but a sister nonetheless. The thought of Célie trapped with her corpse—*months* after burial—made my stomach roll violently. I choked down bile.

"I didn't just steal my father's carriage," Célie whispered into the silence. She gestured to the glittering pile. "I robbed his vault as well. I assumed we would need currency for our travels."

Beau rose for a closer look, dragging Coco along with him. "How did you *carry* all of this?" He eyed Célie's arms with unabashed skepticism as Lou shadowed their footsteps.

Coco toed the coins without interest. "And where is your carriage?"

At last, Célie dropped the leather bag. Her fingers flexed. "I left it with the stable boy at the inn."

"And your footman?" Kneeling, Beau prodded the bag cautiously, like it was crafted from human skin. Perhaps it was. Monsieur Tremblay had once dealt in dangerous magical objects. The witches had killed Filippa for it. "Your driver?"

"I drove myself."

"*What?*" Though Beau whirled, it was *my* voice that cut through the room. "Are you out of your mind?"

Lou cackled again, inordinately pleased with the entire situation.

Shooting her a glare, I stormed back to the group, my own temper brewing dangerously close to the surface. I took a deep breath. Another. "That's it. This is over. I'll speak to Father Achille, and he'll arrange an escort to take you back to Cesarine at daybreak." Roughly, I began shoving the jewelry back into her leather bag. Even filled with heavy jewels, it remained weightless in my hand. Perhaps not human skin, but assuredly magic. Fucking Tremblay. Fucking *Célie.* If a witch had happened upon her with this bag, she would've met the same fate as Filippa. Perhaps that was what she wanted. Perhaps after La Mascarade des Crânes, she had a death wish.

I sure as hell wouldn't indulge it.

"*Hold it.*" Coco seized my arm unexpectedly, her voice the sharpest I'd heard in days. Her fingers shook. Pushing back her hood, she snatched a locket from me. When she lifted it to the candlelight, her face—paler now, nearly ashen—reflected back on its golden surface. Filigree twined around the diamond at the oblong pendant's center. The pattern they created resembled . . . waves. Quietly, coldly, she asked, "Where did you get this?"

Lou appeared at her shoulder in an instant. With the diamonds reflected in them, her eyes gleamed almost silver.

Célie had the sense to yield a step. "I—I told you. I stole it from my father's vault." She glanced at me for reassurance, but I could give her none. I'd never before seen this intensity—this *possession*—in either Coco's or Lou's gaze. Their reactions were . . . unsettling. Whatever relic Célie had inadvertently brought us, it must've been important. "It was my favorite piece as a child, but it—it doesn't open. Father couldn't sell it."

Coco shuddered as if insulted before withdrawing a blade from her cloak. I stepped hastily in front of Célie. "Oh, please," Coco snarled, pricking the tip of her finger instead. A single droplet of blood dripped onto the diamond and beaded into a perfect circle. Then—incredibly—it sank beneath the stone's surface, swirling bright crimson. When the color dissipated, the locket clicked open.

We all leaned closer, entranced, to see a crystal-clear surface within.

Lou recoiled.

"*La Petite Larme,*" Coco said, her voice softening. Her anger momentarily forgotten.

"The Little Tear," Beau echoed.

"A mirror made from a drop of L'Eau Mélancolique." She gazed at her reflection with an inscrutable expression before refocusing on Célie. Her lip curled in distaste once more. "It wouldn't open because it doesn't belong to you. It belonged to my mother."

A pin could've dropped in the sanctuary, and we would've heard its every echo. Even Father Achille—who'd stormed through the scullery doors in an apron, clutching a soapy dish and growling about noise—seemed to realize he'd interrupted a tense moment. His eyes narrowed on Célie and the gold at her feet. "Célie Tremblay," he acknowledged gruffly. "You're a long way from home."

Though she offered him a polite smile, it was brittle. Fraught. "I beg your pardon, *monsieur*, but I do not believe I've had the pleasure of your acquaintance."

"Achille," he said, lips pursing. "Father Achille Altier."

Coco snapped the locket shut. Without a word, she replaced her hood.

"Nice apron." Beau grinned at the hand-painted roses on Father Achille's apron. Brushstrokes large and uneven, they looked as though they'd been painted by a child. In blue and red and green.

"My nieces made it for me," Father Achille muttered.

"It really brings out your eyes."

Father Achille chucked the dish at him. Though Beau managed to catch the slippery plate against his chest, water still splattered his face on impact. Father Achille nodded in righteous satisfaction. "That's the last dish of yours I'll be washing, boy. You can scrub the rest of them yourself—and the scullery, thanks to her." He jerked his thumb toward Lou in irritation. "There's a bucket and a mop waiting for you."

Beau opened his mouth to protest indignantly, but Célie interrupted. "Father Achille." She swept into another curtsy, though not as low this time. Not as grand. She eyed his flowered apron and disheveled robes—the disrepair of the sanctuary—in thinly veiled disapproval. "I am pleased to meet you."

Father Achille shifted awkwardly before her, as if unaccustomed to such pristine manners. If I hadn't known better, I would've said he looked uncomfortable under her scrutiny. Embarrassed, even. "I knew your mother," he finally said by way of explanation. "When I lived in Cesarine."

"Of course. I will pass along your regards."

He snorted again. "Better not. I said I knew her, not that I particularly liked her." At Célie's scandalized expression, he muttered, "The feeling was mutual, I assure you. Now"—he straightened with as much dignity as he could muster—"it isn't my business to ask what you're doing in Fée Tombe, Mademoiselle Tremblay. It isn't my place to tell you how stupid you are for taking up with this lot. So I won't. Because I don't care. Just make sure you don't cause any trouble before you leave."

I stepped forward as he turned on his heel. "She needs an escort back to Cesarine."

"Reid." Célie actually stamped her foot now. "Stop being so—so—"

"Pigheaded?" Beau suggested.

Father Achille scowled at us over his shoulder. "I am not a babysitter."

"See?" Triumphant, she beamed, pointing a finger in the air. "He will not take me, and the journey is far too hazardous to travel alone. I must remain here. With you."

My jaw clenched. "You had no problem hazarding it before."

"Yes, but—" Something akin to nervousness flitted through her eyes, and her smile vanished. "I—I might've . . . fibbed before. A small, inconsequential thing," she added hastily at my expression. "I told you I'd left my coach at the stable, but really, er, in *actuality*, I might've made a wrong turn—"

"A wrong turn where?" I demanded.

"To the lighthouse."

Father Achille slowly turned.

"I lost sight of you all just before dawn." Célie twisted her hands together at her waist. "When I came to the fork in the road, I—I chose the path leading away from the village. I never dreamed you'd seek shelter in a church. Really, I am extraordinarily lucky to have found you at all—"

"*Darling* Célie," Beau interrupted. "Please get on with it."

She flushed again, dipping her head. "O-of course, Your Highness. Forgive me. When I neared the lighthouse, something moved in the shadows. It—it spooked Cabot, of course, and he nearly drove us off the cliff in his haste to flee. A wheel snapped on the bluff. I managed to free Cabot before the whole carriage tumbled into the sea . . . or at least, it *would've* if the creature hadn't wrenched it free." She shuddered. "I've never seen such a monster. Long, matted hair and skin cloaked in shadow. Sharp white teeth. It smelled of rot too. Decaying flesh. I'm quite certain if I hadn't escaped on Cabot's back, it would've eaten us both." She exhaled heavily, lifting her eyes to mine. "So, you see, I left *Cabot* at the stable, not my carriage. I simply cannot return for it while it remains in the creature's possession, and I cannot risk traveling without it either. I *must* stay with you, Reid, or I'll never make it home at all."

"*Cauchemar*," Lou murmured.

I extended a weary hand to her. "What?"

With a small smile, she laced her fingers through mine. They remained like ice. "I didn't say anything."

"Yes, you—"

"A *cauchemar* has indeed taken up residence in the lighthouse." At our blank looks, Father Achille grudgingly added, "A nightmare. That's what the villagers call it, anyway. It found us here in Fée Tombe three days ago, and they're all terrified." He scowled and shook his head. "The fools are planning to raze the lighthouse in the morning."

Something in his scowl made me pause. "Has this *cauchemar* harmed anyone?"

"Aside from me?" Célie asked. "It nearly frightened Cabot and me to death!"

Coco scoffed beneath her hood. "What a tragedy that would've been."

"Coco," Beau admonished. "That was beneath you. If you're going to be spiteful, at least be clever about it."

"Not spiteful at all," she said sweetly. "I would've mourned the horse."

"I beg your pardon?" Célie wheeled around to face her, mouth slack with disbelief. "I—I am terribly sorry about your m-mother's necklace, Cosette, but I didn't *know*—"

I spoke over her. "Has the *cauchemar* harmed anyone?"

Father Achille shrugged. "It hardly matters."

"It matters to me."

"That mob is coming, boy. You'll get yourself killed."

"You don't care."

"That's right." His nostrils flared. "I don't. *Cauchemars* are notoriously cruel, but this creature hasn't yet attacked. Last night, it broke into the boucherie and stole some scraps, but that's the extent of my knowledge." When I exchanged a glance first with Lou, then with Beau, he gritted his teeth and said, as if the words physically pained him, "You should stay out of it. This isn't your fight."

But a mob burning an innocent creature alive sounded exactly like my fight. They would do the same to Lou, if given the chance. The same to Coco. My mother. Me. Familiar anger, thick and viscous, simmered in my gut. These villagers alone weren't guilty. Though they would slaughter this innocent, Morgane had tortured and maimed my siblings, my brothers and sisters—all collateral damage in this war they hadn't chosen. A war this *cauchemar* hadn't chosen.

No more.

A brief stop at the lighthouse wouldn't hurt anything. We could warn the *cauchemar* before the mob struck—perhaps even free it—and still leave by sunrise. It was the noble thing to do. Lou might've chosen the wrong path for us, but this felt a step in the right direction. Perhaps it would set us on a new course. A better one.

At the very least, it would delay our arrival to Chateau le Blanc. And perhaps . . .

"I vote no." Coco's voice cut sharp from beneath her hood. "*Cauchemars* are dangerous, and we can't afford distractions. We should proceed to the Chateau."

Lou grinned and nodded.

"If we help this *cauchemar*," I murmured, "perhaps it'll help us. *Here* is your mysterious ally, Cosette. No trees required."

Though I couldn't see her face, I could feel her glower.

Shaking my head, I handed Célie my blanket before returning to my pew. Lou didn't let go of my hand. Her thumb traced the veins along my wrist. "We need Célie's carriage," I said. "Whether or not she returns home."

Célie's head snapped up. "A carriage would speed our travel considerably."

"Yes." I considered her for a long moment. Rather, I *reconsidered* her. A muscle twitched in my jaw at her hopeful expression, at the determined set of her shoulders. This was not the Célie I'd always known. "It would."

Throwing his hands in the air, Achille stalked to the scullery to be rid of us. "Fools, all of you," he said over his shoulder, voice grim. "A *cauchemar* is strongest at night. Act at first light before the mob attacks. Whatever you do, don't let them see you. Fear makes people stupid." With one last look between Célie and me, he shook his head. "But courage makes 'em stupid too."

AN INSIDIOUS PRESENCE

Lou

From the darkness, a voice arises.

Not *that* voice. Not the terrible one that croons and beckons. This voice is sharper, biting, cutting. Familiar. It does not tempt me. It—it *scolds* me.

Wake up, it snaps. *You aren't dead yet.*

But I do not know this word. I do not understand death.

No one does. That's not the point—or maybe that's the entire *point. You're fading.*

Fading. The darkness offers oblivion. Sweet relief.

Fuck that. You've worked too hard and too long to give up now. Come on. You want more than oblivion. You want to live.

A ghostly chuckle reverberates through the shadows. Through the unending black. It curls around me, caressing the jagged edges of my consciousness, soothing the broken shards at my center. *Surrender, little mouse. Let me devour you.*

I hurt. With each pulse of the darkness, the pain intensifies until I cannot bear it.

It's your heart. The sharp voice returns, louder now. Louder than even the rhythmic drumming. *Tha-thump. Tha-thump. Tha-thump.* Instinctively, I shy away, but I cannot hide from the sound. From the pain. It echoes everywhere, all around me. *It's still beating.*

I try to process this, try to peer through the darkness to where a heart might indeed beat. But still I see nothing.

Don't hide from it, Lou. Own your pain. Use it.

Lou. The word is familiar, like the exhalation on a laugh. The breath before jumping, the gasp when you fly instead. It's a sigh of relief, of irritation, of disappointment. It's a shout of anger and a cry of passion. It's . . . me. I am not the darkness. I am something else entirely. And this voice—it's mine.

There you are, it says—I say—in unabashed relief. *About time too.*

However, on the wings of one realization comes another, and I flex abruptly, pushing against the crushing black. It responds in kind, no longer simple darkness but a sentient presence all its own. An insidious presence. It feels wrong, somehow. Foreign. It shouldn't be here—wherever *here* is—because this place . . . it belongs to me too. Like my heartbeat. Like my name. Though I flex again, testing my strength, spreading myself further, pushing and pushing and *pushing,* I meet only ironclad resistance.

The darkness is unyielding as stone.

A GAME OF QUESTIONS

Reid

Lou's fingertips skimmed my leg in time with the others' rhythmic breathing. With each inhale, she walked them upward. With each exhale, she turned her wrist, trailing downward with the back of her hand. Wind whistled through the cracks in the sanctuary, raising gooseflesh on my arms. I sat rigid beneath her touch, heart pounding in my throat at the subtle friction. Tense. Waiting. Sure enough, those fingers gradually crept up, up, *up* my thigh in slow seduction, but I caught her wrist, slid my hand to cover hers. To pin it in place.

A foreign emotion congealed in my blood as I stared at her hand beneath mine. I should've ached, should've tightened with that familiar hunger, that *heat*, that left me almost fevered when we touched. But this knot in my stomach . . . it wasn't need. It was something else. Something *wrong.* While the others had prepared for bed a half hour ago, a general sense of dread had enveloped me. That dread had only intensified when Beau, the last awake, had finally drifted to sleep, leaving Lou and me alone.

Clearing my throat, I squeezed her fingers. Forced a smile. Brushed a kiss against her palm. "We have an early morning. We'll need to leave Fée Tombe after we free the *cauchemar*. It'll be another long few days on the road."

It sounded like an excuse.

It was one.

A low noise reverberated from her throat. She hadn't worn her ribbon since we left Cesarine. My gaze dropped to her scar, healing yet still puckered, angry. She stroked it with her free hand. "How does one *free* a *cauchemar*?"

"Maybe we can reason with it. Convince it to return to the forest."

"And if we can't?"

I sighed. "We can only warn it about the mob. We can't force it to do anything."

"And if it decides to *eat* the mob? If our warning allows it the chance to do so?"

"It won't," I said firmly.

She considered me with a half smile. "You've developed quite an affinity for us, haven't you?" Her grin spread. "Monsters."

I pressed a kiss to her forehead. Ignored the unfamiliar scent of her skin. "Sleep, Lou."

"I'm not tired," she purred, her eyes too bright in the darkness. Too pale. "We slept all day." When her hand crept up my chest once more, I caught it, lacing my fingers through her own. She misinterpreted the movement. Mistook it for an invitation. Before I could blink, she'd hoisted her knee across my lap to straddle me, lifting our hands awkwardly above our heads. When she arched her lower back, pressing her chest into mine, my stomach dropped like a stone. Shit.

I fought to keep my gaze impassive. Of course she wanted to—to touch me. Why wouldn't she? Less than a month ago, I'd craved her like an addict. The subtle curve of her hip, the thick wave of her hair, the impish gleam in her eyes. I'd been unable to keep from pawing at her every moment of the day—the presence of my own *mother* hadn't stopped me. Even then, however, it'd been so much more than physical.

From the very start, Lou had woken me up. Her presence had been infectious. Even infuriated, exasperated, I'd never stopped wanting to be near her.

Now I glanced at Beau, at Coco, at Célie, praying one of them would stir. Hoping they'd open their eyes and interrupt. But they didn't wake. They slept on, heedless of my inner struggle.

I loved Lou. I knew that. Felt it in my bones.

I also couldn't stand the sight of her.

What was *wrong* with me?

Anger cracked open as she moved her lips against my ear, nibbling the lobe. Too many teeth. Too much *tongue*. Another wave of revulsion swept through me. *Why?* Was it because she was still mourning? Because *I* was? Because she'd attacked her supper like a rabid animal, because she'd only blinked twice in the past hour? I mentally shook myself, irritated with Beau. With *myself.* She'd been stranger than usual, yes, but that didn't justify the way my skin crawled when she touched me.

Worse still, these thoughts—this looming dread, this unsettling aversion—they felt like a betrayal. Lou deserved better than this.

Swallowing hard, I turned to meet her lips. She kissed me back enthusiastically, without hesitation, and my guilt only deepened. She didn't seem to sense my reluctance, however. She pressed closer instead. Rocked her hips against mine. Clumsy. Eager. When she again dropped her mouth to my throat, sucking at my rapid pulse, I shook my head in defeat. It was no good. My hands descended on her shoulders.

"We need to talk."

The words came of their own volition. She blinked in surprise, and what looked like . . . insecurity flickered in her pale eyes. I hated myself for it. I'd seen Lou insecure approximately twice in our entire relationship, and neither instance had boded well for us. It vanished as quickly as it'd come, however, replaced by a wicked gleam. "That involves tongues, yes?"

Gently, firmly, I slid her from my lap. "No. It doesn't."

"Are you sure?" Crooning, she leaned into me seductively. Or at least, that was her intent. But the movement lacked her usual finesse. I leaned back, studying her overbright eyes. Her flushed cheeks.

"Is something wrong?"

Tell me what it is. I'll fix it.

"You tell me." Again, her hands sought my chest. I seized them with tightly leashed frustration, squeezing her icy fingers in warning.

"Talk to me, Lou."

"What would you like to talk about, *darling* husband?"

I took a deep breath, still watching her closely. "Ansel."

His name fell between us like a carcass. Heavy. Dead.

"Ansel." She tugged her hands away with a frown. Her eyes grew distant. Shuttered. She stared at a spot just over my shoulder, her pupils expanding and contracting in tiny, nearly imperceptible movements. "You want to talk about Ansel."

"Yes."

"No," she said flatly. "I want to talk about you."

My own eyes narrowed. "I don't."

She didn't respond right away, still staring intently as if searching for . . . what? The right words? Lou had never cared for the right words before. Indeed, she reveled in saying the wrong ones. If I was honest with myself, I reveled in hearing them. "Let's have another game of questions, then," she said abruptly.

"What?"

"Like in the patisserie." She nodded quickly, almost to herself, before facing me at last. She tilted her head. "You didn't eat your sticky bun."

I blinked at her. "What?"

"Your sticky bun. You didn't eat it."

"Yes, I heard you. I just—" Shaking my head, I tried again, bewildered. "I don't have your sweet tooth."

"Hmm." She licked her lips salaciously. When her arm snaked behind me along the pew, I resisted the urge to lean forward. When her fingers threaded through my hair, however, I couldn't resist. She followed like a plague. "Venison is delicious too. Salty. Tender. At least," she added with a knowing smile, "if you eat it directly." I stared at her in confusion. Then horror. She meant if you ate it *raw*. "Otherwise rigor mortis toughens the meat. You have to hang the animal for a fortnight to break down the connective tissue. Makes it hard to avoid the flies, of course."

"When the hell have you eaten *raw deer*?" I asked incredulously.

Her eyes seemed to glow at the expletive, and she hummed with excitement, leaning toward me. "You should try it. You might like it." Then— "But I suppose a huntsman would have no need to skin a deer in his ivory tower. Tell me, have you ever suffered hunger?"

"Yes."

"*Real* hunger, I mean. Have you ever suffered cold? The kind that freezes your insides and leaves you like ice?"

Despite the hostility of her words, her voice held no contempt. Only curiosity. *Genuine* curiosity. She rocked back and forth, unable to keep still, as she watched me. I glared back at her. "You know I have."

She cocked her head. "Do I?" After pursing her lips, she nodded once more. "I do. Yes, of course. The Hollow. Dreadfully cold, wasn't it?" Her index and middle fingers walked up my leg. "And you're hungry even now, aren't you?"

She giggled when I returned her hand to her lap.

"What"—I cleared my throat—"is your next question?"

I could humor her. I could play this game. If it meant breaking through to her, if it meant unraveling what had . . . *changed* in her, I would sit here all night. I would help her. I *would*. Because if this truly was grief, she needed to talk about it. *We* needed to talk about it. Another stab of guilt shot through me when I glanced down at her hands. She'd clasped them together tightly.

I should've been holding those hands. I couldn't force myself to do it.

"Oooh, questions, questions." She brought her interlaced knuckles to her lips, musing. "If you could be anyone else, who would you be?" Another grin. "Whose skin would you wear?"

"I—" I glanced at Beau without thinking. She didn't miss the movement. "I wouldn't want to be anyone else."

"I don't believe you."

Defensive, I asked, "Who would you be?"

She lowered her hands to her chest. With her fingers still laced together, she could've been praying. Except for the calculated gleam in her eyes, her fiendish smile. "I can be whoever I want to be."

I cleared my throat, fought to ignore the hair lifting on my neck. Lost. "How do you know about *cauchemars*? I've studied the occult my entire life, and I've never heard of such a creature."

"You've *extinguished* the occult. I've lived with it." She cocked her head. The movement sent a fresh shiver down my spine. "I *am* it. We learn more in the shadows than we ever do in the sun." When I didn't answer, she asked abruptly, simply, "How would you choose to die?"

Ah. I eyed her knowingly. *Here we go.* "If I could choose . . . I suppose I'd want to die of old age. Fat and happy. Surrounded by loved ones."

"You wouldn't choose to die in battle?"

A startled breath. A sickening thud. A scarlet halo. I pushed my last memory of Ansel aside, looking her squarely in the eye. "I wouldn't choose that death for anyone. Not even myself. Not anymore."

"*He* chose it."

Though my heart twisted—though even his name brought uncomfortable pressure to my eyes—I inclined my head. "He did. And I'll honor him for it every day of my life—that he chose to help you, to fight with you. That he chose to face Morgane with you. He was the best of us." Her smile finally slipped, and I reached out to grip her hand. Despite its icy temperature, I didn't let go. "But you shouldn't feel guilty. Ansel made the decision for himself—not for you or for me, but for *him*. Now," I said firmly before she could interrupt, "it's your turn. Answer the question."

Her face remained inscrutable. Blank. "I don't want to die."

I rubbed her frigid hand between my own, trying to warm it. "I know. But if you had to choose—"

"I would choose not to die," she said.

"Everyone dies, Lou," I said gently.

She leaned closer at my expression, running her hand up my chest. In my ear, she whispered, "Says who, Reid?" She cupped my cheek, and for just a second, I lost myself in her voice. If I closed my eyes, I could pretend a different Lou held me this way. I could pretend this icy touch belonged to another—to a foul-mouthed thief, a heathen, a witch. I could pretend her breath smelled of cinnamon, and her hair flowed long and brown down her shoulders. Could pretend this was all part of an elaborate joke. An *inappropriate* joke. She would've laughed and flicked my nose at this point. Told me I needed to loosen up. Instead, her lips hovered over mine. "Who says we have to die?"

Swallowing hard, I opened my eyes, and the spell broke.

MY NAME IS LEGION

Lou

There are very few advantages to losing possession of one's body—or rather, losing *awareness* of one's body. With no eyes to see and no ears to hear, no legs to walk and no teeth to *eat*, I pass my time floating in darkness. Except . . . can one even *float* without a body? Or am I merely existing? And this darkness isn't *quite* darkness, is it? Which means—

Oh god. I'm now existing inside Nicholina le Clair.

No. *She* is existing inside *me*, the body-snatching bitch.

Hopefully I'm on my monthly bleed. She'd deserve it.

Though I wait for her response, impatient, no ghostly chuckle answers my provocation, so I try again. Louder this time. Shouting my thoughts—can one have thoughts without a brain?—into the abyss. *I know you can hear me. I hope my uterus is rioting against you.*

The darkness seems to shift in reply, but still she says nothing.

Forcing myself to concentrate, I push against her oppressive presence. It doesn't budge. I try again, harder this time. Nothing. I don't know how long I push. I don't know how much time has passed since I regained consciousness. Time has no meaning here. At this rate, I'll reclaim my body in approximately three hundred years, waking in a grave as more dust than skeleton. At least my mother can't kill a skeleton. At least they don't have uteruses.

I think I'm going mad.

With one last vicious shove, I resist a fit of rage. Emotions seem . . . different in this place. They run wild and unchecked without a body to cage them, and sometimes, in moments like these, I feel myself—whatever form I've now taken—slip into them, unadulterated. As if I *become* the emotion.

Reid would hate it here.

The thought of him lances through my consciousness, and a new emotion threatens to consume me. Melancholy.

Has he noticed I'm not myself? Has anyone? Do they realize what's happened to me?

I refocus on Nicholina, on the darkness, before the melancholy swallows me whole. It does little good to dwell on such things, yet debilitating cold creeps through the mist, my subconscious, at another unwelcome thought: how could they have noticed? Even before La Voisin and Nicholina betrayed us, I wasn't myself. I still feel those splintered edges, those fissures in my spirit I broke willingly.

One bites deeper than the rest. An open wound.

I shy away from it instinctively, though it pulses with whiskey-colored eyes and curling lashes and soft, lyrical laughter. It aches with a lanky arm around my shoulders, a warm hand in my own.

It throbs with empathy, with a feigned accent and a stolen bottle of wine, with shy blushes and not-quite birthdays. It burns with the sort of loyalty that no longer exists in this world.

He didn't make it to seventeen.

Ansel sacrificed everything, cracked me wide open, and I allowed Nicholina to slither into that crack. That's how I repaid him—by losing myself entirely. Self-loathing churns, black and noxious, in the pit of my consciousness. He deserved better. He deserved *more*.

I would give it to him. As God or the Goddess or just the dark of my fucking soul as witness, I would give it to him. I would ensure he didn't die in vain. In response, an unfamiliar voice startles me by murmuring, *Oh, bravo.*

The inky mist contracts with my fright, but I push against it viciously, searching for the new presence. This isn't Nicholina. This certainly isn't *me*. And that means . . . someone else is here.

Who are you? I ask with feigned bravado. Mother's tit, how many people—or spirits, or entities, or *whatever*—can possibly fit within a single body? *What do you want?*

You needn't be frightened. Another voice this time. As unfamiliar as the last. *We cannot hurt you.*

We are *you.*

Or rather, a third adds, *we are her.*

That's not an answer, I snap. *Tell me who you are.*

A brief pause.

Then a fourth voice finally says, *We don't remember.*

A fifth now. *Soon you won't either.*

If I had bones, their words would've chilled them to the marrow. *How . . . how many of you are there?* I ask quietly. *Can none of you remember your name?*

Our name is Legion, the voices reply in unison, not missing a beat. *For we are many.*

Holy hell. Definitely more than five voices. More like fifty. Shit, shit, *shit.* Vaguely, I remember the verse they recited from a passage in the Archbishop's Bible, the one he loaned me in the basement of Chasseur Tower. The man who spoke it had been possessed by demons. But these—these aren't demons, are they? Is Nicholina possessed by *demons?*

Alas, we do not know, the first says amicably. *We have lived here for unknown years. We could be demons, or we could be mice. We see only what our mistress sees, hear only what our mistress hears.*

Mice.

She talks to us sometimes, another adds, and somehow I sense its mischievous intent. I just *know,* as if its stream of consciousness has merged with mine. *We jest, by the way. We aren't called Legion. Stupid name, if you ask us.*

We use it on all the newcomers.

Always gets a rise.

Plucked the verse straight from your memories this time, though. Are you religious?

It is impolite to ask if someone is religious.

She isn't a someone *anymore. She's one of us. We already know the answer, anyway. We're being polite.*

On the contrary, it is quite rude to look through her memories.

Save the sermon for when the memories have gone. Look here. They're still fresh.

An uncomfortable prickling sensation descends as the voices bicker, and again, I instinctively know they're rifling through my consciousness—through *me*. Images of my past flicker in and out of the mist faster than I can track, but the voices only press closer, hungry for more. Dancing around the maypole with Estelle, drowning in the Doleur with the Archbishop, straining at the altar beneath my mother—

Stop it. My own voice cuts sharply through the memories, and the voices draw back, surprised but chastised. As they should be. It's like an infestation of fleas in my own subconscious. *My name is Louise le Blanc, and I am most definitely still a someone. I'd tell you to stay the hell out of my head, but since I'm not sure this even is my head, I'll assume separation is impossible at this point. Now, who's the last newcomer to this place? Can anyone remember?*

Silence reigns for one blissful second before all the voices start talking at once, arguing over who's been here the longest. Too late, I realize the error in my judgment. These voices are no longer individuals but an eerie sort of collective. A hive. Annoyance quickly churns to anger. Longing for hands with which to throttle them, I try to speak, but a new voice interrupts.

I am the newest.

The other voices cease immediately, radiating curiosity. I'm curious myself. This voice sounds different from the rest, deep and low and masculine. He also called himself *I*, not *we*.

And you are? I ask.

If a voice could frown, this one does. *I . . . I believe I was once called Etienne.*

Etienne, the others echo. Their whispers thrum like insect wings. The sound is disconcerting. Worse—I *feel* the moment they manifest his full name from his memories. From *my* memories. *Etienne Gilly.*

You're Gaby's brother, I say in dawning horror, remembering as they do. *Morgane murdered you.*

The voices practically quiver with anticipation as our memories sync, filling in the gaps to paint the entire portrait: how Nicholina possessed him and walked the forest under pretense of a hunt, how she led him to where Morgane lay in wait. How Morgane abducted him, tortured him within the bowels of a dank, dark cave only a handful of miles from the blood camp. And La Voisin—how she'd known all along. How she'd practically delivered Etienne's and Gabrielle's heads to Morgane on a silver platter.

Part of me still can't believe it, can't process my shock at their betrayal. My humiliation. Josephine and Nicholina have allied with my mother. Though I didn't like them, I never suspected them capable of such evil. They sacrificed members of their own coven to . . . what? Return to the Chateau?

Yes, Etienne whispers.

He knows because he saw it all happen through Nicholina's eyes, even after the real Etienne had perished. He witnessed his own desecrated body propped against my tent. He watched helplessly as Morgane kidnapped Gabrielle for the same fate, as my mother tormented his little sister, as Gaby finally escaped from La Mascarade des Crânes.

Except . . .

I frown. There are noticeable *gaps* in his memory. A small hole here, a gaping one there. My own involvement in the skull masquerade, for example. The color of Gabrielle's hair. Each gap fills as I think of it, however, as my memory supplements his own, until the timeline is mostly complete.

Despite being, well, *dead*, he witnessed it all as if he was there.

How? I ask warily. *Etienne, you . . . you died. Why haven't you passed on?*

When Nicholina possessed me, I joined her consciousness, and I—I don't think I ever left.

Holy shit. My shock spreads wildly into outright horror. *Has Nicholina possessed all of you?*

I can feel them sift through our memories once more, piecing together our collective knowledge of Nicholina, of La Voisin, of blood magic. The darkness seems to vibrate with agitation as they contemplate such a fantastical and *impossible* conclusion. And yet . . . how often did Nicholina speak of mice? Gabrielle claimed she and La Voisin ate hearts to remain eternally young. Others whispered of even blacker arts. Their understanding resolves as mine does.

Somehow, Nicholina has trapped their souls in this darkness with her forever.

Yours too, the prim one sniffs. *You are one of us now.*

No. The darkness seems to press closer as their words ring true, and for a moment, I can't speak. *No, I'm still alive. I'm in a church, and Reid—*

Who says we're all dead? the mischievous voice asks. *Perhaps some of us are still alive, somewhere. Perhaps our souls are merely fragmented. Part here, part there. Part everywhere. Yours will shatter soon enough.*

When the darkness shifts once more, heavier now—crushing me beneath its weight—the others sense my mounting hysteria. Their voices turn less amicable, less prim, less mischievous. *We are sorry, Louise le Blanc. It is too late for you. For all of us.*

NO. I lash against the darkness with all my might, repeating the word over and over again like a talisman. I search for a golden pattern. For *anything.* There is only darkness. *No no no no no—*

Only Nicholina's chilling laughter answers.

THE LIGHTHOUSE

Reid

The first light of dawn haloed Father Achille in the sanctuary doors. He waited as I roused the others. No one had slept well. Bags swelled beneath Célie's eyes, though she did her best to pinch color into her pale cheeks. Coco yawned while Beau groaned and cracked his neck. My own ached, despite Lou's fingers kneading the knotted muscle there. I shrugged away from her touch with an apologetic smile, motioning toward the door.

"The villagers won't rouse for another hour or so," Achille said, handing each of us an apple as we filed past. "Remember what I said—don't let them see you. The Chasseurs have an outpost not far from here. You don't want anyone following you to . . . wherever it is you're going."

"Thank you, Father." I tucked the apple into my pocket. It wasn't shiny. It wasn't red. But it was more than he owed us. More than others would've given. "For everything."

He eyed me steadily. "Don't mention it." When I nodded, moving to lead the others through the churchyard, he caught my

arm. "Be careful. *Cauchemars* are heralded as harbingers of doom."
I lifted an incredulous brow, and he added, grudging, "They're
only seen before catastrophic events."

"A mob isn't a catastrophic event."

"Never underestimate the power of a mob." Beau draped his
arm casually across Coco's shoulders as they waited, leaning
against a tree. Mist clung to the edges of their hoods. "People are
capable of unspeakable evil en masse. I've seen it happen."

Father Achille released my arm and stepped away. "As have I.
Take care."

Without another word, he disappeared into the foyer, closing
the door firmly behind him.

A strange sensation twinged my chest as I watched him go. "I
wonder if we'll ever see him again."

"Not likely," Lou said. The thick mist nearly engulfed her
slight frame. Behind her, a white shape slipped through a break
in the haze, and amber eyes flashed. I scowled. The dog had
returned. She hadn't noticed, instead extending her arm down
the hillside. "Shall we?"

The village of Fée Tombe had been named for its sea stacks of
hematite. Black, sparkling, the rocks rose from the sea for miles
on end in the disjointed shapes of faerie wings—some tall and
thin with spiderlike webs of silver, others short and stout with
veins of red. Even the smallest stacks towered over the sea like
great, immortal beings. Waves crashed around the wreckage of
ships below. From our path along the bluff, the broken masts

and booms looked like teeth.

Célie shivered in the icy breeze, wincing as her foot caught and twisted between two rocks. Beau cast her a sympathetic look. "It isn't too late to turn back, you know."

"No." She lifted her chin stubbornly before wrenching her foot free. More rocks skittered from the path and tumbled into the sea below. "We need my carriage."

"Your *father's* carriage," Coco muttered. She kept one hand on the sheer cliff face to her left—the other clenched tightly around *La Petite Larme*—and edged past. Beau followed carefully, picking his way through the uneven terrain as the path narrowed and spiraled upward. At the back of the group, I kept my own hand fisted in the fabric of Lou's cloak.

I needn't have bothered. She moved with the grace of a cat, never slipping, never stumbling. Each step light and nimble.

Color rose high on Célie's cheeks as she tried to maintain our pace. Her breathing grew labored. When she stumbled again, I leaned around Lou and murmured, "Beau was right, Célie. You can wait in the chapel while we deal with the *cauchemar*. We'll return for you before we leave."

"I am *not*," she seethed, skirt and hair whipping wildly in the wind, "waiting in the chapel."

Sweeping past Célie, Lou patted her on the head. "Of course you aren't, kitten." Then she cast a sidelong look down her right shoulder, to where the sea crashed below. "You needn't be worried, anyway. Kittens have nine lives." Her teeth flashed. "Don't they?"

My hand tightened on her cloak, and I tugged her backward, bending low to her ear. "Stop it."

"Stop what, darling?" She craned her neck to look at me. Eyes wide. Innocent. Her lashes fluttered. "I'm *encouraging* her."

"You're terrifying her."

She reached back to trace my lips with her pointer finger. "Perhaps you don't give her enough credit."

With that, she twisted from my grip and strode past Célie without another look. We watched her go with varying degrees of alarm. When she vanished around the bend after Coco and Beau, Célie's shoulders relaxed infinitesimally. She took a deep breath. "She still doesn't like me. I thought she might after . . ."

"Do you like her?"

A second too late, she wrinkled her nose. "Of course not."

I jerked my chin to indicate we should continue. "Then there isn't a problem."

She said nothing for a long moment. "But . . . *why* doesn't she like me?"

"Careful." I moved to steady her when she tripped, but she jerked away, overcompensating and falling hard against the cliff. I fought an eye roll. "She knows we have history. Plus"—I cleared my throat pointedly—"she heard you call her a whore."

Now she whipped around to face me. "She *what?*"

I shrugged and kept walking. "At the Saint Nicolas Day celebrations, she overheard our . . . discussion. I think she took it well, all things considered. She could've murdered us on the spot."

"She . . . she *heard* me . . . ?" Eyes widening with palpable distress, she lifted a hand to her lips. "Oh, no. Oh, no no *no.*"

I couldn't resist this time. My eyes rolled to the heavens. "I'm sure she's been called worse."

"She's a *witch,*" Célie hissed, hand dropping to clutch her chest. "She could—she could *curse* me, or, or—"

"Or *I* could." The smile that carved my lips felt harder than usual. Like it'd been hewn from granite. Even after Lou had risked life and limb to save her in the catacombs, Célie still considered her an enemy. Of course she did. "Why did you follow us, Célie, if you disdain us so?" At her expression, I shook my head with a self-deprecating laugh. A brittle one. Hers wasn't an unprecedented reaction. If Coco hadn't set the tunnels ablaze, would the denizens of La Mascarade des Crânes have returned for us? Would they have brought fire of their own? Yes, they would've, and I couldn't blame them. I'd have once done the same. "Forget it."

"No, Reid, wait, I—I didn't mean—" Though she didn't touch me, something in her voice made me pause. Made me turn. "Jean Luc told me what happened. He told me . . . about you. I am so sorry."

"I'm not."

Her brows lifted, puckered. "You're not?"

"I'm not."

When I didn't elaborate, her frown deepened. She blinked rapidly. "Oh. Of . . . of course. I—" Blowing air from her cheeks, she planted an abrupt hand on her hip, and her eyes sparked again with that unfamiliar temper. "Well, I'm not either. Sorry, that is.

That you're different. That *I'm* different. I'm not sorry at all."

Though she'd spoken in frankness rather than spite, her words still should've hurt. They didn't. Instead, the nervous energy thrumming just beneath my skin seemed to settle, replaced by peculiar warmth. Perhaps peace. Perhaps . . . closure? She had Jean Luc now, and I had Lou. Everything between us had changed. And that—that was okay. That was *good*.

When I smiled this time, it was genuine. "We're friends, Célie. We'll always be friends."

"Well then." She sniffed, straightening and fighting her own smile. "As your *friend*, it is my duty to inform you that your hair is in dire need of a cut and that your coat is missing two buttons. Also, you have a hickey on your throat." When my hand shot upward to the tender skin near my pulse, she laughed and strode around me, pert nose in the air. "You should cover it for propriety's sake."

There she was.

Chuckling, I fell into step beside her. It felt nice. Familiar. After another moment of comfortable silence, she asked, "What will we do after we warn the *cauchemar*?"

The peace I'd felt fractured, as did my smile. "We journey to the Chateau."

Her hand fluttered to her collar once more. A nervous habit. A telling one. "And—and then what? Just how do we plan to defeat Morgane?"

"Watch where you're going." I nodded to a dip in the path. Sure enough, she stumbled slightly. I didn't reach for her this time, and she caught herself without my help. "Lou wants to burn the castle to the ground." The dead weight returned to my chest. To my voice. "And everyone in it."

"How will she do that?"

I shrugged. "How does a witch do anything?"

"How does it work, then? The . . . magic?" Her expression took on a shyer quality, her chin ducking quickly to her chest. She turned to face forward once more. "I've always been curious."

"You have?"

"Oh, don't play coy, Reid. I know you were curious too." She paused delicately. "Before."

Before. Such a simple word. I kept my gaze impassive. "It's a give and take. For Lou to raze the Chateau, she'll have to destroy something of equal value to herself."

Célie's voice held wonder. "And what might that be?"

I don't know. The admission chafed. Lou had provided no details. No strategy. When we'd pressed her, she'd simply smiled and asked, "Are you afraid?" Beau had responded immediately with a resounding *yes.* I'd privately agreed. The entire plan—or lack thereof—made me uneasy.

Like God had plucked him from my thoughts, my brother's shout rent the air. Célie and I looked up in unison to see part of the cliff give way. Rocks rained down upon us, striking first my shoulders, my arms, then my head. Sharp pain exploded, and stars burst in my vision. Reacting instinctively, I thrust Célie out of harm's way, and Beau—he—

Horror unfurled in my gut like a deadly snake.

As if in slow motion, I watched as he lost his footing, as he flailed wildly through the air, as he tried and failed to find purchase among the falling rocks. There was nothing I could do. No way I could help. Lunging forward anyway, I gauged the distance between us, desperate to catch some part of him before he plunged to the sea—

Coco's hand shot through the rockfall and seized his wrist.

With another shout, Beau swung in her grip like a pendulum. He thrust his free hand upward to grip the edge of the rock, and together, the two struggled to drag him back onto the path. I raced ahead to help, my heart pounding a deafening beat. Adrenaline—complete, unadulterated *fear*—coursed through my system, lengthening my stride and shortening my breath. By the time I reached them, however, they lay sprawled in a tangled heap. Their chests rose and fell haphazardly as they too tried to catch their breath. Above us, Lou stood at the top of the bluff. She gazed down with a hint of a smile. Just the slightest curve of her lips. The white dog growled and disappeared behind her. "You should really be more careful," she said softly before turning away.

Beau glared at her in disbelief but didn't respond. Sitting up, he wiped a shaky hand across his brow and glanced at his arm. His mouth twisted in an ugly slash. "Goddamn it. I tore my *fucking* sleeve."

I shook my head, cursing bitterly under my breath. His *sleeve*. He'd nearly plunged to his death, and all he cared about was his *fucking sleeve*. With a convulsive, full-body shudder, I opened my mouth to tell him just what he could do with said sleeve, but an odd choking noise escaped Coco. I stared at her in alarm—then incredulity.

She wasn't choking at all.

She was *laughing*.

Without a word—her shoulders still shaking—she reached out to tear the fabric of his opposite sleeve. His mouth fell open in outrage as he tried to pull away. "*Excuse* you. My mother bought me this shirt!"

"Now you match." She clutched his arms and laughed harder. "Your mother will approve when she sees you. *If* she ever sees you again, that is. You did almost die." She slapped his chest as if the two had shared a hilarious joke. "You almost *died*."

"Yes." Beau searched her face warily. "You mentioned that."

"I can mend your shirt, if you'd like," Célie offered. "I've a needle and thread in my bag—" But she broke off when Coco continued to laugh wildly. When that laughter deepened into something darker. Crazed. Beau pulled her into his arms without hesitation. Her shoulders shook now for an entirely different reason, and she buried her face in the crook of his neck, sobbing incoherently. One of his arms wrapped around her waist, the other across her back, and he held her tightly, fiercely, murmuring soft words in her ear. Words I couldn't hear. Words I didn't *want* to hear.

I looked away.

This pain wasn't for me. This vulnerability. I felt like an interloper. Watching them together—the way Beau rocked her gently, the way she clutched him for dear life—it brought a lump to my throat. Anyone could see where this was headed. Coco and Beau had danced around each other for months. Just as clear, however, was the inevitable heartbreak. Neither was in a position to start a relationship. They shared too much hurt between them. Too much grief. Jealousy. Spite. Even well-adjusted, the two would've been wrong for each other. Like water and oil.

I glanced up at Lou. We'd been wrong for each other too.

And so, so right.

With a sigh, I started up the path, my footsteps heavy. My thoughts heavier. Célie followed quietly behind. When we reached Lou, I laced her cold fingers through mine, and we turned to face the lighthouse.

Beau and Coco joined us several minutes later. Though her eyes remained swollen and red, she no longer cried. Instead she held her shoulders straight. Proud. Riddled with holes, Beau's shirt still smoked slightly, revealing more skin than prudent in January. They didn't speak of what had transpired, and neither did we.

We studied the lighthouse in silence.

It rose from the earth like a crooked finger beckoning to the sky. A single stone tower. Dirty. Dilapidated. Dark against the dawn. No flames flickered in the basin beneath the slanted roof. "The stable boy said no one lights the torches anymore," Célie said, her voice low. I didn't ask why she whispered. The hair on my neck had lifted inexplicably. The shadows here seemed to collect thicker than natural. "He said they haven't been lit for years."

"The stable boy talks a lot." Beau glanced between us nervously. He kept his arm firm around Coco's waist. "Do we . . . has anyone actually *seen* a *cauchemar*?"

"I told you," Célie said. "It was a great hulking beast of tooth and claw, and it—"

"Darling, no." Beau lifted his free hand with a forced smile. "I meant"—he struggled for the right words for a moment before shrugging—"has anyone *else* seen a *cauchemar*? Preferably someone who didn't run away screaming?"

Coco flashed him a grin. Amused. It seemed out of place on her grim face. With a start, I realized I couldn't remember the last time she'd genuinely smiled. Had she ever? Had I seen it? When she pinched his ribs, he yelped and dropped his arm. "You have a beautiful falsetto yourself," she said. "I'd almost forgotten."

Though she grinned wider at his outrage—his surprise—her bravado felt fragile. Delicate. I didn't want to see it break. Buffeting Beau's shoulder, I said, "Do you remember the witch on Modraniht?"

His mouth flattened. "We do not speak of her."

"*I* remember." Coco shot me an appreciative look. It was there and gone in the blink of an eye. So brief I might've imagined it. "She quite liked your little performance, didn't she?"

"I'm an excellent singer," Beau sniffed.

"You're an excellent *dancer.*"

I laughed despite myself. "I remember Beau running away screaming that night."

"What is this?" He looked between us, brows and nose wrinkling in alarm. "What's happening here?"

"She *told* you what a *cauchemar* looks like." Though Coco didn't look at Célie—didn't acknowledge her existence whatsoever—I suspected her admission was the only apology Célie would receive. "Don't be an ass. Listen."

With a long-suffering sigh, Beau inclined his head in Célie's direction. She stood a little straighter. "My apologies, *madame,*" he muttered, sounding like a peevish child. "What I *meant* was has anyone ever *fought* a *cauchemar?* Some actual experience might be the difference between surviving this encounter intact and having our heads thrown to sea."

"Is that your fear?" Lou tilted her own head to study him. She'd grown unusually silent since reaching the lighthouse. Unusually still. Until now, her eyes hadn't wavered from the thick shadows at the base of the tower. "Decapitation?"

His frown matched her own. "I—well, it doesn't seem particularly pleasant, no."

"But do you fear it?" she pressed. "Does it haunt your dreams?"

Beau scoffed at the peculiar question, not bothering to hide his exasperation. "Show me someone who doesn't fear decapitation, and I'll show you a liar."

"Why?" Coco's eyes narrowed. "What is it, Lou?"

Lou's gaze returned to the shadows. She stared at them as if trying to decipher something. As if listening to an unspoken language. "A *cauchemar* is a nightmare," she explained in an offhand voice. Still distracted. "It'll appear differently to each of us, assuming the form of our greatest fears."

A beat of horrific silence passed as her words sank in.

Our greatest fears. An uncanny awareness skittered down my spine, as if even now, the creature watched us. Learned us. I didn't even *know* my greatest fear. I'd never given it thought. Never given it voice. It seemed the *cauchemar* would do it for me.

"Have you—have you fought one?" Coco asked Lou. "A *cauchemar?*"

A sly grin crept across Lou's face. Still she studied the shadows. "Once. A long time ago."

"What shape did it take?" Beau demanded.

Her eyes snapped to his. "That's very personal, Beauregard. What shape will it take for *you?*" When she stepped toward him, he took a hasty step back. "Not decapitation. Not drowning either." She cocked her head and stalked closer, circling him now. She didn't grin. Didn't mock. "No, your fear isn't quite so vital, is it? You fear something else. Something peripheral." When she inhaled deeply, her eyes lighting with recognition, I seized her hand and yanked her to my side.

"This isn't the time or place," I said tersely. "We need to focus."

"By all means, Chass"—she waved to the rotten door—"lead the way."

We all stared at it. No one moved.

I peered behind us to the village, to the dozens of pinpricks of light. The sun had risen. The townspeople had gathered. They'd start their trek soon. We had half an hour—maybe a quarter more—before they ascended on us. On the unwitting monster inside.

You should stay out of it, boy. This isn't your fight.

I squared my shoulders.

With a deep breath, I moved to open the door, but Célie—*Célie*—beat me to it.

Her hand seemed paler and smaller than usual against the dark wood, but she didn't hesitate. She pushed with all her might—once, twice, three times—until the hinges finally swung open with a shriek. The sound pierced the early morning silence, frightening a pair of seagulls from the rafters. Beau cursed and jumped.

So did Lou.

With one last, deep breath, I stepped inside.

LE CAUCHEMAR

Reid

The lower floors had no windows to let in the early morning sun, so the lighthouse's interior remained dark. The air dank. Stale. Broken glass littered the floor, glinting in the narrow swath of light from the door. A small, frightened creature skittered across it, and the shards tinkled under its tiny paws. I looked closer.

Mirrors. Broken mirrors.

They each reflected different pieces of the circular room—rusted hooks on the walls, coiled ropes atop them, bowed beams overhead. A moldy bed sat in one corner, along with a tarnished iron pot. Remnants of the last keeper who'd lived here. I moved farther into the hodgepodge space, watching as the reflections shifted. Now Célie's wide eye. Now Beau's drawn mouth. Now Coco's tense shoulders. Lou kept a hand on my lower back.

Beyond our footsteps, no other sound penetrated the silence.

Perhaps the creature had already moved on. Perhaps Father Achille had been mistaken.

The door slammed shut behind us.

Both Coco and Célie leapt into Beau with identical shrieks. He somehow missed both of them, however, startling sideways with a vicious curse. The two had no choice but to clutch each other as I stormed past, wrenching the door open once more. "We're fine," I said firmly. "It was the wind."

That same wind caressed my cheeks now, bringing with it a soft bout of laughter.

Was that . . . ?

My heart nearly seized.

Looking around wildly, I pivoted in a full circle. The others imitated my movements with panicked expressions. "What is it?" Coco flicked a knife from her sleeve. "Did you hear something?"

My heartbeat thundered in my ears. "I thought I heard . . ." *The Archbishop*, I almost finished, but the words caught in my throat. I thought I'd heard the *Archbishop*. But that couldn't be. He wasn't here. He never laughed. I didn't *fear* him.

It was La Fôret des Yeux all over again. Instead of trees, the *cauchemar* mocked me, twisting my thoughts into nightmares. It could've hidden in the shadows. Célie had described a hulking beast, but perhaps it could change shape. We knew virtually nothing about this creature or its abilities. Its appetite.

I took a steadying breath.

Cauchemars are notoriously cruel, but this creature hasn't yet attacked.

Cruel or no, it hadn't harmed anyone. That laugh—it was a figment of my imagination. A defense mechanism the *cauchemar* had cultivated to protect itself. To *protect* itself. Not to attack. Not to kill or maim or eat.

Still, its tactics weren't exactly endearing. When the laughter returned a second later, I slipped a blade from my bandolier, whirling toward the source.

It hadn't been the *cauchemar* at all.

It'd been Lou.

I slowly lowered my blade.

Oblivious, she leaned around me to peer into the room, still chuckling softly. "I can smell the fear in this place. It's potent. Alive." When we stared at her, nonplussed, she pointed to the walls. "Can you not scent it? It coats the ropes"—her finger turned to the soft floorboards—"paints the glass. The entire room is slick with it."

"No," I said stiffly, wanting to throttle her. "I don't scent anything."

"Perhaps it's *your* fear I smell, then, not the *cauchemar*." When the wind gusted through once more, her grin faded, and she tilted her head again. Listening. "It does feel different, though. It feels . . ." But she kept the words she would've spoken, trailing into silence instead. Her hand clenched on my back. "I think we should leave."

Surprised by her reaction—yet somehow not—I approached the spiral staircase in the center of the room. The wood had half-rotted. Tentatively, I tested the bottom step with my foot. It dipped beneath my weight. "We will. After we warn the creature. After we ask for its help."

For a short moment, she looked likely to argue. Her lip curled. Her eyes darkened. Just as quickly, however, her expression cleared, and she dipped her chin in a slight nod, brushing past me up the stairs.

We ascended the next two floors in a single-file line. One step at a time. Slow. Cautious. We paused only to inspect the dilapidated rooms beyond, but the *cauchemar*—if here at all—remained hidden.

"What was that?" Beau whipped his head to the door on our right, to the ominous groan behind it. "Did you hear—?" Something creaked overhead, and another gust of wind swept up the staircase. He spun to face Coco. "Was that you?"

Her eyes darted all around us. "Why would I be *moaning*?"

It was a mark of Beau's panic that he didn't respond. Instead, he nearly tripped over Célie as she stooped to collect something from the moldy stair. It gleamed through her fingers in the darkness. A shard of mirror. Straightening, she held it out in front of her like a knife.

A beat of silence passed as we stared at her. "What?" she hissed defensively, face nearly white. "No one gave me a weapon."

To my surprise, Coco responded by bending to retrieve her own shard. She held it poised in her free hand, saying nothing of the knife in her other, and nodded once in Célie's direction. Then she nudged Beau. He looked between them, aghast. "You cannot be serious. We're more likely to wound ourselves than the *cauchemar* with such rubbish."

Rolling my eyes, I pressed a dagger into his palm before picking up my own piece of glass. At Célie's incredulous stare, one corner of my mouth quirked up. "What?" I shrugged and continued upward, not looking back. "It was a good idea."

We crept toward the final floor in silence. When the door below slammed shut again, Beau's whisper quickly followed. "I'm as opposed to airing my dirty laundry as anyone, but perhaps— in light of the circumstances—it might help to . . . discuss our fears?" The step beneath him heaved an ominous groan, and he exhaled sharply. "For example, if one of you could reiterate how you'd never *dream* of ignoring or forgetting me, that would be grand. It's a ridiculous notion, I know, but for the sake of—"

"Quiet," Lou snapped. The staircase ended with a door directly overhead. She tilted her head again, hesitating, before pushing it open and slipping through. I followed, nearly flattening her when I climbed to my feet. She'd stopped abruptly to take in the final floor: an open room without walls to shield us from the elements. Only a handful of beams held the roof in place, and sun spilled in from every direction, banishing the last of the shadows. I breathed a sigh of relief. The *cauchemar* wasn't here. *Nothing* was here save an enormous fire basin. Built into the center of the stone floor, it stood empty. No wood or ashes. Except—

Lou stood perfectly still, the wind whipping her pale hair across her face.

Except it wasn't empty at all.

From the basin, an enormous figure rose.

Cloaked in soiled fabric, it charged toward us with blackened, outstretched hands. I lunged to Lou's side, but she'd already moved, surging forward with lightning quickness. When she lashed out with her blade, clipping the creature's midsection, it reared backward like a great bear. Though a hood shielded its hair, its face, its *teeth*, it swiped at Lou with one massive paw, and she sailed through the air. I dove after her—catching her wrist before she could slide from the room's edge—as the others attacked, their knives and mirrors glinting in the sunlight. "Stop!" The wind carried away my shout. "Don't hurt it! We're here to *warn* the creature, not—*stop!*"

The *cauchemar* stumbled back a step, hands still raised, but didn't hesitate to knock Coco's glass aside and roar when she slashed its thigh. She danced out of reach before it could wrap its hands around her neck—and then the first terror came.

Though Lou had warned us, nothing could've prepared me for the horrifying jolt of fear. Of *pain*. My vision flashed white, blinding me, and I slipped, crouching down to one knee. From the others' startled cries, they experienced the same.

A black room, blacker chains. Cold against my skin. Wrong. Blood slides from my wrists to the floor in a steady drip. I count each drop. She returns at the top of each hour. Thirty-six hundred seconds. Thirty-six hundred drops. When the door creaks open at drop thirty-five hundred and sixty-two, I choke back a scream. A saw. A handsaw. She lifts it to the candlelight. "Is it in your bones, I wonder? Like theirs?"

I fell to my hands as the faceless woman advanced. Gasping for breath. Shaking my head. Forcing my eyes to see reality instead of the glint of bone: to see Lou, writhing on the floor beside me, to see Coco in the fetal position, Beau flat on his back, Célie wide-eyed and trembling.

I threw my glass shard, and it stuck, point-first, in the

creature's shoulder. Lurching to my feet, I tore another knife from my bandolier. The *cauchemar* stood its ground. A rumbling noise built in its chest, but I ignored the growl and advanced. The others struggled to join me in vain. Another wave of fear crippled us before we could reach the beast.

Alone. I'm alone. Where is he? Where is he where is he where is he—

I gritted my teeth and continued, disoriented, stumbling against the flickering white like a drunkard.

"Speak." A high, imperious voice. Her voice. "Or I shall pluck out your brother's eyes. It is a fitting punishment, yes? He rendered you mute. I shall render him blind." But I cannot speak. Drugged. The drug. It congeals in my system. The manacle at my throat chokes me. Moan. I try to moan, but she only laughs. His screams fill the air. His pleas.

Oh my God.

This wasn't right. I didn't fear torture. I wasn't *mute*—

More images flashed. Broken pieces, fragmented horror. A swollen jaw. Irrepressible hunger. Empty syringes, the burning pain of infection. A chilling laugh and stale bread. And through it all, an acute, unbearable panic.

Where is he where is he where is he where is he

Wolves howling.

Eucalyptus.

Moonbeam hair.

Moonbeam hair.

I blinked rapidly, my vision clearing with Lou's. With a shrill battle cry, she rushed forward, knife raised. I caught her around the waist, spinning her away from the *cauchemar*. It still waved its hands frenetically, as if—as if trying to tell me something. My stomach churned violently. "Hold. I think—I think it's—"

In a clumsy, disjointed movement, the *cauchemar* pulled back its hood.

I stared at it.

Contrary to Célie's description, the *cauchemar* didn't have shadow-cloaked skin or sharp teeth. Its hair was matted, yes, but its swollen eyes inspired more fear than its namesake. Its broken jaw evoked more rage. My vision tunneled to its lacerated thigh, to the angry red streaks of disease on its russet skin. To the blood crusting its tattered pants. This *cauchemar* had been beaten. Badly.

It also wasn't a *cauchemar* at all.

It was Thierry St. Martin.

Lou twisted from my grasp and sprinted toward him once more. Incredulous, I caught her wrist. "Lou, stop. *Stop.* This is—"

"Let me go," she seethed, still struggling viciously. Frantic. *Distraught.* "Let me kill it—"

Anger flared hot and sudden. Tightening my grip, I dragged her back to my side and kept her there. "Stand down. I won't ask again. This is Thierry. Remember? Thierry St. Martin."

At his name, Thierry sagged with relief against the stone basin. I felt his presence in my mind—saw a picture of my own face—before he slurred a single word.

Reeeiddd.

I resisted the urge to go to him, to sling an arm around his shoulders for support. He looked likely to collapse. Lowering my voice, trying to soothe, I murmured, "I'm here. Everything will be all right. Lou recognizes you now. Isn't that right, Lou?"

She finally, *finally* stopped struggling, and I relinquished my hold on her. "Yes." Voice soft, she looked between Thierry and me for a long moment. I stood perfectly still, wary of the odd gleam in her eyes—savage and bright, like that of a cornered animal. "Yes, I recognize him."

Then she turned and fled.

Barreling into the others, knocking them aside, Lou didn't slow as she reached the door. Célie pinwheeled backward on impact, but Coco caught her elbow before she free-fell down the stairs. Swearing viciously in response, Beau hurled insults after Lou, but she didn't stop. The shadows closed around her as she raced out of sight.

Thierry lifted a weak hand. Two of his fingers appeared broken. Voice hitched with urgency, slow with concentration, he said, *Caaatch . . . her.*

I didn't stop to think. To hesitate. To consider the resolve hardening in my chest. This sensation—this fiery sense of justice, of righteousness—it felt familiar. Unsettlingly so.

She darted down the stairs below me with unnatural swiftness, already near the ground floor. In seconds, she'd be out the door. "Lou!" My shout reverberated with unexpected fury. I didn't understand why my hands shook or my teeth clenched. I didn't understand *why* I needed to catch her. But I did. I needed to catch her like I needed to breathe. Beau had been right—something was wrong here. Terribly, terribly wrong. It went beyond her magic. It went beyond Ansel's death. Beyond mourning.

Like fruit left in the sun to rot, Lou had split open, and something foul had grown inside.

Perhaps it'd happened during La Mascarade des Crânes. Perhaps before, perhaps after. It didn't matter. It *had* happened, and though my instincts had tried to warn me, I'd ignored them. Now they propelled my feet forward faster. Faster still. They told me if Lou reached the door—if she disappeared into the cliffs beyond—I'd never see her again. That could not happen. If I could just catch her, *talk* to her, I could make things right. I could make *her* right. It didn't make any sense, but there it was. This chase had suddenly become the most important of my life. And I wouldn't ignore my instincts any longer.

When she cleared the last stair, I took a deep breath.

Then I gripped the spiral railing and vaulted over it.

Dank air roared in my ears as I plunged to the ground. Eyes widening over her shoulder, Lou bolted for the door. "Fu—" Her expletive ended in a shriek as I landed on top of her. Twisting onto her back, she clawed at my face, my eyes, but I seized her wrists and pinned them to the floor. When she continued to buck and thrash, I straddled her waist, broken glass tearing into my knees as we grappled. My weight kept her restrained, however. Immobilized. She smashed her head into my jaw instead. Grinding my teeth, I pushed my forehead against hers. Hard. "Stop it," I snarled, flattening myself against her. The others descended the stairs in a cacophony of shouts. "What is *wrong* with you? Why are you running?"

"The *cauchemar.*" She struggled harder, panting feverishly. "It—it transformed into—into Thierry—" But the lie crumbled in her mouth as Thierry limped forward. In the shards of mirrors, his very real hatred refracted from every angle. His very real injuries. Coco followed, dropping to the floor beside us. She thrust her bloody forearm to the air above Lou's mouth, the unspoken threat clear. "Don't make me do it, Lou."

Lou's chest rose and fell rapidly beneath mine. Sensing the battle lost, she bared her teeth in a saccharine smile. "Is this how you treat a friend, Cosette? A sister?"

"Why did you run?" Coco repeated. No warmth lingered in her expression as she gazed at her friend. Her sister. Instead, Coco's eyes glittered with frigid, impenetrable cold. The two could've been perfect strangers. No—enemies. "Why did you attack him?"

Lou sneered. "We all attacked him."

"Not after we'd seen his face."

"He startled me. Look at the state of him—"

At this, Thierry's hands curled into fists. Beau winced at his purple fingers. "Perhaps we should return to the chapel, procure supplies," he suggested. "You need medical attention—"

Herrrr, Thierry interrupted, the word strained, breathless inside our minds.

Célie gasped at the mental intrusion, her eyes flicking wildly between Thierry and me.

"*Her,* who?" I asked. "What happened to you?" My voice echoed too loud in the dilapidated room, my flushed cheeks and corded neck reflecting back at me in the broken mirrors. I looked unbalanced. Out of control. "Where have you been?"

But it seemed he couldn't answer. Pictures flickered wildly again, each more incoherent than the last. When his black gaze fixed pointedly on Lou, my stomach plummeted. My hands turned to ice. Sick with trepidation, with regret, I spoke through gritted teeth. "Tell me, Thierry. Please."

He moaned and slumped against the balustrade. *Her.*

Célie shook her head as if trying to dislodge an irksome fly. She couldn't shake his voice from her mind, however. Couldn't impede his magic. Dazed, she stammered, "But—but what does Louise have to do with"—she gaped at his various injuries before hastily looking away—"w-with your misfortunes?"

"He can't answer you. Not yet." Coco's fierce gaze never wavered from Lou. "He's exhausted and injured, and the magic required for speech is too much."

"Was he—do you think he was tortured?"

"Yes."

"But *why?*" Célie asked, clearly horrified. "By whom?"

Coco's eyes narrowed. "He answered the last for us."

As one, we all looked to Lou, but her attention remained fixed on Coco. They studied each other for what felt like an eternity—neither blinking, neither revealing a flicker of emotion—before a slow, uncanny grin split Lou's face. "Two princesses fair, one gold and one red," she sang, her voice familiar yet not. "They slipped into darkness. Now the gold one is dead."

A chill snaked down my spine at the odd words. At her smile.

And her eyes—something shifted in them as she stared back at us. Something . . . sinister. They flickered almost silver, like—

Like—

My mind viciously rejected the possibility.

Lou cackled.

Recoiling, Coco exhaled a breathless curse. "No." She repeated the word like a mantra, her hand flying to her collar, tearing her mother's necklace from her throat. "No, no, no, no, *no*—" When she slid the locket along her bloody forearm, it glowed briefly scarlet before clicking open. She thrust it toward me. "Lift her up. Lift her up *now*."

I hastened to comply, but Lou struck with the speed of an adder, her teeth sinking deep into the soft flesh of my cheek. I reared backward with a roar. Lifting her knee with alarming force, she connected with my groin. I folded instantly at the spike of white-hot pain. Stars dotted my vision, and waves of nausea wracked my frame. Vaguely, I heard Lou spring to her feet. But I couldn't move. Couldn't *breathe*.

Célie nudged my ribs with her boot. "Get up," she said, voice low and panicked. Glass crunched and bodies thudded somewhere beyond me. She kicked my side again. "She's getting away. Get *up*!"

Groaning, I forced myself to my feet. Though my entire lower half ached, I leapt to join Beau and Thierry near the door, where they struggled to contain Lou. She hissed and spat as Coco tried to force blood to her lips. With one man holding her on each side, I stepped behind, wrapping an arm around her waist and seizing her hair in my fist. I forced her head backward. The movement bared her face to Coco, who acted quickly, smearing blood across Lou's mouth.

Lou screamed and seized instantly. Blisters formed where the blood touched her lips.

"What is it?" I asked wildly. My stomach rioted with fear, with regret, with treacherous, treasonous *resolve*. I did not let go. "What've you done?"

"I thought your blood would just *subdue* her—" Beau's frantic voice echoed my own. He watched in horror as Lou's back bowed, as she finally slumped in our arms.

Coco stepped back, eyes blazing with satisfaction. "The blood of an enemy poisons."

The blood of an enemy poisons.

Nonsensical words. Ludicrous ones. And yet . . .

Realization began to take shape in my gut, even as my mind still protested.

Beau shook Lou with rising hysteria, his breath labored. His face red. "What the *fuck* does that mean?" He shook her harder. "Is she—have we just—?" But Coco only grasped Lou's chin in answer, forcing open one fluttering eyelid. *She isn't dead.* I repeated the words, trying to calm the thunderous beat of my heart. To ignore my mounting apprehension. *She isn't dead. She isn't dead. She isn't dead. She's just—*

"You said something was clearly wrong with her." Coco retrieved her locket from where it'd fallen to the ground. Lou twitched in response. "You said it went beyond grief."

"That doesn't mean we *poison* her," Beau said incredulously. "She's still *Lou*. She's still my *sister*."

"No." Coco shook her head with vehemence. "She isn't."

Lifting the mirror in the locket to Lou, she revealed the stark truth at last: I held long black hair in my hand, not white. The waist I clasped wasn't right either. Though I couldn't feel her bones beneath my fingers, I could see each rib in her reflection. Her skin appeared sickly. Alabaster pale. Not the smooth and freckled gold I loved. And scarred—so very scarred.

My pulse slowed to a dull, steady rhythm as I took in the truth. A poison all its own. I felt its cold touch in my chest, felt it crystallize around my heart. When it crept down my spine, my legs—debilitating me—my knees gave out, and I crumpled, dragging Lou's body down with me. I stared at her slack face in my lap. Those dark circles beneath her eyes had deepened since yesterday. Her cheeks had grown sharper. She'd been fighting an altogether different poison. A disease.

Nicholina le Clair.

Fire burst through the ice like lava, melting everything in its path. My hands shook. My chest heaved. "Get her out," I snarled.

NO ROSE WITHOUT A THORN

Reid

Coco crossed to the door swiftly in answer, throwing it open, allowing sun to stream into the dilapidated room. But the sun—it did little to banish the shadows now. Instead, it refracted rainbows of light across broken mirrors, and those broken mirrors . . . they didn't work right either. They reflected Lou back to me.

This wasn't Lou.

"Get her out," I repeated, engulfing the would-be Lou in my arms. My shoulders—my back—rounded to shield her from her own reflection. She didn't stir at the contact. Beneath my fingers, her pulse felt thready and weak. Her skin even colder than usual. "Get her out *now*."

"We need to move." Coco hurried back to my side, looping an arm under mine. She tried to hoist me to my feet as angry voices echoed toward us from the cliffs beyond. The villagers. The mob. "They'll be here any moment." To Thierry, she added, "Is there a back entrance?"

He nodded with supreme effort. He still couldn't speak,

however, instead pointing to the bed. Beau rushed to shift it. Below, a heap of ropes and rusted pots hid a trapdoor. Kicking them aside, he struggled to lift the iron handle. "Thank God you have a carriage, Célie."

"I don't—well, actually, I"—she wrung her hands frantically before finishing in a rush—"the wheel shaft snapped on the rocks."

Beau whipped around to stare at her. "It *what?*"

"The whole mechanism is completely busted. We can't use it."

"You said you had a carriage!" Beau heaved at the door with renewed purpose. "That implies a *functional* one."

Célie stamped her foot, her eyes wide on the door. "Yes, well, no one would have let me come along otherwise!"

"Explain." Ignoring them both, I spoke through numb lips. My voice shook as I looked up at Coco. "Please."

She knelt beside us, face softening infinitesimally as she reached out to brush Lou's forehead. "*La Petite Larme* reflects the truth. It cannot lie."

"How?"

"I told you. Its mirror came from a drop of L'Eau Mélancolique. The waters have magical properties. Sometimes they heal, sometimes they harm." She glanced back at the open door, craning her neck to see beyond it. The sun had fully risen now. We'd run out of time. "But they always tell the truth."

I shook my head in a slow, disoriented movement, even as the villagers' voices grew louder. They'd round the bend at any second. "No. I mean how is *she*—how is she inside of—" But I couldn't finish the question. My throat closed up around the words. I dropped my gaze back to Lou. To the blisters on her lips. Self-loathing churned in my stomach. I hadn't noticed. How could I not have *noticed*?

"There's a spell in my aunt's grimoire," Coco explained quickly. Individual voices could be heard now. Individual words. She renewed her efforts to pull me to my feet. "A spell of possession. Old magic." *Possession.* I closed my eyes as Coco's voice darkened. "My aunt betrayed us."

"But *why*? We promised her the Chateau—"

"Perhaps Morgane did too."

"A little help here?" Beau panted. My eyes snapped open as Célie darted to join him.

"But it makes no *sense*," I insisted, voice hardening. "Why would she ally with the witch who's abused your coven at every turn?"

Hinges shrieked as Beau and Célie finally managed to open the trapdoor. The voices outside grew louder in response. Purposeful. Agitated. When neither Coco nor I moved, Beau waved animatedly toward the earthen tunnel. "Shall we?"

Coco hesitated only a second more before nodding. Célie hesitated longer.

"Are we sure this is safe?" She peered into the dark hole with palpable panic. Twin circles of white surrounded her irises. "The last time—"

But Coco caught her elbow as she passed, and the two vanished into the tunnel together. Beau abandoned the trapdoor—it fell open fully with a thunderous *crack* of wood on wood—to help Thierry navigate the room. The latter's entire chest heaved with each breath. Each step. His body was failing. That much was clear. After passing him to Coco, Beau finally turned to me. "Time to go."

"But Lou—"

"Will die if we stay here. The villagers are going to raze this place to the ground." He extended a hand. "Come on, little brother. We can't help her if we're dead."

He had a point. I gathered Lou in my arms and followed.

Beau slipped in behind us, clumsily maneuvering an arm through the gap between door and floor to wrench the bed back in place. He cursed, low and vicious, when the door slammed shut on his fingers. Footsteps thundered overhead not a second later. We didn't linger, racing after the others without another word.

The tunnel let out about a mile down the cliff's face, where a rocky path led to the beach. Black sand glittered in the early morning light, and the rocks of Fée Tombe leered down at us, macabre and unnatural. Like sentient beings. I shuddered and laid Lou's body across the sand, careful to remain in the shadow of the cliffs. If any villager thought to glance below for their *cauchemar*, they wouldn't see us here. Wouldn't descend with their torches and pitchforks.

I whirled to face Coco, who'd extracted a vial of honey from her pack. She fed it to Thierry carefully before lifting her forearm to his lips. He swallowed once, twice, and the contusions on his face immediately began to fade. With a shuddering sigh, he collapsed back against the rocks. Lost consciousness within seconds.

But he would be fine. He would heal.

Lou would too.

"Fix her." My word brooked no argument. "You have to fix her."

Coco glanced at Lou before bending to rifle in her pack, her face a mask of calm. Her eyes remained tight, however. Her jaw taut. "There is no *fixing* her. She's possessed, Reid. Nicholina has—"

"So cast Nicholina out!" I roared, my own mask exploding in a wave of fury. Of helplessness. When Coco jerked upright, glaring at me in silent rebuke, I clenched my head in my hands. Fisted my hair, pulled it, tore it, *anything* to combat the fierce ache in my chest. Shame colored my cheeks. "I'm sorry. I didn't mean it. I'm sorry. Just—please. Cast Nicholina out. Please."

"It isn't that simple."

"Yes, it is." Desperation laced my voice now. I dropped my hands, pivoted sharply on my heel. Paced. Back and forth. One, two, three, four, five, six. One, two, three, four, five, six. Faster and faster, my footsteps carved a jagged path in the sand. "In the book of Mark, Jesus cast demons into a herd of six thousand pigs—"

"This isn't the Bible, Nicholina isn't a demon, and I'm not the son of *fucking* God." She splayed her hands, facade cracking just slightly, and gestured to the sand and waves around us. "Do you see any pigs?"

I spoke through gritted teeth. "I'm *saying* there's a way to remove her. We just have to find it."

"And what happened to the possessed after Jesus cleansed them?"

"Don't be stupid. They were *healed*."

"Were they?" Her eyes flashed, and she tore a vial of blood from her pack. "The human body isn't meant to house more than one soul, Reid."

I spun to face her, my own hands flying upward. "What are you saying?"

"I'm saying this doesn't end the way we want it to end," she snapped. "I'm saying even if we *miraculously* manage to evict Nicholina, Lou won't be the same. To have touched another soul so intimately—not just in a sonnet or some other bullshit symbolic way, but to have actually *touched* another soul, to have shared the same *body*—I don't know if Lou's will survive intact."

"You mean—her soul could be—"

"Fragmented. Yes." She marched forward, dropping to her knees beside Lou with more force than necessary. Black sand sprayed in Lou's pale hair. I mirrored her movements on Lou's other side, sweeping the sand away. "Part of it might go with Nicholina. *All* of it might go with Nicholina. Or"—she uncorked the vial, and the acrid stench of blood magic assaulted my senses—"Lou could already be gone. She was in a bad way. Nicholina wouldn't have been able to possess her otherwise. Her spirit was weak. Broken. If we force Nicholina out, Lou might . . ." She took a ragged breath. "She might be an empty shell."

"You don't know that," I said fiercely.

"You're being willfully ignorant."

"I'm being *hopeful*."

"You think I don't *want* to believe Lou will be okay?" She shook her head in disgust. No—in pity. She pitied me. My teeth clenched until they ached. "That Nicholina will go easily, that Lou will wake up and smirk and ask for fucking sticky buns? You think I don't *want* to pretend the past three months never happened? The past three *years*?" Her voice broke on the last, her facade finally splintering, but she didn't cower. She didn't look away. Even as fresh tears slipped down her cheeks, as every emotion shone clear in her eyes. Every unspoken fear. Her voice flattened as she continued. "You're asking me to hope, Reid, but I can't. I won't. I've hoped too much and too long. Now I'm sick with it. And for what? My mother left, Ansel died, my aunt betrayed me. The person I love most in this world has been *possessed*." She scoffed through her tears, through the smoke that curled from the sand, and lifted the vial to Lou's lips. "Why should I hope?"

I seized her wrist to still the movement. Forced her to meet my eyes. "Because she's the person you love most in this world."

She stared at me over our hands. Her fingers tightened around the vial. "Let me go."

"What are you doing?"

"*Healing* her." She snatched her wrist back, wiping furiously at her tears. "Because apparently, I can't heal myself. I'm sick with hope, but I can't make it go away. It's still here, even now. Poisoning me." When she looked back at Lou, one of her tears dripped from her cheek to Lou's throat. To Lou's scar. Together, we watched—silent and anxious—as the tear sizzled against her skin, transforming the silver gash into something else entirely.

Into a vine of thorns and roses.

Delicate, intricate—still silver and raised on her skin—the scar looked less a disfigurement now. More a masterpiece.

And it was.

Behind us, Célie gasped. A small, wondrous sound. *"Il n'y a pas de roses sans épines."*

There is no rose without a thorn.

Coco said nothing, staring at the scar with a frightfully blank expression. I hardly dared breathe. One blink. Two. When her eyes opened on the third, resolve had crystallized sharp and bright within them. I nearly wept. "My blood poisoned Lou because Nicholina has assumed control," she said. "I can't use it to heal her." She lifted the vial once more. "We'll use my aunt's blood instead. It won't evict Nicholina, but it'll counteract the effects of mine. It's powerful—more powerful than anything on this earth. It's also rare. I nicked it from her tent at the blood camp." She grinned then. A truly terrifying grin. "I'm sure she won't mind."

Parting Lou's lips, she tipped the entire vial between them. Honey followed.

Color immediately returned to Lou's cheeks, and her breathing deepened. The blisters on her mouth vanished. The transformed scar, however, remained. If I looked too close, it seemed to . . . ripple in the breeze. Unconsciously, I lifted a hand to touch it, but

Beau cleared his throat, startling me. He'd moved closer than I'd realized.

I dropped my hand.

"What happens when she wakes up?" he asked.

Coco's grin faded. "We exorcise Nicholina."

"How?"

Silence reigned in answer. Waves lapped the black sand. A lone gull cried overhead. At last, Célie offered a tentative, "You said . . . you said my father's locket—"

"My *mother's* locket," Coco corrected her.

"Of course." Célie nodded in haste, trying her best not to look horribly, terribly out of her depth. "Y-You said the magic of your mother's locket stems from L'Eau Mélancolique. It showed us Nicholina's true reflection."

"And?"

"You said the waters can heal."

"I also said the waters can harm. They were created from the tears of a madwoman." Coco stood, tucking the empty vials back into her pack. I remained beside Lou, tracking the rise and fall of her chest. Her eyelids began to twitch. "They're volatile. Temperamental. They're just as likely to kill Lou as to restore her. We can't risk it."

Between one breath and another, an idea sparked. My gaze darted to Célie. The empty sheath on my bandolier—right above my heart—weighed heavier than usual. I hadn't felt its absence since Modraniht. "We need a Balisarda, Célie." I scrambled to my feet. Sand flew in every direction as I rushed toward her. "Jean

Luc—you can contact him, right?" She murmured something unintelligible in response, her gaze dropping to her boot with keen interest. "If you ask, he'll bring you his Balisarda, and we can—"

"And we can what?" Beau asked, perplexed. Célie stooped to pick up a whitewashed shell, hiding her face altogether. "*Cut Nicholina out of her?*"

"We'd just need to break her skin with the blade," I said, thinking rapidly. Yes. Yes, this could work. I plucked the seashell from Célie's hand and discarded it. She watched it go with a forlorn expression, still refusing to look at me. "A Balisarda dispels enchantments. It would exorcise Nicholina—"

Beau lifted a casual, mocking hand. "Just how deep would we need to cut, brother? Would it be a simple slice down her arm, or would a spear through her heart suffice?"

I shot him a glare before gripping Célie's freed hands. "Write to him, Célie." Then, in another burst of inspiration, I spun toward Coco. "You could magic him the letter, like you did with your aunt in the Hollow."

"Magic a letter into Chasseur Tower?" Coco rolled her eyes. "They'd lash him to a stake by morning."

Célie pulled her hands from mine. Gentle at first, then firm. She reluctantly met my eyes. "It matters not. He will not come."

"Don't be ridiculous. He's mad about you—"

"No, Reid," she insisted. "The conclave has assembled in Cesarine to elect a new Archbishop. It's why he didn't follow me in the first place. His presence has been requested by the priests, by the *king*. He cannot come here, and I cannot ask him—not for this. Not for Lou. I am sorry."

I stared at her for a beat.

Not for this. Not for Lou. The imperiousness in her voice punctured my hope. My foolish optimism. Had she just . . . dismissed us? As if *this* weren't equally important as the Church's conclave? As if this wouldn't decide the fate of the kingdom in a more tangible way? Lou might not have been the only player on the board, but she was certainly the most critical. Only a fool wouldn't recognize that.

Jean Luc wasn't a fool. Neither was Célie.

When I next spoke, ice coated my voice. My veins. "Lou risked everything for you."

She blinked in surprise at my tone. Her mouth opened and closed like a fish. "I— Reid, of course I am very grateful for that! I would never presume to—to deny her heroism or involvement in my rescue, but she—" Cheeks coloring, she leaned closer, as if speaking a dirty word. "Reid, she is a *witch*. If there were even a *possibility* of Jean abandoning his responsibilities to save her—of forsaking his oath as a Chasseur—of course I would ask, but—"

"But we're a witch," Nicholina cackled gleefully, sitting upright in the sand, "so you will not risk the question. Pity. Such a pretty, pretty pity, you are. Such a pretty, pretty porcelain doll."

I jerked her hands behind her back, holding her wrists captive. Beau joined me, poised to help if she struggled. But she didn't. She merely gazed serenely up at Coco, who crouched in front of her. "*Bonjour, notre princesse rouge.* I must say you look terrible."

"You look better than I've ever seen you."

"Ah, we know." Grinning with Lou's lips and Lou's teeth, she gazed down at herself. "This skin suits us."

Flames erupted in my chest at her words. *This skin.* "She isn't a suit," I snarled, tightening my hold on her wrists until they threatened to snap. I knew I shouldn't. I couldn't help it. I wanted to hurt her, to *force* her out violently if necessary. When she laughed in response—tipping her head back with relish, leaning fully into my chest—I felt my hands twist. Another second, and her bones would shatter. Just one more second. Just *one.*

She moaned in pleasure.

"Yes, Reid. *Yes.*" Tongue flicking out to lick her teeth, she dropped her head to my shoulder. "Hurt me. Hurt this body. This suit. We'll enjoy it, yes. We'll savor each bruise."

I recoiled instantly, hands shaking. Blood roared in my ears. Beau caught her wrists between heartbeats. His mouth firmed when she turned to nuzzle his chest. "Mmm. A *prince.* I tasted your cousin once."

Coco gripped her chin, forcing her to meet her eyes. "Kink is consensual, Nicholina. We're going to remove you one way or another. It won't be kinky. It won't be consensual. But it will hurt."

"Oooh, tell me, with the captain's holy stick? I wonder how he'll help you? Will he prick, prick, prick—"

"There shall be no pricking," Beau interrupted. "Holy sticks or otherwise. No unnecessary force either," he added, glancing pointedly between Coco and me. "Nicholina might be, well, *Nicholina,* but she's hiding behind Lou. Who knows what Lou can see and hear? What she can feel?"

Nicholina laughed again. "I said she's dead, she's dead I said. The gold one is gone. I'm here instead."

I ignored her, nodding with a deep breath. Lou wasn't dead. She *wasn't.* Suppressing a red haze of anger, I took her wrists back from Beau. Though physically repulsed—at her, at *myself*—I rubbed the angry skin there with my thumbs. This was Lou. This was Nicholina. They couldn't be the same person, yet somehow, now, they were.

A golden pattern twined around our hands. Slowly, carefully, I fed it until the red tint in my vision faded. As my anger dissipated, so too did the marks on her wrists. With it, another burst of inspiration struck. I couldn't heal her with a Balisarda, but perhaps I *could* heal her with magic. Closing my eyes, breathless with hope, I cast my net of gold in search of an answer. A cure, a restorative. Anything to purge Nicholina's presence. The patterns coiled and undulated in response, but none connected. They simply drifted outward into nothing. Frustrated, I pulled at each one to examine it, to determine its asking price, but I sensed nothing from them. No gain. No give. These patterns weren't functional. When I plucked one on a whim, snapping my fingers, it fell limp in my hand instead of dispersing.

Concentrating harder, I tried again. Nothing.

Though I hadn't routinely practiced magic, I hadn't expected my patterns to simply . . . wilt. *Could* they wilt? No. No, Nicholina must've been blocking me somehow. As often as I'd tried to dispose of my magic, I knew it *couldn't* go away so easily. Perhaps my intent had been wrong.

I focused anew. *Help me exorcise Lou.*

Nothing.

Help me force Nicholina out of Lou.

The patterns floated aimlessly.

Help me heal Lou. Help me hurt Nicholina. Help me make her like before.

The patterns continued to wander. A vessel nearly burst in my forehead now. I lost track of the others' conversation entirely. *Please.* Please. *Help me save her.*

At the last request, the patterns thrummed, growing brighter and collecting into a single cord. Those familiar voices whispered in my ear—*save her, save her, save her*—as I followed the pattern to a face.

To . . . to Morgane's face.

My entire body recoiled in realization, in horror, and my eyes snapped open. Not that. *Anything* but that. The cost would be too great, no matter the outcome.

Still hovering around Nicholina, the others blinked at me. "Er . . ." Beau's brows dipped. "Are you constipated, brother?"

I cast the pattern from my mind. I couldn't act on it. I *wouldn't.* "My magic won't work."

"If you'd been listening"—he jerked his head to Coco—"she just said the magic of one witch can't undo another. It has to be a different kind. Something old. Something powerful."

"What did she have in mind?"

"What do *I* have in mind, actually." Sniffing, he straightened the lace cuff of his sleeve. A ridiculous display. It still dangled from his shoulder. "You're all quite clearly forgetting we have a god at our disposal."

"Ah, *yes*. King of the forest, the horned god." Nicholina rocked back and forth, still laughing maniacally. "Out of all his names, he chose *Claud*."

Coco ignored her, lips pursing in deep thought. "I *could* magic him a letter, but if he remains in the tunnels, it'll burn before he sees it."

Beau looked at her as if she were stupid. "He is a *god*."

My realization dawned at the same moment hers did. "We pray to him," I breathed.

"No." Beau shook his head in distaste. "*You* pray to him. He likes you better than me."

"Everyone likes me better than you."

"Coco doesn't."

"I don't like either of you," she said irritably. "I also don't pray."

"Why not?" I asked.

"Just do it, Reid."

They all looked to me then: Beau petulant, Coco impatient, Célie apprehensive. Heat crept up my throat at the judgment in her eyes, though she tried to hide it. To her credit, she didn't speak. Didn't express any objection, any disapproval. Nicholina had no problem doing it for her. Her voice floated up on a croon. "Pray, huntsman. Pray to the old gods. Will your god mind, I wonder? Will he open the ground and cast you under?"

I cleared the uncertainty from my throat. "God doesn't deny the existence of other deities. He—He just commands us to worship no other gods before Him." When she tilted her head back, a smile nearly cleaving her face in two, I focused my attention on the waves. The horizon. I had a job to do. Unlike Coco, I *did* know how to pray. I'd done it every day—multiple times per day—for most of my life. Praying to Deveraux would be no different.

Except it was. Deveraux wasn't a nameless, faceless divinity. He was a fiddler, for Christ's sake.

I winced at the apt profanity.

Delicate fingers touched my elbow. Célie's earnest face looked up at me. She swallowed, clearly torn, before whispering, "Perhaps you could . . . start as you would the Lord's Prayer."

I was going to Hell. Still, I nodded, closing my eyes and trying to disassociate. To compartmentalize.

Our Father who art in . . . Cesarine, hallowed be thy name.

I felt the others' stares on my burning cheeks. Felt their fascination. Felt like a complete and total idiot. This wasn't going to work. Deveraux was *a* god, not *the* God, and if I hadn't been damned before, I would be now. No sense in further ceremony. Irritably now, I called, *Deveraux? I don't know if you can hear me. You probably can't. It's me. Reid.* Nothing happened. *Nicholina has possessed Lou, and we need you to exorcise her. Please.* Still nothing. I tried again. *Can you meet us? We're in a small village along the coast of northern Belterra called Fée Tombe. It's about three days from Chateau le Blanc. You probably already know that. You probably already know all of this. Or you don't, and I'm talking to myself like a jackass.*

I cringed again, cracking an eye open.

Beau searched the cliffs for a moment before frowning. "Well, that was underwhelming." He glanced to the sky instead. "He is god of the wilderness, right? I didn't mishear his pretentious little speech?"

Coco squinted down the beach. "King of flora and fauna."

"Frankly, his silence is insulting. He could at least send a bird to shit on our heads or something." Beau harrumphed and turned to me. "Are you sure you're doing it properly?"

I scowled at him. "Would you like to try?"

"Let's not be rash. Perhaps you should give it another go."

I forced my eyes shut. Launched another prayer into the ether with all my concentration. *Please, Claud. Answer us. We need help. We need you.* When he still didn't answer, heat prickled my collar. I opened my eyes. Shook my head. "His silence is answer enough."

Beau's hands fell to his hips. "What are we supposed to do, then? We have an empty bandolier, a negligent god, and"—he gestured to Nicholina in distaste—"an *abysmal* poet. Oh, don't give me that look. Your work is derivative at best and juvenile at worst." His frown deepened as he looked to each of us in turn. "What else is there?"

I'm sick with hope, but I can't make it go away. It's still here, even now. Poisoning me.

Only the sound of the waves answered.

And there it was.

I met Coco's gaze directly. "We don't have a choice."

Shaking her head with regret, she closed her eyes and whispered, "The Wistful Waters."

PART II

La nuit porte conseil.
The night brings advice.
—French proverb

DEATH AT THE WATERS

Nicholina

The huntsman and the princess mean to punish me with their poisoned ropes, but we relish the friction. We rub until our wrists are raw. Until *her* wrists are raw. Because it's the mouse and her huntsman who suffer most—she cannot feel it, no, but *he* can. He knows she's trapped. She knows it too. She doesn't see the gold as we do. Though she summons it, though she pleads, it cannot listen. We will not let it. And if voices not our own murmur a warning, if they hiss—if they know we do not belong—the patterns cannot fix it. They can only obey.

We can only obey.

Even if something *is* wrong. Even if below the gold magic, a newfound presence lingers. A newfound presence waits. I do not like it. I cannot use it. Unknown to the mouse, it coils like a snake preparing to strike, to protect. It is a gift, and it frightens us.

We cannot be frightened.

They were never meant to know, to suspect. Now they gather their packs to find L'Eau Mélancolique. Nasty waters. Cursed waters. They hide secrets but reveal them too, oh yes. But they cannot reveal this one. Not mine. They cannot spill its truth.

The princeling watches me while the others pack, but he watches his princess more. It matters not. We do not want to escape. They seek L'Eau Mélancolique, but Chateau le Blanc is its sister. Its neighbor. We will not struggle. We will not fight. Though our right hand is numb, they do not know our left has sensation. Has pain. We can move through pain. And the gold cannot respond to the mouse, no, but it must respond to us. Though I fear it—though it does not trust me—we will send a message. It is necessary.

The gold bursts in a delicate spray as the letters carve themselves into our flesh. Into our back. THEY KNOW. And then—DEATH AT THE WATERS.

Our mistress will not be pleased with us.

I am disappointed, Nicholina, she will say. *I told you to kill them all.*

We glance at our wrists. At the red smear of blood there. *Her* blood. La Princesse Rouge. *Kill them all,* she will say. *Except the princesses.*

Except the princesses.

More potent than pain—more potent than magic—our fury simmers and bubbles, a poison all its own. Noxious. We must not kill her. Though she has forsaken her family, forsaken my mistress, we must obey.

We must make our mistress proud. We must show her. Then she will realize our worth, yes, she will realize our love. She will never speak of her treacherous niece again. But the others . . .

I will drown them in L'Eau Mélancolique.

They think they've trapped me with their ropes, with their threats, with their bane, but their threats ring empty. They know nothing of pain. No, no, no, *true* pain lies outside the sensation of blood and skin. It lies beyond blisters.

It lies deep within.

The mice continue squeaking as the huntsman pulls me forward. Rocks line the path at the edge of the forest. Above us, thick smoke still darkens the afternoon sky. Below, waves crash tumultuously, oh yes. They warn of a storm. Of calamity. *Do not fret, little mouse,* we tell the princess, inhaling deep. Reveling. *The dead should not remember.*

I am not *dead.*

Soon, we promise. *Very soon, your mother shall devour your body, and we in turn shall devour the rest. Like a mouse in a trap.*

One might say you're the mouse now, Nicholina.

Oh?

My mice press closer, ever curious, and we smile as the huntsman scowls over his shoulder. "Is something funny?" he snaps. Though we smile all the wider, we will not answer. He cannot stand our silence. It aggrieves him, and he expels a sharp breath through his nose, muttering a promise of violence. We welcome it. *Relish* it.

The mouse continues without hearing his words. We laugh because he cannot hear hers either.

It's true, she insists. *The others were never meant to know about La Voisin's betrayal. They were never meant to know about* you. *But you*

*failed at the lighthouse, and Morgane won't forget it. I know my mother.
You've broken her trust. She'll kill you at the first opportunity—like a
mouse in a trap.*

We scoff through her nose, smile vanishing. *Our mistress will
protect us.*

*Your mistress will sacrifice you for the greater good. Just like my mother
will sacrifice me.* As if sensing something within us—she senses
nothing—she pushes brazenly against our consciousness. We feel
each kick, each elbow, though she has no feet or arms. It matters
not. She cannot touch us, and soon she will fade into the others.
Soon she will be ours. *You've chosen the wrong side, Nicholina. You've
lost. Reid and Coco will never allow us near the Chateau now.*

My mice hiss and whisper their uncertainty. *She knows nothing,*
I croon to them. *Hush now, mouses.* "The dead should not remember, beware the night they dream. For in their chest is memory—"

The huntsman jerks us forward viciously, and we stumble. A
crow startles from a nearby fir.

It has three eyes.

*You know what's coming, Nicholina. It isn't too late to stop it. You can
still relinquish my body, ally with us before Morgane and Josephine betray
you. Because they will betray you. It's only a matter of time. Me, Reid, Coco,
Beau—we could protect—*

Bitterness pulses through us at the promise. Promises, promises, empty promises. They taste black, acrimonious, and we shall
choke her with them. We shall fill her throat with eyes, eyes, *eyes*
until she cannot breathe beneath their weight. Her consciousness
does not flinch under our pressure. We push harder. We restrict

and contract and compress until at last she recoils, hardening into a small, hopeless blemish. A blight in our nest. *You think you are clever,* we hiss, *but we are cleverer. Oh yes. We shall kill them all—your precious* family—*and you shall forget each one.*

NO—

But her panic means nothing. It tastes empty, like her promise. She is already dead.

Her friends will join her soon.

A MURDER OF CROWS

Reid

Nicholina stopped walking abruptly. Her face twitched and spasmed as she muttered what sounded like *nasty* over and over again. Her mouth twisted around the word. "What's nasty?" I asked suspiciously, tugging her forward. She yielded a single step. Her eyes fixed on a distant tree at the edge of the forest. A fir. "What are you looking at?"

"Ignore her." Coco glanced at us over her shoulder, huddling deeper in her cloak. Along the coast, the wind blustered stronger than in La Fôret des Yeux. Colder. "The sooner we reach a village, the sooner we'll find black pearls for Le Cœur Brisé."

"Pearls." Beau scoffed and kicked a rock into the sea. "What a ridiculous payment."

"Le Cœur guards L'Eau Mélancolique." Coco shrugged. "The waters are dangerous. They're *powerful*. Without payment, no one broaches their shores."

Beside Thierry, Célie wrinkled her nose as I forced Nicholina another step. Two. "And you think we'll find these ... black pearls in the next village?"

"Perhaps not the *next* one." Coco marched back to prod Nicholina along. She'd seemed to grow roots. She still stared at the fir tree, tilting her head in contemplation. I looked closer, the hair on my neck rising. A solitary crow perched there. "But there are a handful of fishing villages between here and L'Eau Mélancolique."

Worse still—the white dog had reappeared, stalking us with those eerie, silent eyes. With a panicked curse, Beau kicked another rock at him, and he disappeared in a plume of white smoke.

"Aren't black pearls . . . rare?" Célie asked delicately.

Yes. Thierry noticed the crow as well. His brow furrowed. Though he hadn't spoken his plans aloud, I suspected he'd travel with us as long as we continued north. Toward L'Eau Mélancolique. Toward Chateau le Blanc. Morgane had tortured him and his brother—that much had been clear in his memories—yet Thierry was here. Toulouse wasn't. *But anything can be bought for the right price*, he said softly.

"*Move*, Nicholina," Coco snapped, joining me at the rope. Nicholina jolted at the words, and we realized our mistake too late. With a vindictive smile, she curled her pointer finger toward her palm.

A single feather fell from the crow's wing.

"Oh, *shit*—" Hastily, Coco tried to recoat the ropes, but the sharp scent of magic already punctured the air. The feather touched the forest floor. Alarmed now, I pulled sharply on Nicholina's wrists, but she smashed her head into my nose, flinging herself backward on top of me. We both crashed to the ground as the feather began to—to *change.*

"A mouse in a trap," she hissed. "Who are the mice now?"

The delicate black filaments multiplied, slowly at first, gaining momentum. Melting together into a misshapen lump of clay. From that clay, another bird formed, identical to the one perched in the tree. The latter cawed again, and from the former, a second feather fell. Another bird rose. Three now. All identical. Nicholina cackled.

But the birds hadn't finished yet. Within the span of five heartbeats, five more had formed. They multiplied faster. Ten now. Twenty. Fifty.

"Stop it." I crushed her hands in mine—those hands that should've been rendered numb, useless—but she twisted away as the birds rose above us in a horrifying black mass. Scores now. Perhaps hundreds. "Reverse the pattern. Do it *now.*"

"Too late." Laughing in delight, she bounced on her toes. "Look, huntsman. It's a murder of crows. They shall peck, peck, peck all your flesh, flesh, flesh." The plague above us built like a tidal wave preparing to break. "Did you hear me, huntsman? Crows. Murderous ones. Tell me, which shall they eat first: Your eyes or your tongue?"

Then the wave broke.

The birds swooped as one, arrowing toward us with alarming speed. Though I threw up my hands against the onslaught, frantically searching for a pattern, they attacked with single-minded focus. Talons slashed my face, my fingers. Beaks tore into my knuckle. Others drew blood from my ear. Coco tackled

Nicholina to the ground, and the two scrabbled in the snow as the crows descended on the others, pecking skin, pulling hair.

Angry caws muffled Célie's panicked shrieks, Beau's vicious curses, Nicholina's outraged cries. I craned my neck to see her writhe as Coco recoated her ropes with blood. The crows didn't stop, however. My own blood streaked down my forearms, my neck, but I kept my head bowed, searching. Gold rose in a tangled web.

There.

I yanked the pattern with all my might, and a powerful gust of wind blasted the birds backward. I braced as it blasted me too. A necessary sacrifice. I needed space to breathe. To *think.*

I secured neither. More birds darted to replace the others, shrieking indignantly.

It was no good. There were too many of them. Too many *patterns.* Seizing Nicholina, I charged toward the cliffs with talons on my neck. Coco sprinted behind with Beau, and Thierry swooped Célie up in his arms to follow.

"Reid!" I didn't slow at my brother's incredulous shout. "What are we *doing?*"

No. I maintained my focus, searched blindly for the right cord. If we hoped to survive with our eyes and tongues, we'd have to jump. My vision pitched at the thought. Madame Labelle had once said a witch could fly with the right pattern. Deveraux had said a cardinal couldn't if it didn't believe.

Well. We were about to test their theories.

If you're listening, Deveraux, please, please, *help us—*

I didn't get the chance to finish the prayer.

A deafening roar shook the cliffside, the trees, and an amethyst wing parted the clouds of smoke overhead. An *enormous* amethyst wing. Membranous. Razor-tipped. Fire sprayed in a wide arch, silhouetting the great, hulking shape of a serpentine body. A scaled leg appeared. A barbed tail.

An entire dragon followed.

THE DRAGON AND HER MAIDEN

Reid

I could only stare as it dove toward us.

It roared again, and from its great mouth, more fire spilled forth. The heat of it nearly blistered my skin. Finally regaining my senses, I dropped to the ground, covering Lou's body as the crows overhead shrieked in agony. Their burning corpses fell around us like macabre rain—those that fell at all. The dragon incinerated most midair. It snapped vicious jaws around others, devouring them whole.

The others had tumbled with me, covering their heads as if their arms might shield them from the dragon's flames. Except Thierry. He too had fallen, but he didn't cower, instead gazing at the dragon with an unfathomable expression. I could've sworn it looked like—like *relief.* But that couldn't be right. We'd leapt from the pot into the fire. Literally.

Even with magic, with knives—even if I'd still wielded my Balisarda—we couldn't hope to defend ourselves against a *dragon.* We had to flee. Now. While we still had a chance. We just needed a diversion. Quickly, I pulled at the golden web of patterns. Something loud. Something big. Something to slow the beast as we sprinted for the cliff. Could I fell a tree? A *forest* of trees? Yes. A cage of wood for—

For a fire-breathing dragon.

I closed my eyes. *Fuck.*

But I was out of time. It'd have to do. Bracing myself for the consequences, I gathered the golden cords in my hand. Before I could pull, however, the dragon snorted, and fresh smoke engulfed us. I glanced up. Spotted a miniature flame through the haze. My eyes narrowed as I looked closer, harder. It wasn't flame at all, but hair. Red hair. A person.

Seraphine smiled down at me from the dragon's back.

The earth shook as it landed with another roar, tossing its great head. Between one blink and the next, its horns unraveled into lavender curls, and its tail rippled into black satin. Reptilian eyes blinked to brown. Amethyst scales smoothed to skin.

"*Thierry.*" Voice low and hoarse, Zenna caught Seraphine in her arms, transformation complete, before placing her swiftly on her feet. They both hurried toward their fellow troupe member. I gaped at them. We all did. Even Nicholina.

Zenna. Seraphine. He reached them just as Seraphine extended her arms, and he lifted her from the ground to spin her in a circle. *You're here.*

"So are you." Zenna didn't look pleased. "Imagine our surprise when Claud sensed you at last—in northern Belterra, of all places. Not the tunnels we'd been searching for weeks." She seized one of his hands. "We've been worried sick, Thierry. Care to tell us where you've been? Where is Toulouse?"

Thierry's face fell.

I pushed myself to my feet, pulling Nicholina up with me. "You—you're—"

"A dragon, yes." Zenna heaved a long-suffering sigh, and smoke curled from her nostrils. After inspecting Thierry one last time, she casually wiped the blood from her lips. She'd painted them gold today. They matched the blooms embroidered on her gown. "*Bonjour, Mort Rouge.* Shall we all digest together? Go ahead. Take a moment."

"It's going to take a hell of a lot longer than a *moment.*" Beau staggered upright and dusted off his trousers in vain. "This is—I can't believe—we shared the same bed, and you never *told* me? I slept with a dragon!" He whirled to face me as if I hadn't heard him, arms splayed wide. "An actual dragon!"

Coco stood faster than humanly possible. "You *what?*"

He lifted his hands just as quickly. "It was entirely platonic." When her eyes narrowed to dangerous slits, he retreated a step in my direction. I ignored him. Nicholina had wormed away from me. I pulled her back with a scowl. "I was cold," Beau continued defensively, "so Seraphine offered her spot."

Seraphine rested her head on Thierry's shoulder. Refused to release his arm. He squeezed her hand with equal fondness, like a brother might a sister. "Some nights I can't sleep," she said.

"Yes, exactly." Beau nodded to Coco. "She's unusually kind, this one, even read to me until I—"

"She *did?*" Coco clapped her hands together with a terrifying smile. "Do tell me more. Tell me *all about* your cold night between Zenna and Seraphine."

"Well, it wasn't cold after that," Beau said, either woefully ignorant or determined to prove his innocence. "I woke up sweltering. It was terrible. Almost died of heatstroke."

"My temperature does run hotter than a human's," Zenna said.

"You see?" Beau nodded again—as if this settled the matter for good—while I tightened Nicholina's binds. "Tell her, Zenna. Tell her it was platonic."

Zenna arched that brow again. "Does it matter?"

Coco mirrored her expression. "Yes, Beauregard. Does it?"

He stared between them in horror.

"Don't make me tie your ankles too, Nicholina." I planted her in front of me when she tried to wriggle away again. "I'll do it. I'll carry you all the way to L'Eau Mélancolique if necessary."

She leaned back, rubbing her cheek against my chest like a cat. "I think I'd like that, huntsman. Oh, yes. I think I'd like it very much."

Mirroring my own frown, Zenna inhaled deeply. If she detected a new scent from Lou, she said nothing, instead shaking her head and returning her attention to Thierry. "Where is your brother, Thierry? Where is Toulouse?"

Though Thierry stiffened, he exhaled a resigned breath. *Toulouse remains at the Chateau. I . . . escaped.*

"Chateau le Blanc?" Zenna's eyes flashed gold. Her pupils narrowed to slits. "Why? What happened?"

Thierry shook his head reluctantly. *Morgane captured us in the tunnels. Or rather,* she *did.* He jerked his chin toward Nicholina, who giggled and leaned forward, smacking her lips as if blowing him a kiss. Zenna growled. Thierry, however, continued undeterred. *When the lights went out, she attacked. She'd cut my arm before I knew what had happened. She drank my blood. When she commanded Toulouse and me to lock ourselves away from La Mascarade des Crânes— to wait for her return—we had no choice. We had to obey.* He looked to me apologetically. *We heard your screams, but we couldn't intervene. I am sorry.*

I returned his gaze with as much solemnity as I could manage while Nicholina attempted to twirl in my arms. Like we were dancing. "I don't blame you for what happened."

He nodded. *She collected us eventually. She and her mistress. La Voisin. They handed us and the wolves over to La Dame des Sorcières without hesitation. Morgane was . . . interested in us. In our magic. She incapacitated us with her injections and led us to the Chateau.*

Smoke unfurled from between Zenna's clenched teeth.

I cannot relive the horrors she inflicted upon us there. I will not. She wanted to—to discover the source of our magic. To test its limits. To study its differences from hers. I believe she did the same with the wolves. He watched silently as Beau, Coco, and I bore Nicholina to the ground like we'd done in the lighthouse. Coco forced her mouth open. Nicholina smashed her forehead into Coco's face. *Or perhaps now she simply likes to inflict pain. Either way, she experimented on us.*

"Thierry," said Seraphine.

"I will rend her head from her shoulders," said Zenna. "And I will eat it."

Célie waited with bated breath. "How did you escape?"

In the end, my voice saved me. Thierry gave a sardonic laugh. *The witches on duty that night were younger. They'd never tended me before. Some sort of celebration raged above, and they arrived late, tipsy, to administer my injection. I could just feel my hands. My feet. I doused the lantern, waited for them to unlock the door. When they did, I projected my voice down the corridor. It disoriented them. When they turned toward the projection, I—I—* He closed his eyes then. As if he couldn't bear the memory. *I overpowered them.*

"They deserved it," Zenna snapped.

Perhaps. Their last cries alerted others to my escape, however. I couldn't find Toulouse. They'd separated us, used each to torture the other— He broke off abruptly, chest heaving. At last, he whispered, *I had no choice but to leave him.*

Seraphine touched his shoulder. "You could never have saved him without first saving yourself."

I lost my way in the forest. I intended to go back. I need to go back. Unshed tears sparkled in his dark eyes when he finally opened them. *I can't leave him alone.*

Zenna bent to meet his gaze directly. "And we won't. We will return to Chateau le Blanc for Toulouse. For the wolves. Then we will raze that wretched castle to the ground with Morgane le Blanc and her Dames Blanches inside. This I promise you."

"Promises, promises," Nicholina muttered beneath her breath. "*Empty* promises. My mistress will be safe, yes, my mistress will be waiting."

"Your mistress will *keep* waiting." I readjusted my grip to enunciate the point. The crows couldn't happen again. We'd need to be more vigilant. From here until L'Eau Mélancolique, I'd release her only for Coco to recoat her ropes. If she still planned to take Lou to Josephine—to Morgane—she'd have to drag my corpse behind. Exhaling slow, heavy, I asked Zenna, "How are you here? You said Claud *sensed* Thierry?"

She turned those golden eyes toward me. "Claud is not like you. He is not even like me."

"Yes, but—why didn't he sense Thierry before? Why couldn't he have found Thierry in the tunnels? Before Morgane—" I stopped myself from asking the next question. Nicholina asked it for me.

"Before she *tortured* him?"

Fresh smoke erupted from Zenna's nose. "Claud has never claimed to be the supreme deity, huntsman. Only divine. He is not omniscient, and he is not omnipotent. He *did* sense Thierry in the tunnels. When the Hellfire sparked, however"—she cast a baleful look in Coco's direction—"he lost the connection. We believed the fire's magic had cloaked Thierry's presence. We didn't realize it was Chateau le Blanc. When Thierry escaped its enchantment three days ago, Claud felt him once more. I flew north to find him immediately." After blinking with secondary, vertical eyelids, her eyes flicked back to brown. "Seraphine and I have scoured these mountains for days. We couldn't fly low enough to properly search without risking exposure, forcing us to *walk*." Her lip curled at the word.

Seraphine patted her arm. "When we reached Fée Tombe this morning, Zenna finally caught Thierry's scent. Still fresh. We followed it to the lighthouse, where we met with an angry mob."

"They'd already chased you away," Zenna growled, "but we followed." A cruel smile curved her painted lips. "The crows were a tasty coincidence. You are welcome."

"Wait a moment." Lifting a finger, Beau frowned between them, incredulous. Perhaps indignant. "Does this mean Claud didn't send you for *us*? Did he not hear our prayer?"

Zenna arched a brow. "Your arrogance astounds."

"It's hardly *arrogant* to expect the help of a friend—"

"He is not your friend. He is a *god*. If you speak to him, he will listen. He will *not*, however," she added firmly, eyes narrowing, "always answer. You do not have a god at your beck and call, any of you. He is of the Old World, and as such, he is bound by the Old Laws. He cannot directly intervene."

Beau's frown deepened to a scowl. I spoke before he could argue. "Can you help us, then? Nicholina has possessed Lou. We have to exorcise her."

"Do not insult my intelligence." Nostrils flaring once more, Zenna leaned forward to stare into Lou's eyes. "Yes, I recognize the blight you call Nicholina. Long ago, I knew her by a different name. *Nicola*."

Nicholina jerked, snarling, "We do not speak that name. We do not speak it!"

Zenna tilted her head. "But I am only a dragon. I cannot exorcise anyone."

"The Wistful Waters can," I said swiftly. "We're journeying there now. Perhaps you could . . . join us." I held my breath as

I waited, hardly daring to hope. With a dragon on our side, we would reach L'Eau Mélancolique within the day. She could fly us there. She could protect us. Nicholina—even Morgane—wouldn't dare threaten a *dragon*.

Zenna didn't answer right away. Instead she stepped backward, away from us. She straightened her shoulders. Stretched her neck. "Witches are gathering at Chateau le Blanc. We have spied them in the mountains, through the forest. More than we have ever seen. If we are to rescue Toulouse, we must act swiftly. I am sorry."

"But we can help you! No one knows Chateau le Blanc like Lou does. After we find the pearls for Le Cœur, after we exorcise her—"

"After Toulouse *dies*, you mean." Her teeth continued lengthening. Her eyes gleamed gold. "Let me be clear, huntsman—Louise le Blanc may be the center of your universe, but she is not the center of mine. I have made my decision. Every moment I spend arguing with you is a moment Toulouse could lose his life."

"But—"

"Every moment I spend arguing with you is a moment I might eat you instead."

"He understands," Coco said smoothly, stepping in front of Nicholina and me. She raised a hand to motion me backward. Nicholina lunged forward to snap at it. "Go." Coco jerked her head. "Save Toulouse and the wolves. Raze the Chateau. Just—kill Morgane while you're at it." She gestured to the crow carcasses all around us. "Two birds, you know."

Zenna nodded as Thierry moved to clasp my shoulder, considered Nicholina's teeth, and thought better of it. *We shall see each other soon,* mon ami.

I managed a small smile. Zenna was right, of course. Lou *was* my priority. Toulouse was theirs. "Good luck, *frère*. Be careful."

The two of them backed toward the cliff without another word. Seraphine lingered beside us, however, as if searching for words and finding none. At last, she whispered, "I wish we could help more."

Coco kicked aside a burning crow. "You've helped enough."

"We will kill Morgane if we can," Seraphine promised.

Zenna didn't change as the werewolves did. Her bones didn't crack or break. Instead, she shifted with the grace and showmanship of a performer, lifting an elegant arm in the air. The other clutched her train. With a flourish of satin, she whirled, and at the center of her turn, her entire body exploded upward. Outward. Like a flame sparked into existence.

"Beautiful," Célie breathed as Zenna extended a jeweled claw to Thierry. He climbed atop it, and she lifted him to the smooth amethyst scales between her wings.

Seraphine smiled. "She is, isn't she?"

Then the dragon collected her maiden, and they launched into the sky.

LITANY

Lou

Reid, Coco, Beau, Ansel, Madame Labelle. Reid, Coco, Beau, Ansel, Madame Labelle.

I repeat the names like a litany in the darkness. I envision each face. The copper of Reid's hair, the cut of Coco's cheekbones, the arch of Beau's brows, the color of Ansel's eyes. Even the fabric of Madame Labelle's gown when I first saw her: emerald silk.

A pretty color, Legion muses, remembering the gold leaf walls and marble floors of the Bellerose, the grand staircase and the naked ladies. *A pretty . . . brothel?*

Yes. Those are tits.

They press closer, listening to each name in fascination, examining each memory. Except Etienne. His presence lingers apart from the rest, but weaker now. Faded. He's forgotten his own name again, so I remind him. I will *keep* reminding him. *Reid, Coco, Beau, Ansel, Madame Labelle. It's Etienne. You are Etienne.*

I am Etienne, he whispers faintly.

We hoped once too. Legion coils around him, not to bolster but to soothe. They see only one outcome to our situation, but I refuse to accept it. I *refuse.* Instead, I remember the scent of Pan's patisserie, the sweet cream of sticky buns. The wind in my hair as I leap rooftop to rooftop. The sensation of flying. The first light of dawn on my cheeks. *Hope matters not.*

Hope matters most, I say fiercely. *Hope isn't the sickness. It's the cure.*

As they consider my words, the darkness saturates with their confusion, their skepticism. I don't allow it to taint my own thoughts. *Reid, Coco, Beau, Ansel, Madame Labelle. Reid, Coco, Beau, Ansel, Madame Labelle.*

The darkness has thinned in places, however, and within it, I can see glimpses of . . . Nicholina. Her memories. They slip across the surface of the shadows, as slick and bright as oil in water, mingling with my own. Snippets of a lullaby here. Ginger hair and warm hands there, a clandestine smile and an echo of laughter—genuine laughter, not the eerie, artificial kind she uses now. Warmth envelops that particular memory, and I realize it isn't her laughter at all. It comes from another, someone she once held dear. A sister? A mother? Pale skin, freckled flesh. Ah . . . a lover.

Reid, Coco, Beau, Ansel . . .

Panic seizes me at the last. There's someone else, isn't there? I've forgotten—*who* have I forgotten?

Legion croons mournfully. *Hope matters not.*

I am Etienne, he breathes.

The darkness drifts apart in answer, revealing the temple of Chateau le Blanc. But this place . . . I've never known it. Blood runs as a river from the temple down the mountainside, soaking the hair and hems of the fallen witches in its path. I recognize none of them. Except one.

Nicholina stands in the center of the clearing, her hands and mouth dripping blood.

Oh my god.

Never before have I seen such carnage. Never before have I seen such *death*. It pervades everything, coating each blade of grass and permeating each beam of moonlight. It hovers like a disease, thick and foul in my nose. And Nicholina revels in it, her eyes bright and silver as she turns to face La Voisin, who steps down from the red-slicked temple. Behind her, she drags a bound woman. I can't see her face. I can't tell if she's alive or dead.

When I look closer, horrified, the scene returns to darkness, and a familiar voice slithers down my spine.

Do you fear death, little mouse?

I do not recoil, reciting their names. *Reid, Coco, Beau, Ansel.* Then— *Everyone fears death. Even you, Nicholina.*

Her ghostly chuckle reverberates. *If you cannot master this one simple fear, you will not survive L'Eau Mélancolique. Oh, no. Our husband plans to baptize us, but he doesn't realize. He doesn't understand. Our mistress will stop him.* The image of a dragon flashes—there and gone before I can properly see. *Even if not, the waters go down, down, down, down, and there they drown, drown, drown, drown.*

My own surprise and bewilderment stretch between us now. L'Eau Mélancolique? Though I wrack my memory to place the name, the darkness only seems to condense around it. I know those words. I *know* them. I just can't—I can't seem to *remember* them. Fresh panic swells at the realization, but—no. I won't give in. I push against the darkness angrily.

Reid, Coco, Beau, Ansel. If Reid plans to baptize me in these waters, he must have a reason. I have to trust him. *I can swim.*

It has nothing to do with swimming. Another image arises through the inky mist. A woman. She walks with purpose toward an unnaturally smooth sea—a sea so smooth it resembles the face of a mirror. Endless. Gleaming. She doesn't break stride as she crosses into its depths, and the water . . . it seems to absorb her movements. Not a single ripple breaks its surface. She keeps walking, submerging her knees. Her hips. Her chest. When her head slips beneath the water, she does not reemerge. *You aren't the first to seek the waters' embrace. Many have come before you, and many will come behind. She cherishes her lovers. She kisses each to sleep, tucking them in bed and healing them with brine.*

A thought strikes like lightning. *What happens to you if I die?*

You've seen an Ascension, she says. I feel rather than see her turn her attention to Etienne, who trembles beneath her observation. He's forgotten his name again. *The soul can live for an indefinite amount of time without a body.*

Indefinite isn't forever.

No.

So . . . you could *die if I do.*

It will not come to that.

Why not?

Another chuckle. *My mistress resides at the Chateau. She will have brought my body. If you succumb to the waters' lure, I will return to it. You will die, and I will live.*

How do you know your body is there? I ask her, pushing again. Repeating the names. *You've failed, Nicholina. My mother attacked you, and you openly challenged her. Your mistress needs her more than she needs you. Perhaps your body won't be there at all. Perhaps you* will *die.*

I have not *failed.* The darkness writhes in agitation at the words, and Legion hisses and spits. The emotion only partly belongs to them, however. No, they also feel . . . curious, and there—deep within their essence—a sense of longing pervades. A sense of hope. *My mistress tasked me with bringing you to Morgane le Blanc—* Nicholina spits the name—*and I will do so, regardless of your foul family. We will see who dances and who drowns.*

Reid, Coco, Beau.

Laughing again, Nicholina withdraws.

Reid Coco Beau Reid Coco Reid Coco Reid Coco

Hold on, Etienne says.

Then he slips into Legion once more.

Wake up, little mouse.

I rouse as if waking from deep sleep, and immediately, I sense something has changed. Though darkness still shrouds everything, it dissipates into eerie wisps at Nicholina's words, drifting in the wind. Clinging to trees and rocks and—

And people.

I study the man beside me. Copper hair tousled, he stalks along a mountain path with rope in his hand, bickering with the young woman beside him. *Look at them, Louise. Look one last time. Your family.* A hateful pause. *Have you forgotten them?*

Though their names rise slowly, as if through tar, I hold on to each for dear life. Reid and Coco. *No.*

Coco's dark eyes—so dark they're almost black—lift to the sky before landing on me. No. Not on me. On Nicholina. "Even with the pearls, you know we're walking into a trap, right?"

Nicholina giggles.

Shaking his head, Reid pulls us along faster. My vision pitches with each step. "Not necessarily."

They will die, Nicholina croons. *All of them. My mistress will come. She will cut out their hearts.*

They will not. She will not.

"We don't have a choice." Reid's words brook no argument. "The Wistful Waters are our only hope."

"And after? What then, Reid?" They both stare at me for a long moment. "Chateau le Blanc is near. With Lou as herself again—if Zenna doesn't raze the castle to the ground—maybe we *could* slip inside and . . . finish this."

The two walking in front slow their footsteps at the last. Both black-haired. Both unfamiliar.

"It was *Nicholina* who wanted to storm the Chateau," Reid says adamantly, "not Lou. Which means it's the last thing we should do. Morgane and Josephine might be expecting . . ."

But his voice begins to fade as the scene shifts around me.

Say goodbye, Louise. The shadows thicken and solidify into darkness once more. It crushes me beneath its weight, and I'm swept away—away from Reid, away from Coco, away from light. *You will not see them again.*

Yes, I will.

The words are quiet and small, so insignificant that Nicholina doesn't hear them. But others do. Though Etienne is gone, Legion wraps their presence around me, folding me into their depths. Their intent is not to harm, however, not to claim. Instead they hold me apart. They keep me together. *Hope isn't the sickness.* They hum their own litany now. Their own prayer. *It's the cure.*

ANOTHER GRAVE

Reid

Célie emerged from the trees clad in fitted pants and knee-high leather boots. She'd tucked a billowing shirt into them. Jean Luc's shirt. I recognized the stitching on the collar, the sleeves. Deep blue—Chasseur blue—and gold. On her head, she wore a feathered cavalier hat. On her face, she wore a neatly trimmed beard.

Beau burst into laughter.

"What?" Hastily, she looked down at herself, smoothing her shirt. Checking her hair, tucking an errant strand into her hat. "Is it not convincing?"

"Oh, it's convincing," he assured her. "You look like an idiot."

Beside me, Nicholina giggled from her spot on the ground. We'd bound her wrists again, coating her entire hands in Coco's blood. Now she couldn't move a finger if she tried.

Startled, perhaps even scandalized by Beau's bald honesty, Célie's brows shot up. "Cosette often wears trousers—"

"But not a *beard*," Beau said. "You don't need a disguise, Célie. Your face isn't on those wanted posters."

"Well, I—I just thought I might—" Her face flamed. "Perhaps I'm not wanted by the Crown, but my father will eventually search for me. Jean Luc has spies throughout the kingdom. Should I not take precautions?" At our impassive stares, she lifted her chin defiantly and repeated, "Cosette and Louise wear trousers."

Beau spread his hands with a smirk. "And there it is."

Her eyes narrowed. "Your Majesty, please take no offense, but you are a good deal less pleasant than I would have liked to believe."

Still chuckling, he slung an arm over Coco's shoulder. "None taken, I assure you."

Coco pushed him away. "He gets that a lot."

Crooking his finger at Célie, Beau led her into the first village.

We'd decided the two of them would search for black pearls. Though not ideal, Coco and I needed to remain with Nicholina. We couldn't easily drag her through the streets with bound and bloody hands. I shuddered to think of her actually *speaking* if we did find someone who sold them.

By the third village, I'd heard enough of her to last a lifetime.

She reclined atop a rock on the edge of the forest now, moaning and tugging against her rope. Her hands hung limp and useless from her wrists. Like bloody carcasses. "We're *hungry*. Shall we venture into just one hamlet? Just one? Just one, just one, to have some fun?" She cast me a wicked glance. "Just one to find a sticky bun?"

I looked away from her blistered hands. Couldn't bear the

sight of them. "Shut your mouth, Nicholina."

Coco lazed within the roots of a knotted tree while we waited. She picked at the fresh cut on her palm. "She won't stop until you do."

"Oooh, clever mouse." Nicholina sat up abruptly, leering at me. "We don't just live beneath *her* skin, no no no. We live beneath *yours*. It's warm and it's wet and filled with *short— angry—breaths—*"

"I swear to God, if you don't stop talking—"

"You'll do *what*?" With a cackle, she pulled at her ropes again. I pulled back. She nearly toppled from the rock. "Will you harm this pretty skin? Will you strike this freckled flesh? Will you punish us, oh husband, with a good, hard *thrash*?"

"Ignore her," Coco said.

Heat suffused my face. My neck. My hands clenched the rope. I could ignore her. I could do it. She wanted a reaction. I would give her none.

Another handful of minutes passed in silence. Then—

"We need to relieve ourselves," Nicholina pronounced.

I scowled and shook my head. "No."

"Perhaps in the trees?" She continued as if I hadn't spoken. "Perhaps they deserve it. Naughty, naughty trees. Perhaps they'll *observe* it." Rising to her feet, she cackled at her own perverse joke. I tugged her rope irritably.

"I said no."

"No?" Disbelief—still feigned, still disingenuous, as if she'd somehow expected my response—laced her voice. *Lou's* voice.

The sound of it made me ache and rage in equal measure. "You'd have us piss down our leg? Your own wife?"

"You aren't my wife."

A sick wave of regret washed through me at the familiar words. At the memory. The ring I'd once given Lou, golden band and mother-of-pearl stone, weighed heavy in my pocket. Like a brick. I'd kept it with me since Léviathan, anxious to return it to her. To slide it back on her finger where it belonged. I would do just that at L'Eau Mélancolique. I would marry her right there on the beach. Just like last time, except proper now. Real.

Nicholina gave a feline grin. "No, we aren't your wife, are we? Which makes us your . . . what, exactly?" A pause. She leaned closer, brushing her nose against mine. I jerked back. "She fought, you know," she breathed, still grinning. My entire body went still. My entire being. "She screamed your name. You should have heard her in those last moments. Absolutely terrified. Absolutely *delicious*. We savored her death."

It wasn't true. Lou was still in there. We would free her.

"She can't hear you, pet." Nicholina pursed her lips in a sugar-sweet display of sympathy, and I realized I'd spoken the words aloud. "The dead don't have ears. She won't hear your cries, and she won't see your tears."

"That's enough," Coco said sharply. Though I could see her trying to tug the rope from me, I couldn't feel the movement. My fist remained locked. Blood roared in my ears. "Shut the hell up, Nicholina."

She fought, you know.

Nicholina giggled like a little girl. Shrugged. "All right."

She screamed your name.

I took a deep breath. In through my nose. Out through my mouth. One after another. Again and again.

You should've heard her in those last moments. Absolutely terrified.

I should've been there.

It's your fault it's your fault it's your fault

Beau and Célie arrived at that moment, and Coco succeeded in tugging the rope from me. Glowering at their empty hands, she snapped, "Nothing? Again?"

Célie shrugged helplessly while Beau lifted said hands in a lackadaisical gesture. "What would you like us to do, Cosette? Shit the pearls into existence? We aren't *oysters.*"

Her nostrils flared. "Oysters don't shit out *pearls,* you idiotic piece of—"

"Shit?" Nicholina supplied helpfully.

Coco closed her eyes then, forcing a deep breath, before looking up at the sky. Though smoke still obscured the sun, it must've been late afternoon. "The next village is about two hours up the road. It's the last one before L'Eau Mélancolique." Her expression hardened, and she met my gaze. Jaw still clenched, I nodded once. "Reid and I will search it too."

"What?" Beau looked between the two of us incredulously. "Célie and I are *perfectly* capable—"

"I am *sure* that's true," she snapped, "but this isn't the time for a pissing contest. We need to find those pearls. This is our last chance."

"But"—Célie leaned forward, blinking rapidly—"but *Nicholina*..."

Coco lifted her fist. She'd wrapped the rope around it. The movement forced Nicholina closer, and Coco stared directly into her eyes. Every word promised violence. "Nicholina will behave herself. Nicholina doesn't want to die, and she's wearing the face of the most notorious witch in Belterra." She tugged her closer. Nicholina had stopped grinning. "If she causes a scene—if she steps one *toe* out of line—they'll lash her to a stake right there in Anchois. Nicholina understands that, doesn't she?"

Nicholina sneered. "You won't let us burn."

"We might not be able to save you."

Nicholina glowered now but said nothing. Though I reached for her rope once more, Coco shook her head and started forward. "She stays with me," she said over her shoulder. "You can't bring yourself to kick her ass, but I can. It's what Lou would want."

Anchois boasted three dirt-packed streets. One of these led to the dock, where dozens of fishing boats bobbed along black water. One housed the villagers' ramshackle dwellings. Carts and fish stands littered the market of the third. Though the sun had fully set, firelight danced on merchants' faces as they hawked wares. Shoppers slipped arm in arm between them, calling to friends. To family. Some clutched brown paper packages. Others wore seashell necklaces. Bits of agate sparkled in the hair of impish children. Gnarled fishermen gathered at the beach to sip ale in groups of twos and threes. Grousing about their wives. Their grandchildren. Their knees.

Coco peered down the market street, trying to see through the gaps in the crowd. She'd tied one of Nicholina's hands to hers. The sleeves of their cloaks hid all blisters. All blood. "We should split up. We'll cover more ground that way."

I tugged Célie away from a cart of scrying stones. "Fine. You two go to the dock, ask if anyone has heard of black pearls in the area. We'll search the market."

A gleam of wonder entered Célie's eyes as she watched a young man pull a roughly hewn flute from his pocket to serenade another. Some maidens nearby giggled. One even stepped apart from the rest, brave enough to dance. Célie nodded eagerly. "Yes. Let us do that."

Coco eyed us, skeptical. "Is this what you've been doing, Célie?"

Beau scoffed and shook his head. Mutinous.

I gripped Célie's elbow with pointed assurance. "If they're here, we'll find them."

Though Coco still seemed doubtful, she relented with a nod, fidgeting with the locket at her throat. Readjusting her hood. "Fine. But you'd better search the market, not stroll down memory lane." She jabbed a finger at my nose. "And be in plain sight when we get back. I want to see hands." Jerking her chin toward Beau and Nicholina, she left Célie and me standing alone in humiliated silence.

Heat pricked my ears. Her cheeks burned tomato red.

"Thanks, Cosette," I muttered bitterly. Forcing my jaw to unclench, I took a deep breath, adjusted my own cavalier, and guided Célie into the street. When the merchant rattled his scrying stones in our direction—he'd carved them from fish bones—I kept walking. "Don't listen to her. She's . . . going through a lot."

Célie refused to meet my gaze. "I don't think she likes me."

"She doesn't like anyone but Lou."

"Ah." For a split second, resentment flashed across her doll-like features. But then she smoothed her face into a polite smile, squaring her shoulders. Straightening her spine. Always the lady. "Perhaps you're right." Her smile turned genuine as she spotted a shabby confiserie. "Reid, look!" She pointed to the tins of almond candy in the window. Calisson. "It's your favorite! We simply must purchase some." With a pat to her leather satchel—I'd slung it over my shoulder, where it jostled against my own—she tried to steer me toward the confiserie's pink door.

I didn't move. "We're here for black pearls. Not candy."

Still she tugged on my wrists. "It'll take two minutes—"

"No, Célie."

As if Coco's reprimand had struck the ground between us like a bolt of lightning, she dropped my hands. Pink returned to her cheeks. "Very well. Lead the way."

We made it all of two minutes before she stopped again. Anger forgotten, she peered ahead at a group of men huddled around a barrel. Eyes wide and childlike, curious, she asked, "What are they doing?"

I glanced over their shoulders as we passed. A handful of dirty bronze *couronnes* littered the top of the barrel. A pair of wooden dice. "Gambling."

"Oh." She craned her neck to see too. When one of the men

winked at her, motioning her closer, I rolled my eyes. Some disguise. She tapped her satchel again, oblivious. "I should like to try gambling, I think. Please hand over my bag."

I snorted and kept walking. "Absolutely not."

She made an indignant noise at the back of her throat. "I beg your pardon?"

Though I'd barely met Violette and Victoire, I imagined this was how an elder brother felt. Exasperated. Impatient. Fond.

"Reid."

I ignored her.

"*Reid.*" She actually stamped her foot now. When I still didn't turn, didn't acknowledge her inane request, she seemed to snap, tearing after me and latching on to the bag with both hands. Hissing like a cat. Her nails even scored the leather. "You will release my bag this *instant*. This is—you—this is *my* bag. You cannot control it, and you cannot control *me*. If I wish to gamble, I shall gamble, and *you* shall—" Finally, I swung around, and she swung with me. My hand shot out to steady her when she stumbled backward. She swiped it away with an unladylike snarl. "*Give me my bag.*"

"Fine. Here." I tossed the satchel to her, but it slipped from her fingers. Coins and jewelry alike spilled across the snow. Cursing, I knelt to block the gamblers' view with my shoulders. "But you promised to help us. We need your *couronnes* to buy the pearls."

"Oh, I am well aware you need my help." Angry tears sparkled in her eyes as she too knelt, returning fistfuls of treasure to her bag. "Perhaps *you* are the one in need of a reminder." I glared pointedly at interested passersby. My hands swiftly joined hers, and though she tried to swat me away—

I straightened abruptly, my fingers curling around familiar glass. Cylindrical glass. Cold glass. Her nails cut into my knuckles as I moved to withdraw it. "Wait!" she cried.

Too late.

I stared at the syringe in my palm. "What is this?"

But I knew what it was. We both did. She stood perfectly still now, her hands knotted together at her waist. She didn't blink, didn't breathe. I didn't blame her. If she moved, her tearful facade might shatter, and the truth might spill forth. "Where did you get it?" I asked, voice hard.

"Jean gave it to me," she whispered, hesitating briefly, "when I told him I was leaving."

"When you told him you were coming to find us."

She didn't contradict me. "Yes."

My gaze snapped to her face. "Were you going to use it?"

"What?" Her voice cracked on the word, and she clutched my forearm, oblivious to Coco's and Beau's heads bobbing through the crowd. They hadn't yet spotted us. "Reid, I would never—"

"You're still crying."

She wiped her face hastily. "You know I cry when I'm upset—"

"Why are you upset, Célie? Did you think you'd lost it?" My fingers closed around the glass. The hemlock injection didn't warm, however. Devil's Flower, the priests had called it. It'd grown on the hillside of Jesus's crucifixion. When his blood had touched the petals, they'd turned poisonous. "It shouldn't matter if you had. You weren't going to use it."

"Reid." Her hand on my arm crept downward. Even now, she ached to have it in her possession. "It was just a precaution. I never planned to use it on you or—or anyone else. You must believe me."

"I do believe you." And I did. I believed she'd never *planned* to use it. If our reunion had gone wrong, however, she wouldn't have hesitated. The fact that she'd brought it here, that she'd *hidden* it, meant she'd been prepared to hurt us. I tucked the syringe in my pocket. "You know this is poison, right? Standard issue. Witch or no, it'd incapacitate you much faster than it would me. It'd take down Jean Luc. King Auguste. All of them." She blinked in confusion, confirming my suspicions. She'd thought it a weapon unique against witches. I shook my head. "Fuck, Célie. Are you really that afraid of us? Of me?"

She flinched at the profanity, color rising high on her cheeks. But not in embarrassment. In *anger.* When she lifted her chin, her voice didn't waver. "Is that even a question? Of *course* I fear you. A witch murdered Filippa. A witch locked me in a coffin with her remains. When I close my eyes, I can still feel her flesh on my skin, Reid. I can still *smell* her. My *sister.* Now I'm terrified of the dark, of sleep, of dreams, and even awake, I can hardly breathe. I'm trapped in a nightmare without end."

My own anger withered to something small. Something shameful.

"So, yes," she continued fiercely, fresh tears spilling down her cheeks, "I packed a weapon against witches. I hid it from you.

How could I do otherwise? Whether or not I like it, you're a witch now. You're one of them. I'm trying—truly, I am—but you cannot ask me not to protect myself." She took a deep, steadying breath then, and met my gaze. "Truthfully, you cannot ask me anything. I won't live in another grave, Reid. You've moved on. It is time for me to do the same."

Though a hundred words of comfort rose to my lips, I didn't utter one. They weren't enough for what she'd suffered. No words would ever be enough. I handed her the syringe instead. She seized it instantly, lifting it to her eyes with a truly terrifying expression. Not like Lou. Not like Coco. Not like Gabrielle or Violette or Victoire. Like Célie.

"When I next see Morgane, I will stab this needle in her heart," she promised.

And I believed her.

A SIMPLE FAVOR

Reid

Beau, Coco, and Nicholina found us shortly after. I drew them into the shadow of an abandoned stall, away from the whispers of the villagers. "Well?" Coco looked between the two of us expectantly. "Anything?"

Nicholina snickered while Célie stuffed the injection into her pocket. "We, ah—my apologies, but Reid and I got . . . well, *distracted.*"

Coco frowned. "Distracted?"

"We haven't found them yet," I said shortly, hoisting her satchel back over my shoulder. "We need to keep looking."

"The waters go down, down, down," Nicholina sang, her face hidden within the hood of her cloak. "And there you'll drown, drown, drown."

Coco lifted a hand to rub her temple. "This is such a shit show. No one at the dock knew anything, either. One of them threw a *hook* at us when we asked about black pearls. He must've heard rumors about L'Eau Mélancolique." She sighed. "Fishermen. They're superstitious on the best of days, but they fear melusines most of all. I wouldn't be surprised if he calls the Chasseurs. They'll be swarming these streets by morning."

Beau held up a stack of rumpled wanted posters in his hands. "At least he didn't recognize us."

"And we won't be here by morning." I flicked a finger, and the last of my anger leapt onto the papers. Beau yelped when they caught flame, dropping them into the cart. Our faces burned to ash within seconds. "The stalls will be closing soon. Let's turn this market upside down."

An hour later, we regrouped at the end of the street. Bad-tempered. Empty-handed.

Nicholina swayed in the wind. A tendril of white hair swept free of her hood. "Drown, drown, drown."

Scowling, Coco peered through the crowd again. But one could hardly call it a crowd now. Most of the villagers had retired for the night. Only a handful still danced in the street. They stumbled from wine, clutching each other and giggling. By the water, only the staunchest of fishermen remained. And the drunkest. "We should go. There's nothing here. Tomorrow we can circle back—"

Beau slashed a curt hand. "I *told* you. We looked everywhere. There were no pearls in any of those villages."

I too scoured the carts nearest us. Whitewashed coral. Drift-wood chimes. Baskets of woven seaweed, cups of crystallized sea salt, jars of preserved anchovies. Jars and *jars* of anchovies. Beau knocked one to the ground in frustration, and the glass shattered. Célie leapt backward with a startled cry. When the oil soaked her boots, he snorted, and she retaliated by kicking an anchovy at his face.

Children. I was surrounded by children.

"Enough." Voice sharp, I pivoted in one last circle to ensure I hadn't missed anything. But my desperation yielded nothing new. Anchois boasted no pearls, black or otherwise.

"My apologies." Célie sniffed in a dignified way. "It shan't happen again."

"You're going to smell like fish for at *least* a fortnight," Beau said.

Exhaling hard through my nose, I wheeled to face him. "Could you at least *try* to stop provoking everyo—"

A wooden sign behind him caught my attention. A familiar name.

LA CURIEUSE MADAME SAUVAGE
PRICES AVAILABLE UPON REQUEST

I frowned and nudged him aside. Madame Sauvage. I knew that name. How did I know that name? The sign itself— half-hidden and half-rotted—stood between a stall of spindly combs and a barrel of fish oil. I pointed to it. "That wasn't there before, was it?"

Coco's eyes narrowed as she followed my finger. "I don't see anything."

"Well, look. It's right—" I blinked, and the words died on my tongue. I was pointing at the fish oil, not the sign. Because there *was* no sign. Dropping my finger hastily, I shook my head.

Blinked again. "I—never mind."

"Nothing there," Nicholina said, her voice unexpectedly harsh. She tugged on Coco's hand. "Nothing, nothing."

Coco huffed impatiently before drawing her cloak more tightly around her. "If you're *quite* done—" But her eyes widened when she glanced back. "That—that wasn't there before."

Slowly, as if cornering a frightened animal, my gaze returned to the stall and barrel. Sure enough, the wooden sign had rematerialized between them. Emerald and aubergine silk fluttered from the cart behind it. As if it'd been there all along.

"Magic," Célie whispered.

Coco and I shared a wary glance before creeping forward.

Though I clutched a knife in my bandolier, the cart itself didn't *seem* dangerous. Jewelry of all shapes and colors gleamed from the cluttered shelves. Real jewelry. With gemstones and precious metals, not fish bones and octopi tentacles. An assortment of dusty bottles joined them. Dried flowers. Leather-bound books. On a ledge at the back, a crimson-and-gold snake slumbered in a glass cage. Célie approached it in fascination.

I took a deep breath, trying and failing to suppress my unease.

No, it didn't seem dangerous, but there—displayed proudly on the middle shelf—three black pearls nestled in a bed of velvet. It couldn't have been coincidence. When Beau moved toward them, eager, I stilled him with the shake of my head, glancing around for the owner. This mysterious Madame Sauvage. Though nowhere to be seen, she'd tacked a scrap of parchment to the sign:

Coco caught the tail of the emerald silk between two fingers. "Perfect. Makes this easy."

"Too easy," I said before grasping her meaning. Then— "Wait. You want to *steal* them?"

"I'm a thief, Reid." Gaze suddenly alert, she glanced from the cart to the street, assessing the landscape. Tracking the couple closest us. They strolled past hand in hand, oblivious to our presence. When I stepped in front of her, blocking her view, she smirked. "Lou is a thief too, you know. And as soon as we've saved her, you can soak in your virtue until your fingers wrinkle with it. Until then . . ." She slipped past me, lifting a casual shoulder. "We need these pearls. It's better if no one sees our faces." Her eyes lit on something behind me, and she laughed, tossing them my way. "Perfect. A reward for your silence."

I caught the leather pants against my chest. "This isn't funny."

"*Au contraire.* Lou is going to need a laugh after all of this." Her smirk faded then. "You told me to hope, Reid, but hope means nothing without action. I will do whatever it takes to save her. *Whatever* it takes. Are you willing to do the same? Or shall Lou fall on the sword of your principles?"

I glared at her.

"Fabulous. Now. Don't move. You make an excellent shield."

Jaw clenched, I crushed the leather in my fist, watching as she sauntered toward the pearls. When Nicholina moved to knock them aside with her elbow, I caught the rope, untying it from Coco with deft fingers. I wrapped it around my own wrist instead. When Coco glanced back at me, I nodded. This wasn't right, but Lou wasn't right, either. The *world* wasn't right. After L'Eau Mélancolique, I would pay Madame Sauvage back with interest. I would find a dozen black pearls to replace these three, and—

Wait.

Only three?

"There are five of us," I said.

"That shouldn't be a problem." Heart leaping to my throat, I whirled toward the new voice. Coco's hand froze above the pearls. An elderly woman stepped around the cart, her shoulders stooped and her face deeply lined. She wore an olive scarf around her silver hair. Innumerable rings on her ears, her fingers, her toes. Her *bare* toes. An emerald cloak dragged on the ground behind. She grinned, revealing crooked teeth. "Humans can't enter L'Eau Mélancolique. The waters drive them mad."

Nicholina hissed beneath her hood, drawing into me.

I studied the woman. "Have we . . . met before, *madame?*"

"Perhaps? Then again, perhaps not. I have one of those faces, I fear. *Le visage de beaucoup, le visage d'aucun.* The face always seen—"

"—the face never remembered," I finished the old adage by rote. But . . .

Her smile turned knowing. "Hello, dearies. Welcome to my cabinet of curiosities. How may I serve you today?"

Recognition finally dawned at her words, and different shelves rose in rapid succession, each a knife wound in my memory: dancing rats and glass beetles, pointed teeth and butterfly wings. An ugly marionette, a mother-of-pearl ring, and . . . an old woman.

An old woman who'd known more than she should.

Might I interest you in calla lilies? They're said to symbolize humility and devotion. The perfect blooms to end any lovers' quarrel.

Half-healed punctures, all. Still bleeding at the edges.

"Madame Sauvage," I said, lip curling.

She smiled kindly. "*Bonjour*, Reid. What a pleasure it is to see you again." Her smile faded as she took in Nicholina, whose face remained hidden. "Oh, dear." The woman tittered. "I would greet our fair Louise, but it seems another has taken residence—" She stopped abruptly, tilting her head. "Well, well, well . . . more than one someone, I think, and a powerful one at that." Her smile returned full measure, and she clapped her hands in delight. "Louise le Blanc, both cursed *and* blessed. How *riveting*."

More than one someone? I frowned. She meant Nicholina, of course, but—*blessed?*

"You would know," Nicholina snarled with something like fear. "Oh, yes, you would recognize—"

"Ah, ah, ah." With a shake of Madame Sauvage's finger, Nicholina's voice ceased. Her body seemed to grow roots. "That is *quite* enough from you, Nicola. There shall be no blood or secrets spilled in my cart. Please, be still and observe."

"How do you—?" I asked.

"You three know each other?" Célie interrupted, nonplussed.

Madame Sauvage winked. The gesture didn't suit her withered

face. "I suppose one could say that. Last we met, their quarreling nearly shattered my windows." Though she adopted an air of careful indifference, curiosity sparkled in her dark eyes. "I trust our lovebirds have reconciled?"

Still incredulous, confused, I threw the leather pants on a nearby shelf. "It's none of your business."

She *hmph*ed at my tone, but her impish smile didn't waver. Her gaze flicked from me to Célie, lingering on where Beau and Coco hovered near the snake. "Just so, and yet . . . it seems you are once again in need of assistance."

"How much for the pearls?" Coco asked.

"The pearls," Madame Sauvage repeated softly. She looked positively spry. "Well, my dear, the pearls are nearly priceless. What are you willing to give for them?"

Anything.

Nicholina still hadn't moved.

"We have coin," I said automatically. "Lots of coin."

"Oh dear." Madame Sauvage tittered again and shook her head. "Oh dear, oh dear, oh dear. That won't do, will it? I don't sully my hands with money."

A flash of surprise crossed Coco's face. "What *do* you want, then?"

"Whatever it is," Beau muttered, "it can't be good."

Madame Sauvage's entire face split into a grin. "Oh, *no*, Your Highness, you have entirely the wrong idea! Never fear, 'tis nothing nefarious. You see, I deal only in simple favors. Just tokens, really. Trifles."

I scowled. "Nothing simple about a favor."

"What favor?" Coco asked, part apprehensive and part impatient. "Just tell us, so we can do it."

"Of course, of course." If possible, Madame Sauvage's smile widened. "As I said, it's quite simple: one favor for one pearl. My apologies," she added to Beau and Célie, inclining her head, "but truly, L'Eau Mélancolique is no place for humans. 'Tis dark and dangerous, dears. More than monsters lurk within its depths."

Beau scoffed in disbelief. "What are we supposed to do, then? Twiddle our thumbs on the shore?"

"How do you know so much about L'Eau Mélancolique?" Coco asked at the same time.

"Tell us the favors." I raised my voice over theirs. Yes, this strange little cart had appeared from thin air. This stranger little woman seemed to know all our plans, to know Nicholina. Truthfully, she seemed more . . . inquisitive than nefarious, and what choice did we have? We needed the pearls. *Her* pearls. We could deal with the consequences after we'd procured them.

The woman in question rubbed her gnarled hands together. "We'll start with the easy one, yes? Just a kiss."

Just a kiss.

Silence descended like a knife dropped point-first. Instead of lodging at our feet, however, it hovered over our heads. Deadly and sharp. No one dared look at another. I didn't glance at Célie or Nicholina. Neither peeked at me. Beau and Coco stared resolutely at the floor. Finally, I asked, "Between . . . who?"

Cackling, Madame Sauvage lifted a crooked finger to Beau and Coco.

The knife hit its mark.

Beau stiffened. Coco gaped. The tension knotting my own spine, however, left in a rush, and I tried not to sigh with relief. Célie had no qualms. She sagged against a basket of beetles with a shaky laugh.

"The liars, of course." Madame Sauvage nodded with what might've been encouragement. Or glee. "They shall kiss, and the truth shall out. There is truth in a kiss," she added to Célie and me conspiratorially. Célie nodded, though I suspected not because she agreed. No. Because she'd do anything to avoid Madame Sauvage's ire now.

I nodded right along with her.

Coco barely moved her lips as she mumbled, "I'm not lying about anything."

Beau snorted at that.

Though sympathetic to Coco's plight—truly—I reached over to squeeze her shoulder. "Whatever it takes, right?"

She scowled at me.

I smothered a grin. I wasn't enjoying this. I wasn't.

Pushing my hand aside with a muttered curse, she stepped forward. Stopped. Closed her eyes and inhaled deeply. When she opened them again, stony resolve had hardened in their depths. She nodded once to Beau, who looked strangely reluctant. He didn't shrink from her gaze, however. Didn't ease the tension with a joke. He simply stared at her, unmoving. "Just do it," she said. "Hurry up."

He grimaced at the words but took a small step forward, lowering his voice. "If I remember correctly, Cosette, you don't like it hurried." Another step. Coco's fingers still trembled. She fisted them in her skirt. "Not with me."

"I don't like anything with you."

One side of his mouth quirked as he looked down at her, but my own humor faded at his expression. I didn't want to see the emotions in his eyes. I didn't want to see the tenderness. The ache. Even so, his reluctance shone just as clear. He didn't want to kiss her. Not here. Not now. Not like this. "Liar," he whispered.

Then he lowered his lips to hers.

A heartbeat passed as they stood there, bodies rigid and separate. Lips barely touching. Two heartbeats. Three. With a sigh of resignation, Beau moved to pull away, but Coco—

I rolled my eyes.

She wouldn't let him. Her hands crept up his neck, into his hair, holding him there. No. Bringing him closer. Deepening the kiss. When her lips parted on a sigh, he didn't hesitate, his arm snaking out around the small of her back and hauling her flush against him. But it wasn't close enough. Not for Coco. She pressed harder, clutched him tighter, until he chuckled and walked her backward. When her back hit the nearest shelf, he lifted her atop it, spread her knees to push between them. Slow and measured. Unhurried. Until she bit his lip. Something seemed to snap in him then.

Beside me, Célie watched their hands grow frantic—their breaths louder—with round, startled eyes. Her cheeks flamed scarlet. "Oh my," she said.

I averted my gaze. "This has been a long time coming."

"Or *not* coming," Madame Sauvage said, arching a wry brow.

I cringed at the innuendo. "How old *are* you?"

"Young enough, boy. I'm young enough."

Right. With *that* imagery in my head, I cleared my throat. Beau had just slid a hand up Coco's calf, hooking it around her knee to pull her closer. His fingers caressed her skin there. I repeated the sound, louder this time, and grinned despite myself. "Hello! Yes, pardon!" My grin deepened when he pulled back abruptly, as if surfacing from deep water. Blinking slow. Breathing heavy. "As it seems to have escaped your notice, *there are other people here.*"

He still didn't acknowledge us, however. He stared at Coco instead. She stared at him. Neither spoke for several seconds. At last, with infinite gentleness, he brushed his lips against her forehead and stepped away, tugging her skirt back into place. "We'll finish this later."

Her awareness seemed to return then. Her sense. She leapt from the shelf hastily, knocking aside a bin of glass eyes. They scattered across the floor of the cart. When she tripped on one, pinwheeling into Nicholina, Beau caught her arm. She tried to tug it away. "Don't *touch* me. I'm fine." She slipped on another eye, kicking it viciously in response. "I said I'm *fine.*"

His face fell at her outburst, and he scowled, releasing her. "Say it one more time." When she stumbled away, nearly upsetting another basket, he shook his head. "Maybe I'll believe you."

She watched him stalk from the cart with overbright eyes, her arms wrapped tight around her middle. Her shoulders hunched. As if their kiss had inflicted a physical wound. I looked away quickly when her gaze caught mine. "Don't say a word," she snapped, storming past me into the street. She didn't follow Beau.

"Ah, *l'amour.*" Madame Sauvage stared after them with a wistful expression. "I told you the truth would out." When she clapped her hands together once more, turning the full force of her gaze onto me, I recoiled. "Now. It is your turn, young man. Hold out your hand, please."

"I would . . . rather not," I said dubiously.

"Nonsense. You want your pearl, don't you?"

I glanced after Beau and Coco. "That depends."

But it didn't, not really, and we both knew it. Swallowing hard, I extended a hand toward her. To my surprise, she withdrew a small pouch from her sleeve and upended its contents in my palm. Célie inched closer, tilting her head. "Seeds?" she asked in confusion.

And so they were.

Madame Sauvage closed my fingers around them with a pleasant smile. "Just so. Your task is simple, dear boy: plant them."

I frowned down at the mundane things. "Plant them?"

Madame Sauvage turned to bustle around her cart, returning items to their proper places. "What else does one do with seeds?"

"I—" Shaking my head, I stuffed them back in their pouch. "What are they?" *Stupid question.* I tried again. "Where—where do you want me to plant them? When?"

"Those decisions are up to you."

When I cast Célie an incredulous glance, she shrugged, gesturing first to the pearls, then to the street. I swept the black gems into the pouch with the seeds. Madame Sauvage didn't stop me, instead plucking a live mouse from her sleeve and dropping it into the snake's reservoir. She cooed at the snake as it uncoiled. Like a mother with her babe. Célie gestured to the street again. Wilder this time. Emphatic.

But it didn't feel right to just *leave*. And Nicholina—she still stood silent and rooted. Clearly Madame Sauvage wasn't a simple peddler. "Why are you here, Madame Sauvage? How did you—how did you find us?"

The woman looked up as if surprised to find us still standing there. "Why are *you* here, young man? You've collected your pearls. Now be on your way."

She waved her hand once more, and Nicholina gasped. Stumbled. Next second, she lunged at Madame Sauvage with a snarl, but I pulled my wrist sharply, forcing her to a halt. The hood slipped from her face, and she glared between the two of us in silent fury.

"It doesn't feel very nice, does it? To lose bodily autonomy?" Madame Sauvage shooed us from the cart without further ceremony. "A lesson well remembered, Nicola. Now, go. You all have rather more pressing matters of which to attend, don't you?"

Célie clutched my arm when I didn't move, pulling me down the steps.

Yes. Yes, we should go, but—

My gaze caught on a glass display of pastries near the snake. They *definitely* hadn't been there before. Torn between trepidation and interest, between fear and inexplicable ease, I nodded to them. "How . . . how much for the sticky bun?"

"Ah." Madame Sauvage brightened abruptly, plucking the pastry from its case and wrapping it in brown paper. She followed us down the steps before extending it to me. "For you? Free of charge."

I regarded her warily.

"Never fear." She tugged her sign from the mud. An oddly mundane gesture amidst the uncanny circumstances. "We shall meet again soon, Reid Labelle. Plant those seeds."

With a cheery wink, she vanished before our eyes, taking her sign and her strange little cart with her.

LE CŒUR BRISÉ

Reid

"We're here," Coco said softly.

A quarter hour ago, she'd forced us to stop, to bear Nicholina to the ground and tip a sleeping tincture down her throat. It hadn't been pretty. It hadn't been fun. I still had bite marks on my hand to prove it.

We stood beneath the shadow of a lone cypress tree—at least, I thought it was a cypress. Below the smoke and clouds, true darkness had fallen once more. The forest at our backs stood eerily still. Even the wind had ceased here, yet a hint of brine still tinged the air. No waves, however. I heard no waves. No gulls, either. No signs of life at all. Shifting my feet uneasily, I took in the path ahead. Narrow and rocky, it disappeared into fog so thick I could've cut it with a knife. A chill skittered down my spine at what could be lurking within it. Despite no signs of Morgane and Josephine, the hair at my neck lifted. "What now?"

Coco came to stand beside me. "We keep going. Straight down."

"Into *that*?" Beau too stepped forward, halting at my other side. He eyed the fog skeptically. "Can we not?"

"L'Eau Mélancolique lies past it."

"Yes, but surely we can find less overtly ominous access."

"Le Cœur Brisé is everywhere. One doesn't *access* the Wistful Waters without him."

Célie swallowed hard. "But—we only have three pearls. Madame Sauvage said humans aren't allowed near the waters. She said they could drive us mad."

"The waters can drive anyone mad. Human or witch." Coco straightened her shoulders, still staring into the mist. "But you're right. We just have three, so we'll—we'll walk the path as far as Le Cœur allows, but only Reid, Nicholina, and I will continue to shore." Her eyes flashed to mine. "If we can pass his test."

"What *test?*" I asked with mounting unease. "No one said anything about a test."

She waved a curt hand. "You'll pass." Glancing at Nicholina, however, she added, "I'm not so sure about her, but he only tested us the once. Maybe he won't this time either—"

Beau pounced on this new information, whirling to point a finger at Coco. Triumphant. Furious. "I *knew* you were hiding something."

"Lou and I played at L'Eau Mélancolique as children," Coco snapped. "It's hardly a secret. Of course we ran into Le Cœur a time or two. He liked us, so he didn't ask for pearls. We brought him tricks instead."

Célie blinked in confusion. "But you said we needed black pearls."

Huffing impatiently, Coco crossed her arms and looked away.

"We do. We *did*—just not all the time. Lou once magicked them into spiders when he touched them. He's terrified of spiders."

A beat of silence.

"And he *liked* you?" Beau asked, perplexed.

"He liked me better than Lou."

"Enough." I hoisted Nicholina higher in my arms, starting toward the path. Tendrils of fog stretched out to meet me, curling around my boots. My ankles. I kicked them away. We were so close. *Too* close. "We didn't come all this way to leave now."

BUT LEAVE YOU SHALL. An abrupt, unfamiliar voice thundered around me, *through* me, and I stumbled, nearly sending Nicholina face-first into the mist. By the others' reactions—Célie actually screamed—they'd heard it too. The mist at my feet visibly thickened, swirling up my legs now. I felt its pressure like a vise. Panicked, I leapt backward, and the mist released me. It didn't stop thickening, however. It didn't stop speaking. *IF YOU CANNOT DRINK OF THE WATERS AND SPILL THEIR TRUTH.*

I nearly stepped on Célie in my haste to retreat.

"What is it?" She clutched my arm, clutched Nicholina's arm, clutched anything to ground herself in reality. But this *was* our reality—possessions, harbinger dogs, shape-shifting dragons, talking *mist*. It would never end. "Is it Le Cœur?"

In answer, the mist slowly darkened, drawing in on itself as a spider might spin its web. Growing limbs. A head. A pair of chilling coal-black eyes. Despite the ominous voice, those eyes softened on Coco as their owner stepped forth. Powerfully built—taller even than me—the man heaved a booming laugh and opened his arms to her. She hesitated for only a second before rushing forward. Voice hitching with laughter—perhaps tears—she buried her face in his chest and she said, "I've missed you, Constantin."

Beau stared at them, dumbstruck, as they embraced. I might've found his expression comical if I too hadn't felt this revelation like a blow to the head.

Constantin. *Constantin.* I knew the name, of course. How could I ever forget? Madame Labelle had held me captive with it in the Bellerose all those months ago, weaving magic with her tale of star-crossed lovers. Of magic rings and seas of tears and witches and holy men. Of Angelica and *Constantin.* The saint who'd gifted the Church his blessed sword, the original Balisarda. I'd carried a part of him with me for years, unaware his sword hadn't been blessed at all, but enchanted by his lover. She'd wanted to protect him. He'd wanted her magic. When he hadn't been able to take it from her, he'd eventually taken his life instead.

This couldn't be the same man. Of course it couldn't. The story said he'd died, and even if he hadn't, he would be thousands of years old now. Long dead. And Coco—she hadn't spoken a word about knowing Constantin during Madame Labelle's tale. She would have told us. Surely. Lou's life had been tangentially tied with him and Angelica, whose ill-fated love had first sparked the war between the Church and Dames Blanches. She would've told us. She *would've.*

"Constantin." Beau said the name slowly, tasting it. Remembering. "I know that name. Aren't you supposed to be dead?"

Coco stiffened at his brash words, but Constantin merely

chuckled. Ruffling her hair, he gently disentangled himself from her arms. "My reputation precedes me."

"You're Le Cœur Brisé?" I asked in disbelief. "The Broken Heart?"

His dark eyes glinted. "The irony is not lost on me, I assure you."

"But you aren't . . . you aren't *the* Constantin. You're not him." When he simply stared at me, I exhaled a harsh breath and looked at Coco, unable to articulate the sudden, painful flare of emotion in my chest. She hadn't told us. She'd . . . withheld information. She hadn't lied—not exactly—but she hadn't told the truth either. It felt like a betrayal.

"Right." Shaking my head, I tried to refocus. "How?"

"Who cares?" Beau muttered, near indiscernible.

Constantin extended his arms. "I am cursed eternal, huntsman, because I yearned for more."

Coco cast him a slanted look. "I think you went a bit further than that."

"You're right, of course, Cosette. I broke a woman's heart in the process—my one true regret in life."

Rolling her eyes, Coco said, "Constantin leapt from these cliffs. When Angelica wept her sea of tears, the waters . . . revived him." She gestured to the mist around us. The very mist from which he'd formed. "Their magic gives him life. Now he serves as a warning."

We all stared at her. "What does that mean?" Beau finally asked.

"It means Isla poked her nose in like a prying busybody,"

Constantin said, surprisingly pleasant given the circumstances. He swept a hand down his arm, his bare chest. He wore nothing save the cloth around his waist, his lower half obscured by mist. Condensation collected on his skin, curled in his hair. "She watched everything between Angelica and me, and when the waters intervened, she swept in and cursed me to guard the women of these waters—and their magic—forever."

Célie's gaze darted. "The women of these waters?"

"The melusines." Constantin's face contorted with distaste. "Fish women. *Fickle* women."

"Temptresses," Coco added. "The ones who dwell here are also truth tellers. Some are seers. The waters have given them strange abilities."

My arms began to burn, and I readjusted my grip on Nicholina. "Who is Isla?"

Constantin snorted in response. "The queen of the melusines."

"Claud's sister," Coco said at the same time.

"Is she a goddess, then?" Célie asked.

Constantin bowed slightly, inclining his head. "Some would call her such. Others would not. Either way, she is very old and powerful. If you seek an audience, however, I must warn you: she cannot interfere in the affairs of humans. Not without repercussion."

Coco touched his arm. "We aren't here for her, Constantin. Not yet, at least." She looked to Nicholina, to Lou in my arms, and her entire body seemed to wilt once more. Constantin followed her gaze, his sharp eyes tracking over Lou's sallow skin, her gaunt cheeks. He hummed a low note of understanding.

"Louise is ill."

"And possessed," I added a touch desperately.

His eyebrows shot up. "You believe the waters will heal her."

"They healed you," Beau pointed out, "and you were dead."

Constantin parted the mist with his hands, the tendrils curling between his fingers. It struck me as an idle gesture. An apathetic one. "It's true. If anything can heal her, these waters can. Though they started as mere tears, they've become as sentient as the pulse within a Dame Rouge, as connected as a Dame Blanche to this land. Angelica was a seer, and her magic shaped them. The waters see things we cannot see, know things we cannot know. I am part of them now, yet even I do not grasp the future as they. I have lived a hundred human lives, yet even I cannot comprehend their knowledge."

I struggled to extract the pearls from my pack while maintaining my hold on Nicholina. Beau extended his arms instead. Reluctantly, I handed her over before thrusting the pearls at Constantin. To my surprise, his hands felt solid. Warm. He truly was alive. "Our payment," I said.

His fingers curled around the pearls. His eyes flicked to Coco. "Are you sure?"

She nodded resolutely. "She's my best friend."

He shrugged then, and the pearls dissolved into mist. "Very well. On her head be it." To the rest of us, he asked, "Who accompanies the fair maidens?"

I stepped forward. "Me."

"Of course." His gaze swept from my head to my toes. He *hmph*ed as if displeased. As if the mud on my boots, perhaps the bandolier on my chest, offended him. "I've heard of your exploits,

Reid Diggory. I've heard of your glory in my legacy. I've heard all about the death and blood on yours and your brethren's hands." He paused for me to respond, but I didn't give him the satisfaction. I didn't give him any reaction at all. "To be honest, you remind me of a much younger version of myself."

"I am nothing like you."

He tilted his head. "Time changes us all, does it not?"

"La-di-da, mysterious bullshit, ominous warnings." Beau repositioned Nicholina with stiff, awkward movements, exhaling an aggrieved breath. "Should we keep standing around, or—?"

"Point taken." Constantin grinned, and with the wave of his hand, Beau and Célie vanished. Both just . . . vanished. Nicholina's weight landed solidly back in my arms.

"Where did you send them?" Coco asked, voice rising in panic. "I mean—are they safe?"

Constantine's eyes glittered knowingly. "No one is safe here, Cosette. Not even you. I protected you and your friend as children. This time, however, you seek the waters as an adult of your own volition. I can no longer bend the rules. You too must drink and speak truth. Now"—he stepped aside, gesturing to the path before us, the path still concealed by semisolid mist—"shall we?"

She swallowed visibly.

When I strode forward, however, she slipped her arm through mine, hurrying to keep up. "Have you never drunk before?" I asked her quietly. Though I couldn't hear Constantin following, I sensed his presence behind us as we trekked down the path. It sloped gently, evenly, despite the rocks. Silence still coated everything. "In all the times you visited?"

"Just once," she whispered back, "when I tried to see my—" But she stopped abruptly, squeezing my arm tight. "When Lou and I tried to swim in the waters. Constantin never made us drink of them otherwise. We usually just played along the shore."

"And that one time?" I asked.

She shuddered. "It was awful."

"What did you see?"

"What I wanted most in the world."

"Which was?"

She scoffed but didn't withdraw her arm. "Like I'd tell you. I already spoke it once. I'm not speaking it again."

"You aren't serious." An ache started to build in my right temple. "How can I know what to expect if you won't—"

"You can't," Constantin interrupted, materializing directly in front of us. We both skidded to a halt. "None know what the water will show them. Desires, fears, strengths, weaknesses, memories—it sees truth and demands truth in turn. All you must do is acknowledge it."

At his words, the mist behind him began to clear. It moved slowly, deliberately, each tendril creeping apart to reveal a vast, impossibly smooth body of water. It stretched between two mountains, extended as far as the eye could see. To the horizon. Beyond. The moon—silver as a freshly minted coin—shone clear and bright across its glassy surface. No smoke here. No waves either.

Not a single sound.

Constantin flicked his wrist, and from the fog, three chalices formed, solidifying into simple iron. They waited in the sand at the edge of the water. Almost touching it. Not quite. Gently, I lowered Nicholina to the ground. She didn't stir when I lifted her eyelid, checked her pulse. "What did you *do* to her? She's barely conscious."

"It's a simple sleeping solution—lavender, chamomile, valerian root, and blood." Coco shrugged nervously. "It's *possible* that I overdid it."

"She will drink," Constantin said, his form beginning to fade, "or she will die."

I couldn't suppress a snarl of frustration. "You're a real son of a bitch, you know that?"

When he lifted his hands, they dissolved into mist. Another arrogant smile. "I am a simple guardian. Drink of the waters, and spill their truth. If you succeed, you may enter their healing depths. If you fail, you will leave this place, and you will never return."

"I'm not going anywhere—" But even as the words left my mouth, I felt the mist constrict around me like iron manacles, knew staying upon failure wouldn't be an option. The mist—or Le Cœur, or the waters, or the magic itself—wouldn't allow it. Only when I muttered a terse agreement did the manacles dissipate. I still felt their presence, however, hovering over my skin. Their warning.

"Drink of the waters," Constantin repeated, near immaterial now, "and spill their truth." Only his eyes remained. When they found Coco, they softened, and a tendril of fog reached out to caress her face. "Good luck."

He left us standing alone in the moonlight, staring down at our chalices.

THE WATERS' TRUTH

Reid

I still remembered the exact moment I received my Balisarda. After each tournament, a banquet was held to honor the champions, to welcome them into the ranks of brotherhood. Few attended outside of the Chasseurs and Church, and the celebrations never lasted long—a quick address, a quicker meal. No toasts. No music. No revelry. A modest affair. The next morning, however, the real exhibition would begin. The entire kingdom would come to Cathédral Saint-Cécile d'Cesarine to watch the induction ceremony. Aristocrats and paupers alike would dress in their finest. Initiates would line the aisle. At the altar, the Archbishop would stand with the inductees' Balisardas. They would adorn the communion table, polished and resplendent in their velvet boxes.

I'd been the only inductee at my ceremony. Mine had been the only Balisarda.

Jean Luc had stood at the end of the aisle, hands clasped behind his back. His face tight. His body rigid. Célie had sat in the third row with her parents and sister. She'd tried to catch my eye as I'd marched down the aisle, but I hadn't been able to look at her. I hadn't been able to look at anything but my Balisarda. It'd called to me as a siren's song, the sapphire glittering in the filtered sunlight.

I'd repeated my vows by rote. Shoulders straight and proud. After, the Archbishop had broken tradition to embrace me, but his public display hadn't embarrassed me. I'd been pleased with it. Pleased with myself. So, so pleased. And why not? I'd trained religiously for years—I'd bled and sweat and sacrificed—all for this moment.

When I'd reached out to finally accept my Balisarda, however, I'd hesitated. Just for a second.

Part of me had known, even then, this sword—this life— would bring pain. Part of me had known I would suffer.

I'd chosen it anyway.

Just as I chose it now.

My fingers wrapped around the cold metal of my chalice, and I knelt to fill it. No ripples emanated when I broke the waters' still surface. Instead, it seemed to absorb the movement. Frowning, I tried to slip my hand beneath as well, to splash, to create movement, but I met with an invisible wall. I pushed harder. My hand stopped a hair's breadth over the surface—so close I could feel the wintry cold emanating from the waters. I still couldn't touch them. Expelling a harsh breath, I abandoned the attempt. Constantin had said as much.

I eyed the iron chalice warily. This wouldn't be pleasant.

"Wait." Coco clasped my forearm when I moved the cup to my mouth. "Lou first. I don't know what'll happen when we drink, but I doubt we'll be able to help her."

"I don't think we *can* help her." Still, I lowered my hand. "We don't know what the waters will show her. How can we fight an invisible foe?"

"I'm not saying she's incapable of fighting her own battle." Coco rolled her eyes and bent to fill the other chalices. "I'm saying she's unconscious. She'll need help with the actual drinking."

"Oh." Despite the seriousness of our circumstances, heat crept up my throat. I hurried to help her lift Lou, gently pulling her onto my lap. "Right."

"Tilt her head back."

I obliged, fighting the instinct to knock the chalice aside as Coco brought it to Lou's lips. Because Coco was right—if anyone could do this, Lou could. I held her secure, and slowly, carefully, Coco opened her mouth and tipped the water in. "Easy," I warned her. "Easy."

Coco didn't take her eyes from the task at hand. "Shut up, Reid."

Nothing happened when the cold water touched Lou's tongue. Coco poured a little more. It trickled from one corner of her mouth. Still nothing. "She isn't swallowing," I said.

"Yes, *thank* you—" But Coco stopped abruptly when Lou's eyes snapped open. We both stared down at her. Coco placed a tentative hand on her cheek. "Lou? How do you feel?"

Her eyes rolled to the back of her head in response, and her mouth opened on a violent scream—except no sound came out. Silence still reigned. The waters, however, rippled in an eerie sort of acknowledgment. Gripping her shoulders, I watched helplessly as she scratched at her face, her hair. Like she would tear Nicholina out by force. Her head thrashed. "*Shit.*" I struggled to hold her, but Coco pushed me backward, downing her chalice in a single swallow.

"Hurry!" She tossed her cup aside, bracing her hands against the shore. "Drink now. The sooner we spill our truths, the sooner we can dip Lou in the—" But her eyes too rolled backward, and though her body didn't seize as Lou's had, she fell sideways, comatose, her cheek hitting the sand. Eyes still rolling.

She'd looked like this once before. Seeing nothing. Seeing everything.

A man close to your heart will die.

Cursing bitterly—casting one last look at Lou, who'd gone limp on my lap—I tossed back the contents of my own chalice. If possible, the water tasted even colder than it'd felt. Unnaturally cold. Cruelly cold. It burned my throat all the way down, solidifying to ice in my stomach. In my limbs. In my veins. Within seconds, movement became difficult. Coughing, gagging, I slid Lou from my lap as the first tremor rocked my frame. When I collapsed forward on hands and knees, the edges of my vision paled to white. Strange. It should've gone dark, not light, and—

The burn in my lungs vanished abruptly, and my vision cleared. I blinked in surprise. Blinked again. This couldn't be right. Had I not drunk enough? Straightening, I glanced first to my empty cup, then to Lou and Coco. Surprise withered to confusion. To fear. They'd disappeared in the mist as completely as the others. I shot to my feet. "Lou? Coco?"

"I'm here!" Lou called from down the shoreline. Surprised, relieved, I hurried after her voice, peering through the mist and darkness. Though the moon still suffused the scene in soft silver light, it illuminated little now. Shafts of it shone through the mist intermittently. Blinding me one moment. Disorienting me the next.

"Where are you? I can't—"

Her hand caught mine, and she stepped into sight, grinning and whole. I stared at her in disbelief. Where her skin had been wan and sickly, it now shone gold, dusted with freckles. Where her hair had been shorn and white, it now spilled long and lustrous down her back, chestnut and sable once more. I caught a strand of it between my fingers. Even her scars had healed. Except . . . except one.

I traced a finger over the thorns and roses at her throat. At my touch, her eyes fluttered shut. Mist undulated around her face, casting her in an ethereal haze. "Do you like it? Coco could make a killing doing this—transforming the macabre into the macabrely beautiful."

"You're always beautiful." Throat tight, I could barely speak the words. She wrapped her arms around my waist, resting her ear against my heart. "Are you . . . better?" I asked.

"Almost." Grinning anew at my wary expression, she stood on her tiptoes to kiss me. "Come on. I want to show you something."

I followed blindly, my heart in my throat. A voice at the back of my mind warned it couldn't be this easy—warned I shouldn't trust it—but when Lou laced her fingers through mine, pulling me farther into the mist, I let her. Her hand felt warmer than it'd been in ages. And that scent in the air—like magic and vanilla and cinnamon—I inhaled it deeply. An innate sense of peace spread outward from my chest. Of course I didn't hesitate. This was Lou. She wasn't a Balisarda, and I wasn't walking down the aisle. I wasn't pledging my fate. I'd already done that.

"How did you exorcise Nicholina?" I asked dreamily. "What did the waters show you?"

She smiled at me over her shoulder, lit from within. "I don't remember you being so chatty, husband."

Husband. The rightness of the word felt warm. Heady. I grinned and draped my free arm across her shoulders, tucking her firmly against my side. Craving her warmth. Her smile. "And I don't remember *you*—"

—*spilling her truth*, my mind chastised. *You haven't either. This isn't real.*

My smile slipped. Of course it was real. I could feel her against me. Slowing to a stop, I gripped her tighter, spun her around. When she looked up, arching a familiar brow, my breath caught in my throat. Truly, she seemed to be glowing with happiness. I felt like I could fly. "Tell me," I said softly, brushing a strand of hair behind her ear. "Tell me what you saw."

"Let me show you instead."

I frowned now. Was her skin—was it actually glowing? She

waved her hands, and the mist around us thinned, revealing a stone altar behind her. On it, a young woman lay prone, bound, and gagged. She struggled to support her head, which protruded past the altar. Her hair—white as the snow and the moon, white as her gown—had been braided. The plait fell from her nape to the stone bowl beneath her throat. I stepped closer in alarm. The girl looked . . . no, *felt* . . . familiar. With her turquoise eyes, she could've been a sixteen-year-old Lou, but that wasn't right. She was too tall. Too strong. Her skin pale and unfreckled.

"Look at her, darling," Lou crooned with a dagger in her hand. I stared at it, unable to understand where it'd come from. Unable to grasp why she had it. "Isn't she lovely?"

"What are you doing?"

She tossed the dagger into the air, watching it rotate up, down, catching it by the handle. "I have to kill her."

"What? No." I tried to stand between them, but my feet wouldn't move. The mist had crept forward while I'd studied the girl, solidifying around us. My breathing quickened. "Why? Why would you do that?"

She cast me a pitiful look. "It's for the greater good, of course."

"No. That—no, Lou." I shook my head vehemently. "Killing that child won't solve anything—"

"Not just *any* child." She sauntered toward the altar, still tossing her knife and catching it. The girl watched with wide eyes, struggling harder, as the scene around us continued to evolve. The waters disappeared, and true mountains formed. A temple in a meadow. Scores of women all around, dancing wildly in the moonlight. Black-haired triplets and a witch with a holly crown. But the girl on the altar couldn't escape. The mist held her trapped in place like a pig for slaughter while Lou pointed the knife at her throat. "*This* child. I alone am willing to do what must be done, darling. I alone am willing to sacrifice. Why can't you see that? I will save *everyone.*"

Bile rose in my throat. "You can't do this. Not—not her. Please."

She stared at me sadly, knife still poised above the girl. "I am my mother's daughter, Reid. I will do anything to protect those I love. Would you not kill"—she kissed the girl's throat with the blade—"for me?"

Incredulous, angry, I nearly broke my legs trying to wrench free. "I wouldn't ki—"

The lie blackened and cracked before I could finish it. Like ashes on my tongue. My ashes.

I *had* killed for Lou. The Archbishop hadn't been innocent, no, but the others—the ones before him? I'd killed them for less than love. I'd killed them out of obligation, out of loyalty. I'd killed them for glory. But . . . that wasn't quite right either. *Drink of the waters, and spill their truth.*

I could see the cracks in their magic now. Their Lou had been so convincing. So perfect. Like the Lou I'd preserved in my memory. But reality wasn't perfection, and neither was she—not then and not now. She'd once told me it hurt to remember the dead as they were, rather than who we wanted them to be. Memory was a dangerous thing.

Time changes us all, does it not?

I was no longer the boy who'd pined after his Balisarda, who'd first held it with reverence, with pride, yet part of me remembered him. Part of me still felt his longing. Now, perhaps for the first time, I saw the truth clearly. I'd killed the Archbishop because I loved Lou. I'd killed innocents because I loved the Archbishop. Because I'd loved my brethren, my family. Every time I'd found a home, I'd fought tooth and nail to keep it.

Just like Morgane.

A thin line of scarlet wet Lou's blade. It colored the girl's neck like a ribbon. "You once said I'm like my mother." Lou stared at the blood on her knife, transfixed. "You were right." Quicker than I could react, she slashed the girl's neck, turning to face me as the latter choked and gurgled. Her movements slowed within seconds. Scarlet stained the white stone irrevocably. "You were right."

Drink of the waters, and spill their truth.

"Yes." The mist around my feet vanished with the word, and I strode forward purposefully, swallowing bile. I didn't look at the girl. Didn't memorize her face. My chest cleaved in two with the effort. This wasn't real. Not yet. Not *ever*—not if I could help it. "Yes, Lou, you are like your mother." I took her chin in my hand, forcing her to look at me. "But so am I."

The second the words left my lips, a wide grin broke across her face. "Well done, you." And then the ground began to crumble, the altar and temple falling away to white sand and still water. A rushing sound filled my ears, and Lou's chin vanished between my fingers. I clutched only empty air. Sand abraded my knees, and I glanced down to my discarded iron chalice. I touched it gingerly. Still cold.

"You've returned." Constantin's amused voice punctured the silence as I sat backward, stunned. "After Coco, I might add." He winked at her where she sat frozen beside me, clutching her knees.

At my anxious look, she muttered, "I'm fine."

"Did you speak your truth?"

"Every word."

"You aren't going to repeat it, are you?"

"Never."

Constantin chuckled before snapping his gaze to Lou, who started to stir. He rubbed his hands together in anticipation. "Ah, excellent. Right on time."

I moved to her side just as she opened her eyes. Her gaze darted from me to Coco, to the endless sand beyond us, and she bolted upright, craning her neck to look behind. "Lou?" I asked in confusion, lifting a hand to touch her forehead. Her bite hadn't healed—I hadn't expected it to, not yet—and her color looked paler than usual. As white as her hair. She scrabbled backward on her hands, still searching the beach wildly.

"Where are they?" Her voice pitched high, girlish, and my heart dropped. Not Lou at all, then. "Where are they hiding? Where are they waiting? They're near, they're near. They must be here."

I stared at her in disgust. In pity. "No one else is here, Nicholina. Just you."

"No, no, no." She rocked back and forth as Coco had done, shaking her head frenetically. Wincing as she did. "It's a trap. They're here, oh yes, and they're waiting, hiding, creeping through the mist—"

Coco knelt in front of her, grasping her chin in her fingers. "They aren't coming. Accept it. Move on. Better yet—switch sides. Nicholina, my aunt isn't the person you want her to be. Morgane is even worse. They don't value you. They don't accept you. You're a tool to them—a means to an end—just like the rest of us."

"*No.*" The word tore from Nicholina in a guttural snarl, and she clawed at her own face, scoring the skin there. When I leapt to intervene, those nails raked down my chest instead. "*You.* I shall deliver you with the mouse, yes, yes, yes, and we shall cut your heart into thirds—"

Constantin tsked in disapproval and waved his hand. The mist answered by swirling around her in a violent tornado, trapping her in place. Nicholina howled in rage. "They will kill us both, stupid mouse. Stupid, *stupid* mouse. We cannot dance, no, but we *can* drown. Down, down, down, we can drown. There is no hope. Only *sickness.*"

Then she spoke again.

Warmth suffused my entire body.

"I thought you weren't"—her voice pitched lower than before, and she gritted her teeth in concentration—"worried about dying? Or have you—finally—accepted the truth?"

Lou.

I couldn't breathe. Couldn't calm the racing of my heart. It was her. It was *Lou.*

The waters must've weakened Nicholina enough for her to break through, or—or perhaps they demanded truth, even now. They knew Nicholina didn't belong. They knew whose body she inhabited.

Constantin sighed. "The bickering was diverting at first. Now it isn't. Spill your truths, all of you, or leave this place in peace. I don't have all night."

"Really?" Lou fought to smile, still panting. "What else—do you have to do? This is—your sole purpose—isn't it?"

He glowered at her. "Charming as always, Louise."

She bowed, failing to hide her grimace as Nicholina threw them against the cage. "I—try."

"Your truth," he insisted, voice hard.

Her face spasmed, and when she opened her mouth once more, I wasn't sure who spoke: Lou or Nicholina. Either way, their truth spilled from them unapologetically. Strong and without strain. "I am capable of great evil." The words hung in the air between us, as sentient as the mist. They waited, coiled, for my response. For my clarification. For my own truth.

I looked directly in her eyes. "We all are."

As if exhaling on a sigh, the words dissipated. The mist went with it, leaving Lou sprawled unceremoniously in the sand. Constantin nodded. "Very good, each of you. One of life's greatest trials is to acknowledge our own reflections. Tonight, you have seen yourselves. You have drunk of the waters, and you have spilled their truth." He extended his hand to the shore. An emotion I couldn't place shone deep in his eyes. Perhaps sadness.

Wistfulness. "Go now. Let their wisdom flow through your veins and restore you." To Coco, he murmured, "I hope you live your truth, Cosette."

She gazed out at the waters with an identical expression. "I hope so too."

In the stillness of the moment, Nicholina lunged toward the path with a feral cry. A desperate cry. I caught her before she could escape, hauling her over my shoulder. Her fists pounded my back, weaker than they should've been. Her hands still tender and raw. When she moved to kick my groin, I caught her shin, holding it away from me. My own hope swelled in my chest. Bright and savage. "You're going to injure yourself."

"Let me go!" She bit my shoulder like a rabid animal, but the thick wool of my coat prevented much damage. "You'll kill us! Do you hear me? We'll drown! We cannot dance beneath these waters. We are too heavy, too *many*—"

"Enough." I marched her toward the water with steely determination. This time, my feet broke its surface without resistance. We'd been granted permission to enter. To heal. Behind us, Constantin vanished, leaving Coco to stand alone. She gave a curt nod. "We finish this now, Nicholina. Get. The. Hell. Out. Of. My. Wife."

She shrieked as I threw her headfirst into the waters.

MATHIEU

Lou

The water was freezing—shockingly and cripplingly so. My muscles seized on impact, and my breath left in a painful, startled rush. My lungs immediately shrieked in protest.

Fucking fabulous. Fucking *Reid*.

He'd meant well, of course, but couldn't the heroic brute have checked the waters' temperature first? Perhaps taken a dip himself? I certainly couldn't dance as a block of ice. And my eyes—I couldn't see *anything*. Whatever moonlight had shone above hadn't managed to penetrate below, plunging us into pitch blackness. A fitting end for Nicholina, that. A true taste of her own medicine. If possible, she seemed to like the dark even less than me, and in her utter hysteria, she thrashed wildly, vying for control. Sinking us like a brick.

Stop it. Clenching my aching teeth, I struggled to move my arms and legs in unison. She floundered in the opposite direction, and our skirt tangled in our feet, thick and heavy and dangerous. We sank another inch, and another and another, each of our panic feeding the other, heightening to a collective sort of frenzy. *Nicholina,* I said sharply, ignoring the roaring of my heart. It nearly exploded in my chest. *Stop struggling. We need to work together, or we're both going to die. I'm a strong swimmer. Let me lead—*

Never.

The voices echoed her. *Never, never, never.* They swarmed around us, panicked and hysterical, and we sank faster still, weighed down by our heavy cloak and gown. I pulled at the former while Nicholina tried to loosen the latter. Swearing viciously, I joined her instead, and together—miraculously in unison—we unknotted the laces with stiff, clumsy fingers. She kicked at the skirt as I clawed at our cloak. Within seconds, both floated away from us through the black water, ominous and slow, before disappearing altogether.

Still we sank.

Shit. It was like swimming through oil, through tar. My lungs burned as I strained upward, and Nicholina finally, desperately mimicked my movements. *That's it. Keep going. Left foot, right foot, left foot, right foot.*

We dance, we dance, we dance.

But we weren't dancing at all. Already, white stars popped in my vision, and my head pounded from lack of oxygen. Sharp pain pierced my ears. And . . . and something else. Something worse. Too late, I realized that Nicholina's veil—the darkness that had shielded her subconscious—had vanished altogether. The waters had stripped it. At last, her every thought, every feeling, every fear flooded our shared consciousness with startling clarity. Faces flashed. Pieces of memories, bits of sentiment tied to each one. Fervor and affection and hatred and shame. It was too much.

Too many. I didn't want them. Her emotions didn't stop coming, however—so intense, so *painful*—and the full force of her being crashed into me like a tidal wave.

And so did my magic.

Gold and white exploded with blinding intensity, everywhere at once. Though I tried to catch a pattern—a pattern to swim, a pattern to shield, a pattern to *anything*—Nicholina's emotions overwhelmed everything. They buffeted me.

What are you doing? What are you doing? She urged me onward, voice frantic, realizing too late what had happened. She hadn't known her veil had lifted. Though she tried to summon it once more, the waters had shredded it beyond repair. *Dance, little mouse! You must dance! Right, left, right, left, right!*

But the waters didn't drown us now. She did. Unadulterated emotion robbed what little of our breath remained, pulling us both beneath the onslaught. We sank and sank and sank with each fresh wave. No. We sank *into* each fresh wave. The darkness around us pricked with light.

And suddenly, we weren't in the Wistful Waters at all.

Lavender brushed my fingertips. Its scent perfumed the summer air, sweet and sharp and heady, and overhead, a single fat cloud drifted past. I glanced around warily. I knew this place. I knew the mountains all around us, the creek trickling at the edge of the field. As a child, I'd played here often, but it hadn't been filled with lavender then, only grass and the gnarled stumps of pear trees. Manon said a grove had once grown in this valley, but Morgane had torched it in an inexplicable fit of rage before we were born. Had the lavender preceded the trees? Or had it come after?

Something shifted beside me, and I tensed instinctively, whipping around to face it.

My heart leapt to my throat.

"You're . . . *you*," I said in disbelief.

Nicholina stared back at me, her silver eyes wider than I'd ever seen them. Her skin paler. The scars on her chest shone stark and gruesome in the bright sunlight, and her black dress—tattered and dirty—seemed incongruous with this happy place. Glancing down at my own body, I lifted my hands experimentally, and they responded without hesitation. I flexed my fingers. At the sight of them straightening, curling back into my palms, a bubble of laughter rose in my throat—*my* throat. Not ours.

Unable to help myself, I lifted my face to the sun, savoring its warmth. Just for a moment. I didn't know where we were, I didn't know *how* we were, and I didn't care. Instead, I felt . . . whole. Curious sensation flowed through my limbs, as if the waters had not only restored me but strengthened me too. Empowered me. Or perhaps I'd finally died and entered the Summerland. Or was this Heaven? Neither would explain Nicholina's presence, yet what else could it be?

Panic sliced through my reverie, sharp and unexpected, and my smile vanished as quickly as it'd come. Because it hadn't been *my* panic. No, the emotion had come from someone else. I groaned loudly in realization: Nicholina recognized this place too. Though her thoughts came too quickly to untangle, a sense of longing permeated them. A sense of despair.

Fuck.

I shook my head.

Though our bodies had separated, it seemed our consciousness had not, and no god would ever be cruel enough to saddle me with Nicholina for eternity, which meant—which meant this wasn't Heaven at all. I glared up at the crystal-blue skies. The single cloud there seemed to mock me, and I couldn't stop a harsh chuckle. It took the shape of a burning cross.

Worse—now I couldn't feel my magic at all. Cautious, curious, I tried to summon the golden patterns in my mind, but they didn't rise. Though the veil between Nicholina and me hadn't re-formed, they'd simply . . . vanished. Whatever magic fed this place, it clearly wasn't like mine. It wasn't like hers either. It was more powerful than both, and it'd stripped us equally bare.

When a familiar voice crooned a lullaby behind us, we turned simultaneously. Nicholina's panic deepened to dread, interlaced with my own morbid curiosity. "Who is that?" I asked, watching two figures approach. A slender, dark-haired woman—perhaps my age—bounded hand in hand with a sallow-faced little boy. Deep shadows drained the life from his eyes, yet still he laughed, breathless, and tried to keep up. Sensing his struggle, the woman swept him up in her arms. They fell to the ground together, still laughing, rolling amidst the lavender. Neither of them noticed us. "Sing for me, *maman*," he begged her, sprawling across her chest. He wrapped frail arms around her neck. "Sing me a song. *S'il vous plaît.*"

She squeezed him gently. In her pale eyes, adoration and anxiousness shone in equal measure. My heart twisted in response.

Beside me, Nicholina had stilled, her attention rapt on the little boy's face. "And what song shall I sing, *mon bébé*?" the woman asked.

"You know the one!"

Her nose wrinkled in distaste, and she smoothed the hair from his forehead. Black like hers. "I don't like that one. It's too . . . grim."

"Please, *maman*." His pale eyes sought hers earnestly. Indeed, he could've been the woman's miniature. "It's my favorite."

She scoffed in fond exasperation. "*Why?*"

"It's scary!" He grinned, revealing a chipped front tooth and dimples. "It has monsters!"

Rolling her eyes, the woman sighed. "Very well. But just the once. And don't—don't sing it with me this time, all right? Please?" I would've frowned at the odd request if I hadn't felt her unease echoing through Nicholina. If I hadn't known what would happen three weeks hence. This little boy . . . he wouldn't get better. He'd die a slow, painful death in the days to come, and this—this wasn't my hell, after all.

It was Nicholina's.

But she hadn't always been Nicholina. Once, she'd been Nicola.

I couldn't look away.

Closing her eyes, the woman leaned back into the lavender, and the boy nestled his face in the crook of her neck. I knew the words of the song before she sang them. They resounded in my very bones. "*Beneath the moon of harvest, a ripple stirs the leaves.*" With a high, clear soprano, she sang the eerie lullaby slowly, still stroking the boy's hair. "*The veil is thin, the ghouls a'grin, rattling the eaves.*"

He giggled as she continued.

"*A bridegroom hears them calling, wakes from eternal sleep, to seek his love, his Geneviève, who married her Louis. Beyond her glowing window, fair Geneviève doth sing*"—despite his mother's request, the boy began humming along—"*to the babe upon her breast. The bridegroom starts to weep.*" She hesitated now, her hand stilling on the boy's hair as he continued the song without her.

"*The dead should not remember. Beware the night they dream. For in their chest is memory—*"

"Of a heart that cannot beat," the woman said softly, no longer singing. The boy grinned, and together, they finished the disturbing lullaby. "*Beneath the moon of harvest, a ripple stirs the leaves. The veil is thin, the babe a'grins, and even ghouls shalt grieve.*"

The boy let out a loud, delighted cackle. "He was a *zombie*. Right, *maman*? The bridegroom was a zombie?"

"I think a ghoul," she offered, her eyes unfocused. She still clutched the boy's head to her chest, tighter than necessary. "Or maybe a different sort of spirit. A wraith."

"Will I become a wraith too, *maman*?"

She closed her eyes as if pained. "Never."

The conversation drifted from there. Nausea churning in my stomach, I watched as they eventually stood, walking hand in hand back the way they'd come. Nicholina did not blink. She stared at the boy's back with naked longing, unwilling to spare even a glance at the woman. At the boy's mother. Nicola. "What was his name?" I asked quietly.

She answered with equal softness. "Mathieu."

"Mathieu le Claire?"

The boy grew smaller and smaller in the distance. "I was only seventeen," she whispered instead, lost in her memories. I saw the events in her mind as clearly as the field of lavender: how she'd loved a man—a fair-skinned, ginger-haired man from their mountain village—and how they'd conceived a child who they in turn loved without question, completely and unconditionally. How the man had died unexpectedly from the cold, how their son had fallen ill shortly after, how she'd tried everything from magic to medicine to heal him. She'd even taken him to a priest—or the closest approximation to one—in a distant land, but he'd explained Mathieu's sickness as "divine retribution" and turned them away.

Nicholina had killed him. His had been the first life she'd ever taken.

She hadn't known La Voisin then. If she had, maybe Mathieu would've—

"Out of my thoughts, little mouse," she snarled, jerking her head back and forth as if to dislodge an irksome fly. "We don't want to see it, no, we don't want to see—"

"You were seventeen." I repeated her words slowly, pivoting to look around us again, studying the silhouette of the mountains. When I'd played here as a child, one crag had resembled a crone's crooked nose. The rock that had formed its wart, however, wasn't visible now, and that couldn't be right. Mountains didn't simply *move*. "How old *are* you, Nicholina?"

She hissed through stained, too-sharp teeth, anger sparking

like kindling. And I pitied her. Those teeth had once been beautiful. *She* had been beautiful. Not just of face and form, but also of spirit—the sort of spirit that drove a mother to the ends of the earth to save her child, the sort who loved with everything in her being. The sort who held nothing back. Yes, Nicola had been beautiful in all the ways that counted—and all the ways that didn't too—but beauty faded with time.

And Nicholina had lived too long.

How did you become like this? I'd asked her the question once, sitting in the dark and dirt of Léviathan. She hadn't given a proper answer then. She didn't need to give one now. I knew without her opening her cracked lips, without her lifting her girlish, uncanny voice. She'd lived too long, and time had ravaged her to a withered husk of the woman she'd once been.

Rage washed through her at my pity, or perhaps at the memory of her dead son. Like a wild animal, savage and trapped, she spat, "You wish to be in Hell, Louise le Blanc? We shall oblige you. Oh, yes, we shall drag you down, down, down—"

When she lunged, wrapping skeletal fingers around my throat, black waves crashed upon us once more. They flattened the lavender, enveloped the sun, swept us up into their treacherous current. My lungs screamed in agony as our situation resolved with knife-sharp clarity.

We weren't in Hell, and we weren't in Heaven either.

Ears bursting, vision pitching, I scrabbled at Nicholina's hold, but those fingers pressed into more than flesh now. They dug into consciousness, ripped through memory. The two of us foundered, tossed mercilessly through the waves, until Nicholina regained purchase, nearly crushing my windpipe. I felt that pressure everywhere. In my head, in my chest, in my heart. White exploded all around us as I tore free, and we pitched headlong into another memory.

Through a curtain.

A hush fell over the audience as we crashed onto the stage, and insidious fear bloomed at the sight before us: Reid caging me against his chest, my body deathly still in his arms. My hair long and brown, my face bloody and bruised. My dress torn. I glanced, panicked, to the right, where the Archbishop would step out in mere moments. And the crowd—who lay in wait, watching me? Would they recognize me? Would they find me at last?

Nicholina took advantage of my terror, seizing my hair and wrenching my face upward. "Look at yourself, mouse. Smell your fear even now, so thick and delicious. So lovely." She inhaled deeply against the scars on my throat. "And you fear so much, don't you? You fear your own mother, your own father. You fear your own *husband*." When she licked down the column of my neck, I twisted from her grip, smashing my crown into her face and staggering forward. She wiped a hand across her bloody nose before bringing it to her lips. Her tongue flicked out like a snake's. "But you should feel *lucky* you tricked him, oh yes, because if you hadn't tricked him—such a tricky little mouse— he never would've loved you. If he had known what you are, he never would've *held* you beneath the *stars*."

I glanced over my shoulder to where Reid and I still stared at each other, frozen. From the wings of the theater, Estelle moved to help me. Nicholina laughed. "You burned her, Louise. Your fear *burned* her."

When Reid flung me away, I winced, watching as my battered body hit the stage once more.

But there—in his gaze—

He was frightened too.

He was frightened, yet he rose with the stagehands when they came. Though his hands shook, he didn't fight them, didn't cower or plead or flee. And I wouldn't either. Fear was inevitable. We all made our choices, and we all suffered our consequences. We all felt fear. The *trick* was learning to live with that fear, to continue forward in spite of it. "I didn't mean for any of this to happen," I murmured, longing to reach out and touch his face. To smooth the furrow between his brows. To tell him everything would be all right. "But I'm glad it did."

Squaring my shoulders as Reid had done, I turned back to face Nicholina. Her eyes burned with silver light, and her chest rose and fell rapidly. Like me, she struggled to catch her breath, yet this strength in my limbs was hers as well. The waters had healed us both. And suddenly, I understood.

The Wistful Waters *healed*.

They didn't exorcise malevolent presences.

I'd have to do that myself.

Gritting my teeth, I launched myself at her.

WHAT IT IS TO DROWN

Lou

As soon as I touched her skin, she rolled, and the waters swept us up again. Nicholina snapped at my throat. Prying her mouth open—*keeping* it open—I swam with the current this time instead of against. But so many currents swirled around us now, some warm and some cold, some familiar and some foreign. Hundreds upon thousands of them. And I still couldn't breathe, couldn't *think*, as images rushed past in the water: fragments of faces, bits of skyline, sights and scents and sensations. Each beckoned and threatened simultaneously, like crooked fingers in the dark. They pulled me in every direction, clawing at my hair and tearing at my chemise. My panic became a living thing as I struggled to swim, to fend off Nicholina's gnashing teeth. How could I exorcise her without drowning myself in the process?

On the heels of that thought came another, swift and sudden and sure.

I could drown *her* instead—if not in water, then in emotion. Perhaps both.

Instinctively, I kicked down an unfamiliar current, and we spiraled into the temple by Chateau le Blanc.

Blood still coated the mountainside, and there, in the center, Nicholina stood with her maw dripping like a wild animal's—*Nicholina*, not Nicola, because in her hand, she held a human heart.

Triumph flared through us both, hot and heady. Triumph and hideous shame.

I encouraged the latter, fanning it higher as we grappled. Hotter. It became a weapon in my hands, and I wielded it like a knife, cutting through the quick of her. Piercing her very heart. This shame—it might kill her, if I let it.

"What did you do, Nicholina?"

"What was *necessary*." Her teeth finally sank into my fingers, and I cried out, tearing skin as I pulled them away. She spat blood. "We killed our sisters, yes, and we feel no shame," she lied, continuing on a single breath. "We would've killed her too. We would've killed for our mistress."

"Who—?"

But Nicholina attacked me with new fervor as we watched La Voisin drag an unconscious woman from the temple steps. I sidestepped, craning my neck with a powerful, inexplicable urge to see the woman's face. La Voisin obliged by tossing her to the ground, but past-Nicholina sprang toward them, obstructing my view. The present one wheeled and charged at me once more. I thanked any god listening—the very waters themselves—for rescinding our powers in this place. When she lashed out, I caught her wrist and twisted. I had skill enough without magic, but it would've been impossible to fight a wraith.

Will I become a wraith too, maman?

The thought made me hesitate, made me *sick*, and Nicholina spun, her elbow connecting sharply with my chest. When I doubled over, unable to breathe, she seized my throat once more. This time, she didn't let go.

She knew the rules of our game had changed.

Kill me, I whispered to her mind, unable to utter the words aloud. Goading her further, even as agony crescendoed in my lungs, pressure built behind my eyes. The capillaries there ruptured in little bursts of pain before healing once more. It didn't matter. I gripped her wrists and pressed closer with lethal purpose, staring into those sinister eyes. *Kill me, or I'll kill you.*

She snarled, squeezing harder, her own murderous impulse warring against her loyalty to La Voisin, who had told her not to kill me. Who had told her I was for Morgane.

She'll kill you if you do, I hiss. *I'll kill you if you don't. Either way, you die.*

Choking against her rage, she bared her teeth and forced me to the blood-soaked ground. I fed that rage. I fed it and stoked it and watched it consume her.

"She'll forgive us, yes," she breathed, wholly crazed. "Our mistress will understand—"

You stink with fear, Nicholina. Perhaps you were right—perhaps we are alike. Perhaps you fear death too. I forced a grin despite the blinding pressure in my head. Cords hung between us like the strings of a marionette—because Nicholina *was* a marionette. If I cut her free, she would fall. She would drown. The words raked up my battered throat like shards of glass. Like knives. I forced them past my swollen tongue, gasping, "You'll soon . . . join Mathieu . . . in the Summerland."

At his name on my lips, Nicholina made a guttural sound, forgetting her mistress, forgetting everything except her own bloodlust. Pressing her knee into my stomach, she leveraged her entire body, all her strength, against my throat. Her elbows locked.

And I had won.

Bridging upward with all my strength, I punched her arms at the elbow, breaking her grip, and hooked a foot outside hers. Air returned in a dizzying wave as I rolled atop her. I struck her face once, twice, before shoving off her chest to my feet. When I stumbled backward, heaving, La Voisin dropped to one knee beside the unconscious woman. She gripped the woman's chin hard and lifted her face.

I nearly lost my footing.

Coco stared back at me.

I shook my head incredulously, still reeling from lack of oxygen. It couldn't be Coco. It had to be someone else—someone nearly *identical*—

Nicholina tackled me from behind without warning, and we plummeted back into the icy churn of waters. With a high, maniacal laugh, she forced us down an even colder current. I tensed instinctively, fighting the pull, but it was too late.

We landed in a battered bedroom of Chasseur Tower. Bits of broken furniture littered the ground around us. I seized a shard of bedpost as we rolled. When I thrust it at her chest, she lurched sideways, and it lodged in her arm instead. Relentless, I twisted it, relishing her shrieks. "Give up." I lunged for another piece of wood. "You're *alone*. Your lover, your son—they're *gone*. They're *dead*. Josephine is going to kill you too, and if she doesn't, Morgane will. You're in over your head—"

She wrenched the wood from her arm and used it to block my strike. "We are not alone, little mouse. We are *never* alone." Giggling softly, she flicked her eyes behind me. "Not like you."

I wouldn't give her the satisfaction. I wouldn't look. I *wouldn't*—

Like a moth to a flame, my gaze drifted over my shoulder, following Reid's voice. I dreaded the sound of it. The look on his face. Nicholina cackled without moving to attack.

She'd already chosen her weapon.

She was trying to drown me too.

Reid towered over my pitiful form, his voice loud and angry and hurt. Estelle's sister still cooled at our feet, but neither of us looked at her. We had eyes only for each other. "I'm a Chasseur!" he roared, wringing his hands. His knuckles clenched white. "I took an oath to hunt witches—to hunt *you*! How could you do this to me?"

"You—Reid, you also made an oath to *me*." I listened to my own impassioned plea with bitter regret. "You're my husband, and I'm your wife."

His expression darkened, and my stomach rolled. An ache

built at the back of my throat.

"You are not my wife."

Cold, familiar despair chilled my bones at his words. How often had I heard them? How often had this exact scene plagued my nightmares?

"You see?" Nicholina crept closer, blood dripping in her wake. The puncture in her arm, however, had already vanished. I tore my gaze from Reid to study the smooth alabaster skin there. The waters had healed her. Nicholina realized it at the same moment I did, and a heinous grin split her face. She twirled the bloody shard of wood between her fingers. "Lucky you tricked him, really. Lucky, lucky, *lucky*."

I picked up my own shard to match, lifting it high. "He would've loved me anyway."

Then we were drowning again, caught up in fresh currents. When she tried to drive her shard into my skull, the wood burst in a geyser, spraying her face as we left the previous memory. Burning her. She shrieked again, and in that moment, I saw another scene flash: a dark tent and cloaked figures, my mother and La Voisin. They shook hands amidst the smoking sage while Nicholina hovered in the corner. Her heart rioted.

"We cannot do this," she muttered, following her mistress from the tent. Her face and shoulders twitched in agitation. "Not the children."

La Voisin turned without warning and slapped her roundly across the cheek. "We do what is necessary. Do not forget your place, Nicholina. You wanted a cure for death, and I gave you one. My benevolence extends only so far. You will follow me, or I will revoke my gift. Is that what you want?"

Nicholina thrashed in humiliation and hurt, tearing us from the memory. *You see?* My voice echoed cruelly even to my own ears. But we couldn't continue this way forever. The time had come for one of us to end—and one of us *would* end. I would die before I returned to the surface with Nicholina. *She doesn't love you. She isn't a sister or mother or family at all. You mean nothing to her. Give up, and go peacefully. You have nothing to fear in death, Nicholina. Mathieu will—*

She lashed out viciously then, pulling me along the coldest current of all.

Glittering masks.

A cavernous open space.

And—and Ansel.

My stomach bottomed out at her intent. My nails bit into the skin of her arm. No longer to harm her, but to *escape*. Every fiber in my being recoiled from the memory, but it didn't matter. I couldn't stop it.

And I would drown, after all.

She alighted, catlike, at the bottom of the amphitheater, and I landed sprawled at her feet. Dazed, I scrambled away before she could touch me, before she could force my gaze to the group at the center of the primitive stage. But I couldn't look at them. I couldn't spend these last precious moments staring at myself, at Coco or Beau, even at Reid—at the hideous relief on all our faces. We'd thought we'd won. We'd thought Claud had swooped in to save us, that we'd eluded Coco's prophecy, that we'd defeated my mother at last.

We'd thought so many things.

Morgane inched toward the back tunnel, where Ansel stood near. Too near. His beautiful face contorted with concentration as he looked from her to Claud to me.

He'd looked to me, and I hadn't seen it.

I bolted toward him now.

Rationally, I knew this memory would play out regardless of my presence, my interference. My feet, however, weren't rational. My heart wasn't either. Both carried me forward with foolish urgency as Morgane began to applaud. Skidding to a stop in front of him, I looked around wildly for anything I might use to shield him, to protect him. My eyes landed on the fallen knife. I bent to snatch it up, triumphant, but my fingers passed through the hilt, billowing into smoke before re-forming.

"No." I stared down at them. This didn't make sense. I'd—I'd touched the wood in Chasseur Tower. I'd stabbed Nicholina, for Christ's sake. "*No.*" At my vehement refusal, Claud's eyes seemed to flicker in my direction before finding Morgane once more.

"We can't change the past, little mouse, even in our memories. Not truly." Nicholina pursed her lips in saccharine pity. Her silver eyes glittered. "We can't save him, no. He is dead. He is dead, he is dead, with *that* knife in his head." She inclined her chin to the knife, which remained firmly upon the ground. Nicholina sauntered forward as Morgane inched backward. "Such a pity." When she reached out to stroke his cheek, I knocked her hand away, widening my stance between them. She grinned. "Such a pretty pity. He was *your* family, wasn't he, Louise? The only one who never betrayed you."

I scowled without looking at her. My attention remained on Morgane, who blithered about rules and games, still creeping backward. "Coco hasn't—" But Nicholina held knowledge that I did not, secrets of Coco and—and her mother. Nicholina laughed at my wide-eyed expression, at my slack jaw, as those secrets became my own. "No." I shook my head, a cold wave of shock washing over me. "Coco would have—"

Morgane lunged, and I could only stand there, immaterial between them, as she plunged her knife through me. My form rippled at the contact. Bone crunched. When Ansel crumpled to his knees, I went with him, trying and failing to catch his broken body, wrapping invisible arms around him to cushion his fall. Still stunned. Still numb. His blood soaked my dress, and my mind simply . . . fled. "Perhaps you didn't deserve your mother's ire," Nicholina mused, circling us idly as Morgane darted into the tunnel, as my own screams shattered the night, "or your huntsman's hate. But *this*"—she bounced excitedly on the balls of her feet—"this you earned, Louise."

Cutting my own strings mercilessly, she repeated the words I'd told him.

"You wreck everything you touch, Ansel. It's *tragic* how helpless you are." Snip. Snip. "You say you're not a child, Ansel, but you *are*." Snip. "You're a little boy playing pretend, dressing up with our coats and boots. We've let you tag along for laughs, but now the time for games is done. A woman's life is in danger—*my* life is in danger. We can't afford for you to mess this up."

Snip, snip, snip.

As if my life had been worth more than his.

As if his life hadn't been worth all of ours together.

I'd known it, even then. I'd known how much better he was than us. I stared down at his profile now, his eyes wide and unseeing. Blood matted his hair. It slicked down his graceful neck, stained the back of his coat. "Did you *love* him, Louise?" Nicholina echoed my mother's jeer. "Did you watch as the light left those pretty brown eyes?"

Why hadn't I told him? Why hadn't I hugged him one last time?

Closing my own eyes, I crumpled to my knees, pressing my forehead against his cheek. I couldn't feel him, of course. Couldn't feel anything. Was this what it was to drown? How strange. I couldn't even bring myself to cry—not when Coco wrenched the knife from his skull, not when Reid pried his lips apart. Not when Nicholina loomed over me, the discarded knife in hand.

She wouldn't be changing the past by killing me.

Part of me had died here already.

WHAT IT IS TO SWIM

Reid

I didn't pause to unlace my boots, unfasten my coat. When she hit the water, I moved to follow, already ankle-deep.

A low growl rumbled from behind.

Stiffening, I turned. Amber eyes reflected back at me. White fur gleamed in the moonlight.

I swore softly.

The *fucking* dog.

It paced along the path, hackles raised and teeth bared. Snorting, it shook its head before whining once. Twice. Its eyes bored into mine as if trying to . . . to communicate something. When it inched closer, I drew a knife. Unsettled. "Not another step," I said darkly. Flattening its ears, it snarled again, louder now, vicious, and did just that. To Coco, I asked, "How did it get here? Where is Constantin?"

"Leave it." She watched our standoff while hastily shucking off her own boots. "It isn't harming anything."

"Every time something catastrophic happens to us, that dog is there. It's an *ill omen*—"

"Lou is probably *drowning*." Her fingers moved to the laces of her bodice next. I looked away hastily. "Get your ass in there before—"

We both froze, scenting it at the same time: sharp yet sweet, barely there on the breeze. My nose still burned with its familiar scent.

Magic.

Not mine and not hers. Someone else's. Which meant—

Célie's scream split the night. The dog's ears pricked forward in response, but instead of turning toward it, he stared fixedly at a point within the waters. My blood ran cold. Torn with indecision—rooted in fear—I didn't move fast enough. I couldn't block it.

With preternatural speed, the dog careened past me, straight into the heart of the Wistful Waters.

The decision came easily then.

I dove in after it.

THE FINAL VERSE

Lou

Nicholina didn't strike right away. Though I kept my eyes closed, the scene still burned through our shared consciousness. Leisurely, she lifted the knife through the smoke, admiring Ansel's blood along the blade, while I remained bowed over his corpse, my hands clenched desperately around his shoulders. Through her eyes, I saw how pitiful I'd become. And she relished it. She relished this hideous pain inside me, this dark and noxious poison. It was exactly like hers.

I should've forced myself to my feet then—to fight, to flee, to *something.* And if I couldn't have stood, I should've crawled. I should've lifted my fists and raged through the ringing in my ears, should've spat in her face before she drove her knife into my back.

But I couldn't do any of it. I couldn't even lift my head.

"It isn't my birthday until next month," he said sheepishly, but he clutched the bottle to his chest anyway. *The fire cast flickering light on his quiet joy. "No one's ever—" He cleared his throat and swallowed hard. "I've never received a present before."*

He'd never received a birthday present.

"I'm sick and tired of everyone needing to protect me. I'd like to protect myself for a change, or even—" When my frown deepened, he sighed and dropped his face into his hands, grinding his palms into his eyes. "I just want to contribute to the group. I don't want to be the bumbling idiot anymore. Is that so much to ask? I just . . . I don't want to be a liability."

A liability.

"She keeps looking at you." Ansel tripped over a stray limb, nearly landing face-first in the snow. Absalon leapt sleekly from his path.

"Of course she does. I'm objectively beautiful. A masterpiece made flesh." Ansel snorted.

"Excuse me?" Offended, I kicked snow in his direction, and he nearly tumbled again. "I don't think I heard you correctly. The proper response was, 'Goddess Divine, of course thy beauty is a sacred gift from Heaven, and we mortals are blessed to even gaze upon thy face.'"

"Goddess Divine." He laughed harder now, brushing the snow from his coat. "Right."

Gasping now, half laughing and half sobbing, I rocked back and forth, unable to stand it for a single second longer—this great, gaping hole in my chest where Ansel had been. Where Estelle and my mother and Manon and my father and Coco and Beau and even Reid had been. *I* had once been there too. Happy and whole and safe and sound. What had *happened?* What had led us here? Surely we'd done nothing to deserve this life. If someone like Ansel had received only neglect, loneliness, and pain for his efforts, for his *goodness*, what hope could the rest of us have? I'd lied, killed, and cheated—I'd shredded the very fibers of my soul—yet here I was, still standing. He deserved better. He deserved *more*, so much more than he'd ever been given. In another time, I would've screamed and raged at the injustice of it all, at the senselessness, but no amount of anger would change anything now. This was life.

And Ansel was dead.

In another day, another week, another month, this would be Reid's lifeless body I inevitably held, or Coco's. Beau's own father would probably kill him, as my own mother would eventually kill me. There really *was* only one way this story could end. I'd been so foolish to think otherwise. So stupid and naive.

"It'll be quick," Nicholina lied in a whisper, bending over me. Her fingers caressed the back of my head, and her hair tickled my cheek. Around us, the entire cavern succumbed to black flame. "Painless. You will see him soon, little mouse. You can tell him exactly what he meant."

But if I died now, his death would mean nothing.

My eyes snapped open at that cruel reality, and I stared numbly at the flames in front of me. Ansel deserved better. He deserved more than my self-pity. Summoning the final dregs of my strength—the absolute last of them—I lifted my head. She lifted her knife. Our eyes met for one synchronized beat of our hearts.

Then something moved in the tunnel.

Confusion flashed through us both before we turned. Coco's fire had driven everyone in memory into that tunnel, and none should've reappeared. We'd all fled straight to Léviathan after La

Mascarade des Crânes. Could someone have crept back? Could they have returned for Ansel's body? I instantly quelled the thought. Even if someone *had* miraculously traversed the cursed fire, this was *my* memory. It should've ended the moment I'd disappeared in pursuit of Morgane. Why hadn't it?

Through the smoke, a white dog emerged.

Nicholina bared her teeth at it, blasting awareness through me the second before the dog transformed. If I'd been standing, my legs would've buckled. As it was, I rose slowly to my knees, the ringing in my ears deepening to a rushing sound. A roar of blood and hope and fear. This couldn't be happening. This couldn't be *real.*

Ansel ambled toward me.

"Hello, Lou." At my dumbstruck expression, he grinned, the same sheepish grin he'd given a thousand times and the same sheepish grin of which I wanted a thousand more. He wore a pristine powder-blue coat with golden tassels and buttons—my heart ached at the familiarity—with his hands shoved deep into the pockets of his pants. An eternal initiate. No blood marred his person, not his hair or his skin, and his brown eyes sparkled even in the dark. "Did you miss me?"

I stared at him for a second too long, swallowing hard. And then—

"Ansel." My voice broke on his name.

His gaze softened as he came to stand beside me, extending a slender hand to help me to my feet. Hardly daring to breathe, I accepted it tentatively and marveled at its warmth. When he glanced down at his broken body, his smile dimmed slightly, and he shook his head. "What are you doing here, Lou?"

I still didn't have an answer.

It didn't matter, however, as Nicholina's shock had worn off. She whooped with crazed hysteria, reeling backward in glee. "Oh, the baby mouse. The little pinkie, little pup." Her expression hardened. "The boy who doesn't know when it's time to give up."

He met her glare with an equally hostile one, his fingers still bracing mine. "No one is giving up here."

She charged without warning, stabbing her knife at him, and he vanished with a wink in my direction. My heart seized at his absence. When she whirled to find him—slashing her knife through the smoke and spewing a torrent of curses—he reappeared behind her without a sound and tapped her shoulder. She nearly leapt out of her skin.

A snort burst from me unexpectedly.

Ansel grinned again.

Recovering quickly, Nicholina struck out once more, harder and faster this time. Ansel didn't move, but allowed her blade to pierce him—except it didn't pierce him at all. It simply *stuck* an inch from his chest, jammed midair as if she'd plunged it into an invisible brick wall. His grin widened. "You can't kill me. I'm already dead."

"I do not fear the dead," she snarled.

He leaned closer. "You're probably the only one who should. I've recently met some of your enemies, Nicholina—splintered souls and vengeful witches and even a few of the king's children. They're all waiting for you."

I stepped closer, looping my elbow through his and ignoring the chill down my spine at his words. The certainty in them. I focused instead on the euphoric tingle in my chest, the warmth spreading through my limbs. His arm felt solid in mine. Real. I couldn't have stopped my grin if I'd tried. Which I didn't. "I bet they have all sorts of fun things planned for you."

He inclined his head. "Fun is one word."

"You're *lying*." Nicholina lunged again, and he stepped in front of me, blocking her knife. The movement held a sort of grace, or perhaps confidence, he'd never achieved in life. Fascinated, morbidly curious—and something else, something that weighed heavy in my chest—I plucked the knife from midair, paced backward twice, and threw it at him.

He caught it without hesitation—without even *looking*, the cheeky bastard—and I laughed again, unable to help myself. That heavy sensation in my chest lessened slightly when he blushed. "This is an interesting development," I said.

"Lots of those going around." He lifted a brow before pressing the knife back into my hand. Though Nicholina sprang for it, she couldn't seem to move past him to reach me. The wall he'd erected held firm. He didn't acknowledge her efforts, so I didn't either. "The Lou I knew wouldn't have given up," he continued softly. My grin vanished. "She would've fought, and she would've won."

My own words were barely audible. I spoke through numb lips. "Not without you, she wouldn't have."

"You've never needed me, Lou. Not like I needed you."

"Look where that got you." I closed my eyes, a fat tear rolling down my cheek. "I'm so sorry, Ansel. I—I should've protected you. I *never* should've let you come with me."

"Lou."

My chin quivered.

"Lou," he repeated, voice soft. "Look at me. Please." When I still didn't, he turned his back on Nicholina completely, drawing me into a hug. My arms wrapped around his slender torso of their own volition, and though they shook, they held on tight. Too tight. Like they'd never let him go again. "I didn't *want* to be protected. I wanted to help you—"

"You did—"

"I know I did," he said firmly, squeezing me once before drawing back. My arms remained locked around him. Removing them one at a time, he disentangled himself gently, stronger now than before. Strong and graceful and confident. Another tear spilled over. "And I'm going to help you again." He nodded toward Nicholina, who thrashed against the invisible barrier. "You'll have to kill her."

"I've tried."

"Try harder." He squeezed my fingers around the knife's hilt. "A wound to the arm won't do it. The waters have healed you both of superficial injuries. You won't be able to drown her, either." He glanced over his shoulder to where she raged, all but invisible, and a flash of pity crossed his warm brown eyes. "She's lived too long with her emotions. She's numb to them now."

"She isn't numb to her son."

He turned back around to look at me. "You'd rather kill her slowly? Make her suffer?"

"No." The word rose to my lips unbidden. I frowned, realizing its truth. Despite the heinous things she'd done—to me, to Etienne, to God knew who else—I couldn't forget the sense of longing she'd felt in that lavender field with Mathieu, the despair and hopelessness and shame. The fear. *We cannot do this*, she'd said to La Voisin. *Not the children.* Loathing burned up from my stomach to my throat. She'd still done it. She'd still killed them. And perhaps that was punishment in itself.

Will I become a wraith too, maman?

Never.

"I think . . ." I said the words quietly, my thoughts tangling out loud. "I think she's suffered enough." My knuckles clenched around the knife. "But this won't kill her permanently, will it? She said her body is at the Chateau."

"Only one way to find out."

With a sweep of his arm, the barrier collapsed, but Nicholina didn't assail us right away. Eyes narrowed, suddenly wary, she skittered backward as I approached. She felt my resolve. It frightened her. Undeterred, I continued forward with purpose, shifting to block the tunnel, her easiest means of escape. Though she dodged with incredible speed—feinted even faster—we still shared our consciousness, and I matched her every step. Ansel watched our dance in silence, black smoke undulating around his lean frame.

It didn't take long. Not now. Not with him behind me.

Not with Nicholina so incredibly alone.

I anticipated her third bluff, catching her wrist and trapping her against the wall of rock. Flames licked up its face, but neither of us could feel their heat. I pinned my forearm across her throat. She tore at my face, but Ansel appeared, catching her hands and subduing them with ease. She arched off the wall in response, hissing, spitting—eyes bright and rolling with fear—but stilled unexpectedly when I raised the knife. Those eyes found mine and held, and one name radiated through our consciousness.

Mathieu.

I took a deep breath and brought the knife down.

It slid through her ribs in a sickening, viscous movement, and I left it there, protruding straight from her heart. She stared at me, unblinking, as her body collapsed in our arms. "I'm sorry," I said. I didn't know if it was true.

With one last, ragged breath, she clutched me and whispered, "The dead should not remember, but I do." Those eyes found mine again as the light finally left them. "I remember everything."

She slipped from our hold, fading into black mist, and was gone.

We both stared at the spot where she'd disappeared.

In those seconds, a mournful sort of blanket settled over us, deadening the crackling of flames and rumbling of stone. The entire amphitheater would collapse soon. I couldn't bring myself to care. A knot solidified in my throat as I glanced at Ansel, as he looked back with a sad little smile.

"Good riddance." Swallowing hard, I forced a laugh. "She was a huge pain in the ass."

And that was a huge understatement.

"Thank you," I continued, rambling now. "We should really look into procuring you armor for next time. Just imagine—you riding in on a white steed, undoing your helmet in slow motion and tossing all that glorious hair in the wind." I swallowed again, unable to dislodge the lump, and—also unable to look at him—glanced down. "Coco would love it. Hell, Beau probably would too." The fire had completely consumed his body now. Bile rose in my throat, and I tore my gaze away, fresh tears filling my eyes. Surely, *this* was Hell, yet I couldn't bring myself to leave. My feet had grown roots. An inexplicable tug unfurled deep in my stomach the longer we stood there, like an itch I needed to scratch, yet I resisted its pull. It would take me away from here. Away from him. I knew it as fundamentally as I knew that, one way or another, this moment would have to end.

But not yet.

He missed nothing, shaking his head in fond exasperation. "I'll ask again, Lou . . . what are you doing here?"

I bumped his shoulder with mine. "You should know. It seems you've been following us since—since—" The words withered on my tongue, and I tried again. "Since—" *Fuck.* I dropped my gaze once more before quickly regretting the decision. His body still smoldered at our feet. *Double fuck.*

"Since I died?" he supplied helpfully.

My eyes snapped to his, and my expression flattened. "You're an ass."

He bumped me this time, grinning anew. "You can say the words, you know. They won't make me any less dead."

I swatted him away. "Stop *saying* it—"

"Saying what? The truth?" He splayed his hands wide. "Why are you so afraid of it?"

"I'm not afraid."

He leveled me with a frank stare. "Don't lie to me. You can lie to everyone else, but I know better. You're my best friend. Even if I hadn't been following you for the past few weeks, I'd know you're one of the most frightened people I've ever met."

"Everyone is frightened of death," I muttered petulantly. "Those who say differently are drunk." Unable to help it, my eyes drifted back to his body. Fresh gorge rose. I had a finite amount of time left with Ansel, yet here I stood, arguing with him atop his makeshift pyre. Perhaps these waters hadn't healed me, after all. Perhaps whatever was broken inside me couldn't be fixed.

Despite his harsh words, his insistence at our new reality, he lifted my chin with a gentle finger. His brows furrowed with concern. Still Ansel. "I'm sorry. Don't look if it upsets you." He continued in a milder tone. "No one wants to die, but death comes for us all."

I scoffed. It was an angry, ugly sound. "Don't feed me that shit. I don't want platitudes."

"They aren't platitudes." Dropping his hand, he stepped backward, and I couldn't help it. I looked down again.

"Of course they are." Hot tears brimmed over my eyes, burning tracks down my cheeks. I wiped them away furiously. "Death isn't a happy ending, Ansel. It's sickness and rot and betrayal. It's fire and pain and"—my voice cracked—"and never getting to say goodbye."

"Death isn't an ending at all, Lou. That's what I'm trying to tell you. It's the beginning." Quieter still, he added, "You've lived in fear too long."

"Fear has helped me survive," I snapped.

"Fear has kept you from living."

I backed away from his corpse, from the flames, from the knowing gleam in his gaze. "You don't—"

He didn't allow me to finish, however, waving his hand. The scene before us dissipated—as simple as brushing aside the smoke—and another formed instead: a crackling hearth, a smooth stone floor, and a gleaming wooden table. Copper pans hung above it, and flowerpots of eucalyptus cluttered the far windowsill. Snowflakes fell beyond its panes, illuminated by starlight.

At the oven, Reid pulled forth a baking stone, and the sticky buns atop it sizzled and smoked. He'd burned them slightly, their tops a shade too brown, but still he turned to me—exorbitantly pleased with himself—grinning and flushed from the heat. Coco and Beau sat around the table, mixing what looked like cream. Vanilla and spice perfumed the air.

I sank into the chair next to them, limbs trembling. Ansel took the last free seat.

Rapt, I watched as Beau plucked a bun from the stone, dipped it straight into the cream, and shoved the entire thing in his mouth without a word.

"'eez a' burnt," he protested, face convoluting in distaste. Or perhaps pain. Steam still rolled from the buns, and as such, from his open mouth. Coco waved his breath from her face, eyes rolling skyward.

"You're disgusting."

"And you"—he swallowed hard and gripped the back of her chair, yanking her closer and leaning low with a smirk—"are beautiful." She scoffed and pushed him away, plating two buns for herself.

Ansel watched with a surprisingly contented smile.

"Where are we?" I breathed, glancing around the room at large. A black cat curled by the hearth, and in the distance—perhaps in the next room, perhaps in the next house—a woman and her daughter sang a familiar ditty. A game of ninepin bowling echoed upward from the street below, as did the children's shouts and laughter. "I've never been here before."

Still, this place felt . . . familiar. Like a dream I could almost remember.

Reid drizzled cream over two more buns with expert precision, his focus intent, before handing them to me. He didn't wear his Chasseur coat, nor a bandolier around his chest. His boots sat neatly by the front door, and there—on the third finger of his left hand—a simple gold band gleamed in the firelight. When I glanced down at the mother-of-pearl ring on my own finger, my heart nearly burst from my chest. "We're in Paradise, of course," he said with a slow, sultry grin. He even winked.

Verily I say unto thee, today shalt thou be with me in Paradise.

I stared at him incredulously.

Coco snatched up the buns before I could touch them, dumping half the dish of cream over his masterpiece. Smirking at his sudden scowl, she pushed them toward me once more. Her eyes no longer glinted with pain. With heartache. "There. I fixed them."

Ansel squeezed my hand under the table. "This is what you wanted, right? A home in East End, surrounded by family?"

My mouth might've fallen open. "How did you . . . ?"

"It's a bit tame for you, isn't it?" Beau narrowed his eyes at the room. "No naked men with strawberries and chocolate"—Reid shot him a murderous look—"no mountains of gold or fountains of champagne."

"That's your Paradise, Beau." Coco smiled sweetly. "And a hideously clichéd one at that."

"Oh, come on. Don't tell me you weren't expecting something outrageous like dancing bears and fire-eaters." Beau frowned when he spied the cat purring at the hearth. "Is that . . . ? Tell me that isn't supposed to be Absalon."

Bristling at his disparaging tone, I said, "What? I miss him."

Reid groaned. "He was a restless spirit, Lou. Not a pet. You should be glad he's gone."

Coco rose to extricate a pack of cards from a nearby hutch. The familiarity of the movement, the intimacy of it—as if she'd done this precise thing a hundred times before—unnerved me.

We'd never had a real home, the two of us, but here in this place, surrounded by loved ones, it felt dangerously close.

In a different world, I might've been Louise Clément, daughter of Florin and Morgane. Perhaps they would've loved each other, adored each other, filling our home in East End with sticky buns and potted eucalyptus—and children. Lots and lots of children. . . . We could've been happy. We could've been a family.

Family. It'd been an errant thought in the catacombs, surrounded by dust and death. It'd been a simple, foolish dream. Now, however, my chest ached as I glanced from Coco to Reid to Beau. To Ansel. Perhaps I hadn't found parents or brothers or sisters, but I'd found a family regardless. Sitting with them at my table—in my home—that dream didn't feel so foolish, after all.

And I wanted it. Desperately.

"You never know." Coco lifted a casual shoulder as she closed the drawer. "Maybe Absalon has found peace."

Peace.

With a long-suffering sigh, Beau helped himself to another sticky bun in response.

I couldn't shake the word, however, as Ansel's eyes locked with mine, and the levity of the scene fell away. Even the firelight seemed to darken. And that pull in my stomach—it returned with a vengeance. This time, however, I couldn't discern exactly where it led. Part of it seemed to tow me away from this place, away from Ansel, but the other part . . . I tilted my head, studying it closer.

The other part seemed to tow me *toward* him.

A siren's call.

With another sad shake of his head, he leaned forward. His voice dropped to a whisper. "No, Lou."

Beau lifted a finger, pointing it between us accusingly. "Stop it. No secrets allowed."

Coco returned to her seat and cut the deck. The cards snapped between her deft fingers. "I do hate when they whisper." Her eyes flicked to Ansel, and she added, albeit playfully, "*I* am her best friend, thanks very much. If she's going to whisper with anyone, it should be me."

"It *should* be me." Reid crossed his arms, eyes sharp on the deck in her hand. "And I saw that."

She flicked the card from her sleeve, grinning without remorse.

"I'm okay, Lou," Ansel continued softly, ignoring them. He didn't so much as glance in their direction as the protests began anew. When my chin began to quiver—when the room blurred through my tears—he lifted a hand to stroke my back, consoling me. "I'm okay. You're going to be okay too."

The tears fell thick and fast now, salty on my lips, and my entire body trembled. I forced myself to look at his face, to memorize him—the color of his eyes and the shape of his smile, the sound of his voice and the scent of his clothes, like sunshine. Pure sunshine. That was Ansel. Always the warmest of us all. "I don't want you to go."

"I know."

"Will I ever see you again?"

"Not for a long time, I hope."

"Can't I come with you?"

He looked to Reid and Coco and Beau then, who'd just started up a game of tarot. Beau cursed roundly when Coco took the first trick. "Is that really what you want?" he asked. *Yes.* I choked on the word, face hot and wretched, before shaking my head. He smiled again. "I didn't think so." Still he made no move to rise, content to remain sitting with me for as long as I needed. He wouldn't force me to go, I realized. It would have to be my decision.

The tug in my stomach grew stronger, more insistent. I clenched my fists against it and bowed my head in response, shoulders shaking. Not yet. *Not yet not yet not yet.* "I can't just *leave* you, though. I can't do it. I—I'll never see you blush again. I'll never teach you the rest of 'Big Titty Liddy,' and we'll—we'll never go to Pan's or sneak spiders into Jean Luc's pillow or read *La Vie Éphémère* together. You promised to read it with me, remember? And I never showed you the attic where I lived. You never caught a fish—"

"Lou." When I looked up, he was no longer smiling. "I need to find peace."

Peace.

I swallowed hard around the word, my eyes wet and swollen.

Peace.

It felt foreign and strange on my tongue. Bitter.

Peace.

But . . . the ache in my chest expanded to thrice its size. It also felt right. Exhaling softly, I closed my eyes in resolve. I couldn't count the number of times I'd done wrong in my life— and I regretted few of them—but I would do right by Ansel. He wouldn't spend another moment following me, restless, trapped in a world where he no longer belonged. He would fix my mistakes no further. I didn't know how he'd managed to stick around in the first place—whether it'd been his choice or mine—but I couldn't keep him here. I'd finally give him what he needed. What he deserved.

He deserved peace.

Nodding, numb, I allowed the tug in my stomach to pull me to my feet. He rose with me, and the scene around us began to swirl and shift in waves. "Was any of this real?" I asked as Reid, Coco, and Beau continued their card game, oblivious to the waters. Pressure pinched at my shoulders. "Or did I drown and imagine everything?"

Ansel's eyes twinkled. "A little bit of both, I think."

We stared at each other, neither willing to move.

"I don't think—"

"It's funny—"

"You first," I insisted.

A touch of wistfulness entered his expression. "Do you think . . . before you go . . . you could sing me the last verse?" He rubbed his neck, sheepish once more. "If you feel like it."

As if I'd ever had a choice.

"*Their babe they named Abe,*" I sang on a watery chuckle, "*his brother Green Gabe. Then Belle and Adele and Keen Kate. Soon dozens came mewling, but still they kept screwing, even outside the pearly gates.*"

His face burned so vivid a scarlet it rivaled my every memory, but he grinned from ear to ear regardless. "That's indecent."

"Of course it is," I whispered. "It's a pub song."

His eyes shone too brightly now, brimming with tears of his

own. Still he grinned. "You've been to a pub?" When I nodded, smiling so hard it hurt, my chest aching and aching and *aching*, he shook his head in horror. "But you're a *woman*."

"There's a whole world outside this church, you know. I could show you, if you wanted."

His grin faded slowly, and he touched my cheek, bending to brush a kiss across my forehead. "Thank you, Lou. For everything."

I clutched his wrist desperately as the last of the house darkened, as the tug in my stomach deepened to a burn. The pressure at my shoulders increased, and my ears popped. Shouts penetrated the thick haze of my consciousness, echoing all around as if from underwater. "Where will you go?"

He glanced back to where Coco had sat at our table, shuffling cards and laughing. The wistfulness in his expression returned. "I have one more goodbye to make."

The burn in my chest became near unbearable. Icy needles pierced my skin. "I love you, Ansel."

My vision clouded as the waves truly descended, shocking and brutal. Though they pulled me away from him, I'd remember his smile until the day I died. Until the day I saw it again. His fingers slipped from mine, and he drifted backward, a beacon of light in the darkness. "I love you too."

With a powerful kick of my legs, I surged upward.

Toward fear.

Toward pain.

Toward *life*.

ANOTHER PATTERN

Reid

We broke the surface together. Water sluiced from her face, golden and freckled, and her hair, long and brown. She clutched my shirt as she gasped, spluttered, before tipping her face to the sky and grinning. Those clear blue-green eyes met mine, and she finally spoke. "Do you have something in your pocket, Chass, or are you just happy to see me?"

I couldn't help it. I threw back my own head and laughed.

When I'd found her drifting beneath the surface—her body limp and cold, her white hair floating eerily around her—I'd feared the worst. I'd seized her. Shaken her. Kicked to the surface and shouted her name. Nothing had worked. In a fit of rage, I'd even dived back down to find the white dog, but it'd vanished.

As we'd risen the second time, however, something had changed: her legs had started to move. Slowly at first, then swifter. Stronger. They'd worked in synchrony with mine, and I'd watched, amazed, as her hair had grown longer with each kick, as the color had returned to each strand. To her skin.

She'd healed before my very eyes.

Crushing her to me now, I spun us in the water. It didn't ripple with the movement. I didn't care.

"Lou." I said her name desperately, pushing the long locks from her face. "Lou." I kissed her mouth, her cheeks, her throat. I kissed every inch of her I could reach. Still laughing. Hardly able to breathe. She laughed with me, and the sound sparked in my bones. Light. Bright. If I stopped swimming now, I would've floated. I would've *flown*. I kissed her again. I'd never stop kissing her. "Lou, are you—?"

"I'm all right. I'm me." Her arms wove around my neck, and she tugged me closer. I buried my nose in the crook of her shoulder. "I feel—I feel better than I have in ages, honestly. Like I could fly or wield an axe or—or erect a statue in my honor." She wrenched my head up to kiss me once more. When we broke apart, gasping for breath, she added, "It'd be made of sticky buns, of course, because I'm *starving*."

My cheeks hurt from smiling. My head pounded in rhythm with my heart. I never wanted it to stop. "I have one in my—"

Coco's shout at the shore caught us both unaware, and we turned as the world rushed back into focus. She'd sunk to her knees, staring into the waters like she'd seen a ghost. "Ansel," Lou whispered, loosening her grip to better tread water.

I frowned. "What?"

"He wanted to say goodbye." Smiling softer now, she kissed me again. "I love you, Reid. I don't say it often enough."

I blinked at her. Warmth cracked open in my chest at her

words, spreading to the tips of my fingers and toes. "I love you too, Lou. I've always loved you."

She scoffed playfully. "No, you haven't."

"I have."

"You didn't love me when I plowed into you at Pan's—"

"I absolutely did," I protested, brows shooting upward. "I loved your god-awful suit and your ugly mustache and—"

"Excuse you." She leaned back in mock outrage. "My mustache was *magnificent.*"

"I agree. You should wear it more often."

"Don't tempt me."

I leaned closer, brushing my nose against hers. Whispering against her lips. "Why not?"

Her eyes gleamed wickedly in response, and she wrapped her legs around my waist, nearly drowning us both. I couldn't bring myself to care. "You've corrupted me terribly, Chass." With one last maddening kiss—slow and deep—she disentangled herself and flicked my nose. "I'll wear my mustache for you later. For now, we should—"

Then Coco screamed again.

I knew immediately this scream wasn't like the last—knew it before a man's body thudded to the beach, knew it before Lou released me abruptly. I reached for her again, drawing her into a protective embrace.

Because I recognized the man's body.

And Constantin—an immortal being made of water and mist—was dead.

Coco sprinted forward with another cry. "Constantin!" Her hands fluttered over him helplessly while Lou and I treaded water in silent horror. Ice crept up my spine at his wide-open eyes. His slack mouth. The bloody hole in his chest. "Constantin!" Coco shook him fiercely now, clearly unable to process. Her shock, no, *denial,* mirrored my own. Constantin couldn't have died—the melusines had cursed him eternal.

No one is safe here, Cosette.

Lou's knuckles turned white on my arms. "How is this possible?"

My grip tightened on her waist. "I don't know."

When Coco continued to shake him, her hysteria rising, Lou swam forward determinedly. "Right. We can fix this. The waters restored him once, which means—"

I caught the back of her chemise. "Wait—"

A high, chilling laugh echoed over the cliffs, down to the shore, and Morgane le Blanc stepped from the path onto the beach. A dozen witches followed. They fanned out behind her in a defensive formation, eyes sharp and mouths hard. Resolute. Coco scrambled backward into the water, dragging Constantin's body with her.

"Well, isn't this sweet." Hair gleaming in the moonlight, Morgane clapped her hands in applause. Her gaze flicked from Lou and me to Coco, who lifted a silver chalice to Constantin's lips in a final attempt to revive him. Her lip curled. "You must be so proud, Josephine. Look how your darling niece frets over the guardian." To Coco, she said, "He's dead, *mon petit chou.*" She lifted her stained fingers. "Surely you know magic cannot live without a heart?"

"How—how did you—?" Coco's voice stuttered as she stared helplessly at Constantin. "He's the *guardian*. How did you kill him?"

Morgane arched a brow. "I didn't."

La Voisin stepped into view. A dark substance coated her hands. It matched the hole in Constantin's chest. "I did."

Coco rose slowly to her feet.

"Foolish man. We presented our black pearls, of course, but still he put up quite the fight." Though Morgane tutted, the sound lacked her signature melodrama. Deep purple shadowed her eyes, like she hadn't slept in days. Her skin was paler than usual. Burns riddled her face and chest, and her hair appeared singed in places. "Unfortunately for Constantin, we are the two most powerful witches in the world. Now, I will admit, the dragon gave us pause. It stole my broken toys, nearly razed my dollhouse to the ground, but no matter. The dragon has gone, and we shall not be caught unprepared again." She glanced out at the waters, clearly displeased. "We are here now."

"A dragon?" Lou whispered. "Who . . . ?"

"Zenna."

She'd saved the others, after all. She'd flown back to Cesarine.

Coco could've been carved from stone. "What have you done, *tante*?"

La Voisin met her niece's hard stare, impassive. Her expression revealed nothing. With the dip of her chin, however, three blood witches marched forward. Between them floated two gagged and bound figures. Eyes wide, both thrashed against the magic holding them to no avail.

Beau and Célie.

Lou cursed softly.

"What I must," La Voisin said simply.

A beat of silence passed as they stared at each other.

"No." Coco's eyes burned at the word, her hands curling into fists. She took a small step forward, and the waters—they rippled beneath her foot. La Voisin's eyes tracked the movement, narrowing infinitesimally. "That isn't an answer, and neither is Morgane le Blanc. How many times did we ask for her aid? How many of our kin have perished from cold and disease? How many of them have *starved* while she stood idly by?"

La Voisin arched a brow. "As *you* have stood idly by?"

Coco didn't so much as flinch. "I'm not standing idly by now."

"No. You are *actively* standing in my way."

"You betrayed us."

"I am losing patience," Morgane said with quiet malevolence. Her fingers twitched.

"Foolish child." La Voisin spoke as if she hadn't heard her. "You would have us continue to sicken and starve. Why?" Her black gaze found Lou and me. "For them?" Lip curling, she shook her head in a slow, winding movement, like a cobra preparing to strike. "You are the Princesse Rouge. Once, I would have encouraged your voice. I would have respected your opinion. But now your empathy rings hollow. You do not care for our people. You do not claim them as kin. You may protest my betrayal, Cosette, but you betrayed us long before this. Morgane has promised our coven safety in Chateau le Blanc"—her eyes seemed to harden at the name—"in exchange for Louise. I would do far worse than betray you to procure it. The time has come to choose your side."

She stepped beside Morgane at the last, tall and unyielding. Together, the two formed a striking image. Both regal, both beautiful. Both queens in their own right. Whereas Morgane possessed a dark sort of glamour, however—ever the showman—Josephine boasted no decoration. She was stark. A study in harsh reality and bleak truth. The malice in the former's eyes looked comically bright next to the flat, cold cunning of the other. The honesty. She didn't try to hide it.

La Voisin loathed Morgane.

"The ends justify the means," she finally murmured. "If we don't stand together, we will fall."

Coco stared at her aunt as if seeing her for the first time. "You're right." The Dames Rouges on the beach stilled at Coco's unexpected response. I recognized a few of them from our time together in Léviathan. "I *was* a child," she continued, her voice growing stronger with each word. Impassioned. "I was a child scared of my own birthright—of leading everyone, of failing any-one. Of disappointing *you*. I feared the responsibilities such a life would entail. Yes, I ran, and I am sorry for that."

She looked to her kin then, bowing her head, accepting her culpability in their hardship. They regarded her with a mixture of suspicion and admiration. "I am no longer that child. You *are* my kin, and I want to protect you as much as my aunt does. But *her* life"—she pointed a finger in Lou's direction—"is worth just as much as yours." She turned back to her aunt. "Morgane has been hunting the king's children. We found Etienne—the king's son—butchered in our own camp, and Gabrielle disappeared shortly after. Morgane was responsible, *tante*. But you already know that, don't you? Did you offer them up yourself? Your own people?" When Josephine said nothing, confirming her suspicions, Coco exhaled harshly, moving to stand between us and her aunt with deliberate care. "I've chosen my side."

Lou went still at her words. The blood witches, however, stirred. Murmurs rose from a few of them. Whether in support or dissent, I couldn't tell.

La Voisin's expression didn't change at her niece's declaration. Instead, she jerked her head to the witches nearest her. "Take her." When they hesitated, shooting anxious glances at Coco, La Voisin slowly turned to face them. Though I couldn't see her expression, they hastened to obey this time.

Coco skittered backward as they approached, and the waters rippled again. Kept rippling.

The witches halted at the shore, reluctant to follow, until the bravest took a tentative step forward.

When her toe touched the waters, her entire body jolted, and—as if a spectral hand had reached forth to snatch her foot—she slipped, vanishing into their depths. They swallowed her scream without even a ripple. Sinister and still in the moonlight.

The witch might've never existed.

Morgane tsked as the other witches balked. Her voice rang out hard. Ruthless. "I suppose rules are rules, aren't they? Dreadful things. As if any one of us had time to *speak our truth.* Never fear, though, *tata*," she said to Josephine, whose jaw clenched at the diminutive epithet. "The poor dears will have to come out eventually, and we have all the time in the world." She snapped her bloody fingers, and Beau and Célie dropped to their feet. "*These* two, however, don't have much time at all. What say you, darling?" she called to Lou. "How shall I play with them?"

"You're sick," Beau snarled, the veins in his throat bulging as he fought to move.

She only smiled. It held no warmth. From her cloak, she extracted Célie's injection, hurling the syringe into the water. "Though perhaps I tire of play altogether. Come here, Louise, or I shall kill them. Our game is done."

Lou started forward instantly, but my fingers caught her chemise. I didn't let her go. Couldn't let her go.

"Reid, don't—"

Baring her teeth, Morgane snapped her fingers again. Swords appeared in Beau's and Célie's hands. Another snap, and Beau lunged forward, his blade slicing through Célie's side. Blood welled in its wake. With the flick of Morgane's finger, Célie retaliated with a sob, her sword lodging deep in Beau's shoulder. Toy soldiers. "I'm sorry," she gasped, arms trembling as she attempted to combat Morgane's magic. "I'm so sorry—"

"I'm fine." Beau desperately strove to comfort her as he countered her strikes, teeth gritted. Breath shallow. "We're going to be fine—"

Célie stabbed again, this time in his thigh.

Blood poured.

With a wild cry, Coco surged forward as Lou twisted in my arms. Morgane waved a hand, however, and when Coco cleared the water, a glass cage descended around her. She pounded against its walls, furious, and strings wrapped themselves around her wrists and ankles.

Baring her teeth, La Voisin darted forward to intervene.

"The ends, Josephine." Morgane waved another hand, and the strings tightened, stretching Coco's limbs taut to the point of pain. A doll in a box. "They justify the means. Is that not what you said?"

La Voisin stopped dead in her tracks. Her body quivered with fury. "My niece remains unharmed."

"She *is* unharmed." Those glittering emerald eyes found Lou. Beau and Célie continued battling behind her, their blood splattering the sand. "For now."

"You have to let me go, Reid," Lou pleaded. "She won't stop—"

"No." I kept my voice low, shook my head fervently. Tried to ignore my own mounting panic. There had to be another way. My eyes swept over the witches again, assessing. Thirteen in all—six Dames Rouges, judging from the scars on their skin, and seven Dames Blanches. The former would need physical contact to harm, but the latter could attack at any moment. My mind searched wildly for an advantage. *Any* advantage. Could L'Eau Mélancolique affect our magic? Repress it? If we could somehow lure Morgane into the waters . . . I tested my own patterns. The golden cords rose instantaneously. *Shit.*

Worse still, one cord continued to shine brighter than the rest, pulsing with insistence. The same cord that had answered at the lighthouse. The same cord I couldn't pull. I *wouldn't* pull.

Save her, the magic whispered. *Save them all.*

I continued to ignore it.

Coco cried out as her strings tightened, and Lou took advantage of my distraction, finally twisting free. "Look, *maman*, look." She waved her hands in a placating gesture. "I'll play with you now. I'll even trade toys: me in exchange for Beau and Célie." Though I still shook my head, reaching for her, she kicked away and continued determinedly. "But you can't harm them again. I mean it, *maman*. Any of them. Beau, Célie, Reid, Coco—they're all safe from this point onward. No one touches them."

The pattern pulsed. My head continued to shake.

Morgane didn't seem particularly surprised by Lou's request, nor did she laugh or dance or goad as she once would have. "You can see how that might present a problem, daughter. With your death, the prince and huntsman will also perish."

"You assume I'll die."

"I *know* you'll die, darling."

Lou smirked then, and the sight of it struck me like a physical blow. Only days ago, I'd feared I would never see that smirk again. My body tensed with barely controlled restraint. "I guess we'll have to play to find out," she said.

She started for shore once more.

"No." I caught her arm. She hadn't suffered this long—she hadn't sacrificed everything, walked through literal fire, exorcised a fucking *demon*—to give up so easily now. Coco had said one life wasn't worth more than another, but she'd been wrong. Her life meant more. Beau's and Célie's lives meant more. And Lou—her life meant most of all. I would ensure she lived it. I would ensure they *all* lived. "You can't do this."

She kicked upward to kiss me in one last desperate plea. "I can't kill her if I keep hiding, Reid," she breathed against my cheek. "Remember what your mother said—closing my eyes won't make it so the monsters can't see me. I have to play. I have to *win*."

"No." My jaw locked. I couldn't stop shaking my head. "Not like this."

"Either I kill my mother, or my mother kills me. It's the only way."

But it wasn't. It wasn't the only way. She didn't know that, of course. I'd refused to speak the alternative aloud, refused to acknowledge it even in my own thoughts. The golden cord quivered in anticipation.

Lou had already given so much. She'd journeyed to Hell and back to save us, shattering herself in the process. She couldn't die now. And if she didn't die—she spoke of killing her mother lightly, as if matricide wasn't an unspeakably heinous act. As if it wasn't unnatural. As if it wouldn't break her all over again.

"No."

My purpose resolved as I clutched her face. As I brushed the water droplets from her lashes.

So beautiful.

"You test my patience, children." Morgane flicked her hand, and Beau, Célie, and Coco all crumpled in identical movements—like toys crushed underfoot. Beau and Célie lost consciousness completely, and Coco bit her lip around a scream. Morgane's emerald eyes filled with spite. "Perhaps you're right, little blood witch. Perhaps I'll kill all of you instead."

"Do not be foolish," La Voisin snapped. "Accept the terms. The prince and girl mean nothing. They will die soon enough."

Morgane whirled to face her. "You *dare* command me—?"

Faintly, I heard their voices escalate, but my entire world had narrowed to Lou's face. To the golden pattern. It vied for my attention, nearly blinding now, pointing straight and true at its target. Connecting us. Demanding to be seen. Hope and despair warred deep in my chest. Neither existed without the other.

I would find my way back to her. I'd done it once. I could do it again.

And she'd finally be safe.

"I'll find you again, Lou," I whispered, and her brows puckered in confusion. I kissed them smooth. "I promise."

Before she could answer, I clenched my fist in her hair.

The pattern burst in a shower of gold.

I saw no more.

PART III

C'est l'exception qui confirme la règle.
It's the exception that proves the rule.
—French proverb

DOUBT CREEPS IN

Nicholina

The pain fades without a body, as does all sense of touch, of smell, of taste. There is no blood as we spiral from sea to sky. There is no magic. No death. Here we are . . . free. We are a gust of wind. We are the winter cold. We are a flurry of snow on the mountainside—swirling, twirling, whirling—nipping the noses of witches below. Our mistress walks among them. She calls them by name.

She does not call ours.

Anxious now, we sweep onward, up, up, *up* the mountain as snowflakes flit to and fro around us, within us. *It isn't here*, they flutter, they mutter. *We cannot find it.*

Our body, our body, our body.

Our mistress will not have forgotten us.

We move faster now, searching, gusting through the trees. The castle. She will have brought our body to the castle. But there is no castle, only snow and mountain and pine. There is no bridge. There is no one to welcome us, no one to grant us entry. If *she* would've stayed—the one with the nasty words, the one with the golden patterns—if her spirit would've fragmented, we would have found the castle. We would have found our body.

But she did not fragment. She did not stay.

Now she is alone.

You've failed, Nicholina.

Nasty words.

Your mistress needs her more than she needs you.

Our mistress has not forgotten us.

Perhaps your body won't be there at all. Perhaps you will *die.*

We spiral again in agitation, in fear, and streak the mountainside. Already, we feel ourselves spreading, drifting, losing purpose. We cannot linger long without a body, or we will become something else. Something helpless and small. A cat or a fox or a rat. There are many ways to become a matagot, oh yes, but we will not become one. Not us. We are not forgotten.

Something scurries through the foliage, and we dive, eliciting a shriek of fear from the creature. It matters not. We need a body until our mistress returns. Until *her* mistress shows us the way. Nasty woman, like her daughter. Nasty witch.

We crouch inside the mink's body and wait. Time passes differently to animals. We track shadows instead, quivering within the roots of a tree. Hiding from eagles. From foxes. We smell our mistress before we see her, and we hear her sharp, impatient words. She argues with Morgane. She speaks of Morgane's daughter.

We leave the mink and follow behind as towers and turrets

take shape. A bridge. Fire has ravaged each structure. All around, white ladies knit and weave their invisible patterns into stone. Into wood. Into windows and arches and shingles. We do not care about castle reparations. We sweep for the entrance, hiding from their prying eyes, curling through the smoke. We feel the pull of our body now. We feel it here.

Our mistress hasn't forgotten us after all.

Up the stairwell, down the hall, into the small, sparse bedroom. Our body isn't on the bed, however. It isn't on the pillow. *The bed is empty,* we cry in dismay. *The bed is bare.* We draw short, quivering, as we search. As we follow our body's pull. As we find it on the hard stone floor. *But the bed is empty.* Confusion swirls. *The bed is bare.*

Our body looks as a corpse in the shadows of the corner. Sickly and pale. Scarred. We hover above it, regret wafting through us now. A tendril of hurt. No fire warms the chamber. No candlelight. But it matters not. We feel no cold, no, and our mistress knows this. She knows. She knows pain is fleeting. She will relish our greeting.

You've failed, Nicholina.

It matters not.

Your mistress needs her more than she needs you.

Pain is fleeting.

You've chosen the wrong side, Nicholina. But it isn't too late. You could ally with us before they betray you. Because they will *betray you. It's only a matter of time.*

Our mistress would never betray us.

Slowly, we sink into ourselves, first a finger, a toe, then a leg and an arm and a chest until our entire body settles in on itself with a heavy breath. Heavy. So heavy. So weary. Images of lavender and wraiths and sickly, corpselike little boys flicker. Memories of family. The word tastes different now than it did then. Once, it tasted of comfort, of love, of warmth. We do not remember what warm feels like now. We do not remember love. Within *her* we'd felt it—a brief flicker in the shadows, in the dark. She'd felt it so strongly. We hold on to it now, that memory. We hold on to that warmth we'd felt when she looked upon her huntsman, her family.

Our own eyes do not open as we lie upon this hard, cold stone. We do not move to the bed. Our mistress did not want us there.

Sometimes we think our mistress does not want us at all.

ANGELICA

Lou

Without warning, Reid collapsed face-first into the water, and that—

That is when I lost my shit completely.

Fresh shouts erupted from shore as I dove toward him, slinging an arm across his shoulders and spinning him to his back, looping his elbow through mine and cradling his head against my shoulder. The sharp, potent scent of magic clung to him. Though his chest still rose and fell, the movement seemed shallow, harsh, as if he was in terrible pain. "Reid!" I shook him desperately, struggling to stay afloat. We both went under. Water burned my throat, my eyes. Choking on it, I kicked harder, propelling us above the surface for a few precious seconds. I could swim, yes, but towing a limp two-hundred-and-something-pound man was something else entirely. *"Reid!"*

The shouts around us escalated, and I glanced to shore. My heart lodged in my ravaged throat.

Morgane had lost consciousness with Reid.

Whatever magic he'd done, it'd affected her too, and absolute chaos reigned. The Dames Blanches nearest her shrieked and rushed forward, pulling her away from Josephine, from Coco, from us. "Do not be foolish!" Josephine's vehement shouts cut through the mist, which had descended with a vengeance once more. "This is our chance! Get the girl!"

But even the blood witches wouldn't step foot in the waters again—not when they continued to ripple.

Not when Coco rose, her binds having vanished after Morgane's collapse.

Not when she stepped back into the waters, nor when she lifted her hands. Her dark eyes fell first to Constantin, then to Beau and Célie—still blood-soaked and unconscious—and they burned with retribution. "You should've known better than to follow us here, *tante*. I was born in these waters. Their magic is my own."

I foundered beneath the waves, surging up in time to see Josephine clench her fists.

"Their magic is *hers*," she spat. "Not yours. Never yours."

"I am part of her."

"You are *mine*." The last shred of Josephine's control seemed to snap, and she swept a long, crooked dagger from her cloak. Her hands shook. "She abandoned you. She abandoned *me*. She—"

"—is on her way," Coco finished grimly, eyes flicking to her own uplifted hand. A fresh wound I hadn't noticed sliced her palm. Blood dripped from it into the waters, and with a start, I realized Coco's steps hadn't woken L'Eau Mélancolique at all.

Her blood had.

And the waters weren't merely rippling now.

They were *moving*, parting down the center as if the heavens had drawn a line from Coco to the horizon. They swelled on either side of that line, growing and growing and *growing*—like twin tidal waves—until a footpath along the rocky seafloor appeared. Small enough for a single person to walk unhindered. I clung to Reid as the waves battered us, the currents dragging us under before thrusting us upward once more. When I shouted Coco's name, coughing and spluttering and desperately kicking for shore, she turned to look at us. Her eyes widened with panic before we went under again.

When we reemerged, another current swept us up between one breath and the next. This one, however, seemed determined not to drown us, but to deliver us to Coco. I didn't fight or question it, focusing all my attention on keeping Reid's head above water. My arms shook with the effort. My legs seized. "Come on, Chass." I pressed the back of his head into the crook of my neck once more. "We're almost there. Stay with me. Come on, come *on*—"

The current dropped suddenly, and we plummeted with it, straight through the icy water to the seafloor path. When we landed, stunned and shivering, Coco sprinted out to meet us, pulling at my arms, my hands, pushing Reid's soaking hair out of his face, checking his pulse. She ignored Josephine and the blood witches completely. They still didn't dare enter L'Eau Mélancolique, even on the path. "Are you hurt?" Coco demanded, checking every inch of me in harried, clumsy movements. "Are you—?"

I caught her hands and grinned. "You look like shit, *amie.* Those eye bags are as big as Beau's head."

Coco dropped her forehead to our joined hands, exhaling in relief. "You're you."

"I'm me."

"Thank god."

"Thank *Ansel.*"

She chuckled on a weak exhale, lifting her head—then froze. Her stare fixed on something over my shoulder, something farther up the footpath. Its silver reflection, just a speck in the darkness, shone bright in her eyes. Whoever or whatever it was, it approached not from shore, but from the depths of L'Eau Mélancolique. I tensed instinctively. A face drifted in my mind's eye from Nicholina's memories, and suspicion lifted the hair at my neck. Gooseflesh rose on my arms.

When Josephine turned ashen, however, I knew. When she stumbled—actually *stumbled*—back a step, I clutched Reid tighter in my lap, my heartbeat thundering in my ears. Several of the blood witches fled without a word. My gaze remained locked on Coco as the silver speck in her eyes grew larger. Nearer. Too near now to ignore.

I twisted to look over my shoulder at last.

And there she was.

A full-body chill swept through me at the sight of her: tall and statuesque with thick black curls and rich brown skin, nearly identical to Coco in every way. Except for the eyes. At some point between Nicholina's memory and now, they'd turned a pale, icy shade. Her gown matched the peculiar color—the iridescent fabric swirling between white and green and purple and blue—and rippled in the breeze as she approached. Like a goddamn fairytale princess.

She stopped a pace behind me. I might've gaped. My mouth might've fallen open like a bug-eyed fish. Up close, she appeared even more beautiful than from afar: her face perfectly heart-shaped, her lips perfectly bowed. Silver powder dusted her cheeks and nose, as well as her brow and collarbones, and ornate moonstone jewelry gleamed from her fingers, her wrists, her ears, her throat. She'd braided her hair around a teardrop opal headpiece. The precious stone glittered against her forehead.

Her dress and hair continued to undulate gently, even after the breeze waned.

She smiled down at me.

"Angelica," I whispered in awe.

"Sister," Josephine hissed.

But it was Coco's whispered accusation that changed everything. "Mother."

With the graceful incline of her head, Angelica nodded. She stood with impeccable posture, unearthly stillness, her shoulders back and her hands clasped at her waist in a familiar position. How many times had I seen Josephine hold herself that way? How many times had I yearned to wring that long, elegant neck?

It was uncanny how two people with the same features could look so different.

I glanced at Coco.

It was haunting when there was a third.

"*Sœur.*" With a voice smooth as silk, Angelica spoke with calm assurance. "*Fille.*" She lifted a hand as if to touch Coco's cheek before thinking better of it. She let it fall to her side instead. Bereft. "I have missed you."

Though Coco said nothing, her eyes spoke volumes. They glittered with unshed emotion in the moonlight.

I frowned, my own eyes narrowing, and the glow around Angelica's face dimmed slightly.

More than slightly.

I might've even called her hideous now.

Then again, mothers abandoning their children to cruel relatives might've been a sore spot for me. Madame Labelle had left Reid, and he'd ended up with the Archbishop as a father. Morgane had tried to kill me, and somehow, I had too. Though beautiful, Angelica had left Coco in the hands of her aunt. She was no different from them, really. She was rotten inside.

In her case, rot just happened to smell like lilies.

Accepting that her daughter wouldn't or perhaps *couldn't* answer, Angelica returned her gaze to Josephine, who had inched toward Beau and Célie. Those perfect lips pursed. "Do not harm the children, Josie. Your quarrel is with me."

Josephine glowered as she lifted Célie's head. Her hands weren't needlessly cruel, but careful and steady as she held

Célie's neck firm. No. Not careful. Practical. Efficient. She would kill Célie if necessary, just as she'd killed Etienne. "What will you do?" she asked her sister. "You cannot leave the waters."

Coco and I shared a brief, confused look.

Angelica only flicked a jeweled dagger from her thigh sheath—her *thigh sheath*—and sighed. "Must we do this, *sœur*? We both know the damage I can inflict from here." To illustrate her point, she placed the dagger against her chest and sliced down, directly between her breasts, without hesitation. The blade tore through fabric and skin as butter, leaving a thick line of blood in its wake.

Josephine hissed, and her hand flew to her own chest, where an identical wound had formed.

My confusion deepened as I stared at it. Nicholina's memories hadn't revealed anything like this. Not that I'd known to look for it.

"What the hell is happening?" I breathed to Coco. Josephine and Angelica still glared at each other, bleeding, in a silent stand-off. "You said your mother was dead."

"I said my *aunt* said she was dead."

"And now?"

She shrugged stiffly. "Now it looks like they're blood bound."

"Blood bound?"

"It's a dangerous spell between Dames Rouges. It binds their lives together. Their magic."

I looked again at their twin wounds. "Oh shit."

She nodded. "That about sums it up."

On the heels of that unpleasant realization, however, came another. "Does that mean we can't—we can't kill your aunt without killing your mom?"

"Apparently."

My stomach plunged as Josephine readjusted her grip on Célie, pressing the dagger to the back of her head. "Your threat is empty as always, *sœur*," she said, "while you clutch at others' skirts and hide where I cannot reach you." She laughed harshly. The only time I'd heard her laugh at all. "No. You will not inflict real harm on yourself to hurt me, or you would have done so centuries ago."

Right. I couldn't kill her, then. Testing my patterns swiftly, I followed each one to their sacrifice. I just needed to knock the knife from her hand—something simple. A gust of wind, perhaps. A spasm of her fingers. "Wait," I whispered to Coco as I searched. "If you thought your mother was dead, why were you trying to summon her?"

"I wasn't trying to summon her. I just—the waters spoke to me. I listened."

"You gave them your *blood*"—I cut an incredulous glance at her over my shoulder—"because they asked nicely? Did they at least say please?"

"I was born of them," she muttered defensively.

"Surrender Louise," Josephine insisted, ignoring our low, fervent conversation. Angelica kept her blade loose at her side. Her blood dripped from its tip to the seafloor, and black pearls formed from each drop. I glanced again at Constantin.

"Surrender Cosette"—Josephine's fingers tightened around her own dagger—"or I will dispose of this pathetic child. I will dispose of the mortal prince."

Like hell.

Gritting my teeth in a sharp burst of hatred, I clenched my fist, and my anger sparked along a pattern. I watched as it sizzled between us, feeling the heat of it leave me. The cord disintegrated to golden ash as Josephine yelped, dropping her dagger and clutching her burned hand. I grinned in satisfaction and wiggled my fingers. "It's time for you to go, *Josie.*"

Angelica lifted her own hand in emphasis, and the waters responded, surging past the shoreline to reclaim Célie and Beau, depositing each of them at our feet. But they didn't stop there. They continued to flood the sand, to reclaim the beach, sweeping away the silver chalices. They chased Josephine's hem with sentient determination, and she had no choice but to back away quickly. Just as Nicholina had feared the dark, it seemed Josephine feared the strange magic fortifying these waters.

She still refused to cede.

When she turned to shout orders to the remaining Dames Rouges, however—commanding them to hold their ground—her eyes widened, and she finally saw the battle had been lost. The blood witches had already fled into the cliffs. Josephine stood alone.

"Leave this place, *sœur,*" Angelica said. From the steely edge to her voice, I knew this was her final warning. "And never return. I cannot promise your safety if you continue to provoke Isla."

"*Isla*." Josephine's face twisted at the name. The waters kept coming, however, forcing her back until she stood atop the first rocks of the path. Her black eyes bored holes into Angelica's beautiful face. "The Oracle. Your *mistress*."

"My *friend*." With another wave of Angelica's hand, the waters climbed higher, and Josephine leapt backward, away from them. She moved with surprising agility for a thousand-year-old hag. "You would do well to respect her," Angelica continued. "Though she rules below, she has not turned a blind eye to the war above. You do not want her as an enemy." A peculiar light built in those pale eyes as her gaze turned inward. "Though it seems you've already displeased her siblings." For our benefit, she added, "The Triple Goddess and the Wild Man of the Forest."

Do you have a family, Monsieur Deveraux?

As a matter of fact, I do. Two elder sisters. Terrifying creatures, to be sure.

"All these years, I have watched you, Josephine." Sadness softened Angelica's voice, and the ethereal glow slowly faded from her eyes. "I have hoped for you. You think me a coward, but you are a fool. Have you learned nothing from our mistakes?"

Josephine didn't visibly react to her sister's piteous words. She merely continued to walk backward, her face inscrutable, her eyes burning like twin flames in the darkness. "There are no mistakes, sister." She smiled at each of us in turn. "We shall see each other soon, I think."

Then she turned, cloak billowing behind her, and disappeared into the night.

A LIE OF OMISSION

Lou

I collapsed at Reid's side the next moment, and Coco followed suit with Beau and Célie. To my surprise, Angelica knelt too, brushing Constantin's cheek with the back of one slender hand. Unlike her sister, she wore her emotions proudly for all to see. This one looked akin to . . . wistfulness.

I gestured to the floodwater on the beach, both irritated and impressed. "Maybe lead with that next time."

She laughed softly.

Shaking my head and grumbling—her laughter sounded like a goddamn bell—I pressed my ear to Reid's chest to listen to his heart. It beat strong and steady. When I checked his temperature, his skin felt warm—but not too warm—beneath my wrist. I lifted his eyelids next, sparking a light on the tip of my finger with residual anger. His pupils contracted like they should've. Right. I sat back in relief. He was perfectly healthy, just . . . asleep. He'd probably claimed Morgane's consciousness to give us time to flee, sacrificing his own in the process. I only needed to wake him up. As I searched for a pattern to do that, however, I couldn't quash my curiosity. Glancing at Angelica and Constantin, I asked, "Didn't he betray you?"

Her pale eyes rose to mine. "He did."

Coco didn't look up. Tension radiated from her clenched jaw, her taut shoulders. She snatched my dagger to reopen the cut on her palm. Like me, however, she couldn't seem to help herself. "And you still loved him?"

"You needn't do that, darling." Angelica's gaze flicked to the wall of water on our right. In response, a thin stream twisted toward us like a serpent. It reached first for Beau, touching the deep puncture in his leg and flowing into his very skin. The wound closed almost instantly, followed by the one on his shoulder. A second tendril unfurled toward Célie, and a third stretched to Angelica. All of their injuries vanished.

"You see?" Angelica smiled, and my breath might've caught in my throat a little. I forced a scowl to compensate. "Do not fatigue yourself." She looked again at Constantin's lifeless body, her gaze lingering at the hole in his chest, before swallowing hard. The movement made her seem almost human. "But yes, Cosette. I loved him the way we all love things we shouldn't—to excess. He hurt me in the way those things always do." That palpable sadness crept back into her voice. "I am sorry he is dead."

I am sorry he is dead. Just like that, she became something strange and foreign once more.

Coco's hands clenched around Beau's collar as his eyes fluttered open. She didn't thank her mother for healing him. I didn't blame her. Instead, I scooted closer, pulling Reid with me, and braced my shoulder against hers in silent support. She leaned into the touch, dropping Beau's shirt as he sat upright. "What happened? Where's Mor—" His eyes widened when he caught sight of Angelica. To his credit, he only blinked stupidly for about three seconds before turning to Coco. Then he blinked a few times more. "Is this . . . ?"

Coco nodded curtly. When her hand rose to clench her locket in a death grip, Angelica's eyes followed, widening in disbelief. "You . . . wear my locket," she said. It sounded like a question.

"I—" Coco stared at the ground with ferocious intent. "Yes."

A fierce sort of protectiveness pricked my chest at her obvious discomfort. Perhaps I should've been angry with her for never telling me about her mother. How many times had we talked about Angelica together? How many times had she chosen not to tell me? A lie of omission was still a lie. Hadn't I learned that the hard way?

Nicholina had called it a betrayal. Perhaps I should've been upset, but I wasn't. We all had our secrets. I'd certainly kept my fair share. Though I didn't know why she hadn't confided in me, I *did* know Coco had been six years old the last time she'd seen her mother. I knew she didn't need an audience for this reunion. What she *needed* was time to process, time to decide what she wanted her relationship with Angelica to look like. To decide if she even wanted that relationship at all.

Resolute, I settled on a pattern to wake Reid, flicking his nose to wield it, eager to distract the others from this painfully awkward situation. One night of my own sleep in exchange for his consciousness now. Simple, yet effective. Nothing too harmful. With Reid awake, we could move on. We could gather our allies to march on Chateau le Blanc or return to Cesarine or—well, I didn't know exactly, but we could do *something* other than gawk.

I flicked Reid's nose once more, waiting for the pattern I'd enacted to dissipate. It didn't budge. I tried again, clenching my fist this time. It actually recoiled, twisting into a different pattern altogether. And the other patterns in my web—they did too. They grew hopelessly knotted in a way I couldn't trace or understand, as if the magic itself had grown confused.

I frowned down at him.

What the hell had he *done?*

Distracted by my nonsensical patterns, I didn't see or hear Angelica move behind me. Her hand landed on my shoulder. "He will not wake," she said gently. "Not until he is ready."

I shot her an irritated look, shrugging away from her touch. "What does that mean?"

"His mind needs time to heal." She dropped her hand without insult, lacing her fingers together in a maddeningly calm pose. "He is lucky to be alive, Louise. This spell could have done irreparable damage to more than his mind."

"*What* spell?" When she didn't answer, my frown deepened to an outright glower. I pushed to my feet, my cheeks hotter than usual. Claud, Constantin, Angelica—what was the *point* of omniscience, of omnipotence, if one didn't use it? I shook my head. "If his mind has been harmed, why can't you heal him? You healed everyone else!"

She only smiled again, a horrible, pitying smile. "Only he can heal himself."

"That's horsesh—"

"Do not worry, Louise." A hint of that unnatural glow reentered her eyes, and I stepped back despite myself. "His injuries are not fatal. He will wake—of that, I am certain. His path forward, however, cannot yet be seen."

The waters see things we cannot see, know things we cannot know. Constantin's warning repeated in my mind. *Angelica was a seer, and her magic shaped them.*

"Your path, on the other hand, is clear." She gestured down the narrow split in the waters. It led straight into the heart of L'Eau Mélancolique. In the silver light of the moon, the mist from its flowing walls sparkled like flecks of diamond. She looked almost apologetically to Coco. "I am sorry, *fille*, that our reunion is fraught with such complication. When you summoned me—"

"I didn't know I was summoning you," Coco interjected.

Angelica nodded, though something like pain flashed through her eyes. "Of course. When you called upon the *waters*, I heard it. I felt your need, and I—well, I needed to answer it." Her voice gentled as she continued, though she spoke with no less certainty. "There is much you don't understand, Cosette. I know you are angry with me—as you well should be—but we do not have the luxury of time for lengthy explanations and apologies."

Coco stiffened at the straightforward words, and I squeezed her arm. Angelica was right, however; this wasn't the time or place for this conversation. Not with Morgane and Josephine roaming near, not with a corpse at our feet, trapped between colossal walls of water. I eyed them nervously as a long silver fin flicked past.

"To do so," Angelica continued, recapturing my attention, "you must understand three things. First, I am no longer safe outside these waters. Isla's benevolence protects me, and she risked much in allowing me to come here. My sister lives in fear of my magic—in fear of Isla herself—but if Josephine had tried to enter these waters, I would not have been able to stop her. For as much as this magic is yours through birth, it is also hers because of our blood bond."

She didn't give us another chance to interrupt. "Understand this second: all of your life, Cosette, I have watched you." Those blue eyes eddied with white, and fresh gooseflesh lifted the hair on my arms. It lifted Coco's too. "I know where you have been and who you have loved. I know you have scoured the kingdom—from La Fôret des Yeux to Le Ventre to Fée Tombe—for allies against Morgane. You have befriended the Beast of Gévaudan and the Wild Man of the Forest. You have entranced dragons and witches and werewolves alike."

For the first time, she hesitated, the white in her eyes flaring brighter. To me, she said, "You still wish to defeat your mother?"

"Of course I do, but what—?"

"Isla would make a powerful friend."

Coco clutched my arm so hard that I nearly lost sensation in it. But her voice didn't falter. "Whatever you're trying to say, *maman* . . . say it."

"Very well." She waved her hand at the waters once more, and streaming tendrils shot forth, weaving midair to form a liquid lattice. They looked much like the roots of a glass tree, clear and bright and shining. Twining beneath Reid, they lifted his body and suspended it at waist level. I reached out to seize his hand with my free one. When Angelica motioned him down the path, the waters obeyed. He floated away from us, and I darted to keep up, dragging Coco along with me. "Stop it! What are you—?"

Her mother spoke in a strained voice. "I wish I could offer you a choice, *fille*, but truthfully, you have already made one. When you called upon the waters, you asked of them a favor. Now we must ask one of you."

Coco dug in her heels, incredulous. "But I didn't know—"

The waters began to close behind us, blocking our path to the beach. We stared at them in horror. "Isla wishes to speak with you in Le Présage, Cosette—you and your friends." Angelica's beautiful face pinched with regret. "I'm afraid you must all come with me."

A MAGPIE'S NEST

Lou

Le Présage.

I'd heard the name once, spoken amidst breathless giggles at the maypole. Another witchling had suggested we seek it out as we'd twirled and danced in the sweltering midsummer heat. Manon had refused, repeating a story her mother had told her about melusines drowning unsuspecting witchlings. We'd all believed it at the time. Melusines *were* bloodthirsty, after all. Treacherous and uncanny. The boogeyman hiding beneath our beds—or in our backyard, as was actually the case. Some days, I'd been able to see the mist from their shore through my window at sunrise. It wasn't until I'd first played with Coco that I'd realized melusines posed no real threat. They held dominion over an entire world below—a world apart from the rest of us, greater and stranger than our own. They had little interest in the affairs of witches.

Until now, it seemed.

I shot surreptitious looks at the black waters as we trudged along the footpath. They twined beneath Reid, towing him forward, while more water flooded the path behind, forcing us deeper along the seafloor. Within the waves on either side, shadows moved, some small and innocuous and others alarming in their size and dexterity. Beau appeared to share my disquiet. He nearly clipped my heel in his haste to flee the serpentine faces pressing in on the pathway. "Fish women, eh?" he muttered at my ear.

"Legend says they could once walk on land, but I've never seen it in my lifetime."

He gave a full-body shudder. "I don't like fish."

Another silver face flashed through the waters, sticking her forked tongue out at him.

Angelica glanced over her shoulder as she continued to glide forward. "Whatever you do, do not insult them. They're incredibly vain, melusines, but never vapid. They value beauty almost as much as gentility—manners are of utmost importance to a melusine—but they have vicious tempers when provoked."

At Beau's alarmed expression, Coco added, "They love flattery. You'll be fine."

"Flattery." Beau nodded seriously to himself, tucking the knowledge away. "Right."

"Are they very beautiful, then?" Célie asked, clutching her leather satchel over her shoulder with both hands. Dirt was caked beneath her cracked nails, and her hair spilled haphazardly from her chignon. Blood and grime stained her porcelain skin, the once-rich velvet of her trousers. The lace trim at her sleeves now trailed gently behind her in the wind. "Since they value beauty?"

"They are." Angelica inclined her head with an almost impish smile. "They are not, however, human. Never forget that, child— beautiful things can have teeth." Célie frowned at the words but said nothing more, and Angelica turned her attention instead to Coco, who studiously ignored her. She stared at her daughter for a long moment, deliberating, before clearing her throat. "Are you well, Cosette? Have your own injuries healed?"

"It's Coco." She glared at a beautiful fish flitting past, its golden fins rippling behind it. "And I've survived worse."

"That isn't what I asked."

"I know what you asked."

An awkward moment passed before Angelica spoke again. "Are you warm enough?"

"I'm fine."

Then another.

"Your hair looks lovely, I must say," she tried again. "Look how long it's grown."

"I look like a drowned rat."

"Nonsense. You could never look like a rat."

"Though you do look a bit peaky," Beau interjected helpfully. "A bit limp."

They both turned cold gazes upon him, and he shrugged, not at all contrite. When they turned away once more, I elbowed him in the ribs, hissing, "You ass."

"What?" He rubbed the spot ruefully. "That's likely the first time they've ever agreed on something. I'm trying to help."

After a handful more feeble attempts at conversation—which Coco shut down with an ease and efficiency I admired—Angelica cut straight to the heart of it. "We have a long walk ahead of us to Le Présage, daughter. I should like to know you better, if you are willing."

Coco scoffed and kicked an algae-covered rock. It plunked into the water, splashing my ruined hem. "Why? You said you've been watching me. You should already know everything."

"Perhaps. I don't know your thoughts, however." Angelica tilted her head to the side, lips pursed, as if debating something. After another few seconds, she said, "I don't know why you wear my necklace, for example."

Subtle as a brick.

"I wonder what that's like," Coco mused bitterly, still watching the golden fish. "Wanting an explanation and never receiving one. It'd be horribly frustrating, don't you think?"

Angelica didn't force any more horrendously awkward conversation after that.

As for myself, I tried not to think. Angelica had said Reid's injuries weren't fatal. She said he would wake. And Isla—though I knew little about the mysterious woman they called the Oracle, she *would* make a powerful ally against Morgane and Josephine. With our other allies occupied, it made sense to indulge Isla. Josephine clearly feared her.

I didn't know how much time passed before my heels began to ache. It could've been moments. It could've been hours. One second, the moon shone directly overhead, limning Reid's silhouette in silver, and the next, it had dipped below a wall of water, bathing us all in shadow. Only then did I notice the strange phosphorescent glow emanating from the waters.

"What is that?" I whispered.

"A special kind of plankton," Angelica said, her voice equally soft. "Though here we call them sea stars. They light the waters around the city."

The bluish glow reflected in Célie's wide eyes. She reached out to the wall nearest us, where thousands of nearly indiscernible specks of light swirled together to form one bright, pulsing wave. "They're like fireflies."

Angelica smiled and nodded, lifting her chin for us to look down the footpath. What appeared to be a golden gate bisected it, colossal and ornate, expanding into the empty plains of water on either side and rising to the sky. If not for the algae growing along its whorls and spikes, it could've been the gate to Heaven.

Beyond it, there seemed to be no water at all.

"Behold—Le Présage." Angelica's smile widened as we drew to a unanimous halt. "And there, in the center, Le Palais de Cristal."

We all stared, necks craned, at the orb of dry, mountainous terrain in the heart of L'Eau Mélancolique. Huts had been carved into the rock along the city's edge, into the very mountainside, as the seafloor rose to one tumultuous peak. At the top of that peak, spires of sea glass rose—cruel and sharp and beautiful—from the ruins of an enormous sunken ship. Its broken masts and shredded sails glowed blue in the light of the sea stars.

"Is it—is that dry land?" Beau glanced from Coco to me and

back again in search of an explanation, but Coco didn't seem to notice; her mouth had parted slightly as she gazed up at the city, and her free hand had risen to grasp her locket once more.

"I . . . I remember this place," she breathed. Those dark eyes sought mine, brimming with sudden certainty. With hope. Grinning, I released her arm, and she took a stumbling step forward. "I've been here before. Le Présage." She said the words as if tasting them, returning my smile. Her anger, her resentment momentarily forgotten. Memory was a strange and wonderful thing. "The Oracle City. Le Palais de Cristal."

Angelica shadowed her movements, close enough to touch. She still didn't dare. "You were born there."

Coco whirled to face her, nearly breathless in her anticipation, and the dam finally burst. "How? How was I born here if you can't leave? Is my father a merman? Is my father Constantin? Why is the Oracle City built on dry land? How is there dry land in the middle of the Wistful Waters?"

Angelica laughed at Coco's outburst—it really *did* sound like bells—and gestured us onward toward the gate. The sea stars followed in our wake. Though they didn't speak, though I could hardly see them, they seemed almost . . . *curious*. Sprite-like. "It isn't always dry," she said. "I told you. Melusines are courteous to a fault. They wouldn't want their guests to feel uncomfortable."

"So they drained their entire city?" Beau asked incredulously. "Just for us to breathe?"

Even Angelica's shrug articulated elegance and grace. "Why not?"

"Does that mean they *can* walk on land?" I asked, sticking a finger into the waters on impulse. The sea stars clustered around my knuckle, illuminating the shape of my bone through my skin. I flexed it in fascination, watching as they swirled and eddied, desperate to touch me. They left a cold, tingling sensation in their wake.

Angelica's smile vanished, and she slapped my hand away. "Stop it." She lifted my finger to eye level, revealing thousands of tiny bloodred pricks. Teeth marks. "They'll eat you if you let them." I snatched my hand away with an outraged sound, wiping my blood on my chemise and glaring at the carnivorous little beasts. "And we are *not* on land," she continued, resolute. "Make no mistake. We remain on the seafloor, where melusines are free to grow legs."

"Grow legs?" Beau's face twisted in disgust as a handful of humanoid shadows swam toward us from along the gate, their metallic tails flashing. I inched closer to Reid. "Like frogs?"

Angelica's expression grew stony as the melusines' faces took shape through the waters. Three women and two men. Though their bodies ranged in shape—from broad and coarse to fine and delicate—they all seemed somewhat longer than human, as if their limbs had been stretched, and each moved with a sort of liquid grace. Their colors varied from the palest of silver to the deepest of ebony, but all shimmered slightly, monochromatic and dusted with pearlescent scales. Their webbed fingers wrapped around what could only be described as spears. Perhaps tridents.

Whatever they were, they gleamed wickedly sharp in the

phosphorescent light, and I had no interest in meeting the receiving end of them.

"Beau," I murmured, smiling pleasantly at their hostile faces as they swam closer. Closer still. "Apologize, you blithering idiot."

He backed into me, nearly breaking my foot. I stomped on his toes in return. He swore roundly, snarling, "They couldn't have heard me."

Coco spoke through her own fixed smile, imitating Célie, who curtsied low, and elbowed Beau when he didn't do the same. "Good idea. Let's risk it."

"It was an honest question—"

The melusines didn't pause at the walls of water, instead gliding seamlessly through them and stepping—actually *stepping*—onto the footpath, their split tails transforming to legs before our very eyes. The scales on their fins disappeared, and glistening skin wrapped around feet, ankles, calves, thighs, and—

A beat of silence passed as Beau's alarm promptly vanished, replaced by a wide, shit-eating grin.

They were naked.

And, contrary to Angelica's assertion, they looked *very* human. Célie gasped.

"*Bonjour, mademoiselle,*" Beau said to the one in front, bending to kiss her long-fingered hand. He hesitated for only a second when he saw she had one extra knuckle per finger. Each clenched around her spear as she pointed it at his face, hissing and revealing a pair of thin fangs.

"You dare to touch me without permission?"

The male nearest her lifted his trident to emphasize her words. Unlike the female, he wore a thick golden rope around his neck, its emerald pendant the size of a goose egg. Matching twin emeralds glittered at his tapered ears. "He likened us to amphibians as well." When he tilted his head, the movement was predatory. His silver eyes glittered with menace. "Do we appear as amphibians?"

Angelica swept into a deep, immaculate curtsy. "He meant no offense, Aurélien."

Beau lifted placating hands, nodding along hastily. "I meant no offense."

The female slanted her black eyes at him. Against her narrow silver face and her long—*long*—silver hair, they appeared . . . disconcerting. And far too large. Indeed, everything about her and her kin's features seemed disproportionate somehow. Not wrong, exactly. Just . . . strange. Striking. Like a beautiful portrait meant to be studied, not admired. She didn't lower her weapon. "Yet still I hear no apology. Does the human prince think us ugly? Does he think us strange?"

Yes.

The answer rose to my lips, unbidden, but I bit my tongue at the last second, frowning and averting my gaze. The movement attracted the melusine's attention, however, and those black eyes turned to me, flicking over the planes of my face. Studying me. She grinned with dark cunning, and my stomach dropped with realization.

The women who dwell here are truth tellers.
Drink of the waters, and spill their truth.

Oh god.

Beau, who'd quashed his own answer with a strangled sound, cast me a panicked look. I returned it full measure. If we couldn't lie, if we'd been forced into a kingdom of *literal* truth—

If he didn't kill us, I certainly would.

Either way, we'd all be dead by night's end.

Beau tried to speak again, keeping his eyes trained carefully on the melusine's face. His throat bobbed against the tip of her spear. "Of course you do not look like a frog, *mademoiselle*, and I am grievously sorry for the implication. Indeed, you are quite—" The lie stuck in his throat, and his mouth gaped open and closed, like the fish who'd gathered to watch our inevitable demise. "Quite—"

"Lovely," Célie finished, her voice earnest and firm. "You are lovely."

The melusines regarded Célie with open curiosity, and the silver-haired female slowly lowered her spear. Beau swallowed visibly as she inclined her head. The others followed suit, some bowing deeply, others curtsying. The one called Aurélien even extended his hand to her, pressing an emerald earring into her palm. "You are welcome here, Célie Tremblay." The silver-haired melusine's lip curled as she glanced back at Beau. "More so than your companions."

Célie curtsied again, smaller this time. "I am pleased to make your acquaintance, Mademoiselle . . . ?"

"I am Elvire, the Oracle's Hand." The melusine smiled in approval at Célie's impeccable manners, and another of her companions looped a strand of pretty white pearls around Célie's neck. They looked ridiculous against her tattered gown, but Célie didn't seem to mind.

"Thank you." She lifted a hand in surprise, stroking them gently, before pushing the single emerald stud through her pierced earlobe. She looked like a magpie. "I shall treasure each one."

Beau stared at her incredulously.

"They suit you." Elvire nodded before gesturing toward her companions. "We are here to escort you into the Oracle City. This is Aurélien"—she pointed to the bejeweled but otherwise naked merman—"Olympienne"—another mermaid, this one the palest lavender with diamonds adorning her teeth—"Leopoldine"— a third with thin golden chains sparkling along her charcoal torso—"Lasimonne and Sabatay." She finished with two onyx mermen. One boasted rubies in his nipples, while the other's eyes glowed milky white. Seaweed wound through his braided hair. "We are simply enchanted to meet you. If you would be so kind as to walk beside me, Mademoiselle Célie, I would much appreciate your company."

When Célie nodded, Elvire extended an arm, and the two joined elbows, as prim and polite as any two aristocrats strolling through the park in Cesarine. Sabatay gestured for Angelica and Coco to fall in behind them while Leopoldine and Lasimonne flanked Reid on either side. Aurélien stepped in behind without a backward glance. Only his barnacle-crusted trident even glanced in our direction, waving us forward.

And *that* was how Beau and I found ourselves at the rear of the procession into the city.

Le Présage was unlike anything I'd ever seen. Just as I'd suspected, the melusines lived like magpies, building their homes
from the remnants of sunken ships, from coral, from stone,
hoarding sunken treasure to decorate their windows and lawns.
A weathered marble bust sank deep into the silt of a kelp-filled
garden at the edge of the city. The owner had affixed diamonds
to each eye. Farther in, officials ushered melusines to the side of a
bustling thoroughfare. Instead of brick or cobblestones, the road
had been paved with mismatched coins—gold, silver, and bronze
couronnes, as well as foreign coinage I didn't recognize. The occasional gemstone. An errant shell.

"Is it always this . . . crowded?" Beau asked, brows raised.
Scores of melusines gathered to watch us pass, their eyes luminous and skin lustrous. Many wore gowns hundreds of years
out of fashion—ostentatious and ornate—while others, like our
guards, wore nothing at all. A merman with a bone necklace and
pearl hood winked at me from afar. His companion had painted
her entire body gold, donning only a fork in her intricately
braided chignon.

The only thing every melusine had in common, it seemed,
was their legs.

"We have not walked for many years," Aurélien said as means
of explanation.

From around the bend of the street, a team of sienna-colored
octopi surged into view, pulling a gilded carriage behind. Except
its paint had disintegrated in the salty water, and its wood had
mostly rotted, caving in half the roof. Still, the melusines nearest

it clapped gleefully, and the couple inside—one wore a monocle, for Christ's sake—waved as if royalty. And perhaps they were. Perhaps kings and queens in the world below owned octopi and carriages. Perhaps they also sewed shark teeth into veils and wore golden cutlery in their powdered wigs.

The entire city glittered with the air of ludicrous opulence gone to seed.

I adored it.

"I want a wig." I couldn't see enough as we marched past little shops of stone with planter boxes of red algae. One melusine walked his pet spotted turtle on a gold-threaded leash. Another lounged in a claw-footed tub at the street corner, pouring water from a pitcher onto her legs. They transformed back into obsidian fins before our very eyes. Merchants hawked wares of everything from conch fritters and crab legs to oyster-and-pearl earrings and music boxes. The light of the sea stars undulated eerily across each face, the only illumination in the entire city. "*Why* do melusines own wigs?"

"And gowns?" Coco asked, eyeing the couple nearest us. They both wore heavy trains of brocade velvet and . . . corsets. Just corsets. No bodices. No chemises. "How do you wear them with fins? Wouldn't skirts weigh you down in the water?"

"Can a melusine drown?" I asked curiously.

Olympienne tilted her lavender head between us in consideration. She pursed her lavender lips. "Do not be silly. Of course melusines cannot drown. We have gills." She bared her neck, revealing pearlescent slits along the side of her throat. "And lungs." She inhaled deeply. "But yes, unfortunately, such handsome attire can prove quite troublesome underwater. We have much anticipated your arrival for just this reason."

"To wear dresses?" Beau frowned as a young boy strode past in scarlet breeches and billowing cloak. He bared sharp teeth at us. "You drained the entire city to wear . . . dresses."

"We drained the city because we are courteous hosts," Lasimonne said, his voice unexpectedly deep. "That we should also wear our treasure is a pleasant inclusion."

Wear our treasure. Huh. It made sense. Where else would a melusine trapped below water find such sumptuous clothing but sunken ships? Perhaps Lasimonne's ruby nipple rings had come from the ship we approached at this very moment, splintered at the base of Le Palais de Cristal.

"How long does it take to drain an entire city?" I peered down a darkened alley that seemed to drop straight into an abyss, where I swore I saw an enormous eye blink. "And what's down there?"

"A giant squid. No, do not provoke it." Aurélien steered me back onto the main road with the tip of his trident.

"Isla foresaw your arrival months ago." Sabatay tossed his braid over a sculpted shoulder and gestured for us to keep moving. The palace loomed directly ahead of us now. "From the moment you chose to marry the huntsman rather than flee or allow the authorities to lock you away."

Beau cleared his throat, glancing up at the waters far above. The sea stars' reflection pulsed faintly in his dark eyes. "Yet Constantin was quite adamant that Célie and I *not* enter this place.

Indeed, he said humans who drank of the waters would go mad."

Elvire looked at us from over her shoulder. "And *did* you drink of the waters?"

"I—" Beau frowned and looked at Célie. "Did we?"

She shook her head slowly, brow creasing. "I don't know. I did have a rather disturbing dream while unconscious, but I thought..."

Elvire patted her arm knowingly. "Dreams are never dreams, Mademoiselle Célie. They are our deepest wishes and darkest secrets made true, whispered only under cloak of night. In them, we are free to know ourselves."

Beau's skin appeared sallow in the ghostly light, and he swallowed, visibly disturbed. "I didn't speak any truth."

Elvire arched a silver brow. "Didn't you, *Your Highness*?" When he didn't answer—merely stared at her in confusion and dismay—she chuckled softly. "Never fear. You shall not go mad from it. You entered the waters under the Oracle's invitation, and she will protect your mind for the duration of your stay."

My own frown deepened as more guards lowered a rotten gangway for us to board the ship. "The only human entrance into Le Palais de Cristal," Aurélien explained, prodding us forward. Tentatively, we followed the others atop the soft wood. It bowed beneath our weight.

A buxom melusine waited for us above, her silver hair elaborately coiffed and her gray eyes clouded with age. Fine smile lines crinkled the corners of her mouth. "*Bonsoir*," she greeted us with a deep curtsy, her train sparkling behind her on the deck.

She wore no forks or monocles, instead looking every inch the consummate human aristocrat. Even the color and fabric of her gown—aubergine silk embellished with golden thread—would've been the height of fashion in Cesarine. "Welcome to Le Palais de Cristal. I am Eglantine, the Oracle's personal handmaid and lady of this palace. I shall be attending you during your stay in our home."

With the same impeccable grace and innate confidence as Angelica, she turned toward the colossal doors to our left. By some miracle, water hadn't eroded the structure beyond—perhaps the captain's quarters?—as it had much of the quarterdeck. Some boards had splintered or rotted completely, leaving gaping holes through which candlelight flickered from below. Music too. I strained to hear fragments of the haunting melody, but Aurélien prodded me forward once more, through the doors and onto a grand staircase. Covered in moldy carpet and lit by gilded candelabra, the stairs seemed to descend into the belly of the ship.

I glanced at the crystal spires above our head. "Are we not going up?"

"Guests are not permitted in the towers." Aurélien poked me more insistently now. "Only the Oracle and her court inhabit them."

"Are you part of her court, then?"

He puffed out his muscled chest, a peculiar shade between white and gray. Like fog. "I am."

I patted his trident. "Of course you are."

Reluctantly fascinated, I followed Beau down the stairs. The walls had once been papered, but time and water had disintegrated all but scraps of the striped design. The carpet squelched softly underfoot. "When will we meet with Isla?" I asked, grinning as Leopoldine trailed a long finger through the candle flame. She drew it back sharply a second later, examining the fresh burn there with a frown. "Will there be food?"

Though the guards stiffened as if insulted by the question, Eglantine chuckled. "Of course there shall be food. As much as you could possibly eat." My stomach rumbled its appreciation. "A special banquet has been prepared just for you. After you wash, we shall join Isla to dine."

"*Just* her?" Coco asked, eyes narrowed in suspicion.

A knowing gleam entered Eglantine's eyes. "Well, I would be remiss if I didn't mention how eager the entire court is to meet all of you. Especially you, Cosette." She winked at Coco in a conspiratorial fashion, and I decided instantly that I liked her. "Look how you've grown! You've always been beautiful, *chérie*, but I must say your breasts are an exquisite addition."

I definitely liked her.

Coco straightened her shoulders in pride—or defiance—pushing said additions front and center as the guards prepared to leave us. To Célie, Elvire asked, "Won't you sit with us at tonight's feast, Mademoiselle Célie? We would so enjoy your company."

Célie blinked once, glancing between each of their hopeful faces, before smiling wide. "I would love that."

"Excellent." Olympienne flashed her diamond teeth while

Leopoldine unclasped a golden chain from between her breasts, refastening it around Célie's waist. Sabatay tucked a strand of seaweed into her chignon, and Beau, Coco, and I—well, we all watched Célie become a bird's nest in unabashed bewilderment. "Until later, *mon trésor.*"

They left us under Eglantine's watchful gaze. "Your chambers are just around the hall—one for each of you, of course. Unless you and the human prince would like to share, Cosette?"

Beau smirked as tension bolted down Coco's spine. "That won't be necessary," she said tersely. Angelica turned away to hide her smile behind her hand. "Thank you."

"Very well. I shall leave you here." Eglantine halted outside another decaying door. A burgundy curtain had been draped over the threshold, shielding the room from the hall. "This entire wing is completely your own." She nodded to the other doors lining the way. "Ring the bells when you've finished with your wash, and I shall collect you. Might I bring anything else to make you more comfortable?"

Célie reluctantly glanced at her ruined trousers. "Perhaps a clean nightgown?"

"Oh! How silly of me." Eglantine brushed the burgundy curtain aside, pointing to the tarnished armoire beside a hammock of nets. "Each room has been stocked with clothing of all shapes and sizes, hand selected by the Oracle herself. Consider each piece yours."

THE GREEN RIBBON

Lou

Coco followed me into the curtained room while Beau and Célie wandered down the corridor in search of privacy. Already, steam curled from a golden tub in the corner. What had probably once been a silk dressing screen stood furled beside it, but the fabric had decomposed long ago. They'd woven seaweed into the panels instead.

Yawning, Coco unlaced her blouse before stripping it overhead. Though I moved to Reid's side, I didn't bother shielding his eyes. He hadn't so much as stirred since we'd entered Le Présage, and if the sight of even Coco's exquisite assets couldn't tempt him to wake, we might've been in more trouble than I thought.

I snatched a bowl from the dressing table, filling it with bathwater.

Then again, this *was* Reid. If he'd opened his eyes just now, he would've fainted all over again.

He was going to be *fine.*

Coco eyed the bowl as she shimmied from her pants and

plucked a scarf from the armoire, wrapping it around her hair. "Are you bathing him?"

"Nope." Thrusting my shoulder into his, I rolled him onto the hammock, and his magical bed burst beneath us, soaking the carpet once more. "Not yet anyway." She arched a brow and slipped into the tub, scooping sea salt from the pot beside it and scrubbing the gritty substance onto her skin. When I lifted Reid's wrist to submerge his hand in the bowl, she shook her head and sighed.

"Tell me you aren't doing what I think you're doing."

I shrugged. "Your mom said he would wake. I'm just helping him along."

"She said he would wake *when he's ready.*"

"And?" I watched his pants intently, settling into the hammock beside him, my back against the musty wall. My *magic* wouldn't work, but . . . "Perhaps he's ready."

Her lips twitched slightly as she followed my gaze. His chest still rose and fell rhythmically, but otherwise, he didn't move. "Perhaps he's not," she said.

"Well, we'll know in a few minutes, won't we?"

"I expected you to be more worried about this."

"I've spent the entirety of my life worried, Coco. Nothing has changed."

Except it had. Everything had changed. I'd made a promise to Ansel—to myself—when I'd left him in those waters. I wouldn't allow fear to control me for another moment. No. Not even for another second.

Coco's lips twitched harder as she scrubbed her skin. "He'll be furious when he wakes."

When he wakes.

I arched a devilish brow. "Dare I say he'll be . . . pissed?"

She cackled outright now, leaning over the tub to better see the proceedings. "Oh my god. That was *terrible*."

"That was brilliant, and you know it." Absurdly pleased with myself, I pushed to my feet just as a veritable army of maids bustled through the curtain. Each carried pitchers of fresh, scalding water in tow.

"Are you finished, milady?" one of them asked Coco. When she nodded, the maid held out a silk robe, and Coco—shooting a quick, dubious glance in my direction—hesitated before stepping into it. I hid a smile behind my hand. I couldn't speak for Coco, but I hadn't been waited on since I'd left the Chateau at sixteen. Had anyone ever pampered her? My grin spread as another maid presented her with bottles of perfumed oils for her skin and hair. The others set about emptying the tub and refilling it with fresh water.

"From the geysers below the palace," one explained through the steam. She selected a gown for Coco, draping it across the ornate—albeit mildewed—chair in the corner. "We often visit them to bathe ourselves, yet this is our first opportunity to use their waters in such a fashion. How did you find your bath?" she asked Coco. "Was it pleasant?"

"Very." Slowly, Coco trailed her fingers along the lace of her nightgown. "Thank you."

The maid smiled. "Very good. Is there anything else you require?"

Coco touched a tentative hand to her stomach. "I'm actually feeling a little sick."

"We shall send for some ginger tea. Just harvested from a ship on route to Amandine. It will settle your stomach."

I waited until they'd left before shucking off my bloody chemise and sinking into the tub. The water nearly scalded me, but I relished the heat of it, the catharsis. Dipping my head back, I scrubbed at my scalp, loosening the sand and dirt there. I couldn't remember the last time I'd been truly clean.

I glanced again at Reid, who hadn't wet himself and hadn't woken.

Coco removed his hand from the bowl. "We need to get creative. You could—"

A light knock sounded from the threshold, and we both turned. "It's me," Célie said softly. "May I come in?"

At the sound of her voice, Coco and I both froze, exchanging a panicked look. It wasn't as if we *disliked* Célie. Indeed, we'd risked life and limb to save her, but we hadn't . . . spent time with her. Not really. We hadn't bonded outside of La Mascarade des Crânes. We weren't *friends*.

Coco gestured toward the curtain. *Go on*, she mouthed. *Answer her.*

I waved an agitated hand down my naked body.

Coco shrugged, the corners of her mouth lifting. *Who cares? You're hot as f—*

"Come in!" I called, flinging wet sea salt at Coco's smug face. It landed with a *splat*, soaking her robe, just as Célie poked her head into the room. "Hi, Célie. Is something wrong?"

A pretty pink blush spread across her cheeks at the question. She too had bathed, and she wore her own dressing robe, ruffles rising to her chin. "No." Moving the curtain aside tentatively, she stepped forward without looking at either of us, concentrating on the ostentatious gold-and-glass serving tray in her hands. A chipped china set perched atop it. "I just . . . heard you talking. Here"—she thrust the tray toward us abruptly—"I passed a maid in the hall. She ground ginger for your stomach pains, and I—I offered to bring it to you."

Coco cut her gaze to me, clearly waiting to follow my lead. I scowled at her. It made sense, of course, as Célie wasn't *Beau's* clinging ex-paramour, but still . . . how did one react in this situation? Célie had nowhere to go. She had no friends to speak of, and the horrors she'd endured . . . I sighed. The last time I'd spoken to her, she'd loathed my very name, accusing me of stealing Reid away from her with magic. That same night, she'd fled into my arms.

No. Realization twisted my already knotted stomach. Into Reid's.

She'd fled into *Reid's* arms, not mine. She probably still thought me a whore. She'd said as much once, right before kissing my husband at the Saint Nicolas Day ball. The knot in my stomach tangled further, and the silence lengthened as I stared at her, as she stared at anything but me.

Right. I sat forward in the tub, loathing the awkwardness between us. There was nothing for it. I'd have to ask her.

Coco sighed hard through her nose before I could speak. Flicking an impatient look in my direction, she started to say, "Thank you," at precisely the same moment I said, "Are you still in love with Reid?"

Startled, Célie finally looked up, and the blush on her cheeks fanned to an open flame upon seeing me naked. She stumbled back a step, and the tray slipped from one hand. Though she did her best to right herself, one hand still flailed wildly, finding purchase against Reid's—

Oh shit.

My eyes flew wide. With a small cry, she snatched her hand away from him, and the tray went flying, china shattering against the wall, the carpets, while tea sprayed in every direction. It dripped from her beautiful dressing robe as she dropped to her knees, trying and failing to fix it. "I—I'm so s-sorry. How terribly clumsy—"

Guilt reared her ugly head like a bitch, and I swung my legs over the tub, searching for something with which to cover myself. Coco threw another robe my way. I hurried to tie it as Célie continued spluttering on the sodden carpet, collecting the shards of china in vain. "I didn't mean—oh, the maids will be so upset. And your poor stomachs—"

I knelt beside her, stilling her hand before she cut herself. Her gaze swung upward and locked on mine. Tears welled in her eyes.

"Our stomachs will be fine, Célie." Gently, I took the shards from her and deposited them back on the floor. "We'll all be fine."

She said nothing for a long moment, simply staring at me. I looked back at her with feigned calm and waited, though I longed to rise, to seek the ease and familiarity of Coco's presence amidst this painfully awkward situation. Célie had no such person to comfort her. She had no familiarity here. And though we weren't friends, we weren't enemies either. We never had been.

When she spoke again, her voice was a whisper. Barely discernible. "No. I am not in love with him. Not anymore." Some of the tension left my shoulders. She spoke truth. The waters wouldn't have allowed the words otherwise. "And I'm sorry." Her voice fell quieter still, but she didn't lower her gaze. Her cheeks shone brilliant scarlet. "You aren't a whore."

Coco knelt beside us now, a clean robe in hand. She snorted, puncturing the unexpected sincerity of the moment. "Oh, she is, and I am too. You don't know us well enough"—she extended the robe, arching a meaningful brow—"yet."

Célie glanced down at herself, as if just realizing she'd been doused with tea.

"Take it." Coco pressed it into her hands before motioning toward the dressing screen.

Célie blushed again, looking between us. "You probably think I'm a prude."

"So?" I waved a hand over the broken china set, and the golden pattern connecting each shard dissipated. Sharpness pierced my chest as the pieces knit themselves back together. I lifted a hand to rub the spot, torn between sighing and wincing. Forgiveness was a painful thing. A sacrifice in itself. "You shouldn't care what we think, Célie—or anyone else, for that matter. Don't forfeit your power like that."

"Because who cares if you're a prude?" Coco pulled Célie to her feet with both hands. She gestured to me. "Who cares if we're whores? They're just words."

"And we can't get it right no matter what we do." Winking, I slipped a satin ribbon from the armoire, tying it around my throat before falling into the hammock once more. Reid swayed beside me. I ignored the knot of panic in my chest. He hadn't so much as stirred. Instead, I flicked his boot and added, "We might as well do it our own way. Being a prude or being a whore are both better than being what they want us to be."

Célie blinked between us, eyes huge, and whispered, "What do they want us to be?"

Coco and I exchanged a long-suffering look before she said simply, "Theirs."

"Be prudish and proud, Célie." I shrugged, my hand curling instinctively around Reid's ankle. "We'll be whorish and happy." He would wake soon, surely. And if not, Isla—the Oracle, Claud's sister, a *goddess*—would help us fix everything. We just needed to dine with her first. I glared at the brush on the dressing table. Following my gaze, Coco seized it before I could melt its golden handle into ore.

Planting one hand on her hip and grinning in challenge, she said, "It's time, Lou."

I glared at her now. "Everyone knows not to brush wet hair.

The strands are weaker. They could break."

"Shall we summon a maid for a fire, then?" When I didn't answer, she waved the brush under my nose. "That's what I thought. *Up*."

Rolling my eyes, I slid from the hammock and stalked toward the mildewed chair. It sat before a full-length, gilded vanity mirror that had clouded with age. Golden serpents twined together to form its frame. I stared peevishly at my reflection within it: cheeks gaunt, freckles stark, hair long and tangled. Water still dripped from its ends, permeating the thin silk of my robe. I didn't shiver, however; the melusines had cast some sort of magic to keep the air balmy and comfortable.

Before Coco could lift the brush—I suspected she secretly enjoyed tormenting me—Célie stepped forward tentatively, hand extended. "May I?"

"Er—" Coco flicked her gaze to mine in the mirror, uncertain. When I nodded once, part curious—mostly curious—she handed Célie the brush and stepped aside. "The ends tangle," she warned.

Célie smiled. "So do mine."

"I can brush my own hair, you know," I muttered, but I didn't stop her as she lifted a small section and began working the brush through the ends. Though she held the hair firm, she moved with surprising gentleness.

"I do not mind." With the patience of a saint, she set about untangling two gnarled locks. "Pip and I once brushed each other's hair every night." If she felt me still, she didn't comment. "We dismissed our maid when I was ten. Evangeline was her name. I couldn't understand where she'd gone, but Pippa—Pippa was old enough to realize what had happened. We often snuck into our father's safe as children, you see. Pippa liked to steal his ledger, sit at his desk, and add his sums, pretending to smoke his cigars, while I played with our mother's jewels. She knew our parents had lost everything in a bad investment. I didn't know until all of Maman's diamonds disappeared."

Successfully untangling the knot, she moved on to another section of hair. "Père told us not to worry, of course. He said he would make it right." Her smile twisted in the mirror's leaden reflection. "He did just that, I suppose. Slowly but surely, Maman's jewelry returned, along with all manner of other strange and unusual objects. He changed the lock on his safe shortly thereafter—an impossible lock even I could not pick. Not then, anyway."

"Did Evangeline return?" I asked.

"No." She shook her head ruefully. "Evangeline wouldn't so much as step foot through our door after that. She said we were cursed. Another maid took her place, but Pip insisted on brushing my hair regardless. I think she wanted to distract me. Père's contacts always visited at night."

"She sounds like a wonderful sister."

Her smile turned warm and genuine. "She was."

We descended into silence for only a moment—Célie continuing to stroke my hair with expert precision—before Coco surprised me by speaking. "And your mother?"

Célie spoke without hesitation, matter-of-fact, as if Coco had asked her not an exceptionally personal question, but the color of the sky. "My mother tried. She was not particularly maternal, but she gave us what she could: gifts, mostly, but on occasion she'd join us in the parlor while we sewed or played pianoforte. She would read us stories. She could be severe at times, of course—especially after Pippa's death—but . . . it was how she expressed her love."

Coco no longer pretended to be interested in her reflection. "Do you think she misses you?"

"I certainly hope so." Célie shrugged delicately, setting the brush atop the vanity. She swept my now-tidy hair down my back. "But I will see her again soon. Who knows? Perhaps she'll be proud I helped rid the world of Morgane."

Coco and I locked gazes in the mirror. The heartbreak in hers shone clear.

My mother tried.

It shouldn't have been a glowing commendation, yet it was. Célie's mother had tried, and in doing so, she'd given more to her daughter than either of our mothers had given us. Unbidden, my hand crept upward to the satin ribbon around my throat. A mark of my mother's love.

"Why do you hide it?" Célie asked abruptly. I glanced up to find her staring at me—at my scar. Even Coco seemed to return from her thoughts, eyes sharpening on the emerald ribbon. She arched a brow, and Célie nodded to her. "Coco shows her scars."

"Coco's scars aren't shameful." I tilted my head, fixing her reflection with a narrow gaze. "Why don't you show *your* scars, Célie?"

She looked away then. "I don't have any scars."

"Not all scars are visible."

"You are avoiding the question."

"So are you."

Sighing, Coco joined Célie behind me, her hands threading through my hair. Comfortable and familiar. She leaned down, her cheek hovering beside mine, and our reflections met once more. "How many times have I told you? No scar is shameful." Mouth set with determination, she plucked at the end of my ribbon, and it fell from my throat, revealing my scar. Except it wasn't my scar any longer. At least, it wasn't the scar I'd always known.

Gasping, I traced the fine lines with my fingertips, following the graceful curve of leaves, the delicate whorls of petals. Like a silver necklace, it transformed the column of my throat into something rare and beautiful. Something exquisite. When I swallowed, the leaves seemed to wink at me in the candlelight. "When did this happen?"

"When we learned you'd been possessed." Coco straightened, pulling a small stool over beside my chair. From the pile of its fabric, the upholstery had once been velvet, though the original color and pattern had long been lost. It was simply gray now, its curving legs as rotted as the rest of this place. Coco gestured for Célie—who appeared paler than before, her hands knotted together in apprehension—to sit. "When I decided to hope regardless. My tears transformed it."

Hope isn't the sickness. It's the cure.

Coco slipped her hands into Célie's unbound hair next, surprising me yet again. Judging by the way Célie straightened, the way her eyes flew wide, Coco had surprised her too. She wove the black strands into a single plait down Célie's back, tying the end with my ribbon, looping the emerald satin into a perfect bow. "You should both show your scars," she murmured.

Célie dragged her braid across her shoulder to stare at it, fingering the tails of the ribbon in quiet wonder. Coco plopped her cheek atop my head, and her familiar scent—earthy yet sweet, like a freshly brewed cup of tea—engulfed me. "They mean you survived."

THE ORACLE AND THE SEA URCHIN

Lou

Clad in a gown of marigold chiffon with floral appliqué, each rose dark and glittering as gunpowder, I followed Eglantine through a labyrinth of passages that night. Coco walked beside me. Her own gown of ivory satin—slimmer in skirt than my own, with a fitted bodice and golden thread spun into delicate filigree—trailed behind us for miles. The dress of a true *princesse*. Célie glided forward on her other side, regal and elegant and completely in her element. The soft petal pink of her bodice brought color to her porcelain cheeks, and the crawling juniper vines adorning the skirt flattered her slender form.

We cut quite the striking figure, the three of us. More than one head turned as we passed.

Even Beau did a double take as he stepped from his cabin, eyes flitting from the pearl headpiece in Coco's hair to the emerald earring in Célie's ear, the matching ribbon on her wrist.

"Lord help us all." Beau shook his head and stepped behind us, plunging his hands into the pockets of his velvet pants. He whistled low. "Though Heaven never created such a view."

"We know." Coco arched a brow over her shoulder, each step revealing a bit of smooth thigh through the slit in her skirt.

Like the rest of the ship, the hall boasted extravagance with its once-gilded panels and glittering, albeit broken, chandeliers. Unlike our cabins, however, this room rose high above us, the painted ceilings towering unnaturally tall for a sea vessel. The air here smelled not of mildew but of magic, sweet and pleasant and sharp. A golden banquet table ran the length of the enormous room, and atop it, dishes and platters of a strange variety covered every inch. At the door, a liveried melusine bowed deeply and nearly sent his wig tumbling to the floor.

"*Bonjour, mes demoiselles.*" He straightened with the cool hauteur of an aristocrat. On one powdered cheek, he'd drawn a tiny black heart. "Please, allow me to escort you to your seats."

Eglantine winked at us before retreating from the room.

We followed the butler in a single-file line until we reached the head of the table, where a veritable throne of seashells and pearls sat empty, along with two seats on either side. The butler seated Coco and Célie together with practiced efficiency before turning to me. He ignored Beau altogether. With another low bow, he murmured, "The Oracle will join us shortly. She kindly asks for you to sample the salted sea lettuce." He paused to sniff through his long nose. "It is her very favorite."

"Remember"—Célie spoke in a low voice, keeping her expression pleasant as the butler stalked back to his post—"to mind your manners." She smiled at the aristocrats down the table. They watched us openly, some returning her smile, others whispering behind painted fans. "We would not want to disrespect our host."

Elvire appeared without warning at her shoulder. No longer naked, she wore a dress fashioned from faded sails, complete with a belt of rope and a tiara of emeralds. The latter matched Célie's earring. I suspected it wasn't a coincidence. Touching it reverentially, Elvire inclined her head. "*Bonjour*, Mademoiselle Célie. Your gown is exquisite."

Behind her, Leopoldine and Lasimonne leaned forward with comical interest to hang on Célie's every word. Without preamble, the melusines sitting beside Célie rose politely and offered their seats to the guards, who accepted with equal courtesy. It was all very civil. Almost saccharine. "You must try the sargassum," Lasimonne insisted, spooning the yellowish leaves onto Célie's plate and drizzling green sauce over them. "It is the Oracle's favored dish."

I eyed her plate suspiciously, feeling very much like I'd failed to prepare for a schoolroom test. "I thought the salted sea lettuce was her favorite?"

He blinked at me before turning to Leopoldine, who nodded gravely. "It is true. Sargassum was her favored dish *yesterday*."

Oh god.

"Dear me." Lasimonne lifted a horrified hand to his chest before bowing deeply over Célie's plate of sargassum. "My apologies, *mademoiselle*. Of course you must sample the salted sea lettuce instead. Good gracious. The Oracle would not have forgotten such a slight."

Beau and I exchanged wide-eyed glances.

Without another word, I heaped salted sea lettuce onto first my plate, then Beau's. "To the right of the dinner fork," he muttered discreetly as I studied the mismatched cutlery on either side of my plate. I speared a leaf with the tiny fork, but before I could lift it to my mouth, Beau stopped me with the curt shake of his head. "Cut it first. Were you raised in a barn?"

Heat licked at my cheeks as I returned the leaf to my plate, searching for the proper knife.

Elvire sipped at the effervescent liquid in her flute as Célie cut her own lettuce into exemplary pieces. "Yes," the former said, "the Oracle positively banished Guillaumette for the gaffe last week."

"An insipid woman," Leopoldine added conspiratorially. "I never cared for her."

Elvire fixed her with a cool stare, lifting a silver brow. "Verily? Is she not the godmother of your daughter?"

Leopoldine abruptly busied herself with her own drink, unable to answer.

"Where is Angelica?" I focused on cutting my sea lettuce into perfect squares, lest Elvire or Leopoldine or the octopi in the street take offense and feed me to the giant squid. "Will she be joining us?"

Lasimonne stared at me as if *I* were the giant squid. "Of course she is." Though clearly vexed that I'd spoken at all, he didn't hesitate to pour me a flute of the effervescent liquid. So polite. So fascinating. If I spilled my plate in his lap, would he thank me?

"She is the most treasured of the Oracle's companions. I daresay she will arrive with Our Lady herself."

I bit my tongue before I could ask *when* that would be—then ran it over my teeth to check for bits of sea lettuce, just in case. Apparently, tardiness wasn't as heinous a gaffe as forgetting Her Ladyship's favorite food. Lifting the flute to my lips instead, I simply nodded. Then choked.

It was seawater.

With a forced smile, Beau patted my back as I spluttered, pressing his foot atop my own under the table. "There, there." He handed me a folded napkin before saying to the others, "Please pardon my dear sister. She must have a sensitive gag reflex."

I snorted again, unable to help myself, and kicked Beau's foot from mine.

Two more liveried melusines stepped into the banquet hall then, each holding an enormous conch shell. As one, they lifted the shells to their lips and blew. The call reverberated through the chamber, rattling china and chandeliers, as the melusines around us swept to their feet.

The Oracle followed a moment later.

I could only stare at her.

Quite simply, she was the most beautiful woman I'd ever seen.

Her hair rippled like water down her shoulders as she floated into the room, casting her ethereal silver gaze in our direction. When her eyes met mine, I saw not iris and sclera but tranquil moonlight on the sea, silken foam along the shore. I saw cresting waves and flashing scales—primordial creatures of teeth and shadow who awoke with the darkness. I saw tempests to tear apart kingdoms, secrets bared and secrets kept. Secrets drowned in boundless depths.

Then she smiled at me, and a shiver skittered down my spine. In that smile, I saw chaos.

Pure, unadulterated chaos.

Angelica walked behind her, head bowed and hands clasped. She caught Coco's eye as they approached, winking covertly, before resuming her pious stance. The Oracle looked only at me. I straightened as furtively as I could, painfully aware of my damp palms, but otherwise, I didn't cower. Claud had once described himself as the Wild, and in his true form, I'd believed it. The Oracle didn't need to assume her true form for me to understand. From the misty, nameless color of her hair and skin to the liquid movement of her body, she *was* the sea. And the sea drowned those who couldn't swim.

"*Je vous voir*, Louise." To my great surprise, her voice held a calming, tranquil note, like still waters at dawn. "*Bienvenue* to the Crystal Palace. I have long awaited your arrival."

I curtsied with the others. "I'm happy to be here. Thank you for interfering at the beach."

Her silver eyes—so like Angelica's, yet so different—sparkled with amusement. "Ah. The beach. We shall speak at length about that happy coincidence later. First, we must dine." She nodded to another liveried melusine, who hastened to pull back her chair. Her gown—crafted entirely from long, gleaming strands of pearls—clinked softly as she sat. The rest of the court seated themselves with her. When she snapped her fingers, the aristocrat on Coco's right vaulted to her feet without a word, ceding her seat to Angelica. "You have sampled the salted sea lettuce, yes?"

"Yes, my lady." I too returned to my seat, wiping my palms on my thighs beneath the table. "It was . . ." The waters prevented me from lying. I tried again. "A special experience."

"Come now." Her smile broadened, and unbidden, the image of a hungry shark rose in my mind's eye. I clenched my skirt between two fists, mentally chastising myself. "There is no need for clever language amongst friends. How did you find it, truly?"

"I'm glad to have tasted it."

"Glad." She said the word slowly, curiously. "There are uglier designations, I suppose. *I* am glad you found it . . . what clever word did you use?" She tapped her lips. "*Special.* Now"—she snapped her fingers again—"clear it away. I tire of its stench." The servants bustled to remove every plate of salted sea lettuce from the table. "*S'il vous plaît,*" she continued before they'd finished, "I crave heavier fare tonight. Bring the *neige marine* for our *special* guests."

Perhaps not so calming at all.

My palms continued to sweat.

We sat in distinctly uncomfortable silence as more dishes were passed down the table. Isla didn't seem to notice. She merely continued to smile as servants spooned small amounts of gray, sticky substance onto each plate. When she lifted a bite to her lips, she paused, appraising the room to ensure she held everyone's attention. She did, of course. Every melusine's face turned toward her as if she were their very sun. She waved an elegant hand with a laugh. "Eat, *mes enfants*, and be merry."

Her children obliged, and the gentle sounds of clinking cutlery and soft voices soon filled the silence. Elvire, Leopoldine, and Lasimonne immediately engaged in conversation with Célie—and Angelica with a resigned Coco—leaving Beau and me to suffer the weight of Isla's stare alone. "Tell me," she crooned, leaning across him to grasp my clammy hand. He stiffened but didn't complain. "What were your last words to Reid?"

I looked up from my *neige marine* in surprise. "Pardon me?"

"The last words you spoke to your lover—what were they?"

"I—" Glancing at Beau, I frowned. "I don't remember."

Her smile turned positively wicked. "Try."

Feeling increasingly unsettled, I concentrated on recalling the memory, exhaling hard as the threads of our conversation returned. "I said 'Either I kill my mother, or my mother kills me. It's the only way.'"

That smile. Those eyes. Not tranquil water at all, but the calm in the eye of a hurricane. Perhaps the hurricane itself. Inexplicably, I knew the pleasantries had ended. She released my hand and returned to her seat, dabbing her mouth with a napkin. "Is that so?"

"I wouldn't have been able to say it otherwise."

Beau pressed his foot over mine again.

"And . . . do you remember his last words to you?" she asked slyly.

These words I didn't struggle to remember. "He promised he would find me."

"Find you?" When she batted her lashes as if—as if goading me—unease lifted the hair at my neck. Surely this wasn't appropriate table conversation? We'd only just met, and melusines valued etiquette. My suspicion only deepened when she asked, "He sleeps belowdecks, does he not?"

"He does." I forced my voice to remain calm and collected— pleasant even. Still, I couldn't help but search her features for some of her brother's warmth. His good humor. "I've tried to wake him to no avail. Actually . . ." I cleared my throat as delicately as possible, throwing caution to the wind. "I was hoping you might . . . speed along the process."

Inexplicable triumph flashed in those nameless eyes. "Oh?" Though her voice remained light, conversational, her words belied the tone. "You *hope*, or you presume?"

My brows furrowed at the word. "I would never *presume*—"

"No?" Idly, she lifted a hand, and a servant hurried to fill her flute. "Do my mirrors lie, *l'oursin*? Do you not secretly scheme for an alliance?"

"I—" Incredulous, I met Coco's eyes across the table. She didn't intervene, however. She didn't dare interrupt. "I don't *scheme* for anything, my lady. While I would've *liked* to secure your friendship during our visit, I don't expect it."

"*Would've*? Does this mean you no longer desire my friendship?"

"No, my lady. I mean *yes*. It's just"—I splayed my hands

helplessly—"this doesn't seem to be going terribly well."

"What do you *expect*, Louise, when you treat gods and goddesses as your personal attendants?" She sipped at her seawater, still studying me. "To be frank, I cannot fathom what my siblings see in you, nor why they indulge your arrogance. When I sent Angelica to fetch you, I expected . . . some sort of grandeur—a magnetism, perhaps—but now, having met you, I see you possess neither. Aurore has bestowed her blessing on a sea urchin."

The first spark of anger lit in my chest. *Aurore's blessing? A sea urchin?* "Is that why you invited me here? To satisfy your curiosity?"

She didn't answer, instead turning to Beau. "What about you, princeling? Do you find Louise intelligent?"

He carefully returned his spoon to his plate before answering. "I do."

"Do you find her extraordinarily intelligent?"

"Y—" His reply caught in his throat, however, and his gaze cut to mine, abruptly panicked. Rueful. My anger spiked in response. He couldn't lie—not here, not caught in Isla's web of magic—even to spare my feelings. The knowledge hurt, but it didn't cut deep enough to scar. I might not have been *extraordinarily intelligent*, but I had intelligence enough to know Isla wanted to hurt me. To shock and awe me. I just didn't understand why.

"As I thought. Tell me, princeling, do you find her extraordinarily beautiful, then?"

He frowned, eyes still darting between us. Her gaze, however, still didn't stray from mine. It bored into me with disturbing intensity. With disturbing *clarity*. Beau tugged at the collar of his shirt before muttering, "Of course I find her pretty. She's my"—his throat worked again, failing to form the words—"she's *like* my sister."

"How quaint. I asked if you find her beauty *extraordinary*, however. Is Louise among the fairest you've encountered?" When he didn't answer right away, she inclined her head. "Just so. Do you consider her extraordinarily brave instead?" Again, he didn't answer. "No? Extraordinarily true, perhaps? Extraordinarily just?" Still Beau said nothing, swallowing hard around words that couldn't come. Sweat beaded along his forehead at the effort. His foot pressed against mine with enough force to crack my bones.

A peculiar hum started in my ears at the pressure, and my vision tunneled on Isla's superior expression. How *dare* she treat us this way? We were guests in her realm. She'd *invited* us here—and for what? To torment us? To poke and prod until we snapped? An almost childlike indignation flooded my system at the injustice.

Isla was supposed to be an ally.

"I don't—why do you ask such questions?" Beau ground out.

She ignored his struggle, continuing ruthlessly. "Is Louise a leader, Beauregard? A visionary?"

"She—not as such—"

"Has she offered you riches in exchange for your loyalty? Has she offered you magic?"

He nearly choked on his answer.

"Is she extraordinary in *any* way?"

"She—" He looked to me, helpless, color rising in his cheeks. Across the table, Célie shot us covert looks, still pretending to listen to Elvire. Coco didn't pretend at all. She glared at Isla with eyes that blazed with hatred while the hum in my ears grew louder.

"—is just as I feared," Isla finished for him. "She is ordinary. Painfully, intolerably ordinary, yet she inspires the loyalty and devotion of my sister, my brother, *you*." Scoffing, she shook her head and signaled for another course. "A wasted blessing, to be sure."

"I am not blessed."

"You don't even realize, do you? I shouldn't be surprised. Aurore may say what she likes about Morgane, but at least your mother possesses a modicum of awareness."

My fingers shook at the comparison. At the insult. I curled them into fists, staring at the pan-fried dulse without seeing it. "Why did you summon us here?"

Again, she ignored my question, reaching across Beau to seize the diamond pin in my hair. "Help me understand, Louise. Why do they follow where you lead? I have only ever watched you fail—watched you murder, watched you lie, watched you cheat. Indeed, like a sea urchin, the only feat you've managed in all your life is survival. In doing so, you have harmed every person in this beloved family of yours, yet each one remains. Why?"

"Perhaps it's my extraordinary sense of humor." The words fell heavy from my lips. Hard. Heat rippled from my chest through my limbs now, and my entire body trembled. White edged my vision. *Ordinary.* She'd said it as an expletive. Something basic and coarse, something inferior.

"No." With an errant flick of her wrist, my diamond pin clattered to the floor. Vaguely, I realized the table had stilled around us. Every eye had turned in my direction. "I do not think so. Even with Aurore's blessing—even with your precious allies—you are not equipped to win this war, Louise le Blanc. Quite simply, my sister chose wrong."

That heat kept spreading. Hotter than anger now. Hotter than embarrassment. Brows furrowing in alarm, Beau stared at my hand when I slammed it atop the table. "You speak of blessings," I said, the words spilling forth wildly and with abandon, "but what good are the *loyalty* and *devotion* of the Wild Man of the Forest and the Triple Goddess? My mother—my own *mother,* the person who should've loved me most in the world—has tried to kill me three times. She murdered my best friend in front of me. Since then, I've spent days, perhaps *weeks,* possessed by Nicholina. Earlier tonight she almost drowned me in these wretched waters, where my mother also tried to kill me. *Again.* Now Reid sleeps under an enchantment I cannot break while you insult me in front of your entire court." My chest heaved. "If this is the *blessing* of a goddess, I'd hate to see her curse."

Isla only smiled.

With a single finger, she pushed the dish between us—still covered—in my direction. The flippant gesture only enraged me further. I shoved to my feet, prepared to stalk from the hall, to seize Reid's body and *leave,* when my eyes dropped to the silver cloche. To my reflection there.

Too late, I registered the sharp scent of magic.

Coco's eyes held wonder, fear, as she too pushed from the table. "Lou?"

But I didn't recognize my reflection. Round brown eyes stared back at me, and straight, wheat-colored locks replaced my own. Pink cheeks replaced freckles. My gown hung from diminutive shoulders, the excess fabric pooling at my feet. As I stared at it, the heat in my chest morphed slowly to something else—something innocent, youthful, inquisitive, *alive.*

Without realizing, I'd transformed into the Maiden.

When Isla stood to stroll toward me, her entire court stood too. She trailed a casual finger across my throat. Scarless now. "You were saying?"

I swallowed hard against her nail, refusing to look at anyone. Especially my reflection. "How—how is this possible?"

"Claud warned Morgane. He told her what would happen if she continued to defy us. Morgane arranged your possession regardless."

"But that"—Beau pushed his plate away with a slack expression—"that means—"

"Yes, princeling." Isla moved behind me, fanning my hair across my shoulders. "The sea urchin has become La Dame des Sorcières. A pity, if you ask me, but admittedly a useful one."

"Does Morgane know?" Coco asked sharply.

In answer, Angelica tensed, her eyes eddying until she no longer saw the room but something else. *Somewhere* else. "Yes." She returned to us after another moment, shaking her head and wincing. "She is not pleased."

I spoke through numb lips. "Why did you bring us here?"

Her hands tightened on my neck, and at last—at *last*—she answered. "My darling Angelica believes we should ally ourselves with you in this tedious struggle against Morgane." I felt her shrug, as if we discussed the weather and not my very life. "I must confess, I care not for it. Neither your death nor your mother's will affect us here." She moved beside me then, offering a hand. I had no choice but to accept it. Tucking my arm in hers, she led me about the room while the others tracked us with their eyes. No one dared resume eating.

"I am not, however, a fool."

I didn't correct her.

"You present a unique opportunity for me and my people—and most of all for Angelica. I treasure her, you know," she added. The woman in question kept her head bowed and her hands clasped, as all the melusines did. "Twenty years ago, a ring of hers was stolen while she dallied above water, creating your rather beautiful friend." Isla waved a vague hand toward Coco. "You have heard of this ring. You have called it by name." Reaching around me, she lifted my right hand to stroke my empty ring finger. "You have even wielded its magic. You do not, however, know it as we do. It is not a simple ring of immunity and invisibility, as your foolish kin believe. More importantly, it does not belong to them. It does not belong to *any* of you. It is Angelica's Ring—it is her very power—and we shall have it back."

Vindicated, I almost laughed at the realization. At the hard, delicious truth. For all her extraordinary intelligence, beauty, and bravery, here she was . . . in need of me. A sea urchin. "If you know I've used it, you also know I don't have it any longer. My mother does. It's kept under lock and key at Chateau le Blanc."

"Precisely."

"I don't quite grasp what you're implying. Ordinary brain, you know. If her ring is so important, surely you can retrieve it yourself?"

When she turned me to face her abruptly, her smile shone hard and bright, and her nails dug painfully into my forearm, longer and sharper than before. She lifted a finger to my lips when I tried to protest, and the metallic taste of blood followed. *My* blood. "Ah, ah, ah." Her eyes dipped to my lips, to her finger, before flicking back to my own. "Do not disrespect me, or you shall never hear my proposition."

I glared at her in mutinous silence.

She arched a devilish brow. "I cannot retrieve the ring myself because I cannot directly intervene. My melusines cannot do it for me because they cannot leave the waters without it. Do you understand now, *mon pouffiasse*? It is, as you say, a mutually beneficial arrangement."

Her words rang in my ears as the rest of her fingers curled around my face, squeezing my cheeks hard enough to bruise. "Tomorrow, you shall return to the surface, and you shall steal back Angelica's Ring from your mother. Then—and *only* then—will my people join you against her."

THE MOST BEAUTIFUL SHADE OF BLUE

Lou

On deck a scant hour later, Angelica pulled Coco aside as Aurélien, Olympienne, and Sabatay hovered around Célie, bidding
her tearful farewells. Truly. Actual *tears* dripped down Olympienne's lavender cheeks. Scoffing, Beau readjusted his pack and
started down the plank. Halfway to the seafloor, he turned to jerk
his chin at me. "Come on."

I hoisted my own pack over my shoulder. After dinner, Isla
had wasted no time in expelling us from her realm. She might've
been the most conceited creature alive, but she *had* gifted us supplies for the journey ahead, at least. That included fresh clothes.
Sensible ones, this time, and warm ones too. I'd also slipped a
new sheath around my thigh, just in case.

Reid drifted along behind, still comatose, as Elvire and Leopoldine escorted us from the city. With each step, the unease I'd
been avoiding grew impossible to ignore. It set my teeth on edge,
pulsing painfully in my right temple.

Despite my pleas, Isla hadn't woken him. She'd insisted she couldn't intervene. I'd insisted we couldn't rob Chateau le Blanc with a six-and-a-half-foot, two-hundred-pound, *unconscious* man in tow.

Truthfully, I'd expected him to wake by now. He'd been unconscious for hours.

Do not worry, Louise. His injuries are not fatal. He will wake—of that, I am certain.

My head continued to throb.

The others walked toward the gates in silence, seemingly oblivious to our rather giant problem, except for Beau. He threw more than one anxious glance my way.

I assumed he expected me to transform into the Maiden at any moment. I half expected it myself. Even now, I wasn't sure how I'd done it, but I took care not to think too long or too hard about that shiver in my skin—that heady sensation of wild abandon. Curiously enough, it reminded me of . . . rooftops. If I closed my eyes, I could almost *feel* the wind tangling in my hair, my arms stretching wide, as I propelled myself upward, outward, from shingles into empty air. Exhilaration swooped low in my stomach for those precious seconds. Those precious seconds when I might've flown.

When my hands began to ripple, my eyes snapped open.

Beau still stared at me.

"What is it?" I snapped. "Spit it out."

"Are you okay? With"—he jerked his chin toward my hands— "that?"

I eyed him suspiciously. "Are *you?*"

He tipped his head, considering, before a fierce smile broke across his face. "I think it's the most impressive fucking thing I've ever seen. You're a . . . Lou, you're a *goddess* now."

"Goddess Divine." I matched his smirk with one of my own, despite Isla's words ringing loud and true in my ears. *My sister chose wrong.* "Queen of the sea urchins."

His smirk vanished at the last, and he stared resolutely at the back of Elvire's head. "About that. I . . . want to apologize." He cleared his throat. "For earlier."

"Ah." I exhaled with a soft chuckle. "There's no need."

"There is a need—"

"You told the truth."

"It *wasn't* the truth." He shook his head in agitation. "That's what I'm trying to tell you. Isla, she—she twisted my words—" Clearing his throat, he tried again, lowering his voice so the others couldn't hear. "I *do* find you extraordinary. Perhaps not extraordinarily brave or just or true, but extraordinary nonetheless." When I rolled my eyes, politely skeptical, he stepped in front of me, forcing us both to a halt. "Who else would have accepted the spoiled son of a king? The misused aristocrat? The sacrilegious huntsman? In the eyes of the kingdom, we are nothing." His voice dropped lower still. "You've given us all a place, a purpose, when before we didn't have one. *You* are the reason we're here, Lou. And I don't care about the waters' truth—you *are* my sister. Never forget it."

He sped up to walk beside Coco and Célie without allowing me to answer. Probably for the best.

I couldn't speak around the emotion in my throat.

When we finally reached the shores of L'Eau Mélancolique, the water supporting Reid burst—the last of Angelica's magic falling away—and he collapsed upon the sand. I immediately dropped to my knees beside him. "Shit." I checked his pulse again, pried open his eyelids to assess his pupils. All sounded and looked perfectly healthy.

Exhaling harshly, I poked him in the ribs. Nothing. I flicked his nose. Nothing again. I blew in his face, his eyes, unlaced his boot to tickle his foot, even slapped him smartly across the cheek. Nothing, nothing, *nothing.* My chest tightened with frustration as I dragged him to the water's edge. When splashing his face yielded no results, I swore viciously and prepared to dunk his entire head—his entire *body*, if necessary—but Beau stopped me with an impatient hand. "I don't think drowning him is an option."

"It worked for me—"

"You've tried magic, I assume?" His eyes darted up the path and into the mountains. I didn't blame him. Morgane and Josephine could've been watching us at this very moment. Still . . . as much as Isla had insisted she wouldn't get involved, I doubted she'd forgive an attack on her people so quickly. Constantin had been under her protection. It would be a very brave witch indeed—or perhaps a very stupid one—who trespassed on these shores again. Morgane and Josephine were neither brave nor stupid.

Here, we were safe. For now.

"The patterns are in a knot." I resisted the urge to snap at Beau again in light of his confession. It must've been hard to admit such things aloud. I appreciated them. "I can't make any sense of it."

Coco approached tentatively. "I could take some of his blood."

My mind immediately recoiled from the idea. The last time Coco had taken blood, she'd foreseen Ansel's death, and I'd had quite enough of misinterpreting the future.

"Angelica said—" Célie started, but I interrupted impatiently. "We don't have time for cryptic advice. He needs to wake *now*."

Célie crouched beside me in response, placing a comforting hand on my back, and I felt like the world's greatest ass.

"Sorry," I muttered. "I just don't know what to do. If we don't wake him, we can't steal Angelica's Ring, and if we don't steal Angelica's Ring, we can't count on the melusines to join us against Morgane. Without the melusines—"

"I understand." Her hand drew soothing circles. "At least Reid is all right. He is. Look at him." Forcing my eyes open, I watched him breathe, each swell and fall of his chest a small comfort. Célie smiled. "Truly, he could be only sleeping. An enchanted sleep, perhaps, but—"

Her eyes flew wide.

"What?" I lurched upright. "What is it, Célie?"

"One of the stories my mother used to read me," she said breathlessly, clapping her hands together. "It was about a princess cursed with eternal sleep. The only way to break the spell was the kiss of true love."

Coco scoffed and threw herself on the sand. "That's a fairy tale, Célie. It isn't real."

"We just bathed and dined and conversed underwater in the royal palace of melusines, where octopi walked on leashes and the Goddess of the Sea served us salted *sea lettuce*." Célie's cheeks burned pink. "None of this should be real."

Beau arched a brow. "She makes a fair point."

"Fine." With a sigh of fatigue, Coco fell to her back, folding her hands on her chest. "Kiss him, then. Kiss him good. Just do it quickly. And when that inevitably fails, I'll prick his finger, and we can make real progress."

I looked between each of their expectant faces, feeling utterly ridiculous. *True love's kiss.* Célie had apparently mistaken this nightmare for a sweeping romance, complete with the white knight charging in to save his fair maiden. I glared at Reid's lips. To be fair, it *had* started that way, once upon a time. He'd crossed the entire kingdom to save me from Morgane's sacrificial altar. Perhaps the roles could be reversed now that he was in need. And what real harm could there be in a kiss?

Exhaling hard through my nose, I gripped his shoulders and leaned over him.

Here goes nothing.

My lips brushed his in a light caress, and I parted them slowly, touching his tongue to mine. Just for a second. Just a single breath. My eyes fell closed at the simple joy of it—of kissing Reid. God, I missed him. For too long, our lives had been tangled yet separate, intrinsically linked yet forever apart. It was my fault. It was his too.

But mostly, it was Morgane's.

He didn't wake.

Sighing in defeat, I rested my head against his chest and listened to his heart. How many times had I lain in this exact position, counting each beat? He'd often stroked my hair, traced my spine, even when things had been strained between us. When things had been good, however, he'd wrapped his strong arms around me and—

A heavy hand fell upon my back.

My eyes snapped open.

Behind me, Célie gasped, Coco gasped—even *Beau* gasped—as I scrambled to my elbows, staring down at Reid's face in shock. He blinked back at me, and those eyes—they were the most beautiful shade of blue. Giddy laughter bubbled up my throat at his frown. "Sleeping beauty awakes."

His hands landed lightly on my waist. "I beg your pardon?"

Skimming a fingertip along his dark lashes, I leaned down to kiss him once more. He drew back before I could. "You slept for a while, Chass. We worried you wouldn't wake up." I chuckled and brushed my nose against his. His brows puckered. "You aren't going to *believe* where we've been." I didn't pause for him to guess. "We went underwater, Reid. To the seafloor of L'Eau Mélancolique. You were there too, of course, just unconscious." My thoughts whirled in an incoherent blur of excitement. Where to begin? So much had happened in such a short period of time. "We walked with melusines in Le Présage—did you know they can grow legs?—and we dined with the Oracle in Le Palais de

Cristal. The Oracle is Claud's sister, remember? Isla. We met Isla, and she was the world's biggest *bitch*—"

He stiffened abruptly, and his frown deepened to an outright scowl. "My apologies, *mademoiselle*, but I think there's been a misunderstanding. Please"—he lifted me from his lap, depositing me firmly onto the sand beside him—"allow me to introduce myself. I am Captain Reid Diggory." He cleared his throat pointedly. "And I'd appreciate if you'd refrain from using such coarse language around me in the future."

I snorted in disbelief. "That's rich coming from *you*, Monsieur Fuck." His eyes widened comically at the expletive, and I laughed out loud. He didn't. "Fine," I said, still light with giddiness. His prickliness couldn't puncture it. He was awake, I was awake, and we were together. Finally. "I'll play along with this . . . whatever this is. Some sort of foreplay?"

Pushing to my feet, I offered him a hand. He stared as if it might bite him. Shrugging, I brushed off the seat of my pants instead. If his eyes had been wide before, they nearly burst from his face now. "*Bonsoir*, Captain Diggory." Laughing again, I dipped in a theatrical bow. "My name is Louise le Blanc, daughter of the infamous Morgane le Blanc, and I am positively *chuffed* to make your acquaintance. I see you're missing your official uniform, but no matter. Shall we light the stake now, or—?"

His eyes sharpened on my face, and without warning, he launched to his feet. "What did you say?"

My smile slipped at the sudden fierceness in his voice. I glanced at Coco and Beau, who both looked back in bewilderment. Célie rose slowly behind me. "My name is Louise le Blanc," I repeated, less theatric now. For someone as stoic as Reid, he could play-act much better than I'd anticipated. "And I'm chuffed to make your—"

"You're the daughter of Morgane le Blanc? A witch?"

Alarm bells began pealing in my head. "Well, yes—"

He tackled me before I could finish.

We hit the ground hard, rolling, and his forearm collided with my throat. My breath left in a painful rush. "Um—*ow.*" Gasping, I shoved at his chest, but he didn't move. His forearm remained. Combined with the weight of his body, I could scarcely breathe. "Okay, Chass, this role-play thing has officially gone too far—" He only pressed down harder until lights popped in my vision.

Right. This wasn't fun anymore.

Cocking my head back, I smashed my forehead into his nose, thrusting my knee into his groin when he recoiled. When he bent inward with a groan, I scrambled out from beneath him. "What the hell is wrong with you?" I snarled, clutching my throat. "Are you trying to kill me?"

He panted and bared his teeth. "You're a witch."

"Yeah? So?"

Ignoring me, he tore at his bandolier, unsheathing one knife and reaching for another—the one directly above his heart. But it wasn't there. Its sheath remained empty. He checked the others frantically, fingers seizing each one, before he realized what we'd already known. All emotion slid from his face. With deadly calm, he said, "Where is my Balisarda?"

I inched toward Coco. "Stop it, Reid. You're scaring me."

He stalked forward slowly, intently, matching each of my steps with his own. "Where is it?"

"A tree ate it." Coco gripped my elbow and pulled me to her side. We watched him approach together. "In the southern part of the kingdom. Bas and his bandits attacked on the road, and Lou threw your Balisarda to protect me." She paused, uncertain. "Don't you remember?"

"You." Recognition flared as he focused on Coco. "You're a healer in the Tower." His eyes dropped to where she clutched my arm, and his lip curled. "Are you in league with this witch?"

"I—" She stopped short when I shook my head, my stomach plunging with déjà vu. I'd had this exact conversation with Bas after he'd tried to kill me in La Fôret des Yeux. Had Reid—?

No.

My mind seized, unwilling to continue thought. He wouldn't have. He—he *couldn't* have. Could he?

"Who am I?" My voice shook as I stepped in front of Coco, toward him and his knife. The movement seemed to surprise him. He didn't strike right away. Instead, he stared at me with brows furrowed as I carefully pushed down his blade. "How do we know each other?"

He lifted it back to my face. "We don't."

No no no

"If this is a joke, Reid, it's gone far enough."

"I do not joke."

The truth of the words fragmented in my chest, and I exhaled deeply, absorbing their pain. No one was this good at playacting. Which meant . . . he had forgotten me. Just like Bas, he'd forgotten, only this time, I couldn't reverse the pattern. I hadn't cast it. But how far did it reach?

And *why* was he acting this way?

I searched blindly for an answer, remembering the way he'd collapsed in my arms. The way Morgane had collapsed with him on the beach. If he'd truly forgotten me, did that mean . . . ?

Holy hell.

"Are you sure?" I asked. "Think hard, Reid. Please. Just think. I'm Lou, remember? I'm your . . ." I glanced down at my empty ring finger, and the cracks in my chest splintered further. I'd returned his mother's ring. *Stupid. So stupid.* "I'm your wife."

His eyes hardened. "I don't have a wife."

"Easy." I jerked back as he swiped at me, lifting placating hands. "I *am* your wife. Maybe not *legally*, but in the biblical sense—"

Perhaps speaking of his holy book had been a mistake.

With a snarl, he charged again, and I sidestepped, kicking his knee from behind as he went. He didn't stumble as planned, instead pivoting with frightening agility. This time his knife caught my shirt, but I twisted at the last second. It shredded my sleeve instead. "God*damn* it." The fabric fluttered uselessly in the breeze. "Just once, I'd like to keep my clothing *intact*—"

He rushed again with unexpected speed, catching my torn sleeve and yanking me closer, lifting his knife to thrust it deep in my chest. I caught his wrist, but physically, I was no match for his strength. The blade plunged lower and lower, and—not for the first time in my life—I looked death straight in the eyes.

They were the most beautiful shade of blue.

Something hard thudded into Reid's back, propelling his knife the final inch. Blood welled as it pierced my skin, as Beau pounded at Reid's head with both fists. Coco soon joined him, hissing as she punched down on Reid's elbows, breaking his hold. When he turned—dragging Beau over his shoulder and throwing him to the ground—Coco wrenched a knife from his bandolier and sliced open her forearm. The bitter scent of blood magic coated the air. "We don't want to hurt you, Reid," she said, breathing heavily, "but if you don't stop being an asshole, I'll cut you a new one."

His nostrils flared. "Demon spawn."

She bared her teeth in a grin. "In the flesh."

He moved to attack her, but Beau caught his ankle. "Stop this now. I command it as your—as your crown prince," he finished lamely. Reid froze and frowned down at him.

"Your Highness? What are you doing here?"

"That's right." Beau choked on a cough, still struggling to breathe. He pointed to his chest. "I'm in charge. Me. And I'm telling you to concede."

"But you're"—Reid shook his head sharply and winced as if in pain—"you're my . . . are you my brother?" He touched a hand to his temple. "You *are* my brother."

Beau slumped on the ground. "Oh, thank God. You remember." He twirled a hand and coughed again. "Put your knife down, Reid. You're outnumbered if not outmanned, and I have no interest in seeing your second asshole." He turned to Célie, who stood apart from the rest of us, her face ashen. "Do you want to see his second asshole?"

It was Reid's turn to blanch. "Célie." Instead of dropping his weapons, however, he streaked to her side, his righteous anger deepening to outright rage. He pushed her behind him. "Stay back, Célie. I won't let them touch you."

"Oh, good lord," Coco muttered.

"Reid." Tentatively, Célie pushed at his back, but he didn't budge. His eyes found mine, and in them, hatred burned hotter than anything I'd ever seen. I could feel its heat wash over my skin, primal and visceral. Eternal. Like Coco's Hellfire. "Reid, this is unnecessary. These—Louise and Cosette are my friends." She tried showing him the green ribbon around her wrist. "See? They will not harm me. They will not harm you either. Just give us a chance to explain."

"What?" He whirled to face her then, seizing the ribbon and tearing it free. "You call them *friends*? They're *witches*, Célie. They killed your sister!"

"Yes, *thank* you for that kindly reminder." She snatched the ribbon back, scowling and stepping around him. "You'll be surprised to find my ears actually do work. I know who they are. More importantly, *you* know who they are, if you'd stop acting like a barbarian and *listen*."

"I don't—" He shook his head again, eyes narrowing. Confusion clouded his gaze, and stupid, *useless* hope lit in my heart. He sensed the truth in her words. Of course he did. Surely he could feel something had gone terribly wrong. Surely if he followed the thread of his thoughts, he would realize what had happened, and he would reverse the pattern. And he *had* to reverse the pattern. Forgetting me was one thing, but this—this wasn't Reid. This was a murderous *zealot*. He must've botched the magic somehow, perhaps pulled two cords instead of one.

As quickly as the thought came, I dismissed it, knowing in my heart it wasn't true. Reid hadn't botched anything.

He'd simply . . . forgotten me.

Forgotten him.

Forgotten everything.

"Remember, Reid," I whispered, tears thickening my voice. "Please. I don't know what you gained by doing this, but give it back. It isn't worth it." When I reached out to him, unable to stop myself, his knuckles tightened on his knives. He pushed Célie behind him once more.

"I don't know what you're talking about."

"The pattern." The sounds of the beach fell away as I wrung my hands, imploring him to look at me. To *see* me. "It's your magic. Only you can reverse it. You lost consciousness in L'Eau Mélancolique. Think back to that moment. Remember what you chose to forget."

"Lou." Coco shook her head sadly. "Don't."

"He needs to understand. I can help him—"

"He *did* understand. That's the point. He made a choice he felt was necessary. We need to respect it."

"Respect it?" My voice rose hysterically. "How can I *respect* it?

How can I respect *any* of this?" I flung my arms wide, danger-ously close to my breaking point. "If he doesn't love me—if he doesn't even *remember* me—what was the point in all this, Coco? What was the point in *any* of it? All the pain, all the sorrow, all the *death*?"

Tears limned her own lashes as she took my hands in hers. "He did this for *you*, Lou. If Morgane has forgotten, maybe you're—you're finally safe."

I tore my hand away from her. "I will *never* be safe, Coco. Even if Morgane *has* forgotten me, Josephine hasn't. Auguste and his Chasseurs haven't. How are we supposed to win this *war* if Reid can't separate friend from foe?"

"I don't know." She shook her head helplessly. "I really don't. I just know he saved our lives."

Reid wrapped an arm around Célie's waist then, pulling her away from us. I closed my eyes against the sight of it. The sight of them. He'd made a sacrifice for the greater good, yet again, my blood spilled upon the altar. "You're both insane," he said brusquely. "Come on, Célie. We need to go."

Célie's voice rose in protest. "But I don't want—"

"You're making a mistake, Reid," Coco said.

He chuckled darkly. "Don't worry. I'll be back for you, witch. And your friend. I'll even bring some friends of my own. Perhaps we'll build a bonfire."

"Oh, you'll be back all right, brother." Beau rose to his feet. "You have nowhere else to go. But you won't be taking Célie with you."

"With all due respect, *brother*—"

"All due respect means honoring the lady's request," Coco said. "She doesn't want to go with you, and *you* don't want to pick a fight with me, Reid. Not without your Balisarda."

The threat hung heavy in the air.

I finally opened my eyes.

Reid's throat worked with palpable distress as he weighed the situation: two witches against an unarmed huntsman with his blasphemous prince and childhood love caught in the crossfire. The Chasseur inside him—the part ruled by duty, by honor, by courage—refused to leave. The man inside him knew he must. Coco hadn't been bluffing; she *would* hurt him if necessary. He didn't know I wouldn't let her. He didn't know he could wield magic.

He didn't remember me.

Leveling his knives at our faces, he spoke softly, viciously. "I *will* be back."

I watched him disappear up the path with an overwhelming sense of emptiness.

Coco pressed my head upon her shoulder. "He'll be back."

STICKS AND STONES

Reid

My footsteps pounded in rhythm with my heart. Faster and faster. Faster still. My skin flushed with heat, with sweat, as I sprinted uphill, vaulting stone and fern. I'd only traveled this far north once. Right after taking my vows. My captain at the time, a weak-spirited man by the name of Blanchart, had been trying to prove his spine to the Archbishop. He'd heard rumors of melusines in the area, and he'd ordered my contingent to investigate. We hadn't even found the beach, instead wandering for days in this godforsaken mist.

If the freckled witch spoke truth, Blanchart had been right. There were melusines in the area. After I dispatched the demon in question, I'd return and—

Scoffing, I launched from the path.

She was a witch.

Of course she didn't speak truth.

Instead of plunging into the forest, I followed the tree line south. There'd been a hamlet nearby. My brethren and I had rented rooms there each night. Unbidden, I glanced down at my chest. My bandolier. The empty sheath above my heart. Pieces of memory swarmed and stung like insects. Leering faces. Bloodstained snow. Searing pain and painted wagons and bitter honey—

A *tree* had eaten my Balisarda.

I nearly stumbled at the realization. At the onslaught of images. They formed a picture riddled with holes, a puzzle with missing pieces. There'd been lavender hair. Starry cloaks. Troupe de Fortune. The words gored my mind with surprising pain, and this time, I did miss a step. I'd traveled with them, briefly. I'd thrown knives in their company.

Why?

Clenching my eyes against such riotous thoughts, I focused on the one knife that mattered. The one knife I *would* reclaim. I'd burn the whole forest if necessary. I'd hack the demonic tree down to the ground, and I'd dig until its roots became kindling.

Bas and his bandits attacked on the road, and Lou threw your Balisarda to protect me. Don't you remember?

Oh, I remembered. I remembered the scarred witch, who'd slithered into our mists as a healer. I remembered the disgraced Bastien St. Pierre, and I remembered my own gruesome injury. I did *not*, however, remember their coconspirator—the freckled witch. The one who'd looked at me as if someone had died.

I'm your wife, she'd said, her eyes glistening with unshed tears. *In the biblical sense.*

Remember, Reid. She'd known my name. *Called* me by name.

If he doesn't love me—if he doesn't even remember *me—what was the point in all this, Coco?*

Blistering rage further quickened my step. The wind rushed past me now, burning my cheeks and numbing my ears. As if I'd ever debase myself with a witch. As if I'd ever marry *anyone*, let alone a bride of Satan. "*Lou.*" I sneered the name aloud, my breath catching around it. A hideous name for a hideous being, and Célie—

My God.

I'd left Célie alone with them.

No. I shook my head. Not alone. The crown prince, my *brother*—he'd been there too. He'd even shared some sort of absurd camaraderie with the creatures, as if they three were family instead of him and me. Perhaps he could protect Célie. Then again, perhaps he couldn't. Regardless of how he felt toward them, witches held no family. I couldn't risk it. Not with her.

I hurtled around the bend, and sure enough, a familiar hamlet rose to meet me. If one could even call it that. Comprising a single street, it boasted a parish and an inn, complete with pub underneath. The entire settlement had risen only to accommodate sailors in need of work, passing from one port city to the next. A handful of them stared as I hurtled past. It mattered not.

Without breaking stride, I headed toward the parish at the end of the road. My fist nearly leveled the door. Once. Twice. Three times. At last, a tall, spotted boy peeked his head out. His eyes widened at my ruddy cheeks, my towering frame. My palpable fury. He let out a squeak before trying to slam the door in my face. Incredulous, I caught it and wrenched it back open. "I am Captain Reid Diggory, and—"

"You can't be here!" His feeble arms trembled with the effort to shut the door. I held fast. "You—you—"

"—require your services," I finished roughly, losing patience and flinging the door wide. It banged against the weathered stone wall. Men outside the pub turned to stare. "There are witches in the area. Summon your priest. If no Chasseurs are near, I'll need a contingent of able-bodied men to—"

The boy planted himself in the threshold when I moved to step inside. "Father Angelart ain't here. He's—he's in Cesarine, sittin' in on the conclave, isn't he?"

I frowned. "What conclave?" But the boy merely shook his head, swallowing hard. My frown deepened. Though I attempted to pass once more, he flung his arms wide, barring entrance. Impatience roused the anger in my gut. "Step aside, boy. This is urgent. These witches hold both the crown prince and a lady of the aristocracy hostage. Do you want the lives of innocents on your conscience?"

"Do *you*?" His voice cracked on the challenge, but still he didn't move. "Go on. Get!" He jerked his head down the street, waving his hands to shoo me away like I was a mangy dog. "Father Angelart ain't here, but I—I got me a knife too, right? I'll gut you, I will, before the huntsmen arrive. This is a sacred place. We don't—we won't tolerate your sort here!"

I clenched my fists, resisting the urge to knock his hands aside. To force my way through. "What sort is that?"

The boy's entire body trembled now. With anger or fear, I couldn't tell. "Murderers." He looked as if he wanted to spit at me. Anger, then. "*Witches.*"

"What are you talking—" My own angry words broke as the memories rose. A temple. The Archbishop. And—and me. I'd stabbed him to death. Sickening cold swept through me at the realization. It extinguished my rage. My mind continued to skitter over the images, however, leaping from one to the next before scattering. I stumbled back a step. Lifted my hands. I could still feel his blood there, could still feel its slick warmth on my palm.

But it—it made no *sense*. I'd felt nothing but love for my patriarch. Nothing but respect. Except . . . I focused harder on the memory, the parish in front of me falling away.

I'd felt vengeful too. Bitter. The emotions came to me slowly, reluctantly. Like shameful secrets. The Archbishop had lied. Though I couldn't recall it—though the memory rippled somehow as if distorted—I knew he'd betrayed me. Betrayed the *Church*. He'd consorted with a witch, and I—I must've killed him for it.

I was no longer a Chasseur at all.

"Is there a problem here?" A brawny sailor with a beard pressed his hand on my shoulder, jerking me from my thoughts. Two companions flanked him on either side. "Is this man bothering you, Calot?"

Instead of relief, fresh panic widened the boy's features. He looked from the sailor's hand on my shoulder to my face, where my jaw had clenched and my mouth had flattened. "Remove your hand, sir," I said through my teeth. "Before I remove it for you."

The man chuckled but complied. "All right." Slowly, I turned my head to look at him. "You're built like a tree, and I don't want any trouble. Why don't you and I head on up for a pint and leave poor Calot here alone?"

Calot pointed to something beside us before I could answer. A piece of paper. It fluttered in the evening breeze, tacked to the message post beside the door. I looked closer. A picture of my own face glared back at me.

REID DIGGORY

WANTED DEAD OR ALIVE

UNDER SUSPICION OF MURDER, CONSPIRACY, AND WITCHCRAFT.

REWARD.

The sick feeling in my stomach increased tenfold.

It couldn't be true. Though my memory felt—*off,* surely I would know if I—if—

I swallowed bile. There were too many gaps. I couldn't be sure of *anything,* and these men—their amicable nature vanished instantly. "Holy shit," one breathed. His companion hastened to yank the sword from his scabbard. I lifted my hands in a conciliatory gesture.

"I don't want any trouble either. I came to gather men. There are witches three miles up the road. Two of them. They—"

"We know who they are," the bearded man growled, jabbing

a finger at the other posters. More men from the pub headed toward us now. They drew weapons as they came. Calot shrank into the shadows of the foyer. "You travel with them. They even say one is your wife. Mort Rouge and Sommeil Éternel, they call you." He too drew a set of knives from his belt. They gleamed sharp and polished in the setting sun. Well used. "You killed the Archbishop. You set the capital aflame."

My eyes narrowed. A tendril of old anger unfurled. Of disgust. "I would never marry a witch."

"Is this some sort of hoax?" his friend asked uncertainly.

The bearded man jerked his chin. "Ride to Hacqueville. See if that Chasseur is still there. We'll hold him."

"That Chasseur?" My voice sharpened. "Who?"

Instead of answering, the man charged, and the anger simmering in my gut exploded. We collided with bone-shattering impact, and Calot squeaked again before slamming the parish door shut. I threw the bearded man against it. "This is ridiculous. We're on the same—"

His unharmed friend leapt atop my back, wrapping an arm around my neck. Fisting his hair, I wrenched him over my shoulders and drew a knife from my bandolier. Each dove out of reach as I slashed it in front of me. "Fine. You want to challenge me? You'll lose. I'm the youngest captain of the Chasseurs in history—"

"*Were.*" The bearded man stepped around me in a circle. His friend stepped behind. "You *were* a captain of the Chasseurs. Now you're a witch."

"Call them." With a snarl, I unsheathed another knife, pointing one at each of them. Backing into the parish wall. "Call them all. There are witches near, and they've taken someone I—"

They dove at me simultaneously. Though I dodged the bearded man, his friend's sword clipped my side. Gritting my teeth, I blocked his counterstrike, but others joined now—too many. Far too many. Blades glinted in every direction, and where one failed, a fist connected. A boot. An elbow. A scabbard smashed into my skull, and stars blurred my vision. When I doubled over, someone drove a knee into my face. Another my groin, my ribs. I couldn't breathe. Couldn't think. Wrapping my arms around my head, I attempted to bowl through the mob, but I crashed to my knees instead, spitting blood. The blows kept coming. Violent, frenzied shouts echoed from everywhere at once. My head swam with them.

A strange, whispering energy thrummed in my chest, building and building until—

"That's enough!" A familiar voice cut through the din, and the foot on my back vanished. "Stop it! Let him go!" I felt rather than saw him approach. My eyes had swollen shut. Still, two hands gripped under my arms and heaved until I stood vertical, and his arm wrapped around my bloody waist.

"Jean Luc," I croaked, prying my right eye open. Never before had I been so pleased by his presence.

"Shut up," he said harshly.

Perhaps not.

He swung his Balisarda wide, and those nearest us lurched

back with sounds of protest. "This creature belongs to the Church now, and we shall deal with it accordingly—on a stake in Cesarine. Did you think your fists could kill it? Did you think a sword to the heart would do?" He sneered derisively like only he could. "Witches must *burn*. Here now, watch me subdue the creature!" When he lifted a syringe, I pushed away from him, lunging for my fallen knives. He laughed coldly and kicked my knees. I sprawled into the snow. Bearing down on me, bending low, he pretended to stick the needle in my throat and whispered, "Play along."

My muscles sagged in relief.

He rolled me to my back with the tip of his boot. "You there"—pointing to the bearded man, he jerked his chin toward his horse—"help me move the body. It shall burn within the fortnight." Hastily, the man complied, and together, the two heaved my body upward. "Onto the saddle," Jean Luc commanded.

The man hesitated in confusion. "Sir?"

Jean Luc's eyes narrowed as he realized his mistake. "I meant tie him *to* the saddle. I'll drag him behind to Cesarine."

"Him?"

"*It*," Jean Luc snapped. "I'll drag *it* to Cesarine, you impertinent clot. Perhaps you'd like to join?"

They dumped me behind the horse without another word. No one spoke as Jean Luc tied a length of rope around my wrists, as he hoisted himself into the saddle. I watched him in disbelief. "You all can clear off now." He kicked his horse into a trot, and my body rioted with pain as I staggered to my feet. At the last second, Jean Luc called, "Thank you for your service in apprehending this criminal. I shall inform the king of your"—he craned around to look at them—"what is the name of this foul place?"

"Montfort," the bearded man called back angrily.

"What about our reward money?" someone else shouted.

Jean Luc ignored them both, dragging me into the forest.

"You enjoyed that too much," I said darkly.

Rougher than necessary, Jean Luc untied the rope from my wrists outside the village. "Entirely too much." He didn't smile, instead shoving my chest with a murderous expression. "What the hell is wrong with you? Where's Célie?"

I rubbed my wrists, instantly alert. My head still pounded. "She's with the witches."

"What?" Jean Luc's roar shook the birds from the nearest trees, and he advanced on me again. "What witches? *Who?*"

Under normal circumstances, I wouldn't have retreated. As it was, however, I'd sustained two broken ribs, a concussion, and a shattered nose. My pride was bruised enough already. It needn't suffer another defeat at the hands of Jean Luc. "I don't know. Two of them." I started north, careful to navigate *around* Montfort. "Coco and—and Lou. The crown prince was there too. I tried to bring her with me, but she refused. She likes them."

"She *likes* them?" Jean Luc hurried to catch up. "What does that mean?"

"How did you know I was here?" I asked instead.

"I didn't. I've been tracking Célie since she hatched this demented scheme. Did you know she stole her father's carriage?"

"After robbing his vault," I added, surprising even myself.

"She robbed him?" Voice faint, Jean Luc shook his head. "You've been a terrible influence—you and that witch. I can't *believe* you left Célie." He flung his hands in the air, outpacing me in his agitation. "You are the *only* reason I allowed her to go. This place—this entire fucking kingdom—it's dangerous. You were supposed to *guard* her. Now she's God knows where with only an idiotic prince for protection." He exhaled hard, shaking his head frenetically. "This just might be the stupidest thing you've ever done, Reid. I shouldn't be surprised. You haven't thought straight since the moment you met—" He clenched his fists midair, apparently overcome. He took a deep breath. Then another. "Whenever *she's* around, it's like every single coherent thought flies out of your head."

"Who? Célie?"

He whipped around to face me, eyes murderous. "No. *Not* Célie. Lou. Your *wife.*"

My wife. I snapped at the repulsive words, stooping to pick up a stone and hurling it at his face. Eyes wide, he ducked, narrowly missing it. "Stop *saying* that," I snarled.

"What the hell is wrong with you?" He scooped up his own stone then, launching it back at me. I didn't dodge in time. When it grazed my shoulder, I groaned, but he merely reached for another—a stick this time. "Saying *what?* That she's your wife? She *is.* I watched the inane ceremony myself—"

"Shut up!" I tackled him around the knees, and we both went tumbling in the snow. "Shut! Up! I would *never* tie myself to such a creature." We rolled, neither of our blows fully landing. "I would never deign to even *touch* one—"

"You've touched her plenty from what I gather." He bared his teeth and pushed a palm against my face, scrambling free. "What's the matter, Reid? Trouble in paradise? I could've told you it would never work, but you wouldn't have listened. You've been completely obsessed with her—and still are, by the sound of it. Oh no, don't try to deny it, and don't get any ideas about you and Célie either. You made your choice. She's moved on—"

I snorted and shot to my feet. "You're pathetic. You think she *belongs* to you? You think you *allowed* her to come here? You don't know her at all, do you?" When he seized my coat front, enraged, I broke his grip, resisting the urge to break his nose too. "She isn't an object. She's a person, and she's changed since you last saw her. You better prepare yourself."

"If you—"

I elbowed past him. "You don't have to worry about me." The truth in the words shocked me. Where once there had been attraction, even infatuation, when I thought of Célie now, I felt only a familial sort of affection. Frowning, I tried to pinpoint the source of the change, but I couldn't. Though I'd tried to deny it, to rationalize it, something had clearly happened inside my head. Something unnatural. Something like witchcraft. I stormed north, determined to fix it no matter the cost. The witches would know. They'd probably cursed me themselves. Their last act on earth would be undoing it. "Worry about yourself, Jean. Célie won't be happy to learn you've been following her. It implies a lack of trust. A lack of confidence."

He grimaced and looked away. Good.

"Now," I said, taking advantage of his silence, "we should strategize for when we meet them. I don't have my Balisarda, but you do. You'll need to incapacitate the freckled one." I frowned. "Coco's magic is different. She needs to touch us to inflict harm, so I'll handle her. I should be able to disable her before she can draw blood."

Jean Luc shook his head, nonplussed. "Why would we need to incapacitate either of them?"

"Because they're witches."

"So are you."

It was my turn to grimace. "Just stick to the plan."

He squared up to face me at last, straightening his shoulders. "No."

"Excuse me?"

"I said *no*." Though he shrugged, old spitefulness glinted in his pale eyes. "I hate your plan. It's a terrible plan, and I won't be doing any of it. I'm only here to collect Célie. Why would I pick a fight with two witches, one who nearly killed me during our last encounter?"

"Because you're a Chasseur," I ground out. "You swore an oath to eradicate the occult."

"Does that mean I should eradicate you?" He stepped closer, cocking his head. "When shall I do it, Reid? How? Would you prefer I drag you back to Cesarine, or shall I behead you here and now, burning your body to ash? It'd certainly be easier." He took another step, nearly chest to chest with me. "How is that for a plan?"

Red washed over my vision—whether at him or at myself, I didn't know. I inhaled deeply through my nose. Exhaled hard. I concentrated on each breath, counting to ten. Finally, forcing my voice to remain even, I said, "We can't simply let them live. They—they did something to me, Jean. My head, it isn't right. I think they've stolen my memories. Pieces of my life. And the freckled witch, she—"

"Lou," he corrected me.

"*Lou.*" The name tasted sour on my tongue. "I think she's the one who did it."

He rolled his eyes and started forward once more. "She'd die before she'd harm you. No, don't"—he lifted a hand to stop my protest—"don't start. Clearly, something *is* wrong, but killing Lou and Coco won't solve it. It *won't*, Reid. They're the only people who like you. No, I *said* don't interrupt. If you kill them and return to Cesarine, the huntsmen will inevitably find and execute you. You saw the wanted posters. You're one of the most notorious outlaws in the entire kingdom, second only to Lou. It's too dangerous for you to wander the countryside alone—a point you've just proven, by the way—which leaves only one option: you stay with the witches."

"I don't—"

"You stay with the witches," he continued in a hard voice,

"and they will protect you. Perhaps they'll even help undo whatever has gone so *critically* wrong inside your head. Of course, you might need to conduct yourself with a bit more charm to persuade them. A near impossible task, I know—"

"They'll undo it either way," I growled.

He stopped again, turning to face me with an impatient sigh. "You still don't seem to understand, so allow me to make this perfectly clear. You can't kill them. Simply put, I won't let you. You're a dead man walking without them, and beyond that, you'll hate yourself later if you do. Despite what you think now, those women are your friends. Your family. I've watched you all together, and I—" He broke off abruptly, eyes tightening, before turning to stomp through the snow once more. "You're an idiot."

I glared at the back of his head, but I no longer tried to argue. He'd painted a clear enough picture. Yes, perhaps I had nowhere else to go at present. Perhaps my brethren would kill me if they found me. Perhaps I *did* need these witches—to reverse the hex on my mind, to ensure Célie and the crown prince survived. But Jean Luc had been wrong about one thing: I *could* survive alone. I'd been unprepared before. It wouldn't happen again.

And I would kill Lou and Coco at the first opportunity.

THE WAGER

Lou

Coco allowed me to wallow in misery for approximately three minutes—hugging me all the while—before pulling back and wiping my tears. "He isn't dead, you know."

"He loathes me."

She shrugged and rifled through her bag, extracting a bottle of honey. "I seem to remember him loathing you once before. You both rose to the occasion." She combined the amber liquid with blood from her forearm before swabbing the mixture over the wound at my chest. She turned to examine Beau's injuries next. "We might as well be comfortable while we wait."

"Wait for what?" Beau asked mulishly. Sporting a terrific shiner from Reid's ministrations, he swallowed the blood and honey. The swelling disappeared almost instantly.

"For Reid to crawl back with his tail between his legs. It shouldn't take long." She shooed him down the beach. "Now go find some driftwood for a fire. It's colder than a witch's tit out here."

"*Why?*" Though Beau complied, snatching up a stick by our

feet, he glanced around nervously. "Shouldn't we leave? Morgane could be lurking out of sight."

"I doubt it," Coco murmured, "if she doesn't remember Lou."

I jerked my sleeve back in place.

"Here." Célie smiled faintly, reaching into her own bag. She withdrew a needle and thread. "Let me help with that." I frowned as her delicate fingers threaded the eye, as she slowly, carefully reaffixed the fabric.

"We'll leave as soon as Reid returns." Coco walked to the path to gather rocks for a firepit. "If we go before, he might not find us again. We'll need him to help steal the ring before we can return to Cesarine." With an inscrutable look in my direction, she added, "That *is* the plan, isn't it? To rejoin Claud and Blaise with the melusines? Plot a final strike against Morgane? Rescue Madame Labelle from the stake?"

"More or less."

Beau scowled when she snatched his stick, speaking in an aggrieved whisper. "On that note, how on earth are we supposed to *steal* the ring? Chateau le Blanc is a fortress, and *again*— Morgane could be hiding behind that rock even now, listening to our every word."

"*Again*, without Lou in the picture, Morgane could be rallying forces to kill your father as we speak," Coco said pointedly. "Zenna said witches have been gathering at Chateau le Blanc en masse. I doubt they're braiding each other's hair. Perhaps they've already marched toward Cesarine. It'd certainly make our job easier."

"And if not? Couldn't we just . . . dispatch Morgane at the Chateau?"

"Like we could've dispatched her on the beach?" I watched as Célie moved to the gash at my chest. Though the fabric was still wet from my blood—from Coco's blood and honey—she didn't seem to mind. I, however, struggled to remain still. To remain *calm*. "It worked out so well for us the first time. I'm sure it'll be even simpler surrounded by witches en masse." To Coco, I said, "Why didn't we think of that?"

She shrugged. "Who needs gods and dragons, werewolves and mermaids, when we could've just done it ourselves the whole time?"

"Yes, all right." Beau scowled at each of us, stalking down the beach, as Célie finished mending my shirt. "It was just a thought."

He returned a few moments later with an armful of driftwood, dumping it at Coco's feet. She promptly scowled and stacked the pieces into a square. "Genuinely, how have you survived this long, Beauregard?"

"Here." I snapped my fingers, magicking the friction between them to the point of pain. The golden pattern vanished as a flame sparked. Delicious heat washed over me, a welcome reprieve to the icy cold in my chest. I glanced to the path instinctively.

He'll come back.

"Lou." As if reading my thoughts, Coco turned my chin with a single finger. "You forgot to include one key component in our plan: seducing Reid." She smirked at my deadpan expression. "Fortunately you happen to know a master in the art of seduction.

Don't worry, Célie," she added, winking. "I'll teach you in the process as well. Think of it as your first lesson in debauchment."

My heart sank miserably, and I shook my head. "We have more important things to worry about. Besides," I added, loathing the note of bitterness in my voice. "It won't work. Not this time."

"I don't see why not. He fell in love with you before." She dropped her hand. "And I would argue it's the *most* important thing."

"He didn't know I was a witch then. He thought I was his wife."

"Nuance. Your souls are bound. Magic can't change that."

"You can't really believe in soul mates?"

"I believe in you." At my incredulous look, she shrugged again, watching the flames crackle. "And *perhaps* I'm willing to make an exception when it comes to the two of you. I've been here this whole time, you know," she added. "I watched Reid take his forefather's life to save yours. I watched him throw his entire belief system out the window and learn magic for your sake—and wear leather pants in a traveling troupe. I watched you sacrifice pieces of yourself to protect him. He fought an entire pack of werewolves to return the favor, and *you* fought tooth and nail in these waters to return to him. You've befriended a god, swum with mermaids, and now you can even transform into a three-form shape at will. You can probably do a whole slew of other fun new things too." Her brows lifted with her shoulders. "I'm certainly not betting against you—unless you're too afraid to try?"

Nicholina's hateful voice filled my mind. *But you should feel lucky you tricked him, oh yes, because if you hadn't tricked him—such a tricky little mouse—he never would've loved you. If he had known what you are, he never would've held you beneath the stars.*

Goddamn it.

Beau, who'd been listening in silence, watched me too closely to be comfortable. He arched a brow. "I don't know, Coco. I don't think she can do it."

I glared mutinously at the fire. "Don't start with me, Beau."

"Why not?" His dark eyes searched my face and missed nothing. "You just said as much yourself. It won't work. He'll never love you again. I'm merely concurring with the sentiment."

"I'm not doing this."

"Yes, you've made that perfectly clear. Better not to try at all than to fail, right?" He shrugged dispassionately. "I couldn't agree more."

"Beau!" Célie's eyes widened in protest. Perhaps she was too naive to see Beau's manipulation, or—more likely—perhaps she insisted on being the voice of optimism despite it. "How can you say such wicked things? Of course Reid will love her. The bond they share is *true*. You saw their kiss—it woke him up despite the magic!"

"Oh, Célie, enough with this *true love* nonsense." He returned his cool attention to me. "You want truth, sister mine? I shall give you truth. You were right before. Without memories of your relationship, you are only a witch to Reid, and he hates you. You are no longer his wife. As far as he knows, you were *never* his wife. Indeed, he's probably plotting creative ways to kill you at this very moment." He leaned forward to whisper conspiratorially.

"My money is on strangulation. He never has been able to keep his hands off you."

Célie's eyes flashed. "*Really*, Beau, you shouldn't—"

I mimicked his movement with a black smile, leaning toward him until our noses nearly touched. "Let's sweeten the pot. I bet it'll be a knife to heart."

Coco rolled her eyes as Beau shook his head. "Not intimate enough."

"There's nothing *more* intimate—"

"Oh, I disagree—"

"You're both ridiculous," Célie snapped, shooting to her feet in a spectacular display of temper. "You want to sweeten the pot? I wager all the riches in my father's treasury that Reid *does* fall in love with you again, *despite* knowing you're a witch."

A beat of silence passed as she glared at me. Pink tinged her cheeks.

"I thought you stole all of your father's treasure?" Beau asked suspiciously.

"Not even close."

He pursed his lips, considering, while I quietly seethed. They were treating this like a game, all of them. But this wasn't a game. This was my *life*. And why did Célie care so much, anyway? Reid had wrecked their own relationship for the sake of *true love* with me. As if reading my thoughts, she whispered, "The two of you have something special, Louise. Something precious. How can you not fight for him? He has certainly fought for you."

You've lived in fear too long.

Fear has helped me survive.

Fear has kept you from living.

"I think I'd like to accept that wager, Mademoiselle Tremblay," Beau mused before turning to Coco. "What do you think, Cosette? Does the fair maiden stand a chance of seducing her gallant knight? Shall true love win the day?"

Coco carefully stoked the fire. "You know what I think."

"It would seem we have a wager." Beau held out a hand to Célie, clasping her wrist and shaking it. "If Lou fails to seduce her husband, you will give me all the riches in your father's treasury." His teeth flashed in a hard smile. "And if she succeeds, I will give you all the riches in *mine*."

Célie blinked, the indignation in her eyes winking out. Her mouth parted in awe. "King Auguste's entire treasury?"

"Indeed. Unless, of course, our fair maiden objects?" He extended his free hand toward me, but I knocked it aside with a scowl. Ass. "As I thought." He tutted softly. "You *are* too afraid."

Paralysis crept up my spine as I looked between them all. Though I opened my mouth to speak—to *vehemently* object to this foolish game—the words caught, and different words altogether spilled out instead. Honest ones. "I'm not afraid. I'm *terrified*. What if he does try to strangle me or stick a knife through my heart? What if he doesn't remember at all? What if he doesn't . . ." I swallowed hard and blinked back fresh tears. "What if he doesn't love me?"

Beau wrapped an arm around my shoulders, pulling me close. "Then I will become a rich man."

"You're already a rich man."

"A *very* rich man."

"You're an ass, Beau."

He brushed a brotherly kiss across my temple. "Do we have a wager?"

I rested my head on his shoulder as noise sounded from the path, and Reid stormed into sight, right on time. Jean Luc followed at a wary distance. *Jean Luc.* It was a mark of the last twenty-four hours that I didn't bat an eye.

"Yes," I said. The word tasted like hope. It felt like armor. I allowed it to wrap around me, bolstering my spirit and protecting my heart. Reid *had* fallen in love with me once, and I still returned that love fiercely. It was special. It was precious. And I would fight for it. "Yes, we have a wager."

HOLES IN THE TAPESTRY

Reid

The witch called Lou stepped from the crown prince with a smirk as I approached. I did a double take. Whereas before her eyes had shone with grief—with near unfathomable loss—they now sparkled with wicked intent. I frowned as the other witch, Coco, stepped in front of her, breaking my line of sight.

Was she—I stared at them incredulously—was she pulling Lou's neckline down?

I averted my eyes, furious, but glanced back as Célie leaned over to pinch Lou's cheeks.

Beside me, Jean Luc broke into a jog. He didn't seem to notice Lou's décolletage. He saw only Célie. Spinning her around, he cupped her face and kissed her. Straight on the mouth. In front of us all. Though Célie's eyes flew open in surprise, she didn't protest. Indeed, she even wrapped her arms around his neck, smiling against his lips. "You're here," she said happily.

He returned her smile before resting his forehead against hers. I stared at them. I hadn't seen Jean smile since we were children. "I'm here," he breathed.

Something shifted in her expression. Her smile faltered. "You're here." She blinked up at him in confusion. "Why are you here?"

"Yes, Jean." I stalked forward, careful to keep one eye on Lou. She kept both on me. Unease snaked down my spine, further inflaming my fury. "Why *are* you here?"

Lou sauntered forward, still grinning. I refused to retreat a step. Not a single one. "I could pose the same question to you, Chass." She batted her lashes and trailed a finger across my chest. "Just couldn't stay away, could you?"

I caught her wrist and stepped closer. Baring my teeth. I longed for my Balisarda. "Hardly. You've clearly tampered with my memories, witch. I want them back."

She tilted her face toward mine, unperturbed. "Hmm. I don't think I can help you with that."

"You can, and you will."

"Only the witch who cast the enchantment can break it." Coco's hip knocked into Lou as she swept past us, pushing Lou flush against me. She winked. "In this case, that means *you.*"

My jaw clenched, and I lifted my hands to Lou's shoulders to forcibly remove her. "You lie."

"Why would we lie? Trust us when we say you aren't exactly fun to be around—not like this anyway. If there was a way for us to reverse your memory, we would've already done it." Coco lifted a shoulder as she stepped on the path. "You'll need to do it, or no one will."

"A pity, that." Lou thrust her pack against my chest. I caught it instinctively. "Guess you'll have to stay with us until you figure it out." She followed Coco without a backward glance, swaying her hips as she went. My lip curled in disgust. She wore trousers. Fitted ones. Leather. They adhered to her delicate shape in a distasteful way—indecent, even. Shaking my head, I tore my gaze away to stare at the pack in my hands.

I suspected she was anything but delicate.

"Answer the question, Jean." Célie's voice reclaimed my attention. She scowled up at Jean Luc, fierce and unrelenting. "You said the priests—the *king*—requested your presence at the conclave."

"They did."

"You *disobeyed* them?"

"I . . ." He tugged at his collar. "I had to see you."

Her eyes narrowed in suspicion. "Why? Why are you here? Did you"—those accusing eyes cut to mine—"did he think I couldn't do this? Did he think I would die at the first opportunity?"

"You did almost fall from a cliff," Jean Luc muttered defensively. When Célie's face contorted in shock, in outrage, he added, "What? You *did*. I spoke with Father Achille."

"You spoke with Father Achille?" Célie's voice could've frozen water. Abruptly, she stepped away from him, her neck and spine snapping impossibly straight. Taut as a bow. "Have you been following me?"

"I—well, I—of course I have." He rubbed a sheepish hand across his neck. "How could I not?"

"For how long?"

He hesitated, clearly reluctant. "Since . . . since Cesarine."

Her expression emptied of all emotion. "You abandoned your post. You forsook the conclave."

"*No.*" Jean Luc shook his head vehemently. "I delegated my duties before I left. I ensured the king and your parents would remain protected—"

"Do my parents know? Did you tell them that you planned to follow me?"

He looked deeply uncomfortable now. "Yes." At her intense, cold stare, he hastened to add, "We had to know you were safe, Célie. They—*I*—couldn't bear the thought of anything—"

She didn't allow him to finish. Instead, she bludgeoned him in the chest with her own pack, turning on her heel to follow Coco and Lou. He staggered beneath its weight. "Célie." When she didn't turn, his voice grew louder, imploring. "Célie, please, wait—"

She whirled suddenly, fists clenched. "I do not need a *keeper*, Jean. This may come as a surprise, but I can take care of myself. I may be a woman—I may be gentle and meek and refined, like a *pretty doll*—but I have survived more in my eighteen years than you and my parents combined. Do not mistake me for porcelain. Do not mistake me for *weak*."

She left without another word.

Struggling to hold her bag, Jean Luc tried to follow, but the crown prince clapped his shoulder, further upsetting his balance. He pitched forward with a curse. "Bad luck, man." Beau didn't lift a finger to set him right. "I think there might be actual bars of gold in there." He shrugged. "The melusines liked her best."

"She's wearing trousers," Jean Luc said incredulously, panting now. "*Célie.*"

Tension radiated across my face, shoulders, neck. I cared for none of this—the witches, their lies, their *clothes.* Tasteless wardrobes aside, however, the women had disappeared around the bend. We couldn't afford to lose them. *I* couldn't afford to lose them. Not with my memory at stake. Despite their deceit, they would help me restore my memories, or I would cut the very lies from their tongues. I just needed patience. Scowling, I hitched Lou's bag higher. "Where are we going?"

Beau started after them without waiting for either of us. "I believe to pillage a castle."

Jean Luc acquired two additional horses at the next village to speed our travel. When he extended a hand to Célie to help her mount his own, she knocked it aside and ascended herself. She now sat formal and straight in his saddle while he perched behind her.

That left four of us.

I glared at the witches, prepared to tie them behind as Jean Luc had tied me. Beau had a different idea. Without giving me a chance to speak—to protest—he ushered Coco astride the second horse, hoisting himself up after her.

That left two of us for the last horse.

And it was unacceptable.

"Give me the rope." I stomped to Jean Luc's side, seizing

his bag. The coil sat at the top. Right. Squaring my shoulders, I turned to face the witch. The others watched in rapt fascination. "Don't make this difficult."

Her eyes fell to the rope in my hand. Her smile faltered. "You're kidding."

"I don't kid. Give me your wrists. You can walk behind the horse."

"Fuck you."

Coco slid from her own horse now, coming to stand beside Lou. "Don't make us tie *you* to the horse, Reid." She lifted her wrist to place a thumbnail upon it. A threat. "If you talk to her like that again, it would be my pleasure."

My hands tightened on the rope. "Try."

Beau rolled his eyes. "Honestly, brother, will you insist on this asshattery at every turn? If so, it's going to be a very long trip."

"I'm not riding anywhere with that witch."

Without my Balisarda, I was virtually defenseless. She could attack me even now, and I wouldn't be able to stop her. As if sensing that thought, Lou snorted. "You aren't in any more danger on the horse." Stepping into the stirrup, she swung her leg over its back. "Don't be stupid, Chass. Climb up. You can tie me up later if you'd like, but I'm not walking anywhere."

I glared up at her. "I don't trust you."

Her answering smile was hard. "I don't particularly trust you either, which is why you should know"—she brushed the sheath at her thigh—"I'll gut you like a fish if you try anything."

I didn't move. Coco didn't either. Her eyes narrowed on my

bandolier. "Not good enough. Give me your knives."

"That isn't going to happen."

Lou tipped her face up to the sky, exhaling heavily. "It's fine, Coco. I've kicked his ass before. I can do it again."

"We're wasting time," Célie urged.

Jean Luc shot me an impatient look. "Just get on the horse, Reid."

Judas.

Reluctant, furious, I hoisted myself behind her, reaching around to take hold of the reins. She relinquished them freely. "Be very careful," I warned her, voice low. "You may have magic, but you aren't the only one who can gut a fish."

She turned her face toward mine. "I'm not the only one who has magic either." When I nudged our horse into a trot, following the others, she asked, "Have you heard them yet? The voices?"

I glared straight ahead. "I am sound of mind."

"For now."

I ignored the bait. Ignored her altogether. Until— "Beau said we're riding toward a castle?"

"Chateau le Blanc." She settled between my arms, heaving a terse sigh when I shoved her forward once more. "My ancestral home."

"You're going to rob it?" I tried to keep my voice casual. Cold. Only a Dame Blanche could locate the infamous Chateau. Finally, I'd found one to lead me to it. How many years had my brethren searched? How many witches would I snare there, unsuspecting and defenseless? Would I unearth the great pythoness herself, La Dame des Sorcières? One could only hope.

If Lou couldn't return my memories, perhaps this was the next best thing.

"*We* are going to rob it." She didn't lean against me again. Unfortunately, her forward position fitted her backside more firmly between my legs. I gritted my teeth against the sensation. "It'll be locked in the treasury, up in the highest room of the tallest tower. That's where my coven hides all their relics—cursed books and eternal flowers and magic rings alike."

"Your father would shit a brick, Célie," Beau called over his shoulder.

"Shut up, Your Highness," Jean Luc fired back.

Célie spoke through her teeth. "I can speak for myself, Jean."

Lou chuckled before continuing. "My mother allowed me inside only once, and the door was guarded by a powerful enchantment. We'll have to break it somehow—if we even manage to reach it. Eyes surround the castle itself from all sides. Hundreds of witches live there year-round." She paused. "Even more now."

Hundreds of witches.

"You said only the witch who casts the enchantment can break it."

"That's right."

I clenched my jaw in irritation. In disappointment. "How will we break the enchantment on the door?"

She merely shrugged, her hair tickling my face. Long and thick and brown. Wild. Against my better judgment, I inhaled its scent. She smelled sweet in a way I almost recognized—like vanilla and cinnamon. A warm coat on a cold winter day. Snow on my tongue. I shook my head, feeling thoroughly stupid. "You have no strategy at all, do you?"

"I bottled several pints of L'Eau Mélancolique." The wind carried Coco's voice in an upward spiral. Lou strained forward to hear her, and I shifted away, cursing inwardly. Heat crept into my cheeks. My body didn't realize, of course. This wasn't a woman but a witch. "Maybe the waters will restore the door to what it was before the enchantment," Coco continued. "If not, my blood might. It's a different magic than yours."

Jean Luc didn't hide his scorn. "It's a door. We break it down."

I scarcely heard the exchange. With each stride of the horse, the witch's backside moved against my lap, up and down, rhythmic, until heat suffused my entire body. I glared determinedly at the sky overhead. The situation had grown dire. Soon, she would notice, and soon, I would have to kill her for it.

"Is there a problem, Chass?" she murmured after another moment.

"None," I snapped.

She said nothing for several seconds. Then— "You can tell me if there is." She cleared her throat. It sounded suspiciously like a laugh. "It must be *hard*, riding with me like this."

I would have to kill her.

"Seriously, Reid." Lowering her voice, she turned to look at me in the saddle. I exhaled harshly at the movement. "Do I need to move?" The sudden earnestness in her expression startled me. As did the flush in her cheeks. The dilation of her pupils. "I can sit behind you."

Ahead of us, Beau glanced back at me before winking and whispering in Coco's ear. She laughed. Feverish with rage or—or something else—I shook my head. Their sly behavior chafed. All of it. Though truthfully, one couldn't call them sly at all. Each communicated openly if not clearly, which made it all the more infuriating. They were laughing at my expense.

I just didn't know why.

And I wouldn't be humiliated by a witch.

I jerked my chin behind me. "Move."

She stood in the stirrups without hesitation. Or tried. She couldn't reach both, instead standing on tiptoe atop each of my boots. She nearly lost her balance. I didn't help her. Didn't touch her. Not until she pivoted to face me, her breasts at eye level. I nearly choked. Though she shimmied to maneuver around, they still brushed my cheek, and I lurched backward. She smelled sweet. Too sweet. Swiftly, I wrapped an arm around her waist, propelling her behind me. She clutched my shoulders for balance. Her thighs cradled mine. I held back a groan.

At least her breasts weren't in my face anymore—they were pressed into my back.

God was trying to kill me.

She slid her arms around my torso. "Is this better?"

"How do I restore my memories?" I asked instead. Hideous shame tightened my chest. This physical response—I'd never felt it with such intensity. Worse, the ache didn't ease. It only strengthened with each passing moment. My body felt . . . unfulfilled. Like it knew what came next. Like it craved it. But that was nonsense. It didn't know anything, didn't *crave* anything, and it certainly didn't recognize that sweet smell.

"It'll be painful. I've only done it once."

"And?"

"And I just sort of . . . focused on the holes in the tapestry. I followed the loose threads."

I scoffed. "Riddles."

"No." She squeezed me tighter, her wrist dangerously close to one of my knives. I didn't warn her. "It isn't a riddle at all. Think of a specific gap in your memory. Focus. Remember everything around it—the colors, the scents, the sounds. Logically, your mind will try to fill in the missing pieces, but subconsciously, each explanation will feel wrong." She paused. "That's when you move on to the illogical ones. The magical ones."

Are you sure? Think hard, Reid. Please. Just think. I'm Lou, remember? I'm your wife.

Wanted dead or alive under suspicion of murder, conspiracy, and witchcraft.

I viciously rejected each thought. They simply weren't true. And despite what this creature claimed, they didn't feel *right*. They felt wrong in every way. Unnatural. I gripped the reins tighter, spurring our horse faster. I needed to recenter. To refocus. Plunging a knife in a witch's heart should do the trick. A simple, logical solution.

Even better if she had freckles.

WINTER WONDERLAND

Lou

I wasn't prepared to return to Chateau le Blanc. A chill skittered down my spine at the familiarity of the wind here, the taste of the salt and pine and magic. Beyond the eerie mist of L'Eau Mélancolique, waves crashed and gulls cried. The former had lulled me to sleep every night as a child—and the latter had woken me each morning. My bedroom window had overlooked the sea.

"Stop." Though I said the word quietly, Jean Luc pulled on the reins of his horse, turning to face me. "We should walk from here. My sisters stalk these trees at night."

To my surprise, he nodded and complied without argument or scorn. Reid, however, stiffened and shook his head. "Your *sisters.*"

"Do you have any?" Sliding from the saddle, I voiced the question with casual nonchalance. I knew the answer, of course, but *he* didn't know that. I'd spooked him before with talk of wives and magic. His physical response to me hadn't helped. If I had any chance of rekindling what we'd once had, it would take more than seduction. More than pleas. I'd need to fall in love with him all over again—the person he was now—and he would need to fall in love with me. When he didn't answer, I tried to clarify. "Sisters, I mean."

"I knew what you meant," he said shortly.

Right.

I'd forgotten he was now an ass.

Jean Luc and Coco worked on tying the horses to trees while Célie and Beau approached. Beau rubbed his hands together against the cold. "What's the plan? We charge in, swords drawn, banners flying?"

"Morgane would kill us before we even crossed the bridge." My eyes snagged on Célie's hands. She'd clasped them at her waist, the picture of propriety—except for the needle sticking between them. "What is *that*?"

Slowly, she uncurled her fingers, revealing a crude metal syringe. She didn't cower or flinch beneath my black gaze as she said, matter-of-fact, "An injection. I lost it at the beach, but Elvire returned it to me. I plan to stab it in your mother's throat."

"Ah." Coco and I shared an incredulous glance. "Well, if that's all."

Reid's eyes gleamed as he stepped forward, but Célie snatched it away before he could take it. "Don't even think about it. It belongs to *me*."

Jean Luc and Coco joined us now. "What *is* the plan?" the former asked. "Do we have any strategy at all?"

"How did you sneak in on Modraniht?" I asked Coco.

"Madame Labelle transformed our faces." She shrugged helplessly. Reid, however, frowned at the name, his gaze turning inward, distant, as he found his mother in his memories. When his frown turned to a scowl, I knew he'd remembered her a witch. "Can you do the same? If witches have gathered from all over the kingdom, we could slip inside without suspicion."

"It's possible, but . . ." I shook my head with mounting apprehension. "Morgane might not remember me, but she'll remember how you infiltrated the castle. Others will remember too. I doubt they'll fall for such a trick again—especially after Zenna's attack. Everyone will be on high alert. Every stranger in the castle will be counted."

"How did *you* sneak in?" Coco asked Jean Luc. "You and the Chasseurs?"

"We waited on the beach until Madame Labelle led us through the enchantment. We had no need to disguise ourselves. We wanted the witches to see us approach—to know ours would be the last faces they ever saw."

Célie wrinkled her nose at the gratuitous explanation. "Lovely."

His expression turned solemn. "I'm still a Chasseur, Célie. I still eradicate the occult. What I'm doing now—I'd lose my Balisarda if my brethren caught me here. I'd burn at the stake myself." He gestured between us. "We all would."

"Unless we bring them La Dame des Sorcières's head." Reid looked pointedly at Coco and me. "And those of her *sisters*."

Beau jutted a finger at him. "*You* don't get to talk anymore—"

"Just be sure this is what you want." Jean Luc clutched Célie's hands, ignoring them both. "We can still walk away. You have a choice. You don't have to do this."

Célie's knuckles whitened around the injection. "Yes, I do."

"Célie—"

"And you are not called to eradicate the occult, Jean. You are called to eradicate *evil*." She pulled away from him, stepping backward to stand beside me. "There is evil in this chateau. Truthfully, we have no choice at all."

They stared at each other for several seconds—neither willing to blink—before Jean Luc finally sighed. "If we must enter from the bridge, we need some sort of cover." Reluctantly, he unbuckled his scabbard, retreating briefly to his horse to hide it within his pack. The sapphire of his Balisarda's hilt winked as he withdrew a set of knives instead.

Reid's eyes widened incredulously. "What are you doing?"

"Think, Reid." He tucked one knife into each boot. "The only viable cover available to us is magic." He waved a hand in my direction, refusing to look at me. "Magic will not work if I carry my Balisarda."

Together, they all turned to stare at me. As if I knew the answers. As if I held each of their fates in the palm of my hand. Stomach rolling, I forced myself to return their gaze—because in a way, they were right. This was my ancestral home. These were my kin. If I couldn't protect them here, if I couldn't *hide* them from my sisters, they would indeed die.

"Perhaps I should . . ." I cleared my throat. "Perhaps I should go in alone."

The thought met instantaneous and decisive objection, each of them speaking over the other. Coco and Beau refused to leave me. Célie demanded a chance to prove herself, and Jean Luc insisted I would need his expertise. Even Reid shook his head in stoic silence, his eyes communicating what his mouth did not.

Nothing would stand between him and his conquest.

At the moment, that conquest was Morgane le Blanc. Soon, he would realize his target had shifted, and the fleeting impulse to kill me would solidify into something very real and very dangerous. When he learned I'd become La Dame des Sorcières, I would no longer be safe with him. Not until he remembered. Not until I recaptured his heart.

"We go where you go," he said with dark resolve.

My heart twisted with the words, and I turned away, closing my eyes. A web of golden patterns rose up to meet me. Studying them carefully—my lids fluttering in concentration—I discarded one after another, unsatisfied with each. This sort of magic, the sort to hide six people, would exact a heavy cost. Perhaps I could transform their bodies instead of their faces. They could become birds or squirrels or foxes. A rock in a badger's mouth.

Expelling a sigh of frustration, I shook my head. Such transfiguration would probably kill me. Beau would have to live the rest of his life as a rock—or, more likely, live as a rock forever because rocks didn't die. After another moment or two of my own fruitless searching, Coco said softly, "Could you make us invisible?"

I didn't open my eyes, instead widening my inner sight for such a pattern. My skin tingled at the effort. My chest ached, an uncomfortable pressure building there. These cords—they felt simplistic somehow. Inadequate. Almost weak. Had something happened to my magic? Had Nicholina ... altered me somehow? I frowned and pushed harder, stamping a metaphorical foot at the injustice of it all. Heat fanned across my face in humiliation.

Here I was, La Dame des Sorcières—famed and all-powerful, Mother, Maiden, and Crone—yet I couldn't even cast an enchantment to protect my friends.

My sister chose wrong.

I could feel their expectant eyes on me now, waiting for a miracle.

I stomped my foot again, this time in desperation, and the web beneath me bowed and rippled outward. Startled, I instinctively stomped once more.

This time, the web broke.

A web of pure, blinding white lay below it, and the tingle in my skin exploded in a wave of raw power. No. *Awareness.* Every blade of grass, every flake of snow, every *needle* of *pine* I felt with such an intensity that I stumbled backward, breathless. Célie caught my arm. "Lou?" she asked in alarm.

I didn't dare open my eyes. Not when the web below offered so much more. I tracked each pattern eagerly, feverish with possibility. I'd thought my magic infinite before. I'd thought it limited only to my imagination.

I'd been wrong.

My magic had flowed through the land, but this magic—it *was* the land. *This* land. The Triple Goddess hadn't merely bestowed her form. She'd bestowed the heart of our entire people. My finger twitched, and the web rippled outward, connected to my every thought, every emotion, every memory. My ancestors' too. I didn't just feel the grass. I *was* the grass. I'd become the snow and pine.

"Lou, you're scaring me." Coco's sharp voice cut through my wonder, and unbidden, my eyes snapped open. She stood directly in front of me. In the brown of her irises, my skin reflected back at me, bright and burnished. Luminous. "What happened?"

"I—" The ache in my chest towed me forward through the trees. I couldn't resist its pull. "I'm fine," I called over my shoulder, chuckling at their wide eyes and parted mouths. Reid had drawn a knife from his bandolier. He regarded me with open suspicion. I couldn't bring myself to care. "I can hide everyone. Follow me."

Coco rushed after me. "*How?*"

I grinned at her. "White patterns."

"Like the one at the blood camp?" Her hopeful expression fell. "The one that led you to Etienne?"

My smile slipped, and I shuddered to a halt, suddenly unsure. "Do you think it's Morgane?"

"I think we should consider the possibility. Your patterns have never been white before, have they?"

"You've never been La Dame des Sorcières before either," Beau pointed out. Though Coco and I both glared at him, it was too late. The damage had been done, and Reid's menacing presence loomed behind me.

"*You're* La Dame des Sorcières?"

With my newfound awareness, I could feel the weight of his footsteps. I could feel the snow and moss tamp beneath his boots. His presence was heavier than the others', harder and stronger. Darker. I scoffed. "Barely." Turning to Coco, trusting Beau and Célie and even Jean Luc to protect my back, I said, "It doesn't feel like Morgane. It feels familiar, yes—almost familial—but it also feels like me. I . . . I think I trust it."

She nodded once in understanding. But how could she? I hardly understood myself. Though I implicitly trusted the wholeness of this magic, the purity, I felt much like a rowboat at sea. The ache in my chest kept building, pulling me adrift. Dragging me beneath the current. "Then do it," she said firmly. "Do it quickly."

Closing my eyes, ignoring Reid's vehement protest, I spread my awareness outward, farther and faster than before. There. A mile north, beneath the infamous bridge, a river crashed into the ocean. With the wave of my hand, the water solidified to ice, changing state of matter. The white pattern burst, and my friends and I dissolved into shadow.

With our first steps on the bridge, my body attempted to rematerialize, limbs accumulating and dispersing with violent shudders. Except it wasn't my body at all. Gritting my teeth in concentration, I glanced down at my unfamiliar, disembodied hand. The Maiden's hand.

"Shit."

My whisper floated in the darkness as said hand dispersed to shadow once more. "What is it?" Coco asked sharply. I could just see her shadowed form beside Beau's, though the finer details of their appearance—such as the expressions on their faces, the gleam in their eyes—had been lost to the enchantment. Now they simply appeared pieces of night darker than the rest. Human-shaped shadows. None would notice us unless they looked, and even then, the smoke obscured all traces of moonlight. We were near invisible.

"Nothing. I just—feel weird." Though incorporeal, my head still swam at the magnitude of power before me. At the sheer breadth of it. How had my mother withstood this? How had it not crushed her? "It's too much. It's like I can't breathe."

"So don't," Reid offered.

If I'd had hands, I might've strangled him. Perhaps I still would've tried if I hadn't looked up, past the gatehouse, to the empty expanse of mountain all around the Chateau. I blinked slowly, unable to believe my eyes. Where before a mighty forest had prospered, now only rocks and dirt greeted me. "Where are the trees?"

Someone bumped into me from behind. Jean Luc. "What do you mean?"

"The trees." I gestured to the rocky incline above us, for-getting he couldn't see me. "There used to be trees here. Trees *everywhere*. They covered this entire mountain face."

"It's true." Reid's heavy footsteps stopped beside me. "I remember."

We all crept forward, slower and warier now. "Perhaps they chopped them down," Beau said. "And recently. Look—no snow."

I instantly disagreed. "They didn't."

"How do you know?"

"I just *do.*"

"There are no stumps," Coco said, leaning forward. "See? The ground does look disturbed, though."

"Perhaps Zenna scorched them all, then." Beau pointed to the charred markings on the bridge, on the gatehouse ahead. Evidence of Zenna's wrath. Still, the hair on my neck lifted. These trees hadn't been burned. Of that, I was certain.

"They look like they just . . . uprooted and walked away."

Reid made a low, disparaging sound at the back of his throat. I ignored him. Instead, I started for the gatehouse once more, focusing on the sound of my feet on the wood.

Whatever damage Zenna had caused with her attack, little evidence remained. The structural integrity of the Chateau remained intact, and even the facade bore little sign of fire. Magic was helpful that way. I supposed Morgane wouldn't have liked the soot underfoot. We paused inside the crumbling entrance to listen. Though the air in the courtyard could chill bone, the temperature within felt warm and balmy, despite the overgrown ruins of the hall. And the castle—it came alive at night. Voices echoed from all around: beyond the grand stairwell, through the corridors, within the great hall. Two lovers swept past hand in hand, and soon after, a manservant bustled through with a tray of what smelled like custard tarts. A handful of witchlings passed us a moment later to make shapes in the snow outside. Though I recognized none of them, the familiarity of it all made me smile. Nothing had changed.

Reid unsheathed another knife beside me, and my smile faded. Everything had changed.

At least Morgane hadn't deployed forces to Cesarine. Not *yet*, anyway.

"Keep close," I murmured, starting toward the staircase. Though my body remained like shadow, I kept to the edges of the room. Smoke had obscured the moonlight outside, yes, but inside, lit candles dripped from their candelabra and cast flickering light. I would take no chances. "Morgane and Josephine are here somewhere. Perhaps Nicholina too."

"And the treasury?" Reid murmured.

"Follow me."

I led them through a narrow door beneath the staircase, into the winding passage beyond. Though it would take longer to reach the treasury's tower this way, few others traveled it, and I . . . I couldn't explain the creeping dread in my chest. The longer I concealed my friends in shadow, the more agitated I became. Like the magic itself was—was rebelling against me. Against *them*. It made little sense, yet wasn't the purpose of La Dame des Sorcières to protect her home?

We were trespassers here, all of us, intent on thieving a sacred treasure.

My magic didn't trust us, I realized in a burst of clarity.

The air in the passage tasted stale, damp, and the moss on the stones muted our footsteps. A good thing too—for at that exact moment, a door cracked open ahead, and three figures spilled out into the semidarkness. I froze mid-step, my heart pounding in my ears. I heard their voices before I saw their faces.

Morgane, Josephine, and Nicholina.

They strode forward, deep in harried conversation, and I seized Reid before they could see us, pushing him into the nearest alcove. Célie and Jean Luc barreled in behind as Coco and Beau did the same across the hall. The space was too small, however. My cheek smashed against Reid's chest, and behind me, Jean Luc's knee stabbed my thigh. Célie trembled visibly. Contorting my arm, I wrapped it around her to hide the movement and comfort her in equal measure. No one dared breathe.

"I do not *care* what you say," Morgane hissed at Josephine, visibly agitated. She'd swept her white hair into a tangled braid, and her eyes remained shot through with blood. Fatigue lent a grayish hue to her skin. "The time is now. I tire of these incessant games. The trees have mobilized, and we shall follow, striking hard and true while the conclave deliberates."

Josephine shook her head curtly. "I do not think this wise. We must proceed with the plan as scheduled. Your daughter, the king's children, they will—"

Morgane wheeled to face her, nostrils flaring with sudden rage. "For the last time, Josephine, I do not *have* a daughter, and if I must repeat myself again, I shall rend your tongue from your miserable throat."

I do not have *a daughter.*

Ah. My heart twisted unexpectedly. Though I'd suspected she'd forgotten me, suspecting the truth versus knowing it—versus *hearing* it—were two entirely different things. It shouldn't have hurt as much as it did, but here, in my childhood home—surrounded by sisters who'd cheered as my blood had spilled—it... pinched. Just a bit. I searched Reid's shadowed face. This close, I could see the shape of his eyes, the set of his mouth. He glared back at me.

I looked away.

Cackling, Nicholina sang, "The dead should not remember. Beware the night the dream. For in their chest is memory—"

Morgane struck her across the face without warning. The angry *crack* resounded through the passage.

"You do not speak"—a vein pulsed in my mother's forehead—"you do not *breathe* unless I will it. How many times must I punish you before you understand?" When she lifted her hand once more, Nicholina flinched. She actually *flinched.* Instead of striking her, however, Morgane rapped her knuckles across Nicholina's forehead. "Well? How many? Or are your ears as addled as your brain, you worthless imp?"

Nicholina withdrew visibly at the insult, her expression emptying. She stared past Morgane as a red handprint bloomed on her cheek.

"As I thought." With a sneer, Morgane proceeded toward us up the corridor, her own mottled cheeks visible even in the candlelight. "I should've killed you when I had the chance."

Josephine only arched a brow at her ward and followed.

Célie wasn't the only one trembling now. My own hands shook as Nicholina drifted after them—as vacant and lifeless as the wraiths outside—and even Reid's heart beat an uneven tattoo against my ear. He stood rigid as she passed, but I felt his hand creep slowly up my back. I felt his knife. Whether he meant to kill me or Nicholina, I never discovered. Because before she disappeared around the corner, Nicholina turned toward our alcove.

Her eyes met mine.

And I knew—as instinctively as I'd known the trees had walked and my magic wanted to protect Chateau le Blanc—I *knew* that she'd seen me.

Reid's knife stilled with her footsteps. "Hello, mouse," she whispered, her fingers wrapping around the bend. Pure, unadulterated fear snaked through me at the words. I could do nothing but stare. Paralyzed. A single shout from her could kill us all.

We waited, breaths bated, as Nicholina tilted her head.

As she slipped around the corner without a sound.

"What are we doing?" Reid's voice sounded in my ear, low and furious. "We can still catch her. Move."

I stared at the spot from which she'd vanished, my mind reeling. She didn't reappear, however, and no sounds of alarm rent the silence. No sounds of pursuit. "She let us go."

"To kill us later."

"She could've killed us just then, but she didn't." I scowled now, thoroughly disenchanted with his single-minded intensity. It bordered on pigheaded. Had he been this stupid when I'd first met him? Was *his* mind the addled one? "I don't know why, but I *do* know I won't be looking a gift horse in the mouth. She's with Morgane and La Voisin," I added when he tried to move around me. I planted my feet. "Now isn't the time for this confrontation. We made a deal with Isla—we get in, we get out, and we give her the ring."

"Unacceptable." That knife finally pressed between my shoulder blades. "I am not here for a magic ring, Louise. If you don't move out of my way, I will find another witch to kill."

I poked him in the chest. Hard. "Listen to me, jackass." My voice rose at the word, and I hastened to lower it once more. "Isla needs that ring. *We* need the melusines. The sooner we finish here, the sooner we can unite our allies, the sooner we can formulate a plan of attack—"

"I have a plan—attack. Morgane is here, not in Cesarine."

"Your *mother* is in Cesarine."

"I don't care about my mother," he snarled, shouldering past me at last. I stumbled into Jean Luc, who overcorrected, knocking Célie into Reid and plunging me into the corridor alone.

I whirled to face him, swearing loudly—then froze.

Manon stared back at me.

"Hello?" Her eyes narrowed suspiciously, flitting over my dark shape, and she lifted a hand as if to touch me. I scuttered backward. I had no choice. If she touched me, she'd realize without a doubt that I was human. When her frown deepened, I winced, realizing too late that shadows didn't *scutter.* "Who's there?" She flicked a thin blade from her sleeve. "Show yourself, or I'll summon the sentries."

Why did every plan I ever made go to complete and total shit?

Lips flattening, I cracked open that door of power in my chest, beneath which the white web shimmered. It would be a risk to change forms, but Morgane was clever. Though she'd undoubtedly realized the Triple Goddess had revoked her blessing, perhaps she hadn't yet told our kin. Either way, I couldn't simply stand here with a knife in front and a knife behind, and I couldn't reveal my true form either. This newfound power would make it easier, surely.

I sought to remember my childhood classroom, wracked my mind for everything I knew of the Triple Goddess and her forms.

Her final counterpart is the Crone, who embodies aging and ending, death and rebirth, past lives and transformations, visions and prophecies. She is our guide. She is dusk and night, autumn and winter.

Fitting, as we'd probably all die here anyway.

I focused on those traits, tried to center myself around them, as other memories consumed—my life in this castle, my blood in the basin, my farewell to Ansel. That feeling of bone-deep acceptance. My transformation into the Maiden had happened easily, without intent, but this transformation came easier still. Perhaps once I would've empathized most with the Maiden—and I still did, to an extent—but that joyous season of light had passed. I'd lived in winter for too long. To my surprise, I didn't regret the change. I relished it.

My hands withered and cracked as the shadows around them dissipated, and my spine bowed beneath years of fatigue. My vision clouded. My flesh sagged. Triumphant—exorbitantly pleased with myself—I lifted a gnarled finger to Manon's startled face. I'd done it.

I'd transformed.

"Out for a moonlit stroll, dearie?" My voice warbled, unfamiliar and deep and unpleasant. I cackled at the sound, and Manon retreated a step. "Not much moonlight tonight, I'm afraid." My tongue flicked past the gap in my eyeteeth as I leered at her. "Shall I join you?"

She sank into a hasty curtsy. "My lady. I am sorry. I—I didn't recognize you."

"Some nights I must pass unseen, Manon."

"Of course." She ducked her head. Too late, I realized she'd been crying. The kohl around her eyes had tracked down her cheeks, and her nose still ran. She sniffed as quietly as possible. "I understand."

"Is something wrong, child?"

"No." She spoke the word too quickly, still backing away. "No, my lady. I am sorry to have bothered you."

I didn't need the Crone's Vision to see her lie. Truthfully, I needn't have asked at all. She still grieved her dead lover, Gilles, the man she'd killed with her own hands. All because he'd been a son of the king. "A cup of chamomile tea, my dear." When she blinked, confused, I clarified, "In the kitchens. Brew and steep a cup. It will settle your nerves and send you to sleep."

With another curtsy and word of thanks, she departed, and I sagged against the nearest wall.

"Holy shit," Beau breathed.

"That was *incredible*," Coco added.

"Release me." Reid broke Jean Luc's hold swiftly, efficiently, his throat corded with strain. He whirled on him in a storm of fury. "She was isolated. The situation controlled. We should've *struck—*"

"And then what?" Flinging my hands in the air, I hobbled toward him. "Really, what's the next step in this master plan of yours, Chass? We hide her body for someone to stumble across? We stuff her in the closet? We can't risk anyone knowing we're here!"

"You're jeopardizing the mission, Reid," Jean Luc agreed darkly, "and you're endangering everyone here. Follow her orders, or I'll incapacitate you."

Reid stepped toe to toe with him. "I'd like to see that, Jean."

"Oh, shut it, or I'll stuff *your* body in the goddamn closet." Losing patience completely, I whirled—though in reality, it looked more like a shuffle—and doddered up the passage once more. "We've wasted enough time here."

Reid followed in mutinous silence.

DEADLY AND BEAUTIFUL THINGS

Reid

Chateau le Blanc was a labyrinth. I hadn't ventured beyond the Great Hall on Modraniht, so I could do nothing but follow Lou. *Lou.* She hadn't told me who she was. Of course she hadn't. She hadn't told me she'd inherited her mother's power—that *she* had become La Dame des Sorcières.

She struggled to climb a set of rickety stairs now. Coco and Beau supported her on either side. Their shapes remained dark. Unnatural. Like shadows. "You could always change back," the latter muttered, catching her stout frame as she stumbled.

"This is better. If we meet anyone else, they won't look too close."

The stairs wound up a narrow tower. Here, however, the ceiling had collapsed in places. As in the Great Hall, the elements had overcome most rooms. Snow fell gently in the solar, where an ornately carved fireplace crackled. Its light danced on tapestries of magical beasts and beautiful women—each of their eyes seemed to follow us as we passed. I swore one even craned her elegant neck.

"This room is for Morgane's personal use." Lou pointed to the wooden desk in the corner. A peacock-feather quill scratched at parchment of its own volition. The falling snow didn't mar the paper, nor the carpets or tapestries. It didn't stain the decorative woodwork. It simply melted into nothing in the warm, balmy air. In the corner, a harp plucked itself gently.

The entire scene was eerie.

"Her bedchamber is also in this tower." She gestured to a room beyond the harp. "And her oratory. She forbade me from entering this part of the castle, but I snuck in anyway."

"And the treasury?" Jean Luc asked.

"Directly above us." Shuffling to the bookcase beside the desk, she studied the tomes there. Her silver brows furrowed in concentration. "The door is somewhere . . ." Her fingers stilled on an ancient book bound in black cloth. On its spine, letters had been stamped in gold: *L'argent n'a pas d'odeur.* She tapped it with a wicked grin. "Here."

When she pulled the book toward her, the entire wall groaned. Gears clanked. And the bookcase—it swung open. Beyond it, a steep, narrow staircase disappeared into the dark. She bowed slightly, still grinning, and snapped her fingers. The scent of magic burst around us—fresher than before—and a torch on the wall in the stairwell sprang to life. "After you."

Beau removed the torch warily. A shadow bearing light. The unnatural sight of it lifted the hair on my arms. My neck. "You didn't tell us the treasury was in her personal chambers."

"I didn't want to scare you."

"Oh, yes." Tentative, Beau stepped onto the first plank. It creaked under his weight. "The shadows, wraiths, and murderous witches would've paled in comparison to Morgane's bed." He hesitated and glanced back. "Unless—do you think she'll be returning soon?"

Coco followed before the coward could reconsider. "I think she's busy plotting the end of the world."

"This place . . ." Célie stared longingly over her shoulder as she too ascended. Her eyes lingered on the peacock quill before settling on the harp. Its golden strings. Her body swayed slightly to the haunting melody. "It's so beautiful."

I rolled my eyes. "You almost died outside, Célie."

"I haven't forgotten," she snapped, suddenly defensive. I bristled at her tone. "Believe me, I remember what magic is. It's just—" Tearing her gaze from the room, she turned instead to Jean Luc, to me. Her hand rose to catch a snowflake between us, and we all watched it melt on her fingertip, transfixed. No. *Not* transfixed—revolted. "You never told me it could be beautiful too," she finished, softer now.

"It's dangerous, Célie," Jean Luc said.

She lifted her chin. "Why can't it be both?"

We both heard what she really meant. *Why can't I be both?*

Jean Luc stared at her for several seconds, tilting his head in contemplation. When at last he nodded, affirming her unspoken question, she kissed his cheek and ascended the stairs with the others. He followed behind like a devoted, lovesick puppy, and my stomach plunged as if I'd missed a step. His response shouldn't have surprised me. Nor hers. Célie had clearly suffered from the witches' influence, and Jean Luc would never utter a word against her.

Still, I felt . . . off, somehow—disjointed—as I jerked my chin toward Lou. She alone remained. The others had left in more than the literal sense. "Go."

Her gap-toothed smile slipped. "Forgive me, but I'd rather not end the night with a knife in my back. You understand, I'm sure." She wiggled her fingers in silent threat, motioning me forward.

Scowling, I followed Jean Luc. Though she'd been right in her suspicions—I *did* want to end her depraved existence—I had no choice but to obey. I'd lost my Balisarda. "I thought the door was guarded by a powerful enchantment."

Her footsteps fell heavy and clumsy behind me, her breath growing louder with each tread. Labored. I didn't offer assistance. If she insisted on this foul magic, she would reap the reward. "That was *a* door," she panted. "It wasn't *the* door. Did you really think my mother would protect her most treasured possessions with only a bookshelf?"

Her most treasured possessions. The words sent a thrill of anticipation through me. Surely, something beyond this door would be useful in eliminating her—in eliminating *all* of them. Perhaps if I liberated it, delivered it to the new Archbishop, I could renew my vows and rejoin my brotherhood. It was where I belonged.

As quickly as the thought materialized, however, I cast it aside. If this new Archbishop accepted me so readily—me, a man guilty of murder and conspiracy—he would be no leader at all. I could not follow him. No, from this point onward, I could seek only atonement. I would kill these witches, yes, but I expected no reward. If the wanted posters had been true, I deserved none.

I would kill them nonetheless.

At the top of the staircase, the others halted before a simple, nondescript door. Lou pushed past me, still wheezing. She clutched her chest with one hand and the door handle with another. "My god. I think my knees might've actually cracked."

"My *māmā rū'au* can predict the weather with hers," Beau offered.

"She sounds like a fascinating woman, and I mean that genuinely." Straightening as much as possible, Lou twisted the golden handle experimentally. It didn't move. At my derisive snort, she muttered, "No harm in checking."

A beat of silence passed as she stared at the door, and we stared at her.

Impatience sharpened my tone. "Well?"

Flattening her palm on the handle, she cast me a cutting glance. "I was right. A nasty enchantment has been cast on this door, and it'll take time to break—if I can break it at all." She closed her eyes. "I can . . . feel it there. Like a sixth sense. The magic—it pulls at my chest even now." She shook her head, opening her eyes once more. "But I don't know if I can trust it."

Coco's voice turned grim. "I don't think we have a choice."

"It wants to protect this place, even from me."

"You control the magic, Lou. It doesn't control you."

"But what if—"

"Shift your perspective." The response startled even me, and it'd come from my own mouth. Beneath their startled gazes, I immediately regretted I'd spoken. Heat crept into my cheeks. Why *had* I spoken? I needed to get into this room, of course, but—no. That was the only explanation. I needed to get into this room. Looking each one of them directly in the eye, I continued, "This new magic, it wants to protect the Chateau. Why?"

Lou frowned. "Because it's my home. My sisters' home. It's been ours for all of living memory."

"That isn't quite true," Coco whispered.

Lou blinked at her. "What?"

"My aunt remembers differently." Coco shifted in obvious discomfort. "She speaks of a time when Dames Rouges walked these halls instead of Dames Blanches." At Lou's bewildered expression, she hastened to add, "It doesn't matter. Forget I said anything."

"But—"

"She's right," I interrupted, my voice hard. "What matters now is whether you—La Dame des Sorcières—still consider this place your home." When she didn't speak, only stared at me intently, I shrugged. Shoulders rigid. "If not, it stands to reason your magic won't protect it anymore. It'll shift to your new home. Wherever that is."

She continued to stare at me. "Right."

I crossed my arms and looked away, distinctly uncomfortable. "So? Is it?"

"No." After another long, uncomfortable moment, she finally did the same, murmuring, "No, it isn't."

Then she closed her eyes and exhaled. Her entire body

relaxed into the movement, shedding its withered skin until she no longer resembled the Crone but a young woman once more. A vibrant young woman. *A witch*, my mind chastised. A vibrant young *witch*. Still, with her eyes closed, I couldn't help but study her. Long brown hair and elfin features. Sharp-cut eyes. Sun-kissed freckles. At her throat, a ring of thorns circled her golden skin. Roses too.

Why can't I be both?

The inexplicable urge to touch her nearly overpowered me. To trace the delicate curve of her nose. The bold arch of brow. I resisted the mad impulse. Only fools coveted beautiful and deadly things. I wasn't a fool. I didn't covet. And I certainly didn't want to touch a witch, regardless of how she looked at me.

She looked at me like I belonged to her and she belonged to me.

"It's a lock," she breathed eventually, her face contorting with strain. Sweat glistened on her brow. "The magic. I'm the key. La Dame des Sorcières cast the enchantment, and only she can break it. But I"—her eyes screwed tighter—"the webs, they're all fixed—I can't move them. They're like iron."

"You believe it a lock?" Célie approached the door hesitantly. "Pin and tumbler or warded?"

Eyes still closed, Lou pursed her lips. I tore my gaze away. "I'm not sure. It's like—it's like I'm inside it, if that makes sense—"

"Description, please!"

"I can't describe the inside of a lock, Célie! I've never seen one!"

"Well, I have, and—"

"You have?" Jean Luc asked incredulously. "When?"

"Everyone needs a hobby." Resolute now, she shouldered past him to face Lou, grasping her hands. "I picked the lock on my father's vault, and I can help you pick this one too. Now, tell me, do the patterns have notches and slots, or do they more resemble a counting frame? Are there three or more parallel rows?"

Lou grimaced. So did Jean Luc. "No rows," she said, her knuckles white around Célie's. "They might be notches. I—I can't tell." She inhaled sharply as if in pain. "I don't know if I have the control for this. The magic—it's stronger than me. I . . ." Her voice trailed off, growing faint, and she swayed on her feet.

"Nonsense." Célie steadied her with a firm hand. "In my sister's coffin—when I felt like I might float away—I counted the knots in the wood to ground myself. There were thirty-seven that I could see. I would count them, over and over, and I would take a breath with each one." She squeezed Lou's hands. "Listen to my voice and breathe." Then— "You need a skeleton key."

I couldn't help it. I stepped forward, eyes rapt on Lou's face.

"A skeleton key?" she asked.

"It's a warded lock. Those notches you see are meant for false protrusions, which prevent the mechanism from opening. A skeleton key has none. Form the key in your mind—long and narrow, with none but two true protrusions on the end. Shape them to fit the last notches, and push."

Coco shifted from foot to foot, her expression bewildered. "I don't understand. Why would Morgane have created simple keys and locks when she has magic?"

"Who the hell cares?" Beau hovered anxiously by the stairs, keeping watch. "It's an enchanted lock for an enchanted door in an enchanted fucking castle. None of this makes sense. Just hurry up, will you? I think I heard something."

Lou gritted her teeth, pale and trembling now. "If one of you had tried to open this door, you wouldn't have seen a lock. It's meant for La Dame des Sorcières alone, but it's also—it's the previous matriarchs' magic testing mine. I can feel their challenge. Their treasures lie within, and I must—earn—entry." Her head twitched abruptly with each word, and her eyes flew open, snapping to the doorknob. It responded with a simple click. Heavy silence descended as we stared at it.

Lifting a single finger to the wood, Lou pushed tentatively.

The door swung inward.

We stepped into a room of gold—or at least, it appeared so at first glance. In reality, the vaulted ceiling and octagonal walls had been erected from plates of mercury glass. They reflected the golden *couronnes*. Hundreds of them. Thousands of them. The coins spilled forth from every corner, stacked precariously into piles, forming towers of their own. Narrow footpaths wove between them as roads and alleys in a colossal, glittering city.

"This . . ." Beau craned his neck to study the highest crest in the ceiling. Built at the top of a tower, the room stretched taller than wide—cylindrical—like we'd walked into a music box. A basin of fire sat atop a pedestal in the center of the chamber. No logs fed the flames. They emitted no smoke. I inhaled deeply. Though magic coated everything, it tasted almost stale here.

Like a thick blanket of dust. "Is not what I expected," he finished at last.

Lou examined a set of rusted chains near the door, the links thicker than her fists. A dried substance flaked from the metal. Brown, almost black. Blood. "What did you expect?"

He picked up what looked like an ancient human skull. "A dusty cupboard full of creepy dolls and old furniture?"

"It's a treasury, Beau, not an attic." She pointed to a heap of gold across the path. A wooden figurine sat atop a stained settee. Beside it lay a golden comb and a rose-handled mirror. "Though there is a doll there. Morgane once said it was cursed."

Beau blanched. "Cursed *how?*"

"Just don't look it in the eye." Replacing the chains, she seemed to choose another path at random and strode forward. "Right. We should split up. Give a shout if you find something that resembles a golden ring, but *don't* touch anything else." She arched a brow over her shoulder at us. "Here there are many deadly and beautiful things."

I slipped behind her as the others scattered to search. At the sound of my footsteps, she turned with a small smile. Here, in this dark room with its cursed gold and magic fire, she looked more a witch than I'd seen her. Strange and mysterious. Almost surreal. "Just couldn't stay away, could you?"

I didn't know why I'd followed her. I didn't respond.

When she slipped behind a wardrobe—its black cabinets painted with tiny flowers—I drew a knife from my bandolier. Her ghostly chuckle echoed through the thickly scented air. It seemed to shimmer where she'd disappeared, firelight illuminating the dust motes gold. A fingertip brushed my nape. Whirling, I found her standing directly behind me. Her eyes gleamed unnaturally bright. Blue. No, green. "I won't let you kill me, you know," she said. "You wouldn't be able to live with yourself later."

My fingers ached on the hilt of my knife. My throat tightened. I couldn't breathe. "I just want my memories back, witch."

Those haunting eyes fell to my blade, and she stepped forward. Once. Twice. Three times. She walked until her chest met its tip, and then she leaned farther still, drawing a bead of blood. Only then did her eyes return to mine. Only then did she whisper against my lips, "I want that too."

I stared at my knife. At her blood. A quick thrust would do it. One simple movement, and La Dame des Sorcières would be dead. Incapacitated, at the very least. She'd be helpless to stop me from pitching her body in the fire—the *magic* fire. It'd be almost poetic to watch her burn upon it. She'd be ash before the others could save her.

A quick thrust. One simple movement.

She would drive me mad unless I did it.

We stayed that way for another second, another hundred seconds—tense, poised—but a shout sounded from across the treasury, breaking our standoff. "It's here!" Célie's laughter swelled between us. "I found it!" With a smirk, Lou stepped backward. Away from me. In her absence, I could breathe again. I could *hate*.

The woman would drive me mad *until* I did it.

"You're lucky," I said darkly, sheathing my knife.

"Funny. I don't feel lucky at all."

Her smirk seemed brittle as she turned to follow Célie's voice, gifting me her back. Every fiber in my being longed to lunge. To attack. I even bent my knees, stopping only when a sapphire glinted in my periphery. I froze. From within a drawer of the wardrobe peeked the silver hilt of a Balisarda. It looked as if it'd been stuffed there haphazardly. Stowed away and forgotten. A jolt seared through my body. A lightning strike.

Carefully, quietly, I slipped the Balisarda into my bandolier.

We found Célie, Jean Luc, and Beau congregated beside the fire. Coco converged on them the same moment we did. Immediately, Célie thrust the unexceptional ring into her palm. "I found it," she repeated, breathless with excitement. With something else. When her eyes flicked to Coco's collar near imperceptibly, I followed the movement. A locket glittered there. "Here. Take it."

Coco examined the ring for a long moment before she smiled. "You *would* be the one to find it." With an appreciative nod to Célie, she handed it to Lou, who slipped it on her finger like it belonged there. I frowned. "Thank you, Célie."

"We should go," Beau urged. "Before Morgane comes back."

In agreement, we retreated down the stairs, but it wasn't Morgane who met us at the door.

It was Manon.

ASK ME NO QUESTIONS

Reid

Feet planted wide—arms gripping each side of the threshold—she met us with a frighteningly blank expression. Trapping us here. All traces of her tears had been scrubbed away since the corridor below. "Chamomile tea, Louise?"

Lou edged to the front of our group, her hand brushing mine as she passed. The touch tingled. I jerked away. "You looked like you needed it," she said, gesturing to Manon's general dishevelment. Her airy tone felt forced, as did her smile. "I'm assuming you didn't heed my advice and drink it. When have you last slept?" Manon didn't answer. Shouts below wiped the smile from Lou's face all the same. Her eyes flew wide. "You—did you tell my mother—?"

"Not yet. I had to be sure of the intruder. But I told others. They will inform Our Lady soon."

"Shit, shit, shit. *Shit.*" Exhaling a harsh, incredulous breath, Lou clenched her fists before seizing Manon's collar and yanking her into the stairwell. Beau slammed the door behind them. "This is fine. They don't know *I'm* here specifically. We can still—"

"You will not escape again, Louise," Manon said, her eyes still flat and unexpressive.

"Just—just—" Lou wrung a fist in the witch's face, and Manon stiffened like a board, unable to move. "Just shut up for a second, Manon. I need to think." To Coco, Jean Luc, and me, she said hastily, "We can't go out the way we came in. Any brilliant ideas?"

"We fight our way out," I said instantly.

Jean Luc's brow furrowed as he considered strategy. "There are six of us. Enemy numbers unknown. We've claimed the higher ground, but we'd need to form a choke point—"

I pounded my fist against the door. "We have one. They can't break the enchantment—"

"You're both idiots." Lou turned imploring eyes on Coco. "Was there anything in the treasury we could use?"

"Can't you just *show* them the Goddess has revoked Morgane's blessing?" Beau waved his hands wildly. "You *are* their queen now, correct?"

"Again, why didn't *I* think of that? I'll tell you what, Your Highness, why don't *you* command your people to stop burning witches, so all of our problems go away?" She turned back to Coco before he could answer. "There was magic fire."

Clenching her own eyes shut, Coco rubbed her temples. "And plated glass. I also saw chains and swords and—" Her gaze snapped to Lou's once more, and realization passed between them like a bolt of lightning.

"The window," they said together.

Lou nodded frenetically. "We'll need to climb."

Coco was already dragging Beau and Célie back up the steps. "It'll be risky—"

"No riskier than a choke point—"

The implication of their words finally settled in. My stomach churned. "*No.*"

"You'll be fine." Patting my arm in a distracted way, Lou raced toward the stairs. "I won't let you fall." When I made no move to follow—when the shouts behind grew louder—she lost patience, doubling back and yanking at my hand. I yielded one step. Not another. She spoke with frantic cajolement, still tugging. "*Please,* Reid. We have to climb, or we're never getting out of here. They won't just kill me. They'll kill you too. Horribly. Slowly. You want a *choke point*? You don't have a Balisarda, so you'll feel every single moment."

I bared my teeth in a grin. "I'll risk it."

Frustration flared in her eyes, and she lifted her hand once more. "If you don't move, I'll *make* you move."

"Please"—triumphant, I swept my coat aside, revealing the Balisarda and pivoting between her and the stairs—"do."

When her mouth fell open, astonished, I relished it. Relished her surprise, her fear, her—

The hilt of another knife smashed into my crown, and I staggered forward, into her. She tried to catch me. We both nearly broke our necks. Behind, Beau stood panting, knife still raised. "I don't need magic to knock your ass out. I'll *drag* you onto the roof if necessary. You aren't dying like this."

Jean Luc appeared beside him. They stood shoulder to shoulder, towering over me. As if they could intimidate. As if they could *threaten*—

"We can't defeat an entire castle of witches by ourselves," Jean Luc said, treacherous and cowardly in equal measure. Judas incarnate. "This is our best option. Get up the stairs, or I'll help him drag you."

Footsteps pounded louder now. Biting back a curse—because they were *right*—I seized Manon and sprinted past them. The scent of magic burst behind me as Lou relocked the door. Upstairs, she swung her arms in frantic movements. The treasure complied, settees and wardrobes shifting, stacking, to form a precarious ladder. "It's fine." Beau bent double, hands braced against his knees. "They can't get through the door. We have time—"

I flung Manon into an empty chair. "We don't."

Still rigid, she slid sideways to the floor. "They'll surround the castle soon." To Lou, she whispered, "I told you that you won't escape again."

"Oh, for fuck's sake." Lou stomped over as Jean Luc boosted Célie on top of the wardrobe. Beau and Coco scrambled up behind her. Crouching beside the witch's prostrate body, Lou flipped her over with another wave. Manon relaxed instantly, and Lou—I stared incredulously—she helped the witch sit up with gentle hands. "Morgane ordered you to kill your lover, Manon. Gilles is *dead* because of *her*. How can you still serve such a woman? How can you stand idly by as she tortures and kills *children*?"

Her words acted as a spark to kindling. Manon lurched forward with a feral snarl, snatching Lou's shoulders. "My *sister* is one of those dead children, and Morgane did not kill her. *I* did. Gilles died at no other's hands but my own. I made a *choice* in that ally— a choice I cannot undo. I have gone too far now to turn back." Tears spilled freely down her cheeks at the confession. When she spoke again, her voice broke. "Even if I wanted to."

I watched, stricken, as Lou hastily wiped her tears. "Listen to me, Manon. No, *listen.* Look around you"—she motioned to the others, to herself and to me—"and tell me what you see."

"I see *traitors*—"

"*Exactly.*" Lou reached up to clutch Manon's wrists, eyes wide and imploring. "I betrayed my coven. Reid and Jean Luc have betrayed their Church, and Beau and Célie have betrayed their Crown. All of us—we're fighting for a better world, just like you are. We want the same thing, Manon. We want *peace.*"

Manon's entire body trembled with emotion as her tears continued to fall. They stained Lou's lap. Stained the dirty floor between them, glittering bright in the firelight. At last, Manon dropped her hands. "You'll never have it."

Lou studied Manon's face wistfully for a moment— regretfully—before rising to her feet. "You're wrong. There are very few choices in life that can't be unmade, and the time has come for you to make another one. I won't restrain or otherwise harm you. Go. Tell Morgane you saw me if you must, but don't try to stop us. We're leaving."

Manon didn't move.

Lou stalked to the furniture without another word—then

hesitated. She glanced over her shoulder. Instead of Manon, however, her eyes found mine, and she spoke in a murmur. "You've stalled long enough, Reid. Climb up. I promise you won't fall."

I swallowed hard. Somehow, she knew my chest had tightened and my vision had narrowed. She knew my palms had started to sweat. She knew I'd hesitated beside Manon not to protect the group from her wrath, but to prolong the inevitable. To think of some way—*any* way—out of this room except the window. And that meant she knew my weakness, my vulnerability. Anger blazed through the thick paralysis of my thoughts, spurring me toward the furniture.

"Why did you get to keep yours?" Manon whispered behind us.

Sadness clouded Lou's face as she gazed back at me. "I didn't."

One by one, we squeezed through the window onto the roof. My head pounded. My heart raced. Twice on the furniture, my foot had slipped, and I'd nearly crashed to the floor. Though Lou had maintained a steady stream of encouragement, I longed to wring her neck. This rooftop could've been a steeple, a needle, so pitched was its slope.

"I *will* kill you for this," I promised her.

Crouching low, she peered over the eave to where the others scaled rock with their knives. Their limbs trembled with effort. With strain. "I look forward to it, believe me." She slipped her own knives from her boots. "Until then, do you think you can reach that turret?"

I followed the direction of her knife. Directly below us, at the base of the tower, a spire jutted from the side of the castle. It looked likely to collapse at any moment. "This is madness."

"You go first. I'll follow."

Peeling each finger from the shingles—they'd become my lifelines—I scooted down the slope. Lou crab walked beside me. "That's it." She nodded with excessive cheer, her eyes too bright. Her smile too wide. She either worried more than she said, or she enjoyed this more than she should. Both were unacceptable.

When I inched over the eave, my foot slipped a third time.

A rush of wind.

A sickening, weightless sensation.

And a hand.

Her hand.

It caught mine as it slipped from the edge, and her second followed, wrapping around my wrist. My vision swam with black spots as I dangled midair. As the wind roared past my ears. My heart thrashed wildly. I couldn't see her properly, couldn't hear her panicked instructions. There was only the ground looming beneath me, my body suspended midair. Helplessly, I clawed at her. Her arms shook beneath my weight.

"Lift me up!" My shouts sounded delirious to even my ears. "Lift me up *now*!"

A shadow shifted in her eyes at the command. She flashed a feline grin. "Tell me I'm pretty."

"I—*what*?"

"Tell me," she repeated in a hard voice, "that I'm pretty."

I stared at her for one heart-stopping moment. She couldn't be serious, yet she was. From her weak arms to her spiteful eyes to her sharp smile, she was *serious*. She could drop me—she *would* drop me—if I didn't appease her soon. She couldn't support my weight indefinitely. But what was she asking? For me to lie? To flatter her? No. She wanted something else. Something I couldn't give her. Through gritted teeth, I spat, "You said you wouldn't let me fall."

"You've said a lot of things."

I'd told her the truth. I wanted to kill her. To kill all of them. I couldn't concede to this heresy—this *grand romance* she'd dreamed up between us. As if it were possible. As if a witch and witch hunter could be more than enemies. I remembered none of it. I wanted to remember even less. In that second, however, the wind swept past with terrifying glee, and I glanced down. A mistake. Black edged my vision. My hand slipped a millimeter within hers. "Fine," I said quickly, loathing myself. Loathing her more. "You're . . . you are very pretty, Lou."

"The prettiest you've ever seen?"

I nearly wept in frustration. "Prettier, even. I can't think when I look at you."

She beamed, and the tension melted from her face as quickly as it'd come. Her arms stopped shaking. Too late, I realized her game: her magic couldn't work on *me* because of the Balisarda, but she'd used it to strengthen her own body instead. She'd been pretending to struggle this entire time. Stoking my fear. She probably could've lifted me with a single finger. Fresh anger burned white-hot in my chest. "Now," she said, immensely pleased with herself, "tell me that I'm an excellent singer."

"You—you—"

"I'm waiting," she trilled.

"You're an excellent singer. You sing like a bird. An angel. And if you don't lift me up this *second*, I'm going to snap your pretty neck."

She waited another second just to spite me. Then another. And another. "Well, now that we've sorted *that*." With a mighty heave, she pulled me over the eave once more. I collapsed beside her in a pool of shaking limbs, nearly retching at her feet.

"Don't you *ever* lie to me again."

She poked my cheek. "I wouldn't have dropped you."

"Lies!"

"Well"—she lifted an easy shoulder—"maybe I would've, but I wouldn't have let you splatter." Her smile turned almost self-deprecating. "Come on, Chass. I would've moved the entire castle before I let you die."

"*Why?*" The word burst from me, sudden and unbidden. This wasn't the time for such a question. This wasn't the place, either—not with witches crawling within and without. They probably gathered below even now, waiting to devour us. Manon would've told them. She would've pressed their advantage. No shouts sounded from the ground, however, and no magic ensnared us. "Why did you save me? Why did you let the witch go? You—you comforted her. You wiped her *tears*. We both want to *kill* you."

The realization shocked me into silence. Manon had wanted to kill her. I didn't know *how* I knew, but I did. Manon and La

Voisin and even Morgane, her own mother, wanted her dead. But—my thoughts congealed like mud—that wasn't quite right either. *I do not have a daughter*, Morgane had claimed. Could she too have forgotten her daughter, as I had forgotten my wife? Or had Lou lied about both? I regarded her suspiciously as she rose. "Why?" I repeated firmly.

Patting my cheek, she slipped over the eave without me. Her voice drifted upward with the wind. "Ask me no questions, *mon amour*, and I shall tell you no lies."

I frowned at the simple words. Then winced. These felt different than others, biting and snapping like insects. I shook my head to dislodge them, but they remained. They burrowed deeper. Familiar and painful and jarring. *Ask me no questions*. Though I remained on the rooftop, my vision pitched abruptly, and instead of shingles and smoke, I saw trees, gnarled roots, a bottle of wine. Blue-green eyes. Sickening déjà vu. *And I'll tell you no lies*.

No. I shook my head, wrenching free of the imagery, and stabbed my knife into stone. This was here. Another stab. This was real. I swung myself lower. This was now. *Stab, stab*. I didn't remember her. *Stab*. It hadn't happened. *Stab, stab, stab*.

I repeated the mantra the entire way down. I repeated it until those blue-green eyes faded with the trees and the wind and the Hollow. Fresh pain cleaved my head at the last. I ignored it, focusing on the world below me. The others waited for me in silence. No witches hid in the shadows. Manon, it seemed, had not betrayed us. I didn't understand it. Without looking at anyone, I jumped, landing heavy on my feet.

"Are you all right?" Lou steadied me instinctively. When I cringed away without answering, she sighed and motioned us toward the rocks behind the tower, slipping through the shadows like she'd been born there. I watched her go with a pang in my chest.

Ask me no questions, mon amour, *and I'll tell you no lies.* Another half-formed memory. Useless. Broken.

Like a witch hunter who couldn't kill a witch.

TRUTH OR DARE

Lou

Halfway through our return to L'Eau Mélancolique, Célie fell asleep on her horse. Jean Luc—who'd succumbed to a stupor hours ago—hadn't been able to catch her in time, and she'd plummeted face-first into the mud, bloodying her nose in the process. We'd quickly agreed a rest stop was necessary. Jean Luc had procured two rooms at the next inn, sneaking us in a back door under cover of darkness.

"I'll be back with food," he'd promised. Though smoke still obscured the night sky, it must've been between midnight and dawn. We'd made excellent time, all things considered—in and out of Chateau le Blanc in just over an hour. Still, few inns served supper at three in the morning. I suspected the sight of Jean Luc's blue coat, however, might've helped the innkeeper forget the aberrant hour.

Coco, Célie, and I claimed one of the rooms for ourselves while we waited, and Reid and Beau disappeared into the one next door. Almost immediately, Célie collapsed facedown on the hay-filled mattress, her breath deepening and her mouth falling open. The trickle of drool on her pillow painted her the quintessential gentlewoman. Coco and I each tugged a boot from her foot.

"I don't think I can make it to supper," Coco said, hiding a yawn behind her hand.

My stomach growled audibly. "I can."

"Save me some food, will you?"

I grinned as she flopped onto the bed beside Célie. It was a tight fit. Neither of them seemed to notice. "Will do."

Jean Luc edged the door open a few moments later, carrying a tray of dried figs, brioche, and comté. From the silver tureen at its center, the heavenly scent of beef stew drifted outward, curling around my nose. I immediately began to salivate, but he stopped short when he saw Coco and Célie. Lifting a finger to my lips, I plucked the fruit, bread, and cheese from the tray and left it on the table beside the bed. I motioned him back into the hallway, hesitating for only a second before breaking off a piece of cheese.

I loved cheese.

"They're exhausted." Closing the door behind me, I popped the morsel into my mouth and nearly moaned. "They can eat when they wake."

Though clearly irritated at the prospect of dining with me and not Célie, Jean Luc nodded and led me into the men's room. Beau had lit a candelabra on the dressing table, and it cast soft, ambient light over the sparse furnishings: a single bed, as in our room, and a porcelain bowl for washing. The entire place had a worn yet welcoming atmosphere, probably aided by the colorful quilt on the bed and warm wooden floors.

"The girls are asleep," Jean Luc grunted, kicking the door shut.

"Should I be insulted?" I pirouetted onto the bed, landing dramatically across Beau's lap. He sat with his back against the headboard and his legs stretched out in front of him, taking up more than his fair share of space. Snorting, he shoved me off the bed.

"Yes."

Unperturbed, I crossed the room to investigate the contents of the tureen, but Jean Luc knocked my hand aside. Ladling it into cracked wooden bowls, he jerked his chin behind him. "Go wash, for the love of God. Your hands are filthy."

Unfortunately, Reid stood beside the washbowl. He scowled as I approached, shifting subtly so as not to touch me. When I *accidentally* splashed him with water, he stalked to the other side of the room. "If we leave after breakfast, we'll reach L'Eau Mélancolique this afternoon," I said to no one in particular. Jittery energy coursed through me as I accepted my stew, and I inhaled it greedily—standing over the basin like a rat—to stop from filling the dead air between us. If this was the inner sanctum of masculinity, I wanted no part of it.

My eyes slid to Reid.

Well. I wanted *little* part of it.

We ate in silence until none of the stew remained. Then a light knock sounded on the door.

"Captain Toussaint?" a thin, unfamiliar voice asked. Jean

Luc's eyes flew wide, and he wheeled to face us, mouthing, *The innkeeper.* "My humblest apologies, but might I enter for just a moment? My wife scolded me for my appalling lack of manners below, and she's quite right. I have a bottle of whiskey as recompense—we distill it here with my brother's own wheat"—his voice rose with pride—"and I'd be delighted to pour you a drink personally."

"Er—" Jean Luc cleared his throat. "Just—just leave it at the door."

It sounded like a question.

"Oh." It was a gift of this innkeeper, surely, to pack so much disappointment into one small word. "Oh, well, yes. Quite right. How rude of me. It is very late, of course, and I'm sure you need your rest. My humblest apologies," he said again. The bottle plunked against the door. "Good night, then, Captain."

His footsteps didn't recede. I could almost picture him hovering in the corridor beyond, perhaps leaning an ear against the wood, hoping the great captain would pity him and change his mind. Reid and I exchanged an anxious glance.

As if on cue, Jean Luc groaned quietly. "Er—Monsieur Laurent?" He shot us an apologetic look before hastily stacking our bowls and chucking them behind the washbasin. My eyes narrowed in disbelief. Surely he couldn't mean to—? "I'd love a drink. Please, come in."

Reid, Beau, and I could do nothing but scramble for hiding places, except the room held very little. As the smallest of the three, I dove beneath the bed. As the stupidest, Beau crouched behind the dressing table in plain sight. And Reid, unable to find another spot—not at all small but perhaps stupider than even Beau—rolled under the bed after me, snaking an arm around my waist to prevent me from spilling out the other side. The movement squashed my face against his chest, and I reared back, clutching his collar furiously. *What the hell is wrong with you?*

He rolled to his back, glaring at me, as Monsieur Laurent strode into the room.

"Oh, you can't imagine how pleased Madame Laurent will be, Captain, to know you're tasting our whiskey. She'll be ever so pleased. Thank you, thank you."

Reid's enormous body blocked my view of the room, so slowly, carefully, I leaned over his chest, peering out from across his shoulder. He held very still. He might've even stopped breathing.

Monsieur Laurent was a tall, reedy fellow in his nightclothes and slippers, and he fussed with two tumblers at the dressing table. Jean Luc shifted covertly to hide Beau. "I am honored to taste it, *monsieur.* Thank you again for providing us lodging at such an untimely hour. My companion sleeps in the next room," he added, accepting the proffered glass of amber liquid. He sipped it quickly.

"I must say"—Monsieur Laurent sampled his own glass, leaning against the table with the air of a man getting comfortable—"I was quite shocked to see you on my doorstep, Captain." He chuckled. "Well, I don't have to tell you, do I? Apologies again for the less than warm welcome. One can never be too safe these days. The witches are getting bolder, and they're thick in these

parts. You should hear the ghastly sounds of the forest at night."
Shuddering, he readjusted his nightcap, revealing a high, balding
forehead. Despite his casual tone, beads of nervous sweat gleamed
there. He feared Jean Luc. No—my eyes narrowed shrewdly—
he feared Jean's blue coat. "Anyway, I assumed most Chasseurs
would be in Cesarine with the conclave." He took another hearty
drink of whiskey. "I assume you heard news of the trials?"

Jean Luc—who, to my knowledge, hadn't heard news of any
such thing—nodded and emptied his glass. "I'm forbidden to
speak on such matters."

"Ah, of course, of course. Very good of you, sir." When Monsieur Laurent moved to refill his glass, Jean Luc shook his head,
and the innkeeper's expression fell. He recovered from his disappointment almost immediately, however, perhaps a touch
relieved, and downed the rest of his whiskey in a single swallow.
"I shall leave you to it, then. Please accept the bottle as a mark of
our thanks—it isn't every day one houses a hero. We are honored,
sir, just *honored*, to have you here."

Reid lay so still and so tense he might've grown roots beneath
this bed. Jaw clenched, he glared at the slats overhead without
blinking as Monsieur Laurent showed himself from the room,
and Jean Luc closed the door once more. The key clicked in the
lock.

Reid didn't move for a second, clearly grappling with his
desire to flee from me and his desire to hide from Jean Luc forever. I studied his rigid profile in the backlight. I supposed it . . .
hurt. To hear Monsieur Laurent's reverence for the person he

used to be, the person he could never be again. Jean Luc held that honor now, though truthfully, if he kept hiding witches under his bed, that privilege wouldn't be his for much longer either. Unable to help it, I brushed a lock of copper hair from Reid's forehead. "He doesn't know."

"Who doesn't know what?" he snapped.

"The innkeeper. He doesn't know who he has here." When he shook his head, disgusted—at me, at himself, at the entire situation—I said firmly, "He doesn't know what heroism means."

"And you do?" He turned to sneer at me. "Are you a hero, Louise le Blanc?"

"No. But you are."

Though he pushed my hand away, he still didn't move to leave. "I used to be. Now I'm hiding under a bed with a witch. Did you know I was found in the garbage?" When I said nothing, he scoffed, shaking his head again. "Of course you did. You know everything about me, don't you?" His eyes blazed with emotion in this small, shadowed sanctuary—and a sanctuary it was. Here, cramped and hidden from the rest of the world, we could've been the only two people alive. "Then you know I grew up lost. I grew up alone. They called me trash boy, and I fought tooth and nail for respect—I bloodied noses and broke bones to get it—and I killed the one person who called me family. Does that sound like a hero to you?"

A lump rose in my throat at his expression. He could've been that lost, lonely little boy all over again. "Reid—"

Beau's head popped under the bed. "What are you two whispering about under here?"

As if I'd lit a match in his trousers, Reid surged away from me, up and out of sight. Beau watched him go with a startled expression before extending a hand to me. In his other, he held the neck of the whiskey bottle. "Any luck with the seduction?"

"None, thanks to you."

"I have to protect my investment. But his memories . . . ?"

I frowned. "Coco thinks—"

"I know what Coco thinks." He hooked an arm around my neck, pulling me closer. Reid watched us sullenly from the farthest corner of the room. "I want to know what *you* think. Wager aside, would you rather we focus on restoring his memories? I know we can't force him to reverse the pattern, but perhaps we could help him along."

The weight of his words settled heavy in my chest. A choice. He'd offered me a choice. Free of judgment or disapproval, free of guidance, he'd led me to a fork in the road, and he now waited patiently for me to step left or right. He would follow whatever direction I chose. Except . . . I glanced at Reid. He'd already made a choice—a *stupid* choice, but a choice nonetheless. He'd stepped without consulting me, but he'd obviously thought it necessary. *Had* it been necessary? Morgane had forgotten me, yes, but she hadn't forgotten her wrath against the Church and Crown. The kingdom was in more danger now than ever.

I'll find you, Lou. I promise.

I feigned a smile and flicked Beau's nose. "Don't think you're getting out of our wager."

"I'd never dream of it, sister mine." Still speaking low, he released me with a wink and a grin of his own—our understanding implicit—and wagged the bottle of whiskey in my face. "Perhaps an olive branch, just for tonight? I don't much feel like sleeping."

Snatching the bottle, I downed a gulp. The whiskey burned all those unspoken words from my tongue. All the fear and doubt and restlessness. I swallowed another. "Nor I."

"Now who's whispering," Reid grumbled.

We both looked to Jean Luc, who'd thrown his coat on the dressing table. I lifted my voice and the bottle simultaneously. "What about you, dear captain? Can we tempt you?"

"I'm going to bed. Poison yourselves all you'd like."

I lifted a hand to my mouth, addressing Beau in a mock whisper. "He doesn't want to play."

Jean Luc paused in pulling back the quilt. "Play what?"

"Truth or dare." Batting my lashes, I took another long pull before handing the bottle to Beau. "Just a couple of questions to pass the time until we fall asleep."

"Until you pass out, you mean." He flicked the quilt back and began to climb beneath it. "No, thank you."

"That's probably for the best." I leaned into Beau conspiratorially, my limbs already pleasantly warm. He chuckled in response, a sturdy and familiar presence at my side. An anchor against my riotous thoughts. *You know everything about me, don't you? They called me trash boy.* "I've been spending *lots* of time with Célie lately, so I have all sorts of juicy secrets I might've let slip."

He lurched up instantly—then narrowed his eyes. Slowly, he sank back onto the bed. "I know what you're doing."

"What do you mean?"

"I know what you're *doing*," he repeated, voice emphatic, "and it isn't the reason why I've decided to humor you. Give me the bottle." Beau slapped it in his outstretched hand, and his throat worked on an enormous swallow. Wiping his mouth, he handed it to Reid next. "You start."

Reid examined the bottle in distaste. "I'm not playing."

"Oh, come on, Chass." I rose to my tiptoes, clasping my hands together at my chest and swaying. "Please? I *promise* I won't make you measure your dick against Jean Luc's."

Jean Luc smirked. "Now that *is* for the best. I wouldn't want to embarrass anyone."

Spluttering, Reid's knuckles whitened on the bottle. "You— you can't—" He grimaced. "What are the rules?"

"Rules are simple." Beau plucked the bottle from his hand before draping himself across the end of the bed. I sank to the floor, still cackling with triumph, and curled my legs beneath me. "You choose a truth, or you a choose a dare. If you choose neither"—he lifted the whiskey meaningfully—"you drink. Sound fair?"

Reid remained standing, crossing his arms and glaring down at us like some sort of pink-cheeked, vengeful god.

I sort of liked it.

"I'll go first." Jean Luc cleared his throat and rested his elbows on his knees. His light eyes found mine. "Lou: Truth or dare?"

"Dare."

His shoulders slumped. Clearly, I hadn't given the answer he'd wanted, and clearly, he hadn't prepared a dare in advance. He waved a flippant hand. "I dare you to cut your hair with one of my knives."

I laughed and took a shot of whiskey without a word.

"My turn." Rubbing my hands together, I turned to Reid— then hesitated. This was my first real chance to woo him outside of our usual circumstances, outside of L'Eau Mélancolique, the heist, the rooftop. Outside of danger. I needed to make it count, yet every thought fled my mind as I stared at him. That suspicious gleam in his eyes—the clench of his jaw and the flex of his arms—he might as well have been impenetrable. Like Jean Luc, he knew my game, and he didn't want to play.

How *had* I wooed him in Cesarine?

I wracked my brain, trying and failing to remember. Trapped in Chasseur Tower, surrounded by my enemies, I'd been jagged and sharp and guarded most days, lashing out at the slightest provocation. I'd tried to embarrass him, demean him. I'd mostly succeeded in that endeavor, yet still he'd softened toward me. Still I'd softened toward *him*. How? When? Already, the whiskey slurred my thoughts if not my words, eddying them into a single memory of warmth and nostalgia. There'd been a bathtub and a shared bed in Chasseur Tower, and there'd been books and plays and gowns—

I fought a frustrated groan. Through the thin walls, Coco's snores echoed. She hadn't yet trained me in the subtle art of seduction—if such a thing existed. I hadn't needed it before. He'd simply . . . loved me—despite everything—and that love had led him to this heinous choice, to forget me, to save me.

I would honor it.

It wasn't as if I could reverse the pattern anyway. Even as La Dame des Sorcières. If he couldn't remember our past, I would forge a new future, and I sealed the promise with another swig. "Truth or dare, Reid."

He didn't miss a beat. "Dare."

Shrugging, I pointed the bottle at him. "I dare you to strip naked and dance the *bourrée*. While we watch," I added swiftly when he moved toward the door. I couldn't help my grin. He'd always been unexpectedly quick. "Not out in the hallway."

He scowled and halted mid-step. "Truth."

"Tell me how you're feeling in this exact moment."

"Give me the bottle." He seized it before I could protest, and I smothered my disappointment. Perhaps this was better. Alcohol was its own sort of truth. With a few more shots, he'd become a plethora of information.

"Well, this is going to get ugly early," Beau mused. "I should like to go next. Louise, darling"—he flashed me a charming smile—"truth or dare? And please pick truth."

I rolled my eyes. "Truth."

He gave a feline grin. "Who is the most attractive person here? Be honest, mind you, or it's two drinks."

Winking lewdly, I extended my entire arm toward Reid, condemning him with a finger. "That man there. The copper-haired fellow. He's the one."

Reid scowled and interrupted immediately. "My turn. Lou, what is your deepest fear?"

"You didn't ask truth or dare," I pointed out.

His scowl deepened. "Truth or dare."

"Dare."

"I *dare* you to answer my question."

I chuckled and sat back, crossing my feet at the ankles. *Unexpectedly quick.* Still, his question itself left much to be desired. Of course he'd try to weaponize a game. Of course he'd press every advantage to weaken me. *Well, tough shit, buddy.* "It used to be death," I said conversationally, "but a quick chat with our dear friend Ansel changed that. He's thriving, by the way." All three of the men stared at me with slack jaws. Beau in particular seemed to blanch. "He spoke with me in L'Eau Mélancolique. He'd been following us the entire time, you know—"

"What?" Beau asked incredulously. "*How?*"

"He was a white dog."

"Oh, good Lord." Beau fell back against the quilt, pinching the bridge of his nose. "You mean *the* white dog? I thought he was an *ill omen.*" At my snort, he exclaimed, "He was always there when calamity struck!"

"Probably to *warn* you."

"I didn't realize that he'd—I haven't seen him since—" He swallowed hard. "What happened to him?"

"He found peace." The room fell silent at my gentle words, and I stared intently at my hands, knitting them together in my lap. "But he also made me realize I don't fear death at all. Or at least, it isn't the dying itself that I fear. It isn't the pain. It's the parting with my loved ones forever." I looked up. "But I'll see him again. We all will."

Reid looked as though I'd struck him across the face. He remembered Ansel too, then, if only as an initiate. He remembered his death. Perhaps he just hadn't expected I would mourn, that I'd be capable of such deep feeling for another person—me, a *witch*. I cleared my throat. "I believe it's your turn, Jean Luc."

He immediately looked to Beau. "Truth or dare."

"Truth."

"Did Célie mention me on your travels?"

"Yes." He turned to Reid without expounding on the answer, despite Jean Luc's vehement protests. "Truth or dare."

"Dare."

Another grin. This one harder. "I dare you to magic that copper hair blue."

Reid's face flushed puce. "I can't—how dare you—"

"Compartmentalization isn't healthy, brother. You saw your face on that wanted poster with the naughty W-word, yet I don't think you've acknowledged it." He arched a brow in challenge. "Denial is the first stage of grief."

"Truth," Reid said through gritted teeth.

"Yes, it is." Beau leaned forward earnestly. "Why can't you stop looking at our lovely Louise?"

If possible, Reid's face flushed deeper. It looked physically uncomfortable now, the amount of blood in his cheeks. I started giggling. "Because I want to *kill* her—"

"Ah, ah, ah." Beau wagged a reproving finger before tapping the bottle in Reid's hand. "A lie means two."

When Reid furiously swallowed two shots—without hesitation, without denying his falsehood—an entirely different kind of warmth cracked open in my chest, flowing through my limbs. I sat up on my knees, bouncing with exhilaration. The room swirled with a lovely, rosy hue. "Truth or dare, Jean Luc."

He didn't even pretend to be interested. "Truth."

"Do you regret what happened on Modraniht?"

A beat of silence passed.

Reluctantly, his eyes flicked to Reid, who looked downright murderous now. Or downright nauseous. Still, he didn't interrupt the game, and the sudden sharpness in his own eyes betrayed his interest. He wanted to know this truth. He wanted to know it very much. After a moment, Jean Luc scrubbed a hand down his face and muttered, "Yes and no. I don't regret following orders. The rules exist for a reason. Without them, we have chaos. Anarchy." He heaved a sigh, not looking at anyone now. "But I do regret the rules themselves." Dropping his hand, he asked Reid, "Truth or dare?"

"Truth."

"Is your heart still with the Chasseurs?"

They stared at each other for another long moment. I leaned forward eagerly, holding my breath, while Beau pretended not to listen and hung on every word. Reid tore his gaze away first, breaking the silence. "Is yours?"

Jean Luc leaned over and plucked the whiskey from his hand. After swallowing, he climbed to his feet and handed me the bottle on his way out. "I think I'm done for the night."

The door clicked shut behind him.

"And then there were three," Beau murmured, still toying

with the edge of the quilt. He winked at me abruptly. "I dare you to lick the bottom of my shoe."

Another half hour of antics ensued. The dares from Beau and me grew more and more ridiculous—*serenade us, do four cartwheels, curse like a sailor for twenty seconds straight*—while the questions grew more personal—*What's the grossest thing you've ever had in your mouth? To come out of your body?*—until Reid was good and thoroughly drunk. He staggered over to me at his next turn, crouching down and dropping a heavy hand on my shoulder. Grayish light tinged the window.

His voice slurred. "What's the biggest lie you've ever told?"

I might've snorted whiskey from my nose. "I never told you I was a witch. In Chasseur Tower. You never knew."

"That's stupid. How could I not have known?"

"An *excellent* question—"

"Lou, my darling sister"—Beau flung an arm over his face in a truly dramatic fashion, still lounging on the bed—"you must tell me: Do Coco and I stand a chance?"

"Of course you do! She's head over heels for you. Anyone can see that."

"Does *she* see that?" He peered at me through bleary eyes. The bottle in his hand held an alarming amount of whiskey now—which was to say, not much at all. "She called me Ansel, you know. The other day. She didn't mean it, of course, but it just sort of slipped"—he began to tip the bottle over the quilt, but I crossed the room and snatched it from him just in time—"out. She'd been laughing at a joke I'd made." He looked up at me suddenly, his gaze sharper and clearer. Calmer. "She has a lovely laugh, doesn't she? I love her laugh."

Gently, I pressed him back against the pillow. "You love more than her laugh, Beau."

His lashes fluttered. "We're all going to die, aren't we?"

"No." I pulled the blanket to his chin, tucking it around him. "But I dare you to tell her anyway."

"Tell her . . ." His voice drifted on an enormous yawn. ". . . what?"

"That you love her."

He laughed again as his eyes finally closed, and his body succumbed to sleep.

And then there were two.

I turned to face Reid, startled to find him directly behind me. His eyes fixed on mine with a deep, unsettling intensity that hadn't been there before. "Truth or dare."

Butterflies erupted in my belly as he stepped closer still. Heat washed across every inch of my skin. "Truth."

He shook his head slowly.

I swallowed hard. "Dare."

"Kiss me."

My mouth parted without volition as I looked up at him—as I saw that primal fascination in his eyes—but even through the fugue of alcohol, of keen, desperate *want*, I forced myself back a step. He followed intently. His hand lifted to cradle the nape of my neck. "Reid. You don't—you're drunk—"

The tips of his boots met my bare toes. "What is this between us?"

"A lot of alcohol—"

"I feel like I know you."

"You did know me once." I shrugged helplessly, struggling to breathe at his proximity. At his heat. This glint in his eyes—he hadn't looked at me like this since before the beach. Not on the horse, not on the bridge or in the treasury, not even beneath this very bed. My gaze darted to the whiskey in my hand, and that heat in my belly felt more like nausea now. *Alcohol is its own form of truth.* "But now you don't."

His hand edged to the side of my throat, and his thumb brushed my jaw. "We were . . . romantic."

"Yes."

"Then why are you frightened?"

I clutched his wrist to prevent his thumb from moving to my lips. Every instinct in my body raged against me. Every instinct craved his touch. *Not like this.* "Because this isn't real. You'll wake up with a throbbing headache in a couple of hours, and you'll want to kill me all over again."

"Why?"

"Because I'm a witch."

"You're a witch." He repeated the words slowly, languidly, and I couldn't help it—I leaned into his palm. "And I know you." When he swayed on his feet, my own hands shot to his waist, steadying him. He leaned down to bury his nose in my hair and inhaled deeply. "I've never been drunk before."

"I know."

"You know me."

"I do."

"Truth or dare."

"Truth."

His fingertips traced my scar, and he leaned lower, brushing his nose along the curve of my neck and shoulder. "Why do you have roses on your throat?"

I clung to him helplessly. "My mother disfigured me with hate. Coco transformed me with hope."

He paused then, drawing back slightly to look at me. A nameless emotion shadowed his gaze as it flicked from my scar to my lips. "Why do you smell so sweet?"

Though pressure built behind my eyes, I ignored it, hoisting one of his arms over my shoulders. He would collapse soon. Clumsy with alcohol, his movements lacked their typical grace—lacked even basic coordination—and he continued to sway on his feet. Fervently, I prayed he wouldn't remember any of this tomorrow. I shouldn't have let him drink so much. Pain spiked through my right temple. *I* shouldn't have drunk so much. With slow, heavy footsteps, I lugged him across the room toward the bed. "What do I smell like, Reid?"

His head fell upon my shoulder. "Like a dream." When I deposited him carefully beside Beau—his entire leg spilling free from the mattress—his hand caught my own and lingered there, even after his eyes had fluttered shut. "You smell like a dream."

THE HANGOVER

Reid

I felt as if I'd been hit by a runaway horse.

Our own horses shifted nervously in the alley behind the inn, snorting and stamping their feet. I gripped their reins tighter. Dull pain throbbed behind my eyes. When my stomach rose suddenly, I turned away from them, clenching my eyes against the weak morning light. "Never again," I promised them bitterly.

I would never imbibe another ounce of liquor for as long as I lived.

The horse nearest me lifted his tail and defecated in response.

The smell nearly undid me. Pressing a fist to my mouth, I struggled to tether their reins to the post and fled to our rooms once more. Inside, the others packed the last of their belongings with slow, sluggish movements. Except for Coco and Célie. Smirking, Coco watched from the bed, while Célie flitted to and fro in an effort to help. But she didn't help. Instead, she talked. Loudly.

"Why didn't you wake me?" She swatted Jean Luc's arm before bending to search under the bed for his missing boot. "You know

I have *always* wanted to try whiskey, and you all drank an entire bottle without me! And played truth or dare too! How could you leave me to sleep in the next room while you had all the fun?"

"It wasn't fun," Beau muttered, accepting his shirt from Lou. Sometime in the course of the night, it'd ended up in the washbowl. He wrung it out now with a miserable expression. "Fun is the last word I'd use to describe it, actually. Can you stop talking now, darling?"

"Oh, nonsense!" Abandoning her search beneath the bed, Célie rose and planted her hands on her hips. "I want to know every single detail. What questions did you ask? What dares did you undertake? Is that"—her eyes fell to a dark smear on the corner of the dressing table—"is that blood?"

I strode to wipe it away, cheeks hot, mumbling, "Fell doing a cartwheel."

"Oh my goodness! Are you all right? Actually—never mind. Forget I asked. Clearly, you all had a *grand* time without me, so a little blood can be your penance. You *do* have to tell me everything that transpired, however, since you couldn't be bothered to invite me. Fortunately, we have plenty of time to recount every detail on our way to L'Eau Mélancolique—"

Jean Luc seized her shoulders then, his eyes bloodshot and pleading. "I love you, Célie, but please—shut up."

"Hear, hear," Beau said, lifting his shoe.

Though she narrowed her eyes at each of them, it was Coco who interrupted, her voice rising to a shout. "What's that?" She grinned wider at our collective wince. Each word was a spike through my eyes. "You can't hear us? Célie, darling, we must speak up for them."

Célie grinned now too. "Of *course*, Cosette. How abominably rude of us! Shall I repeat everything I've just said?"

"I think that would be the courteous thing to do."

"You're right. It would be. What I *said* was—"

"Please—" Beau turned helplessly to Lou, who sat on the floor at the foot of the bed, folding her soiled clothes and replacing them in her pack. My stomach twisted anew at the sight of her. Fresh bile rose in my throat. She hadn't acknowledged anyone this morning. Including me. I could've been sick from shame alone—from the memory of her skin, soft and sweet. Its scent haunted me still.

I'd dared her to *kiss* me.

Stalking to the washbowl to splash my face, I swallowed acid.

When she didn't answer, Beau tapped her shoulder, and she looked up with a vacant expression. Her face wan. Her freckles stark. "Can you force them to shut up somehow?" he asked her. "Perhaps solder their vocal cords?"

Lou lifted a hand to her ears, pulling a small piece of fabric from each of them. "What's that?"

We all stared at her.

Earplugs. She'd made *earplugs* from a piece of the innkeeper's quilt. Beau snatched them from her with an air of reverence, stuffing them into his own ears. "You're an evil genius."

But Lou didn't laugh. She only blinked. Her eyes focused on the room slowly, as if she'd been lost in thought. She still held an undergarment in one hand when she asked, "Should we send word to Claud somehow? About Morgane?" The hateful woman's words echoed between us: *The time is now. The trees have mobilized, and we shall follow, striking hard and true while the conclave deliberates.* "We should really warn Blaise too, and both should know about Isla. We can coordinate some sort of defense—"

I couldn't prevent a scoff. "You think mermaids and were-wolves can coordinate anything?"

Her gaze sharpened abruptly. "I think every plan we've ever *coordinated* has been complete and utter shit and ended in total disaster."

"We need them," Coco agreed firmly, cinching her bag and standing. "I'll send word to them from the beach." She paused. "After Isla agrees to help us."

As one, we all looked to the ring on Lou's finger. She twisted it nervously. "Do you think we can trust her?" Her eyes met Coco's across the room. "Can we trust your mother?"

"We held up our end of the agreement." Coco shrugged. "And the waters prevent falsehood."

"Right." Lou continued twisting the ring. Twisting and twist-ing and twisting. "And—what's the conclave? What are they *deliberating?*"

It was Jean Luc who answered. "Religious leaders from throughout the kingdom have gathered in Cesarine to elect a new Archbishop. They're also"—he cleared his throat, abruptly busy with his satchel—"they're *eliciting* information from Madame Labelle."

The word fell heavy with meaning.

"Eliciting," Lou repeated.

Jean Luc still wouldn't look at her. "Hellfire continues to ravage the city."

"What does *eliciting* mean?" Coco asked him, undeterred.

"You know what it means."

They all stared at me in the ensuing silence. Heat prickled my neck. My face. "I don't care."

Lou pushed to her feet. "She's your mother."

"I *said* I don't care." With a snarl, I pivoted to return to the horses—regretting my decision to rejoin the group, to rejoin *her*—but Célie pointed to my bag with a frown.

"Erm . . . Reid? Your satchel is moving."

My satchel is . . . Her words pierced my thoughts a second too late. I glanced down.

Then I threw my bag across the room.

Something within it shrieked as it hit the wall. Seeds and clothing and weapons spilled forth, along with what looked like a pastry and a—and a *rat*. Célie screamed and leapt atop the bed. Beau joined her. Lou, however, swooped to seize the pastry as the rat bolted through a crack in the wall. She held it up between two fingers. "Is this what I think it is?"

"How should I know?" Furious, I swept the seeds back into their pouch. Jean Luc handed me my shirt. My pants. I stuffed them away without ceremony. Then I snatched the pastry from her. "Whatever it is, it's mine."

"This is a sticky bun." She didn't let go. "Have you had this with you the entire time?"

The bun tore between our fingers. "I don't remember."

"Do you remember buying it?"

"No."

"Clearly you bought it for me, then. It's *mine*."

"It isn't yours—"

Célie cleared her throat as we continued to grapple over the admittedly stale pastry. "A rat *was* just eating that, correct?"

"Not all of it." Eyes blazing, Lou tugged hard, and the bun tore in two. She moved to take a mighty bite.

Fire lit in my own chest, and I swiped at it. "Give that back—"

Coco slapped the bun from her hand before I could. "No," she said, matter-of-fact. "We won't be doing that." Dropping the pouch of seeds into my bag, she turned to resume her own packing. "Get along, children."

Lou and I glared at each other.

THE RIFT

Lou

The mist enveloped us later that afternoon.

We dismounted into it at the edge of the path, glancing around for signs of life. Constantin had died; did that mean the waters held no guardian? Could we simply . . . walk to shore? *Should* we?

"Beau, Célie, and Jean Luc, you should all stay here, just in case," I whispered. "Isla's magic protected you before, but we don't know if she'll extend the same courtesy this time. I'll take the ring to her." I looked to Coco. "Will you come too?"

Without a word, she looped her arm through mine in an admirable effort of normalcy. But there was nothing normal about this place. Nothing normal about how we simultaneously bent to draw knives from our boots. Despite the daylight hour, smoke still clouded the sun, and mist darkened the land to perpetual twilight. The latter clung to us as we stepped forward, dense as water, and limited our visibility—which was why we both shrieked when Reid's hand snaked out and caught my elbow. "Don't even think about it."

I shook him off with an indignant cry. "Don't *do* that! If you want to tag along, fine, but *announce* yourself next time. I could've chopped off your hand!"

Coco's eyes narrowed. "He might plan worse."

He glared at her, the fog undulating around his towering frame. "I don't trust either of you. You aren't leaving my sight."

"You aren't exactly endearing yourself to us," Coco said, poisonously sweet.

"I have a Balisarda. There could be witches here."

"Oh, there *are* witches here."

He gritted his teeth. "Manon could've told them what we stole. They could be waiting."

She pretended to consider this for a moment before shrugging. "Fine. As long as you don't stick that Balisarda into *me* instead." It was a mark of how far they'd both come that she turned her back on him, pulling me forward. He followed without comment.

We walked the path as quietly as possible, listening for any sound, but there were none. Not the rustle of leaves or the crash of waves or the cries of gulls. No, this silence was a living creature all its own, unnatural and thick and oppressive. When we stepped onto the beach, we hesitated, blinking into the abrupt sunlight and standing closer together than we normally would've.

"Do we just throw the ring in, or—?"

As if my whisper had broken some sort of spell, Angelica materialized from the water like a specter, silent and ethereal, water streaming from her gown of pure silver. When her eyes landed on Coco, her tranquil face broke into a breathtaking smile. "Cosette. You've returned."

"I told you I would."

Tugging the golden ring from my hand, I hastily extended it to her. "Here. It's yours."

"Thank you, Louise." Her smile faded as she examined the simple band in her palm. Though it sparkled innocently in the sun, we both knew better. Its history had been forged in death and magic until the two had become one. "It has been a long time since I've seen this ring." Regretfully, her eyes lifted to Coco. "Almost twenty years, in fact."

"Does this mean Isla agrees to help us?" I asked.

She ignored me, instead moving to clasp Coco's hands. "Daughter. Events have been set in motion. I fear this is the last opportunity we shall have to speak."

Coco pulled away halfheartedly. "I told you I don't want to talk."

"You must."

"No—"

Angelica dropped her voice to a fervent whisper, drawing closer, but in the silence, her voice still carried. We heard every word. "Please understand. I *never* wanted to leave you, but the thought of you trapped underwater for your entire life—like a fish in a bowl, examined and admired and wooed—I couldn't bear it. You deserved so much more. Believe me. I have watched you always, desperate to join you on the surface."

Now Coco did tear her hands away. "So why didn't you?"

"You know that answer."

"I know you're *afraid*."

"You're right," Angelica continued to whisper, "I abandoned

you to a cruel woman in hopes that she would love you, that she would give you the tools to chart your own path—and she did. You outgrew her. You've outgrown us both."

"Talk to me, Chass," I hissed, wishing desperately that Beau hadn't thieved my earplugs.

He regarded me with open suspicion. "About what?"

"Anything. Whatever comes to—"

"You can try to justify it all you'd like." Coco didn't bother to lower her voice. "How many times did I visit this beach, crying for you? How many times did you ignore me?"

"You would've lived a half life with me, Cosette. I wanted more for you."

Unable to help myself, I glanced behind to see Coco staring at her mother incredulously. "What about what *I* wanted, *maman*? You and *tante*—all either of you have ever cared about is this stupid feud. I'm the collateral damage, aren't I? I'm the one who suffers."

"We *all* have suffered," Angelica said sharply. "Do not mistake me, Cosette. Your aunt and I were among the very first of witchkind. Yes"—she nodded at Coco's dumbfound expression—"I have lived a hundred lives. Perhaps more, even. Time passed differently then." To me, she lifted an impatient hand. "Come, Louise le Blanc. You should hear this too. A battle brews on the horizon more catastrophic than this world has ever seen, and we must all play our parts. This is mine."

I crept closer tentatively. "We really don't have time for this. Morgane has already started for Cesarine—"

"If you wish to defeat your mother—and my sister—you will make time."

Her tone brooked no argument, and in the next second, she'd drawn a thin blade from her sleeve, slicing it across the palm of each hand. Her blood spilled thick upon the sand, and from it, black vines curled upward into the shape of chairs. She pointed to them, blood still trickling down her wrists. Tiny blooms of purple aconite sprouted where it dripped to the beach. "Sit. Now. I will not ask again."

Aconite meant *caution.*

I grabbed Reid's sleeve and forced him to sit, sinking into my own chair without further argument. Opposite me, Coco did the same, and Angelica stood in the center of our macabre little circle. She pivoted slowly to look each of us directly in the eyes. "This is your story—all of yours—so listen now and listen well. In the beginning, magic lived within all witches. Yes, you heard me correctly, Louise," she added when I tried to interrupt. "Though you call us Dames Rouges now, your ancestors' magic was closer to ours than to yours. It coursed through their blood, hummed in their veins. They lived in harmony with nature, never taking more than they gave and never defying the natural way. They lived. They died. They thrived." She bowed her head. "I was one of these original witches, as was my twin sister, Josephine."

"What happened?" Coco whispered.

Angelica sighed. "What always happens? In time, some among us desired more—more power, more freedom, more *life*. When a sect of my kin began experimenting with death, a great rift rose between us." Angelica knelt before Coco now, clasping her hands once more. "Your aunt was among them. I pleaded with Josephine to turn back, to forget this obsession with immortality, but when I caught her eating an infant's heart, I could ignore her sickness no longer. I had to act." A new vine crept up Coco's chair from Angelica's tears. Like the aconite, its petals bloomed purple, but this wasn't aconite at all. It was deadly nightshade. "I forbade my sister from returning to Chateau le Blanc."

"You lived there?" I asked in astonishment.

"We all did. That is what I'm trying to tell you, Louise— this is the great rift between Dame Blanche and Dame Rouge. Though I forbade Josephine from returning, she did not heed my warning, instead gathering the like-minded and organizing a rebellion." Shuddering, she pushed to her feet, and the bella-donna vine slithered higher, curling around the back of Coco's chair. "I've never seen such blood."

I stared at her, heart pounding, as another memory resur-faced: blood running as a river from the temple, soaking the hair and hems of fallen witches in its path. *The Rift.* And suddenly, it made sense—I hadn't seen Coco within this memory at all. I'd seen Angelica. *Angelica* had been the faceless woman.

She closed her eyes now. "They killed them. Our kin. Our mothers and sisters and aunts and nieces—all gone within a sin-gle night, butchered like animals. Despite everything, however, Josephine couldn't kill me. Not after our blood oath."

"She couldn't torture you," I said in dawning realization.

"No, but she *could* banish me, and she did so without hesitation. We would not meet again for many years." Her hands shifted to her elbows, and she seemed to bow into herself. "I watched from afar as her Dames Rouges reaped their just rewards, as they realized the steep cost of their victory—all witchlings born after the massacre held no magic within them. Whether their slain sisters or the Goddess herself had cursed them, I do not know. Forced to draw their magic from the land—and follow the natural order—their daughters, the first Dames Blanches, soon outnumbered their foremothers. My sister's influence dwindled as her experiments continued, growing darker and darker in nature. The Dames Blanches grew suspicious of her, and when the time was right, I capitalized on their hatred, on their fear, returning to the Chateau and driving Josephine from the throne."

Shooting to my feet, I began to pace, my thoughts sporadic and incomplete. "But I didn't know you *were* a blood witch."

"No one ever knew. I guarded the secret jealously for fear of persecution, concealing the truth of my magic with painstaking effort. I was a coward—I always have been—but in the end, it mattered not. When I leapt to my doom in L'Eau Mélancolique, Isla saved me—or rather, she saved my ring." She rubbed her thumb along the band. "My magic. Without it, I am not whole, and without me, neither is L'Eau Mélancolique. For this reason, Isla wishes me to avoid involvement in your war. She does not understand that it is *my* war as well."

Voice raw with unshed emotion, Coco whispered, "If Josephine dies, you will too."

Her words sank like bricks in my stomach.

Abruptly, Angelica turned, her knife a blur as she slashed the nightshade from coiling around Coco's neck. I gasped, Reid startled, and Coco leapt to her feet with a small shriek. None of us had noticed its creeping tendrils, the fruits of Angelica's grief and anger. When she spoke, her voice was soft. "We must all play our parts."

Coco stared at her.

I crossed the circle to squeeze Coco's hand. "Does this mean Isla *won't* join us?"

Angelica's hand closed around her ring. "Isla is many things." Brushing past us, she glided toward the waters. Her chairs of vine withered as Reid joined us, and her aconite flowers blackened to wisps of ash. "But she is not a liar. You returned my ring, and you bested Morgane. You have proven yourself a worthy ally, Louise. Though she cannot directly intervene in the events to come, she allows her melusines to choose for themselves whether to walk by your side in Cesarine. She allows *me* to choose."

"Will they?" I asked.

"Will *you*?" Coco asked at the same time.

She inclined her head. "I will lead the willing to Cesarine myself in three days' time."

"What's in three days?" Reid said, his voice strained.

Angelica merely continued toward the waters, which remained calm and still. At their edge, she drew to a graceful halt, clasping her hands at her waist. "The Oracle offers a final gift." When three iron chalices materialized before us, dread bloomed in my belly. Reid's brows dipped low, and he knelt swiftly to examine one. "Drink of the waters," Angelica said, "and you shall see."

HOLY MEN

Reid

The iron chalice felt familiar in my hand as I lifted it to my lips. *Too* familiar. Like I'd descended a flight of stairs but missed the bottom step. The second the ice water touched my tongue, an invisible force sucked me forward, and I tipped straight over the horizon.

The next second, I resurfaced in the cathedral's formal courtroom. The hard benches and wood-paneled walls I recognized immediately. The honeyed notes in the air. Beeswax candles. They cast the room in flickering light, as curtains had been drawn over its pointed stained-glass windows. I'd guarded those vaulted doors—behind the podium, behind the Archbishop—at least a dozen times while the guilty had awaited verdict. We hadn't committed many inside these halls. King Auguste and his guard had dealt with common criminals, while witches themselves hadn't been afforded trial at all. No, those who testified here had been charged with the crimes in between: conspiracy, aiding and abetting the occult, even attempted witchcraft. In my years with the Chasseurs, only a rare few had openly sympathized with witches. Some had been tempted by power. Others beguiled by beauty. Still others had sought magic for themselves.

To the last man and woman, all had burned.

I swallowed hard as Lou and Coco landed beside me.

Stumbling slightly, Coco knocked into the silver-haired man beside us. He didn't acknowledge her. Indeed, when her shoulder passed through his arm, incorporeal, I frowned. They couldn't see us, then. "Pardon her, sir," I murmured, testing another theory. He didn't respond.

"They can't hear us either." Contrary to her words, Lou spoke in a whisper. Her eyes fixed on something in the center of the chamber. I turned. Blanched. Scowling and fierce, Philippe—once a comrade in arms—dragged my mother to the podium. She'd been gagged and bound. Blood, both crusted black and fresh scarlet, stained the entirety of her gown, and her body hung limp. Drugged. Her eyes fluttered between sleep and wakefulness.

"Oh my god." Coco lifted a hand to her mouth in horror. "Oh my *god*."

Philippe didn't bother to unbind her hands. He simply nailed her ear to the podium. Shrieking, she lurched awake, but the movement only exacerbated her position, tearing the cartilage. Her screams soon morphed to sobs at Philippe's laughter. Under the drug's influence, she couldn't support herself, and when she sank to the floor, her ear tore free completely.

Red washed over my vision. I started forward before I

could stop myself, halting only when another man rose across the chamber. As with the iron chalice, I recognized his face—grizzled beard, gaunt cheeks, stormy eyes—though it took me several seconds to place him.

"Was that necessary, huntsman?" His hard voice cut sharp through the din of the room. At once, every other voice fell silent. Every eye turned to him. His attention didn't waver from Philippe, however. "If I'm not mistaken, this woman has been incapacitated with hemlock, per healers' guidance. She poses no threat in her current condition. Surely such additional measures are cruel and unusual?" Though he posed the last as a question, no one mistook it as such. The censure in his tone rang clear.

And that was when I placed him—standing between pews, holding a pot of stew in his gnarled hands. *Most in the Church wouldn't welcome their own mother if she was a sinner.*

Achille Altier.

Gone was the stooped, cantankerous old man from the graveyard parish, however. He'd combed and oiled his beard. Trimmed it neatly. His robes, too, shone resplendent even in the semidarkness. More so, he held himself differently—straighter, taller—and commanded the room with an ease I envied.

Philippe bristled, squaring his shoulders. Glancing around at the conclave's hard, impassive faces. "It's a witch, Father. Surely no precaution is too great."

"Are you saying you know better than the priests in our infirmary?"

Philippe's face paled. "I—"

"Now, now." The man beside us rose to his feet as well, standing nearly as tall and broad as me. Despite his silver hair—thick and shining as a younger man's—he radiated youth and vitality. Golden skin. Classic features. Some might've even considered him handsome. In his pale blue eyes, however, malice glittered. God had created him as Achille's opposite in every way. "Let us not rush to condemn Chasseur Brisbois for protecting us against the Devil's mistress, whose very power lay within her deceit." He arched a thick brow. "Though I must rebuke the blood he spilled upon our podium."

Philippe hastily bent his head. "My apologies, Father Gaspard."

Father Gaspard. My mind quickly filled the gap. Father Gaspard *Fosse*. I recognized the name from my time spent north in Amandine. There, he'd cultivated the largest parish in the kingdom outside of Cesarine, creating a name for himself in the process. The Archbishop hadn't cared for his ambition, his guile. His clever tongue. I'd adopted the Archbishop's opinion at the time. I'd disliked Father Gaspard on principle. But now—having met the man myself—I realized the Archbishop had spoken truth. At least in this instance.

Father Gaspard wasn't a holy man.

I frowned at my own abrupt conclusion. What had I seen to form such an assumption? He'd defended a Chasseur from open criticism. He'd grown his parish. Both should've been admirable behaviors, biblical ones, but they weren't. They *weren't*, and I didn't understand—not him, not the Church, not this growing heat in my chest or this pricking sensation along my skin. Like it'd grown several sizes too small.

"You are forgiven, child," he said, despite Philippe's gray-streaked beard. "*All* is forgiven in pursuit of our noble cause. The Father knows your heart. In violence against these creatures, he compels your hand."

Gaspard ambled down the steps toward Philippe. Slowly. Almost leisurely. Sleek and proud and superior. Father Achille might've rolled his eyes. Regardless, he hobbled down his own stairs, following Gaspard's lead across the chamber. The two met on either side of the podium. Of my mother.

Achille stepped in front of her. His robes shielded her comatose body. "He never compels our hands to violence."

"Stand down, old man." Though murmured, Gaspard's voice still reverberated through the quiet room. One could've heard a pin drop. "We are here to burn the witch, not coddle it."

My cheeks flushed with anger, with inexplicable hurt. But I *shouldn't* have been agitated, I shouldn't have been *hurt*, and I definitely shouldn't have felt concern for the witch below. As with Célie and Gaspard, however, I couldn't explain my own decisions.

I didn't love her anymore.

I didn't like Father Gaspard.

And I didn't want my mother—a witch—to suffer. I didn't want her to burn.

Sick shame washed through me at the last, and I sank onto the nearest bench. Desperate to regain my composure. When Lou followed, touching a hand to my back, I forced myself to count to three, to five, to ten. Anything to focus my turbulent thoughts. I knew what I should do. I pictured it clearly—unsheathing my knife to lop off her hand. To plunge it into her heart.

Equally clear, I pulled her close and buried my nose in her neck. I tasted her scar. I spread her legs across my lap, and I touched her gently, touched her not gently, touched her any way she wanted. When her lips parted, I stole my name from them, and I kept it forever—not a scream of pain, but a cry of longing.

This is how you touch a woman. This is how you touch me.

Pain cleaved my skull in two at the stark imagery, and I pitched forward, seizing my head. Expelling the hateful words. The hateful voice. As they scattered and drifted, the pain receded, but my shame fanned hotter than before. Intolerable. I moved to fling her hand away from me. I stopped at the last moment.

When she leaned over my shoulder, her hair tickled my cheek. "Reid?"

"No decision has been made," Achille growled.

Gaspard smiled. A cat with a juicy secret. "Of course it has. I cannot blame you for this ignorance, of course, as your idealism has hardened many against you. They dare not speak freely in your presence for fear of censure." When Achille didn't give him the satisfaction of a reply—not a frown, not even a blink—he continued, "By all means, however, let us wait for His Majesty to tally the vote. He arrives at any moment." He leaned forward to whisper something in Achille's ear then. A real whisper, this time. Not a feigned one. Stiffening, Achille muttered something back. As if given permission, the conclave broke into low conversation of their own, all waiting for my father to arrive.

Lou sat beside me. "They won't *really* burn her. Don't worry."

Her thigh pressed into my own. I forced myself to scoot away. "They will."

Coco grimaced and slid beside Lou, bouncing her own leg in agitation. "Unfortunately, I think he's right. Auguste will probably burn her with the Hellfire out of spite."

Lou glanced at me in alarm, eyes wide. "What do we do?"

"Nothing." When she arched a brow, unimpressed, I scowled and added, "There's nothing we *can* do. Even if I wanted to help her—which I don't—there isn't time. My mother is a witch, and she'll burn for her sins."

"*You* are a witch," Lou snapped. "And even if you weren't, you've conspired with us plenty." She ticked off my crimes on her fingers, each a knife coated in poison. "You've married a witch"—I didn't remember—"slept with a witch"—I wished I did—"hidden and protected a witch, multiple times"—I closed my eyes, innards clenching—"and best yet: you've *murdered* for a witch. Four of us, to be precise." My eyes snapped open as she rotated a finger between the three of us. Then jabbed it toward the chamber floor. "And the most important of those is bleeding out on the carpet right now. Because of you, might I add. She sacrificed herself for *you*. Her *son*. Whom she *loves*."

Most in the Church wouldn't welcome their own mother if she was a sinner.

But I wasn't a holy man either.

I clenched my fists and looked away. "I can't do magic."

"You can." Voice conversational, Coco examined a scar on her wrist. "And many times, you practiced when Lou wasn't directly involved, which means you're *choosing* to forget." When I opened my mouth to answer, to snarl, she merely flicked a finger at me. "Shut up. I'm not interested in excuses. Isla gifted us this vision, so we need to pay attention. We're here for a reason."

I glared at her as she glared at me. Crossing her arms, Lou exhaled hard through her nose. Still angry. We had that in common too, apparently. After a moment, she asked, "What does Madame Labelle have to do with electing a new Archbishop?"

"They're using her indictment as their own sort of tribunal." I shouldn't have explained anything to her. I couldn't stop. Jerking my chin toward Achille and Gaspard, I added, "Those two are positioning themselves for the title."

Coco grimaced and scanned the chamber. Presumably for whatever Isla had wanted us to find. "Achille had better win."

Lou glanced between us. "Do you know him?"

"He was the priest in Fée Tombe. He recognized us from the wanted posters, yet he still sheltered us for the night, even fed us his breakfast. He didn't like Beau much," Coco added, as if this were another mark in the man's favor. "He'll make the first decent Archbishop that Belterra has ever seen."

"He won't." To prove my point, I gestured to the men clustered directly below us. They'd pressed their heads together to whisper. Necks tense. Voices strained. Lou and Coco exchanged a glance before leaning toward them to listen.

"...not doing himself any favors," the balding one hissed. "Not with his history."

"What history?" his younger, equally bald companion asked.

The third—also bald, but with a long beard—shook his head. "I suppose you wouldn't know, would you, Emile? It happened before you were born."

"This isn't his first campaign." The balding one sneered down at Achille with unaccountable hostility. "Achille lobbied alongside Florin for support during the last conclave, but he rescinded his candidacy at the last moment."

"Never gave an explanation," the bearded one added. "Just relegated himself to that dismal little parish up north."

"Old Florin took the title, and no one heard from Achille for nearly thirty years—until now."

A knock sounded on the vaulted doors, and the men paused, watching as Philippe slipped into the hall, closing them behind. The balding man snorted and resumed his malicious gossip. "I heard his brother fell in with a witch. I can't remember his name."

"Audric," the bearded one supplied, his expression thoughtful. Unlike his peer, he seemed less inclined to loathe Achille. He peered down at the man in question almost curiously. "My father said Achille helped the whole family slip past the border."

The younger's lip curled. "I didn't know he sympathized with witches."

"How could you not?" The balding man pointed to where Achille still shielded my mother. "He stands no chance of procuring the vote. Not with the way he carries on—all this talk of peace and civility with the *creatures* of this kingdom. The conclave will never appoint him. Clearly, his seclusion has altered his senses."

Lou scoffed with unexpected vehemence. "Do you think he'd feel it if I cut out his tongue?"

Unable to remain still, I stalked down the steps toward my mother. "You will not touch them."

"Why?" She hurried to trail after me. "He's clearly a *bastard*—"

The vaulted doors burst open before she could finish.

Clad in a cape made of lion's fur—the mane draped across his shoulders—my father strode inside the courtroom. Philippe and three huntsmen I didn't recognize accompanied him. As one, the entire congregation rose and bowed at his arrival. Every man. Even Achille. My stomach turned as I lurched to a halt by the podium.

He'd threatened torture the last time I saw him. Threatened rats. Immediately, my gaze dropped to my mother, who lay very still. Though her dress had once been emerald green, I couldn't now place its color—an unpleasant shade of brown, perhaps. I knelt to examine her stomach. When her eyes fluttered at the movement, I froze.

"Yes, yes, *bonjour*." Auguste waved an agitated hand. He offered no smiles today. No empty platitudes. I surveyed him with mounting hatred. His hair remained immaculate, of course, but shadows deepened his eyes. His fingers trembled inexplicably. He hid them in his cape. "I cannot stay long. Though this damned fire has abated slightly"—several around the room stared at the expletive, but Auguste didn't apologize—"the healers at last believe they've discovered the solution: a rare plant in La Fôret des Yeux." Sweeping forward, he motioned for Achille to move away from my mother. "Let us be done with this."

Coco snorted and muttered, "There is no *solution*, fruit or otherwise."

I frowned. "How do you know?"

"Because the fire stemmed from my grief." Expression solemn, she met my eyes directly. "And there is no solution for grief. Only time. The fire might abate, yes, but it will never truly die."

Lou nodded in agreement, staring at my mother, and my mother—I swore she stared back. Crouching beside her, Lou laid a hand on her arm as Auguste continued his tirade.

"We all know the crimes of the creature." Pointing, he sneered at her soiled form. "From its own lips, it admitted its guilt. It is a witch. A powerful one. It promised to douse this lake of black fire in exchange for its life, but *God* has found our cure. The healers have already begun testing. By the end of the week, they promise an extinguishant to the Hellfire, and at such time, this witch shall burn for her sins."

This witch. The words shouldn't have chafed. She *was* a witch. But she was also my mother and *his* former lover. He'd laid with her. He'd even loved her once, if she were to be believed. She'd certainly loved him. Now her stomach bled from rat bites, and she lifted a ruined hand to Lou's cheek. Lou tried and failed to hold it, her own hand passing through without purchase.

Only then did I grasp the rest of his words: *by the end of the week.*

My heart sank like a stone. She would burn by the end of the week. Too soon for us to reach her. Much too soon.

Several in the audience applauded the king's outburst—including the balding man—but only Achille made a noise of protest. "Your Majesty, there are protocols in place. Without an Archbishop elect, the conclave must cast an official vote—"

"Ah." Auguste's nose crinkled as he turned. "You again, Father . . . ?"

"Achille, Your Majesty. Achille Altier."

"Achille Altier, you do realize the support of the Crown is necessary to obtain bishopric?"

"Preferable. Not necessary."

Auguste arched a brow, scrutinizing him with new eyes. "Is that so?"

"Please, Achille," Gaspard interrupted smoothly. "His Majesty's word is divine. If he proclaims the witch shall burn, the witch shall burn."

"If his word is divine," Achille grumbled, "he should have no qualms putting the matter to vote. The outcome will comply."

"*Something* ought to." Auguste glared at him before lifting his arms to address the room at large, his voice curt and impatient. Out of bounds. "You heard the man. Your Father Achille would like a vote, and a vote he shall have. All those in favor of burning the witch, raise your hand."

"Wait!" Achille lifted his own arms, eyes widening in panic. "The witch could still prove valuable! The healers have not yet perfected their extinguishant—if it fails, if we burn this woman, what hope have we of dousing the fire?" He spoke to Auguste alone now. "Her knowledge has proved valuable to the healers. I can bring in another to testify."

August spoke through his teeth. "That will not be necessary. This conclave has heard enough of your ludicrous ramblings."

"With all due respect, Your Majesty, the pursuit of knowledge isn't ludicrous. Not when a woman's life is in jeopardy—"

"Careful, Father, lest I deem it heretical instead."

Achille's mouth snapped shut in response, disappearing into his beard, and Auguste addressed the congregation once more. "Let us try this again, shall we? All those in favor of burning the witch?"

Every hand in the courtroom rose. Every hand but one. Though Achille watched his peers decide my mother's fate with an inscrutable expression, he kept both hands fixed at his sides. Firm. Implacable. Even under the king's baleful gaze. "It seems you have been outvoted," Auguste sneered. "My word *is* divine."

"We'll rescue you," Lou whispered furiously to Madame Labelle. "I don't know how, but we will. I promise."

Madame Labelle might've shaken her head.

"Why wait until week's end?" Achille's voice shook with restraint. "You've made our decision. Why not burn the witch now?"

Auguste chuckled and clapped a threatening hand on Achille's shoulder. "Because she is only the bait, you foolish man. We have much bigger fish to catch." To Philippe, he said, "Spread word far and wide throughout the kingdom, Captain. Madame Helene

Labelle *will* burn"—he cast a pointed look at Achille now—"and any who object will meet the same fate."

Achille bowed stiffly. "You must follow your conscience, Your Majesty. I must follow mine."

"See that your *conscience* leads you outside the cathedral in three days' time. At sunset, you shall light her pyre." With that, he strode through the vaulted doors once more, and the courtroom vanished into smoke.

PART IV

Qui sème le vent, récolte la tempête.
He who sows the wind shall reap the tempest.
—French proverb

WHAT HAPPINESS LOOKS LIKE

Lou

Though Angelica and her iron chalices had gone when we resurfaced, Beau, Célie, and Jean Luc floated atop the inlet in a fishing boat. A *fishing boat*. Célie grinned with palpable excitement from the flybridge, gripping the helm with both hands. Her smile quickly fell at our grim expressions, however, and she called out, "What's wrong?"

I waited until we'd climbed aboard to answer. "Isla's gift was shit."

We wouldn't be able to reach Cesarine before Madame Labelle burned to ash. When Coco said as much—explaining the conclave's decision, Father Achille's involvement, and Auguste's last words—Beau patted the stern. "*This* is her gift. Or at least, this is Angelica's. It'll get us there in time." He shrugged and added, "I wouldn't worry about my father. He has a flair for dramatics, but he knows what he's doing even less than we do."

"You didn't see him." I wrung out my hair, cursing at the cold. The strands had already started to freeze, and gooseflesh steepled my entire body. "He wasn't acting. He knows we'll come to rescue Madame Labelle. He plans to trap us, like he did before." I glanced around the ramshackle boat. "And *this* won't get us to Cesarine anytime soon."

"It will." Nudging Célie aside, Beau nodded as Jean Luc dropped the sail, and we slipped through the waters with speed. "I learned to sail when I was three." He arched a smug brow at Coco, adding, "The admiral of the Royal Navy taught me himself."

Beside me, Coco rubbed her arms, and Reid clenched every muscle, refusing to shiver despite his lips turning blue. Célie hurried to fetch us blankets in the cabin belowdecks. But blankets wouldn't help. Not really. Reluctantly, I reached for the white patterns, bracing as they shimmered into existence. I frowned at the sensation—the breadth of possibility still startled, but after a second or two of adjustment, it felt . . . good. Like stretching after sitting too long in one position. More curious still, instead of pulling me toward Chateau le Blanc, the magic seemed to be pulling me toward—

What matters now is whether you—La Dame des Sorcières—still consider this place your home. If not, it stands to reason your magic won't protect it anymore. It'll shift to your new home. Wherever that is.

It was too easy to pluck a cord now. A burst of hot air enveloped Reid and Coco—then me—and I watched, bemused, as the snow along the path melted. Warmth for warmth. The white pattern dissipated with it.

"How did you do that?" Coco asked suspiciously.

"I melted the snow."

"I thought nature demanded sacrifice?" Her eyes narrowed, skimming my face and body for signs of damage. "How is melting snow a sacrifice?"

I shrugged helplessly, struggling to articulate this strange new power even to myself. Morgane had seemed limitless as La Dame des Sorcières, and—at least in this natural way—perhaps she had been. "I *am* the snow."

She blinked at me in response. They all did. Even Célie, as she returned with slightly moldy blankets. I wrapped mine around my shoulders, burrowing into its warmth. The pattern had dried us, yes, but the bitter wind still remained. I tried and probably failed to clarify. "It's like . . . before, my magic felt like a *connection* to my ancestors. I gained my patterns through them. Now, as La Dame des Sorcières, I *am* them. I'm their ashes, their land, their magic. I'm the snow and the leaves and the wind. I'm . . . bound-less." It was my turn to blink, to stare. I probably sounded like a raving lunatic, but I didn't know how else to describe it. Perhaps words *couldn't* describe it.

"But"—Coco cleared her throat, visibly uncomfortable—"you heard what happened to my aunt without checks and balances. She and her followers pushed too far. They slaughtered their coven as a result, and the Goddess punished them. She—she punished your mother too."

"The Goddess gave my mother a chance to redeem herself at La Mascarade des Crânes. She gave her a warning. When Morgane didn't heed it, Aurore revoked her blessing. See? There *are* checks and balances. And I can't"—I turned my sight inward, examining the patterns there—"I can't do anything *unnatural* with it. At least, I don't think I can. I can't kill anyone, or—"

"Death is natural." Reid stared determinedly over the gunwale. As we hadn't yet cleared L'Eau Mélancolique, the waters below didn't ripple. He clutched his blanket tighter and swallowed hard. "Everyone dies eventually."

"Yes," I said slowly, recalling Ansel's previous words. His had somehow felt comforting, like a benediction. Reid's, however, did not. They felt more like a threat—no, like a promise. I frowned again, eyes narrowing on his heavy brow, his downcast expression. For the first time since he'd lost his memories—aside from our drunken encounter—he didn't project malevolence. He didn't keep one hand on his bandolier. "Death is natural, but murder is not."

Shrugging, he said nothing.

I fought the urge to move closer. "Are you okay, Chass? Beau is right. We *will* reach your mother in time—"

He turned on his heel and stalked belowdecks before I could finish. The door slammed behind him.

Awkward silence descended in his wake, and heat crept up my cheeks.

Coco rummaged in her pack, turning her back to the frigid wind. "You shouldn't need a lesson to know he wants you to go after him." She withdrew a scrap of parchment, a pot of ink, and a quill before sinking to the boat's floor. Without ceremony, she used her knee as a table and began to pen a message. To Claud, probably. To Blaise. "Unless you *do* need a lesson? I could teach you an excellent way to relieve stress—"

"I know *plenty* of ways to relieve stress, thank you." When the wind made it impossible to keep the parchment steady, I waved a hand. It stilled for just a moment, stilling the boat as well. We'd just reached the broader expanse of sea, and waves finally broke against the helm. "He wouldn't be interested in any of them."

"Oh, I think he's *very* interested." Her smirk faded as she looked up, and she tapped her quill upon the paper pointedly. "What am I telling Claud?"

Resigned, I plopped down next to her, spreading my blanket over her as well. Across the small deck, Beau manned the helm while Célie perched atop the boat's single bench. Jean Luc joined her. "My father might plan to trap us," Beau conceded, "but we still have one thing in our favor." He pointed to Célie and Jean Luc in turn. "We have these two this time. He doesn't know about them."

"He knows I abandoned my post," Jean Luc muttered.

Coco shook her head. "But he doesn't know *why*. If he's learned of Célie's absence—which I doubt, knowing Tremblay—he might suspect you followed her, but no one would ever believe she'd seek us out, let alone ally with us. Not after everything that's happened."

"We do have the element of surprise." At the edge of my thoughts, the beginning of a plan began to take shape. I didn't look at it too closely, instead worrying a loose thread in the blanket. Allowing it to form. It wouldn't solve the Morgane problem— though in truth, *problem* seemed too mild a word for the picture Angelica had painted. *A battle brews on the horizon more catastrophic than this world has ever seen.*

We couldn't focus on that now. The plan had changed. Madame Labelle would come first, and then—*then* came catastrophic battles. I tugged at the thread viciously, unraveling part of the blanket. "We won't be able to slip into the city undetected. We couldn't manage it before, even when no one knew we were coming. Now they'll be expecting us."

"Do I hear a *but?*" Beau asked.

I looked up at him then. Looked up at them all. "Maybe we don't *need* to slip in undetected. Maybe we announce our arrival." I grinned slightly, though I didn't particularly feel like grinning. "Maybe we let them arrest us."

"*What?*" Beau exclaimed.

"No, listen." I leaned forward, pointing again at Célie and Jean Luc. "We have an aristocrat with a death wish and a huntsman madly in love with her. A *captain*. He's deadly skilled and highly trained, and—more importantly—he has the respect of the Crown and Church. If Célie struck out on a quest for vengeance—against me, against Reid, against all witches—*of course* he would catch up with her. *Of course* he would incapacitate us, and of course he would bring us back to Cesarine to burn. He would even arrest the lawless crown prince in the process."

"They'll throw you all in prison." The wind ruffled Coco's wild curls as she considered. "The same prison where they hold Madame Labelle."

"Exactly. Jean Luc can relieve the guard, and I'll magic us all out."

"They'll inject you with hemlock," Jean Luc said.

"Not if you've already done it." I slumped as if incapacitated to demonstrate, my head lolling on Coco's shoulder. "You forget I'm an accomplished liar, and your brethren trust you."

"If you escape under my watch, they'll know I've helped you. They'll strip my captaincy."

Coco, who'd been penning our plan—scratching out and writing anew as it formed—looked up with a dark expression. "They'll do a lot worse than that." Slipping a knife from her cloak, she cut a fine line on her forearm, positioning the cut over the paper. With each drop, the paper sizzled and vanished. To me, she said, "I asked Claud—and I assume Zenna and Seraphine—to find Blaise and meet us at Léviathan afterward. If they managed to heal Toulouse, Liana, and Terrance, they'll be able to heal Madame Labelle."

When Jean Luc said nothing, Célie scooted closer, threading her fingers through his. "It's the right thing to do, Jean. Chasseurs are meant to protect the innocent. Madame Labelle has done nothing but love her son. If not for her sacrifice, the king would've tortured Reid instead."

"Also," Beau said, pursing his lips, "not to be *that* person, but your captaincy won't matter after Morgane kills everyone."

"He has a point," Coco said.

Jean Luc closed his eyes, his face tight and strained. Overhead, gulls cried in the filtered sunlight, and to starboard, waves crashed upon the distant shore. Though I didn't know Jean Luc, he still wore his emotions like he wore his coat—a coat he'd worked hard to receive. Harder than most. And all that hard work—all that pain, all that envy, all that spite—it'd be for nothing if he helped us now. In doing the *right thing*, he'd lose everything.

No, I didn't know Jean Luc, but I understood him better than most.

After another moment, he dipped his chin in assent. In sorrow. "Of course. Just tell me what to do."

"Thank you, Jean," Célie said, pressing a kiss upon his cheek.

The last of the parchment vanished with Coco's blood, and the message was sent.

Instead of relief, however, fresh dread crept through me. Fresh dread and stale anger. The latter simmered just beneath my skin as I stared at the cabin door. Jean Luc would help us, yes, and Claud and Blaise would too. We had a dragon on our side, as well as an original witch. Melusines and loup garou. A *goddess* had gifted me the magic of La Dame des Sorcières, so I could change shape—could alter the very fabric of nature—with the wave of my hand. Morgane didn't know I existed, and Auguste didn't know of our plan. Never before had we enjoyed such elements of surprise—indeed, never before had we been quite so prepared for what was to come. Our plan was an excellent one. The best we'd ever concocted.

Except for one very tall, very *obnoxious* problem.

My eyes could've bored holes in the door now.

Following my gaze, Coco nudged my shoulder. "Go talk to him."

"He'll never agree."

"You won't know until you try."

I scoffed. "You're right. He'll probably *love* this plan. It'll give him a chance to act out his martyr fantasies. Hell, he'll probably want to be lashed to the stake out of self-loathing or shame or—or some sense of misplaced *duty*."

She cast me a sideways grin. "That isn't what I said."

"It's what you meant."

"It really wasn't." Wrapping an arm around me now, she leaned close and lowered her voice. "Here's your first lesson in seduction: honesty is sexy as hell. No, not like you're thinking," she added when I scoffed again. "Honesty goes beyond telling him who you used to be, who *he* used to be, who you used to be together. You've tried that, and it hasn't worked. You need to *show* him. Allow yourself to be vulnerable, so he can be vulnerable too. That kind of honesty—*that* kind of honesty is intimate. It's raw."

I plunked my head against the hull, sighing deeply. "You forget I'm a liar. I don't *do* honesty."

Her smile spread. "You do with him."

"He's fucking infuriating."

"That he is."

"I want to gouge his eyes out."

"I completely agree."

"I might steal his Balisarda and shave his eyebrows with it."

"I wish you would."

"I'll be honest if you will."

Her face snapped toward mine then, confused, and I met her gaze steadily. "What do you mean?" she asked suspiciously. From the way her eyes flicked to Beau, however—so quick I might've missed it—she knew *exactly* what I meant. I pretended to ponder my words, tapping my chin with a finger.

"Well . . . Célie told me about a certain kiss."

Those eyes narrowed in warning. "Célie needs to mind her business."

"It sounds like *you* need to mind your business too." I fought a grin at her abruptly murderous expression. "Come now. I thought you said honesty was sexy as hell?"

She yanked her arm from my shoulders, crossing it with her other. Huddling deeper within the blankets. "Don't project what you and Reid have onto Beau and me. Ours isn't a grand, sweeping romance. We aren't star-crossed lovers. *We* were a casual hookup, and that's all."

"Coco, Coco, Coco." I bumped *her* shoulder this time. "Who's the liar now?"

"I'm not lying."

"I thought you said honesty was *raw*? I thought you said it was *intimate*?"

She grimaced and looked away, clutching the locket at her chest. "Too raw. Too intimate."

My grin slowly faded at the hurt in her words. "When was the last time you were vulnerable with anyone?"

"I'm vulnerable with you."

But I didn't count, and she knew it. I wracked my memory for each of Coco's serious relationships—a witch named Flore, Babette, and Beau himself. I didn't know if I should count Ansel. Those emotions had been serious, yes, but unrequited on both sides. "Is this . . . is this about Ansel?" I asked tentatively.

She shot me a sharp look. "No." Then— "Well, not anymore."

Her shoulder slumped, and her arms fell loose at her sides. She stared at her palms in her lap. "It was, at first. But he—he visited me in the Wistful Waters, Lou."

Moisture gathered in my eyes. "I know."

She didn't seem shocked by the revelation, her gaze instead turning inward. As if she hadn't heard me at all. "He told me he wanted me to be happy. He said if Beau could do that, I shouldn't hesitate." She shook her head sadly. "But I don't even know what happiness looks like."

"Of course you do—"

"What I *know*," she continued determinedly, speaking over me, "is that it isn't Beau's job to show me. It isn't anyone's job but mine. If I can't make myself happy, how can he? How can my mother or my aunt or my kin?"

Ah. A beat of silence pulsed between us as the pieces clicked into place. I stared, longing to wrap my arms around her tense shoulders. Whether intentionally or unintentionally, Coco had been abandoned by everyone she'd dared to love. Except me. It was no coincidence she allowed herself to be vulnerable with just one person. Still . . . my heart ached when I looked to Beau, who cast covert looks in our direction every few seconds. "He isn't them," I whispered.

She sniffed in response. "He's a *prince*."

"You're a princess."

"We lead two different peoples. His will need him, and mine will need me. Look around, Lou." She splayed her arms wide, as if Morgane and Josephine and Auguste stood here with us now.

"Regardless of how this plays out in Cesarine, our kingdoms are not aligned. They never will be. We can have no future together."

I arched a brow, parroting her own words. "You won't know unless you try." When she glared at me, saying nothing, I took her hands. "No, listen to me, Coco. If you don't want Beau, fine. I promise I won't say another word. But if you *do* want him—and if he wants you—the two of you will find a way. You'll make it work." Unbidden, I glanced back at the cabin door. "Only you can decide what your happiness looks like."

She squeezed my hands tighter, tears sparkling. "I told you, Lou. I don't *know* what my happiness looks like."

"It's fine not to know." Abruptly, I pulled her to her feet, throwing my arms around her at last. Beau, Célie, and Jean Luc ceased their murmured conversation to watch us, startled. I ignored them. I didn't care. "It isn't fine to stop trying. We have to *try*, Coco, or we'll never find it."

Coco nodded against my cheek, and her words echoed in my ears.

Honesty goes beyond telling him who you used to be, who he used to be, who you used to be together. You need to show him.

Again, I looked to the cabin door. The anger remained, of course—ever stale—but the dread had been replaced with steely resolve. With newfound purpose. My happiness included Reid, and I would never stop fighting for him. Never stop trying. Coco followed my gaze with a small smile. Pushing me forward gently, she whispered, "Here's to finding our happiness."

TAKE ME TO CHURCH

Reid

I stooped to enter the cabin, nearly cracking my skull in the process, before straightening to inspect my sanctuary. A cluttered galley full of pots and pans to the right. A threadbare sofa straight ahead. A circular table. I crossed the cabin in two strides. A bed had been tucked behind tartan curtains at the bow of the ship. Two more strides. A second set of curtains hid another bed in the stern. The linens smelled faintly of mildew. Of salt and fish.

When my stomach gave an audible growl, I rummaged through the cabinets in search of food. It gave my hands purpose. My mind focus. Hunger had a solution. A clear, tangible solution. That pain could be cured with a loaf of hard bread, a jar of pickled vegetables. I stacked them both on the counter now. I cut the loaf with my knife. I uncorked the carrots and radishes. I searched for a plate, for a fork, without truly seeing. When I found them, I ate swiftly, determinedly, every movement efficient. Focused.

The pain in my stomach didn't ease.

Guilt continued to churn until I shoved the plate away,

disgusted with the carrots. With the boat. With myself.

I couldn't stop thinking about her.

We'll rescue you. I don't know how, but we will. I promise.

I'd thought myself convicted. I'd never heard conviction until this day.

You *are a witch, and even if you weren't, you've conspired with us plenty. You've married a witch, slept with a witch, hidden and protected a witch—multiple times—and best yet: you've* murdered *for a witch. Four of us, to be precise. The most important of those is bleeding out on the carpet right now.*

I'd never heard such vehemence. Such passion.

I hated it.

I hated *her.*

I hated that I didn't hate her at all.

My thoughts spun circles as I washed my plate. The empty jar. As I replaced them in the cupboard, along with the bread. Sinking onto the couch, I stared endlessly at the cabin door. I couldn't kill her. I couldn't touch her in that way. In *any* way. When I thought of it now—thought of giving in to temptation, of trailing my lips down her ribs, or perhaps sliding my knife between them—bile rose in my throat. Maybe I could leave her instead, leave *all* of them, as originally planned.

The thought brought physical pain.

No, I couldn't leave her, couldn't kill her, couldn't *have* her, which left only one solution. One clear, tangible solution. If I were honest with myself, I should've done it already. I should've done it as soon as I saw my face on that wanted poster. It should've been easy.

The right thing rarely was.

The door crashed open before I could finish the thought, and Lou burst into the cabin. Hair wild. Chin determined. She still wore those *filthy* leather pants, and the top lace of her blouse had loosened. Her neckline had slipped over her shoulder. It revealed a single collarbone. Long and delicate. My gaze lingered there for a second too long before I tore it away, furious at myself. At her. I glared at the floor.

"That's *quite* enough sulking, I think." Her boots came into view. They stopped an inch from my own. Too close. Trapped on the couch, I couldn't move away without standing, without brushing my body past hers. This cabin was too small. Too hot. Her sweet scent engulfed it. "Come on, Chass," she needled, bending at the waist to catch my eyes. Her hair fell long and thick between us. I clenched my hands on my knees. I wouldn't touch it. I *wouldn't*. "I know things got a bit—well, *bad* in the courtroom, but we have a plan to save her now. We're going to trick Auguste."

"I still don't care."

"And I still don't believe you." When I didn't look at her, she straightened, and my treacherous eyes followed the movement. She planted her hands on her hips. "We're going to trick Auguste," she continued, determined to tell me whether or not I wanted to hear, "by pretending Jean Luc has arrested us."

Abruptly, my attention sharpened on her face. On her words. "We're going to turn ourselves in?"

"*Pretend* to turn ourselves in." Her brows flattened at whatever she saw in my expression. "We're just pretending, Chass. After we free your mother, we too will be getting the hell out of there.

Coco will round up Claud and Blaise and hopefully even Angelica, and we'll meet them all at Léviathan."

Claud and Blaise and Angelica. Gods and werewolves and witches and mermaids.

I shook my head.

"Stop it." Lou snapped her fingers to reclaim my attention. Her eyes narrowed in suspicion. "I know what you're thinking—I can see it all over your stupid face—and the answer is *no*."

I scowled at her finger. "Yeah? What am I thinking?"

"You want to *ruin* this brilliant plan of mine—"

"It *is* a brilliant plan."

The praise should've placated her. Instead, it stoked her ire. She jabbed her finger in my chest. "No. No, no, no. I *knew* you would try this martyrdom bullshit, as if you rotting in prison or burning at the stake will somehow solve everything. Let me clue you in, Chass—it won't. It won't solve anything at all. In fact, it'll complicate an already complex situation because on top of saving your mother and battling Morgane—and La Voisin, Nicholina, and a whole slew of other fucking unpleasantness—I'll also have to rescue *you*."

My skin flamed hotter at her profanity. At her *mouth*. "Language," I snarled.

She ignored me, prodding my chest again. Harder this time. "I know you're experiencing some *big feelings* right now, but you aren't going to do anything stupid with them. Do you understand? You aren't going to *prison* because you love your mother. You aren't going to *die* because you want to fuck a witch. Get—over—your—self."

Each pause she enunciated with a poke.

My blood nearly boiled now. Ears ringing, I shoved past her toward the door. If she insisted on staying belowdecks, I would return above. I could endure the others, but she—*she* spoke to me as if I were a child. An errant, *petulant* child in need of scolding. Of discipline. It was too much. Wheeling to face her at the last moment, I snapped, "What I do or don't do is none of your concern." A brief pause. "And I don't want to *fuck* a witch."

"No?" Like lightning, she closed the small distance between us. In her eyes, anger glinted brutal and bright and beautiful. And something else—something like resolve. When her chest brushed my stomach, my muscles contracted near violently. "What *do* you want, then?" She leaned closer still, her face tipping toward mine. A hard edge crept into her voice. "Make up your mind. You can't string me along forever, blowing hot one minute and cold the next. Do you want to love me, or do you want to kill me?"

I stared down at her, heat creeping up my neck. Flushing my cheeks.

"It's a fine line, isn't it?" Rising to her tiptoes now, she practically whispered the words against my lips. "Or . . . perhaps you don't want either. Perhaps you want to worship me instead. Is that it, Chass? Do you want to worship my body like you used to?"

I couldn't move.

"I can show you how if you've forgotten," she breathed. "*I* remember how to worship *you*."

Red swept across my vision at the image. Whether rage or lust or sheer *madness*, I didn't know. I didn't *care*. I was damned either way. My hands seized her shoulders, her jaw, her hair, and my lips crashed against hers. She responded instantaneously. Flinging her arms around my neck, she surged upward. I caught her leg as she did, hoisting her higher, wrapping her body around mine. My back collided with the door. We rolled. I couldn't slow my hips, my tongue. Pressure built at the base of my spine as I ground into her. As she tore away on a ragged breath. As she clenched her eyes shut and threaded her fingers through my hair.

I didn't stop.

My knee slid between her legs, pinning her against the door. I caught her hands above her head. Trapped them there. Worshiped her neck with my tongue. And her collarbone—her *fucking* collarbone. I bit it gently, relishing how her body responded beneath me. I'd known it would. I didn't know *how*, but I'd known she'd make that exact sound. Like my body knew hers in a way my mind didn't. Oh, and it knew her. It knew her intimately.

I can show you how if you've forgotten. I remember how to worship you.

The words incited me to a fever pitch. Instinct guided me, and I tasted her throat, her shoulder, her ear. I couldn't touch enough of her. The wood groaned beneath my knee, the skin there already chafed and abraded from the pressure, the friction. Instinctively, I transferred her wrists to one hand, using the other to yank her closer, away from the door. I trailed that hand down her back, soothing it, as she rolled her hips along my thigh. Along the hard ridge there.

"Is this how I did it?" I traced her collarbone with my nose, near delirious at the scent of her. My own hips bucked involuntarily. The pressure built. Though a voice at the back of my mind warned me to go no further, I ignored it. We would burn for our sins, the two of us, here and now. I tugged at the laces of her pants. The laces of mine. "Is this how I *worshiped* you?"

Her eyes remained closed as she arched against me, as her entire body shuddered. I savored the sight. I craved it. When her mouth parted on a gasp, I caught the sound hungrily, plunging my hand lower. Fingers curling. Thrusting. Seeking. In this moment, I could have her—I could *worship* her—and pretend she was mine.

Just this once.

My throat constricted inexplicably at the thought, and my chest tightened. I moved my fingers faster now, chasing that empty promise. Pressing her into the door once more. "Show me," I whispered on a ragged breath. "Please. Show me how we used to be."

Her own eyes snapped open, and she stopped moving abruptly. "What's wrong?"

I didn't answer. I *couldn't* answer. Shaking my head, I kissed her again, desperate to try. Desperate to relieve this *ache* between us—this yearning I'd once known and almost remembered. I wanted it. I feared it. I kissed her until I couldn't tell the difference.

"Reid." Her fingers curled around my wrist. With a start, I realized she'd pulled free. She eased my hand from her pants now, her eyes fixed steadily upon mine. They shone with keen emotion. Though I wanted to name the feeling I saw there, to acknowledge it, I wouldn't. I *couldn't*. "Not . . . not like this. You aren't ready."

"I'm *fine*—"

"I don't think you are." Leaning forward, she pressed a kiss upon my forehead, featherlight. The tenderness in the movement nearly broke me. The intimacy. "Slow down, Reid. We have time."

Slow down, Reid. We have time.

We have time.

Defeated, I withdrew at the words, my forehead falling to the crook of her neck. My hands bracing against the door. She sank slowly to the floor as silence descended. When I didn't break it, only clenched my fists against the wood, she nuzzled her cheek against my hair. She actually *nuzzled* me. I closed my eyes. "Talk to me," she whispered.

"I can't." The words fell thick from my tongue. Clumsy. "I'm sorry."

"Never apologize for being uncomfortable."

"I'm not *uncomfortable.* I'm—I'm—" *Adrift.* Though I wrenched my face up to stare at her then, I immediately regretted the decision. Her eyebrows, her nose, her *freckles.* And those eyes— I could drown in those eyes. Light from the windows sparkled within their turquoise depths. This close, I could see the ring of icy blue around her pupils. The sea-green flecks of her irises. She couldn't keep *looking* at me like this. She couldn't keep *touching* me like she—like she— "Why don't I remember you?" I demanded.

Those beautiful eyes blinked. "You chose to forget."

"*Why?*"

"Because you loved me."

Because you loved me.

Throwing my hands in the air, I stalked across the cabin. It made no sense. If I'd loved her, why had I left her? If I'd embraced her as a witch—if I'd embraced *myself*—why had I given it up? Had I been happy? Had *she*? The way she said my name . . . it spoke of more than a fleeting moment of lust.

It spoke of more.

Like a moth to a flame, I faced her once more. "Show me."

She furrowed her brows in response, her hair wilder than when she'd first entered. Her collar lower. Her lips swollen and her pants undone. Through the laces, an inch or two of taut golden skin teased me. When I moved to close the distance between us—again—she tilted her head to one side, catlike. "What are you saying?"

Swallowing hard, I forced myself to stop. To repeat the words. "Show me how we used to be."

"Are you asking me . . . do you *want* to remember?" When I only stared at her, she shook her head slowly, drifting closer. Still studying me. She seemed to be holding her breath. "Silence isn't an answer."

"I don't know."

The words came in a rush, as honest as I could give. Just speaking them aloud stripped me bare. I could hardly look at her. But I did. I looked at her, forced to acknowledge my own indecision. My despair and my hope.

A pause as she considered. A small, wicked smile. "All right."

"What?"

"Sit"—she pointed a finger behind me—"on the couch."

I sank onto the cushions without another word, eyes

wide—heart pounding—as she followed, leaning against the table to face me. As she hoisted herself up on its edge. Close enough to touch. Something in her expression stilled my hand, however, even as she flicked her wrist, locking the cabin door. The scent of magic erupted around us. "There. No one can see us. No one can hear us, either."

"Is that supposed to frighten me?"

"Does it?"

I leveled her with a dark look. Whether intended or not, I'd involved myself with a witch—a witch I wanted in every sense of the word. A witch I wanted to taste and feel and *know*. All of it should've frightened me. The last most of all. But— "It doesn't."

"Tell me where you'd like to touch me, Reid. Tell me, and I'll do it for you. I'll show you how we used to be."

I stared at her hungrily, hardly daring to believe it. She stared back at me. After another moment, she arched a brow, slipping each foot from her boots. Her stockings came next. "If you'd rather not, of course, I understand. There are two beds. We could rest for a while instead."

"No." The word tore from me instinctively. Quick and thoughtless. Cursing my own eagerness, I exhaled an uneven breath. *Slow down, Reid. We have time.* She'd given me this opportunity to master myself. To regain some semblance of control. Obviously she'd underestimated her appeal. My thumbs itched to rub along her bare soles, to slip over her toes and up her ankles. I glanced at the door.

She feigned a yawn.

My eyes locked on hers, searching, and in them, I saw the truth. She wanted my thoughts clear, yes, but not just for my sake. For hers as well. *Make up your mind, Reid*, she'd said before. *You can't string me along forever, blowing hot one minute and cold the next.*

Scooting to the edge of the couch, careful not to touch her, I said, "I want—I want you to—" But the words wouldn't come. Honesty choked me. Honesty and fear. For how far I'd go, how far she'd go, how far we'd gone already.

She cocked her head, her gaze alight with fire. It threatened to devour us both. "Whatever you want, Reid." Softer, she said, "Tell me."

My fear melted at the depth in her voice. The pure, unbridled emotion.

Love.

I quickly shook away the thought. "Take off your pants."

If my request surprised her, she didn't show it. She didn't hesitate. Slowly, torturously, she peeled her pants down her legs. Her eyes never left mine. Not until she'd stripped the leather fabric away completely.

My mouth went dry at the sight.

I'd been captivated by her collarbone. Now the whole of her bare legs stretched out before me. Still perched atop the table, the tips of her toes barely reached the floor. Her shirt billowed around her, however. It hid her from me. Resisting the urge to lean forward, I curled my fingers into the cushion and watched, silent, as she leaned back on her hands, swinging her feet as if bored.

She wasn't bored.

"Now what?" she asked. The hitch in her voice revealed the lie. The breathlessness.

"Your shirt."

"You're supposed to tell me where you'd like to touch me."

"I want to see you first."

And I did. I wanted—no, *needed*—to see her like a starving man needed sustenance. Her eyes narrowed, but she gradually lifted the hem of her top, revealing more of that golden skin. Inch by torturous inch. After sliding it overhead, she tossed it in a pool at my feet. "And now?"

And now she was naked. Gloriously so. Though I longed to touch her, to reach out and trace the curve of her waist, I kept my hands fisted in the cushions. She wanted me to dictate each touch. She wanted to hear every word for what it was—a decision. Small decisions, yes, but decisions nonetheless. Honest ones. There could be no lies between us here. Not like this.

Not like this.

"Your thigh," I said, unable to tear my gaze away from her ankles, her calves, her knees. Unable to think coherently, to speak more than a handful of syllables. Too enthralled to be embarrassed. "Touch it."

Her belly undulated with laughter at the command. Her shoulders shook with it. I feasted on the sound, on the *sight*—each intake of breath, each exhalation. Though each bout rang high and clear, delighted, she had no business sounding so innocent. Not when her body burned as sin incarnate.

"I need more than that, Chass. Be specific." Leaning forward, she swept her hand casually to the middle of her thigh. "Here?" When I shook my head, swallowing hard, she trailed a single finger higher. Higher still. "Or . . . here?"

"What does it feel like?" Unable to help myself, I pitched upright, swift and unsteady. My hands trembled with the need to replace hers, but I resisted. I couldn't touch her now. I'd never stop. "Imagine it's my hand, and tell me exactly how your skin feels."

With a wink, she closed her eyes. "It feels . . . warm."

"Just warm?"

"Feverish." Her other hand drifted to her throat, her neck, as she continued to caress her thigh. Her smile faded. "I feel feverish. Hot."

Feverish. Hot. "Your finger. Move it higher." When she complied, sliding it between her legs, I nearly tore through the cushions. My heart beat rapidly. "What does it feel like there?"

Her breath left in a whoosh as that finger moved. Her legs trembled. I ached to grab them. To pin her to the table and finish what we'd started. But this—this wasn't like before. This was different. This was *everything.* "Tell me, Lou. Tell me how hot you feel."

"It feels"—her hips rocked in slow rhythm with her finger, and her head fell back, her spine arching—"good. It feels so good, Reid. I feel so good."

"Be specific," I said through gritted teeth.

When she told me what it felt like—slick and sensitive, aching and *empty*—I fell to my knees before her. She'd spoken of worship. I understood now. I still didn't touch her, however, not even when she added a second finger, a third, and said on a sigh, "I wish it was you."

I wish it was too. "Part your legs." Her legs fell open. "Show me how you touch yourself."

And she did.

Her thumb made delicate circles first. Then indelicate ones. More and more, her movements growing faster, graceless, as her legs tensed and spasmed. I felt each press of her thumb myself—the building pressure, the sharp ache. The need for release. I managed one breath. Two. Then—

"Stop."

The curt word startled her, and she stilled, her chest heaving. A fine sheen of sweat glistened there. I longed to taste it. Rising on my knees, I gripped the table on either side of her. "Open your eyes." When she did so—still panting softly—I said, "Look at me. Don't hide. I said I want to see you."

Those eyes locked on mine with unerring focus then. She didn't so much as blink as her fingers resumed between us. Slow at first, building faster. And on her lips . . . I leaned closer still, almost touching her now. Never touching her. When she breathed my name—a condemnation, a plea, a *prayer*—the sound virtually undid me. My hand plunged into my own pants. At the first touch, I nearly broke.

"Do I—" Lou rested her forehead against mine, near frantic now. A bead of sweat trickled between her breasts as she moved. I tracked its path mindlessly. "Do I make you feel *wanton*, husband? Does this—make you feel *ashamed*?"

No. *God*, no. Nothing about this felt shameful. My chest constricted tighter at the word—too tight, too small to contain the emotions rioting there. I couldn't describe them, except that they felt—*she* felt— "You make me feel right. Whole."

A shiver swept my spine at the confession. At the truth. My skin tingled in anticipation. Her voice might've broken on a sob, on my name, and the moment she came undone, I did too. One hand rose to clutch my shoulder. Mine seized her knee. Our eyes remained open as we shuddered together, and when I sagged into her—gutted—she brushed her lips against mine. Gentle, this time. Tentative. Hopeful. Her chin quivered. Without a word, I engulfed her in my arms, holding her tight.

She'd seemed so strong since the beach. So tough and unyielding. Impervious to hurt or harm. But here—after breaking, shattering beneath my gaze—she seemed fragile as glass. No, not glass.

My *wife*.

I couldn't remember. Those memories had disappeared, leaving great cracks of emptiness in my identity. In my mind. In my heart.

No, I couldn't remember.

But now I wanted to.

THE BELLY OF THE BEAST

Lou

As the sun crested the horizon on the third morning, we slipped into Cesarine's waters.

Jean Luc gripped the helm tighter than necessary, fingers twisting the wood in an agitated gesture. "This is going to get very ugly, very quickly." His eyes flicked to me and Reid, who stood behind me at the rail. He'd hovered since that first day in the cabin, speaking little and frowning often. I'd expected as much. Reid wasn't the type for casual flings. Our time on the table had meant something to him.

He just didn't know *what*.

Still, when he thought no one could see, I'd catch him furrowing his brows and shaking his head, as if in silent conversation with himself. At times, his face would even contort with pain. I didn't dare speculate at the cause—didn't dare *hope*—instead focusing on what he'd freely given me. Though his words had been few, they'd been precious.

You make me feel right. Whole.

Despite the bitter cold, warmth suffused my body at the memory.

It hadn't been the final decision—not by any means—but it had been *a* decision. In that moment, he'd chosen me. In all the moments since, he'd chosen to stand near me, to sleep beside me, to listen when I spoke. When he'd offered me the last of his food yesterday, scowling and confused, Beau had even offered to pay Célie what he owed her.

It felt too good to be true.

I held on to it for dear life.

"When we dock at port, the harbormaster will call for His Majesty's Guard," Jean Luc said, "who will in turn alert the Chasseurs. I'll order an escort to the castle to request an audience with the king. He'll grant it once he discovers who I've captured."

Célie lifted her injection. "Lou and Reid will feign incapacitation whilst in the city."

"They'll still need to be bound." To Beau, Jean Luc added, "As will you, Your Highness."

"When Célie's parents come to collect her at port, I'll slip beneath their carriage." Coco stared at the skyline of the city as we approached. Though still small and indistinct, it grew larger every moment. "I'll wait with Claud and the others at Léviathan for the signal."

Reid towered behind me, his presence warm and steady. An uncanny sort of calm overtook his features whenever we discussed strategy. Like he'd slipped into another state of consciousness, separate from the chaos and turmoil of his emotions.

I chuckled quietly, hiding the sound behind my palm. The compartmentalization was strong in this one. "After they deposit us in our cells, Coco will create a distraction large enough to merit Chasseur attention," he said. "Jean will insist our guards intervene, and he'll take up their post temporarily."

"I'll magic us all out of our cells," I continued, "including Madame Labelle. Beau and Jean Luc will slip us from the castle undetected via the tunnels."

Jean Luc seemed agitated. "Auguste knows of the tunnels."

"He doesn't know them like me," Beau said grimly. "I can get us out."

Jean Luc's gaze flicked to Reid and me now. His fingers kept twisting. "There will be quite a bit more between the *escort you to the castle* and *deposit you in your cell* parts of the plan. You know that, correct?"

This is going to get very ugly, very quickly.

"Yes." Not for the first time, Estelle's anguished face skipped through my mind's eye. Her limp body. A boot on her cheek and a fist in her hair. Other faces quickly followed, other whispers. *Viera Beauchêne escaped after they tried to burn her and her wife—acid this time instead of flame. An experiment.* And— "I believe His Majesty has an affinity for rats."

"I'll do what I can to protect you, but . . ."

"If this is to work, your performance must be believable," Reid finished for him, voice hard. "All of ours must."

Jean Luc nodded. "It's going to hurt."

"Pain is fleeting." I didn't know where the words came from, but they held true. "And if we slip up—even for a moment—the pain will be much worse. The *stake* will be much worse." Heavy silence descended as I remembered the torment of flames licking up my limbs, of blisters rupturing my skin, of heat peeling muscle from bone. I shuddered slightly. "Trust me."

When we grew close enough to see individual buildings—to see people bustling like ants between them—Jean Luc tossed us the rope. He didn't look at any of us. "It's time."

"Do it tightly," I told Reid, who wrapped it around my ankles a moment later. Crouched before me, he kept his touch gentle, *too* gentle, and seemed loath to tighten the binds. His thumb traced a small vein in my foot up to my ankle, where it disappeared. His thumb kept traveling, however. He stared at it in concentration.

"You'll be feigning incapacitation," he muttered at last. "I don't need to cripple you."

"It needs to be convincing."

"No one will be looking at your ankles."

"Reid." When I sat forward to cup his cheek, he reluctantly met my gaze, and his composure slipped. Just a little. He leaned into my palm, unable to help himself, as emotion finally stirred in his eyes. It looked like dread. "If this goes poorly, I won't be the only one to burn. Your mother will. *You* will too. And that—that is unacceptable."

His throat bobbed. "It won't happen."

"You're right. It won't. Now"—I offered a halfhearted smirk—"can you bind me like a Chasseur binds a witch, or shall I have Coco do it?"

Reid stared at me for a single heartbeat before glancing over his shoulder. Behind us, Coco helped Beau with his own binds while Célie fluttered around them, trying and failing to help. He lowered his voice. "Tell me how to remember."

A pulse of silence—of *shock*—both mine and his.

"What?" I asked dubiously, sure I'd misheard him amidst the commotion. The wind swept past in a gale as we approached shore, and voices rose from the docks. Seagulls cried overhead in the bright morning sunshine. And my heart—it nearly pounded from my chest. "Did you say you want to—?"

"Remember, yes." Again, he looked to Coco and the others, shifting himself slightly to block their view. "You said—earlier, you said only magic could help me. *My* magic. You said I could reverse the pattern. What does that mean?"

"It means"—I forced a deep breath, nodding to him, to myself, to God or the Goddess or anyone who might've been playing such a heinous joke on me—"it means that you—"

"It means nothing for now," Coco said, dropping beside us abruptly. She squeezed my hand before turning to Reid. "Please, think about this. We don't need Morgane to remember Lou while we're all in the city. We have enough working against us without adding vengeful mother to the list."

"But—" I said desperately.

"When you remembered Bas, it almost killed you both." Coco grasped both of my hands now, her expression earnest. Perhaps just as desperate as I was. "We're mere *moments* away from Cesarine's shore, and we have a plan in place to rescue Madame

Labelle. Afterward, if this is what you both choose, I'll help him remember any way I can. You know I will. Right *now*, however, we need to get you both bound, or all seven of us will see the stake before nightfall."

All seven of us.

Shit.

Swallowing hard, I kept nodding even as Reid scowled and began tying his own ankles. This was bigger than us now. It'd always been bigger than us. "There *will* be an after, Lou," Coco whispered fiercely, turning to bind my hands behind my back. She did the same for Reid. "We'll get through this together—*all* of us—and we'll start anew. We'll carve out that piece of paradise. Together," she repeated firmly. "I promise."

Together.

I let my body go limp against the floorboards as she slipped belowdecks, as voices called out to Jean Luc in recognition, as our small boat slipped into port and men leapt aboard to help him tie it down. Reid pressed his head atop mine. The only show of comfort he could give me. Heightened sensation rose like needles along my skin as my magic fought to rise, to protect him, to protect my *home*, but I tamped it down. It was too late to turn back now. We'd entered the belly of the beast.

ALL SEVEN OF US

Lou

Mostly everything went according to plan.

It took a moment for anyone to notice us there, lifeless and forgotten on the floor, but when a hook-nosed gentleman nearly trod on Reid's foot, he yelped in surprise—then yelped louder in fear, recognition dawning over his swarthy features. "Is that— that isn't—?"

"Reid Diggory, yes," Jean Luc said with a sneer, materializing beside us. He nudged my ribs with his boot, and I slipped sideways into Reid. He stiffened subtly. "And his wife, the heiress of La Dame des Sorcières. I apprehended them in a small village north of Amandine."

The sailor's eyes boggled. "All by yourself?"

"I disabled Morgane le Blanc by myself, did I not?" Jean raised an arrogant brow at the man's spluttering. "I think you'll find anything is possible with the proper motivation." He jerked his chin toward Célie, who cowered in proper fashion near the helm, and added, "They had something that belonged to me."

Others had gathered around us now, wide-eyed and curious. Fear hadn't yet taken root. These men lived predominantly on the seas, where witches were little more than fairy stories compared to the very real danger of Isla and her melusines. "Who is that, then?" another asked, staring at Célie.

"Mademoiselle Célie Tremblay, daughter of the viscount. Her father is personal advisor to His Majesty." Jean Luc's jaw hardened. "You might've heard of him in connection to his eldest daughter, Filippa, who was murdered by witches last year. Célie fancied herself a vigilante and went after these two herself." At the sailors' derisive snorts, Célie straightened her shoulders defensively—just for a second—before remembering her role. Casting her eyes downward, she heeded Jean Luc's command when he called her over, tucking her under his arm. His hand on her shoulder clenched tighter than necessary, the only visible sign of his strain. Still, his voice oozed conceit as he added, "She's a foolish girl, but what can we expect from one so pretty?" When the men laughed—like brainless *sheep*—he snapped his fingers at one on the edge of the group. "Send word to her father. He shall collect and discipline her as he sees fit."

The messenger glanced at Beau with a frown. "Hers ain't the only father who'll be administerin' discipline." Then he leapt from the boat and disappeared, replaced almost instantly by the harbormaster. A short, portly man with a spectacular handlebar mustache, he held himself with the ferociousness of a badger as he seized my face to examine it. He wasn't gentle. Reid's muscles tensed beneath me.

"I didn't believe it," the harbormaster growled, jerking my chin this way and that, hard enough to bruise. "But it's her, after all. The bitch witch's daughter in the flesh." He grinned and straightened once more, turning to address Jean Luc. "We'll alert your brethren straightaway, of course, if they're not already on their way. Word like this travels quickly." With the jerk of his hand, another sailor departed. "I'll expect some sort of commendation for allowing you to port. A dual capture, if you will."

Jean Luc glared at him. "You dare to extort a captain of the Chasseurs?"

"Not a captain, no." Undaunted by Jean Luc's ire, the man crossed his arms, still grinning. "Auguste is an old friend of mine, did you know? Rumor has it you've been missed, *Captain*."

Jean Luc's eyes narrowed as my own stomach plunged. "What are you saying?"

The man simply shrugged and glanced behind at the commotion up the street. "I expect you'll find out soon enough."

A virtual battalion of Chasseurs thundered toward us on horseback, eliciting shrieks from pedestrians in their path. More and more people—sailors, fishermen, peddlers—collected around our boat now. All craned their necks from the dock to see what the fuss was about, some clapping hands over their mouths when they spotted us, others hissing through their teeth. One woman even threw a fish with unerring aim. It struck Reid's cheek before falling, dead, to the floor. Beau pretended to struggle in his binds. "That's enough," he snarled.

The harbormaster clicked his tongue. "Well, well, well, Your

Highness." He squatted before him, examining Beau's face from every angle. "The last time I saw you, you were in nappies—" Before he could finish the rest of his humiliating diatribe, however, the first of the huntsmen reached us. I recognized him from La Mascarade des Crânes.

"Philippe." Jean Luc scowled as the man in question—a rather large, frightening man, though not nearly so large and frightening as Reid—shouldered past him with a pointed lack of respect. Indeed, he knocked into Jean Luc like he was a piece of furniture, sending him back two steps. "Have you lost your mind?"

"Secure the area." Philippe snapped and pointed as his brethren fell into place around the boat, around *us*. He ignored Jean Luc completely. To the harbormaster, he said, "His Majesty arrives posthaste."

"He's coming *here*?" Jean Luc lifted his voice above the tumult, determined to be heard. Boots jostled as the King's Guard arrived—the constabulary too—heedless of my fingers. When Philippe stepped on Reid's intentionally, I heard the cruel *crack* of bone. Reid didn't so much as flinch. "*Why?*"

"To secure the prisoners, of course," the harbormaster said.

"No." Jean Luc shook his head wildly. "No, he shouldn't travel out in the open like this. Morgane is here. She's in the city—"

Philippe's smile chilled my very bones. "It isn't up to you, Jean. Not anymore."

The king arrived the next moment—at precisely the same time as Monsieur and Madame Tremblay. Absolute pandemonium ensued. The Tremblays' carriage screeched to a halt beyond the dock, and Madame Tremblay barreled straight into the barricade of soldiers, shouting for her daughter without decorum. "Célie! Célie!" She hardly noticed the guards chasing after her. Jean Luc stepped in front of them, blocking their advance, as she enveloped her daughter in her arms. "Oh, thank *God*—"

"*Control* yourself, woman!" Monsieur Tremblay snarled as he too bolted on deck, skirting around Reid, me, and the barricade of Chasseurs encircling us. "Have you no *shame*? You will *apologize* this *instant*—" I would've laughed at the spectacle they'd created if the king hadn't followed. If his eyes hadn't locked on Reid's. If he hadn't reached into his velvet pocket to extract two metal syringes.

Oh, shit.

"*Rebonjour, fils.*" His eyes moved from Reid to me, and something predatory sparked in them. Something poisonous. A broad, brilliant smile transformed his face from attractive to breathtaking. Quite literally, my breath caught in my throat. That smile belonged to Reid. To Beau. I knew it like the back of my own hand. "*Fille.*"

Chasseur, soldier, and constable alike parted at his approach, and even Madame Tremblay quieted, finally realizing the precariousness of the situation. People didn't smile like that for no reason. Especially kings. I hardly dared breathe as he crouched before me. As he too gripped my chin between thumb and forefinger. His touch was lighter than the harbormaster's. Indeed, he handled me like fine china, his thumb sweeping over the welts as if to soothe them. "Shh, shhh. Fret not, Louise. You cannot know how I have longed for this moment."

Jean Luc hurried to intercede. "Your Majesty, please allow me to—"

"I will allow you nothing." Auguste's coldly spoken words stopped Jean in his tracks. The former's gaze didn't stray from mine, however. He studied my lips as he continued. "You are henceforth stripped of your captaincy, Chasseur Toussaint. All future duties will be handled by your new captain, Philippe Brisbois."

"*Philippe?*" Jean Luc's face twisted, and he glanced between the two, his chest swelling with rage. "I have apprehended and incapacitated two of the most notorious witches in the kingdom. I have returned your *son*—"

"What you have *done*," Auguste snapped, "is disobey my direct command. Your presence at the conclave was not requested. It was required. In forfeiting your responsibilities, you have forfeited your title. I do hope she was worth it." His lip curled as he glanced to Célie. "She *is* very pretty."

Jean Luc opened and closed his mouth, near apoplectic now. Even amidst the dire circumstances, I felt a twinge of sorrow for him. In the breadth of a single moment, he thought he'd lost everything. When Auguste dropped his hand from my chin, however, flicking the first syringe, fear surpassed all other emotions. I cast a panicked glance at Jean Luc, willing him to pull himself together.

"I met your mother once, Louise," Auguste said, still *tap, tap, tapping* the syringe. "Now she—*she* is exquisite. A diamond of the first water. It's too bad, really, that she's a soul-sucking demoness. Just like *your* mother," he added to Reid, tilting his head to examine the quill. A bead of hemlock trickled from its tip. My magic reared its head at the sight, white patterns unfurling all around me. They hummed with the need to protect Reid. To protect all of them. I nearly trembled with restraint. Oblivious, Auguste stroked my hair and pulled my limp body to his lap. "You look nothing like her, of course, poor thing. All your father, aren't you?" He leaned so close that I could smell the mint on his breath. "I loathed that man. Makes this easier, I suppose—a bit *too* easy. When I announced Helene's execution, I knew you'd come, but I never expected this sort of weakness."

He pressed the syringe to my throat.

"Your Majesty." Though Jean Luc didn't dare step closer, his voice rose urgently. "I re-injected the prisoners only moments before docking. If you dose them again so quickly, I fear they'll die before the stake."

Auguste lifted a golden brow. "You *fear* their death?"

"A poor choice of words." Jean Luc ducked his head. "Please forgive me."

But Auguste's gaze had already sharpened with suspicion. "There is only one way to kill a witch, huntsman, and it is not poison. You have nothing to *fear*. Still, however, I am benevolent. I will not dose the prisoners again."

I breathed a long, slow sigh of relief.

Perhaps Auguste felt the movement. Perhaps he didn't. Either way, he gestured Jean Luc toward us, pressing the injection into his palm before rising to his feet. He brought me with him, cradling me within his arms. My limbs dangled helplessly. "*You* will."

Shit, shit, *shit.*

Jean Luc blinked, his expression flattening. "Me, Your Majesty?"

"Yes, huntsman. You. A great honor, is it not? To apprehend *and* incapacitate two of the most notorious witches in the kingdom?"

The implication rang clear in the ensuing silence. Even the wind had fallen silent to listen. As if hoping to prove his suspicions, Auguste pinched the flesh of my thigh and twisted—hard. I clenched my teeth against the pain. He would not break us with a pinch, nor a bruised chin or broken finger. The white patterns still writhed in fury, however. They demanded retribution. I wouldn't use them. Not yet. If I did, all would know Jean Luc had been lying. They would know he'd betrayed them, and he really *would* lose everything—his coat, his Balisarda, his *life.* Célie would be implicated too.

All seven of us.

No, our plan could still work. Jean Luc could fake the injection somehow, and we—

"I am waiting," Auguste said darkly.

Though Jean Luc fought to keep his face impassive, panic flickered within his eyes' pale depths—panic and remorse. They met mine for only a second before dropping to the syringe. In that second, I knew. He would fake nothing. He *could* fake nothing—not with so many eyes on us now. Not under the king's very nose.

Which left me with two options.

I could attack the king now, and we could *likely* fight our way out, condemning Jean Luc, Célie, and Madame Labelle in the process. *Or* I could allow the injection and trust the others to rescue us. Neither option was foolproof. Neither option guaranteed escape. With the latter, at least, we'd be in a centralized location with Madame Labelle. If they rescued one, they could rescue us all. And though Claud claimed he couldn't intervene, he wouldn't truly leave us to die, would he?

I had a split second to decide before Jean plunged the quill into my throat.

Sharp pain flared on impact, and the hemlock—as cold and viscous as I remembered it—spread like mire through my veins. I could just feel the warm trickle of blood before numbness crept in, before my vision faded, before Coco slipped unnoticed from the water to the Tremblays' carriage.

The white patterns resisted the darkness, blazing brighter and hotter as I dimmed.

Auguste held one of my eyes open, even as it rolled back into my head. "Do not fret, *fille*. This pain shall pass. At sunset, you shall burn with my son and his mother in a lake of black fire." When he stroked my cheek—almost tenderly—the white patterns finally softened, finally succumbed, finally dissolved into nothing.

We'd gone from the belly of the beast straight into the shitter.

OUR STORY

Lou

My body awoke in increments. First a twitch of my hand, a tingle in my feet, before lights danced on my eyelids and cotton grew on my tongue. Both felt thick and heavy as my stomach pitched and rolled. My consciousness followed shortly after that—or perhaps not shortly at all—and I felt cold stones beneath my back, hard ridges, dull pain blossoming across my ribs, my temple. Sharper pain at my throat.

Realization trickled in slowly.

Jean Luc had poisoned us. We'd been thrown in prison. We would burn at sunset.

My eyes snapped open at the last.

What time was it?

Staring at the ceiling overhead, I tried to move my fingers, to breathe around the suffocating nausea. I needed to find Reid and Beau. I needed to make sure they were all right—

Only then did I realize two things, like cards flipped over in a game of tarot: warm skin pressed against mine on the right, and wooden bars intersected the ceiling in a cross pattern overhead. Swallowing hard, I turned my head with enormous difficulty. *Thank God.* Reid lay beside me, his face pale but his chest rising and falling deeply.

Wooden bars.

A muffled cough sounded from nearby, and I slammed my eyes shut, listening intently. Footsteps shuffled closer, and what sounded like a door creaked open. After a few more seconds, it clicked shut once more. I opened my eyes carefully this time, peering out through my lashes. The same wooden bars across the ceiling and floor ran perpendicular as well. Smooth and hand planed, they bisected the room and formed a sort of cage around us.

A cage.

Oh god.

Once more, I forced myself to breathe. Though the room beyond remained dark, lit only by a single torch, it didn't look like a dungeon. A colossal table dominated the center of the room—circular and covered in what looked like a map, scraps of parchment, and—and—

Realization didn't trickle now. It rushed in a great flood, and I rolled to my left, away from Reid. We weren't in the castle dungeon at all, but the council room of Chasseur Tower. I would've recognized that table anywhere, except now—instead of charcoal drawings of my mother—portraits of my own face stared back at me. Portraits of Reid. Clearing my throat of bile, I tentatively sat up on my elbows, glancing around the cage. No cots or even chamber pots filled the space. "Beau?" A hoarse whisper, my voice still reverberated too loud in the darkness. "Are you here?"

No one answered.

Cursing quietly, I crawled back to Reid, feeling steadier with each moment. I didn't know why. By all accounts, I too should've been unconscious on the floor, not moving and thinking with relative ease. It made little sense, except . . . I took another deep breath, summoning my magic, both gold and white. Though the golden patterns curled sluggish and confused across the cage, the white ones burst into existence with a vengeance. Their presence soothed the sickness in my body like a balm. My vision cleared, and my stomach settled. The stabbing pain in my temples eased. Of course. *Of course.* These patterns had been gifted by a goddess. They were greater than me, eternal, stronger than my own human flesh and bone.

They'd saved me.

We were going to be fine.

With a triumphant smile, I checked Reid's pupils, his heartbeat, and his breathing. I could sense the poison polluting his blood, could almost *see* it beneath his skin like a black, noxious cloud. Gently, a white pattern coiled around him, illuminating his wan features in a subtle glow. At the brush of my hand, it pulsed and began to sieve the hemlock from his body. The stone around him absorbed the sap like a sponge, returning it to the earth where it belonged. When the last of the poison had gone, the pattern dissolved into white dust, and Reid's eyes fluttered open. I sat back on my heels as he oriented himself with the room. With me.

He reached up to touch a strand of my hair. "You're glowing."

I shrugged, grinning impishly now. "Goddess Divine, you know."

"Such arrogance."

"Such beauty and grace."

He scoffed, sitting up and rubbing his neck. It might've been my imagination, but I thought a rueful grin played on his lips. "Why don't I feel sick?"

I grinned wider. "I *healed* you."

Groaning, he shook his head, and I didn't imagine it now—he definitely smiled. "You really don't know the meaning of humility, do you?"

"And *you* really don't know the meaning of gratitude—"

Footsteps again, quicker this time. We flung ourselves down, feigning unconsciousness, just as the door burst open. "What is it?" a voice asked, unfamiliar and deep.

"I thought I heard someone."

Discomfort seeped into the first's voice. "Should we dose them again?"

The other cleared their throat. "They still *look* incapacitated."

"Philippe will skin us if they die on our watch."

"The hemlock is merely a precaution. The bars will keep them in here." A pause. "Philippe said the wood is . . . special. They harvested it from La Fôret des Yeux."

After another few seconds of anxious silence, they closed the door once more. "Keep your voice down next time," I hissed, poking Reid in the ribs.

His face snapped toward mine in outrage. "I wasn't—"

"I'm joking, Chass."

"Oh." He frowned when I snorted. "Is this really the time to joke?"

"It's *never* the time to joke with us. If we waited until we were out of life-or-death situations, we could only laugh in our graves." Hoisting myself to my feet, I inspected the bars closer. Though clearly wooden, they still felt . . . unnatural. Both made and unmade. The torchlight caught veins of silver in the wood. *The hemlock is merely a precaution. The bars will keep them in here.* I leaned in to sniff them as Reid rose behind.

"What are they?" he asked.

"I don't know. The tree smells like alder, but the timber is . . . metallic? I can't recall any metallic trees in La Fôret des Yeux. Can you?"

"A metallic tree," he echoed slowly.

Our eyes snapped together in dawning horror. "It couldn't be—?"

"It's not—?"

"Oh my god," I breathed, recoiling. The bars felt abruptly cold beneath my touch. Oppressive. "They cut it down. Your Balisarda."

Beside me, Reid closed his eyes in acknowledgment, in defeat, pressing his forehead against the wood. Voice strained, he asked, "How did they even find it?"

"It was along the road. Bas and his cronies called for the Chasseurs when they found us." On a hunch, I pressed a finger to one of the bars. The white patterns dimmed almost instantly in response. No. No, no, *no.* "They would've seen it straightaway—a great tree with silver bark and black fruit and lethal thorns."

"Can you magic us out?"

I released the bar again, returning to the middle of the cage, equal distance from all sides. Though the white patterns flared once more, they floated untethered when they reached the bars, unable to touch them or move past them. Not a promising sign. Closing my eyes, focusing my energy, I sought the lock on the bars—simpler than the one on the treasury door of Chateau le Blanc, made of iron, yet strategically placed outside the magic wood. The harder I tried to reach it, the more the pattern frayed until it disintegrated completely. "Fuck."

To his credit, Reid didn't even flinch. Instead he gripped the bars in earnest, testing their weight. "I can break them."

"You have a broken finger."

That didn't stop him from trying to snap the wood for the next ten minutes. Knuckles bloody, arms shaking, he finally punched the bar with all his might, succeeding in only breaking another finger. When he cocked his fist to strike again, furious, I rolled my eyes and dragged him back to the center of the cage. "Yes, *thank* you. That was helpful."

"What are we going to *do?*" He tore a frustrated hand through his hair. I caught it before he could damage it further. His broken fingers had swelled to twice their normal size, and blood welled dark and purple beneath the skin. He turned away. "This *brilliant* plan of yours has a few holes."

I repressed a scowl, wrapping another pattern around his hand. "I can't control every variable, Reid. At least *this* one didn't involve mustaches and crutches. Now shut it, or I'll give you a real hole to complain about." An empty threat. The Chasseurs had disarmed both of us before throwing us in here.

"Is that supposed to be innuendo? I can never tell with you."

I jerked at the pattern, and it snapped his fingers back into place, shattering my irritation in the process. He winced and wrenched his hand—now completely healed—out of mine. "Thank you," he muttered after another moment. "And . . . sorry." The word sounded pained.

I almost chuckled. Almost. Unfortunately, without irritation to distract me, panic crept back in. I couldn't magic us out of here, and Reid couldn't break the bars physically. Perhaps I could shield us within the cage somehow, like I'd done on the bridge. If they couldn't see us, they couldn't march us to the stake. Even as the thought formed, I knew it was no real solution. We couldn't hide here indefinitely, invisible. Perhaps if they opened the cage to investigate, however . . . "The others will come for us." Whether I spoke to him or myself, I didn't know.

"Philippe won't let Jean Luc within fifty feet of this room."

"It's fortunate, then, that Jean Luc isn't our only ally. Coco will know where we are. She'll bring Claud or Zenna or Blaise, and they'll break us out."

He leveled me with a frank stare. "I don't think you grasp the number of huntsmen living in this tower, Lou."

Leaning forward, I rested my elbows on my knees. "I don't

think *you* grasp that I lived here too."

"You did?" Surprise colored his tone. "How?"

"I was your *wife*. The Archbishop couldn't have separated us, even if he wanted to—which he didn't. He arranged the whole marriage."

"Why?" Now he leaned forward too, his eyes trained on mine. Hungry for information. His earlier words echoed back to me: *Tell me how to remember.* If we were going to die at sunset, Coco's argument hardly applied anymore, did it? Another mad idea formed on the heels of that realization. If Reid remembered, Morgane would too. If the others didn't come for me, *she* would. She'd tear this tower apart brick by brick if she learned the Chasseurs intended to burn me.

Of course, Reid still had a point. She'd never been able to tear it apart before. Stripped of her title, she'd hardly be able to do it now.

"You know why." I shrugged, the thoughts tangling into a helpless knot of confusion. My foot tapped restlessly. "I'm his daughter. He wanted you to protect me."

He scoffed again, an angry sound, and gestured around us. "I've done an excellent job."

"Our friends will come for us, Reid. We have to trust them."

"Where are they, then? Why aren't they here?"

"Hopefully they're out rescuing your mother and brother. That *was* the whole point of the endeavor, if you remember."

His face flushed, and he looked away. "Of course I remember."

The guards flung the door open unexpectedly this time.

In the split second it took for the knob to unlatch, a third idea formed, and impulsively, I transformed into the Maiden as two Chasseurs stepped through. Their eyes flew wide when they saw me. "Oh, please, *messieurs*!" I wrung my hands with a cry, pacing before the bars without touching them. "The witch—she tricked me. I'm a scullery maid upstairs, but while I was washing the linens, I heard a voice singing the most beautiful song." I spoke quicker now, disliking the calculated gleam in the older one's eyes. "I just *had* to follow it, *messieurs*—like some outside force compelled me to do it, like I was in a *trance*—and I didn't wake until I'd unlocked the door and let her go. Please, *please*, let me out while the other still sleeps." Gesturing to Reid on the floor, I allowed my lip to quiver and tears to spill down my cheeks. It was easier to feign distress than I'd anticipated. "I'm so sorry. You can dock my pay, you can relieve me of service, you can *lash* me, but please don't let him hurt me."

Though the younger looked likely to leap to my rescue, the older stilled him with a smile. It wasn't a compassionate one. "Are you finished?"

I sniffed loudly. "Will you not help me?"

In two strides, he crossed the room to the circular table, rifling through the papers there. He pulled one from beneath a crucifix paperweight and held it to the light. Though sketched with rudimentary lines, the drawing portrayed my face—the *Maiden's* face—well enough. My distraught expression fell flat as I leaned against the bars. My form reverted once more. "Good for you."

"Yes," he mused, examining me curiously. "It rather is. It

seems you've inherited your mother's gifts. His Majesty will be pleased to know it."

"That—that's La Dame des Sorcières's daughter?"

"It appears *she* is La Dame des Sorcières now."

The younger's concern vanished instantly, replaced by what looked like awe. Perhaps a touch of fear. Of hunger. "We caught her?"

"You didn't catch anyone." My own fear sharpened my voice. I pushed it down. The others would come. They *would.* "May I inquire as to the time?"

The older replaced the picture before approaching the cage. Though he kept his posture casual, sweat had collected along his upper lip. I made him nervous. *Good.* "You can ask. I won't answer, though. Better to watch you squirm." When I thrust my face at the bars, swift and sudden, he stumbled backward. To his credit, he didn't curse, instead clutching his chest with a low chuckle.

"Shall we inject it?" The younger drew fresh syringes from his coat. "Teach it a lesson?"

"No." The older shook his head and backed from the room. "No, I think we're inflicting just the right amount of torment, don't you?"

The two closed the door behind them with a resounding *click.*

Now Reid pulled *me* away from the bars. "The others will come," he said.

Some time later, a scuffle broke out in the corridor to prove his words. Voices rose to shouts, and the sound of steel against steel rang out in the sweetest harmony. We both launched to our feet, staring at the door and waiting. "This is it." My fingers wrapped around the bars in anticipation. "They're here."

Reid frowned at the high-pitched, feminine voices. Unfamiliar, they didn't belong to Coco or Célie or Zenna or even Seraphine. They sounded like the voices of . . . *children.* "Leave us alone!" one cried, indignant. "Let us go!"

"I don't think so," a Chasseur snarled. "Not this time."

"Your father won't be pleased, Victoire."

"My father can swallow an egg!"

"This isn't *right*," another child cried. "Remove your hands at *once.* That's our *brother* in there, and he hasn't done anything wrong—"

Their voices faded as the Chasseurs dragged them away.

"Violette and Victoire." Reid stared at the door as if sheer will alone might open it. At the intensity of his gaze, I might've believed it too. "They sprang us from the dungeon before La Mascarade les Crânes."

"Follow the memory," I said desperately. If even the king's daughters couldn't enter Chasseur Tower unimpeded, the chances of others doing so had just vanished in a puff of smoke.

"What?"

"You want to remember. This is how." Unable to escape this *hideous* prison, ignorant of the time, of our friends, of our very lives, this suddenly became the most important thing in the world. The most urgent one. He had to remember. If we were going to die at sunset, he had to remember me. The wager, the seduction, the plan—it all fell away in light of this one critical moment. "Follow it forward or backward until you hit a wall. Then *push*."

His mouth twisted grimly. "I—I've *tried*. These past few days—I've done nothing but try to piece it back together."

"Try again. Try harder."

"Lou—"

I crushed his hands in my own. "What if they don't come?"

He clutched mine with equal fervor, his voice low and ferocious as he pulled me closer. "They *will*."

"What if they can't? What if they fail to sneak inside undetected? What if they have to fight? What if Claud can't intervene, or they were captured at the castle, or—" My eyes widened in alarm. "What if they're already dead?"

"Stop, *stop*." He seized my face, bending low to look me directly in the eye. "Breathe. Tell me what to do."

It took a moment to collect myself, to calm my racing heart. He waited patiently, his thumbs kneading my temples. The intimacy of the gesture both agitated and soothed me. At last, I pulled away and said, "After Violette and Victoire rescued you from the dungeons, you returned to Léviathan. Do you remember that?"

He shadowed my footsteps. "Yes. I took a bath."

"And then?"

"And then I"—his face contorted—"I spoke with Claud. I told him about my mother's capture."

Lacing my fingers through his, I shook my head. "You didn't. 'They took her, Lou. They took my mother, and she's not coming back.' That's what you told me."

He stared at me, nonplussed. "What happened next?"

"You tell me." When he said nothing, only stared, I reached up to kiss his cheek. His arms wrapped around my waist. "After I took Bas's memories," I whispered against his skin, "I didn't realize what I'd done until I saw him again. There were these— these gaps in my thoughts. I didn't scrub him away completely, only the romantic moments, but he didn't recognize me at all. I had to find a trigger to help me remember—one memory to spark the rest."

He pulled back to look at me. "But that could be anything."

"For me, it was the moment I met Bas in Soleil et Lune."

"Where did I meet you?"

"Outside of Pan's patisserie." I spun him toward the lock hastily. "Imagine a door. You were blocking the whole thing like a giant asshole, watching Beau's homecoming parade in the street." He turned to scowl at me over his shoulder. "What? You *were*. It was completely discourteous. I tried to move past you"—I imitated the movement—"but there wasn't room for both of us. You ended up turning and nearly breaking my nose with your elbow." When he pivoted to face me in real time, I lifted his elbow and snapped my head back, pantomiming the injury. "Does any of this ring a bell?"

He looked thoroughly miserable. "No."

Fuck. "Maybe this isn't your trigger." I fought to keep my voice even. "It could be something else—like when you chased me in Soleil et Lune, or when we married on the bank of the Doleur, or—or when we had sex for the first time on the rooftop."

His eyes narrowed. "We consummated our relationship on a rooftop?"

I nodded swiftly. Too swiftly. "Soleil et Lune again. It was so cold—try to imagine it. The wind on your bare skin."

When fresh guards popped in to check on us, we ignored them, and after a taunt or two, they left. The clock ticked onward. Every second, it brought us closer to sunset. No other shouts rose from the corridor. No second rescue attempt. Where *were* they? Reid shook his head, scrubbing a hand over his face as he paced. "I don't remember any of this."

"But you—I've seen you as you've started to remember. I've seen the pain in your expression. It *hurts*."

He threw his arms in the air, growing more and more frustrated. Or perhaps flustered. Perhaps both. "Those times have been few and far between, and even then, when I try to push through—to follow the memory—it's like I'm jumping into a void. There's nothing *there*. No wall to break. No door to open or lock to pick or window to smash. The memories are just *gone*."

Wretched tears gathered in my eyes. "The pattern can be reversed."

"What *pattern*?" His voice rose to almost a shout as he whirled to face me, jaw clenched and cheeks flushed. "The entire *world* seems to think I'm a witch—and I'm about to burn at the stake, so it must be true—but I can't—I don't—I've never *seen* a pattern, Lou. Not a single speck of gold or white or fucking indigo. It's like this person you know—he doesn't *exist*. I'm not him. I don't know if I'll ever be him again."

When the tears fell freely down my cheeks, he groaned and wiped them away, moisture glistening in his own eyes. "Please, don't cry. I can't stand your tears. They make me—they make me want to rend the world apart to stop them, and I can't—" He kissed me again, fierce with abandon. "Tell me again. Tell me all of it. I'll remember this time."

Within the hard shield of his arms, I repeated everything. I told him the story of us: the slashed arm and spattered sheet, the book called *La Vie Éphémère*, the trip to the theater and the market, the temple, the troupe, the shop of curiosities. I told him of Modraniht and La Mascarade des Crânes and every moment spent together in between. Every momentous shift in our relationship. The bathtub. The attic. The funeral.

I told him of magic.

He remembered nothing.

Yes, his face twisted occasionally, but upon embracing the pain, chasing the memories, he'd find only smoke and mirrors.

We gradually realized the guards rotated in two-hour shifts—Reid *could* remember that—checking in every half hour. When the last set appeared, I wept openly as Reid cradled me in his lap. "Not long now," one of them had jeered. The other hadn't wanted to linger, however, pulling his companion from the room with a discomfited expression.

Still no one came for us.

I hoped they'd survived. I hoped they'd rescued Madame Labelle and Beau, and I hoped they'd fled the city. I couldn't bear the thought of them watching us burn. Though it wouldn't be their fault, they'd never forgive themselves, and Coco—she'd suffered enough. She'd *lost* enough, as had Madame Labelle and Beau and Célie and even Jean Luc. Perhaps we'd been stupid to dream of something more. Something better. I still hoped they'd found it.

If anyone deserved peace, it was them.

Reid rested his cheek against my hair. "I'm so sorry, Lou." Silence stretched between us, tautly strung like a bow. I waited for it to snap. "I wish—"

"Don't." Slowly, I lifted my head to look at him. My heart contracted at the anguish on his familiar face. I traced the shape of his brows, his nose, his lips, staring at each feature in turn. Deep down, I'd known how this would end all along. I'd sensed it from the moment we'd first met, from the time I'd first glimpsed the Balisarda in his bandolier—two star-crossed lovers brought together by fate or providence. By life and by death. By gods, or perhaps monsters.

We would end with a stake and a match.

Waving my hand, I shielded us from any huntsman's gaze. Magic erupted around us. "Kiss me, Reid."

CONFESSIONAL

Reid

I stared at her tearstained face, chest aching. She didn't need to convince me. I'd do anything she asked. If kissing her would stop another tear from falling, I'd kiss her a thousand times. If we survived the night, I'd kiss away every tear for the rest of her life.

Where you go, I will go. Where you stay, I will stay.

She'd whispered the words to me like a prayer. And I still felt them. I felt each one.

How could I have ever thought this emotion between us wasn't sacred? This connection. What I felt for Lou was visceral and raw and *pure*. It would consume me, if I let it. Consume us both.

But I stared for too long. With fresh tears, she flung her arms around my neck and buried her head in my shoulder. Cursing my mistake, I cradled her face in both hands. Gently. So gently. I tipped her face up to look at me. And then—with deliberate care—I pressed my lips to hers.

I couldn't soothe this ache. I couldn't right this wrong. In all likelihood, we'd both burn at sunset.

But I could hold her.

"I love you," she breathed, lashes fluttering as I brushed soft kisses along her cheeks. Her nose. Her eyelids. "I loved you then, I love you now, and I'll love you after." My lips trailed down her throat. Toward her scar. Her head fell back in response, baring it to me. Completely vulnerable. "Before my mother slit my throat on Modraniht"—the words sounded like a confession—"I thought I'd never see you again. A witch and a witch hunter can't have each other in the afterlife."

I lifted my head then. "I'll find you again, Lou." The words came readily, as if they'd been waiting on the tip of my tongue. A confession of my own. Perhaps I'd said them before. I couldn't remember. It didn't matter. Though I'd lost our past, I refused to lose our future too. Even death wouldn't take it from me. "I promise."

She met my eyes with languorous heat. "I know."

Despite the urgency of our situation—the huntsmen patrolling outside, the sun setting over the city—Lou didn't rush as she slipped her palms into my collar, as she slid them down my back. My own hands moved leisurely to the hem of her shirt. Peeling the fabric from her belly inch by inch, I lowered her to the floor. She stripped my own shirt overhead. Heat pooled between us as she traced the scar on my torso, as I eased down her body. As I tasted each curve. With every breath, every touch—sultry and slow, as if searching—the intensity built. The quiet desperation.

Her fingers curled in my hair.

My tongue stroked her hip.

"You called me your heathen," she said on a sigh, arching and shifting my mouth lower. Lower still.

I would find her again, yes, but we still had this moment. This last breathless hour. "You still are." Sliding her pants down her legs, I flipped her over. Trapping her. Her nails raked against the bars on the floor as I lifted her hips to kiss her. As I stroked her there instead. Her trembling built and built until at last she fractured—biting her hand to stifle the sound—and I hauled her flush against my chest. Pressed her against the bars. Waited with ragged breaths.

Her head fell back on my shoulder, and she snaked an arm around my head. Her lips slanted up to meet mine. "Don't you dare stop."

I plunged into her without another word—unable to speak if I'd tried—snaking one arm around her waist. Heat ripped through my entire body. Overcome, my other arm wrenched her backward, wrapping around her shoulders. Holding her to me. When her fingers braced against my forearm, I couldn't look away from them. Smooth and golden atop my own paler, rougher skin. The simple sight of it tightened my chest to the point of pain. So similar. So different. I couldn't take it. I couldn't *breathe*. She felt—she felt like heaven, but I forced myself to move slowly. Deeply. To savor her. At her moan, I clapped a hand to her mouth. "Shh. They'll hear."

She had other ideas.

Twisting in my arms, she bore me back to the floor and pinned my hands above my head. Leaning low, she bit my lower lip. "Let them."

The last of my breath left in a rush. I fought to remain still as she moved atop me, pressure building until I clenched my eyes shut. Until I couldn't help it. Until my hands descended on her hips, and I coaxed her to move faster, adjusting her angle. Watching as her lips parted, her breath quickened. Though the pressure at my core swelled to physical pain, I gritted my teeth against it. *Not yet.* Her body moved in perfect unison with mine. *She* was perfect. I'd been so foolish to not realize before. So blind.

When she shuddered in release a moment later, I let go too—and in that moment, gold winked in my periphery. Just a flash. There and gone before I could fully register it. A figment of my imagination.

A fragment of memory remained, however. A handful of words. *My* words.

It heeds those who summon it.

Pain wracked my senses at the realization, and I bowed over with it, nearly toppling sideways. Lou's eyes shot open in alarm. "Reid?" She shook me weakly. "What is it? What's wrong?"

"Nothing." The pain passed just as quickly as it'd come. Just as inexplicably. When she remained unconvinced, I shook my head. "I'm fine. Truly."

"A memory?"

"It's gone now."

With a weary sigh, she wrapped her arms around me. I crushed her in my own. We sat like that for several minutes, simply holding each other. Breathing. Her cheek fell heavy upon my shoulder. "You should dress," I murmured at last. "The huntsmen . . ."

"I don't think I can move."

"I can help."

Her arms constricted briefly, but she didn't protest as I slipped first her shirt overhead, then mine. I tugged her pants into place next. She didn't bother lacing them. Instead, she collapsed back against my chest. Her eyelids fluttered. Swallowing hard, I stroked her hair. "Sleep. I'll wake you if anything changes."

"They could still come, you know." She smothered a yawn, her eyes drifting shut. "The others. They could still rescue us."

"They could."

I held her tighter than necessary as she slipped under. The silence seemed to grow and stretch in her wake. The torchlight flickered. "They could," I repeated firmly. To her. To myself. To anyone who would listen.

They could still rescue us.

But they didn't.

A SINGLE SPARK

Reid

When the door opened an hour later, I knew immediately the time had come.

Two huntsmen followed the first, shoulders rigid and Balisardas drawn. Two more filed in after that. Another set. Another. They kept coming until they filled the council room completely. Others waited in the corridor beyond. Dozens of them. Though I scanned their faces in search of Jean Luc, he wasn't there.

Lou startled awake at the footsteps, her eyes still heavy with sleep. "What is—?"

She inhaled sharply as she took in the room, jerking upright. The Chasseur nearest us dropped his eyes to the laces of her trousers. He barked a laugh. Swiftly, I twisted to block her from sight—pulling her to her feet—but she merely leaned around me and flashed a catlike smile. "See something you like?"

Despite her bravado, her eyes remained red-rimmed and puffy. Overly bright. Her hand trembled against my arm.

The huntsman's lip curled. "Hardly."

Sniggering, she surveyed his trousers pointedly. Stepped around me to lace up her own with casual nonchalance. "I doubt that very much."

"You little—" He lunged for the bars, but when Lou met him there, moving with lethal speed, he changed his mind mid-step. Pointing his Balisarda at her face instead, he said, "You'll sing a different tune soon, witch. Your last word will be a scream."

She beckoned him closer. "Why don't you come in here and show me?"

"Lou." Voice low in warning, I pulled at the back of her shirt. She yielded only a step. Around us, the Chasseurs shadowed the movement, pressing closer. "Don't provoke them."

"It's a bit late for that, I think."

"That it is." Philippe's deep rumble preceded him into the chamber. At his appearance, the Chasseurs separated in two waves on either side. Lou's grin turned feral. Dressed in an impeccable suit of royal blue and gold—captain's medal shining on his lapel—he regarded her as a bug beneath his boot. Then he smiled coldly. Bowed. "The sun has set, *ma Dame*. Your funeral pyre awaits."

Lou retreated another step. Her arm brushed mine. Though her smirk remained fixed in place, her gaze darted from the room to the corridor. From Philippe to his Chasseurs. My heart pounded violently as I counted. A score of them in all. An entire squadron. "There are too many."

Lou gestured to the cage's door with a brittle laugh. "Good thing we have a choke point."

I glanced down at her. Her chest rose and fell in shallow breaths. My own limbs shook with adrenaline.

A Chasseur behind us sneered, "You have to come out eventually."

She whipped around to glare at him. "We really don't."

"You'll *starve*."

"Come now. His Majesty won't exhibit such patience. He decreed we would burn this evening." Her grin widened. "It won't reflect well on him if this execution doesn't go to plan, will it? I imagine his denizens are already rather restless about the Hellfire. Rather frightened." She addressed Philippe directly now. "It won't reflect well on *you* either."

On sudden impulse, I added, "Especially after my mother escaped."

Low murmurs broke out across the room at the allegation, and Philippe's face hardened. His expression said everything. Short-lived relief swept through me. They'd saved her. Coco and Jean Luc and Célie—somehow, they'd saved my mother. She was safe. Lou practically cackled now, casting me an appreciative look from the corner of her eye. "She will be apprehended," Philippe said tersely. "Make no mistake."

"You need a win, Phil. You can't afford to wait." Lou waggled her fingers at him. "I think you'll be coming in sooner rather than later."

A different Chasseur—this one younger than the others, practically an initiate—wielded his Balisarda like a crucifix. "You think your magic can harm us, witch?"

"I *think*," she said slowly, "that it won't be terribly difficult to disarm you, *mon petit chou*. I believe you've all met my husband." She hooked her thumb at me. "Youngest Chasseur in the brotherhood. Youngest captain too."

"He is no captain," Philippe said darkly.

Lou arched a brow. "Well. He did kick *your* ass."

I placed a hand on her shoulder, distinctly uncomfortable. Cold sweat trickled down my spine. When she glanced up at me, I shook my head. Near indiscernible. *What are you doing?* I tried to ask.

When she lifted said shoulder—so slight no one else could see—I had my answer. She didn't know. The bluster, the jeers, the threats—all desperate bids for time. For help. For *anything*.

We'd run out of ideas.

"Come on, Phil," she coaxed, and at her words, the faint scent of magic enveloped me. The others smelled it too. Some snarled and stiffened, knuckles tightening on their Balisardas, and looked to Philippe for instruction. Others shifted uneasily. A few, however, studied Lou in fascination as her skin began to glow. "Open the door. Play with me."

Different words resounded in my head. Still her voice, but soft and scared. *Reid.*

I stared at her.

When they open the door, she said, still watching Philippe, *stay close to me. I can't harm them directly with magic, but I can bring this tower down on their heads. It's the best chance we have.* Then— *Do you think Beau escaped too?*

I didn't know, and I couldn't answer. Not as Philippe accepted a bow from the Chasseur next to him. A quiver of blue-tipped arrows. "Not today," he growled, notching one with expert precision. When he pointed it directly at Lou's face, her eyes narrowed. She no longer smiled. "As you've pointed out, I have little time for games. The kingdom awaits."

He loosed the arrow without warning. Before I could vault forward—before I could even shout—it shot toward her with unerring aim. She whirled at the last second, however, faster still, and dropped into a crouch as the shaft lodged into the wall behind us. The Chasseurs there had already moved. They formed ranks on the front and sides of the cage, forming a sort of corral. A bull's-eye.

More bows emerged around us. More arrows.

I hurtled toward her, seizing her hand and dragging her to the back of the cage. I had to do something. *Now.* Lou had spoken of magic, of willing golden cords into being. I focused on them now—on a shield, on a weapon, on a fucking *key.* Anything to escape this cage. No patterns answered. Of course they didn't. I rolled sideways as Philippe launched a second arrow.

"Why bother with the stake?" Snarling, Lou lifted her hand, and the bolt fractured midair. When it fell to our feet, I seized it, spearing a foolish Chasseur who'd tried to creep behind. He fell like a stone. Eyes rolling. Limbs twitching. Lou stared at him in horror. "What the—?"

Philippe notched another arrow. "Hemlock."

This one nearly clipped my shoulder. So close it split the sleeve of my shirt. Lou's eyes blazed at the torn fabric. Her skin pulsed with unnatural light. When she stepped in front of me, her voice rang with deadly calm. *Ethereal* calm. Not a single voice, but many. They reverberated together in a chilling timbre. "You will not touch him."

Immune to the enchantment, Philippe motioned for the others to raise their bows. All twenty of them.

Lou bared her teeth.

At his sharp command, arrows hurtled from two sides. More than twenty. More than *forty*. They cut through the air with lethal precision, but each turned to dust in a three-foot radius around us. They simply—disintegrated. I sensed the barrier in the air rather than saw it. A thin film, like the soap of a bubble. A shield. Lou's fists shook with the effort to maintain it as more arrows flew. "How do I help? Tell me, Lou!"

"A pattern," she said through gritted teeth. "You can strengthen—my magic."

"How?"

"Focus." The air rained thick with arrows now, each Chasseur notching and firing at different times. A constant onslaught. Lou winced at the strike—as if she could *feel* each poisoned tip—and the shield rippled in turn. "You *are* a witch. Accept it. Focus on the outcome, and—the patterns will appear."

But they didn't—they *weren't*—no matter how hard I focused. No gold sparked. I focused harder. On her. On her shield. On the arrow tips tearing it apart. A strange thrumming started in my ears. Voices. Whispers. Not mine or Lou's but *others'*. Still no gold surfaced, however, and I let out a roar of frustration, of *rage*.

"You can do it, Reid," Lou said urgently. "You've done it

before. You can do it again. You just have to—"

She didn't finish her words. Unnoticed, two Chasseurs had succeeded where their fallen brother had not. Hands snaking between the bars—using her shield to their advantage—they seized Lou's shirt and wrenched her backward against the wood.

Her shield vanished instantly.

Shouting her name, I dove forward, prying one's arm from her neck, but sharp pain pierced my thigh. I didn't look. I *couldn't*— not as they plunged a syringe, two syringes, *three*, into Lou's throat simultaneously. Not as her back bowed, her body thrashed, her hands reached for me. "Reid! *Reid!*" Her voice sounded as if from a tunnel. At last, she tore free, catching me as my knees gave out. The Tower shook around us. Her body jolted from impact as she shielded me from arrow after arrow. More than one protruded from her back now. Her arms. Her legs. Still she dragged me toward the cage's door, which Philippe had flung wide.

Hands pulled at our clothing, our hair, flinging us to the council room floor. My vision faded as they descended on Lou like ants. As she collapsed, unmoving, under their syringes. They would kill her before she reached the stake. *Lou.* Clenching my teeth, delirious with pain—with fear—I focused on her dimming skin harder than I'd focused on anything in my life. Hard knees pressed into my back.

She'll die she'll die she'll die

Gold exploded in my vision—and I to my feet—but it was too late.

A quill stabbed into my neck, and the world went dark once more.

I woke to shouts.

To smoke. The scratch of hay at my feet and hard wood at my back. Tight binds on my wrists. Stomach lurching, I pried my eyes open. It took a moment for them to focus. My vision swam.

Torches.

They flickered in the darkness, casting an orange haze over the scene. Over the faces. So many faces. The entire city pressed together in the street below. With a start, I realized I stood above them. *No.* I closed my eyes, pitching forward with a heave. The ropes kept me upright. They held me in place. I didn't stand at all. My eyes snapped open again at the realization.

The stake.

They'd tied me to the stake.

Details rushed in quickly after that, disorienting my senses— the steps of the cathedral, the wooden platform, the warm presence at my back. "Lou." The word slurred on my tongue from the hemlock. My head pounded. I struggled to crane my neck. *"Lou."* Her hair spilled over my shoulder, and her head lolled. She didn't respond. Unconscious. I strained in earnest now, trying to see her, but my body refused to obey. Someone had removed the blue-tipped arrows, at least. They'd clothed her in a clean chemise. Anger fanned as quickly as the drug at that fresh injustice. A Chasseur had undressed her. *Why?*

I glanced down at my own simple shirt and woolen trousers. They'd removed my boots.

Leather doesn't burn.

Blue coats lined the streets, forming a barricade. They kept the crowd at bay. My eyes narrowed, and I blinked slowly, waiting for the scene to sharpen. Philippe stood among them. Jean Luc too. I recognized his black hair. His broad neck and bronze skin. He didn't look at me, his attention focused on Célie, who stood at the front of the crowd with her parents. No Coco. No Beau. No Claud or Blaise or Zenna.

No one.

"Lou." Careful not to move my lips—to keep my voice quiet—I tried to nudge her with my elbow. My arms wouldn't move. "Can you . . . hear me?"

She might've stirred. Just a little.

More shouts sounded as a child broke free of the line. A little girl. She chased a . . . ball. She chased a ball. It rolled to a stop at the base of the platform. "You aren't as tall as I thought you'd be," she mused, peering up at me beneath auburn fringe. Familiar. My eyes fluttered. There were two of her now. No—another child had joined her. A pale boy with shadows in his eyes. He held her hand with a solemn expression. Though I'd never seen it before, I almost recognized his face.

"Do not lose hope, *monsieur*," he whispered.

Another shout. A Chasseur strode forward to shoo them away.

My mouth couldn't properly form the words. "Do I . . . know you?"

"*Le visage de beaucoup*," he said with an unnerving smile. It pitched and rolled with my vision. Garish in the firelight. "*Le visage d'aucun.*" His voice faded as he trailed away.

The face always seen, the face never remembered.

Meaningless words. Nonsensical ones. "Lou," I pleaded, louder now. Desperate. "Wake up. You have to wake up."

She didn't wake.

Imperious laughter beside me. Golden patterns. No—hair. Auguste stepped into my line of vision, a torch in one hand. The flames burned not orange, but black as pitch. Hellfire. Eternal fire. "You're awake. Good."

Behind him, Gaspard Fosse and Achille Altier climbed the platform, the former with an eager smile and the latter with a sickened expression. Achille glanced at me for only a second before murmuring something to Auguste, who scowled and muttered, "It matters not." To me, Auguste added, "Your Balisarda's fruit may not have curbed this wretched fire—not yet—but its wood certainly carried this momentous day." He lifted his hand to catch a strand of Lou's hair. "We had the cage crafted just for the two of you. A bittersweet end, is it not? To be killed by your own blade?"

When I said nothing—only stared at him—he shrugged and examined the torch. "Though I suppose it will not be the Balisarda to deliver the final blow. Perhaps I should be grateful the priests have failed. Now you shall burn eternal."

"As will your . . . city," I managed.

The words cost me. Achille flinched and looked away as I choked on bile, coughed on smoke. He didn't intervene this time. He didn't say a word. How could he? The pyre had been built. He would burn next.

With one last sneer, Auguste turned to address his kingdom.

"My loving people!" He spread his arms wide. His smile wider. The crowd quieted instantly, rapt with attention. "Tonight, at last we eradicate a great evil plaguing our kingdom. Behold—Louise le Blanc, the new and nefarious La Dame des Sorcières, and its *husband*, the man you once knew as Captain Reid Diggory."

Boos and hisses reverberated from the street.

Though I tried to summon my patterns, they shimmered in and out of focus in a golden blur. The hemlock had served its purpose. My stomach rolled. My hands refused to move, to even twitch. They'd coated the ropes. *Concentrate.*

"Yes, behold," Auguste continued, quieter now. He lifted the torch to our faces. "A witch and a witch hunter, fallen in love." Another chuckle. Some in the crowd echoed it. Others did not. "I ask you this, dear subjects—" The torch moved to Achille now, illuminating his dark eyes. They simmered with revulsion as he stared at his king. With rebellion. "Did it save the kingdom? Their *sweeping romance*? Did it unite us, at last?" Now he gestured to the smoke overhead, the charred stone of the church, the blackened and broken buildings that littered the street. Chasseurs stood at every ruin, containing the flames. "No," Auguste whispered, his gaze lingering on their blue coats. "I think not."

When he spoke again, his voice lifted to a shout. "Do not think I haven't heard your whispers! Do not think I haven't seen your doubt! Do not fear that the Peters and Judases among you, the forsakers and betrayers, will continue to roam free! They will not. Ours is a nation divided—we stand at the very precipice—but allow me to elucidate the truth, here and now: we shall not fall."

He seized Lou's chin. "This witch, this *she-devil*, may resemble a woman—your mother, perhaps. Your sister or daughter. It is not them, dear ones. It is not human at all, and it is certainly not capable of *love*. No, this demoness has cursed our kingdom with death and destruction. It has stolen your children and livelihoods, corrupted our once great and noble protector." Dropping her chin, he turned to me, lip curling. I fought for sensation in my hands. *Any* sensation. The golden patterns flickered.

"Reid Diggory." He shook his head. "Traitor. Murderer. *Witch*. You are this kingdom's greatest disappointment."

Behind him, Achille rolled his eyes.

I frowned at the incongruent gesture. The first needle of awareness pierced my palm as Lou's head lifted.

"Lou," I whispered desperately.

It fell once more.

"Hear me and hear me well!" Auguste raised his arms, the torch, with wild passion in his gaze. The people watched with bated breath, following the torch's trajectory hungrily. "I shall not be deceived again, loving people! I have captured this great foe, and with their deaths, we shall alight on a path of victory and salvation. *I* shall lead you through it. The Lyon legacy shall endure!"

Great cries rose from the crowd at the last, evoked by Father Gaspard. They stomped their feet, clapped their hands, even as Philippe and his Chasseurs exchanged cautious glances. Moonbeam hair flashed. Thrusting the torch toward Achille, Auguste said, "Do it, Father. Kill them—kill these creatures you so pity—or you shall join them in Hell."

Though Achille hesitated, he had no choice. His fingers curled slowly around the torch. My frown deepened. They looked . . . straighter than I remembered. The skin younger. Tawny and smooth. When my gaze snapped to his face, his cheeks seemed to broaden, to *move*, the bones inching higher. His eyes lengthened. His nose too. His grizzled beard fell out in pieces, his hair deepened, and his skin—the wrinkles faded as he winked at me.

Then he turned to the king. "You know, *père*," he drawled, the last of Father Achille's features melting with the words, "it's rich of *you* to speak of great disappointments."

Disgusted, Beau shook his head.

I gaped at him.

Beau.

"But you—you were—" Mouth slack, Auguste raked his eyes over his son before his teeth snapped together audibly. A vein bulged in his forehead. "*Magic.*"

The real Father Achille emerged from an alley behind the cathedral. Expression hard, he held the hand of the auburn-haired girl from earlier. With a cheery wave, Claud Deveraux stepped from behind, and—and Coco. She grinned at me in triumph, blowing a kiss. The cut on her palm still bled.

They'd come.

Relief so keen I nearly laughed swept through me.

Lou expelled a ragged breath. "Reid . . ."

The tingling in my palm spread to my fingers. The patterns began to sharpen. "I'm here, Lou. They're all here."

"Sorry we're late, sister mine." Beau darted to her—careful of his torch—as the Chasseurs surged forward, their shouts lost amidst the sudden mayhem. Philippe gestured wildly as those in the crowd fled. As they screamed. As they pulled children away or pressed closer to watch, shoving past the King's Guard, the constabulary. One man even vaulted to the platform with a fierce "Burn the king!" before Philippe caught his collar and threw him back to the ground.

"Maintain the line!" he roared.

When Chasseurs charged the platform, Blaise materialized from beneath it—and Liana and Terrance, Toulouse and Thierry. The werewolves had half-changed, their eyes glowing and their canines lengthening. Dozens more spilled forth from the crowd to join them. Snapping. Snarling. Fully transformed wolves hurtled from every alley. They met the Chasseurs' steel with claws and teeth.

Beau tugged at Lou's ropes with one hand. Hasty. Clumsy. "Turns out Chasseur Tower is a bit of a fortress. Who knew? We couldn't reach you there, but *here*—" His rapid explanation broke off at Lou's moan, and his gaze dropped to the blood on her chemise. The punctures in her arms, her chest. His voice dripped with quiet menace. "What the hell happened to her?"

Though my hands twitched and spasmed, I couldn't readily move them. Couldn't *help*. I strained to regain control. "Poisoned arrows. Hurry—"

"You dare to choose them?" Auguste hissed. Another vein throbbed in his throat. He looked less handsome now. More deranged. "Over your own *father?*"

Before Beau could answer, Philippe finally breached the platform, and Auguste lunged.

It happened in slow motion.

Beau whirled to drive him back, sweeping the torch wide, and a single spark snapped into the air. It hung motionless for a second—for a thousand seconds—before drifting almost lazily to the platform. To the hay.

I could do nothing but watch, horrified, as we went up in flames.

A SHOWER OF LIGHT

Reid

The fire spread quicker than natural, licking up the haystack, our feet, within seconds.

The Hellfire. The eternal flame.

There is no solution, Coco had told me, *fruit or otherwise.*

How do you know?

Because the fire stemmed from my grief. And there is no solution for grief. Only time.

Despite the sweltering heat, cold dread seized me. Shouting Lou's name, I twisted toward her, determined to shield her. To protect her from the inevitable. I would not give up. I would not cede. If we could free ourselves, we could jump to safety—

Panicked, Philippe crashed into Auguste, knocking him from the platform. A flame caught the king's sleeve. It engulfed him instantaneously, and he fell to the ground—writhing, shrieking—as Philippe swiftly stripped the king of his lion's cloak, attempted to strip him of his burning shirt. But the fabric had already melted into his skin. Philippe recoiled instantly, recognizing the battle lost. "Oliana!" Auguste flung a hand toward his wife, who stood beside the platform. Without a word, she turned and entered the church. Blanching at the havoc on the street, Father Gaspard followed quickly behind.

Philippe crushed Auguste's hand underfoot as he too fled.

"Get . . . out of here." Barely audible, Lou jerked her head toward Beau. He still grappled with the rope, grimacing against the flames. They curled up his boots. His leather boots. "*Leave.*"

"No," he snarled.

The heat was all-consuming now. The pain. Below us, Auguste's shrieks stopped abruptly. His limbs stilled. Skin and flesh melting into bone. With empty eyes, he stared at his burning city forevermore.

The flames danced on his corpse.

"I can't—I can't extinguish them." Adrenaline roared through my ears, deadening Lou's voice. Though her face contorted with concentration, I could scarcely see through the smoke, could scarcely *breathe*. The fire raged on. It crept from the alleys, the hidden doors, the cracks and the crannies as Chasseurs left their posts. It snaked up drainpipes. It slithered through windows. Devouring the city inch by inch. Homes. Shops. People.

A keen cry sounded from the street.

Coco.

She fought to reach us, knives flashing, plunging into anyone foolish enough to block her path. The crowd compounded to a mob around her. Bodies collided. Women pulled their children from the street, shrieking and pounding on the nearest doors, while foolish men attempted to enter the fray.

"The magic—it's too—" Lou shuddered on a cough, still immersed in her patterns, as Coco finally broke through the crowd. "It isn't *mine*."

Coco circled the platform frantically, seeking a gap in the flames. Her cries were lost amidst the tumult.

"I've almost"—Beau's fingers scrabbled at the ropes—"got them."

Lou's voice rose to a scream now. It tore from her throat, raw and vicious. Terrified. "It's too late—"

"Just *leave*, brother!" My own voice joined hers. "GO!"

The fire climbed up our legs now. Up his. It consumed all in its path: rope, clothing, *skin*. Without the stake to support him, Beau fell against us. "I'm *not* leaving you." But his knees gave out with the words, and he crumpled. His face contorted as he bellowed in pain, as blisters ruptured his throat, his face.

"Yes, you are," Lou said through gritted teeth. She looked to Coco with tears in her eyes. "Take care of each other."

The ropes at her ankles had disintegrated, and she lifted a leg, kicking him squarely in the chest. He stumbled backward from the platform—a pillar of flame—and fell straight into Coco's arms.

Coco stared at him in horror.

"No." She shook her head frantically, dropping to the snow. Packing it over his skin. He thrashed helplessly. "Beau. Beau, look at me—" Tendrils curled up her arms now, but she ignored them. My own muscles jerked and twitched as I watched, helpless. The snow did nothing to suppress the flame. There was no escape from this, no extinguishant, no magic to help us now. Not even Lou's. "No, no, *no*. Please, Beau. *Beau*."

"I'm so sorry, Reid," Lou gasped. "I can't stop it, but I can—I can help—" She twisted to look in my eyes. "I love you. Find peace."

Find peace.

The words snapped and cracked between us, out of place. Surely I'd misheard her. They couldn't be right. Because here—burning in a lake of black fire—there could be no peace. Not for her. Not for me. Not as our bones melted and our skin peeled.

She flexed her hand.

The ropes on my wrists snapped in response, and I flew from the platform in a rush of hot air. Landing hard on the street, I twisted to look at her. But I could no longer see, no longer *hear*. Pain stole my senses, and my golden patterns scattered into dust, settling as a veil over the scene.

Except it wasn't *this* scene any longer.

The mob dimmed amidst the gold, replaced by another crowd. The black fire vanished. A different stake pierced the sky, and a different witch writhed against it. Her cornsilk hair burned first. I stood before the platform, hands clasped, with the Archbishop beside me. A Balisarda gleamed at my chest.

Witch killer witch killer witch killer

The memory dissipated before I could fully grasp it.

But the pain—the excruciating *heat*—it vanished abruptly as new magic burst around us. Its scent overpowered the smoke.

The cooked flesh. Though flames still devoured my clothing, blistered my skin, I felt only cold snow. Beside me, Beau's eyes snapped open. He settled in Coco's arms.

Then Lou began to scream.

She screamed, and she screamed until her throat should've torn open at the sound. Until her heart should've stopped. The agony on her face shone clear as she writhed. Like her pain had tripled. Quadrupled.

Understanding dawned.

I struggled to my feet.

She'd taken our pain from us. It was all she could do.

"*Lou.*" Coco sobbed her name, rocking Beau as they burned. Pleading. When her tears fell, they hissed against his face. Instead of stoking the fire, however, the drops quenched it. His skin sizzled. *Healed.* Thunder rumbled overhead. "Don't do this, Lou, *please*—"

Another memory resurfaced without warning. Stronger than the first. I fell to my knees once more.

When? When did you know?

During the witch burning. When—when Lou had her fit. Everyone thought Lou was seizing, but I saw her. I smelled the magic.

A deeper pain than fire erupted at the memory, even as Coco's tears thickened. As the first drops of rain fell—Coco's rain. She'd said all along her grief had sparked this fire. Now it seemed her love would soothe it. Wherever the drops touched, the ground sputtered and steamed. The flames quelled. But Lou's screams—they continued. They cleaved me in two. Clutching my head, I pitched forward. The rain soaked my shirt. My skin.

My blisters closed.

She was burning, Reid. I don't know how, but she took away that witch's pain. She gave it to herself.

But I'd already known. In the deepest part of me, I'd drawn the connection. I'd recognized Lou's selflessness, even then. Her sacrifice. I'd been unable to admit it at the time. Unable to confront the truth, even as I'd nursed my dying wife back to health. Because she *had* almost died to save another.

In that moment, I'd fallen in love with her.

The pain in my head built to a crescendo at the realization. I couldn't bear it. Incoherent—aching, roaring—I clawed at my hair. Tore at my face. Vaguely, I heard the platform collapse, felt urgent hands on my shoulders. "Reid! *Reid!*" But Beau's and Coco's shouts couldn't pierce the turmoil of my mind. Darkness edged my vision. Unconsciousness loomed. The ground rose up to meet me.

A pattern shimmered into existence.

At first look, it appeared gold, winding from my chest to the wreckage of the platform. To where wood and smoke and fire had engulfed Lou. When I lifted a trembling hand, however, I realized I'd been wrong. The cord glimmered with dimension.

The blue of my coat. The white of snowflakes. The red of blood in a blacksmith's shop.

A hundred more colors—*memories*—all twining together, pressed into a single strand.

I pulled it.

Energy pulsed outward in a wave, and I collapsed beneath its weight, ears ringing with silence. *Bleeding* with it.

A high-pitched, primal scream shattered the street.

Not from Lou. Not from Coco. Struggling to lift my head—to see through the hysterical crowd, the pouring rain—I recognized the pale features and moonbeam hair of Morgane le Blanc. She too had crumpled. Those nearest her bolted when they saw her, slipping in the melted snow. The mud. Weeping and crying out for loved ones. Their faces smeared with soot.

Josephine crouched beside Morgane, her brow furrowed in confusion.

Behind them, Nicholina smiled.

I hurtled toward the platform without a backward glance. My voice broke on Lou's name. I remembered her. I *remembered.* The Doleur, the attic, the rooftop—the entire story she'd woven in the wooden cage. It'd all been true. It'd all been *real.*

I'll find you again, I'd told her.

She'd taken the promise to heart. She hadn't given up on me. Not when I'd insulted her, threatened her, envisioned a thousand different ways to kill her. I'd think of a thousand others to atone. I'd never leave her again. My voice gained strength. It gained hope. "Lou! LOU!"

She still didn't answer. With the fire at last extinguished by Coco's rain, the wreckage smoked gently. Diving into it, I tore through the charred boards, the ash, the remnants of the stake. Beau and Coco followed hot on my heels. "Where are you?" I asked under my breath, wresting aside plank after plank. "Come on. Where *are* you?"

Pale hands joined mine as I searched. Célie. Darker ones. Jean Luc. They met my gaze with determined expressions and terse nods. They didn't falter, even as my own body shook. *Please, please, please—*

When a board to my right shifted, untouched, I wrenched it free. She had to be here. She *had* to be—

Lou exploded upward in a shower of light.

THE FINAL BATTLE

Lou

Power flooded my limbs and lungs, and I burned not with fire, but light. It shone through my bloody chemise, through the wounds across my body, bursting outward in blinding rays of magic. Though Coco's rain still fell thick and heavy around us, the drops didn't soak me as the others—no, my skin and hair absorbed each one, and they healed me, strengthened me, soothed my aching heart. They tasted of hope. Of *love*.

I found her tearstained face amidst the wreckage, grinning and descending gently beside her.

She'd done it. Though the city still smoked around us, undulating softly—though she would *always* grieve for Ansel—the black fire had gone. She'd conquered it. She'd conquered *herself*.

Returning my grin, she clasped Beau's hand and nodded.

"Lou." Still crouched with a board in his hand, Reid looked up at me, his eyes brimming with tears. With love and relief and— and *recognition*. Awareness. It sparked between us like a living thing, as shining and bright as a pattern. He rose slowly to his feet. We stared at each other for a long moment.

"You found me," I whispered.

"I promised."

We moved at the same time, each staggering toward the other, our limbs tangling until I couldn't tell where his ended and mine began. Breathless, laughing, he swept me into the air, and we whirled round and round again. I couldn't stop kissing his smile. His cheeks. His nose. He didn't protest, instead laughing louder, tipping his face toward the sky. The smoke cleared as Coco watched us—the rain clouds too—until only a crystal winter night remained. For the first time in weeks, the stars glittered overhead. The waning moon reigned supreme.

The beginning of the end.

When at last Reid placed me on my feet, I punched his shoulder. "You absolute *ass*. How *could* you?" I seized his face between my hands, near feverish with laughter. "Why didn't you give me that sticky bun?"

His own cheeks remained flushed, his smile wide. "Because it wasn't *yours*."

A fresh wave of screams sounded behind us, and we turned simultaneously, our giddiness puncturing slightly. The scene returned in degrees. Chasseurs and loup garou still battled in the street—soaked to the skin, bleeding—while pedestrians fled or fought. Some sobbed and clung to fallen loved ones in the mud. Others pounded relentlessly on shop doors, seeking shelter for the injured. For themselves.

On either side of the street, witches had risen, barring all exits.

I recognized some of them from the Chateau, others from the blood camp. More of them than I'd ever believed existed. They must've crawled forth from every inch of the kingdom—perhaps the world. My skin dimmed as gooseflesh rose.

Worse still—across the street, Morgane climbed to her feet.

"Here." Célie slung her bag from her shoulder and upended it. Reid's bandolier spilled across the ground. His knives and seeds. Her own injection. Coco and Beau swooped to retrieve their daggers, and I followed suit, my magic pulsing with eagerness. It sensed the danger here. It yearned to attack, to *protect*, as Morgane squared her shoulders. As she lifted her chin and met my gaze.

Though the sounds of clanging steel and snapping teeth should've muted her voice, I still heard it crystal clear. Like she stood right beside me. "Hello, Daughter."

My own words rose calmly. "Hello, Mother."

I glanced at Reid's bare feet. His sodden chest. My own pitiful chemise. Even the others wore only woolen garments—and Célie a *gown*, at that—leaving them woefully vulnerable to attack. Perhaps not from magic, but steel could cut just as deep. I took a deep breath. We couldn't fight like this. Not yet.

Waving my hand, I scanned the white web of patterns for something more suitable, something defensive, something like—something like a *web*. I grinned anew as the idea took hold. Nicholina had spoken of a spider deep within La Fôret des Yeux. L'Enchanteresse, a cannibalistic creature with silk among the lightest and strongest materials in the natural world.

I searched for the spiders now, spreading my awareness north, east, toward the ancient trees around the city. Their homes. The patterns didn't follow, however, instead plunging directly into the street. I hesitated. Trees didn't live below. Perhaps—perhaps the spiders had burrowed underground for winter. I didn't have time to speculate, however. Not with Morgane across the street, flanked on either side by Josephine and Nicholina. Not with witches closing in.

With another deep breath, I pulled six identical cords. The patterns stretched width-wise until myriad fibers appeared—as thin as webs—and knit themselves tightly into armor.

Dark and fitted, light and flexible, it replaced our clothing in a burst of glittering dust.

Somewhere below, six spiders withered.

Morgane clapped her hands in applause. "How clever you are, darling. How prettily you wear my magic. At last, you suit the company you keep—thieves, all."

"I've stolen nothing from you, *maman*."

"You have stolen *everything*." Her emerald eyes glittered like broken glass. Jagged and sharp. The emotion within them transcended malice into raw, unadulterated hatred. "But do not question—I am here to reclaim what is mine, and I will butcher every last man, woman, and child who attempts to keep it from me." She jerked her chin, and the witches advanced in earnest. "Kill them all."

A mighty roar shook the city in response, and a dark wing shadowed the moon.

Zenna landed beside me a second later. The cobblestones cracked beneath the sheer weight of her. When she snorted derisively, flame spewed forth. Witch, werewolf, and huntsman alike leapt from its path. From atop Zenna's back—dressed in armor of her own—Seraphine drew an ancient longsword.

I couldn't help it. I laughed in delight.

Coco had told me of Toulouse's and Thierry's torture. She'd told me of Zenna's promise to *eat* my mother. Leaning around Zenna's haunch now, I asked her, "What about dragons?"

Zenna punctuated the challenge with a fresh bout of flame.

Snarling with rage, Morgane scrambled backward as Chasseurs and witches charged. Balisardas flashed. Magic erupted. Zenna snorted again, launching into the air, plucking them from the street one by one and—

And eating them.

"Oh, that is *disgusting*," Beau said, grimacing. "The indigestion alone—"

Before he could finish, Morgane brought her palms together one last time. The sharp scent of magic flared.

The ground trembled in answer.

All across the fray, people fought to keep their footing. Even Philippe paused, staggering slightly, with his Balisarda an inch from Terrance's lupine throat. Reid tensed. His eyes narrowed. Then—

"Get down!" He tackled me from the platform, and we landed hard, whirling as branches shot forth from the very earth, splintering the church steps. They didn't stop there. Dozens more surfaced rapidly, larger than life, growing trunks and roots, shattering the beautiful stained-glass windows. Growing *through* them. Stone rained down on our heads, forcing us to scatter into the crowd. I immediately lost sight of Coco and Beau, Célie and Jean Luc. Too short, too slight, I couldn't navigate the tide of people. I couldn't tell friend from foe.

Only Reid's hand in mine kept a loup garou from knocking me back to the ground.

The trees kept growing. They crushed spires and mangled arches until Cathédral Saint-Cécile d'Cesarine crumbled in ruin. Until the forest reclaimed it.

That explained the spiders.

But it didn't make *sense*. The forest belonged to *Claud*, not Morgane. How had she—?

The trees have mobilized, and we shall follow, striking hard and true.

The trees around the Chateau. My stomach twisted. She'd brought her own soldiers.

They didn't stop there, however, fracturing the street now, their branches catching hair and cloaks as they stretched toward the sky. The woman next to me screamed as one hooked her skirt. As it lifted her higher and higher until the fabric tore. The branch snapped.

She plummeted toward the street.

My magic darted wildly. Panicked, I fought to calm it, to concentrate, but the woman fell too quickly—

Scant seconds before she hit the ground, the tree seemed to shudder. I stared incredulously as Claud Deveraux strolled into view. As he whistled a merry tune. As the tree itself *bent*—creaking and groaning—and its branches curled to catch the woman midair. To cradle her in a macabre embrace.

Claud winked at me. "Fancy meeting you here, poppet. How did you like my sister?"

I choked on a laugh while the woman shrieked, contorting her limbs to escape the tree. It had ceased moving. "I thought—I thought you couldn't intervene?" And if not— "Where have you *been* all this time?"

He clicked his tongue playfully. His mere presence seemed to act as a shield; the crush of bodies waned around us, parted, as if all instinctively knew to change direction. "Tut, tut, Louise," he said, "or I shall think you self-absorbed. Though it pains me to admit, you and your friends manage quite well without me, and I have an entire realm of the natural world to govern."

"Like *hell* we can." Bemused, I helped Reid untangle the woman from the tree. Self-absorbed. *Pfft.* "But *again*, I thought you couldn't—"

"Oh, you thought correctly, peach." Though Claud still smiled, the air around us thickened with the scent of rot. Of decay. Poisonous toadstools split open at his feet. The loup garou nearest us swelled with rage, snarling as if possessed, and attacked with newfound savagery. "I am not intervening. Indeed, I am governing said realm as we speak." His smile darkened at the last, and he turned to search the street. His eyes flashed catlike. "And defending it from trespass."

I knew without asking for whom he searched.

And Morgane had called *me* a thief.

"How does she control them?" Reid yielded a step as the woman shoved him and fled up the street, still screaming hysterically. "The trees?"

"They loved her once too."

With those forbidding words, Claud's frame nearly doubled in size, and he transformed in full: enormous stag antlers burst from his head. Cloven hooves shredded his shoes. And the trees—they bowed to him as he advanced up the street as the Woodwose.

Their king.

Their god.

"Wait!"

He paused at my shout, arching a brow over his shoulder. The gesture seemed too human on his animalistic features now. "My mother," I continued with both anticipation and dread. "What will you do to her?"

Those yellow eyes blinked. His voice rumbled deep, like that of a bear's roar. "She has invaded my realm. My being. I will punish her."

Punish her.

He turned and disappeared in the trees without another word. Too late, I realized I should follow. He'd left little doubt of his intention—he was a god, and she had exploited him. Though he'd warned her—though the Triple Goddess herself had stripped her of power—she hadn't listened. She hadn't surrendered. My battle had become their battle. Claud would lead me straight to Morgane, and together, we could—

Reid pulled me in the opposite direction, where the crowd flowed thickest. "We need to evacuate these people."

"What? No!" I shook my head, but without Claud to protect us, the crush resumed. "No, we need to find Morgane—"

"Look around, Lou." He didn't dare let go of my hand, even as those nearest us fled a Dame Rouge who'd torn the beating heart from a man's chest. Though they hammered against shop windows—pleading for entry—the merchants barred their doors. On both ends of the street, blood witches had cut open their arms. Where their blood spilled, black vines twisted skyward, forming a thick hedge. A barricade. "These people—they have nowhere to run. They're *innocent*. You heard Morgane. She won't stop until all of them are dead."

"But I—"

"Claud is a *god*. If he intends to kill Morgane, he'll kill her. We have to mitigate the casualties."

My magic pulsed beneath my skin, urging me to listen. To go with him. He was right. Yes. Of course, he was right.

With one last anxious glance at Claud's back, I nodded, and we sprinted toward Father Achille and Gabrielle, Etienne's sister, who'd been trapped in a circle of vines. A blood witch coaxed the thorns tighter around them. Behind, Célie rushed Violette and Victoire to safety in the nearest shop—a patisserie manned by none other than Johannes Pan.

At Gabrielle's cry, he burst into the street with a rolling pin, shouting and swinging it wildly. It struck the blood witch's head with a sickening crunch. When she crumpled, her thorns shriveled, and Father Achille and Gaby leapt free.

"Come, come!" Pan ushered Gaby toward him while Reid, Jean Luc, and Father Achille converged.

Other witches did too, their eyes intent on the three little girls.

It seemed they still planned to exterminate the Lyon line, regardless of Auguste.

Drawing a deep breath, I plucked a pattern, and it shimmered and expanded like a film over the patisserie. The same protection existed over Chateau le Blanc, over the door to the castle's treasury. It was a piece of my magic itself—a piece of all Dames des Sorcières who'd come before me. As it left my body, the white patterns dimmed. Just a bit. My connection to them weakened. A worthy sacrifice.

None would enter the patisserie but those I permitted. I caught Gaby's hand as she passed, squeezing fiercely. "Stay inside," I told her. My eyes met those of Violette and Victoire. Beau's sisters. Reid's half sisters. "All of you."

Though Gaby and Violette nodded fervently, I didn't like the stubborn set of Victoire's chin. Célie pushed all three into the shop before ushering a hysterical couple in after them.

"Cut down the barricades!" Father Achille pointed to the thorn hedges. A handful of Chasseurs fought to drive the witches back. "Anyone with a blade!"

"We *have* no blades," a panicked man said, pushing forward.

Reid thrust his Balisarda at him in answer. "You do now. *Go.*" When more men clambered forward, hands outstretched, Reid tore another knife from his bandolier. Another and another until none remained.

"What are you doing?" I asked in alarm.

Voice grim, he lifted his hands. "I am a weapon."

Each man turned and fled toward the vines, hacking at the thorns with all their might.

Without pause, Reid pointed at the neighboring shops. To Jean Luc, he said, "Break down the doors. Get these people inside every building. Lou and I will follow behind to enchant them locked—"

He broke off as Philippe and a score of huntsmen blasted through the witches' line, slaughtering them with brutal efficiency. Bite wounds bled freely on his leg. Leveling his Balisarda at Reid and me, he snarled, "Kill them."

I lifted my own knife and stepped in front of Reid. We *were* weapons, yes—our magic sharper than any blade—but only as last resorts. If he'd taught me anything, it was not to cut myself. He wouldn't either. Before I could strike at Philippe, however, Jean Luc planted his feet before both of us. To my surprise, his handful of Chasseurs did too. "Don't be stupid, Philippe. These people are not our enemies."

Philippe's eyes bulged. "They're *witches.*"

"They're *helping* us," another Chasseur snapped. I didn't recognize him. I didn't care. "Open your eyes before you kill us all. Do your duty."

"Protect the kingdom," the one beside him added.

"Children." Achille pushed roughly between them. "We don't

have time for this, nor the forces to stand divided. Those with Balisardas *must* strike against our attackers."

"He's right." Reid nodded, already scanning the street beyond. Huntsmen fought witch, fought werewolf, while both sides fought each other. Pandemonium reigned. "Chasseurs, if you cannot kill, aim for their hands. Dames Blanches cannot cast accurately without dexterity—cut them off at the wrist, but do not draw blood from a Dame Rouge under any circumstance. Unless dead, their blood will maim you."

"How do we tell the difference?" the first Chasseur asked.

"Dames Rouges are heavily scarred. Strike quickly, and strike true. Leave the werewolves, and leave the trees."

"*Leave* the—?" Philippe's face flushed puce. He jerked his head back and forth. "We will not. Chasseurs—to me. Do not listen to these heretics. I am your captain, and we *will* strike fast and true." To prove his point, he stabbed his Balisarda into the heart of the nearest tree. Claud's roar reverberated from somewhere beyond the cathedral. Face twisting in delight, Philippe thrust deeper. "Cut them down! All of them! Tree, werewolf, and witch alike!"

"*No.*" I pushed past Jean Luc as Philippe's huntsmen obeyed, goring the trees with brutal efficiency. Roots snapped upward like the crack of the whip to ensnare them. "No, *stop*—"

But agonized shouts soon sounded from the hedges, and I turned to see witches impaling men on the thorns. *Shit.*

Reid tore after them without hesitation. His hands moved in the air, searching, pulling, as fresh magic burst around us. Three of the witches screamed in response, and fresh burns licked up

Reid's arms. But he couldn't save the men. Without Balisardas, each person here stood vulnerable—including Reid.

The fourth witch clenched her fist, and Reid stumbled, clutching his chest.

Shit, shit, *shit.*

My feet moved instinctively. Seizing the Balisarda from a trapped Chasseur, I sprinted toward him. Veins bulged in his neck, his face. His hands moved instinctively to his bandolier for a knife. They came away with only seeds. Tossing them aside, he collapsed on his hands and knees.

I hurled the Balisarda straight through the witch's forehead.

Zenna took care of the rest. Her jaws snapped viciously as she swooped low, incinerating witch and thorn alike. When the flame abated, I wrenched the Balisarda from the witch's skull and shoved it at Reid. "*I* am a weapon." Panting, I imitated his stupid voice. Breathless laughter rose. I didn't fight it, despite the gruesome circumstances. Despite the charred witches at our feet. I'd never fight laughter again. Not for their sake. "The world shall *tremble* and *fear me*—"

"Shut"—his own voice broke on a gasp of laughter—"up."

I dragged him to his feet. "My enemies shall *rue* the day they ever dared to challenge—"

"I'm fine." He shook his head as if to clear it. "Go help the others."

"I am." Pressing a hard kiss to his lips, I shoved him back toward the patisserie. "I'm helping them by helping *you*, you great selfless prick. If you give that Balisarda away again, I'll make you swallow it. Consider chivalry dead."

He huffed another laugh as we rejoined the fray.

The next moments passed in a blur of magic and blood. Following Reid's instruction, free huntsmen hacked at witches' hands, while those trapped in Claud's trees hacked at roots. Father Achille led a party of able-bodied men and women to the nearest smithy for weapons. Those unable to fight followed Célie into boucheries and confiseries, any shop that would open its doors. Jean Luc and Reid kicked down the rest. I followed behind, feeding my magic into each lock.

The witches were undaunted. I felt them attack each door, each window, their patterns hissing and striking like snakes against my magic. They taunted those within—taunted *me*—whispering the ways they would kill them. Reid and Jean Luc hacked their way through them, leaving a trail of bodies behind.

Halfway down the street, Reid noticed my pale face, and his brows furrowed. I only shrugged and continued. It didn't matter. Fewer allies littered the ground than foes. Though Zenna couldn't breathe fire freely—not without roasting us in the process—she snatched witch after witch from the street. When they backed Coco and Toulouse into a corner, she plucked the two free. When they pursued Beau and Thierry—the former shouting for Coco at the top of his lungs—Seraphine cut them down from above. We'd prepared for this. Blaise and his pack, Troupe de Fortune, even Jean Luc and his Chasseurs—all around, they exacted their vengeance. Liana and Terrance gnawed hands from wrists while Toulouse and Thierry injected a trio of witches with hemlock.

Still, overwhelming unease crept down my spine. It near paralyzed me.

Morgane had vanished without a trace.

As the battle spread down the streets, I searched for her. For Claud. Any sign of horn or moonbeam hair. He could've disposed of her already, but for some strange reason, I didn't think so. The air in the city remained foul with the stench of magic and rot. Where Balisardas had pierced the trees, dark sap wept like blood. Fungi crept up the front of homes. Of the castle itself. The entire atmosphere felt charged—*angry*—and continued to build.

More than once, I swore I heard Morgane's laughter. My unease deepened to dread.

For his part, Reid had procured three more Balisardas—from where, I didn't know—for Gaby, Violette, and Victoire, who cropped up every few minutes, hissing and spitting and bloody in their pursuit of those who pursued them. He and Beau had exploded, near apoplectic with rage, on the third time.

"They are trying to *kill* you!" Beau had torn open the door of Soleil et Lune and thrust them inside. "I swear to God, I will tie you to those seats—"

"They're trying to kill *you* too," Victoire had snarled as Reid slammed the door behind. She'd pounded on the door. "Let us out! Let us fight!"

Another bout of laughter drifted on the wind, and I whirled, searching. The hair rose on my neck. I hadn't imagined it that time. She'd sounded close enough to touch. In proof of my point, Reid frowned at the theater door. "What was that?"

"Lock them in."

"What?" His gaze snapped to mine. Sensing my intent, he stepped forward, but Victoire flung the door open once more. He hesitated. "Lou, what are you—where are you *going?*"

I didn't answer, already racing down the street, ignoring his shouts. It didn't matter how many times Beau interceded, how many people Reid led to safety. No one was safe here, not truly—not with Morgane still pulling the strings. Every move she'd ever made had been calculated. Tonight was no different. She'd *known* Claud and Zenna would join us—she'd known about the loup garou too—and she would've taken offensive action. The witches would keep coming. They wouldn't stop until they'd finished this, destroying the Crown, the Church, their persecutors at last. But witches alone couldn't down a dragon. They couldn't kill a *god.*

No, these witches were the defense, not the offense.

And this was undoubtedly a trap.

"Where are you?" I slid down a side street, following a flash of moonbeam hair ahead. Reid's voice faded behind. "I thought you didn't want to play anymore? Come out. Come out and face me, *maman.* That's what you want, isn't it? Just the two of us?"

Another street. Another. I gripped my dagger in one hand, white patterns coiling and twisting through cobblestones, trash bins, wooden doors and broken windows and herb gardens. She laughed again. When I darted after the sound—bursting into Brindelle Park—a hand snaked out to catch mine.

I nearly stabbed Manon straight in the eye.

"She isn't here, Louise." Voice quiet, she didn't meet my gaze, hers darting all around us. Twin gashes slashed each cheek.

Though one bled freely—fresh—the other looked older. It'd started to scab. She backed away, pulling her clammy hand from mine and melting into the shadows. "You must turn back."

"What are you doing here? Shouldn't you be with our *sisters*?"

She hesitated at the bitter note in my voice. Quieter still, she said, "You speak as if we have a choice."

"Where is she? Tell me, Manon."

"She'll kill us." When she brushed the healing wound with her fingertips, I understood. Though Manon hadn't revealed our identities to Morgane, she *had* let thieves escape. Backing away once more, Manon touched her other cheek now. The one with fresh blood. "Or your huntsmen will."

My stomach sank. Conscious of every step, every sound, I followed after her, extending a hand. A lifeline. "Come with me. I won't let anyone hurt you."

She only shook her head. "The dragon will fall, but still we're outmatched. Morgane knows this. Don't allow her to manipulate the—"

A branch snapped behind us. I jumped, slashing my knife backward, but Coco's voice rose in a shout. She lifted her hands wildly. "It's me! It's only me! What's going on? I saw you tearing past earlier. Is it Reid? Is it *Beau*? I lost track of him, and—"

"They're both fine." I clutched my chest with insidious relief. "It's Manon. She said—she said that—"

But when I turned to face her once more, she wasn't there. She'd vanished.

In her place stood Josephine and Nicholina.

WHEN A GOD INTERVENES

Lou

It happened too quickly to stop. Snarling, Coco pulled me behind a tree, slashing open her arm in the same movement. The instant my back touched the trunk, I registered two things: first, a warm, wet substance coated the bark—mixed with stinging nettles—and second, it melted my armor instantly.

Then came pain. *Violent* pain.

It ripped through my limbs as serrated branches pierced my hands and my feet, lifting me in the air like Jesus to the cross. Though I tried to scream for Claud, for Zenna, for *anyone*, thorns shot forth across my mouth. They lacerated my lips, my cheeks, gagging me with poisoned tips. Helplessly, I thrashed, but the spikes and thorns bit deeper.

Though Coco reached for me in horror, Nicholina pounced, giggling when Coco sprayed blood across her face—then punching her fist into Coco's rib cage. No. *Through* it. Straight toward her heart. Choking on a gasp, Coco clawed at Nicholina's wrist, her eyes wide and unseeing.

When Nicholina squeezed, she fell frighteningly still.

"Nicholina." Josephine's deep voice cut through the night. "Enough."

Nicholina glanced back at her mistress, laughter fading. They held gazes for a second too long before—reluctantly—Nicholina withdrew her hand from Coco's chest cavity. The latter's eyes rolled, and she collapsed, unconscious, to the ground. "Nasty," Nicholina muttered.

Josephine didn't react. She only stared at me. No longer impassive, she lifted her chin with the chilling words, "Bring me her heart."

If Nicholina hesitated—if a shadow crossed her expression— the movement was near indiscernible. I could do nothing but watch, delirious with pain, as she took a single step in my direction. Two. Three. My heart pounded savagely, pumping more of Josephine's blood through my veins. More poison. I wouldn't close my eyes. She would see her reflection in their depths. She would *see* this monster she'd become, this perversion of the person she'd once been: her own features, her *son's* features, twisted into something sick and wrong. Four steps now. Coco's blood still dripped from her hand. It scorched the skin there.

She ignored it.

On the fifth step, however, her eyes flicked to the Doleur. It wound behind us though the city, the river where the Archbishop had almost drowned me, where Reid and I had spoken our vows. Josephine followed her gaze, snarling at something I couldn't see. I strained to hear, but the dull roar of the water revealed nothing.

"Do it," Josephine said quickly. "Do it *now*."

Though Nicholina moved with renewed urgency, her entire body shuddered with the next step. Her foot lurched. Slipping, she crashed to her knees in a graceless movement. Confusion warped her ghastly face. Confusion and—and *panic*. Gritting her teeth, she struggled to stand as her muscles spasmed. As they rioted against her.

I stared at her now, hardly daring to hope.

"Naughty, nasty." Each word burst from her in a sharp exhale, as if she suffered terrible pain. Her entire body bowed. Still she crawled forward, her nails tearing through earth. "Tricky—little—*mice*—"

"Useless." Lip curling with disgust, Josephine strode toward me, kicking Nicholina's ribs as she went. Hard. "I will do it myself."

Nicholina's head lifted with a frighteningly blank expression.

On my first day in Cesarine, a stray dog had meandered into the garbage where I'd hidden. Shivering and alone, his only possession had been a bone. I'd watched as a cruel child had stolen it from him, as she'd beaten him with it until the dog had snapped, lunging forward to bite her hand. Later that day—after the girl had scampered away, crying and bleeding—a man had patted the dog's head as he passed, feeding him a bit of calisson. The dog had followed him home.

Like a stray dog in the garbage, Nicholina snapped, plunging her nails into her mistress's calf.

Josephine jerked as if startled, her eyes narrowing with incredulity—then widening with rage. With a feral snarl, she swooped to seize Nicholina's hair, wrenching her attendant upward and sinking her teeth deep into her throat. Bile rose in my own as those teeth crunched and snapped—feasting hungrily— while Nicholina kicked helplessly. Her screams ended in a gurgle.

Josephine had torn out her vocal cords.

Even then, she didn't stop. She drank and drank until Nicholina's hands slackened and her feet fell limp. She drank until splashes sounded behind us, accompanied by piercing undulations. Battle cries. When the first naked woman sprinted past—silver hair rippling and trident flashing—I never thought I'd be so grateful to see Elvire's backside.

Dropping Nicholina's body, Josephine whirled with wild eyes. Blood poured from her mouth, but she caught Elvire's trident before it connected with her skull. Aurélien felled my tree with the single stroke of his club. He caught me with surprising tenderness, while Lasimonne dropped to his knees beside us. "My lady sends her regards," he rumbled. "Forgive me. This is going to hurt."

He peeled the thorns from my mouth, drew the spikes from my hands and feet, as Olympienne, Leopoldine, and Sabatay fell upon Josephine. Dozens of others streaked past, finding prey within the trees—the blood witches who'd gathered to watch my execution.

As I coughed and spluttered, Aurélien and Lasimonne dragged me from harm's way. "What can we do?" the former asked. "How may we heal you?"

"You can't do anything unless you're hiding an antidote to poison in your . . . not pocket." I coughed on a laugh, cradling my hands in my lap. They'd rested me against another tree. This one thankfully free of blood. "Go. My body will heal."

Just slowly.

They didn't need to be convinced. With two impeccable bows, they charged into the fray once more. I tried to breathe, to anchor myself in my magic. It had purged the hemlock from my body. It would cleanse Josephine's blood too. Though the patterns shone dimmer than before—stretched too far and too thin across the city—the Brindelle trees helped. Even now, the power of this sacred grove flowed through me, deepening my connections. Restoring my balance.

I just needed time.

With a jolt of panic, I remembered Coco.

Trying and failing to stand, I searched for her amidst the chaos—blood witches and melusines weaving through the shadows of the trees—and found her sitting up amidst the roots of another sapling. At her back, Angelica helped her stand.

I heaved a shaky sigh of relief—until the two turned to face Josephine.

She fought with blood and blade, slicing and swiping at the melusines with preternatural strength and speed. If their blood didn't spill, hers did, and she spattered it in their eyes, ears, noses, and groins. Every vulnerable spot in their human bodies. When Elvire fell backward, tangling in another witch's black thorns, Angelica cut her free with equal skill.

Josephine snarled.

With the shake of her head, Angelica cleaned the thorn's sap from her blade, wiping it on her gown. She'd worn a gown. "You've chosen the wrong side, sister."

"At least I've chosen a side." Josephine didn't cower as Angelica approached. Coco crept behind, her eyes wide and anxious. I tried again to stand. "For too long, you have spoken of right and wrong, of good and evil, of facile concepts that do not exist. Not truly." She prowled around Angelica, who waved her hand to still Elvire's approach. "There is only pursuit, dear sister. Of knowledge. Of power. Of *life*. But you have always been afraid to live, haven't you? You craved power, yet you betrayed your own people. You sought love and affection, yet you abandoned your child. Even now, you yearn for freedom, yet you remain trapped beneath the sea. You are a *coward*." She spat the word and continued circling.

Angelica turned with her, keeping Coco at her back. "You're such a fool," she whispered.

"*I* am the fool? How do you envision this ends, sister?" Josephine's mouth twisted as she gestured between the two of them. "Shall we carry on the pretense? Will you cut yourself to cut me? We both know it cannot go beyond that. One cannot live without the other. I cannot kill you, and you cannot kill me."

"You're wrong."

Josephine's eyes narrowed at the words. "I think not."

"We must all play our parts." Lacing her fingers through Coco's, Angelica glanced back and squeezed. "For a new regime."

Josephine stared between them. Perhaps it was the way Coco shook her head, the tears in her eyes, or perhaps it was the profound acceptance in Angelica's smile. The way she touched Coco's locket and whispered, "Wear it always."

Whatever the reason, she yielded a step. Then another. Indeed, when Angelica faced her once more, advancing slowly—knife in hand—Josephine abandoned all pretense. She turned and fled.

Nicholina caught her ankle.

Unseen by all, she'd dragged herself forward, throat mangled, each breath a wet, hollow sound. Her skin had grayed beyond pale. Corpselike. Even now, she struggled to keep her eyes open as her lifeblood poured freely.

She didn't let go.

Appalled, Josephine tried to kick free, but she slipped in Nicholina's blood, falling hard to the ground. The movement cost her. Mustering the last of her strength, Nicholina crawled up her legs as Angelica advanced. "Get *off* of me, you disgusting little—" Though Josephine scrambled backward, kicking harder, she couldn't dislodge her attendant.

"Miss . . . tress . . ." Nicholina gurgled.

Josephine's eyes widened in true panic now. Turning, she attempted to push to her feet, but Nicholina held on, trapping her legs. Angelica loomed behind. When Josephine crashed back to the ground—twisting, snarling—Angelica knelt beside her, sliding her blade neatly through her sister's neck.

Right at the base of the skull.

The three of them died together.

It wasn't poetic. It wasn't grand or heroic or momentous, like one might've expected. The heavens didn't part, and the earth didn't swallow them whole. These three women—the oldest and most powerful in the world—died just like anyone would: with their eyes open and their limbs cold.

Coco pulled her mother apart from the rest, fighting tears. Heedless of the fighting around her.

I staggered to her side. When she saw me, she gasped my name, flinging her arms around me. "Are you all right?" She pulled back to look at me, frantic, wiping her tears. Her fingers touched my face. "Oh my god. Here—let me—let me heal you—"

"Save your strength. I'm already healing."

Her eyes dropped back to her mother. "We need to finish this, Lou."

Slowly, I knelt to the ground, closing each of their eyes in turn. Even Nicholina's. Even Josephine's. "And we will."

She supported my shoulders as we hobbled through the trees to the street. To Coco's surprise—and less to mine—a handful of blood witches ceased fighting when they recognized Josephine's corpse on the ground. Some knelt beside her. Others fled. Still more looked to Coco as if lost, mirroring her own unnerved expression. At the blood witches' abrupt withdrawal, the melusines moved on, following the sounds of shouts and steel.

Claud—still shaped as the Woodwose—thundered around the corner at the far end of the street. When he saw us, he moved faster, raising his voice to shout, "What is it? What happened? I heard your call—"

Something moved too quickly behind us.

A flash of white. Of moonbeam hair.

"LOOK OUT!" Célie's unexpected shriek nearly rent the sky, but it was too late. We couldn't stop it. Paralyzed with fear, we stood rooted as Morgane rose up to meet us. As she lifted her hand to thrust a dagger in my heart. As Claud blasted us backward, and her lips curled into a macabre smile.

"Oh no." Her ghostly laughter reverberated through the grove. "Oh no, no, no."

The ground beneath us began to quake.

"It seems you've broken the rules, darling." Tutting, she shook her head. "Old ones."

Sickening realization dawned. "He's intervened," I repeated on a whisper.

As one, Coco and I turned to Claud, who stood alone in the street, his face a mask of calm. The cobblestones cracked and fissured around him. The earth trembled. He looked us squarely in the eyes. "Run."

THE CHASM

Reid

"Would you *run?*" Incredulous, I glanced over my shoulder at Beau, who lagged behind. He clutched his ribs with one hand. With each stride, he nearly impaled himself with his Balisarda.

He'd stolen it from Philippe.

We hadn't bothered to free him.

"*You* run." Panting, he gestured around the empty street with his other hand. It held another knife. "I can't fucking *breathe*, and if you haven't noticed—there's no one here!"

I scowled and pushed onward.

He had a point.

This street—that street, every street we'd passed for the last quarter hour—had been virtually empty. We'd succeeded in sequestering most pedestrians inside their homes, inside shops. Inside any buildings we could fortify. Father Achille and Johannes Pan had converted the boucherie next door into an infirmary. They treated the injured there. They gathered the dead.

The witches had . . . withdrawn.

It'd happened slowly. Almost imperceptibly. One moment, we'd fought scores of them. Too many to count. Werewolves and huntsmen, men and women—even melusines, rising up from the Doleur like sea serpents—had fought tooth and nail to contain them. As the hour had passed, however, each had slipped from the fray one by one. Slipped through our fingers. As if answering some unspoken call.

My own breath quickened with each step. They couldn't have simply *vanished*.

My voice hardened with resolution. "We need to find them."

"We *need* to find our wretched little sisters." Waving his knife for me to stop, Beau clutched his knees. I scowled, doubling back, and pulled him onward. We would find them. If not, we'd regroup with Lou and Coco, with Father Achille and Jean Luc and Célie, and we'd determine another strategy.

When we rounded the corner, however, all plans of *planning* fled.

At the end of the street, a horde of witches collected in the shadows.

Beau hissed as I shoved him behind a garbage can, but it mattered not—dozens of heads snapped in our direction. I exhaled a heavy breath. A resigned one. Slowly, I rose to my feet. Beau followed with a curse, muttering, "Have you ever heard of manifestation?"

"Shut up."

"*You* shut up." He lifted his Balisarda and knife with white knuckles as three witches broke apart from the rest. The others refocused their attention on something at the center of the group. Something that . . . rattled. Eyes narrowing, I stepped closer. "Actually, don't. I'd love to hear the next step in your *let's find the bloodthirsty witches* plan—"

The clink of metal. Thick rings.

A chain.

My brow furrowed as the three witches moved shoulder to shoulder, blocking my view. It was a chain. An ancient, crusted *chain*. From the glimpse I'd gotten, it'd looked long enough to encircle half of Cesarine. Wide enough too. A memory harried my subconscious, half-realized. I'd seen this chain in Chateau le Blanc's treasury. "Hello, princelings," the middle witch crooned.

With a jolt of shock, I recognized her amber face from Modraniht. It felt like years ago. "Elaina."

"No." Beau winced as they drew to a halt before us. Identical black hair and narrow noses. Full lips. They twisted with identical menace. "That one is Elinor. I'd recognize her aura of disdain anywhere." He pointed a finger to his teeth, flashing a charming smile. "Do you remember me now, sweetheart? Do you *see* the opportunity you missed?"

"Oh, I remember you, *Burke*. You made me look a *fool* in front of the entire coven."

"It doesn't matter now," her sister said, either Elaina or Elodie.

"We've been looking for you both all night," the other finished. "Thank you for making this easy."

Though all three crooked their fingers at once, nothing happened. No patterns reared to strike. Beau waggled his Balisarda at them, grinning anew. "Something wrong?"

Elinor bared her teeth. "Ask your sister."

"What does that—"

They attacked before he could finish, slipping knives from their sleeves and launching toward us. Elaina and Elodie at me. Elinor at him. Though quick—though furious—the sisters clearly hadn't trained for physical combat sans magic. With a sense of dread at those chilling last words, I dispatched the first of them swiftly while Beau battled Elinor strike for strike. Her sister's blood still dripped from my blade when I turned to face Elodie.

The earth beneath us rolled.

I staggered at the movement, glancing down incredulously. Cobblestones broke to pieces. All around, foundations cracked. Tiles littered the street. And Zenna—from somewhere above, she let out a mighty roar. The witches ahead tensed, renewing their efforts with haste. Half had climbed the drainpipes, stringing the chain taut between rooftops, like a wire. Magic coated everything.

I couldn't make sense of it. Couldn't think. The ground kept shaking. Sensing my distraction, the sister slashed her blade down in a mighty strike. Though I recoiled, though I lifted my own blade to parry, another knife whizzed past my face—close enough to feel its heat on my cheek—and lodged in the sister's chest.

With a squeak of surprise, she sank to her knees, slipped sideways, and moved no more.

Behind us, Beau stood triumphant. Elinor stilled at his feet. "Did you *see* that?" Though he waved his Balisarda at the vengeful witch's body, he glanced away quickly. He swallowed hard. "I saved your life."

I blocked his view of their corpses. Knocked his shoulder with my own. Forced him to turn. "You also set me on fire."

"Perhaps you could conjure some up for the rest of these—"

With another thunderous roar, Zenna swept into view. The sight of her wings against the sky, of her white-hot flame, stole the breath from my throat. And I remembered. A torch-lit stage. A starry cloak. And Zenna—Zenna weaving a heart-wrenching tale of dragon and maiden.

A magic chain, her kin doth wield to stay him on an even keel.

And when Tarasque did spiral down, her father felled him to the ground.

With Seraphine atop her back, Zenna dove low—too low— scouring the streets for persons unknown. When she saw us, she swooped even lower. She didn't see the chain until it was too late.

"Wait! No, STOP!"

At the desperate wave of my arms, she banked, but her foot still caught the links. The chain moved of its own volition, slinging rapidly around her leg, up her haunch. With a bellow of rage, she began to fall, and as she did, her leg—it transformed into that of a human. Gruesomely. The witches descended like ants when she crashed to the ground. The impact threw Seraphine through the air with frightening speed. She collided with the trash cans nearest us.

"Oh my god," Beau said. "Oh my god, oh my god, oh my *god*."

Zenna's roars transitioned to screams as Seraphine struggled to move. I bolted toward her, kicking the trash cans aside. "Seraphine—"

She pushed my hands away with surprising strength. "*Go.*" Though Beau attempted to drag her upright, she shook him off too, unsheathing another sword from down her back. She swung both equally with surprising dexterity. "Find Claud and the others. Find Lou. He *intervened.*"

"What?" Beau asked, perplexed.

My gaze darted toward Zenna, who the witches had lashed and beaten with the chain. She'd fully transformed now. Human once more. Vulnerable. "Let us help—"

"I am no damsel." Springing to her feet, she knocked us aside and streaked toward her mate. "Find Claud. Leave Zenna to me."

The ground gave a mighty lurch in response, and we had no choice.

We sprinted up the street.

"Where are we *going?*" Though Beau's shout tore through my senses, I ignored him, pressing harder. Faster. Blood roared in my ears as we followed the fissure, tracking its path through West End, past the Tremblays' townhouse, and skidding to a halt outside Brindelle Park. Buildings crumbled now. Witches and melusines alike scattered.

Claud stood in the middle of the street, completely and carefully still. He faced the spindly Brindelle trees.

He faced Coco and Lou.

The fissure ran directly between them, cracking wide, forcing them to leap apart. "LOU!" Her name shredded my throat, but I shouted it louder. I shouted it crazed. When her face jerked up— her eyes meeting mine—a cold fist of fear gripped my heart. Though I cast for a golden pattern, none could've prevented this. None could've stopped it. She tried anyway, flinging both hands toward the ground. Her entire body strained. Trembled. The sharp scent of magic exploded over the grass, the rocks, the trees—stronger than ever before—but this fissure was stronger, deeper, *older*, than even La Dame des Sorcières.

Together, helpless, we watched as the earth broke open completely.

As Claud plummeted into its depths without a word.

As the fissure kept growing, kept *spreading*, until Brindelle Park—until half of the entire *city*—fractured from the rest, separated by a yawning chasm. Still it grew. Coco's voice rose to join mine, and she backpedaled, preparing to take an impossible leap—

Beau caught her shirt at the last second. He ripped her toward him. "Are you *crazy?*"

"Let me *go!*" She pounded his chest, stomped on his feet, twisted to elbow him viciously. Only then did he release her with a gasp.

"Please, Coco, *don't*—!"

But she didn't leap this time. Instead she dove to the chasm's edge, hands latching onto a blood witch's wrist. Another. Screaming, they dangled hopelessly. Their nails clawed at rock, at Coco's skin. Realizing her intent, Beau dashed to help, and together, they pulled the witches to safety, collapsing together in a heap.

When the dust settled, Beau, Coco, and I stood on one side of the chasm.

Lou and Célie clutched each on the other.

Behind them loomed Morgane le Blanc.

AS WE STARTED

Lou

The horror on Reid's face, the absolute *terror*, was an image I'd never forget. Though he charged up and down the chasm's edge, searching for the narrowest lip, for a pattern, for a *miracle*—it was better this way. Truly. Whatever happened now, it would be between my mother and me.

Just as we'd started.

In line with my thoughts, Morgane swept her hand in a burst of magic, and Célie soared through the air, crashing into a Brindelle tree. Two blood witches who'd been trapped here dropped to seize her, to—no. Hope burned savage and bright in my heart. To *help* her. They were helping her. In that split second, I thought of Manon, of Ismay, or Dame Blanche and Dame Rouge alike who'd been harmed by Morgane's hatred. Who'd felt trapped between Church and coven. Who'd lived in fear as debilitating as mine.

Hope isn't the sickness. It's the cure.

Of all people, of course it had been Célie to find Morgane.

To stalk her unseen as she slipped through the city. My mother never would've suspected it. She never would've believed such a pretty porcelain doll could grow teeth. If she thought Célie would shatter, however—if she thought *I* would—it would be the last mistake of her life.

This time, I wouldn't hesitate.

"Lou! LOU! *Célie!*"

Reid, Coco, Beau, Jean Luc—they called our names in a frenzy, voices blending into one. Resolve hardened to a sharpened point in my chest as I looked at them. We'd already lost so much, each of us. Fathers and mothers and sisters and brothers. Our homes. Our hope. Our very *hearts*.

No more.

I found Reid's gaze last, holding it longer than the others. When I shook my head slowly, determinedly, he drew to a swift halt, chest heaving. We stared at each other for the span of a single heartbeat.

Then he nodded.

I love you, I told him.

As I love you.

Morgane sneered, lowering the hood of Auguste's lion-skin cloak as she advanced. She'd stolen it from his corpse at the cathedral. Though charred black in places, she wore it as a trophy now. Its teeth glinted around her throat in a gruesome smile, and its mane spread proudly across her shoulders. "No more running, Louise. No more hiding." She jabbed a finger across the chasm, where Blaise and the remains of his pack had gathered. Where

Elvire and her melusines still attempted to cross, where Claud had fallen to fate unknown. "Your god has fallen, your dragon has perished, and your precious *allies* cannot reach you here. I must admit . . . you are far cleverer than I ever gave you credit. How cunning it was to hide behind those more powerful than yourself. How *cruel*. We are more alike than you realize, darling, but the time has come at last. You are alone."

But I wasn't alone. Not truly. In life or in death, I'd have someone to meet me. Someone to *love* me. My stomach curdled at Nicholina's congealed throat. At Josephine's empty expression. Though the former might've found peace with her son, could the latter say the same? Could Morgane? She stepped over their corpses without acknowledgment. Already, they meant less to her than the mire beneath her boots. "Your generals are dead," I said quietly. "I think *you* are the one alone."

The blood witches stiffened as Morgane paused, turning to kick Josephine's vacant face. "*Good riddance.*"

With a crippling sense of sorrow, I stared at her as my white patterns undulated weakly. I couldn't kill her with them. Not outright. Death was natural, yes, but murder was not. It hardly mattered now either way. When I'd clasped two sides of the very world, trying to save Claud—a god, a *friend*—from his own magic, I'd nearly rent myself apart. My patterns had distended past the point of reparation. Some had snapped altogether. Those remaining had grown dim with weariness.

Morgane didn't know that.

I searched each carefully now, seeking a distraction, something to allow me near. Something to debilitate her long enough for me to strike. Gently, I fed the patterns outward. "Have you loved anyone in this world, *maman?*"

She scoffed and lifted her hands. "*Love.* I curse the word."

"Has anyone loved you?"

Her eyes narrowed on mine. Her mouth twisted in question. "It's true," I admitted, quieter still. "I did love you once. Part of me still does, despite everything." I twitched my finger, and the water of the Doleur trickled steadily, silently, through the grass beneath our feet. It melted the snow. It cleansed the blood. If Morgane noticed, she didn't react. Though her features remained riddled with spite, she studied me as if enthralled. As if she'd never heard me say it, though I'd told her a thousand times. A single tear slid down my cheek in response, and the pattern dissipated. A tear for a river. Both held endless depths.

"You gave me life," I continued, stronger now, the words spilling faster than I'd intended. Cathartic. "Of course I loved you. Why do you think I allowed them to *chain* me to an *altar?* At sixteen years old, I was willing to *die* for you. My mother." Another tear fell, and the water flowed faster. It touched her hem now. "You never should've asked me. I'm your daughter."

"You were never my daughter."

"You gave me life."

"I gave you *purpose.* What should I have *done,* darling? Cradled you in my arms while others' daughters perished? While they *burned?* Should I have valued your life more than theirs?"

"Yes!" The confession burst from me in a shock of cold regret, and I capitalized on it, clenching my fist. The water around Morgane's feet froze to solid ice. It trapped her. "You *should* have valued me—you should've *protected* me—because I am the *only* person in this world who still loves you!"

"You are a *fool*," she snarled, fire lashing from her fingertips. "And a predictable one at that."

With the slash of her hand, the ice melted, and the ground itself desiccated in a fiery path toward me. It didn't burn my skin, however, instead passing through it—straight to my organs. My body temperature spiked as my blood literally began to boil, as my muscles cramped and my vision spun. Crying out, Célie attempted to leap to my aid, but the blood witches held her back, recoiling from Morgane. In fear. In hatred.

With seconds to react, I seized another pattern, and the Brindelle tree nearest me withered and blackened to ash.

The lion of Auguste's cloak began to reanimate.

I fell to my knees, smoke curling from my mouth, as its teeth sank deep into Morgane's neck. Screaming, she whirled, pulling a knife from her sleeve, but the half-formed lion clung to her back. Tendon and muscle continued to regenerate with gruesome speed. Where sleeves had been, mighty paws rose to grip her shoulders. Its hind legs kicked at her back.

Morgane's fiery hold dissipated as she struggled, and I fought to rise. To *breathe.*

When she buried her blade in the beast's chest, it gave a final snarl before falling limp. She heaved its carcass between us. Blood poured from wounds on her neck, her shoulders, her legs, but she ignored them, clenching another fist. "Is that the best you can do?" Beneath my armor, against my skin, arose an alarming tickle. The skitter of legs. "You may call yourself La Dame des Sorcières—you may kill trees and steal rivers—but you will never know this magic as I have known it. You will never conquer its power as I once did. Just *look* at yourself. Already, it has weakened your feeble spirit." She advanced in earnest now, a lethal gleam in her eyes. "The Goddess has chosen wrong, but I do not need her blessing to conquer *you*."

Scrambling backward—hardly hearing her words—I pulled hastily at my armor.

Hundreds of spiders burst from the woven fabric. From their own silk. They scuttled over my body in a wave of legs, piercing my skin with their fangs. Each bite brought a prick of pain, a tingle of numbness. Shrieking instinctively, heart palpitating, I crushed all within reach, sweeping their wriggling corpses from my arms, legs, chest—

"You were born to be immortal, Louise." Morgane lifted her hands, pouring her rage, her frustration, her *guilt* into another bout of fire. I rolled to avoid it—squashing the last of the spiders—and seized the lion's skin as a shield. "Though destined to die, your name would have lived forever. We could have written history together, the two of us. You may scorn me now, you may hate me always, but I gave everything—I *sacrificed* everything—for you. For *love*."

Feeding strength to the fur through another pattern, I crouched lower. The grass beneath her feet ignited instead. She leapt away from it with a hiss. "You cannot imagine the grief of your birth. Even *you* cannot imagine the bitterness I felt. I should have killed you then. I'd even lifted the knife, prepared to plunge it into your newborn heart, but you—you clasped my finger. With the whole of your fist, you clutched me, blinking those sightless eyes. So peaceful. So content. I couldn't do it. In a single moment, you softened my heart." Her flames subsided abruptly. "I failed our people that day. It took sixteen years to harden myself again. Even then, I would have gifted you everything. I would have gifted you *greatness.*"

"I didn't *want* greatness." Casting my shield aside, I pushed to my feet at last. Her heart might've softened for a newborn babe, but she hadn't ever loved me—not *me*, not truly, not the person. She'd loved the idea of me. The idea of greatness, of salvation. I'd mistaken her attention for the genuine thing. I hadn't known what real love looked like then. I glanced across the chasm to Reid, Coco, and Beau, who stood hand in hand at the edge, pale and silent.

I knew what it looked like now—both love *and* grief. Two sides of the same wretched coin. "I only wanted *you.*"

When I clenched my fist, exhaling hard, my grief ruptured into a storm wind: grief for the mother she could've been, grief for the good moments, for the bad moments, for all the moments in between. Grief for the mother I had lost, truly, long before this one.

The wind blasted her backward, but she twisted midair, and the momentum carried her closer to Célie. Wicked intent flared in Morgane's eyes. Before I could stop her, she jerked her fingers, and Célie skidded from the blood witches as if pulled by an invisible rope. Morgane caught her. She used her body as a shield, pressing her knife to Célie's breastbone. "Foolish child. How many times must I tell you? You cannot defeat me. You cannot *hope* to triumph. Once upon a time, you could've been immortal, but now, your name will *rot* with your corpse—"

She broke off inexplicably, her mouth falling open in a comical O.

Except it wasn't funny. It wasn't funny at all.

Stumbling backward, she thrust Célie away with a noise of surprise and—and glanced down. I followed her gaze.

A quill lodged deep in her thigh, its syringe quivering from impact.

An injection.

I stared at it in shock. In relief. In horror. Each emotion flickered through me with wild abandon. A hundred others. Each passed too quickly to name. To *feel*. I could only stare, numb, as she slid to her knees in a smooth, fluid motion. As her hair rippled down her shoulders, less silver now than bloody scarlet. Eyes still rapt on the syringe, she slipped sideways. She didn't move.

Cold metal touched my palm, and Célie's voice drifted from afar. "Do you need me to do it?"

I felt myself shake my head. My fingers curled around the hilt of her dagger. Swallowing hard, I approached my mother's limp body. When I brushed her hair from her face, her eyes rolled back to look at me. Pleading. I couldn't help it. I pulled her across my lap. Her throat worked for several seconds before sound came out. "Daugh . . . ter . . ."

I memorized those emerald eyes. "Yes."

Then I drew Célie's blade across my mother's throat.

IT ENDS IN HOPE

Lou

The first time I'd slept beside Reid, I'd dreamed of him.

More specifically, I'd dreamed of his book. *La Vie Éphémère.* He'd gifted it to me that day. His first secret. Later that night, after Madame Labelle had issued her warning—after I'd woken in a fit of tangled sheets and icy panic—I'd crawled next to him on the hard floor. His breathing had lulled me to sleep.

She is coming.

Fear of my mother had literally driven me into his arms.

The dream had crept over me slowly, like the wash of gray before dawn. As in the story, Emilie and Alexandre had lain side by side in her family's tomb. Their cold fingers had touched forevermore. On the final page, their parents had wept for them, mourning the loss of life so young. They'd promised to set aside their blood feud, their prejudice, in the name of their children. It was of this scene I'd dreamed, except it hadn't been Emilie's and Alexandre's bodies, but mine and Reid's.

When I'd woken the next morning, unease had plagued me.

I'd blamed it on the nightmare. On the memory of my mother.

Now, as I held her in my arms, I couldn't help but remember that peaceful image of Emilie and Alexandre.

There was nothing peaceful about this.

Nothing easy.

Yet still Reid's voice drifted back to me as he'd clutched *La Vie Éphémère* in hand . . .

It doesn't end in death. It ends in hope.

PAN'S PATISSERIE

Reid

Lou held her mother for a long time. I waited at the chasm's edge, even after Coco and a handful of blood witches built a bridge of vines. Even after Célie and her newfound friends—two witches named Corinne and Barnabé—crossed on shaky legs. Jean Luc had enveloped Célie in a desperate hug, while Coco had tentatively greeted the witches. She'd remembered them from childhood. They'd remembered her.

They'd even bared their throats before leaving to find their kin. A sign of submission.

Coco had watched them go, visibly shaken.

Not all had been so courteous. One witch—a sobbing Dame Blanche—had attacked my back as I'd waited. Jean Luc had been forced to inject her. To bind her wrists. He hadn't killed her, however, not even when Célie had stepped aside to speak with Elvire. Aurélien had fallen. Others too. As the Oracle's Hand, Elvire had begun to collect their dead, preparing to depart for Le Présage once more.

"We cannot leave our lady waiting," she'd murmured, bowing low. "Please say you will visit us sometime."

Beau and Coco hurried to find Zenna and Seraphine.

Though I started to follow, Coco shook her head. Her gaze drifted to Lou, who hadn't moved from beneath her mother. "She needs you more," Coco murmured. Nodding, I swallowed hard, and after another moment, I took a hesitant step on the bridge.

Someone shouted behind me.

Unsheathing my stolen Balisarda, I whirled, prepared for another witch. Instead, I met two: Babette supporting Madame Labelle as they hobbled into the street. An enormous smile stretched across my mother's face. "Reid!" She waved with her entire body, presumably healed by Babette's blood. The lesions and bruises from the trial had vanished, replaced by vibrant skin, if a touch pale. I exhaled a sharp breath. My knees weakened in a dizzying wave of relief.

She was here.

She was *alive*.

Crossing the street in three great strides, I met her halfway, crushing her in my arms. She choked on a laugh. Patted my arm. "Easy, son. It takes a bit more time for the insides to heal, you know." Though she still beamed, clapping my cheeks, her eyes tightened at the corners. Babette looked unusually grave behind.

I met her gaze over my mother's head. "Thank you."

"Do not thank me." She waved an errant hand. "Your mother supplied my first job in this city. I owed her one."

"And still owe me many more," Madame Labelle added, turning to eye the courtesan waspishly. "Do not think I've forgotten, Babette, the time you dyed my hair blue."

Only then did Babette crack a sheepish grin. After another moment, she glanced around us covertly. "Pray tell, huntsman, have you seen our lovely Cosette?"

"She's with Beau. They headed north."

Her smile fell slightly. "Of course. If you'll excuse me."

She left without delay, and I wrapped a steadying arm around Madame Labelle's waist. "Where have you been? Are you well?"

"I am as well as possible, given the circumstances." She shrugged delicately. "We took a leaf out of your wife's book and hid in Soleil et Lune's attic. No one bothered us there. Perhaps none knew of its importance to Lou. If they had, I suspect Morgane would've razed it out of spite." When I nodded to them across the chasm, her expression crumpled. She shook her head. "Oh, dear. Oh, *dear*. How sickening." Those piercing blue eyes flitted up to mine, filled with regret. "Babette told me that Auguste perished by his own fire. Stupid, *arrogant* man." As if realizing the tactlessness of her words, she patted my arm again. "But he—he was very—"

"He tortured you," I said darkly.

She sighed, crestfallen. "Yes, he did."

"He deserved worse than death."

"Perhaps. We must content ourselves that wherever he is, he is in great pain. Perhaps with *rats*. Still . . ." She wobbled slightly, unsteady on her feet. My arm tightened around her. "He was your father. I am sorry for it, but I am never sorry for you." She touched my cheek once more before glancing at Lou. "You must go. If you could walk me to the nearest bench, however, I'd be most grateful. I should like to watch the sun rise."

I stared at her incredulously. "I can't leave you on a bench."

"Nonsense. Of course you can. No witch with any sense would attack us now, and those that do—well, I believe more than one Chasseur survived, and that Father Achille has *quite* a nice—"

"I'll stop you there." Though I shook my head, one corner of my mouth curled upward. Unbidden. "Father Achille is off-limits."

It wasn't true. She could have whoever she wanted. I would personally introduce them.

After situating her on a bench—beds of winter jasmine blooming on either side—I kissed her forehead. Though night still claimed the sky, dawn would come soon. With it, a new day. I knelt to catch my mother's eyes. "I love you. I don't think I've ever told you."

Scoffing, she busied herself with her skirt. Still, I saw her eyes. They sparkled with sudden tears. "I only expect to hear it every day from this moment onward. You shall visit at least thrice a week, and you and Louise shall name your firstborn child after me. Perhaps your second too. That sounds reasonable, does it not?"

I chuckled and tugged on her hair. "I'll see what I can do."

"Go on, then."

As I walked back to Lou, however, I heard low voices down

a side street. Familiar ones. A keening wail. Frowning, I followed the sound to Gabrielle and Violette. They stood huddled on a stoop between Beau, who'd wrapped one arm around each of them. Coco hovered behind, one hand clapped to her mouth. At their feet, Ismay and Victoire lay sprawled unnaturally, face-down, surrounded by a half-dozen witches. None stirred.

Stricken, unable to move, I watched as Beau's face broke on a sob, and he pulled the two girls into his chest. Their shoulders shuddered as they clutched him. Their tears raw. Anguished. Intimate. The sight of them punched me in the gut. My siblings. Though I hadn't known Victoire as well as Beau, I could have. I *would* have. The pain cut unexpectedly sharp.

It should've been me on those cobblestones. Morgane had wanted *me*, not her. She'd wanted Beau. Not Victoire, a thirteen-year-old child.

Guilt reared its ugly head, and I finally turned. I walked back to Lou. I waited.

This time, she lifted her head to greet me.

I held her gaze.

Nodding, she smoothed Morgane's hair, her touch tender. Full of longing. She closed her mother's eyes. Then she rose heavily to her feet—bent as if bearing the weight of the very sky—and she left her there.

When she crossed the bridge, I extended my arms to her at last, and she fell into them without a sound. Her face pale and drawn. Broken-hearted. I leaned to rest my forehead against hers. "I'm so sorry, Lou."

She held my face between both hands. Closed her eyes. "Me too."

"We'll get through this together."

"I know."

"Where you go—"

"—I will go," she finished softly. Her eyes opened, and she brushed a kiss against my lips. "Who survived?"

"Let's find out."

As I'd suspected, the chasm split the entire city in two. Lou and I walked it hand in hand. Near the cathedral, we found Toulouse and Thierry. They stared into the chasm's depths with Zenna and Seraphine. No one spoke a word.

"What do you think happened to him?" Lou whispered, slowing to a stop. This wake wasn't meant for us. It was meant for them. Troupe de Fortune. Claud's family. "Do you think he . . . died?"

I frowned at the prospect. Pressure built in my chest. Behind my eyes. "I don't think gods *can* die."

When we turned to go, Terrance stepped forward from the shadows. Like us, he, Blaise, and Liana hovered a respectable distance away. Ignoring Lou and me, he caught Toulouse's and Thierry's eyes. "You could come with us." His voice resonated deeper than I'd remembered. Blood dripped down his bare chest. The side of his face. His ear had been torn off completely— whether in battle or before, I couldn't tell. With a start, I realized he must've met Toulouse and Thierry at Chateau le Blanc. When they'd all been . . . tortured together. Liana too.

The thought turned my stomach.

Blaise stepped to his son's side, clasping a hand on his shoulder. "We would be honored." He cleared the emotion from his throat. "My children . . . they have spoken of how you comforted them. How you gave them hope. I can never repay either of you for this kindness."

The twins cast subtle glances at Zenna and Seraphine. The former shrugged. Though link-shaped burns marred her visible skin—she'd somehow donned a sparkling fuchsia gown—the rest of her appeared relatively unscathed. Seraphine too. Blood coated her armor, but it didn't seem to belong to her. I stared at them both incredulously. "How did they escape?"

"Who?" Lou asked. "What happened?"

"The witches—they felled Zenna with a magic chain."

"Ah." A hint of a smile touched her lips. "Tarasque's chain."

"Like in Zenna's story."

"She *did* say that wasn't her real name."

I frowned as she pulled me away in search of the others.

We ended up in Pan's patisserie.

Outside the boarded windows, Father Achille and a score of huntsmen attempted to free their brethren. Philippe still bellowed orders within his cage of roots. None listened. When at last they freed him, he swiped wildly at Achille, who dodged with the speed of a much younger man before knocking Philippe to the ground. It took five huntsmen to subdue him. Another to clap irons around his wrists.

"You can't *do* this!" Veins throbbed in his forehead as he thrashed. "I am a *captain* of the Chasseurs! *Father Gaspard!*" He'd nearly burst blood vessels. "Someone summon him—FATHER GASPARD!"

Father Gaspard hadn't heeded his summons, instead remaining crouched behind a tree in the sanctuary. The Chasseurs had flushed him out while searching for Queen Oliana, who they'd found trapped beneath the pulpit. Though her leg had been fractured, she would face greater pain soon. I didn't envy the Chasseur who would tell her about her child. For the first time in a long time, I didn't envy any Chasseur at all.

Unsure what to do with Philippe, Jean Luc and Célie settled on chaining him to a horse post down the street. Out of hearing distance. Thankfully.

They joined us in the patisserie moments later.

Collapsing in a vacant chair, Jean Luc scrubbed a hand down his face. "We'll need to coordinate shelter as soon as possible. Petition citizens to open their homes to those without."

Célie sat beside him with quiet calm. Soot smeared her white cheeks, and her hair hung lank from Coco's rain. From sweat. A gash still bled from her temple. She gestured next door to the boucherie. "The injured will need treatment. We must summon healers from the nearest metropolises."

"Oh God." Jean Luc groaned and shot to his feet. "Were there priests in the infirmary? Has anyone checked for survivors?" At our blank looks, he shook his head and stalked outside to find

Father Achille. Instead of joining him, Célie looked between us anxiously. She knitted her hands in her lap.

"Er—Lou? Do you think—I'm terribly sorry, but—might you be able to return my gown now?"

Lou blinked in confusion. With a breathy laugh, Célie gestured to her armor.

"*Oh.*" Lou chuckled too and waved her hand. The sharp scent of incense erupted. "Yes, of course."

From her feet, Célie's armor unraveled into a black mourning gown, and she patted her waist anxiously. At whatever she found, tension left her shoulders, and she relaxed. Just a little. "Right. Thank you so much." A bright smile at Lou. A quick glance at me. It seemed . . . inexplicably significant. When Jean Luc shouted for her a moment later, however, she grimaced and strode toward the door. "I shall return in just a moment."

Lou watched her go with a bemused grin, stretching to watch her through the window. "What was *that* about?"

"She must . . . really like dresses?"

Lou rolled her eyes.

Coco and Beau found us next. Though tears still stained my brother's face, he rubbed them away with a weak smile, pulling a chair around to sit beside Lou. Then he wrapped her in a headlock and ruffled her hair. "Did Reid tell you I saved his life?"

She didn't push him away. "He *didn't.*"

"Then he is a *spectacular* ass. I threw a knife with such precision that it would've put Mort Rouge to shame—"

"You also caught me on fire," I said scathingly. "Her too."

"Nonsense. Also—nuance." Sighing dramatically, he held Lou there for another moment. They locked eyes, and both of their grins gradually faded. "How are you, sister mine?" he asked seriously.

Her hands came up to grip his forearm. "I'm . . . better now, I think. The shock is starting to wear off. It's like—like I can finally take a breath." Her fingers squeezed, and she blinked rapidly. "I'm so sorry, Beau." When she looked to Coco, he released her from his grip. "To all of you."

Coco traced a pattern in the tabletop's grain. "I lost my mother a long time ago."

"My father too," Beau added, his voice quiet.

But not Victoire. The guilt resurfaced with a vengeance. I'd survived enough to know it always would. There'd been no sense in that little girl's death. No explanation to make it right. There'd been none when we'd burned the witches' children, either. Victoire had deserved better. They all had.

We did too.

Pushing to my feet, I craned my neck in search of Pan. He'd disappeared into a back room at my arrival, but he couldn't hide from me forever. I strode to the counter and rang the bell. I rang it again. If a small voice in my head chastised me—if it called me rude for harassing a baker after he'd risked life and limb for mine—I ignored it. The witches hadn't doused his hearth. I would bake the pastries myself if he couldn't. Surely I could figure it out.

"What are you doing?" Lou eyed me suspiciously from the

table. "You need to be nice to Pan."

"I'm always nice to—"

"You're ringing his bell."

"Isn't that why it's here?"

"He isn't a *cat*, Reid," Beau said with a smirk.

"It's rude to ring the bell," Coco agreed.

Lou nodded. "Also annoying."

"Very," Beau said.

I grimaced at them all. "I am *trying* to purchase us sticky buns." To Lou, I grumbled, "I think I owe *you* one, in particular."

Her face cleared instantly, and she leaned forward with bright eyes, knitting her fingers together atop the table. "Have I told you today how absolutely and completely attractive I find your ass?"

I snorted just as Pan strode into view. Scowling, he snatched the bell from his counter. "What is it? What do you want? Can you not see I am closed for business?" He gestured a wild hand at the window. "There was a *war*, young man. Wake up!" When he snapped his fingers beneath my nose, I fought the urge to roll my eyes. "We cannot all cower and tremble, forsaking our loved ones. Oh no! Some of us must protect this great kingdom of ours. You treat our fair Lucida like a princess now, yes?"

I cast a scathing look over my shoulder. Both Beau's and Coco's shoulders shook with laughter. Lou gazed back at me with a perfectly placid expression. She batted her lashes. "Like a queen," I said wryly.

Pan frowned at me as if considering. "Very well. I shall make you the sticky buns"—he snapped his fingers again—"but you shall pay full price."

I flashed a hard smile. "Thanks."

Back at the table, Lou pressed her foot over mine. "A truly spectacular ass."

A moment of silence stretched between us. Then another. Outside, Father Achille still coordinated with Jean Luc. With Célie. They'd sent word to neighboring villages for supplies. For healers. Two had survived Morgane's attack on the Tower, but they needed medical treatment themselves. At least, I thought they'd said two. Behind the counter, Pan bustled ostentatiously, banging every pot and slamming every utensil. "Double price," he'd muttered at one point.

At last, Beau heaved a shattered sigh. His smirk had faded. His eyes gleamed anew. "What are we supposed to do now? The cathedral is destroyed. The castle too, by the looks of it. The Archbishop is dead, the king is dead, La Dame des Sorcières is dead—er, the old one, anyway." He shot Lou an apologetic glance.

She shrugged stiffly, tracing the lines on my palm. "The Chateau remains standing. I suppose it's mine now. We can . . . live there." Her eyes flashed to Coco. "All of us."

A wide smile spread across Coco's face. "I don't think Father Achille will give us any trouble."

"*If* he's elected."

"He will be," Beau said. "Father Gaspard nearly pissed down his leg when Morgane showed up. He's a politician." He jerked his head to the window. To Father Achille. "Not a leader."

"Are you a leader, Beau?" Coco asked quietly.

He studied her for a moment, his lips pursed. Undecided. "I don't know yet."

She smirked at him. "We have that in common."

"You can say that again," Lou muttered. "I couldn't manage an attic, let alone a fucking *castle*."

We lapsed into silence until Célie poked her head into the patisserie once more. With a quick wave, she motioned me forward. I kissed Lou's hand before rising to meet her. Jean Luc stood on the other side of the door. Leaning past me, he pushed it closed behind us, and Célie—she actually *bounced* on the balls of her feet. "I have something for you." She spoke over me before I could answer. "When Jean Luc stole your items from the Tower, I chose not to keep it with the rest—your bandolier and knives and such—because it looked too important. I didn't want you to lose it in the heat of the battle."

Jean Luc nodded. "I told her it belonged to your mother."

Realization sparked. Anticipation.

"Of course, when Lou enchanted our clothing, I thought *I'd* lost it." She shook her head, grinning but frazzled. Reaching into the band at her waist, she extracted a familiar ring with a thin golden band and mother-of-pearl stone. It gleamed even in the grayish light. Her smile widened as she placed it in my hand. "Here. Do as you wish with it. It's yours."

I stared down at it in wonder. Warmth radiated through me at the point of contact. My heart pounded. "Thank you, Célie."

"That isn't all." Jean Luc touched the hilt of the Balisarda in my bandolier. Its sapphire winked through the leather. "I spoke with Father Achille. We agreed, both of us—you have a place within our ranks if you want it. That Balisarda is yours."

The happiness in my chest punctured slightly. But—no. I wouldn't let it. Not this time. Unsheathing the Balisarda with one hand, I extended it to Célie. "I think there are others better suited." When her fingers curled around it, her eyes widening in shock, I said, "Two clever little girls once told me they wished to be huntsmen. Not as they are now, but as they should be: proper knights riding forth to vanquish evil. Defending the land and protecting the innocent. One of them even swore she'd wear a dress."

"Oh, I can't"—she shook her head swiftly, attempting to return the Balisarda—"I don't know how to wield a sword. I couldn't possibly use this."

"You don't need to wield a sword to protect the innocent, Célie," Jean Luc said, nodding to me in appreciation. In respect. He glowed with pride as he looked at her. "You've proven that more than anyone."

I nodded too, stepping away from the door. Opening it wide. "The Tower is broken. It's time to rebuild."

She flashed a tentative smile before Jean Luc swept her through it.

I didn't follow. Not right away. Instead I stared at the ring in my hand.

"What are you doing out here?" Lou touched my shoulder,

and I turned, tucking the ring into my pocket. She looked left and right with a pointed smirk. "Having fun with all your friends?"

At her inquisitive gaze, I couldn't help it. A broad smile split my own face, and I kissed her full on the mouth. When I pulled back, she flicked my nose before soothing the spot with her thumb, her hand lingering on my cheek. "Come back inside. Pan says the sticky buns are done."

I brushed my lips across her palm. "That sounds like paradise to me."

EPILOGUE

Ansel

Summer bloomed slow and languorous at Chateau le Blanc. Wild sage and lavender rippled across the mountain in dusky purple and blue; white and yellow marguerites grew rampant between rocks, along creek beds, joined by the blushing pink of thrift and clover. I'd never seen such colors in life. I'd never felt such warmth on my cheeks, like the kiss of a mother, the embrace of a friend. If the voices—no, the *laughter*—of my own friends hadn't called to me, I could've stood within the peace of those wildflowers forever.

Lou wore a spray of each on her wedding day.

Sitting cross-legged atop her childhood bed—the golden thread of her quilt sparkling in the late afternoon sunlight—she waited impatiently for Coco to weave the blooms into a crown. "Stop squirming," Coco chided, grinning and tugging a strand of Lou's hair. "You're shaking the whole bed."

Lou only wriggled her hips more pointedly. "Oh, it'll be shaking tonight."

Célie's cheeks warmed along with my own. When she swept a simple ivory gown from the armoire to cover her embarrassment, I smiled, settling on the chaise beside Madame Labelle. She couldn't see me, of course, but from the way her eyes sparkled, from the way they danced, I thought she might feel me instead.

"You, my friend, are delectably depraved."

"Oh, I'm sorry." With another wide grin, Lou twisted to face Coco. "*Who* was it who lost her virginity atop a—?"

Coughing delicately, Célie asked, "Might I suggest we postpone this conversation for more appropriate company?" Her eyes flicked to Violette and Gabrielle, who flitted about the room, examining anything and everything. The gold leaf across the ceiling. The moondust on the sill. The gilded harp in the corner and the tin soldiers beneath the chaise. Lou had etched mustaches on them as a child. A trunk at the foot of her bed still held toy swords and broken instruments, half-read books and a white rabbit. Stuffed, of course.

The very real cat at my feet hissed at it.

Melisandre, Lou had named her. The cat. Not the rabbit. With her broken tail and crooked teeth, the gray tabby wasn't beautiful, but one wouldn't know it from the way Lou looked at her. She'd found the cat yowling indignantly in a back alley after the battle of Cesarine, and she'd promptly adopted the pitiful creature, much to Reid's chagrin.

Melisandre didn't like Reid.

"Please do not worry yourself, Mademoiselle Célie." With poppy blooms braided into her black hair, Violette giggled and bounced on the balls of her feet as Madame Labelle cackled beside me. "We know all about the birds and the bees. Don't we, Gaby? It's *terribly* romantic."

"*I* think the euphemism is silly." Gabrielle now sat beside me on her knees—wrinkling her olive dress—and attempted to coax Melisandre closer with a piece of string. The cat hissed again before glancing at me with a pained expression. Grinning, I knelt to scratch her ears, and the hiss transformed to a purr. "As if we *need* the imagery of a bird laying eggs to understand ovulation, or a bee depositing pollen to understand fertiliza—"

"Oh, dear." Célie's cheeks washed as pretty a petal pink as her dress, and she draped the ivory gown across the foot of the bed. "That is *quite* enough talk about that, I think. It's almost time for the ceremony. Shall we help you don your gown, Lou?"

When Lou nodded and rose to her feet, Melisandre abandoned me instantly, darting to her mother's side. Lou didn't hesitate to scoop her up and cuddle her against her chest. "And how is my *darling* honeybee? So fetching." She nodded appreciatively to Célie, who'd woven a miniature version of Lou's flower crown for the cat. Melisandre purred under Lou's praise, craning her neck, exorbitantly pleased with herself.

Snorting, Coco helped Célie unlace the wedding gown. "You know Reid is currently plotting her demise."

Madame Labelle rose to join them with a chuckle. "It was his own fault. Vanity, thy name is cat, after all."

Even Manon—who'd hovered silently in the corner, unsure of her place among these people—inched forward tentatively, clutching the handfasting ribbons. When Lou winked at her, she smiled. It was a small, unsure sort of smile, but a smile nonetheless. I recognized it well. I'd worn it many times. Pushing to my own feet, I strode to stand beside her.

She would find her new place here. They all would.

"He'd insulted her!" Lou pressed a kiss to Melisandre's scarred nose, undeterred. "Besides, the piss washed right out of his pillow. No harm done." To Melisandre, she crooned, "He won't mock your singing again, will he, honeybee? No, he won't."

Melisandre yowled in answer, rubbing her head against Lou's chin.

I looked away as they helped her into her gown.

Though heat still suffused my cheeks, it was no longer embarrassment but . . . pride. I nearly burst with it. For too long had Lou deserved this moment—*all* of these moments, the large ones and the small ones and the ones in between. She'd suffered more than most, more than any one person ever should. I could only hope that she'd delight in just as much from this day forward.

Hope.

It wasn't the sickness.

God, she'd done so beautifully. They all had.

Reid would cherish her, I knew. He would do everything in his power to ensure her happiness, and she would return his efforts tenfold. Though I'd known little of life when I'd walked beside them, even then, I'd recognized theirs was a love that would change everything. A love that would break the world. A love that would make it new.

Their love had been the cure.

"What do you think?" Lou's low murmur brought pressure to my eyes. "Will it do?"

I waited to hear Madame Labelle's and Célie's exclamations, Violette's and Gabrielle's laughter, Coco's sniffle, even Manon's soft inhalation before turning to look at my dearest friend.

Reid paced in the early evening sunlight of the old pear grove. It burnished his hair more golden than copper, caught the fine stitching of his jacket and made the threads shimmer. He'd forgone his bandolier for the occasion, instead buckling a single sword at his waist. He steadied it with one hand as he trod a well-worn path in the grass. His other he dragged through his hair.

Beau watched him with unabashed amusement. "Tell me you aren't nervous."

"I'm not nervous." Reid scoffed as if insulted, but his eyes still darted to the opposite end of the grove, where guests had already begun to arrive. It would be an intimate ceremony. They'd invited only those they loved or trusted: Zenna and Seraphine, Toulouse and Thierry, Johannes Pan and his wife. Babette mingled with a handful of other witches, all of whom kept one eye on Jean Luc and Father Achille. Blaise and his children hovered at the edge of the grove, speaking little, until Toulouse beckoned them to come sit. Even Elvire and Lasimonne were in attendance, lounging regally with their diamond gowns and fishhook earrings.

Reid, Beau, and Jean Luc had spent the morning filling the grove with chairs. On the backs of each, they'd painstakingly looped brightly colored ribbons and flowers—poppies, marigolds, peonies, and cornflowers. Scarlets and golds and blushes and blues, all nestled in beds of deep green. More blooms spilled from the stumps of pear trees throughout the grove, where lush moss crept over gnarled wood.

Reid glared at the stumps, the only piece of the scene out of place. Only yesterday, he'd painstakingly constructed the arbor of vines and florets overhead. Every detail had been planned. Every flower plucked to perfection.

Beau followed his gaze with a wistful expression. "If only Claud were here. He could've grown new trees."

Reid looked at him incredulously. "He could also be *dead*."

"We don't know that. He's a god. Perhaps after he's served his time—"

"The ground opened up and swallowed him."

"—he will return to us, good as new," Beau finished determinedly, clasping Reid's shoulder. Forcing him to a halt. "Loosen up, brother mine. It's your wedding day."

"I know." Reid nodded to himself, shaking free to pace again. "I *know*. I just want it to be perfect."

"And it *is*."

He was right. Lou would love it.

If my heart ached that I too couldn't be part of this moment, this memory, the pain eased when I caught sight of an empty chair in the front row. In a burnished oval frame, a picture of my likeness had been affixed to a bouquet of sunflowers. Warmth radiated through me as I knelt to study it.

They'd saved me a seat, after all.

When Coco swept forward in her own gown of ivory—with flowers braided into her black curls—the warmth in my chest bloomed tenfold. Exertion flushed her cheeks, and her dark eyes sparkled with excitement as she looked to Reid and Beau, lifting the sunflower bouquet from my seat. "It's time." She dipped her chin to Beau. "She's waiting."

With a smirk, Beau straightened his jacket and smoothed his immaculate waves. "Finally." He clasped Reid's shoulder before turning on his heel. "My moment to shine."

Snorting, Coco rolled her eyes and said, "No one will be looking at you."

He arched a wicked brow. "*You* will be."

She lifted a casual shoulder, speaking over it as she strode back up the aisle. "We'll see."

"*Yes*, we—" He skidded to a halt in his pursuit of her, his eyes falling on Jean Luc. The spray on the latter's chair had loosened, and he was attempting to reattach it. "Honestly, Jean, what did I tell you? We want it to appear *artfully* strewn, as if the daisies sprang up from this very chair. You're tacking them on too neatly." When Jean Luc scowled, unimpressed, Beau elbowed him aside to do it himself. "Like tits on a boar."

"Careful, Your Majesty." With a wry grin, Jean Luc tossed a handful of fallen edelweiss at his head. The King of Belterra lurched away with a violent curse, finger combing his hair frantically. "You'll muss those luscious locks."

"I will *kill* you—"

Coco caught his hand and dragged him up the aisle before they could brawl. Grinning despite myself, I followed them around the bend, where Lou stood out of sight with Madame Labelle, Célie, and Manon. Beau shook his head when he saw her, whistling low and appreciative. "Reid is going to lose his mind."

Lou winked and shimmied her shoulders. "That's the plan."

Madame Labelle fixed one of her soon-to-be daughter's curls, arranging it artfully around Lou's freckled cheek. "You look beautiful, *fille*. I shall see you soon. Come." She motioned for Célie and Manon to join her, leaving Lou, Coco, Beau, and me alone in the shadow of a withered pear tree. The only one that'd survived. When Reid had suggested holding the festivities here, Madame Labelle had protested, explaining again how Morgane had torched these trees in a fit of rage. Reid knew that, of course. He knew how love could twist even the most beautiful of people, of places, into cruel and dark things. He also knew how special this grove had once been to his mother—to all the Dames Blanches.

Lou had agreed, and together, they'd made it beautiful once more.

When Coco extended the sunflower bouquet, Lou's grin dimmed slightly. Her finger traced the curve of the frame. "Do you think he's watching?"

Coco looped an arm through hers. "I think he wouldn't miss it for anything."

"He should've been here. He should've given me away too."

Beau claimed Lou's other arm, tapping my face in the frame. "He still is."

"I still am," I whispered with a smile. In response, a soft breeze rustled the branches overhead, bringing with it a pleasant warmth, a low hum of bees, a faint scent of daffodils. Of new beginnings.

I walked beside them as they led Lou up the aisle.

Though Claud had gone, his empty seat remained next to mine, and Seraphine crooned a lovely ballad of love lost and love found while Reid waited beneath the arbor. Madame Labelle stood beside him, the handfasting ribbons woven between her fingers. She winked at Father Achille in the audience.

Beau cleared his throat, and every person—every human, witch, werewolf, and mermaid—turned as one to look at us. To look at Lou. Her breath caught in her throat, and her hands tightened instinctively on Coco and Beau. "Breathe, sister mine," the latter murmured. "Just breathe."

"Go on, Lou." Though she couldn't see me, couldn't hear me, I spoke the words regardless, pushing her forward gently. "Find peace."

She seemed to relax at the warm touch of wind on her face.

Then her eyes found Reid, and the entire world faded to that blinding, soul-deep connection. Anyone could see it. Everyone could *feel* it. If I reached out a hand now, I sensed I could've touched it. Though I knew not of magic patterns, this thread that connected Lou and Reid—this gravitational pull, this *cosmic* one—it was a magic in itself. It pulled them together. It would keep them there.

He gazed at her with the most brilliant, devastating smile.

She blinked at the sight of it, her own slightly dazed, slightly awed, as Reid took in her ivory gown, her trailing sleeves, the rich flowers atop her long, loose hair. The scarred roses at her throat. Summer sun had gilded her skin once more. It burnished the freckles across her nose. When he stepped forward to take her hand, he brushed his lips across them, trying to kiss each one. "See something you like?" he murmured in her ear.

She eyed him appreciatively. "Let's make this quick."

Their vows were not traditional. Not this time. Nor was their ceremony. It ended just as the sun touched the mountains, its golden light lengthening the shadows of the grove. Fireflies winked into existence. Ever curious, feu follet soon followed, their eerie glow lighting a path through the gnarled trees. Twice, Beau snatched an inquisitive Gabrielle away from them, much to her indignation. "You *rotten* brother! I just want to *see* them!"

Her protests could barely be heard over the music.

Several more witches had trekked from the castle with mandolins, lutes, and lyres underarm. Others had brought wine. Indeed, most who'd remained at Chateau le Blanc gathered in the grove now, curious and wary. Though they gave Jean Luc and Father Achille a wide berth—and Elvire and Blaise too—no one lifted a hand against them. Toulouse even managed to charm a pretty young witch into dancing with him. Another asked Liana for a turn.

It took little for the rest to follow.

Except for Lasimonne, who—with a cry of "It has *four* legs!"— chased after Melisandre with abject fascination. The cat hissed and yowled and streaked toward the safety of the castle. With the roll of her eyes, Elvire continued to examine the flowers, taking a tentative bite of a peony. Pan swatted her hand away in horror. "No," he said sternly, wagging his finger. "Absolutely not, *ma douce.* You come to Cesarine, and I will bake you something sweet, yes?"

Turning away, I watched Coco and Beau dance for one long, bittersweet moment. He said something to make her laugh— *really* laugh, the sort of laugh that transformed her entire face. The sound of it made him giddy. He twirled her closer next time, his attention rapt on her expression. Drinking in the sight. "I could do more than sail at the age of three," he told her imperiously. "Sir D'artagnan Delmore le Devere taught me to dance as soon as I could walk."

Unfortunately, he chose that moment to spin directly into Jean Luc and Célie. Jean Luc compensated seamlessly, twirling Célie outward with one hand while catching Coco's waist with the other. Beau, who'd slipped on impact, reeled into a stump and nearly lost his footing. Jean Luc smirked. "Sir D'artagnan Delmore le Devere is my godfather, Your Majesty."

Coco howled with laughter.

I hoped she never stopped laughing.

At the center of it all, Lou and Reid whirled with flushed cheeks and bright eyes. When she stepped on his toes for the third time—tipsy with drink—he swept her up in his arms and spun wildly, round and round until Lou shrieked with delight, tipping her head and urging him faster. He never lost his footing. He never loosened his grip.

He even joined her when she belted out "Big Titty Liddy."

Though both sang horribly off-key, all applauded their efforts when they'd finished, and Lou swept into a dramatic bow. Cheeks red, Reid chuckled and tried to move away—out of the limelight—but Lou pulled him back. "Wasn't he *marvelous?*" She crowed the words with pride, cackling as his flush deepened. Madame Labelle whistled from Father Achille's arm. "Everyone tell him how marvelous he is. Tell him how *impressive.*"

Shaking his head, he tucked her firmly into his side and dragged her toward the nearest stump. "You're embarrassing me, wife."

"Look how red your face is." She cackled and wrapped her arms around his waist. "Just wait until the honeymoon—those few blissful days where I'll have you all to myself."

Reid smirked. "I'll believe it when I see it. Your sisters can't leave you alone for more than an hour."

"That's why we're leaving the Chateau."

He raised a brow. "Oh?"

"*Oh,*" she confirmed, matter-of-fact. "There's an old cottage on the beach. It belonged to my grandmother. I've cleaned it out for the two of us." She nuzzled his chest, much like her cat. "Coco can handle the castle without me."

Reid shrugged, the corner of his mouth still quirked. "You're probably right. She's much more diplomatic."

"*Excuse* you." Lou elbowed him in the ribs in feigned outrage, raising her voice for the others to hear. "Should I tell them about your *impressive* foot size? What about those other *marvelous* things you can do with your tongue?"

Reid actually clapped a hand over her mouth.

Shoulders shaking, the two devolved into laughter as a wizened old woman hobbled into the grove.

I didn't recognize her, but the others clearly did: Lou and Reid straightened, Coco and Beau stilled, and even Célie stepped closer to Jean Luc. Though none appeared outright alarmed, a definite current of tension had materialized with the woman. Curiously enough, Zenna smiled.

"Hello, dearies!" Bracelets clinked on the woman's wrist as she waved gaily, heedless of her less-than-warm reception. Her scarlet robes billowed around her. "What a *sublime* evening for a wedding. And truly, you could not have chosen a more fortuitous locale."

"Madame Sauvage." Reid cast a quick, nervous glance toward Coco, Beau, and Célie. His next word sounded a question. "Welcome."

Lou's eyes narrowed. "How did you find this place?"

"Ah." Madame Sauvage clasped Lou's hands in her own, pressing a kiss to them. "Felicitations, my dear, on your recent nuptials. It seems I missed quite a delightful evening, and you, in turn, missed my winsome company." Her clouded eyes lingered on the witch with the mandolin. "I trust you provided the correct designation this time? None of this *Larue* business?"

Lou's frown deepened, but she didn't pull her hands away. "How do you know about that?"

Madame Sauvage ignored the question, instead turning to Reid. She pinched his cheek. "And you, young man? Did you plant those seeds as you promised?"

"I"—he looked again to Lou, more panicked now than before—"I'm sorry, Madame Sauvage, but I—I misplaced them."

"You *lost* them, you mean?" When Reid nodded, she clicked her tongue in disappointment. I inched closer, studying her face. She seemed . . . familiar, somehow. Like I'd met her before. And her disappointment—I glanced around, uncertain—it felt staged. Zenna still smiled behind us, and that smile had spread to Seraphine, Toulouse, and Thierry. Madame Sauvage winked at them. "Well, Monsieur le Blanc, just how should we proceed? We made a *bargain*, you remember."

Reid nodded grimly. "I'll procure another pearl for you, *madame*. I promise."

"You promised"—Madame Sauvage unfurled her fingers slowly, revealing a handful of seeds in her palm—"to plant the seeds."

We all stared at them.

"How did you—?" Reid started.

Her dark eyes gleamed. Pressing the seeds into his hand, she said, "A fortuitous location, indeed. If you plant them—if you *care* for them—they will grow." When Reid didn't move, when he only studied the seeds with open suspicion, Madame Sauvage poked his chest. "Well, what are you waiting for? Do it now! I'm not getting any younger."

"I don't have a *shovel*—"

With an impatient sigh, Lou waved her hand, and the seeds flew outward in a sharp burst of magic, scattering across the grove. In the next second, they burrowed into the ground of their own accord. "There." She thrust her arm through Reid's. "Are we settled? Have we honored this ridiculous bargain?"

Trees burst from the ground as Madame Sauvage's answer.

Pear trees.

They climbed skyward at a rapid pace, white blossoms blooming and falling to reveal hard green fruit. A dozen in all—one tree for each seed planted. Lou gasped as Reid stared, as Beau leapt backward, and Madame Labelle stretched incredulously to touch one of the low-hanging fruit. Shaking her head, she whirled to face the old woman. "Who *are* you?"

Madame Sauvage bowed, looking meaningfully at Lou. "A friend."

She turned without another word, and as suddenly as she'd hobbled into our presence, she hobbled out, leaving only the peculiar scent of . . . of *earth* in her wake. Of fresh grass and pine sap and pears. Still smiling, Zenna, Seraphine, Toulouse, and Thierry followed after her.

Lou watched them go, slack-jawed, until unexpected laughter burst from her. Until she was breathless with it. She turned to Reid, tears of mirth lining her turquoise eyes. "That nosy son of a *bitch*—"

I didn't hear the rest, however. Because at the edge of the grove, Madame Sauvage looked back to meet my gaze. *My* gaze. With a small smile, she inclined her head toward something behind me.

"Ansel."

I turned at that voice, at that presence. I recognized it now as innately as my own.

Two figures stood on the path down the mountain. His hair and his jaw were my own. Her eyes and her skin, as well. "Are you ready, darling?" The woman extended an olive hand to me, and her smile—it was as warm as I'd always dreamed it. As warm as this summer night.

"That boy is asking after you again," the man said, wrapping an arm around her shoulders. "Etienne."

Butterflies erupted at the name.

Unbidden, my feet drifted toward them, my lips lifting in a smile. I couldn't help one last look, however—at Lou, at Reid, at Coco, at Beau. They milled around the pear trees, feeling each trunk, testing the leaves. Laughing at themselves with Terrance and Liana and Manon.

If you plant them—if you care for them—they will grow.

My smile widened. Madame Sauvage had vanished, leaving them to life anew.

Taking my mother's hand, I did too.

Pickup By:
10/20/2021

BENN

1642

*

*

*

*

ACKNOWLEDGMENTS

I owe a great debt to many people for not only the creation of this book, but also for the creation of this entire series. To cut straight to the heart of it, the most important of them is *you*. The reader. *Thank you* seems too commonplace an expression to convey my gratitude, but truly, no words can describe the emotion in my chest when I think of how kind you've all been, how enthusiastic. Though the pandemic struck just months after *Serpent & Dove* was published, each one of you went above and beyond to support these books. The beautiful photos, illustrations, cosplays, lyrics, reels—I have a lump in my throat thinking of them now. The past three years have changed my life, and readers continue to be the heart of that. From Lou and Reid, from Coco, Ansel, Beau, and *me*, thank you, thank you, *thank you*.

Jordan, I've told you a million times, but I'll tell you again—I couldn't have written this book without you. When writers ask me for guidance, I often tell them to find what they love and lean into it unapologetically. You give me permission to follow my own advice. This book—*all* my books—wouldn't contain half the wit, half the kissing, half the *fun* without your input. Are you my muse? Probably. I love you to the moon and to Saturn.

RJ, Beau, James, and Rose, words will never be able to convey the depths of my love for you. This deadline could've been a burden, but it wasn't. Thank you for your patience. Thank you for your understanding. Thank you for your love and respect and support as together, we chase our crazy dreams. Zane and Kelly—and Jake, Brooke, Justin, Chelsy, and Lewie—we don't get to choose our family, but even if we could, I would choose you anyway. Thank you for being my collective rock. I love you all more than you know.

Jordan, Spencer, Meghan, Aaron, Adrianne, Chelsea, Courtney, Austin, Jamie, Josh, Jake, Jillian, Aaron, Jon, and Kendall, you are my favorite people on this earth, and your wholehearted support of both me and my books has been so precious to me. I don't deserve any of you. Katie, Carolyn, Isabel, Kristin, Adrienne, Adalyn, and Rachel, there is something so special about writing friends who become real-life friends, and I couldn't be more honored to call you mine.

Sarah, I feel so incredibly grateful to have such a warm and approachable agent in my corner. Erica, editor extraordinaire, I can't thank you enough for your unending patience and your infallible vision for this series. (And I promise I'll make my next deadline! I promise!) Stephanie Guerdan, it was so wonderful to work with you. Alexandra Rakaczki and Jessica White, I'm so grateful for your sharp eyes, and I similarly promise there will be no Célie or Philippe in my next book! Allison Brown, thank you for all the time and energy you poured into this series. Jessie Gang and Alison Donalty, these covers have continued to blow my mind; I attribute so much of this series' success to your and Katt Phatt's skills. Rachel Horowitz, Sheala Howley, and Cassidy Miller, as well as Sophie Kossakowski, Gillian Wise, Sam Howard, Karen Radner, and the entire sales team, thank you for working behind the scenes to make these books successful.

Mitch Thorpe, Michael D'Angelo, Ebony LaDelle, Audrey Diestelkamp, and the entire team at Epic Reads—you are all rock stars. Truly, I can't thank you enough for your enthusiasm and support of this series, as well as the resources and opportunities you provided.

SNARE OF SERPENTS

By Victoria Holt

SNARE OF SERPENTS

THE CAPTIVE

THE INDIA FAN

THE SILK VENDETTA

SECRET FOR A NIGHTINGALE

THE ROAD TO PARADISE ISLAND

THE LANDOWER LEGACY

THE TIME OF THE HUNTER'S MOON

THE DEMON LOVER

THE JUDAS KISS

THE MASK OF THE ENCHANTRESS

THE SPRING OF THE TIGER

MY ENEMY THE QUEEN

THE DEVIL ON HORSEBACK

THE PRIDE OF THE PEACOCK

LORD OF THE FAR ISLAND

THE HOUSE OF A THOUSAND LANTERNS

THE CURSE OF THE KINGS

ON THE NIGHT OF THE SEVENTH MOON

THE SHADOW OF THE LYNX

THE SECRET WOMAN

THE SHIVERING SANDS

THE QUEEN'S CONFESSION

THE KING OF THE CASTLE

MENFREYA IN THE MORNING

THE LEGEND OF THE SEVENTH VIRGIN

BRIDE OF PENDORRIC

KIRKLAND REVELS

MISTRESS OF MELLYN

VICTORIA HOLT

Snare

of Serpents

DOUBLEDAY

New York • London • Toronto • Sydney • Auckland

PUBLISHED BY DOUBLEDAY
a division of Bantam Doubleday Dell Publishing Group, Inc.
666 Fifth Avenue, New York, New York 10103

DOUBLEDAY and the portrayal of an anchor with a dolphin are trademarks of
Doubleday, a division of Bantam Doubleday Dell Publishing Group, Inc.

Library of Congress Cataloging-in-Publication Data

Holt, Victoria, 1906–
Snare of serpents/by Victoria Holt.—1st ed.
p. cm.
I. Title.
PR6015.I3S588   1990
823'.914—dc20   89-71453
CIP

ISBN 0-385-41385-8

Printed in the United States of America
October 1990
First Edition

Edinburgh

A Thief in the House

I HAD NEVER SEEN ANYONE look less like a governess. I was watching from a window when she arrived. She stood for a moment looking up at the house and I saw her face clearly. Her reddish hair—Titian, I think it was called—was visible under a black hat with a green feather. That air of genteel poverty which her predecessor, Lilias Milne, had had in common with most of her kind was completely lacking. There was a flamboyant quality about this woman. She looked as if she were about to join some theatrical group instead of coming to teach the daughter of one of Edinburgh's most respected citizens.

Moreover Hamish Vosper, son of the coachman, had been ordered to take the carriage to the station to meet her. It was too long ago for me to remember the arrival of Lilias Milne, but I was sure she had not been brought here by the family carriage. Hamish helped her out of the vehicle as though she were an important guest; then he collected her baggage—of which there was a considerable amount—and brought her to the front door.

At that point I went down to the hall. Mrs. Kirkwell, the housekeeper, was already there.

"It's the new governess," she said to me.

The governess was standing in the hall. She had very green eyes, their colour no doubt accentuated by the green feather in her hat and the silk scarf at her throat; but what made her face so startling were the dark brows and eyelashes which contrasted vividly with the colour of her hair; she had a short rather pert nose with a long upper lip which gave her a playful kittenish look. The full red lips made another contrast; they revealed slightly prominent teeth which suggested an eagerness, a greediness for what—I was only just sixteen—I was not quite sure.

She was looking straight at me and I felt I was being closely scrutinised.

"You must be Davina," she said.

"Yes, I am," I answered.

The green eyes were speculative. "We're going to get along," she said, in a coy voice which did not quite match the look she gave me.

I knew she was not Scottish.

My father had spoken of her only briefly. He had said: "There will be a new governess. I myself engaged her so I am sure she will give satisfaction."

I had been dismayed. I did not want another governess. I should be seventeen soon and I thought it was time I finished with governesses. Moreover I was still very upset by what had happened to Lilias Milne. She had been with me for eight years and we had become good friends. I could not believe that she was guilty of what they had accused her.

Mrs. Kirkwell was saying: "Perhaps you'd like to show Miss . . . er . . ."

"Grey," said the governess. "Zillah Grey."

Zillah! What a strange name for a governess! And why did

she tell us? Why not say just Miss Grey? It had been a long time before I discovered that Miss Milne was Lilias.

I took her to her room and she stood beside me looking round, studying it intently as a few moments before she had studied me.

"Very nice," she said. She turned her luminous eyes on me. "I think I am going to be very happy here."

THE EVENTS which had led up to the arrival of Miss Zillah Grey had been dramatic and the fact that they had burst so unexpectedly into our peaceful existence made them more so.

It began that morning when I went into my mother's bedroom and found her dead. After that, a sinister influence began to creep into the house—vaguely, insidiously at first until it culminated in the tragedy which threatened to ruin my life.

I had risen that morning as usual and was coming down to breakfast when I met Kitty McLeod, our parlourmaid, on the stairs.

"I cannot get an answer from Mrs. Glentyre," she said. "I've knocked two or three times. I dinna like to go in without her saying so."

"I'll come with you," I said.

We went up the stairs to the master bedroom which for the last year or so my mother had occupied alone, for she had not been in good health and my father sometimes was away on business until late and, not wanting to disturb her, he occupied the room next to hers. There were even nights when he could not get home at all.

I knocked. There was no answer so I went into the room. It was a very pleasant one. There was a large double bed with highly polished brass knobs and flounces which matched the curtains. It had tall windows from which one could look out onto the grey stone, dignified houses on the other side of the wide street.

I went to the bed and there lay my mother—white and very still—with a look of tranquility on her face.

I knew that she was dead.

I turned to Kitty who was standing beside me and said: "Get Mr. Kirkwell at once."

Kirkwell the butler was there almost immediately with Mrs. Kirkwell beside him.

"We'll send for the doctor," he said.

We were shocked and stunned, but we could only wait for the arrival of the doctor.

When he came he told us that she had died in her sleep. "It was very peaceful," he said, "and not unexpected."

We could not send for my father because we did not know where he was. We believed he was on a business trip to Glasgow, but that was too vague. He returned later that day.

I had never seen such horror in any face as I saw in his when he heard the news. Strangely enough I had just a fleeting fancy that I detected a look of guilt.

It would be because he had not been at home when it happened, of course. But could he blame himself for that?

THEN THE CHANGE set in.

I had lived the sixteen years of my life in an orderly fashion and could never have suspected that it would change so drastically. I learned that peace, security, happiness, when we have them, are taken for granted and we do not value them highly enough until we have lost them.

Looking back, there is so much to remember: a roomy comfortable house where warm fires appeared as soon as the cold winds of autumn reminded us that winter was on the way. I had no need to fear the cold. I enjoyed the stimulation of going out walking in warm gaiters, coat tipped with fur at the neck and sleeves, woollen muffler, gloves and a fur muff for added protection. There was the knowledge that I was a member of one of the most highly respected families in Edinburgh.

My father was head of a bank in Princes Street, and I always felt a glow of pride when I walked past it. When I was very young I thought that all the money which went into the bank was his. It was a wonderful thing to be a Glentyre—member of such an illustrious family. My father was David Ross Glentyre and I have been named Davina which was the nearest they could get to David. If I had been a boy, which I supposed they would have preferred, I should have been called David. But there was never a boy; my mother had been too delicate to risk a second childbirth.

Such memories there were for me in that house which had become one of mourning.

Until a year or so before her death my mother and I had often ridden out in the carriage to the shops or to visit friends. Much homage was shown to her in all the big shops. Men in black coats came hurrying forward rubbing their hands in unctuous delight because she had deigned to visit them. "When would you like this sent, Mrs. Glentyre? Of course, of course, we can get it to the house today. And Miss Davina . . . quite the young lady now." It was all very gratifying.

We would visit friends—people as comfortably situated as ourselves, living in similar houses. We would take tea, bannocks and Dundee cake and I would sit and listen docilely to the accounts of the trials and triumphs of our neighbours; and sometimes there would be hints—although only hints because of my presence, with pursed lips seeming to hold back words which threatened to escape and so sully my ears—that there were fascinating details to come at a more suitable time.

How I loved driving along the Royal Mile from the castle on the rock to that most delightful of all palaces, Holyrood House. Once I had been inside the palace. I had stood in the room where Rizzio had been murdered at the feet of Queen Mary; I had shivered and dreamed of it for months afterwards. It was all so frighteningly wonderful.

Every Sunday I went to church with my mother and with my father if he was not away. In that case my mother and I went alone and after the service we would pause outside the church to chat with friends before we got into the carriage which Vosper, the coachman, would have waiting for us. Then we would drive through the streets with their Sunday quietness to the house and Sunday lunch.

That would have been a solemn occasion but for my mother; she laughed a good deal and could be a trifle irreverent about the sermon; when she talked about people she had a way of

imitating them so accurately that it was as though they themselves were speaking. She did this affectionately rather than
maliciously; and we were very amused. Even my father allowed his lips to twitch and Kirkwell would put his hand discreetly to his lips to hide a smile; Kitty would smirk and my
father would look with mild reproach at my mother who only
laughed.

My father was a very solemn man, very religious and anxious
that everyone in the house should be the same. He conducted
prayers every morning in the library when he was at home,
and all must attend, except my mother. She had been told by
the doctor that she needed rest, so she did not rise until ten
o'clock.

After church Sunday lunches would be going on in all those
tall granite houses. Most of them would have the requisite
number of servants, similar to ours. We had Mr. and Mrs.
Kirkwell, Kitty, Bess and the tweeny. Then there were the
Vospers. They did not live in the house but had their own
quarters in the mews where the horses and carriage were kept.
There were Mr. and Mrs. Vosper and Hamish their son. Hamish was about twenty. He helped his father and if old Vosper
was not able to drive the carriage, Hamish did.

There was something about Hamish which puzzled me. He
was very dark-haired with eyes which were almost black. Mrs.
Kirkwell said: "There's more than a touch of insolence about
young Hamish. He seems to have a notion he's a cut above the
rest of us."

He certainly swaggered. He was tallish and broad; he towered above his father and Mr. Kirkwell, and had a habit of
lifting one eyebrow and the side of his mouth at the same time
as he surveyed people. It made him appear supercilious, as
though he were looking down on us because he knew so much
more than we did.

My father seemed to like him. He said he had a way with
horses, and he rather preferred the younger Vosper to the elder
when it came to driving the carriage.

I loved those sessions when my mother and I were alone and
we talked. She was fascinated by what she called the olden days

and talked of them constantly. Her eyes would glow with excitement when she discussed the conflicts with our enemy below the border. She grew passionate about the great William Wallace who had stood against the mighty Edward when he had wreaked such harm on our country that he was known in history as the Hammer of the Scots.

"Great Wallace was captured." Her eyes would glow with anger and then with bitter sorrow. "They hanged and quartered him at Smithfield . . . like a common traitor."

Then there was Bonnie Prince Charlie and the tragedy of Culloden; there was the triumph of Bannockburn; and, of course, the ill-fated and ever romantic Mary Queen of Scots.

Enchanted afternoons they were and I could not bear to think that they had gone forever.

How I loved our grey city—so austere and so beautiful when the sun shone on the grey stone buildings. Such a comfortable, cosy life that was. The affairs of the household ran smoothly, or if they did not it never reached our ears but was sorted out by the excellent Kirkwells. Meals were always on time. Prayers when my father was in residence, with everyone except my mother and the Vospers attending. The Vospers were excused, of course, because they did not live in the house. I was sure no prayer ritual was conducted in the mews rooms.

Until I was fourteen I had taken my meals with Miss Milne. After that I joined my parents. It was as I was beginning to grow up that I became such good friends with Lilias Milne. I learned a great deal about her, and it was through her that I understood something of the precarious and often humiliating life these ladies were forced to live. I was glad Lilias had come to us. So was she.

"Your mother is a lady in every sense of the word," she said on one occasion. "She has never made me feel that I am a sort of servant. When I first came here she asked me questions about my family and I could see at once that she understood and cared. She took an interest in other people; she saw what their lives were like and could put herself in their places. She always tried not to hurt people in any way. That's what I call a lady."

"Oh, I am so glad you came, Lilias," I said. I was calling her

Lilias then when we were alone. I reserved Miss Milne for when we were not. I was sure Mrs. Kirkwell would have objected to my use of the governess's Christian name—my father, too. My mother would not have cared.

Lilias told me about her family who lived in England in the county of Devon.

"I was one of six," she said. "All girls. It would have been better if some of us had been boys, although, of course, they would have had to be expensively educated. We were really very poor. We had the big house to keep up. It was always cold and draughty. How I love these warm fires here. You need them up here, of course, where it is so much colder. But in the house I'm warm. That's what I like."

"Tell me about the vicarage."

"Big . . . draughty . . . right close to the church. The church is ancient, as so many of them are, and there is always something going wrong. Deathwatch beetle, woodworm and leaking roof. We have it all. It's beautiful though. It's in the heart of Lakemere, which is one of our English villages, with the old church, the cottages and the manor house. You don't have them up here. You notice the difference as soon as you cross the border. I love the English villages."

"And the draughty old vicarage? You must admit it's warmer in our house."

"I do. I do. I appreciate it. Then I say to myself, how long? That's something I have to face, Davina. How much longer will you be needing a governess? I've been wondering that for a long time. They will send you away to school, I suppose."

"They won't now. Perhaps I'll get married and you can be governess to my children."

"That's a little way ahead," she said wryly.

She was ten years older than I and I had been eight when she came to us. I was her first pupil.

She told me about life before she came.

"Six girls," she said. "We always knew we should have to earn a living if we did not get married. We couldn't all stay at home. The two eldest, Grace and Emma, did marry. Grace to a clergyman and Emma to a solicitor. I was next and then there were Alice, Mary and Jane. Mary became a missionary. She's out in Africa somewhere. Alice and Jane stayed at home to help keep house, for my mother had died."

"And you came here. I'm glad you did, Lilias."

Our friendship was growing closer. I, too, was afraid that one day my father would decide that I was no longer in need of a governess. When would that be? When I was seventeen? That was not far-off.

Lilias had come near to marriage once. She talked of it sadly, nostalgically. But her lover had "never spoken."

"I suppose it was all implication," I said. "How did you know he might . . . speak?"

"He was fond of me. He was the son of the squire of Lakemere, the younger son. It would have been a good match for the vicar's daughter. He had a fall when he was riding. It crippled him very badly. He lost the use of his legs."

"Didn't you go to him? Didn't you tell him that you would look after him forevermore?"

She was silent, looking back into the past. "He hadn't spoken. Nobody knew how it was, you see. There would have been opposition, I daresay. What could I do?"

"I would have gone to him. I would have done the speaking."

She smiled at me indulgently. "A woman cannot do that."

"Why not?" I demanded.

"Because . . . she has to wait to be asked. He wouldn't ask me, would he . . . when he was in that state? It couldn't be. It was ordained."

"By whom?"

"By God. By Fate. By Destiny . . . whatever you like to call it."

"I wouldn't have allowed it. I would have gone to him and told him I would marry him."

"You have much to learn, Davina," she said, and I retorted: "Then teach me."

"There are some things," she said, "which people have to learn through experience."

I thought a good deal about Lilias and I sometimes wondered whether it was the idea of being married, of not having to be a governess, always wondering when she would be looking for another post in a strange household, that she had been in love with . . . rather than with the man.

I was growing very fond of her, and I knew she was of me and, during those weeks before my mother died, her fear of what the future held drew her close to me—and after my mother's death we were more friendly than ever.

But I was growing up. I was facing facts and I knew that Lilias would not be in the house much longer.

Nanny Grant had left only a short time before. She had gone to live with a cousin in the country. Her departure had saddened me deeply. She had been my mother's nurse and had stayed with her until her marriage and then she had come to this house and eventually nannied me. We had been very close in those early days. She was the one who had comforted me when I had my nightmares and fell and hurt myself. There would always be memories of those days. When the snow came she would take me out into the garden at the back between the mews and the house, patiently sitting on a seat while I made a snowman. I remembered her suddenly picking me up and crying: "That'll do. Do you want to turn your old nanny into a snowman? Look at you now. Your eyes are dancing at the thought. Ye're a wee villain, that's what ye are."

I remember those rainy days when we sat at the window waiting for it to clear up so that we could go out. We would sing together:

> *Rainy rainy rattle stanes*
> *Dinna rain on me*
> *Rain on John o' Groaties' hoose*
> *Far across the sea.*

And now Nanny Grant had gone, leaving those wonderful memories—all part of a life over which a shutter was drawn on that tragic day I had gone into my mother's room and found her dead.

"MOURNING FOR A DAUGHTER is a year," announced Mrs. Kirkwell. "For us I reckon it should be from three to six months. Six for Mr. Kirkwell and me. Three months will be enough for the maids."

How I hated my black clothes. Every time I put them on I was reminded of my mother lying dead in her bed.

Nothing was the same. Sometimes I had a feeling that we were waiting for something to happen, waiting to emerge from our mourning. Lilias, I knew, was waiting for the summons to my father's presence to be told that as I was growing up her services would no longer be needed.

As for my father, he was away more than ever. I was glad of this. I dreaded meals with him. We were both too conscious of that empty chair.

Not that he had ever been communicative. He had always seemed encased in a demeanour of formality. My mother, though, had been able to break through it. I thought of how his lips twitched when he felt amusement which he tried hard to suppress. I guessed he had cared for her deeply, which was strange because she was so different from him. She would have thrust aside the conventions to which he adhered so strongly. I remembered his gently reproaching voice when she said something which he considered rather outrageous. "My dear . . . my dear . . ." I had heard him murmur, smiling in spite of himself. If it had been left to her, our household would have been a merry one.

Once my mother said: "Your father is a man of high principles, a good man. He tries so hard to live up to his high standards. Sometimes I think it is more comfortable to set them slightly lower, so that one does not have to disappoint oneself."

I did not quite understand what she meant and when I asked her to explain she just laughed and said: "My mind's wandering. It's nothing . . ." Then she shrugged her shoulders and murmured: "Poor David."

I wondered why she should be pitying my father. But she would say no more on the subject.

Some three weeks after my mother's death my father's sister, Aunt Roberta, came to stay with us. She had been ill at the time of the funeral and unable to attend, but at this time she had recovered her good health.

She was quite unlike my father. He was a reserved man who kept aloof from us. Not so Aunt Roberta. Her voice could be heard all over the house, high-pitched and authoritative. She surveyed us all with the utmost disapproval.

She was unmarried. Mrs. Kirkwell, who greatly resented her presence in the house, said she was not surprised that Miss Glentyre had not been able to find a man bold enough to take her on.

Aunt Roberta announced that she had come to us because my father, having lost his wife, would need a woman to supervise his household. As my mother had never supervised anything this was unacceptable from the start. Moreover it sent shivers of apprehension through the house, for it implied that Aunt Roberta intended to make her stay a permanent one.

From the moment she arrived she began to disrupt the household. Resentment was brewing, and it occurred to me that the servants might soon be looking for new places.

"It's a good thing that Mr. Kirkwell is a patient man," Mrs. Kirkwell told Lilias, who imparted the information to me. Lilias added: "I really think that, comfortable as they have all been here, this might be too much for them."

How I wished she would go.

My father, fortunately, was less patient than Mr. Kirkwell. There was an acid conversation between them one evening at dinner.

The conversation was about me.

"You should remember, David, that you have a daughter," began Roberta, helping herself from the dish of parsnips which Kitty was offering.

"It is something I am not likely to forget," retorted my father.

"She is growing up . . . fast."

"At the same rate, I have always thought, as others of her age."

"She needs looking after."

"She has a perfectly adequate governess. That, I believe, will suffice for a while."

"Governess!" snorted Aunt Roberta. "What do they know about launching a girl?"

"Launching?" I cried in dismay.

"I was not talking to you, Davina."

I felt angry that she should consider I was still at the stage of being seen but not heard, yet not too young for launching.

"You were talking about me," I retorted sharply.

"Oh dear me. What is the world coming to?"

"Roberta," said my father calmly. "You are welcome to stay here, but I cannot have you attempting to rule my household. It has always been efficiently managed, and I do not care to have it changed."

"I cannot understand you, David," said Aunt Roberta. "I think you forget . . ."

"It is you who forget that you are no longer the elder sister. I know that you are two years older than I, and that may have had some significance when you were eight and I was six. But at this stage I do not need you to look after my household."

She was taken aback. She shrugged her shoulders philosophically with an air of resignation, murmuring: "The ingratitude of some people is beyond all understanding."

I thought she might have left the house then, but she seemed to persuade herself that, unappreciated as she was, it was her duty to steer us away from disaster.

Then something happened which shocked me deeply—as it did all of us—and made her decision for her.

Hamish was driving my father almost all the time now. The position in the mews had been reversed. It was not Hamish who now stood in when his father was otherwise engaged, but the father who was called when Hamish was not available. Hamish was swaggering more than ever. He made a habit of coming into the kitchen. He would sit in a chair at the table watching everyone . . . even me if I happened to be there. It was clear that Kitty, Bess and the tweeny found his presence exciting; and he indulged in condescending flirtation with them.

I could not understand why they liked him so much. I thought his hairy arms were revolting. He seemed to find great pleasure in displaying them, and his sleeves were invariably rolled up to the elbow so that he could stroke his arms caressingly.

Mrs. Kirkwell regarded him with suspicion. He had tried to be jolly with her, but without success. He had a habit of laying his hands on the girls which they seemed to like; but the charm he exerted so easily over them did not extend to Mrs. Kirkwell.

Once he touched her shoulder as she passed and murmured: "You must have been a bonny wench in your day, Mrs. K. A bit of a wee handful, if you asked me . . . but perhaps not so wee, eh?"

She replied with the utmost dignity: "I'd thank you to remember who you are talking to, Hamish Vosper."

At which he made cooing noises and said: "So it's like that, is it? I've got to mind me pints and quarts here, I can see."

"And I can't have you lying around in this kitchen either," retorted Mrs. Kirkwell.

"Oh aye. But I'm waiting for the master, you see."

"Well, the sooner he sends for you the better in my opinion."

Lilias Milne came into the kitchen at that moment, I remember. She wanted to speak to Bess to ask her if she had seen a packet of pins on her table that morning. She had left them there and now they were gone. She thought Bess might have put them in with the rubbish.

I noticed that Hamish was watching her with a look of speculation—not as he looked at the young girls, but intently . . . differently.

IT WAS A FEW DAYS LATER when the trouble arose.

It began when I met Aunt Roberta on the stairs. It was after luncheon and I knew she had a rest in the afternoon. It was the one time when the house settled down to a peaceful quietness.

Aunt Roberta had been a little subdued since her altercation with my father, but she still supervised all that went on in the house and her eagle eye constantly alighted with disapproval on most things around her.

I was on the point of hastily returning to my room when she saw me.

"Oh, it's you, is it, Davina? You are dressed for going out?"

"Yes. Miss Milne and I often take a walk at this time of day."

She was about to pass some comment when she stopped suddenly, listening.

"Is anything wrong?" I asked.

She put her fingers to her lips and I went quietly to stand beside her.

"Listen," she whispered.

I heard the sound of a stifled laugh and strange noises. They were coming from behind one of the closed doors.

Aunt Roberta strode to that door and threw it open. I was standing beside her and I saw a sight which astonished me. The tangled bodies of Kitty and Hamish were on the bed and both of them were in a state of seminudity.

They started up. Kitty's face was scarlet and even Hamish looked a little taken aback.

I heard Aunt Roberta's quick intake of breath. Her first thoughts were for me. "Leave us, Davina," she cried.

But I could not move. I could only stare in fascination at the two on the bed.

Aunt Roberta advanced into the room.

"Disgusting . . . I never saw . . . you depraved . . ." She was spluttering, for once unable to find the words she needed.

Hamish had risen from the bed and began struggling into his clothes. He assumed an air of truculent bravado. He grinned at Aunt Roberta. "Well," he said, "it's only human nature, after all."

"You disgusting creature," she said. "Get out of this house. As for you . . ." She could not bring herself to say Kitty's name. "You . . . you slut. You'll pack your bags immediately and get out . . . get out, both of you."

Hamish shrugged his shoulders, but Kitty looked stunned. Her face, which had been as red as holly berries, was now as white as paper.

Aunt Roberta turned and almost fell on me.

"Davina! What is the world coming to? I told you to go. It is quite . . . disgusting. I knew something was going on in this house. As soon as your father comes in . . ."

I turned and fled. I shut myself in my room. I, too, was

shocked. I felt nauseated. "Human nature," Hamish had said. I had never been so close to that sort of human nature before.

THERE WAS SILENCE in the house. The servants had congregated in the kitchen. I pictured them sitting round the table whispering. Lilias came to my room.

"There is going to be trouble," she said. "And you were there."

I nodded.

"What did you see?"

"I saw the two of them . . . on the bed."

Lilias shivered.

"It was so repulsive," I said. "Hamish's legs are hairy . . . just like his arms."

"I suppose a man like that would have some sort of attraction for a girl like Kitty."

"What sort of attraction?"

"I don't know exactly, but I can see that he is . . . virile. He could be quite overpowering to a young girl. They'll dismiss her, of course. They'll dismiss both of them. I wonder where Kitty will go. And what will they do with him? He lives there . . . in the mews. There's going to be great trouble over this when your father comes home."

I could not forget Kitty's face. There had been such terrible fear there. She had been with us for four years and had been fourteen when she had come to us from the country.

"Where will she go?" I asked. Lilias shook her head.

I knew that when my father came home Aunt Roberta would insist that Kitty left. I could not get out of my mind a picture of her standing on the pavement surrounded by her few possessions.

I went up to the room she shared with Bess and Jenny the tweeny. She was there alone, sent there by Aunt Roberta. She was sitting on the bed looking desperately afraid.

I went in and sat beside her. She seemed like a different person in her skirt and blouse from that half-nude creature on the bed.

"Oh, Miss Davina, you shouldn't be here," she said. Then: "Is the master home?"

I shook my head. "Not yet."

"Her?" she asked.

"You mean my aunt? My father has made it clear that she does not run the household."

"I'll have to go when he comes."

"How could you . . . do that?" I demanded. And added: "With him?"

She looked at me and shook her head. "You don't understand, Miss Davina. It's natural like . . . with him."

"Human nature," I said, quoting him. "But it seems so . . ."

"Well, there's something about him."

"All that hair," I said with a shiver. "On his legs as well as his arms."

"Maybe . . ."

"Kitty, what will you do?"

She shook her head and started to cry.

"If they send you away . . . where will you go?"

"I just don't know, Miss."

"Could you go to your home?"

"It's miles away . . . near to John o' Groats. I came down because there's nothing for me up there. There's only me old dad now. He couldna keep me up there. There's nothing. I canna go back and tell him why."

"Then where, Kitty?"

"Perhaps the master will give me another chance," she said hopefully, but I could see she thought there was little chance of that.

I thought of his reading the Bible . . . all the little bits about the vengeance of the Lord, and it occurred to me that he would consider Kitty's sin too great for forgiveness. I had always liked Kitty. She had been jolly and merry. I wanted to help her. I had a money box in which I put the odd coin saved from my weekly pocket money. She could have what I had there. It was not much, and the problem was where could she go?

"You must go somewhere," I said.

She shook her head in despair.

What happened to girls who had sinned as Kitty had? They were driven out into the falling snow. There was no snow at this time, but that was small consolation.

I had heard of a nun being walled up for a similar offence. It appeared to be one of the greatest sins. Because of it some girls had babies and were shamed forever.

I did my best to comfort Kitty. I hoped my father would not come home that night, which would give her a little respite— time to think of some solution.

I went to Lilias and told her that I had been with Kitty and what a state of desolation she was in.

"She's a fool," said Lilias, "to behave so . . . and particularly with a man like Hamish. She can't be quite right in the head."

"She really is desperate, Lilias. She has nowhere to go."

"Poor girl."

"What will she do? She might kill herself. Lilias, what if she did? I should never forget that I hadn't helped her."

"What could you do?"

"I could give her the little money I have."

"I doubt that would last long."

"I went to talk to her about having to go. *You* could go back to your vicarage. *You* do have a home. It's different for Kitty. She has nowhere to go. They wouldn't be so cruel, would they, to turn her out when she has nowhere to go?"

"She's committed the cardinal sin, it seems. They stoned people like that, according to the Bible. I think some people would do the same today."

"What can we do for her?"

"You say she has nowhere to go."

"That's what she says. If they turn her out she will just wander about the streets. Lilias, I can't bear it. She was so happy here. I can't forget the way she laughed when he looked at her and joked . . . and it has all led to this."

Lilias was thoughtful. She said suddenly: "I feel as you do about Kitty. She's got caught up with that man. He's a rake and she . . . well, she's a silly flighty girl. He overwhelmed her

. . . and she gave way. It's easy to understand. And for that her life will be ruined, while he goes merrily on his way."

"If my father dismisses Kitty he'll have to dismiss Hamish, so Hamish will have to go away."

"How can he dismiss the whole family? I've thought of something: I'll send Kitty to my home."

"To your home? What could they do?"

"My father is vicar of Lakemere. He is a real Christian. By that I mean he practises what he preaches. Few do, you know. He is truly a good man. We're poor . . . but he wouldn't refuse Kitty shelter. He might be able to find a place for her. It wouldn't be the first time he's helped a girl in trouble. I'll write and tell him about it."

"Would he take her in . . . after what she's done?"

"If I wrote to him he would understand."

"Oh, Lilias, wouldn't that be wonderful!"

"It's a hope anyway," said Lilias.

I threw my arms round her neck. "Will you write that letter? Will you tell her where she can go? I'll see how much money I've got. If we could get her fare."

"I daresay she will be given the wages which are due to her and with what we can muster . . ."

"I'm going to tell her. I must. I couldn't bear to see that awful lost look on her face."

I went and told Kitty what we were planning and I had the pleasure of seeing her abject despair turn to hope.

IT WAS LATE THAT NIGHT when my father returned. Lying in bed, I heard him come in. The storm would not break that night.

The next morning Kitty was sent for. Pale, shame-faced, but not so desperate as she had been, she went to his study. I was waiting on the stairs for her when she emerged. She looked at me and nodded.

I went with her to her room where Lilias joined us.

"I'm to pack my box and leave. I've already packed."

"At once?" I asked.

She nodded. "He said I was a disgrace to the house and he had a young daughter to think of."

"Oh, Kitty," I said. "I'm sorry you're going like this."

"You've been an angel, Miss Davina, you and Miss Milne." Her voice broke. "I don't know what I'd have done without your help."

"Here's the letter," said Lilias. "Take that. And here's some money."

"I've got my wages due to me."

"Then you'll have a little. It'll get you to Lakemere. My father is a good man. He would never turn anyone in distress away. He will pray a lot, but it won't be all prayers. He'll do his best to help you. He's done it for people in trouble before."

Kitty broke into tears and embraced us both.

"I'll never forget you two," she sobbed. "What I'd have done without . . ."

A cab had been ordered to take her to the station and solemnity reigned over the house. Kitty had been dismissed in disgrace. A lesson to foolish girls. And now it was the turn of Hamish.

He was to go to see the master. He swaggered into the house, hands in pockets. There was no sign of repentance.

He went to my father's study and the door was shut on them.

Lilias came to my room. "What will happen?" she asked. "It's going to be very awkward . . . his family living in the mews."

"He'll be dismissed, of course. He won't be able to come into the house. Well, we shall see."

The whole house was waiting for what would happen next. The interview was long. No one heard any raised voices coming from the study, and finally Hamish emerged and walked calmly out of the house.

It was not until the following day that we realised that Hamish was to drive my father just as usual, and that the punishment meted out to his partner-in-crime was not to be inflicted on him.

•   •   •   •

THERE WAS BEWILDERMENT. Hamish went about nonchalant as ever, whistling "Ye Banks and Braes" or "Loch Lomond" just as though nothing had happened. We could not understand it.

Aunt Roberta was not of a nature to allow the matter to rest there.

She raised it at dinner that evening.

"The girl has gone," she said. "What about him?"

My father pretended to misunderstand. He raised his eyebrows and assumed that cold manner which intimidated most of us. But not Aunt Roberta.

"You know to what I am referring, David, so please don't pretend you don't."

"Perhaps," he said, "you would be good enough to elucidate."

"Surely incidents such as that which has recently taken place in this household are not lightly passed over."

"I understand," he said, "that you are referring to the maid's dismissal."

"She wasn't the only culprit."

"The man is one of the best coachmen I ever had. I don't propose to dispense with his services . . . if that is what you mean."

Aunt Roberta forgot her dignity and screamed: "What?"

My father looked pained. "I have dealt with the matter," he said coldly, "and it is closed."

Aunt Roberta could only stare at him.

"I cannot believe I am hearing aright. I tell you I saw them. They were caught in the act."

My father continued to look at her coldly and then gave a significant glance in my direction, meaning that they could not discuss such a matter when I was present on account of my youth and innocence.

Aunt Roberta shut her lips tightly and glared at him.

The rest of the meal was conducted in near silence. But afterwards she followed him into his study. She was there for quite a long time and when she came out she went straight to her room.

The very next morning she left, with the air of the righteous leaving Sodom and Gomorrah before disaster descended.

She could not stay another night in a house where sin was condoned because one of the sinners was "a good coachman."

THE MATTER was discussed at length belowstairs—not in my presence, but much of what was said was imparted to me by Lilias.

She said: "It's very strange. No one understands it. Your father sent for Hamish and we thought he was going to be dismissed as Kitty had been. But Hamish came out of that room, even more sure of himself, it seemed. What was said no one knows. But he is just carrying on as usual. And to think that poor Kitty was turned out as she was! It doesn't make sense. But then they always blame the woman in cases like this, and the men get off, scot-free."

"I can't understand it," I said. "Perhaps it's because he doesn't live in the house."

"He comes into the house. He corrupts the servants."

"I wonder why . . . I wish I knew."

"Your father is not a man to be easily understood."

"But he is so religious and Hamish . . ."

"Is a rogue. It didn't take this to tell me that. We could all see what he was. A pity Kitty was such a little idiot as to be tempted by him. I admit there is something about him. She must have found him irresistible."

"I know one who thinks he is wonderful."

"Who?"

"Himself."

"That's true enough. If ever a man was in love with himself that man is Hamish Vosper. But the servants don't like it, you know. Kitty was a good worker . . . and she was well thought of."

"I do hope she will be all right."

"I know she won't be turned away. My father will do what he can. As I told you, he's a real Christian."

"My father is supposed to be one and he turned her out."

"Your father is good at saying prayers and looking like a

Christian. My father is good at being one. There is a difference."

"I hope so, for Kitty's sake."

"He'll write to me and tell me what happened."

"I am so pleased you are here to help, Lilias."

That caused a frown to appear on her brow. For how long?
she would be wondering. My father had ruthlessly dismissed
Kitty, and Lilias would have to go when her services were no
longer required. She was right. My father was very good at
showing a Christian demeanour to the world, but he had his
own creed of right and wrong. Lilias had summed up his attitude; and I had seen what had happened to Kitty.

But what was the true reason why Hamish had been forgiven? Because he was a good coachman? Because he was a
man?

AFTER A WHILE the affair ceased to be talked of continuously. A
new parlourmaid was employed to replace Kitty. She was Ellen
Farley, a woman of about thirty. My father said she had been
personally recommended to him.

Mr. and Mrs. Kirkwell were somewhat put out. The engag-
ing of staff was their province and they did not like members of
it to be introduced over their heads, as Mrs. Kirkwell put it. It
was a reflection on her and Mr. Kirkwell that Kitty had been
their choice. But the main culprit in that affair, if you asked
Mrs. Kirkwell, was Hamish Vosper, and why he was allowed
to stay on she would like to know.

However, Ellen came. She was quite different from Kitty—
quiet, efficient and, said Mrs. Kirkwell, kept herself to herself.

Hamish still came into the kitchen and sat at the table, seemingly amused because Mrs. Kirkwell pretended that he was not
there. He had an eye for Bess and Jenny but, remembering
Kitty, they were wary.

Hamish's opinion seemed to be that he was unassailable; he
could act in whatever way he pleased because it was natural
that he should. It was human nature, as he had once said. A
man such as he was, irresistible to the female sex, could not be
expected to behave in any way but that which came naturally

to him. But I fancied he would have to look elsewhere for his conquests because he would not find them in our house. The example set by Kitty was very fresh in everyone's mind.

In due course there was a letter from Lakemere vicarage. Lilias took it to her bedroom and I went with her that we might read it together.

Kitty had arrived and the vicar had behaved in exactly the way that Lilias had said he would.

"She is so grateful," he wrote. "She cannot say enough in praise of you, Lilias, and your charge Davina. I am proud of you. The poor child, for she is little more, was in acute distress. She has been useful to Alice and Jane in the kitchen and about the house. Mrs. Ellington up at Lakemere House needs someone in the kitchen. You remember Mrs. Ellington, a very forceful lady but with a kind heart. I went to see her and told her the story, which of course I had to do. She promised to give Kitty a chance and I am sure the poor child will not slip up again. It seems that one of her maids is leaving in a few weeks to get married so there will be a vacant place. While she is waiting, Kitty can stay and help Alice and Jane. Lilias, I am so glad you did what you did. What would have happened to poor Kitty otherwise I cannot imagine . . . ."

I gazed at Lilias and I felt the tears in my eyes.

"Oh, Lilias," I said, "your father is a wonderful man."

"I agree with you," she replied.

But the response of the vicar of Lakemere set me thinking about my own father. I had always regarded him as an upright and honourable man. But to have dismissed Kitty as he had and inflict no punishment on Hamish, except perhaps a verbal reprimand, had made me change my image of him. He had always seemed so remote, but now he was less so. In the old days I had thought he was too noble to be considered as one of us; now my feelings towards him had begun to change. How could he have cared so little as to what would become of another human being and send Kitty out into a harsh world, while he kept her partner-in-crime because he was a good coachman? He was acting not out of righteousness but for his own comfort. The image of the good and noble man was fading.

If my mother had been there I could have talked with her. But it would not have happened if she had been with us. She would never have allowed Kitty to be sent away having nowhere to go.

I felt bewildered and apprehensive.

My father sent for me one day and when I arrived in his study he looked at me quizzically. "You're growing up," he said. "Nearly seventeen, is it not?"

I agreed that it was, terrified that this was a prelude to the departure of Lilias whose services would no longer be required so that she would be as cursorily dismissed as Kitty had been.

However, it was not to be just then, for he turned to a casket which was on the table. I knew it well. It contained my mother's jewellery. She had shown it to me on more than one occasion, taking out each piece and talking to me about it.

There was the pearl necklace which her father had given her on her wedding day. There was the ruby ring which had been her mother's. There were the bracelet set with turquoise, a turquoise necklace to match, two gold brooches and a silver one.

"You shall have them all when you are grown up," she had told me, "and you'll be able to give them to your daughter. It's rather pleasant to think of these trinkets going on through the generations, don't you think?"

I did.

My father picked up the pearl necklace and held it in his hands. My mother had told me that there were sixty pearls in it and the clasp was a real diamond surrounded by seed pearls. I had seen her wear it on several occasions, as I had most of the jewellery in the box.

My father said: "Your mother wished you to have these. I think you are too young for the jewellery as yet, but the necklace is different. You could have that now. They say that if pearls are not worn they lose their lustre."

I took it from him and my first thought was one of relief. He considered me too young to wear jewellery; therefore I would not yet be ready to dispense with Lilias. But I was pleased to have the pearl necklace.

I put it round my neck and when I thought of my mother I was overwhelmed with sadness.

When I joined Lilias, she noticed the necklace at once.

"It's beautiful," she cried. "It really is."

"It was my mother's. There are several brooches and things. They are for me, but my father doesn't think I am old enough to wear them yet. But it's not good for pearls if they are not worn."

"I've heard that," she said. She touched the pearls lovingly and I took them off and handed them to her.

"The clasp is lovely," she said. "That in itself would be worth a good deal."

"Oh . . . I shouldn't want to sell them."

"Of course not. But I was just thinking . . . they'd be a nice little nest egg."

"You mean if I fell on hard times."

"Well, it's a comfort to have such things."

I saw that sad, rather faraway look in her eyes. She was looking into a future where a nest egg would be a great comfort to her, I guessed.

I went down to the kitchen to find out whether my father had said he would not be in for dinner that evening. He usually left a message for Mrs. Kirkwell. There was that uneasy atmosphere down there because Hamish was sitting at the table, sleeves rolled up, pulling idly at the hairs on his arms.

I went over to Mrs. Kirkwell who was stirring something in a basin. She noticed the pearls at once.

"My word," she cried. "They do look fine."

"Yes. They are mine now. They were my mother's. I have to wear them because they get dull if they are shut away too long."

"Do they now?" said Mrs. Kirkwell.

"That's what my father said."

"Well, he would know, would he not?"

"I think I have heard it before."

"Well, they look very nice. They suit you, Miss Davina."

"The clasp is valuable, too," I said. "It's a diamond with little pearls round it."

"There now."

"Miss Milne said it would be a nest egg . . . if ever I was in need."

Mrs. Kirkwell laughed. "Oh, not you, Miss Davina. But she would think of that, wouldn't she? Poor wee soul. Governesses . . . well, I've always said I wouldna be one."

"Has my father said whether he would be in to dinner tonight?"

Before she could answer Hamish looked up and said: "Nay, he'll nae be in. I know. I'm driving him."

Mrs. Kirkwell answered as though he had not spoken.

"He left a message that he would not be in."

And soon after that, I left.

THE NEXT DAY there was consternation. My necklace was missing. I had kept it in its blue case in the drawer of my dressing table and I could not believe it when I discovered that the case was there but not the necklace. Frantically I searched through all the drawers, but they revealed nothing. The necklace had disappeared. It was a mystery because I would not have dreamed of not putting it away in its case.

Everyone was shocked. When a valuable article like the necklace disappeared, said Mrs. Kirkwell, it was not very nice for those close by.

She was right. The necklace had been in my room. Now it was no longer there. Where was it? "Necklaces don't walk," said Mrs. Kirkwell. Therefore the inference must be that someone had taken it. Who? No one could feel entirely free from suspicion.

My father had not returned until late that night, driven home by Hamish, and as the household had retired he had not heard of the missing necklace until the next morning.

I don't suppose I was the only one in the house who had a sleepless night. We had a thief in the house and my suspicions naturally turned to Hamish. If he were capable of that other thing, might he not believe that it was "human nature" to take a necklace from someone who did not need it and give it to someone who did—himself in this case?

But Hamish did not go beyond the kitchen. Since he was discovered in one of the bedrooms with Kitty it had been a tacit agreement that the upper floors were out of bounds to him unless he was summoned there by my father. Of course, there was always a possibility that he had not kept to the rule; but I had never seen him anywhere except in the kitchen since that affair. Yet it was not impossible that he might have crept up to my room and taken the necklace. If he had been caught there I was sure he would have had a ready explanation for his presence.

During the night when I was trying to sleep I went over what had happened since I last put the necklace on and I was sure I had put it back in the case when I last took it off.

My father was naturally horrified. He ordered that my room be thoroughly searched. He fired questions at me. Did I remember taking off the necklace? Did I remember putting it into the case? Who had been in my room since then? Only the maid to clean and Miss Milne, of course. She came to discuss something with me. I forgot what.

He said that everyone should assemble in the library.

"This is a grievous matter," he said to the company. "A valuable piece of jewellery is missing. Someone in this house knows where it is. I am going to give that person a chance to hand it over now. If this is done, I will consider the matter. But if it is not brought to me this day I shall inform the police. Is everyone here?"

"Where is Ellen?" asked Mrs. Kirkwell.

"I don't know," said Bess. "She was giving me a hand with the rooms. I called out to her when we had the order to come to the library."

"Someone should be sent to tell her," said Mrs. Kirkwell. "I'll go myself."

Mrs. Kirkwell did not have to go for just at that moment Ellen appeared. In her hand she held the pearl necklace.

"Ellen!" cried Mrs. Kirkwell.

"I heard Bess calling that we were to come here," said Ellen. "But . . . I was finding this. I couldn't shut the drawer . . . it looked untidy . . . half open. I thought something in the drawer below might have caught up somehow. So I opened the lower drawer. It was a petticoat. I pulled it out and as I did this fell out. Is it the one that's been lost?"

"In what drawer did you find this?" demanded my father.

"It was in Miss Milne's room, sir."

I looked at Lilias. Her face had turned scarlet; and then it was deathly pale. It was as though a voice was clanging in my head. "A nest egg . . . a nest egg . . ."

It could not be Lilias.

Everyone was looking at her.

My father said: "Miss Milne, can you explain how the necklace came to be in your drawer?"

"In . . . my drawer . . . it couldn't have been."

"But Ellen has just told us it was. And here it is. Come, Miss Milne, an explanation is needed."

"I . . . I didn't put it there. I . . . can't understand."

My father was looking at her severely. "It won't do, Miss Milne, I want an explanation."

I heard myself say in a high-pitched hysterical voice: "There must be some reason . . ."

"Of course, there is a reason," said my father impatiently. "Miss Milne will give it to us. You took the necklace, did you not, Miss Milne? Unfortunately for you, you did not shut the drawer properly so Ellen saw that something was wrong. That was fortunate for us . . . but not for you."

I have never seen such horror in any face as I saw in Lilias' then.

How could you? I thought. I would always have helped you. Why did you take the necklace? And my father knows! My father is the sort of man who will not tolerate any sin—and stealing is a great sin. "Thou shalt not steal." It is one of the commandments. Think of Kitty. Hamish, of course, was all right, but then he was a good coachman.

I wanted this nightmare to be over. The silence was terrible. It was broken by my father. "I am waiting for an explanation, Miss Milne."

"I . . . I do not know how it came to be there. I did not know it was there . . ."

My father laughed softly but derisively.

"It will not do, Miss Milne. You have been discovered. I could, of course, hand you over to the police."

She caught her breath. I thought she was going to faint. I had to restrain myself from going to her and putting my arms around her and telling her that whatever she had done she was my friend.

She raised her eyes and looked at me . . . pleadingly . . . asking me to believe her. And in that moment I did. I could not believe that Lilias would ever have stolen my necklace even though she so longed to have some bulwark against a needy future . . . a nest egg. I marvelled that I could ever have doubted her innocence and loathed myself for having done so.

"This is a crime," went on my father. "All these years you have been in my household and I have been harbouring a thief. It is very distressing to me."

"I did not," cried Lilias. "I did not. Someone put it there."

"Indeed someone put it there," retorted my father grimly. "You, Miss Milne. You are the daughter of a vicar. You must have had a religious upbringing. That makes the matter so much worse."

"You are condemning me without question." Lilias' eyes flashed. It was the spirit of desperation. Who could have put the necklace in her room? What was the point of it? If someone had taken it, of what use would it be to steal it and give it up . . . just to accuse Lilias?

"I have asked you for an explanation," went on my father, "but you have none."

"I can only say I did not take the necklace."

"Then explain how it came to be in your room."

"I can only say that I did not put it there."

"Miss Milne, as I said, I could prosecute you. You could then give your explanations in a court of law. But because of your family and the fact that you have been in this house for so many years during which time no thefts have been discovered against you, I am taking a lenient view. I will say that you were overcome by a sudden temptation . . . and you submitted to it. So . . . I am going to ask you to pack your bags and leave this house at once. Mrs. Kirkwell will accompany you and make sure that you take nothing with you which does not belong to you."

She looked at him with hatred. "How can you? How can you judge me so unfairly? I will not be treated like a criminal."

"You would prefer to have your case judged in court?"

She covered her face with her hands, and then, without another word, turned and went out of the room.

My father said: "This is regrettable but the matter is closed."

Closed? With Lilias dismissed for theft! Her reputation was tarnished. She would live her life in fear of the fact that she had been accused of stealing would be brought to light.

I went to her room. She was sitting on her bed staring gloomily before her. I ran to her and put my arms about her.

"Oh, Lilias . . . Lilias," I cried. "This is awful. *I* believe you."

"Thank you, Davina," she said. "Who could have done this to me? What could be the point?"

"I don't know. First poor Kitty and now you. It's as though there is some horrible curse on this house. It's ever since my mother died."

"I shall have to go home and tell them. How can I do that?"

"Your father will understand. He will believe you. He is a Christian."

"I shall be a burden to them. I shall never be able to get another post."

"Why not?"

"Because they will want to know where I have been . . . why I left."

"Couldn't you say I was getting old. It's true."

"They would get into touch with your father."

"Perhaps he would say nothing."

She laughed mirthlessly. "Of course he would say something. He would consider it unrighteous not to. He is so holy that he cannot give a woman a chance to defend herself. People like him love to find sin in others. They are so eager to find it that they see it where it does not exist. It makes them feel even more good . . . thanking God they are not like other men."

"Oh, Lilias, it is going to be so miserable without you. I wish I had never seen that necklace."

"I should have stood up for myself. I should never have allowed myself to be accused of something of which I am completely innocent. I should have dared him to prove it."

"Oh, Lilias, why didn't you?"

"It could have been even worse. He didn't believe me. Perhaps others wouldn't. If he had called in the police . . . people would have known. The disgrace would have been terrible . . . for my father. I could see that I had to get away . . ."

"You must write to me, Lilias. Give me your address. You did tell me, but I want it written down. I'm going to find out who took the necklace out of my room and put it in yours. I know someone did. Perhaps it was Hamish."

"Why? Just because he was caught with Kitty? This isn't the same thing. I could understand his stealing the necklace, but if he had done so he would want to sell it right away. There isn't any reason why he should try to incriminate me."

"Perhaps he wanted revenge. Had you done something he didn't like?"

"I hardly know him. He never even looks at me."

"Someone must have done it. What about Ellen?"

"Why? What would be the point?"

"Whichever way you look at it, there seems to be no reason."

"Thank you, Davina, for your trust. I shall never forget it."

"Oh, Lilias. It's what I've dreaded . . . your going away. Though . . . I never thought it would be like this."

"Write to me and I'll write to you. I'll let you know what happens."

"At least you have your family to go to. They'll be kind and understanding."

"They will believe in my innocence. They will never believe that I could be a thief."

Mrs. Kirkwell came in. She looked grim and resolute.

"Miss Davina!" she said reprovingly, surprised, I supposed, to find me there.

"I think this is a great mistake," I said.

Mrs. Kirkwell ignored that and said: "What about this packing? I see you haven't begun yet."

I went back to my room. I thought of all that had happened in a short time: my mother's death, Kitty's misdemeanour which had resulted in her dismissal—and now Lilias.

How DREARY the house was without her. She had been my special friend for so long, and I had known that I would miss her; what I had not realised was how much. I felt very melancholy.

A few days after Lilias had left, my father sent for me. He was in his study, unsmiling and forbidding.

"I wanted to speak to you, Davina," he said. "It is about a governess."

I stared at him. For the moment I thought he had discovered the real thief and let myself fancy that Lilias was coming back.

"You are not yet fully educated," he went on. "I had considered the idea of sending you away to a finishing school, but I have decided against that. So there will be a governess."

"A new governess, but . . ."

He looked at me with faint exasperation.

"A new one, of course. I myself will make sure that this time I engage someone who is reliable and is not going to shock us all by stealing our property."

I flushed and began: "I do not believe . . ."

He went on as though I had not spoken: "This one will be able to teach a great deal you should know. Deportment, good manners. It will not be so much a schoolroom governess as someone who will be able to equip you with social graces."

I was not listening. How foolish of me to think even for a moment that he was going to say that Lilias was coming back.

"Miss Grey will be arriving at the end of the week."

"Miss Grey . . ."

The irritation showed again. "I am sure that Miss Grey will give every satisfaction."

I came out of the study, dazed and very sad.

I knew I was not going to like Miss Grey. How should I stop comparing her with Lilias?

And a few days later Miss Zillah Grey arrived.

The Governess

THE HOUSEHOLD was in a state of disbelief. Miss Zillah Grey astonished them all; and what was most amazing was that my father had engaged her.

She was the sort of person whom people would turn to look at when they passed her in the street. She had what I can only call a flaunting manner. Her clothes, her gestures, everything about her seemed to be saying "Look at me."

She was definitely not what Mrs. Kirkwell would call "lady-like" but she was very affable to everyone and within a short time of our acquaintance she was calling me "dear." I had thought I should hate Lilias' successor, but I could not hate Zillah Grey. I could only marvel at her.

She had brought a great many clothes with her . . . all of them quite unsuitable, I should have thought.

When I had taken her to her room on her arrival she had looked round and said she knew she was going to be happy. Then she had taken off her hat and removed the pins from her hair; she shook it out so that it fell in seductive waves about her shoulders like a reddish cloak.

"That's better," she said. "You see I'm making myself at home."

I was amazed by the pots and bottles which were soon arrayed on the dressing table. I had thought there might have been some books in her baggage, but there was no sign of even one. She hung up her clothes and asked for more coat hangers.

Bess was amazed. I could imagine what she was telling them in the kitchen.

When my father came in he asked if Miss Grey had arrived and when he was told that she had, he said he would see her in his study at once.

I saw her going down the stairs. She had piled her hair high on her head, which made her look very tall, and I noticed that she had reddened her lips.

I was certain that he would decide she was most unsuitable. I was sorry in a way for, although I deeply regretted Lilias' departure, I felt it would be more interesting to have a governess like Miss Grey than the normal kind.

I wondered what the servants were thinking. Lilias was no longer there to tell me what they said. But I was sure there would be marked disapproval from the Kirkwells.

The interview with my father lasted over an hour. I was surprised, expecting it to be brief. When it was over my father sent for me.

He was looking rather pleased, I thought, and I wondered what that meant.

"So," he said. "Your new governess is here. She has met you, she says."

"Yes. I took her to her room and we talked a little."

"Good. I am sure she will be of great benefit to you."

I was astonished. How could he think that?

He said to me: "She will dine with us. It seems to me the most suitable arrangement."

"You . . . er . . . approve of her?"

He looked pained. "I am of the opinion that she will teach you a great many things you should know."

It was extraordinary. Was it because I was comparing her with the really rather conventional Lilias that I found her so strange? My father, obviously, did not.

She appeared at dinner that night in a black dress which fitted her figure rather closely. She had what Lilias had referred to as "an hourglass figure." Her red hair was wound round her head in what was meant to be a severe fashion—but somehow it was quite the reverse on her.

My father was gracious. It was more like having a guest to dinner than a governess.

He said: "Of course, you have not yet had an opportunity to assess Davina's capabilities, but when you have you will be able to decide what is best for her."

"Davina and I are going to get along wonderfully," she replied, smiling at him.

"Her governess left in rather a hurry. I fancy she was not entirely competent."

I could not resist cutting in. "Miss Milne was a very good governess, Papa. She made learning interesting."

"And that is what it should be, of course," said Miss Grey. "And that is how I intend to make it."

"I suppose my daughter will be having some sort of season. But that, of course, is a little way ahead. We can wait until after her seventeenth birthday before we need to consider that."

"I am sure you are right."

The conversation went along on conventional lines. I gathered Miss Grey had recently come to Edinburgh. Her home had been in London.

"And what do you think of our Scottish ways?" my father asked almost playfully.

"I think they are divine," she answered.

I glanced at him, wondering whether he would think this blasphemous in some way. It was a strange word to use. But she lowered her eyes so that the fanlike black lashes lay demurely against her skin; the full red lips smiled and the little nose and long upper lip looked more kittenish than ever. My father's look was indulgent. His lips twitched a little as they used to when my mother said something which amused him and at the same time shocked him a little.

"I hope," he said, "that you will continue to do so."

I left them together over coffee in the drawing room.

It was an extraordinary evening. Everything seemed so different now . . . even my father.

DURING THE NEXT WEEKS, although I spent a good deal of time with Zillah Grey, I felt I did not really learn a great deal about her. She seemed like two different people . . . no, more than two. She appeared to be able to slip into different personalities with the greatest of ease. With my father she played the lady-like person who is suddenly confronted with the need to earn a living. That was characteristic of most governesses; but with her it was different. They were usually quietly retiring, very much aware of their reduced circumstances, unsure where they belonged, poised between upstairs and down. Zillah Grey, although she had a habit of lowering her eyes, did not strike me as modest. I suspected she did it because it was an excellent way of calling attention to those long thick eyelashes. She was certainly not without guile. She knew exactly how to behave with my father and he approved of her wholeheartedly.

With me her attitude was more volatile. Sometimes she threw off all pretence. She would laugh uproariously and I noticed her accent changed a little—her words became more racy.

It soon became clear that there were to be no set lessons.

"What I have to do is prepare you for society, so your father tells me," she announced.

I was amazed. I could not imagine her being a great success in Edinburgh society, or even being accepted into it. What was she going to teach me?

I asked her what I needed to know.

"Clothes for one thing," she said. "You have to make the best of yourself. You could be quite good-looking."

"Could be?" I said. "Surely one either is or one isn't?"

She winked at me. She had a habit of doing that when she

was in certain moods. "That's one of the things I'm going to teach you. Oh, we're going to have a lot of fun together."

She said I ought to learn to dance. "Ballroom dancing, of course," she added. "Is there anyone here who can play the piano?"

"I don't think so. I've had lessons. Miss Milne, my last governess, played well."

"Well, you can't play and dance at the same time, can you? I'll have to see what we can do about that. I can knock out a bit of a tune myself. I wonder if there's someone who could partner you."

"You mean one of the maids?"

"We'll see about that. I'll teach you how to walk."

"To walk?"

"Gracefully. How to make the best of yourself."

"What about lessons . . . books and all that?"

She wrinkled her kitten's nose and laughed. "We'll see about that, shall we?"

She made her own rules. Often she went out and stayed out for several hours. I had no idea where she went.

"It's a funny way of going on, if you ask me," said Mrs. Kirkwell. "I mentioned it to the master and got a flea in my ear for my pains. I don't know what the world's coming to."

It was certainly a strange situation.

Only a week after she arrived she asked that the carriage should take her somewhere one afternoon. Hamish arrived at the door just as though she were a member of the family.

The Kirkwells were watching from one of the windows when I came upon them.

"What's all this about?" she was demanding of her husband, unaware of my presence.

"It's a wee bit fishy to me," he replied.

Then they saw me.

"That Miss Grey's gone off in the carriage," said Mrs. Kirkwell.

"Yes, I know."

"Seems to think she owns the place. I wonder what the master will have to say about this."

She need not have wondered, for nothing was said.

During the carriage drive she must have decided that Hamish would make a dancing partner for me.

When she sent for him I was horrified. I had always found Hamish repulsive and the intimacy of the dance would be most unpleasant. I could not shut out the image of him with Kitty on the bed.

Miss Grey demonstrated the dance, first with me and then with Hamish. She sang as she danced and I had to admit that she did it with the utmost grace. She floated by herself . . . her arms outstretched, muttering: "See. One two, one two three . . . the lady turns . . . the gentleman guides her . . . there. Let me try it with you, Hamish, while Davina watches. Then I'll take Davina while you watch . . . then you two can do it together. Oh dear, I wish we had someone who could play the piano."

She turned to me and held me loosely. She smelt of musk and attar of roses. I could see her white teeth and greedy lips closely—but it was wonderful to dance with her. It was much less so with Hamish.

He grinned at me. I believe he understood my feelings and they amused him.

I could have enjoyed the dancing lessons but for Hamish.

Mrs. Kirkwell was shocked when she heard that he was my partner in these lessons—so much so that she bearded my father in his study to tell him what was going on.

She was so bemused and indignant when she emerged that she forgot my youth for once and while I was present told Bess what had taken place.

"I said to him, 'There he was . . . dancing with Miss Davina . . . that man who was as much to blame as Kitty for what happened.' And what do you think he said to me? He said, very cold like, 'I wish to hear no more of the matter, Mrs. Kirkwell.' I spoke up bold as brass because I knew it were the right and proper thing to do. I said to him, 'Well, sir, to see that man holding Miss Davina . . . as they have to do in this dance . . . well, it's more than flesh and blood can stand after . . .'

He wouldn't let me finish. He said: 'I trust Miss Grey to do what is best for my daughter. She needs a dancing partner for the practise apparently and he is the only young man available. That is an end to the matter.' He was as cold as a fish. Well, there's nothing more I can do. But I've made my feelings known and I reckon I've done my duty."

And Hamish continued to practise with me.

There were a great many demonstrations, though, and Miss Grey danced more often with Hamish than I did.

I had a letter from Lilias.

My dear Davina,

I am very unhappy. I feel I have brought a blight on my family. Sometimes I cannot believe this has happened and I am filled with hatred towards that person who played that trick on me—for I am sure it was a trick. Someone must have hated me almost as much as I hate that person now, although I don't know whom I am hating.

My father has been wonderful. He makes me pray with him. He says I must forgive this enemy, but I cannot, Davina. I feel this wicked person has ruined my life.

I know you believe me and that gives me great comfort. But I am home now and I shall never be able to take another post. This terrible stigma will hang over me for ever.

I am helping Alice and Jane at the moment and Alice is going to take a post as governess . . . so I shall step into her shoes. I shall remain at the vicarage. Although my family believe in me, I am very unhappy. I should be grateful for their trust, I know, and I am, but I suffer still from this malicious accusation.

I saw Kitty the other day. She is settling in at Lakemere House, which is one of the two big houses here—the other being the Manor. Kitty seemed to be getting along quite well. We are the two disgraced ones, but I think she will be better able to get over her shameful humiliation, even though guilty, than I, innocent, ever shall be.

My dear Davina, I shall always remember you. Write to me

and tell me how you are getting on. Perhaps we shall be able to meet one day.

All happiness to you and my love,

LILIAS

I wrote back.

Dear Lilias,

Thank you for your letter which I was delighted to receive. I think of you a great deal. I am going to try and find out who did that terrible thing. You know where my suspicions are, but I can't think of a reason.

I loathe him. He has been brought in by my new governess to partner me. I am learning dancing and need a partner. There isn't anyone else, Miss Grey says. I could enjoy dancing lessons but for that.

Miss Grey is the new governess. She came very soon after you left. It is hard to describe her because she is more than one person. She is beautiful in a way that makes people look at her. She has reddish hair and green eyes. My father seems to approve of her. That surprised me because we don't do lessons in the ordinary way. She tells me what to wear . . . how I should walk . . . and, of course, I am learning to dance. I think it is a sort of preparation for launching me into society. I'm getting old, I suppose.

Oh, Lilias, how I miss you! I wish you could come back.

My love as ever,

DAVINA

MISS GREY said I was not to wear black anymore.

"It doesn't become your colouring, Davina," she said. "You are too dark. Dark hair and blue eyes . . . an attractive combination, but not for black. I can wear it, though it is not my favourite colour. It's too sombre. I'm fair skinned, you see. There is hardly any skin fairer than redheads. So I can get away with black . . . but it is not for you."

"Mrs. Kirkwell said I should wear it for a year."

She held up her hands in mock horror. "But I say no black . . . and no black there shall be."

I was not displeased. I hated the black clothes. I did not need them to remind me of my mother.

Of course, the Kirkwells were very shocked, but my father raised no objection.

I discovered that Miss Grey was very interested in the family. She wanted to hear about my mother and all the relations I had. There was little family except Aunt Roberta, I told her. I found myself talking quite frankly, for she had a way of drawing me out. I was soon telling her how Aunt Roberta had descended upon us after my mother's death and how she had discovered Hamish and Kitty together in one of the bedrooms. I thought that might make her realise that Hamish was not a fit person to be my dancing partner.

She was thoughtful. "The young devil," she said at length.

"Yes. It was very shocking. Aunt Roberta and I were together at the time. She opened the door . . . and there they were."

"Caught in the act! And you a witness. Oh, Davina, what a sight for you!" She laughed and went on laughing, the greedy mouth open, the green eyes full of tears, so great was her mirth. "And little Kitty was given her marching orders, eh? 'Don't darken these doors again.'"

"It was not very funny for Kitty."

"No. I suppose not."

"Lilias . . . Miss Milne . . . has a father who is a vicar. He took Kitty in."

"God's good man, eh?"

"He was good to Kitty. He found her a post in a house near him."

"Let's hope there aren't any good-looking young men around like Hamish."

"Do you call him good-looking?"

"He's got something. There's no doubt about that. I don't suppose Kitty was the only one who couldn't say no."

I did not want to talk about Hamish. I felt I should say too much and that I suspected him of stealing the necklace and putting it in Lilias' drawer. I must not tell anyone of my suspicions as I had no proof.

She asked a lot of questions about what had happened when my mother was alive. I told her how we used to go shopping and visiting friends.

"It was not so long ago," she said.

I discovered that she kept a flask of brandy in her room. It was in a cupboard which she kept locked. She let me into the secret once. She had been out to luncheon on that day. I did not know with whom, but she did now and then make these mysterious excursions and on this occasion she came back rather flushed and extremely talkative. Her speech seemed different and she was more affectionate than ever.

I went to her room on some pretext—I forget what—and found her lying fully dressed on her bed, propped up by pillows.

"Hello, Davina," she said. "Come and sit down and talk to me."

I sat down and she told me she had had a very good luncheon . . . too good in fact . . . with a very great friend.

"I feel sleepy," she said. "I could do with a little tonic. Here. Take the key in that drawer and open that little cupboard. There's a bottle in there and a glass. Just pour out a little, will you? It's just what I need."

I could smell that the tonic was brandy.

I poured it out and took it to her.

She drank it quickly.

"That's better," she said. "Leave the glass, dear. I'll wash it later. Put the key back in the drawer. Now sit down. There. Let's talk. I've had a lovely meal . . . and the wine was delicious. I like people who know how to choose a good wine. It's one of the things I'll have to teach you, Davina."

"I didn't think I had to learn things like that. I know absolutely nothing about wines."

"When you're in a big house with a nice husband and he brings his guests home . . . you'll have to know how to entertain them."

"So that's what I have to learn as well!"

"Well, it's as good a reason as any . . ."

"What do you mean, 'as good a reason as any'?"

She hesitated. I could see how sleepy she was. She seemed to rouse herself.

"I'm just babbling on. I like to talk to you, Davina. I think we've become friends . . . and that's nice. That's how I wanted it. You're a nice girl . . . a nice *innocent* girl, and that's how young girls should be, shouldn't they?"

"I suppose so."

She went on: "What a nice cosy time you must have had, Davina, my dear. Living all your life in this house . . . with kind Mama and stern Papa, the worthy banker, pillar of society in a great city." She laughed. "You ought to see London."

"I'd like to."

"We've got our grand houses, you know. Grander than this even. But we've got some which are not so grand."

"That is so here. I suppose it is like that everywhere."

"In big cities the contrasts are greater."

"This is a big city."

"I was thinking of London."

"It's your home, is it?" I asked. "Why did you come up here?"

"I came for a little while and decided to stay . . . awhile at least."

She sounded as though she would soon be asleep.

"Were you a governess before?" I asked.

She laughed. "Governess, me? Do I look like a governess?"

I shook my head.

"I was on the boards," she said.

"Boards?"

She was laughing again. "Music hall," she said in a slurred voice. "Song and dance act. It went down well for a time . . . as that sort of act goes. Quite a long time really."

"You mean you were on the stage?"

She nodded dreamily. "Those were the days . . ."

"Why did you come here then?"

She shrugged her shoulders. "I like a change. Besides . . . well, never mind. I was in Glasgow with the Jolly Red Heads. Three of us there were . . . all red-haired. That was what gave us the idea. We'd come on stage with our hair flying loose.

Brought the house down . . . to start with. People get tired.
That's the trouble. Fickle, that's what they are. We toured the
provinces and then we came to Glasgow. Did quite well there.
It's a hard grind, though. There comes a time when you feel
like settling . . ."

"And are you going to settle, Miss Grey?"

"Yes," she murmured.

"I'll leave you, then you can sleep."

"No, don't go. I like to hear you talking. You're a nice girl,
Davina. I like you."

"Thank you. I had no idea you were on the stage."

"Didn't you, dear? That's because you're a nice little innocent."

She was changing again, but her voice was getting fainter. I
was sure she was almost asleep.

I said: "When I first saw you, I thought I had never seen
anyone less like a governess."

"Thank you, dear. That's a compliment. How am I doing
then?"

"What do you mean?"

"Governessing," she said.

"You are a very strange governess."

"Hm," she murmured.

"You are quite different from Miss Milne."

"The one who stole the necklace?"

"She didn't steal it. It was put in her drawer . . . by someone."

She opened her eyes and some of the sleepiness dropped
from her. "You mean, someone planted it?"

"I mean that someone did it deliberately to make trouble for
her."

"Who told you that?"

"Nobody told me. I just knew."

"How could you know?"

"Because Miss Milne couldn't possibly have stolen anything."

"Is that the only reason you know?"

I nodded. "I wish I could find out the truth."

"You never know people, dear. They do the oddest things. You never know what's going on inside people. They go on and on . . . in the same old way and then suddenly they break out and do something you couldn't have believed they ever would."

She was growing dreamy again.

"You don't seem to be interested in the usual things," I said.

"Like what, dear?"

"Mathematics, geography, English, history. Miss Milne was ever so keen on history. My mother was, too. She knew a lot about what happened in the past and she used to talk to me about it. It was very exciting. Once I went to Holyrood House."

"What's that?"

I was astounded.

"Surely you know. It's the old palace. Mary Queen of Scots was there, Rizzio was murdered there. And then there's the castle where King James was born . . . the Sixth of Scotland and the First of England. His mother was Mary Queen of Scots."

She was almost asleep. Then suddenly she began to sing:

> *Wasn't it pitiful what they did to Mary Queen of Scots?*
> *Of her emulsion I have taken lots and lots and lots.*
> *They locked her up in Fotheringay,*
> *Fotheringay was not so gay,*
> *Mary, Mary, Hanover Squarey, Mary Queen of Scots.*

I listened in amazement. Then I thought: she is drunk.

How COULD MY FATHER, who was so stern and so conventional, allow such a woman to remain in the house, and moreover to have brought her in in the first place?

Of course, he had never seen her lying on her bed singing "Mary Queen of Scots." She changed her personality when he was there. She wore the black dress often. It seemed to me that she could adjust herself to fit the occasion.

She did refer to that afternoon.

"I don't know what I said, dear. You see, I had been to lunch with a dear friend. She'd been in trouble . . . it was a love affair and suddenly everything came right. I was so happy for her. She wanted to drink. She told me what had happened . . . how it had nearly gone wrong and then come right. And there was champagne . . . to celebrate, you see. She made me drink with her. Well, I'm afraid I'm not used to it."

I thought of the brandy in the locked cupboard and she must have guessed my thoughts for she went on quickly: "I just keep a little something in case I'm off-colour. I know I look robust, but I have my little weakness. Internal, dear. I get quickly upset if something doesn't agree with me and a spoonful always puts me right. I had to drink with her. It would have been sort of unkind not to. You understand?"

"Oh, yes," I reassured her.

"I must have said a lot of silly things, did I?"

"You sang a song about Mary Queen of Scots."

"It was . . . awful?"

"Well, it was joking about Fotheringay, which was very sad really, and something I didn't understand about 'hanover squarey.' I didn't know what that meant."

"It's a well-known place in London. Hanover Square, actually Squarey, to rhyme with Mary. That's why that's there. It was silly. An old music hall song. Was that all? Did I say anything else?"

"Only that you used to be with the Jolly Red Heads."

She looked a little grave. "People talk a lot of nonsense when they have been so foolish as to be persuaded to drink too much. I'm sorry, Davina, my dear. Forget it, will you?"

I nodded again and she swept me into her perfumed embrace.

"I'm getting very fond of you, Davina," she said.

I felt a sense of uneasiness and a desperate longing came to me for the old days with Lilias.

Soon after that we were in Princes Street shopping and she said to me: "It's beautiful, isn't it? Doesn't the castle look grand? You must tell me about all that history sometime. I'd love to hear."

Certainly she was the most unusual governess any girl ever had.

She bought a dress that afternoon. It was green with the tightly fitting bodice which she favoured and the skirt billowing out from the nipped-in waist. It was piped with ruby velvet.

She tried it on and paraded before the shop girl and me.

"Madam is . . . entrancing," cried the girl ecstatically.

I had to admit that she looked startlingly attractive.

Before we went down to dinner that night she came into my room wearing the dress.

"How do I look?" she asked.

"You look beautiful."

"Do you think it's suitable for dinner tonight? What do you think your father will say?"

"I don't suppose he will say anything. I don't think he notices one's clothes."

She kissed me suddenly. "Davina, you are a little darling."

A few nights later she wore the dress again and during dinner I noticed that she was wearing a very fine ruby ring.

I could not stop looking at it because I was sure I had seen it before. It was exactly like one my mother had worn.

The next day I mentioned it to her.

I said: "I noticed that lovely ring you were wearing last night."

"Oh?" she said. "My ruby."

"It's a beautiful ring. My mother had one just like it. It's going to be mine one day. My father just didn't think I was old enough to wear it yet."

"Yes . . . I see what he means."

"I don't suppose it's exactly the same. But it is very like it."

"I suppose one ring can look like another. There are fashions in rings, you know."

"Are there?"

"They were probably made about the same period."

"It is lovely anyway. May I see it?"

"But of course."

She went to a drawer and took out a case.

"The case is like my mother's, too," I said.

"Well, aren't all those cases rather alike?"

I slipped the ring on my finger. It was too big for me. I remembered there was one time when my mother had been wearing her ruby ring. I had admired it and she had taken it from her finger and slipped it on mine. "It will be yours one day," she had said. "Your fingers will be a little fatter perhaps by that time."

Miss Grey took it from me and put it back in the case.

I said: "The ruby matched the piping on your new dress."

"Yes," she said. "I thought that. It was the reason why I wore it."

She shut the drawer and smiled at me. "I think we should practise our dancing," she said.

The next time she wore the dress I noticed that she did not put on the ruby ring.

THERE WERE TIMES when I felt that I had been thrust into an entirely different world. Everything had changed so much since my mother's death. The servants were different; they were aloof and disapproving. When my mother was alive it had seemed as though life went on just as it had been doing for generations. Now it was all changed.

Lilias' departure had helped to change it. Lilias had been what one expected a governess to be. She and I had had a close friendship, but that did not mean that our lives had not been conducted in a strictly conventional way. When I thought of the old days . . . Sunday church . . . Sunday lunch . . . prayers . . . the amiable but regulated relationship between the upper and lower sections of the house . . . it was all so natural and orderly . . . just as it must have been for generations.

Now it was as though a whirlwind had struck the house and left the old order in ruins.

There were prayers every morning; the whole household attended, Miss Grey, discreet and demure, praying with the rest of us. But it was different. My father went to church on Sundays and I went with him, Miss Grey—as Lilias used to—accompanying us. But there was no chatting outside the church, only the occasional "How do you do" from my father and myself.

There was smouldering resentment in the kitchen, often openly displayed by the Kirkwells. They did not understand, any more than I did, why Miss Grey was allowed to remain in the house, or why she was chosen in the first place. She was a disruptive influence, not so much because of the manner in which she behaved—indeed she seemed to want to be on good terms with all of us—but because she was so different and people are suspicious of anything that does not conform to the rules.

It was at this time about nine months after my mother's death. I felt bewildered. How often I wished that Lilias was with me so that I could have talked frankly to someone. I was caught up in the general uneasiness which pervaded the house; and then suddenly I stumbled on a clue which explained a great deal to me. It was like finding a key which opened a door to . . . knowledge.

It was night. I was in bed. I could not sleep and lay tossing and turning when suddenly I heard a faint noise. I sat up in bed listening. I was sure I heard light footsteps going along the corridor past my room.

I got out of bed and opened my door very slightly. I was in time to see a figure on the stairs. I tiptoed to the banisters and saw quite clearly that it was Miss Grey. She was in her night attire—very different from mine which buttoned up to the neck. Hers was diaphanous, pale green with lace and ribbons. Her hair was loose about her shoulders.

What was she doing? Walking in her sleep? I must be careful not to wake her. I had heard somewhere that this could be dangerous to sleepwalkers. Very quietly I started to follow her.

She had descended the staircase and was walking along the corridor. She paused at the door of the master bedroom. It was where my father slept.

She opened the door and went in. I stood still, staring after her. What was she doing? What would happen now? She would awaken my father.

I waited in trepidation. Nothing happened. I stood there staring at the door. He must be awake by now.

I waited. My bare feet were cold. Nothing happened.

I mounted the stairs and stood at the top looking down. Minutes passed . . . and still she was there.

Then I knew, of course, why she had come here . . . why she was unlike any other governess. The truth came to me in a flash of understanding.

She was no governess. She was my father's mistress.

I LAY IN MY BED thinking of what this meant. But he was so religious! He had been so outraged by Kitty's conduct. How could he when he was acting in a similar way himself? How could anybody be so hypocritical? I felt sick with disgust.

So he had brought her here for this. She went to his room at night. He had given her my mother's ruby ring which was to have been mine. And this was my father—the worthy citizen, whom the people of this city so respected. Already he was putting Miss Grey in the place of my mother.

I did not know how I should act. I wanted to go to that room and burst in on them . . . as Aunt Roberta had on Kitty and Hamish. I wanted to tell them what I thought of them. Not so much for what they were doing—that was something I knew nothing about—but because it was despicable to stand in judgement against people who did the same.

What could I do? My impulse was to leave the house. How foolish! Where should I go? To Lilias? Again foolish. The Lakemere vicarage was not a home for all those in trouble. In any case, what I suffered from was not that sort of trouble.

I had a home, plenty to eat, comfort, and I felt I could never look my father in the face again.

And Miss Grey. What of her? I did not mind so much about her. She was not a lady. I knew that. That she was exceptionally beautiful and attractive I had to admit. I supposed she would be considered quite fascinating. But my father . . . how could he?

What should I do? What should I say when I met them? Say

nothing, was the wise answer. Certainly not yet . . . not until I had thought how I must act.

If only Lilias were here how different it would be. But Lilias had gone. If she had not, Miss Grey would not be here.

My father had wanted Miss Grey to come to the house. It was fortuitous that Lilias had been dismissed for a crime of which I was certain she was innocent.

I was getting entangled in the maze of my thoughts. I felt lost, bewildered, completely shaken by this sudden understanding.

I WISHED that I could get away . . . out of this house. I was writing to Lilias but, of course, I could not mention in a letter what was in my mind. It would have been different if I could have talked to her.

My father did not notice the change in my attitude. It was different with Miss Grey. She noticed at once.

"Is anything troubling you, Davina?" she asked.

"No," I lied.

"You seem . . ."

"How do I seem?"

She hesitated for a moment. "Different . . . as though you have something on your mind."

I looked at her and I could not stop myself seeing her and my father on that bed as I had seen Kitty and Hamish. I felt sick.

"Do you feel all right?"

"Yes."

"I think you might be sickening for something."

Yes, I thought. I feel sick when I think about you and my father.

I hated him more than I did her. I thought: that is her way of life. She wasn't really so shocked about Kitty and Hamish and didn't pretend to be. She would say with Hamish: it's human nature. Human nature for people like her and Hamish . . . and it seemed my father. He only held up his hands in horror when girls like Kitty succumbed to it. He went to church and prayed and thanked God that he was not as other men.

Then I started to think about Lilias. How strange that she

should have been dismissed just when he wanted to bring another governess into the house. But Zillah Grey was not a governess. She was a Jolly Red Head. She was really a loose
woman. That was what they called them. She was one of those
and my father was by no means the good man he pretended to
be.

My mind kept going back to Lilias. Who had put the necklace in her room? The more I thought of it the more strange it
seemed. Could it be that my father had wanted Lilias out of the
house so that he could conveniently bring Zillah Grey in . . .
so that she could share his bed at night with the greatest ease?

He himself had selected her. He had said that. And it would
have been impossible for her to masquerade as an educated
woman, a proper governess, one of those genteel ladies who
had fallen on hard times. So she had come to teach me the
social graces. That was really amusing. I felt waves of bitterness sweeping over me.

What had this done to Lilias? She would have to go through
life with that stigma upon her. People would say she had been
dismissed for theft because a missing necklace was found in her
room. I had always believed that someone had put it there.
Now it seemed that someone might have had a reason for it,
and I had a burning desire to find out who.

I could not imagine my father's stealing into my room, taking the necklace and putting it into a drawer in Lilias' room.
That was beyond my imagination. But a short while ago should
I have been able to visualise my father in positions which I
could not get out of my mind?

I often found Miss Grey looking at me speculatively. I was
betraying myself. I was not as skilled at subterfuge as they
were.

I wondered whether Zillah Grey had guessed that I had discovered the truth about her relationship with my father. She
was clearly a little anxious and I was not subtle enough to hide
my feelings.

One afternoon my father arrived home early and very soon
afterwards Miss Grey came to my room.

She said: "Your father wants you to go to his study. He has something to say to you."

I looked surprised. I fancied he had been avoiding me lately. When we dined he seemed determined not to meet my eyes, but as he rarely addressed a remark to me it was not really necessary to do so.

She came with me to the study and shut the door behind us.

My father was standing leaning against his desk. She went and stood beside him.

"Sit down, Davina," he said. "I want to tell you that Miss Grey has promised to become my wife."

I stared at them both in astonishment.

Miss Grey came to me and kissed me.

"Dear Davina," she said. "We have always got on so well. It is going to be wonderful." She turned to my father. "Wonderful for us all," she added.

She held out her hand and he took it. He was looking at me rather anxiously I thought.

"The wedding will not take place for another three months," said my father. "We must wait the full year . . . and a little more, I think."

I wanted to laugh at him. I wanted to cry out: "But you did not wait. This is a pretence. It's all a pretence. There is sham everywhere."

But "I see" was all I could manage to say.

"I am sure," he went on, "that you will realise this is the best thing possible. You need a mother."

And I thought, you need someone . . . as Hamish did.

It was disturbing how I heard myself speaking inwardly . . . saying things which I would never have dared say aloud, things which I would never have believed possible a year ago.

How I hated them standing there, pretending . . . both of them. But I hated him more than I did her.

"There will be a wedding," I heard myself say stupidly; and that other voice within me said, of course there will be a wedding. A quiet one . . . all very right and proper . . . just as it should be . . . and no one will know.

"A quiet one naturally," said my father.

"Naturally," I repeated and wondered whether they noticed the sarcasm.

"Are you going to congratulate us?" asked Miss Grey archly. I did not answer.

"It is something of a surprise, I have no doubt," said my father. "But it will be the best thing possible . . . for us all. You will have a mother . . ."

I looked at Zillah Grey. She grimaced and somehow I liked her for that. She was not the hypocrite he was, whatever else she might be; and I think at that time it was the hypocrisy which was the greatest sin in my eyes.

"Well then," said my father. "I want us to drink to the future."

He opened a cupboard and took out three glasses and a bottle of champagne.

There was a little for me, less than half a glass. I kept thinking of Miss Grey lying on her bed singing "Mary Queen of Scots"; and I began to laugh.

My father smiled quite benignly, not understanding. When had he ever? I asked myself. But I think Miss Grey was aware of my feelings.

AT FIRST the news was received with dismay throughout the household, but after a few days they all seemed to accept it.

Mrs. Kirkwell had a little talk with me.

She said: "A lot has happened in this house lately, Miss Davina. Mr. Kirkwell and I were beginning to look on you as the mistress of the house. Of course, you are young as yet. We had thought that Mr. Glentyre might marry again, but we hadn't thought it would be so soon."

"It will be a year since my mother died when they marry."

"Oh yes. Well, they couldna very well do it before. That wouldn't have been right and Mr. Glentyre, he's one who'll always do what's right. It's soon . . . but it will be the full year. And we shall have a new lady of the house." Mrs. Kirkwell wrinkled her brows. I knew she was thinking that it would be difficult to imagine Zillah Grey as the mistress of a staid Edinburgh residence.

"There'll be changes," she went on. "I'm sure of that. Well, we must take them as they come, I suppose. A man needs a wife . . . even a gentleman like Mr. Glentyre, and having a daughter to bring up."

"I think I am brought up by now, don't you, Mrs. Kirkwell?"

"Well, there'll be things to arrange and a woman's best for that even if . . ."

"I am glad you and Mr. Kirkwell are not too upset by all these changes."

She shook her head sadly and I guessed she was thinking of the days when my mother was alive. I wondered if she were aware of Miss Grey's nightly excursions. Mrs. Kirkwell was shrewd and she had always liked to be aware of what was going on in the house.

I imagined she and Mr. Kirkwell might have decided that when there were certain "goings-on" in a respectable house— men being what they were—it was as well to have them legalised.

And so the house settled down to a mood of greater serenity than it had enjoyed since my mother died.

Later I heard Mrs. Kirkwell's comments on the mistress-of-the-house-to-be. "She's not the interfering sort. That's the kind neither Mr. Kirkwell nor me would work for."

So, unsuitable as the match might seem to outsiders, it was— if somewhat grudgingly—accepted in the house, largely because it was recognised that a man needed a wife and the chosen one in this case was "not the interfering sort."

THE WEDDING was, as had been decided, quiet—just a simple ceremony performed by the Reverend Charles Stocks who had been a friend of the family all my life.

There were few guests, chiefly friends of my father. Aunt Roberta did not appear, for the feud between her and my father continued. There were no friends of Zillah Grey present. The reception at the house was brief and very soon my father, with his bride, left for Italy.

I went at once to my room to write to Lilias.

"I have a stepmother now. It seems incongruous. So much has happened in the last year. Sometimes I wonder what is going to happen next . . ."

Jamie

WHEN THEY HAD GONE the house seemed very quiet and the strangeness of everything that had happened struck me afresh. I could not get out of my mind the fact that just over a year ago my mother had been alive and Lilias had been with me.

I had reached my seventeenth birthday in September and had left my childhood behind me—not only because of my age. I had learned so much—chiefly that people were not what they seemed to be. I had learned that a man like my father—outwardly a pillar of virtue—was capable of urges as powerful as those which had lured Kitty to abandon herself recklessly to disaster. They had carried my father so far that he had not only brought a woman like Zillah Grey into the house but had actually married her. So there was no doubt that I had grown up.

A sense of aloneness came over me. I had lost my best friends. There was no one now. Perhaps that was why I was so ready to welcome Jamie into my life.

I found a great pleasure in walking. In the old days I should not have been going out alone, but now there was no one who could stop me. In the absence of my stepmother I was the mistress of the house. I was on the way to becoming eighteen years old . . . an age, I supposed, when one could, in some circumstances, take charge. Mrs. Kirkwell had made it clear that she would rather take orders from me than from the new Mrs. Glentyre.

It will be different when they return, I reminded myself.

There was comfort in exploring the city, and the more I saw of it, the more captivated I became by its inimitable charm.

I was struck by the Gothic buildings which had been infiltrated with a touch of the classic Greek which gave an added dignity. In the first place, the situation was impressive. From one point it was possible to overlook the estuary of the Forth flowing into the ocean, and away to the west were the mountains. Such a superb position must be paid for, and the toll demanded was the bitter east wind and the snow from the mountains. But we had grown accustomed to that and it made our warm houses the more luxurious.

The coming of spring was particularly welcome and it was during that delightful season when I was able to indulge in my explorations. How beautiful it was then, with the sun shining on the tall grey buildings lighting them to silver. Sometimes I would sit in the gardens looking up to the castle or along Princes Street; and at others I would wander into the old town and listen for the bell of the university which rang out every hour.

It was a revelation to discover what a great divide there was in our city between the comfortably situated and the wretchedly poor. I suppose it is so in all big cities, but in ours it seemed more marked, I think, because the two were so close together. A few minutes' walk could take one from the affluent to the needy. One could be in Princes Street where the carriages rolled by carrying the well-dressed and well-fed, and very soon be in the wynds, where dwellings huddled together, where many lived in one small room, where the lines of pitiful garments hung out to dry and bare-footed, ragged children played in the gutters.

It was called the old town; and that was where I met Jamie.

Of course, if I had been wise I should not have been there. A well-dressed young woman could only be visiting such a neighbourhood out of curiosity. But I had become fascinated by my discoveries, and, contemplating on what I saw, I forgot my own dilemma, for my discoveries broke into my brooding on what the future might bring.

When I went out on my walks I carried a small purse with a chain handle which hung on my arm. In it I carried a little money. Since I had visited the poorer parts of the city I liked to have something with me to give to people. There were quite a number of beggars to be encountered and I was very moved to see children in such circumstances.

I knew that I should not venture deep into these streets. For one thing, there was such a maze of them that it was easy to lose one's way.

I had come to a street which was full of people. There was a man with a barrow selling old clothes, children squatting on the pavement and several people standing at their doors gossiping.

I turned away and started to go back as I thought the way I had come, but I soon realised how unwise I had been to enter these streets. I came to a small alley. At the end of it was a young man; he was just about to turn the corner. He looked respectable, out of place in these streets and I thought I might ask him the way back to Princes Street.

I started after him and just at that moment two young boys darted out of a side alley and approached me. They barred my way. They were poorly clad and obviously undernourished and they said something in an accent so broad that I could not understand them, but I knew they were asking me for money. I took the purse from my arm and opened it. One of them immediately snatched it and ran towards the young man who was about to turn the corner.

"Come back," I called. The young man turned. He must have guessed what had happened. No doubt it was a common occurrence. He caught the boy with the purse. His companion darted away and disappeared.

The young man came towards me, dragging the boy with him.

He smiled at me. He was young . . . not much older than I, I guessed. He had light blue eyes and fair hair with a reddish tint; he looked clean and healthy, which struck me as it was such a contrast to the boy he was dragging with him. He smiled; he had very white teeth.

"He has taken your purse, I believe," he said.

"Yes. I was going to give him some money."

The boy let out a stream of words, some of which I understood. He was terrified.

"Give the lady her purse," commanded the young man.

Meekly the boy did so.

"Why did you do it?" I said. "I would have given you something."

He did not answer.

"Poor little devil," said the young man.

"Yes," I said. And to the boy: "You shouldn't steal, you know. You'll get into trouble. My mother gave me this purse. It would have hurt me to lose it and it wouldn't have been worth much to you."

The boy stared at me. He was beginning to realise that I was not going to be harsh. I saw hope flicker in his eyes. Poor child, I thought.

I said: "You're hungry, are you?"

He nodded.

I took all the money in the purse and gave it to him. "Don't steal again," I said. "You could get caught and someone might not let you go. You know what that would mean, don't you?"

He nodded again.

"Let him go," I said to the young man.

He lifted his shoulders and smiled at me. Then he released the boy, who darted off.

"So," said the young man. "You've let a thief loose among the people of Edinburgh. It's only just postponed his stay in jail, you know."

"At least I shall not be responsible for it."

"Does it matter who is? He'll be there, sure enough."

"Perhaps he's learned his lesson. He was hungry, poor child. I felt so desperately sorry for them."

"But . . . may I ask what a young lady like you is doing in this part of the city?"

"Exploring. I've lived in Edinburgh all my life and I have never seen this part before."

"Perhaps we should introduce ourselves. I'm James North . . . known as Jamie."

"I'm Davina Glentyre."

"Should I escort you back to a more salubrious part of the town?"

"I wish you would. I'm lost."

"May I make a suggestion?"

"Please do."

"If I were you I would not venture into these parts alone again."

"I shall certainly be more careful in future."

"Then our young vagrant has done some good in his criminal life."

"Do you live in Edinburgh?"

"I have rooms. I'm at the University."

"A student?"

"Yes."

"How interesting. What do you study?"

"Law. But at the moment I'm doing a thesis on this city. I find it the most fascinating project I have ever undertaken."

"Were you researching in the wynds when you rescued me?"

"Yes. I want to see all aspects of the city—its glories and its horrors. This place reeks of history. You can feel it everywhere you go."

"Is that why it is called Old Reekie?"

He laughed.

"Why did they?" I asked.

"I am not sure. Perhaps it is because it is set on a hill. It may have started when someone saw the city from a distance with the smoke from chimneys rising over the buildings. That's the sort of thing I probe for. I want to recreate not only the city as it is today but as it was throughout its history."

"That must be exciting work. I'm only just starting to know it."

"Yet you say you have lived here all your life."

We had come to the end of the narrow streets.

"You know where you are now," he said.

I was disappointed because I thought he was implying that now he had safely delivered me, he was going to say goodbye.

"It was very kind of you to come to my rescue," I said.

"Oh aye," he replied with a laugh. "I did not exactly have to face a fire-breathing dragon, you know. You could hardly call it a rescue."

"I should have hated to lose my purse."

"Because your mother gave it to you. And she is dead now?"

"Yes."

"I'm sorry."

We had come to the gardens. "If you are not in a hurry . . ." he began.

"I'm not in a hurry," I replied eagerly.

"Shall we sit down for a while?"

"I'd like that."

So we sat and talked and an hour slipped by. It was the most stimulating hour I had spent for a long time.

I learned that his father was a minister and he had lived all his life in the manse north of Edinburgh—a small place which I had never heard of before—Everloch. Great sacrifices had been made to send him to the University and he was determined to make a success and repay his parents for all they had done for him.

I liked him more every moment. It was so pleasant to talk to someone near one's own age. I told him about my mother's death and what a shock it had been. "I had had a governess who was a great friend of mine, but she . . . left. And now my father has married again."

"And you are not happy about that?"

"I don't know. It all happened so quickly."

"And your stepmother . . ."

"She is rather . . . different. As a matter of fact she came as my governess."

"I see. And your father fell in love with her. I expect he was lonely after your mother died."

"I don't know. There are some people one doesn't under-stand very well. Whereas this morning I hadn't met you and now I feel I know quite a lot about you . . . much more than I do about Zillah Grey."

"Zillah Grey?"

"She is the governess . . . my stepmother now."

He said: "I suppose it all happened so quickly that you are not used to it yet. I think it can be quite a shock when a parent remarries . . . particularly if you have been close to the one who has departed."

"Yes, that is so. You see, if my old governess were there . . ."

"The one who left. Why did she go?"

I stammered: "She . . . er . . . she just had to."

"I see . . . her family or something, I suppose . . ."

I was silent and he went on: "Well, it is not as though you are a child. You'll make your own life."

"They are going to be away for three weeks," I said. "One of them has already gone."

"I expect it will work out all right. These things usually do."

"Do they?"

"Yes, if you let them."

"That's a comforting philosophy. I'm glad we talked."

"Yes, so am I."

"Do you have a lot of spare time?"

"For a week or so, yes. It's a break now. I could go home, but it's cheaper to stay here. I'm just exploring . . . making notes, you see . . . and writing it all up in the evenings."

"What an interesting life you must have."

"It has its moments." He smiled and added, "Like today." He turned to me suddenly. "You've got an interest in the city . . . exploring the wynds, seeing parts you have never seen before. I'm doing the same. Is it possible . . . ?"

I looked at him eagerly, questioningly.

"Well," he went on, "if you have no objection . . . and

when it fits in with your arrangements . . . I don't see why we shouldn't do a little exploring together."

"Oh," I cried, "I should love that."

"Well then. It's settled. When is your best time?"

"This, I think."

"Of course, there are some places to which I should hesitate to take you."

"It would be better for two to go to those places than one."

"Well, for all those that are not safe there are dozens that are."

"Let's go to those places together."

"It's a promise."

"Where shall we meet?"

"Here on this seat."

"Tomorrow morning?"

"Ten o'clock. Is that too early?"

"That would suit me very well."

"Well, that's settled."

I thought it better if he did not escort me right to the house. It would be difficult to explain who he was if I were seen by the Kirkwells or any of the servants and, of course, they would start to speculate.

It had been a pleasant morning, the most enjoyable for a long time. I wondered what my father would think if he knew I had talked with a stranger and, moreover, arranged to meet him the following day.

I simply do not care, I told myself.

GETTING TO KNOW JAMIE—we had become Jamie and Davina to each other very quickly—was a wonderful and stimulating experience. The morning after our first meeting we met again and it became a custom.

There was so much to talk about. He had made me see the manse and his younger brother Alex, who was going into the ministry, his father and mother, the aunts and cousins all living close by, the family reunions. It seemed a very jolly life, quite different from mine.

And then there was Edinburgh which came to mean something special to me, probably because of Jamie.

He loved every stone of the place, and memories of those days when we explored the place together will always be with me. I lived through them with an intensity, for I knew they could not last. When my father returned with Zillah there would be enquiries. They could hardly be shocked because I had strayed a little from conventional behaviour. I felt that if this were suggested I should not be able to restrain my anger and I might let him know that I was aware that he had not always kept rigorously to the paths of virtue. But then, of course, I was not facing him.

I shall never forget the banner floating over the castle . . . the wonderful view we had of the Pentland Hills when the air was clear. I shall always remember strolling along the Royal Mile from the castle to Holyrood House. The cathedral, the house where John Knox had lived. How I hated that man! I could grow angry to think of his thundering abuse at the Queen. Was he such a good man? I wondered. What secret vice had he? I was suspicious of all men who boasted of their virtues. Jamie was amused by the way in which I fulminated against John Knox.

Jamie was entranced by the past. He knew so much more about it than I did. It was wonderful to have my eyes opened by such an exciting companion.

He made me see Bonnie Dundee with his dragoons riding behind him; Queen Mary fresh from the splendour of the French court coming to dour Scotland; those Covenanters who had died there in the Grass Market for what they believed; he told me stories of the fabulous thief Deacon Brodie and Burke and Hare, the body snatchers.

Then my father, with Zillah, returned from Italy. They looked sleek and satisfied. They were affable to everyone. Zillah was excited in a rather childlike way, but I felt in my heart that there was really nothing childlike about her. My father was indulgent, as besotted by her as ever.

She had brought presents for everyone: a blouse from Paris for Mrs. Kirkwell, for they had stopped there on the way home, a statuette for Mr. Kirkwell and embroidered handkerchiefs for the others. They were all delighted and I thought, she certainly knows how to please people.

For me there were clothes. "My dear, dear Davina, I know your size and exactly what suits you. I spent hours choosing, didn't I, dear?"

My father nodded with an expression of mock exasperation which made her laugh.

"We're going to try them on at once," she announced. "I can't wait."

And there we were in my room while she fitted the dress on me, the coat, the skirt, the blouses—one frilly, the other plainish but stylish. She stood back admiring.

"They do something for you, Davina. They really do. You're quite good-looking, you know."

I said: "It *was* good of you to remember everyone. The servants are delighted."

She grimaced. "A little bit of bribery. I sensed disapproval before." She laughed and the pretence dropped from her. "Governess marries the master of the house! I mean to say . . . a little bit of a disturbance in the servants' quarters, eh?"

I found myself laughing with her.

Perhaps, I thought, it is going to be all right after all.

I was right when I thought the gifts from Paris would have a good effect. The servants were almost reconciled now.

I heard Mrs. Kirkwell remark: "Like a pair of turtledoves, they are. Well, there's no harm in that and she's not the interfering sort."

My thoughts were, of course, with Jamie. It was difficult now to slip out of the house without saying where I was going. We had to get messages to each other which was not easy.

I was always afraid that a note from him might come to me at an awkward moment, when my father was present. Fate was perverse and it could happen. I could imagine Kirkwell coming in with it on one of the silver salvers. "A young man left this for you, Miss Davina." A young man! Suspicions would be aroused. It was easier for me to drop a note into Jamie's lodgings.

However, we did manage to meet, though it was not the same as it had been in those idyllic weeks.

It was always a joy to see his face light up when I arrived. He would get up and run towards me, taking my hands and looking into my face. And I felt a great exhilaration.

We talked endlessly during those mornings, but I always had to watch the time, which I was sure passed more quickly than it had before.

I believe Zillah was aware that I harboured some secret. I called her Zillah now. She had been Miss Grey in my thoughts, but I could not call her that now. In any case, she was no longer Miss Grey.

"You must call me Zillah," she said. "I refuse to be called Stepmama." She appealed to my father. "That would be quite ridiculous, wouldn't it, darling?"

"Quite ridiculous," he agreed.

And so she had become Zillah.

She was given to those coy moods, especially when my father was present; but I was always aware of the sharpness beneath them. She was as shrewd and watchful as she had been on the day of her arrival.

I knew there was something not quite natural about her; she had been an actress—well, a kind of actress, if one could call the Jolly Red Heads that. In any case, she would know how to play a part. It seemed to me that she was playing a part now.

She fussed over my father, giving the impression that she was worried about his health.

"Now you must not overtire yourself, dearest. That journey was quite exhausting."

He shrugged off her cosseting, but he liked it. She continued to play the ingenue when I was certain that a very mature woman lurked beneath.

One day Jamie and I arranged to meet on our seat in the gardens. When he saw me he came hurrying towards me as usual, his face alight with pleasure.

He took my hands. "I was afraid you wouldn't come . . . that something might prevent it."

"Of course I'd come."

"Well, I'm never sure nowadays. I wish . . . it weren't like this. I can tell you're uneasy. They were wonderful days we had."

"Yes," I sighed and we sat down.

He said seriously: "I think we have to do something, Davina."

"What do you suggest?"

"Your people don't know you are meeting me."

"Good heavens, no. My father would think it was quite improper to pick up an acquaintance in the street."

"Well, what are we going to do about it? I want to call at your house. I don't like this hole-and-corner business."

"I don't like it either. I agree with you. They could discover sooner or later. So far we have kept our meetings secret . . . but one of the servants might see us . . . and there would be talk. They would all be wondering who you are and why you don't call at the house."

"Davina, do you think it is possible to fall in love in a short time?"

"I think I do," I answered.

He turned to me and took my hands. We laughed together happily.

"I'd have to pass exams and get out of the University before we could marry," he said.

"Of course."

"So would you . . . will you?"

"I think it would be wonderful," I said. "But do you know me well enough?"

"I know all I want to know about you. Haven't we talked and talked . . . as much in these few weeks as people do in years?"

"Yes, we have."

"And isn't that enough?"

"It's enough for me. I was wondering about you."

He kissed me then. I withdrew, embarrassed. It was not the kind of behaviour expected on a seat in public gardens in mid-morning.

"People will be shocked!" I said.

"Who cares?"

"Not us," I said recklessly.

"Then we're engaged?"

A voice broke in on us. "Davina!"

Zillah was coming towards us. She stood there, her green eyes glowing, her reddish hair bright under a black hat. She looked very elegant in her black coat with the green scarf at her neck.

She was smiling at Jamie. "Please introduce us."

"This is James North and . . . er . . . this is my step-mother."

She put her face close to his and whispered: "But we don't usually mention that. I am conceited enough to think I don't look the part."

"No . . . no," stammered Jamie. "Of course you don't."

"May I sit down?"

"Please do," said Jamie.

She was between us. "You two seem to be good friends."

"We met while you were away," I said. "I wandered into the old town and got lost in the wynds. Mr. North rescued me and showed me the way to go home."

"How interesting! And you became friends."

"We were both enormously interested in the city," said Jamie.

"I'm not surprised. It's fascinating . . . historically and otherwise."

I was surprised. She cared nothing about the city. "Mary Mary, Hanover Squarey." I could hear her singing.

"Well," she went on. "So you are good friends . . . apparently. That's very nice." She smiled beguilingly at Jamie. "I daresay my stepdaughter has told you all about me."

"All?" I said.

"Well, I daresay she has mentioned that I have lately come into the family."

"She did mention it," said Jamie. "I know you have recently come from your honeymoon in Venice and Paris."

"Venice! What an enchanting place. Those fascinating canals. The Rialto. Full of wonderful treasures. Paris, too . . ."

the Louvre and all that history . . . Davina, why do you not invite Mr. North to come to the house?"

"Well, I didn't think . . . I didn't know . . ."

"Oh, you foolish girl! I'm very cross, Mr. North, that I have not met you earlier. Davina has been keeping you to herself. You must meet my husband. He will be delighted to meet you. What about tomorrow evening? Come to dinner. Are you free? Oh . . . good. It won't be a big party. Just the four of us. Do say you'll come."

Jamie said: "I should like that very much."

"Wonderful!"

She sat back on the seat and I saw she intended to stay until I left. She talked a great deal with animation and much laughter. Jamie joined in. I was longing to ask him what he thought of her.

Moreover I was a little dismayed to have been so discovered, and also faintly annoyed. She had broken into a moment when we desperately wanted to talk about ourselves.

IT WAS AN UNEASY MEAL. Jamie was clearly a little overwhelmed by the formality. I imagined meals were very different in the manse. My father's dignified appearance and cool manner did not help.

He was polite. He thanked Jamie for rescuing me when I was lost and asked a great many questions about his studies and his home.

"You must find Edinburgh quite different from your little country village."

Jamie admitted that he did and that he was quite fascinated by the city.

"Mr. North is doing a thesis on the city," I said. "It means delving into history."

"Very interesting," said my father. "And you were brought up in the manse and your parents are still there?" he went on.

Jamie confirmed this. It was all very stiff and stilted.

Zillah, of course, introduced a light note into the evening and I was glad of her help.

She talked about Venice and Paris, to neither of which places

Jamie or I had ever been; but she was so pleasant to him and did her best to make him feel that he was a welcome guest, which softened the ordeal to which my father appeared to be subjecting him.

I knew it was more serious than it appeared to be and that my father was very disapproving of the acquaintance.

He would be thinking that it was very remiss of me to talk to a stranger in the street. I suppose if one had lost one's way there might be some excuse for doing so; but the proper procedure after that would have been for the rescuer to have taken me back to my home and called the next day to enquire how I was. Then it would have been for my family to decide whether he was worthy to be invited to the house to resume his acquaintance with me.

Jamie was clearly pleased when the ordeal was over and when I asked him what he thought about the meeting he replied: "I don't think your father approves of me. He doesn't know, of course, that we are engaged and what his reaction to that will be I can well imagine."

"I don't care what he says."

"Well . . . I think it would be better for us to say nothing as yet. I am sure he has not reckoned on having the penniless son of a manse as his son-in-law."

"It is something to which he will have to grow accustomed."

"He is the sort of man who would want everything according to convention."

Inwardly I laughed. I thought of Zillah, selected by him, creeping along to his bedroom. I said nothing. But I would remember it if he ever reproached me for unconventional behaviour.

"So," went on Jamie, "for the moment we'd better plan in secret."

I knew he was right and we had a wonderful time talking about the future.

He did say during the course of that conversation: "That stepmother of yours . . . she's quite different, isn't she?"

"Different from what?"

"From your father. She's jolly. Good fun. I don't think she

would be cluttered by conventions. Do you know, I had a feeling that she would be on our side."

"I never know with her. I have a feeling she is not all she seems."

"Who of us is?"

We parted with a promise to meet in two days' time.

Before I saw him again, Mr. Alastair McCrae, who had been a widower for five years, came to dine.

He was between thirty-five and forty, tall, upright and quite good-looking. He was a colleague of my father; and I knew he was wealthy for he had a private income and there was a family estate not far from Aberdeen.

I had seen him once some years before when he had come to the house to dine. I, of course, had not been present at the dinner party, but I had taken a peep through the banisters and seen him arrive with his wife who had been alive at that time.

My mother had mentioned him to me. "Your father has a high respect for Mr. McCrae. He comes of a very good family and I believe the estate he owns is very large."

I was interested to see the gentleman with the large estate and I must have been quite unimpressed because all thought of the gentleman went out of my mind until the recent mention of his name.

Zillah said: "This is going to be a rather special dinner party. You know that dress I bought for you in Paris? It's most becoming. Your father has asked me to make sure you are presentable."

"Why should he be interested in what *I* look like?"

"Well, you are his daughter and he wants you to grace the dinner party with me." She grimaced. "Between us, my dear, we'll open this fine gentleman's eyes."

There were two other guests, my father's solicitor and his wife; and rather to my surprise I was seated next to Alastair McCrae at dinner. He was quite attentive and we talked pleasantly together. He told me about his estate near Aberdeen and how he liked to escape to it whenever possible.

"It sounds delightful," I said.

He then told me how much land he owned and it seemed

considerable. The house itself was quite ancient. "It needs propping up from time to time," he said, "but what ancient house doesn't? The McCraes have been there for four centuries."

"How exciting!"

"I should like to show it to you one day. Perhaps we could arrange something."

My father was smiling quite benignly at me.

"Davina is very interested in the past," he said. "History has always fascinated her."

"There is plenty of that here," said Alastair McCrae.

"There's plenty of it everywhere," I said.

Zillah laughed loudly and everyone joined in. My father was very affable, smiling at me as well as at Zillah. It was very different from that other evening when Jamie had been our guest.

I found Alastair McCrae quite a pleasant man and I was glad to see my father in such a mellow mood. I would ask Zillah if Jamie could come to tea. It would be more friendly than dinner as my father would not be there to assess him.

I asked her the next day.

She looked at me and laughed. "I don't think your father would approve of that."

"Why not?"

"Well, dear, we have to face facts, don't we? You're what they call of a marriageable age."

"Well?"

"Young men . . . particularly young men who meet you in romantic places . . ."

"In those squalid wynds! You call them romantic?"

"Romance springs up everywhere, dear child. Those streets may not have been romantic, but the rescue was. And then seeing each other every day . . . looking at each other in such a charming way . . . well, that tells a good deal . . . especially to an old warhorse like me."

"Oh, Zillah, you are very funny."

"I'm glad I amuse you. To be able to amuse people is one of the gifts from the gods."

I thought how she changed. I wondered if my father ever saw Zillah as the woman she was now.

"So," I said, "you want me to ask my father if he can come to tea? This is my home. Surely I can have my friends here?"

"Of course you can and of course you shall. I was merely commenting that your father wouldn't like it. Let us ask the young man to tea. We won't worry your father with telling him. That's all."

I looked at her in astonishment. She smiled at me.

"I understand, dear. I want to help you. After all, I am your stepmother—only don't call me that, will you?"

"Of course I won't."

I wondered what my father would have said if he had known she was in league with me to keep Jamie's visit to the house a secret.

Jamie came. It was a very happy time. There was a great deal of laughter and I could see that Jamie enjoyed Zillah's company.

I saw him the next day. It was easier to arrange our meetings now that Zillah knew and clearly wanted to make things easy for us. He told me how kind he thought her and it was wonderful that she was so helpful.

As for Zillah, she said he was a charming young man.

"He dotes on you," she said. "He's clever, too. I am sure he is going to pass all those exams and become a judge or something. You are a lucky girl, Davina."

"My father doesn't know we're meeting," I reminded her. "I don't think he will approve of Jamie . . . not for Jamie himself, but because he isn't rich like . . . like . . ."

"Like Alastair McCrae. Now, there is a fine man and, as we used to say, 'well padded,' which in the vernacular of the halls, my dear, means that he has a nice little fortune stacked away. I have to admit that your father would approve of him . . . most heartily."

I looked at her in horror. "You don't think . . . ?"

She lifted her shoulders. "Fond parents will plan for their daughters, you know. Your future is very important to him."

"Oh, Zillah," I said. "He mustn't. Jamie and I . . ."

"Oh, he has spoken, has he?"

"Well, it's all very much in the future."

She nodded gravely and then a smile curved her lips.

"If my father objected," I said fiercely, "I wouldn't let that stand in the way."

"No, of course you wouldn't. But don't you worry. It'll all come right in the end. Don't forget you've got me to help you."

Alastair McCrae came to dinner with other friends of my father. He was seated next to me as before and he and I chatted in a very friendly way. He was quite interesting and less dignified than my father and he seemed to want to hear all about me.

The day after he called he asked us to spend the weekend at his country house.

Zillah told me that my father had agreed that it would be an excellent idea to accept.

It was a very pleasant weekend we spent at Castle Gleeson. I was rather taken with the place. It was small as castles go, but because it was of ancient grey stone and had a battlemented tower I thought it worthy of the name. It faced the sea and the views were spectacular. There was a sizeable estate and Alastair was quite proud of it. That was made clear when we drove through it in the carriage which took us from the station to the castle.

He was frankly delighted that we were paying this visit. It was the first time my father had been there in all the years of their friendship. That was significant, of course.

I enjoyed being shown the castle and listening to the history of the place and the part the family had played in the conflicts between Regent Moray and his sister Mary, of the troubles with the English enemy. I was fascinated by the hardy Highland cattle I saw in the fields. The country was grand, majestic and awe-inspiring.

But everything was particularly cosy within the castle. I had a room in a turret and there was a fire in the grate in spite of the fact that it was summer.

"The nights can get cold," the housekeeper told me. I learned that she had been born in the castle; her parents had been servants to the McCraes; now her son worked in the stables, her daughter in the house. There was an air of serenity about the place. I was not surprised that Alastair was proud of it.

Dinner was served in a dining room which led from a hall which must have been the same as it had been for centuries, with stone flagged floor, whitewashed walls on which ancient weapons hung. It was darkish, for the windows were small and set in embrasures.

"When we are a large company we eat in the hall," Alastair explained, "but this dining room is more comfortable for small parties."

"What a pity," I said, "that you are not here more often. I suppose the greater part of your time is spent in Edinburgh."

"That has been the case. Business, you know. But I escape on every opportunity."

"I can understand that."

He looked at me intently. "I'm so glad you like the old place. I enjoy playing the laird when I can, but mostly the affairs of the estate have to be left to my manager."

"You have the best of both worlds," said my father. "It's a very pleasant house of yours in Edinburgh."

"But I always think of this as my home."

Over dinner he asked me if I rode.

I said I greatly regretted that I did not. "There would not be much opportunity in Edinburgh."

"One needs a horse in the country."

"It must be wonderful to ride," I said. "Galloping over moors and along by the sea."

He smiled and leaned towards me. "Would you like me to teach you?"

"Well, I think that would be most exciting, but I couldn't learn in one lesson."

"One can learn the rudiments. It takes practice, of course, before you are able to handle a horse properly. But somehow I think you would be a receptive pupil."

I laughed. "Well, one lesson will not take me very far."

"It would be a beginning."

"What are you two concocting?" demanded Zillah.

"Miss Davina and I are arranging a lesson in riding."

"What a wonderful idea! An excellent opportunity for you, Davina dear."

"Miss Davina is protesting that she cannot get very far in one lesson."

"You never know," said Zillah slyly, "there might be more."

The next morning I was in the paddock, seated on a small horse on a leading rein, chosen for its gentleness, with Alastair beside me. He looked very distinguished in his riding coat. The housekeeper had found a riding habit for me. It belonged to Alastair's sister, who visited the castle occasionally but hadn't worn it for some time.

"She used to ride all the time," the housekeeper told me. "The family has always been one for the horses. But since she had her children she doesn't ride so much. I'm sure she'd be glad for you to use her old habit."

The fit was not too bad. It was a little large for me, but it served its purpose and I was equipped for the exercise.

I must say I enjoyed it. Round the paddock we went. Zillah and my father walked in the gardens and came to watch us for a few minutes. They seemed very pleased.

At the end of the lesson, Alastair said: "You're a wonderful pupil. We must have another lesson tomorrow."

"I think we are leaving tomorrow."

"I'm hoping to persuade your father to stay another day. Why not? We can travel back together on Tuesday."

And so it was arranged and the next morning I spent in the paddock with Alastair.

At luncheon Alastair said to my father: "Your daughter will soon be a champion rider."

I laughed. "You exaggerate. Besides, I shall not have the opportunity for all the practise I should need."

"You must come again . . . soon, before you forget what I have taught you. We'll arrange something."

"That is most hospitable of you," began my father.

Alastair raised a hand. "Please . . . the pleasure is all mine. What about the weekend after next?"

My father hesitated. Zillah gave him a sideways glance. He turned to her and said: "What do you say, my dear?"

"It seems delightful," she answered.

"Well, Alastair, if you are sure we shall not be encroaching . . ."

"Encroaching, my dear fellow! As I have told you, the pleasure is all mine."

"Not *all* surely," said Zillah with a little laugh. "David dear, you know we should love to come. The week after next, is it?"

"That is settled then," said Alastair.

We travelled back to Edinburgh on the Tuesday.

When I was unpacking Zillah came into my room. She sat on the bed regarding me slightly sardonically.

She said: "The McCrae affair progresses with speed. What a charming gentleman he is. Is he beginning to wean you from the impecunious but oh so charming Jamie?"

"What do you mean?"

"Oh, just is it going to be Papa's choice or yours?"

I was alarmed. It was obvious, of course, but I had refused to think of it too seriously.

Alastair McCrae would be a suitable husband. He had wealth and standing in the city. Jamie was a humble student. He had his way to make and there was the question as to whether he would make it.

I had been stupid, while I was enjoying my riding lessons under the benevolent eyes of my father, not to accept the fact that this was part of a well-laid scheme.

How incredibly innocent I was! My father disapproved of Jamie, whose existence had brought home the fact that it was time I married and settled in life out of the path of penniless students who in his view were in all probability grasping adventurers.

There would be no questioning that with Alastair McCrae; he was probably more wealthy than my father.

Zillah was watching me through half-closed eyes. There was a smile about her lips.

I should be grateful to her. She was making me see life through her somewhat cynical but highly sophisticated eyes.

• • • •

IT WAS SOON AFTER OUR RETURN that my father was taken ill. It happened during the night, but I did not hear about it until the morning.

Zillah said he had awakened her at about three o'clock feeling very sick. She had been up with him half the night. She had given him a powder to settle his stomach, she said. It was a well-known recipe for that sort of trouble. It had not been effective immediately, but after a while he had felt better; and now he was sleeping peacefully.

"Shall I send for the doctor, Madam?" asked Kirkwell.

"I think we might wait awhile," said Zillah. "You know how he hates the thought of the doctor coming. He kept saying he didn't want him. He'd be better soon. I'll watch him carefully. And if there is a return of the symptoms . . . yes, certainly we'll get the doctor. It's just that he hates a fuss and we don't want to upset him. It's something he's eaten most likely, so . . . let's wait awhile."

She kept him in bed all day.

I heard Mrs. Kirkwell mutter something about old men's marrying young wives. Sometimes it was too much for them. "A man's as old as his years and it's not going to do him much good to fancy he's a young one . . . when he is not. He's going to pay for it . . . sooner or later."

I think everyone was surprised by how assiduously Zillah played the nurse; and he had recovered the next day, except that he felt a little weak, which was natural.

"You were wonderful, my dear," he told Zillah. "I'd never thought of you as a nurse, but you played the part perfectly."

"I'm good at playing parts," she replied lightly. "There's a lot you have to discover about me, my dear husband."

The next day I met Jamie.

He was working hard, he said. He had had to forget the thesis for a while. He had to think of passing his exams with honours and setting out on his career as soon as possible.

He asked about the weekend and I told him of the riding lessons.

He was somewhat gloomy.

"What castle was this?"

"It belongs to Alastair McCrae, a friend of my father."

He wanted to know about Alastair; and I told him we should be going to the castle again the weekend after next.

"If my father is well, of course," I added. "He has been ill."

"He'll recover in time for this visit, I daresay. What is the man like?"

"Alastair McCrae? Oh, he's quite pleasant. He's old, of course."

"Your father's age?"

"Oh . . . not quite. Late thirties, I imagine."

"Oh," said Jamie with relief. "Some twenty years older than you."

"About that, I imagine."

That seemed to satisfy him. I did not tell him of Zillah's hints and what was becoming more and more obvious to me.

He asked after Zillah. She had clearly made a great impression on him.

I told him how she had looked after my father when he was ill . . . not seriously ill, of course, only mildly so, but it had left him a little weak. It seemed she had been very efficient in the sickroom.

"There's something very nice about her," he said.

"Yes, I'm beginning to think so. I resented her, of course, when she first came. It was because I was so fond of Lilias . . ."

And then I was telling him about Lilias' departure.

He listened intently. "Do you really think that someone put the necklace in her room to incriminate her . . . deliberately?"

"I have to think that because I know Lilias would never have stolen anything. She had been brought up in a religious way. Similar to your upbringing, I should say. She came from an English vicarage . . . you from a Scottish manse. People like Lilias don't steal, do they?"

"People do strange things . . . unexpected things. You can never be sure what anyone will do."

"Well . . . she did say something about the necklace's being a nest egg for me. I keep remembering that. What she wanted desperately was a nest egg for herself, for she was always worried about the future."

"Most people whose future is insecure worry about it. You mean that perhaps in a moment of temptation she took it? It had not all that material value to you. Sentimental, of course, because it had belonged to your mother. But you were not in need of a nest egg."

"All that has occurred to me, but nothing will make me believe that Lilias stole the necklace."

"If she did not, the implication must be that there was someone in the house who did this terrible thing. Ruined her life to a large extent, you could say. Who could have done that?"

"Why should anyone? There seemed to be no reason."

"Reasons can often be obscure."

"I can think of nothing. But at the same time I am convinced that Lilias did not take the necklace."

"It has to be one thing or the other. Either she took it or someone put it there."

"Oh, Jamie, I can't bear to think of it. I can't get anywhere . . . Don't let's talk of it. One just goes over and over the same ground. But I had to tell you. I don't want there to be any secrets between us."

"I wish that I were two years older," said Jamie.

"They say it is foolish to wish your life away."

"Well, I can't help wishing the next two years away. If they were over I should be in a different position. I wish we could be at least officially engaged."

"You mean announce it?"

"I do not think your father would approve. I think he would try to stop us."

"Zillah is on our side."

"She knows?"

"She guessed. She'll help us."

"I daresay she has a great deal of influence with your father."

"He dotes on her. I have never seen him with anyone as he is with her. What of your family?"

"I've written to tell them."

"And what do they say?"

"My father has sent me a long letter. He wishes me all that is good. They want to meet you, of course. I am sure you will like them. The manse is a bit shabby."

I turned to him indignantly. "You think I would care about that?"

"Well, your home is rather grand . . . and you visit castles . . ."

"There was only one castle, and that was quite a small one. But tell me about your father."

"They are all delighted. I told them about our meeting and they enjoyed hearing about that. I said that I had dined at your house. I may have given the impression that I have been accepted by your family."

"Zillah thinks it better if we don't say anything just yet."

"She's probably right. Oh, how I wish everything was settled. You see now why I wish I were two years older."

"Are you working very hard, Jamie?"

"Yes, burning the midnight oil. Trying not to think too much of you because that is very distracting."

"Isn't it wonderful that we have met? If I hadn't happened to be in the wynds that day . . . lost . . . you would have gone on with your walk and we should not have known each other."

"You haven't any regrets?"

"What a foolish question! Everything is going to work out well for us, Jamie. I believe that, don't you?"

"Yes, I believe it. I'm sure of it . . . because we are going to do everything to make it come right. And because of that we can't fail."

WE WENT TO CASTLE GLEESON for another weekend as we had arranged and the second visit was as successful as the first. I had some riding lessons and Alastair said that during our next weekend he would take me out hacking. If he were with me I should have nothing to fear.

I must say that I did enjoy being in the saddle. He was a wonderful teacher and it gave me a sense of security to have him riding beside me.

"You're doing amazingly well," he told me. "You must come down again very soon so that we can continue."

My father smiled indulgently when he heard this. He said he could think of no way of spending a weekend more agreeably than at Castle Gleeson.

And, of course, when we were in Edinburgh Alastair was frequently asked to dine with us.

Zillah watched it all with an amusement which bordered on the cynical.

"We are working up to an interesting situation," she said. "I have no doubt of the worthy Alastair's intentions, have you?"

I was afraid she was right.

"Do you think I ought to let him know that I am secretly engaged to Jamie?" I asked.

"Oh no. That would be most unmaidenly. It would suggest you knew to what he was leading. Society's rules demand that you, an innocent young girl, know nothing of what is in his mind. Remember the approved surprise of the well brought up young lady when she is confronted with a proposal of marriage. 'La, sir, but this is so sudden.'"

She could always make me laugh.

"Perhaps I should not accept invitations . . ."

"My dear, it is for your papa to accept invitations. We all know they are offered because of you, but modesty forbids you to betray you know."

"What am I going to do?"

"That is for you to decide. Do you want to be the wife of a doting older husband with a castle in the north of this land and comfortable house in this city? Or do you want to be the wife of a young man who is not yet a struggling lawyer, hungry for briefs which might not come his way with great speed, even when he first sets out for a career at the bar? It lies in your hands."

"You know I am going to marry Jamie."

"And renounce the bawbees?"

"Of course. I love Jamie. It's love that is important, isn't it?"

"Providing you have the roof over your head to cover you and food to sustain you that you may enjoy it."

"If there is any difficulty . . . you'll help me, won't you, Zillah?"

She put her hand on my shoulder and, drawing me towards her, kissed my cheek.

"That's what I want to do, my dear," she said.

EVER SINCE Zillah had discovered Jamie's existence she and I had grown closer together. I was getting more and more worried. It was clear now that my father looked upon Alastair McCrae as a suitable husband for me and was delighted that Alastair was paying such attention to me in accordance with the accepted custom. I was sure Alastair would conform as rigorously as my father to the rules and this could only mean that a proposal of marriage was imminent.

My father knew of my friendship with Jamie. Had he not been invited to the house? And after that . . . nothing. Did my father think the friendship had ceased because I, as a dutiful daughter, recognised his wishes for me? In his opinion we were now waiting for Alastair to make his proposal . . . and then we should go on from there.

It would all seem so predictable and so suitable to my father. He would dispose of his daughter to a man in a position similar to his own; and she could be expected to continue in that state to which she had been accustomed. What more could any father do or any daughter ask? It was all natural, convenient and traditional.

So I was pleased to have Zillah in the house because she understood my feelings, laughed at the conventions and could advise me what to do.

She often came to my room to talk to me and would sit where she could see herself in the mirror, finding, I was sure, her image of immense interest. I would watch her as she talked.

I said to her one day: "You are very beautiful, Zillah. I am not surprised that you like to see yourself reflected there."

She laughed. "I am really just looking to make sure everything is all right. You could say that I am conscious of my appearance and not confident about it—that is why I have to keep looking to check up."

"I don't believe that. I think you like to look."

"Well, a little bit of both, I daresay."

"I think you are the most beautiful person I have ever seen."

She patted her hair complacently. "I work hard at it," she said.

"What do you mean?"

"Well, you don't think all this is quite what Nature bestowed on me, do you?"

"Well, yes. How else . . . ?"

She raised her eyebrows. "Mind you, I will say that Nature was *kind* to me. I came into the world rather well endowed in that respect. But when you have been given special gifts you have to cherish them . . . cultivate them."

"Well, naturally. But your hair is a glorious colour."

"There are means, you know, of keeping it so."

"Means?"

"My dear, a little something out of a bottle when it is washed."

"You mean it's not naturally that colour?"

"It's not far-off. Inclined more to the ginger. I keep it up to standard, you might say."

"Oh, I see. And your skin . . . it is so white and beautiful. What are you laughing at?"

"You are an adorable little innocent, Davina. But I do have a wonderful secret to keep my skin clear and beautiful. It's daring, but it works."

"What do you mean . . . daring?"

"You won't believe it, but it's due to arsenic."

"Arsenic? Is that a poison?"

"In large doses it kills people . . . but a lot of things if taken to excess are dangerous. In small doses it is beneficial."

"Where do you get it? Don't you have to go to a chemist?"

"Well, yes . . . but there's a bit of fuss about buying it over a counter. I resort to other methods. Ellen is wonderful at that sort of thing. She gets it from flypapers."

"Flypapers? Those sticky things you hang up to trap the flies?"

"The very things. She soaks them in boiling water. The result is a liquid which looks a little like weak tea."

"And you drink that?"

"Only in very small quantities."

I was looking at her in horror.

She said: "You see what people will do for beauty. But beauty is a weapon. If you're beautiful people do things for you. It's a gift, like being born wealthy. You see what I mean?"

"I do. But I believe that without the arsenic and that stuff which makes your hair brighter, you'd still be beautiful."

"Do you know, I rather imagine I would . . . but slightly less so."

"And you think it worth it?"

"If God gives you a gift, He expects you to make the most of it. Isn't there a parable of the talents or something?"

"Yes," I said. "I see what you mean."

"Don't you start trying things," she cautioned. "I shouldn't want you to start soaking flypapers and drinking the solution. It could be dangerous."

"Perhaps for you, too."

"I'm wise. I know what I'm about. Ellen's a bit of an old witch. She knows a lot about this and she's become an ally of mine. They don't like her very much belowstairs . . . and in a way that makes two of us. I know they tolerate me because I don't bother them, but your father did step out of line when he married the governess. Now you've got a nice skin as it is. Yours is untouched . . . perfect. It won't need any attention for some time."

"I'm glad you let me into the secret."

"Well, didn't you let me into yours? How is Jamie? Don't you dare tell him about my aids to beauty. I shouldn't have confessed to you, but we're such good friends, aren't we?"

"Yes, good friends. Jamie's all right. He's getting impatient. He doesn't like those weekends at Castle Gleeson."

"I'm not surprised. Oh, Davina, I hope it will all come right for you and Jamie."

"If you were in my place you would marry Alastair McCrae if he asked you."

"Why should you think that?"

"You would think it was wise."

"I'm a romantic at heart, dear. That's why I'd do anything I could for you and Jamie."

"I think you would have a lot of influence with my father."

"In some ways, yes. I'm not sure about this matter. He's a stickler for conventions, you know."

"Not always," I said.

She laughed again. "Well, hardly anyone is . . . always. Sometimes it suits them not to be and then they forget how important they've always thought them. But never mind. Trust me. I'll do my best for you and Jamie."

SHORTLY AFTER THAT my father was ill again. This time Zillah had a mild form of the illness. She recovered first and gave herself up to the task of looking after my father with my help.

"It must have been something we ate," said Zillah.

Mrs. Kirkwell was indignant.

"Does she mean something which came out of my kitchen?" she demanded.

I reminded her that they had both dined at the home of one of my father's business colleagues on the night when they had been taken ill. "It couldn't have been here," I added, "because I dined at home on that night and I was all right."

That mollified her. She said: "I think Mr. Glentyre ought to see a doctor. This is not the first time he's been taken ill in a little while."

"I'll suggest it," I told her.

When I did, Zillah said: "It might not be a bad idea, although I'm sure it was something we'd eaten, and that sort of thing soon passes. Moreover, I was ill, too. Admittedly I was not *very* ill, but I eat a good deal less than your father. I think it was the veal we had at the Kenningtons. Veal, I've heard, can be a little tricky. I'll see what he says about seeing a doctor."

He was firm in his refusal at first, but she managed to persuade him.

When Dr. Dorrington called my father was back to normal. The doctor came at about eleven-thirty and was asked to stay to luncheon. He had been a friend of the family for years. He must have been quite sixty and we had been wondering for the last year when he would retire. There was a young nephew in the offing who was just passing through the last stages of his training and was at the time working in one of the hospitals in Glasgow. It was an understanding that in due course he would take over his uncle's practise.

I heard my father greeting the doctor in the hall.

"Oh, come on in, Edwin. This is all very unnecessary. But I've at last given in to my wife . . . for the sake of peace."

"Well, it can't do any harm to have a little check."

They went upstairs to the bedroom.

When I went down to lunch, the doctor greeted me warmly. He had, as he was fond of saying and did so almost every time we met, brought me into the world. This seemed to give him a kind of proprietary interest in me. He had attended my mother through her illness and had been very upset when she died.

I could see that he was a little fascinated by Zillah.

"Is everything all right?" I asked.

The doctor replied: "Oh yes . . . yes." But he did not sound altogether convincing.

However, it was a very pleasant luncheon. Zillah was in good spirits and made much of the doctor. She flirted with him mildly, which he seemed to like, and my father looked on with amusement.

Afterwards I talked to her.

"Is anything wrong with him?" I asked.

"Well, he's not a young man, is he? But there's nothing to worry about."

"You don't seem very certain."

"Well, I made old Dorrington tell me the truth . . . the absolute truth. I made sure he knew that this was the second attack your father had had. It must have been the food the second time . . . because I had it, too. He said your father should take care. There could be a weakness . . . an internal weakness. His heart's all right, but the doctor kept stressing his age."

"He's not so very old."

"He's not so very young either. People have to be careful as they advance in years." She laid a hand on my shoulder. "Never mind. I'll look after him. I'm discovering a hidden talent. Do you think I'm rather a good nurse?"

"My father seems to think so."

"Oh, he'd think anything I did was good."

"That's nice for you."

"Indeed it is, and I intend to keep it so."

MATTERS CAME TO A HEAD soon after that when Alastair McCrae came to the house to see my father.

He was taken to the study and was there some time. He left without staying to lunch or seeing anyone else.

My father sent for me and when I arrived in his study he smiled at me benignly.

"Shut the door, Davina. I want to talk to you."

I did so.

"Sit down."

When I was seated he went to the fireplace and stood, his hands in his pockets, rocking on his heels as though he were about to address a meeting.

He said: "I have some very good news for you. Alastair has been to see me. He has asked my permission to marry you."

I stood up. "It's impossible."

"Impossible! What do you mean?"

"I'm engaged to someone else."

"Engaged!" He was staring at me in horror, words on his lips which he was too shocked to utter. "Engaged," he said at length, "to . . . to . . ."

"Yes," I said. "James North."

"That . . . that . . . student!"

"Yes," I said. "You met him."

"But . . . you are a fool . . ."

"Maybe." I was feeling bold. I was not going to be intimidated. I loved Jamie. I was going to marry him. I was not going to allow my father to rule my life. How dared he, who had brought Zillah into the house . . . who had kept her here in the pretence that she was a governess to me? I thought of her creeping into his bedroom. It gave me courage.

"You will forget this nonsense," he said.

"It is not nonsense. It is the best thing that has ever happened to me."

He raised his eyes to the ceiling as though speaking to someone up there. "My daughter is an idiot," he said.

"No, Father. I am not. This is my life and I will live it as I want to. You have done what you want and I shall do the same."

"Of all the ingratitude . . ."

"Gratitude for what?"

"All these years . . . I have looked after you . . . made your welfare my chief concern . . ."

"Your chief concern?" I said.

I thought he was going to strike me. He came towards me and then stopped abruptly.

"You've been meeting this young man?"

"Yes."

"And what else?"

"We have discussed our future."

"And what else?" he repeated.

I was suddenly angry. I said: "I don't know what you are suggesting. James has always behaved to me with the utmost courtesy and in a gentlemanly fashion."

He laughed derisively.

"You must not judge everyone by yourself, Father," I said.

"What?"

"It is no use playing the virtuous citizen with me. I know you brought your mistress into this house. I know she visited your bedroom before you were married. As a matter of fact, I saw her going to your room."

He stared at me, his face scarlet.

"You, you . . . brazen . . ."

I felt I was in command. I said: "Not I, Father. You are the brazen one. You are the one who poses as virtuous, self-righteous. You have your secrets, do you not? I think you should be the last one to criticise my behaviour and that of my fiancé."

He was aghast. I could see he was deeply embarrassed. I had unmasked him and he knew that I must have known this of him for some time.

His anger burst out suddenly. There was hatred in the look he gave me. I had cracked the veneer. I had exposed him as an ordinary sinful man; the aura he had always tried to create about himself had been destroyed by those few words of mine.

"You are an ungrateful girl," he said. "You forget I am your father."

"I find it impossible to do that. I am sorry I shall have to refuse Alastair's offer, but I shall tell him that I am already engaged to Jamie."

I opened the door and was about to go. He had lost control. He shouted: "Don't let that student think he is going to live in luxury for the rest of his life. If you marry him, you'll not get a penny of my money."

I ran upstairs to my room and shut the door.

It was about an hour later when Zillah came to me. I was still in my room, shaken by the shock of the encounter and wondering what was going to happen next. I longed to see Jamie and tell him what had taken place between my father and me.

Zillah looked at me in horror.

"What have you done?" she asked. "Your father is raving against you. He says he's going to cut you out of his will."

"Alastair McCrae is coming to ask me to marry him. He has asked my father if he might and, of course, my father has said yes. He has already given him his blessing and was prepared to do the same to me. Then I told him I was engaged to Jamie."

"Yes. I gathered that from him. Rather rash, wasn't it?"

"What else could I have done?"

"Nothing, I suppose. But what are you going to do now?"

"I shall not marry Alastair McCrae just because my father says I must."

"Of course you won't. Oh, Davina, what a mess! You'll have to talk this over with Jamie."

"I shall send a note to his lodgings and ask him to see me tomorrow."

"Give it to me and I'll send one of the servants over with it."

"Oh, thank you, Zillah."

"Don't fret. It will all come right."

"I don't think my father will ever forgive me."

"He will. He'll get used to it. These things happen in families."

"Oh, thank you, Zillah."

"You know I want to help, don't you? Besides, I'm a little anxious about your father's health. I know old Dorrington says there is nothing to worry about, but I don't want him too upset."

"Yes, yes, I know. I'm so glad you're here."

"Well, write that note and we'll get you and Jamie together. See what he has to say. He might suggest a runaway match at Gretna Green."

"Do you think he might?"

"It would be very romantic."

"But where should we go? Where should we live?"

"They say love conquers all."

"I feel I want to get away from my father, and I feel he'd want me to go."

"What he wants is a nice rich marriage for you with a man of solid worth like Alastair McCrae. After all, that's what all fathers would want for their daughters."

"But if the daughter loved someone else . . ."

"Well, write that letter to Jamie. Tell him what's happened, and if he suggests Gretna Green, I'll do all I can to help you get there."

"Thank you, Zillah. I am so glad you're here."

"So you said, dear, and so I am glad I'm here. You want someone to look after you."

I wrote the letter and it was despatched for me.

THE NEXT DAY Jamie was waiting for me at the seat in the gardens.

When I told him what had happened he was aghast.

"So this man is coming to ask you to marry him and he has your father's approval?"

"I shall explain to him at once that I am engaged to you."

"And your father?"

"I don't know what he'll do. He might turn me out of the house. He says he will cut me out of his will if I marry you."

"Good heavens! What a terrible thing to do!"

"He means it. He will never forgive me for what I said to him . . . even if I agreed to marry Alastair McCrae. Jamie, what are we going to do?"

"I can't see what we can do."

"Zillah said we might run away and get married at Gretna Green."

"Where would we go? You couldn't live in my lodgings. I've yet to go through those two years before I can take my exams. How could we live?"

"I don't know. I suppose some people manage."

"You've always lived in comfort. You don't know what it would be like."

"Perhaps your people would help."

"They are desperately poor, Davina. They couldn't help in that way."

"Well, what are we going to do?"

"I can't see what we can do."

I was dismayed. I had thought he would be so delighted that I had admitted to my father that we were engaged and that I had stated so firmly that I would not marry anyone but him. It seemed that romance was crumbling before the mediocre problem of how we were going to live.

"There is only one thing to do," he said gloomily at length. "We can't afford to marry. We've got to wait until I'm through. I'm taking help from my family now. I can't ask them to keep a wife as well."

"I can see that I shall be a burden."

"Of course you won't. But you see it simply isn't possible yet."

I was deflated. I realised I had been rash.

"What can I do then? I've told him now."

"You'll have to hold him off for a while. Wait until we can work something out."

"Zillah said she would help. I think she thought you would suggest our running away together."

"It's not practical, Davina. I wish it were. Oh, why did this have to happen now?"

"Things don't happen when we want them to. How can I go back and refuse Alastair McCrae? My father is furious. He has decided that I shall marry him."

"Surely he'll allow you to have some say in the matter."

"My father never allows anyone—except Zillah—to have any say in any matter. His word is law and he expects everyone to accept that."

"We must think of something, Davina."

"But what?"

He was silent for a moment. Then he said: "It's distasteful, and I hesitate to say it, but . . . I think you will have to play this fellow along."

"What do you mean?"

"Well, tell him that you can't give him an answer. You have to think about it. It's so unexpected and all that. Ask him to give you time to think. It will be giving us time really. I'll see what can be managed. Who knows, there might be something. We might live in rooms . . . find something cheap until I'm through. I don't know whether it's possible. I'd have to have time to work things out . . . I need time . . ."

"You think that you could work something out so that we could be married?"

"I can talk it over with my family. They might come up with something. But I must have time."

"We *must* work something out, Jamie."

"What sort of man is this Alastair McCrae?"

"He's a very good man, I am sure. He's pleasant. I quite like him. He's very courteous and gentlemanly. I think it would be possible . . . as you say, to hold him off. I don't like doing it. It seems dishonest because I know I'm not going to marry him . . . and to pretend I might."

"I know, I know. But so much depends on this. I'll soon get us out of it. We'll be married . . . but in my position . . . I have to give a lot of thought to it."

"Of course. I wish Alastair McCrae would find someone else. I wish he would fall hopelessly in love with someone and forget all about me."

"We can always hope," said Jamie.

ZILLAH WANTED TO KNOW what had been said. I told her.

"He's hardly the reckless knight, is he?" she said. "I thought he'd dash you off to Gretna Green right away."

"It wouldn't make sense, Zillah. Where should we live?"

"He has lodgings in the town, hasn't he?"

"There's only room for one."

"Love knows no boundaries, as well as laughing at lock-smiths."

"Oh, Zillah, you must see his point of view."

"Of course I do. He's right to be practical. But I thought he might have been carried away by the romance of it."

"I am sure *you* would always be most practical."

"In such circumstances?" she said, as though questioning herself.

"In all circumstances," I insisted, and I told her what Jamie had said about not giving Alastair McCrae a positive answer.

"It's a wise plan," she said. "Alastair will understand. He'll say he'll wait. Your father will be mildly placated. He'll think you're coming to heel and want to save your pride by taking a little time over it. I'll drop a little whisper of this into his ear. And in the meantime we'll go on as normal, hoping something will turn up."

"I suppose I shall have to see what I can do," I said.

"You will," she told me.

And when the time came I did.

Alastair was charming, and I hated deceiving him. He proposed marriage in a dignified manner.

He began by saying: "I have been a widower for over six years, Davina, and never thought to marry again, but when I saw you at Gleeson, I said to myself, 'It is time I took another wife.' And I knew that there she was. Will you marry me?"

It was difficult. I drew away and he looked at me tenderly. He went on: "You think I have spoken too soon."

"We have not really seen a great deal of each other."

"For me it is enough."

"I hadn't thought that you . . . felt like this," I forced my-self to say untruthfully.

"No, of course not. My dear Davina, forgive me for speaking too soon, but I wanted you to know in what esteem I held you. What do you say?"

What could I say? It was hard enough not to shout out the truth. I shall never marry you. I am engaged to Jamie and as soon as he is able to marry me he will. But I must not say that. There was so much at stake. Jamie needed time and my father in his rage might turn me out. I must prevent that at all costs.

I steeled myself to say: "I can't . . . not yet . . . please."

"Of course I understand. This has been thrust on you. You need time to consider. My dear Davina, of course you shall have time. And while you are thinking I shall be patient. I shall try to persuade you what a blessing it would be for us both . . . to marry."

"You are very kind and understanding, Mr. McCrae."

"Oh, Alastair, please—and kind and understanding is what I intend to be for the rest of our lives."

It had been easier than I imagined although I could not help despising myself for what I was doing.

Alastair went up to my father's study and as I made my way to my room I heard his first words before the door shut on them.

"Davina was a little taken aback. I'm afraid I have been rather hasty. It's going to be all right. She just needs time."

I could imagine the look of satisfaction on my father's face.

I soon discovered that he was not displeased. It was not out of place for a young girl to show a certain amount of hesitancy; and although I must have proved to him that I was not quite the docile innocent daughter he had previously imagined me to be, he did regard me with a little more favour.

My outburst and the fact that I had caught him in a compro-mising situation could not be forgotten and it would always be there between us; but if I gave in to his wishes and married Alastair McCrae, he would be mollified to a certain extent.

• • • •

Zillah insisted that he rest. She made a great show of forbidding him to go out when she considered he was not fit to do so. He protested but obviously liked her attentions.

"You're making an invalid of me," he grumbled in mock irritation.

"No. No. I'm nursing you back to the strong man you really are. Give it a little longer. Don't be impatient like some naughty little boy and I tell you you will soon be quite well again."

It was extraordinary to hear someone talk to him like that, but he enjoyed it . . . from Zillah.

She took to going out more frequently, sometimes with me and sometimes in the carriage driven by Hamish. She talked vaguely about shopping or just going for a drive round the wonderful old city. She said she thought Hamish was rather amusing.

One day I went to the kitchen on some pretext. Mrs. Kirkwell was there talking to Ellen when Hamish came in.

He said: "Rats."

"What's that?" demanded Mrs. Kirkwell.

"Rats in the mews. I saw one . . . black it was and nigh on as big as a cat."

"Get away with ye," said Mrs. Kirkwell, sitting down and looking shocked.

"Running round the stables," said Hamish, "having a rare old time. Bold as brass. Saw me and just looked at me . . . brazen like. I threw a stone at it and it just glared at me."

"I don't like the sound of that," said Mrs. Kirkwell. "I hope they don't start coming into my kitchen."

"Dinna fash yeself, Mrs. K. I know how to get rid of the little beggars."

"How will you do that?" I asked.

"Arsenic, Miss."

"Arsenic!" cried Mrs. Kirkwell. "That's poison."

"You don't say! Well, that's what I'm giving to the rats. I'm going to poison the lot of them. That's what."

I said: "Where will you get the arsenic?"

He grinned at me and winked. "I can get it from Henniker's."

"Will they sell it over the counter?" I asked.

"Yes. You tell them what you want and put your name in a book. That's it."

"You can get it from flypapers," I said unguardedly.

"Flypapers!" cried Mrs. Kirkwell. "Oh, yes. I remember that case. Forgotten who it was. Woman murdered her husband. Soaked flypapers or something like that. It was what gave her away. She said she soaked the flypapers to get stuff for her complexion."

"Yes, that's right," I said. "Some ladies do that."

"I'm surprised you know about such things, Miss Davina. As for you, Hamish Vosper, you get those things away from me. Rats indeed! I wouldn't want to see the likes of them in my kitchen, I can tell you."

"I heard," said Hamish, touching his forehead. "You leave the rats to me."

ALASTAIR McCRAE came to dine with us and we went to dine with him. He had a fine town house in a quiet square similar to our own. It was very comfortable, tastefully furnished and contained the requisite number of servants.

My father was pleased and, I think, becoming a little reconciled to the fact that I knew something of his private life, though of course he would much rather have kept it secret. He believed that I was, as he would say, "coming to my senses."

The same thoughts were in Zillah's mind, I guessed from the looks she gave me. I felt ashamed of myself for continuing with this farce. I felt I was betraying myself, Jamie, Alastair . . . everyone.

I kept reminding myself that I had to do so. Jamie had suggested it. I had to think of our future together. That was more important than anything.

Jamie had changed. Some of the joy had gone out of our relationship. He was thoughtful, a little melancholy. He told me that he hated to think of my meetings with Alastair McCrae and the subterfuge I was forced to practise.

"But what can we do?" he demanded. "It's this wretched poverty. If only I were as rich as Alastair McCrae."

"Perhaps you will be one day, Jamie, and we shall laugh at all this."

"Yes, we will, won't we? But this happens to be *now*, when I am as poor as the mice in my father's kirk. Does he talk to you . . . about marriage?"

"No. He is very kind really. He thinks that in time I shall agree to marry him. He thinks of my being young . . . younger than I really am. He wants to wait until I am ready. He is sure that in time I will agree. He's trying to tell me how good he will be to me. I feel terrible really. It's all such deceit. How I wish I could get away. I don't want to stay in the house anymore. I don't know what it is, but . . ."

"You get on very well with Zillah, don't you?"

"Yes. She is a comfort in a way, but . . . I don't always feel that I know her very well. I think she's an actress at heart, and I never quite know when she is acting."

"She's a good sort."

"My father dotes on her."

"I'm not surprised."

"Oh, Jamie, what are we going to do?"

"Just wait. Something will happen. We'll think of something."

We tried to cheer ourselves by talking of what we would do as soon as we were able, but the joy had gone and had been replaced by a deep apprehension; and we could not shake it off, however much we pretended to.

THE NEXT DAY I was on my way to see Jamie and as I came into the hall I met Ellen.

She said: "Oh, I'm glad I've seen you, Miss Davina. Are you going out? I don't like to ask you, but I wonder if . . ." She hesitated, frowning.

"What is it, Ellen?"

"I'd go myself, but I can't get out just now, and I don't want Mrs. Kirkwell to know. It will upset her. She'll be in a real panic. I did ask Hamish . . . but he's run out of it and he asked me to get it. He'll show me how to use it, he said."

"What is it you want, Ellen?"

"Well, this morning when I went to the dustbin which you know is just outside the kitchen door, I lifted the lid and a rat jumped out."

"Oh dear!"

"Yes. I'm glad I was the one who saw it . . . not Mrs. Kirkwell. I told Hamish and he said he can't get to the shop today. Mr. Glentyre wants him on duty. But he said it ought to be seen to right away. He's killed two or three in the mews already and he thinks they are trying elsewhere. He said rats are clever things."

"Mrs. Kirkwell will be horrified."

"Yes, Hamish said you have to take prompt action; otherwise they'll be in the house and they multiply quickly. I thought . . . as you are going out . . . you might drop in at Henniker's and get some of that arsenic."

"Is that what you ask for? Arsenic . . . just like that?"

"Yes. Sixpennyworth of arsenic. They'll ask you what it's for and you can tell them it's for the rats. Lots of people use it for that. Then you have to sign a book, I think. That's what Hamish said."

"Of course I'll get it."

"Oh thanks. Don't tell anyone. People get so panicky about rats and if it got to Mrs. Kirkwell's ears she'd be hysterical."

"All right. Don't worry. I'll get it and say nothing."

"And as soon as you come back, I'll put it in the dustbin. Thanks so much, Miss Davina."

I went straight to the drug shop. There was a young man behind the counter. He smiled at me.

"I want sixpennyworth of arsenic," I said.

He looked at me, faintly surprised. "Oh . . . er . . . Miss, I have to ask you what you want it for. It's a sort of rule . . . if you know what I mean."

"Of course. We have rats in the garden. They have been round the mews quarters and seem now to have come closer to the house."

"It will do the trick," he said. "But as it's poison, I have to ask you to sign the book."

"I understand that."

He went to a drawer and brought out a book with a red cover. A label had been stuck on it which stated: "Henniker's Sale of Poisons Registration Book."

"Do you sell a lot of arsenic?" I asked.

"No, Miss. But people use it for vermin and things like that. It's very effective. One lick and that's the end of them. They do say it does something for the complexion and that ladies use it for that. I couldn't say. Men take it, too." He looked at me slyly. "They say it has powers."

"Powers?"

"When they are not so young, you know."

He opened the book, and wrote the date and my name and address which I spelt out for him. "Sixpennyworth of arsenic for vermin in garden. Now you sign here, Miss."

I did and came out of the shop with a small packet in the pocket of my skirt.

I found Jamie waiting for me, and we talked as usual and I felt frustrated, for I knew it would be a long time before he could take me out of this difficult situation.

When I came back to the house Ellen was waiting for me. Surreptitiously she took the packet.

"I haven't seen any more yet," she said. "I'll use this right away."

A FEW DAYS LATER when I saw Ellen she told me that it had worked beautifully, she was sure. She had not seen anything since and Mrs. Kirkwell had no idea that the rats had been so close. She impressed on me not to mention it to her.

It was later that afternoon. Zillah had gone out in the carriage as she often did. She enjoyed going to the shops and sometimes, she told me, Hamish took her for a tour of the town. Listening to my talk of it she had become interested and was finding it fascinating.

Usually she was home before five o'clock when she would change for dinner—by no means a short operation with her.

I fancied my father had been weaker since his last bout of illness. Zillah thought so, too. Sometimes when he came home he seemed very tired and needed little persuasion to have his meal in his own room. Zillah would, of course, take hers with him.

"It makes him feel less of an invalid and he likes me to be there," she said.

On this particular occasion it was getting late and Zillah had not returned.

I went over to the mews. The carriage was not there. Mr. and Mrs. Vosper were in. They told me that Hamish had taken Mrs. Glentyre out as he often did and they expected him to be back at any moment.

Mrs. Kirkwell was wondering whether to serve dinner. The master was having his in his room, but he would expect Mrs. Glentyre to have it with him there.

"He'll have to be told," said Mrs. Kirkwell. "You'd best tell him, Miss Davina."

I went to his room. He was dressed for dinner and was sitting in a chair.

"Is that you, my dear?" he said with relief.

"No," I replied. "It is I."

"What's wrong?"

"Zillah has not returned."

"Where is she?"

"I thought she went shopping."

"In the carriage?"

"Yes."

"She wouldn't be shopping at this hour surely?"

"No."

"Then where is she?"

He was clutching the sides of his chair and had half risen. I thought how ill he looked. He had lost weight and there were dark shadows under his eyes.

I remembered Mrs. Kirkwell's saying how he had changed and repeating her conviction that it was not good when old men married young women.

It was just at that moment when I heard the sound of carriage wheels. I rushed to the window.

"It's the carriage. She's here."

"Oh, thank God," said my father.

In a few moments Zillah rushed into the room.

"Oh, my dears, what an adventure! Were you wondering where I was? The carriage broke down. We had driven out to take a look at Arthur's Seat. I wanted to see it—hearing you talk about it, Davina . . ."

"Didn't Hamish know what was wrong?" asked my father.

"Oh yes. He tried to put it right. He discovered that he needed something . . . I don't know what. He said he would get a cab for me to come back . . . but it was so difficult right out there to get one. Anyway . . . he managed to fix it up . . . enough to get us home. But it made this terrible delay."

"I have been so worried," said my father.

"Oh, how sweet of you!"

"But of course I was worried."

"He's only just heard that you hadn't come back at the time," I said.

"I was wondering what could have happened to you," went on my father.

She ruffled his hair. "Well, here I am. And we are going to have our cosy little meal for the two of us. You'll excuse us, Davina . . . I think that's how it should be tonight."

"But of course," I said.

I left them together and went downstairs and ate a solitary meal.

The next afternoon Miss Appleyard called. Zillah had not gone out. I thought she was a little shaken by the carriage incident of the previous day. She and I were in the drawing room together when Miss Appleyard was announced.

We knew her only slightly. In the old days my mother had exchanged a word or two with her after church. I had heard it said that she was a rather malicious gossip who thrived on scandal. My mother had once said that she was a person from whom one should keep one's distance.

Why should she come calling on us? I wondered.

Bess said: "She's asking for Mr. Glentyre. I was sure she said Mr."

"Doesn't she know he is at the bank at this hour?" said Zillah.

"I wouldn't know, Mrs. Glentyre. But that's what she said."

"I suppose you'd better show her in."

Miss Appleyard came into the drawing room and looked abashed when she saw us.

"I asked to see *Mr.* Glentyre," she said.

"Good afternoon, Miss Appleyard," I began.

She nodded in my direction and then looked rather venomously, I thought, at Zillah.

"I wanted to speak to Mr. Glentyre," she reiterated.

"Is it banking business? He's at the bank at this time, you know," said Zillah, regarding her coldly.

"Well, I know he's home quite a lot."

Now how did she know that? I wondered. But she was the sort of woman who would make other people's business hers.

"Can we help?" asked Zillah.

For a few moments Miss Appleyard stood biting her lips as though making a decision.

"I'll have a word with Mrs. Glentyre," she said, looking significantly at me.

I said: "I'll leave you."

Miss Appleyard nodded approvingly and I went out, wondering what this was all about.

Some ten minutes later I heard her leave the house and I went back to Zillah.

She was sitting in the sofa staring ahead of her. She looked troubled.

"What was that all about?" I asked.

"Oh, she was indignant about somebody's 'goings-on.' I didn't know what she was talking about half the time. Silly old fool!"

"She seems to have upset you."

"Oh no. I just can't stand that sort of person. They pry into other people's affairs and try to make trouble."

"Why did she want to see my father?"

"Oh, it was something about money . . . I don't know. Somebody at the bank. I'm glad he wasn't in. He wouldn't have much patience with that sort of thing."

"She evidently thought it was too shocking for my ears."

"Silly old gossip! What's the time? Your father will be home soon. I think I'll go up and have a bath and get ready. Would you tell them to send up some hot water?"

"Of course. You sure you're all right?"

"Certainly I'm all right." She sounded a little irritated, which was unlike her. I wondered why Miss Appleyard's visit had upset her so much.

I left her then and did not see her again until we were at dinner, which we took together in the dining room that night.

My father was unctuous. His anxiety of the previous evening over her late return to the house had no doubt made him feel how very important she was to him.

She remarked that he was looking tired and if he were not better in the morning she was going to insist that he spend a day in his room.

"Zillah!" he said.

"But I shall," she said firmly. "I shall keep you here . . . and dance attendance on you all through the day. It's no use protesting. I shall insist."

He shrugged his shoulders and looked at her with great tenderness.

I thought what a change she had wrought in him. He was a different man with her.

TRUE TO HER WORD, she insisted on his staying home next day.

"He's all right," she said. "All he needs is rest."

It was mid-morning when Ellen knocked at the door of my room.

She said: "Miss Davina, I must speak to you. I've bad news."

"Bad news?" I echoed.

She nodded. "From my cousin. She lives near my mother. My mother is very ill . . . as a matter of fact, not expected to live. I must go to her."

"But of course, Ellen."

"I'll leave today if I can, Miss. There's a train to London at two-thirty. If I could leave in that . . ."

"Can you be ready? It's such short notice."

"I must."

"Have you spoken to Mrs. Glentyre?"

"Well, she's up with the master. I wanted to have a word with her, of course, but I thought I'd tell you and see if it was all right."

"I'll go and tell her you want to see her. In the meantime you get on with your packing. Hamish can take you to the station."

"Oh, thank you, Miss Davina. That's a great weight off my mind."

I went to the master bedroom and knocked. Zillah came to the door. I glimpsed my father. He was sitting in his chair in his dressing gown.

I said: "Ellen's in trouble. Her mother is very ill. She has to leave today for London. She wants to see you."

"My goodness. Poor Ellen. I'll go to her right away. Where is she?"

"In her room packing."

I left and she turned to my father and said something to him.

Ellen left that afternoon.

THAT EVENING I dined with my father and Zillah. He was wearing his dressing gown, but Zillah had said she thought it would be better for him to come to the dining room.

"She treats me like a child," said my father, pouting like one.

Zillah talked with her usual animation throughout the meal, and it seemed that the day's rest had been good for my father.

"We shall do this more often," announced Zillah.

When we had finished eating my father was impatient for his glass of port which he always took at the end of the meal. Kirkwell was not there. After the last course had been served he would disappear and come back later to pour out the port. But on this occasion it seemed we had finished more quickly than usual.

I said: "I'll get your port wine, Father," and I went to the sideboard. There was very little left in the decanter. I poured out a glassful and as I did so Kirkwell came into the room.

"Ah," he said, "you are already at the port. I'm sorry. I noticed the decanter was almost empty, so in case there was not enough I went down to the cellar for another bottle. I have decanted it and here it is. Have you enough in that one, Miss Davina?"

"Oh yes," I said. "Would you like a glass, Zillah?"

"Not tonight," she said.

Kirkwell looked questioningly at me. I shook my head and said: "No thanks."

He set the full decanter down beside the empty one.

When my father had finished his port Zillah said: "We'll say goodnight, Davina. I don't want your father overtaxed."

Again that exasperated and loving look.

I said goodnight and went to my room.

It must have been about two o'clock in the morning when there was a knock on my door.

I sprang out of bed and Zillah came in. She was in her night-dress, her hair loose about her shoulders, her feet bare.

"It's your father," she said. "He's very ill. He's terribly sick and in pain. I wonder whether we ought to send for Dr. Dorrington."

"At this hour?"

I was seeking for my slippers and putting on my dressing gown.

"I don't know," she said. "I don't like the look of him."

I went to their bedroom with her. My father was lying on the bed, his face ashen; he was breathing with difficulty and his eyes were glassy. He seemed to be in some pain.

"It's one of his bad turns again," I said.

"It's worse than the others, I think. We must send for the doctor."

"I'll wake Kirkwell. He's very capable. He'll go for the doctor. We can hardly send one of the maids at this hour."

"Will you do that?"

I went to the Kirkwells' room, knocked and went straight in. Kirkwell was already getting out of bed.

"I'm sorry to wake you like this," I said, "but Mr. Glentyre seems very ill."

Kirkwell, slightly embarrassed at my seeing him in his nightshirt, was hastily reaching for his dressing gown.

As we went out Mrs. Kirkwell was hastily rising to follow us.

Kirkwell took one look at my father and said he would only stop to put on a few clothes and go for the doctor. He thought it was necessary.

Then Mrs. Kirkwell joined us. There was very little she—or any of us—could do.

It seemed a long time before we heard the sound of the brougham bringing Kirkwell with the doctor. But by that time my father was dead.

The Accused

THAT WAS THE BEGINNING of the nightmare. The weeks which followed seem now to have been quite unreal. I felt I had stepped into a mad world which was full of menace. And it had begun on that night.

The doctor had stayed with my father for a long time and when he finally came out he looked very grave. He did not speak to me. He walked straight past as though he did not see me. He seemed deeply shocked.

I soon realised why.

When he had gone Zillah came to my room. She was a little incoherent, unlike herself.

She stammered: "He . . . he thinks it could be some sort of poison."

"Poison?"

"Something he took . . . or . . ."

"Or what?"

"Was given to him."

"Poison given to my father?"

"He says there will be a postmortem. Then . . . an inquest."

"But . . . why . . . he'd been ill. It was not so unexpected."

She looked at me fearfully and shook her head. Then she said: "There is nothing for us to be afraid of." She looked at me intently and added: "Is there?"

"But," I cried, "it's horrible. Why . . . why?"

"They do when people die mysteriously."

"It's . . . horrible," I said.

She came to my room and lay on my bed with me.

We did not sleep all through that night and spoke little. I guessed she was as preoccupied with her horrified thoughts as I was.

The next day they came and took my father's body away.

THERE WERE the thick black headlines: "Mysterious Death of Edinburgh Banker. Postmortem on Body."

It was discussed everywhere. The house had become an object of interest in the town. From my window I glimpsed people passing—and a great many more than did usually—and they would pause and look up at the house staring at the windows. The servants whispered together. I felt they were all watching us furtively.

"It's horrible," said Zillah. "I wish they'd get on with it and let us know the worst. It's the suspense I can't bear."

The day of the inquest was fixed. The entire household must attend. Many of us would be called as witnesses.

They were all in a state of nervous tension, fearful yet half-revelling in the excitement of being at the centre of the drama but still dreading it.

Dr. Dorrington gave evidence first. He said he had suspected poison when he had visited Mr. Glentyre and found him dead. Then the doctors who had carried out the postmortem were questioned. Dr. Dorrington had been right. There was evidence of arsenic in Mr. Glentyre's body. They had found definite inflammation of the stomach and bowels due to an irritant poison. The liver and content of the stomach had been placed in sealed bottles for further investigation, but there was no doubt in the minds of both doctors that doses of arsenic had been taken—or perhaps administered—probably in port wine, and this was the cause of death.

There was a hush in the court.

They had discovered a great deal. They knew that I had bought sixpennyworth of arsenic at Henniker's. The young man who had served me was there with his red-covered book, and there was my name and the date of the purchase.

He had previously sold sixpennyworth of arsenic to another member of the household, Hamish Vosper. First they wanted to know why Hamish had bought it. There were rats in the mews and Mrs. Vosper had seen them. She had also seen Hamish using the poison. She told the court that she did not like the idea of having poison around but she disliked the rats more. One of the boys who cleaned out the stables had also seen the rats and watched Hamish putting down the poison.

It was my turn. They wanted to know why I had bought the arsenic. I told them it was because there were rats just outside the kitchen. One had been seen in the dustbin. Who else had seen the rat? I told them I had not seen it. It was Ellen Farley who had seen it and asked me to buy the poison that day because she was unable to go out herself. This Ellen Farley was no longer employed at the house. Where had she gone? I did not know and I was muddled about which day it was. I thought it was the day before . . . or two days before my father had died.

I could see the looks of disbelief and sensed that the coroner was suspicious.

I was asked about a quarrel with my father. I was engaged to marry a student, was I? And at the same time a gentleman of Edinburgh was courting me?

"Well, er . . . not exactly. We were only secretly engaged . . ."

"But you liked having two strings to your bow?"

"It was not like that."

"Your father had threatened to disinherit you if you married your student?"

"Well . . ."

"Was that so?"

"I suppose so."

"Did he say in no uncertain terms that the relationship with the student must cease? Was there a scene between you?"

Of course they knew it all. They only asked the questions to trap me.

Hamish Vosper gave evidence. He said he did not know about rats being near the kitchen. They had had them in the mews and he had got rid of them with sixpennyworth of arsenic. Had he used all the arsenic on the rats? Yes, he had. You didn't get all that much for sixpence and they were quite big rats.

"And you never heard of them being near the house. Did you tell Ellen Farley to get arsenic for rats?"

He looked bewildered and shook his head.

"Did you talk about rats to Ellen Farley?"

"Not special to my recollection. I mentioned them in the kitchen once and Mrs. Kirkwell was all shook up."

"Was Miss Glentyre there when you mentioned them?"

"Yes . . . come to think of it, she was."

I felt they were all looking at me accusingly. Zillah, who was sitting next to me, took my hand and pressed it comfortingly.

She looked beautiful, rather pale and her reddish hair was plaited neatly. It was just visible under the black hat. She looked terribly sad—the tragic widow.

They asked her about the port wine. She said her husband usually took a glass after dinner. He kept some in his bedroom and if he did not feel tired he had a glass. He said it made him sleep.

"Did he take some on the night he died?"

"Not in the bedroom. He was very tired, he said. And then . . . he started to be ill."

"So the glass he had was at dinner."

"Yes."

"Was there anything special about the wine?"

"Special? I . . . er . . . don't understand. Oh . . . it was near the end of that in the decanter. I remember Mr. Kirkwell, the butler, came in with another . . . freshly decanted."

Kirkwell was called. He told how he had found there was very little in the decanter and had gone down to get another. When he came back I had poured out the wine and given it to my father.

"What about the rest of the wine in the decanter?"

"I threw it away. There was a little sediment and I thought they wouldn't want that."

"Where is the decanter?"

"In the cupboard. They are always washed and put away when they are empty . . . till we want them again next time."

The coroner's jury agreed unanimously that my father had died from the administration of arsenic and gave a verdict of murder against some person or persons unknown.

As we drove back to the house in the carriage, sitting well back lest we should be seen and recognised, both Zillah and I were limp with shock. We did not speak. Our thoughts were too horrifying to be put into words.

A small knot of people were gathered on the other side of the road. When the carriage stopped and we alighted they moved a little closer.

As we went to the door I heard a voice say: "Murderess." It was terrible.

We went to our separate rooms. I lay on my bed and tried to recall all that had happened, all that had been said in that dreadful courtroom.

How had this happened? Just a sequence of events . . . which . . . when fitted together, created a suspicion of guilt. My relationship with Jamie. What was Jamie thinking now? He would not doubt me, I was sure. My quarrel with my father . . . that outburst which had been heard by the servants. The simple act of pouring out a glass of port wine. And then, of course, the most damning of all—buying the arsenic. It seemed as if some evil spirit were at work, determined to destroy me, turning what had seemed the most insignificant acts into those of vital importance. And where was Ellen Farley, who could have told them that she had asked me to buy the arsenic? Indeed, I could believe some malevolent fate had made her mother ill so that she was spirited away when it was so necessary that she corroborate my story.

What had they implied? That I had bought arsenic that I might kill my father? And all because he had threatened to disinherit me if I married Jamie?

I felt sick and very frightened.

That night I wrote to Lilias. I had always found comfort in writing to her and receiving her letters. She was becoming reconciled to her fate now; she had settled down to village life; one of her sisters had become a governess and Lilias had stepped into her shoes.

Now there seemed a special bond between us. We were both wrongly accused, for there was no doubt in my mind that all in the courtroom had made up their minds that I had murdered my father.

And murder was a far more serious matter than theft.

I was exaggerating, I told myself. They could not believe that of me.

I told Lilias the details, how I had quarrelled with my father, how he had threatened to cut me out of his will.

"I don't care about the money, Lilias. I really don't. Nor does Jamie. We just want to be together and we shall be when he is a fully fledged lawyer. We'll set up in Edinburgh and have lots of children. That's what I want. But in the meantime there is this thing. People were waiting for us when we came home from the court. I can't tell you how upsetting it was. The worst thing is the matter of the arsenic. I did go to Henniker's. I did sign my name. They've got it all, Lilias. And Ellen isn't here to confirm what I tell them. If only she would come back. Perhaps she will . . ."

Yes, it was comforting to write to Lilias. It was like talking to her.

I sealed the letter and left it to be posted next day.

I went to bed, but sleep was impossible. Scenes from the courtroom kept flashing before my eyes. I could hear the voices droning on, the questions . . . the answers that seemed like betrayal.

Two days later, on the orders of the Procurator Fiscal, I was arrested on suspicion of having murdered my father.

OFTEN DURING THOSE DARK DAYS which followed, I told myself, if this had not happened I should never have met Ninian Grainger.

I was taken away by two men in a closed carriage. Several spectators saw me leave the house and I sensed the excitement among them. I wondered what the headlines in the papers would be now. I found I did not greatly care. I could not believe that I, hitherto insignificant, could be the subject of headlines in the newspapers. I could not believe that I was not only involved in a case of murder but at the heart of it. It seemed years since my mother and I had ridden out in the carriage together and taken conventional tea in the discreetly curtained rooms of neighbours as prosperous as ourselves. It even seemed a long time since Zillah had come to us. Could such things happen to ordinary people such as I was?

So many unusual events and the most unusual was that I, Davina Glentyre, daughter of a respected banker of Edinburgh, was in custody accused of his murder.

How could this have come about? It began when Zillah came to us—no, before that—when Lilias was dismissed. If Lilias had stayed, Zillah would never have come. My father would not have been married. I should have told Lilias that I had bought the arsenic. She would probably have come with me to the shop. Why hadn't I told someone? Zillah . . . Jamie . . . ?

I was put in a little room. I was glad to be alone, and it was there that Ninian Grainger came to see me.

Ninian Grainger was a tall, rather lean man, about twenty-eight, I should say. There was about him an air of authority and what I needed most at that time—confidence.

"I'm Ninian Grainger," he said. "Your stepmother has arranged for my firm to defend you. You are going to need someone to help you. I am that one."

He was pleasantly friendly from the start and I was soon

aware of the compassion he felt for a young girl accused of murder before she really knew a great deal about the world. He said that he had been convinced of my innocence from the moment he saw me. At that bewildering and horrifying time, this was what I needed more than anything and I shall never forget he gave it to me.

His approach was, I am sure, quite different from that of most advocates. From the beginning not only did he give me confidence but that fearful feeling of being alone in a hostile world began to disappear. I felt better even after our first encounter.

Oddly enough, he told me a little about himself so it was rather like a social meeting between two people who would become friends. His father was the senior partner in Grainger and Dudley. One day it would be Grainger, Dudley and Grainger and he would be the second Grainger.

"I have been in the business for five years . . . ever since I qualified. Do you remember the Orland Green case? No, I suppose you wouldn't. Things looked very black against Mrs. Orland Green, but I got her off, and that was a feather in my cap. I'm telling you all this so that you don't think my firm is sending you an inexperienced fellow."

"I wasn't thinking that."

"Well . . . let's get down to facts. You won't be allowed to go into the witness box. A pity. I'm sure you would have done well. No one looking at you could believe you guilty."

"That's because I am not guilty."

"I know that and you know it, but we have to convince other people of it. You'll have to make a Declaration. That's what I want to talk to you about. It's a pity you bought that arsenic and this Ellen Farley is not around to confirm your story. If we could find her, it would help enormously. It's too bad she's disappeared. Never mind. We'll find her. How long had she been with you?"

"I'm not sure whether she came before or after Zillah. Just before, I think."

"Zillah is your stepmother, Mrs. Glentyre."

"Yes. She came as my governess when the previous one left."

"And married your father. That was rather romantic, wasn't it? She does not look like a governess."

"That is what I have always told her."

"A most attractive lady. I am not sure what impression she will make in court."

"She will have to be there, I suppose."

"She'll be a major witness. She was with your father when he died. Oh yes, she will be very important. But we must try and find this Ellen Farley to confirm that she asked you to buy the arsenic for her. You bought it, you gave it to her, and that was the end of the matter as far as you were concerned."

"Yes, that's true."

"Then we must find her."

"I know she went to London. She caught the London train. Hamish Vosper took her to the station."

"London is a big place, but we must find her. It's imperative to your case that we do. Now tell me about the student."

"His name is James North. We met when I was lost in the wynds and we became friends."

"I see. And it went on from there. You met secretly."

"It was only my father who did not know of the meetings."

"Your stepmother knew?"

"Yes, she was very sympathetic. Jamie came to dine. I think she suggested it."

"And it was then that matters came to a head with your father who wanted you to marry Mr. McCrae?"

"Yes. Mr. McCrae had invited us to his house and was a fairly frequent visitor to ours."

"He came to see you?"

"Well, he had not come much before."

"He was the husband your father had chosen for you and he threatened to disinherit you if you married the student. You did not tell Mr. McCrae of your attachment to the student?"

"No . . . I was afraid of what my father would do and Jamie said we needed time."

"I see. And this was the state of affairs when your father died of arsenic poisoning?"

He was frowning. I knew he was thinking that the case was black against me.

"Well," he said, "we'll get to work on this Declaration. We'll marshall the facts . . . just as they really happened. We'll present them simply and go on from there. The important thing is to find Ellen Farley. I'll go and see your stepmother."

He rose, smiled at me and held out his hand. I took it and said: "You do believe me, don't you?"

He looked at me earnestly and replied: "I do indeed, and I am going to bring you out of this. Never fear."

WHILE I WAS AWAITING my trial I saw Ninian Grainger frequently and he continued to be of more comfort to me than anyone. He had an air of buoyant confidence. Never once would he allow himself to visualise failure. It meant a great deal to me that he showed his belief in my innocence, though when I considered my declaration of what had led up to the tragedy there was so much which seemed to suggest my guilt.

But that had to be proved and I was awaiting the trial which was to take place two months after my arrest.

One cannot remain in a state of shock forever; and when I awoke in the morning it was no longer to unfamiliar surroundings. There was no longer that feeling of blankness as realisation of what had happened swept over me.

An ordeal lay before me and the passing of each day was a relief to me because it brought it nearer; and I longed for it to be over.

I had no idea what the outcome would be. Ninian Grainger was wonderful. He filled me with hope which I could not entirely believe in unless he was there. In his presence I had the utmost faith in him and myself.

I was allowed visitors, but I was never alone with them. There was a woman with sharp eyes and an alert manner sitting in a corner watching me all the time. She was not unkindly, just impersonal. I never knew whether she thought I was a murderess or an innocent victim of an evil fate.

She saw to my creature comforts to a certain extent, but there was no warmth in her. I began to regard her as an inanimate object, which was just as well in a way because it enabled me to talk more freely to my visitors when I had a chance to do so.

Zillah came. She was full of compassion. "This dreadful, dreadful business," she said. "But it must come out right, Davina. Your very nice barrister seems to think so. He's been to see me several times. He's very eager to find Ellen. I told him that she'd come from London and I thought her mother was there."

"And London's a big place," I said, echoing Ninian Grainger.

"Yes, I'm afraid so. Mr. Grainger did go to London. He's put a notice in the papers to see if he can trace her."

"Do you think he will?"

"I expect so. These people do a marvellous job, don't they? Oh, Davina . . . I do hope you'll soon be home."

"There's the trial first. And do you think they'll believe me?"

"I think that Ninian Grainger is very good. He's young and full of energy. It means a good deal to him to get you off."

"Yes, he's in his father's business. He hopes to be a partner and I suppose he wants to prove himself."

"He wants that, of course. But it's more than that. He really believes in you."

"He has been very good to me. I don't know what I should have done without him."

She was silent.

"Zillah," I said. "What's it like at home?"

"It's awful. They rush out and get the papers as soon as they hear the boys in the street. They're always hoping there'll be some news."

"And you're bearing it all!"

"*You*'re doing very well, Davina."

"I don't know. I feel it is all so strange. I feel like another person. I keep going over it all. I keep thinking of everything that happened. Have you seen . . . Jamie?"

"He did come to the house. He seemed absolutely broken-hearted. He'll come to see you, I think. He didn't know whether he should . . . whether it would be right. He's just so shocked by the whole thing."

"Who is not?"

"I wish there were something I could do."

"They'll ask you a lot of questions, Zillah."

"I know. I'm dreading it."

"I'm longing for it. I think waiting is one of the worst things about it. I want to get it over . . . even if . . ."

"Don't say that," said Zillah. "I can't bear it."

We were seated at a table facing each other, which was according to the regulations, and the watchdog was seated in a corner, her eyes discreetly averted.

Zillah gripped my hands.

"I'm thinking of you all the time," she said. "It's got to come out right. It *must*. Everyone must see that you couldn't possibly do such a thing."

JAMIE CAME. He looked like a different person. All the joy had gone out of him. He was pale and there were shadows under his eyes.

"Davina!" he said.

"Oh, Jamie, I'm so glad you came to see me."

"This is terrible."

"I know."

"What will be the outcome?"

"We have to wait and see. The advocate is very optimistic."

He put his hand to his forehead covering his eyes.

"Davina . . . they are saying the most terrible things."

"I know."

"You bought that arsenic. You signed for it. Your name is in that book with the date and everything . . . and soon after your father is dead . . . after you bought it."

"I know that, Jamie. I've explained it all."

"People are saying . . ."

"I can guess what they are saying, but Ninian Grainger is going to prove them wrong. He's going to make them see the truth."

"Can he?"

"He says he can, Jamie. And he must because it is the truth, Jamie. I believe you think . . . I did it."

He hesitated for too long before he protested that of course he did not believe that.

"Your family?" I said. "What are they thinking?"

He bit his lip and did not answer.

"I suppose," I went on, "it is not good for a minister to be caught up in this sort of thing . . . even if it is remotely."

"Oh," he said after a pause, "it is not good for anyone, is it?"

"I'm sorry, Jamie . . . so sorry to have involved you in this."

He said: "I shall be called to give evidence at the trial. Everyone is talking about it. My fellow students . . . they think I know something. It's horrible."

"Yes, horrible things have happened to us both. But Mr. Grainger is sure everything will come right."

"But . . . it will always be there, won't it? People will remember."

I stared at him in horror. I had not thought of that. I imagined that once Ninian Grainger had made the court agree with him that I was innocent, that would be an end of the matter. I would return home, marry Jamie and this would all become like a dream . . . not a recurring nightmare.

He had changed. He was remote. He was not the warm-hearted lover I had known. Whatever he said there was doubt in his heart. I recoiled from him.

He was aware of this, but there was nothing he could do to hide his true feelings. We had changed towards each other.

The doubt was in his mind. It hung like a cloud between us; and for me there was the knowledge that the love he had had for me was not strong enough to bear this strain.

Jamie's visit had not made me happier.

Alastair McCrae did not come to see me. I fancied he was congratulating himself that he was not sufficiently involved for the glare of publicity to alight on him; and he wanted to keep it like that.

· · · ·

MY TRIAL TOOK PLACE in the High Court of Justiciary. I felt dazed. The courtroom was crowded and it seemed that the object of everyone present was to scrutinise me. I had been prepared by Ninian Grainger for what I must expect. I should stand at the bar and the Crown would state the case against me when the Defense would endeavour to prove the accusation wrong.

My feelings were so tumultuous that it is impossible to describe them. They changed from moment to moment. Innocence is the greatest defence. It gives courage. If one tells the truth, surely that must prevail. That thought remains with one all the time. It is the greatest ally.

I looked at the members of the jury—those who would decide my fate; and they gave me confidence.

Even at this stage, after the weeks of waiting for this day, there was an element of unreality about it all. I . . . . Davina Glentyre, the young girl who had gone to church with her mother, was now the prisoner at the bar in a court of law accused of murdering her father.

How could it have come about? It must be a wild mad dream.

There was silence through the court while the indictment against me was read.

"Davina Scott Glentyre, now or lately prisoner in the prison of Edinburgh, you are indicted and accused at the instance of Her Majesty's Advocate for Her Majesty's interest: that albeit by the laws of this land and of every other well governed realm, the wickedly and felonious administering of arsenic, or other poisons, with intent to murder, is a crime of a heinous nature and severely punishable. Yet true it is that you, Davina Scott Glentyre, are guilty of the said crime . . ."

It went on detailing the evidence against me—most damning of which was, of course, my buying the arsenic at Henniker's shop, my signature in the poison book being an important piece of evidence.

Then came the witnesses.

Dr. Dorrington explained how Mr. Kirkwell, the butler, called him in the early hours of the morning. He was not surprised because Mr. Glentyre had, over a few months, suffered from bilious attacks. He had expected to find this just another, perhaps more severe than the previous ones, and he had felt it was unnecessary to call him out at such an hour. However, he had been shocked on arriving at the house to find Mr. Glentyre dead.

"Did you examine him?"

"Briefly. I saw at once that there was nothing I could do for him."

"Did you suspect poison?"

"I thought there was something unusual about his sudden death."

Other doctors followed. There was Dr. Camrose, professor of chemistry at the University. He had examined certain of the deceased's organs and had found undoubted traces of arsenic. Another doctor was called and confirmed this. He said there had been a final dose which had resulted in death and which had obviously been taken in port wine. But there were traces of arsenic in the body which suggested that it had been taken over some little time.

There followed a great many scientific references which I was sure none but the specialists understood; but the fact emerged that my father had died through arsenical poisoning and that he had been taking it in smaller quantities over some time.

The doctors were asked if it were a common practise to take arsenic.

"It is said to have rejuvenating powers," replied the doctor. He had known men take it for that reason. Women used it here and there, he believed, because it was thought to be good for the complexion. It was a dangerous practise.

At length it was time for the people I knew to take their places. I was alert, watchful of them. It seemed so strange to see them there, though stranger still for them, I supposed, to see me where I was.

On trial for murder! It was not the sort of thing one would think could ever happen to oneself. That sort of drama was for other people. And now here we all were . . . people who had known each other over the years . . . ordinary, simple people

. . . all here in the centre of the stage, with the whole of Scotland . . . and perhaps beyond . . . watching us.

I could imagine the excitement which people were feeling. A young girl on trial for her life!

Mr. Kirkwell was questioned about being called by me in the early morning and dashing off to get the doctor.

"Did you go to the bedroom where Mr. Glentyre was dying?"

"Yes, sir."

"Did it occur to you that it was strange that he should be so ill?"

"Well, sir, he'd had one or two of these attacks. I thought it was just another . . . only worse."

Mrs. Kirkwell followed her husband into the witness box.

"Mrs. Kirkwell, you were worried about the rats which had appeared near the house, were you?"

"Yes, sir. They were in the mews. I never had them in the house, sir."

"Did you ever see any near the house?"

"Oh no. I couldn't have borne that. Rats near my kitchen! Horrible things. Dirty. Hamish told me they were in the mews . . . stables and all that. But he got some arsenic and finished them off."

"Was there any mention of getting arsenic because he had seen them near the kitchen door?"

"Never in my hearing, sir. I never knew they were in the dustbin. I would have been out of my mind, I can tell you, if I'd heard that."

"So you would undoubtedly remember. Now I want you to cast your mind back. A young man, a Mr. James North, had been invited to the house, had he not?"

"Yes. He came once or twice. He was sweet on Miss Davina."

"And Mr. Glentyre did not approve of the young man. Is that it?"

"I don't reckon he had anything against him, but he was poor and wasn't what Mr. Glentyre had in mind for her."

"And there was a scene."

"Well, sir. I just happened to be on the stairs with Bess . . .

that's one of the maids. The door of the study opened. I heard them shouting and Miss Davina flounced out. He was going to cut her out of his will if she married Mr. North."

"And Miss Davina was upset, was she?"

"Oh terribly. She shouted back at him. She said he could cut her out if he wanted to. It wouldn't change her mind . . . or something like that."

Ninian rose and said: "Do you often listen to your employer's private conversation, Mrs. Kirkwell?"

"No, I do not, sir. I just happened . . ."

"Just happened to be conveniently placed when Miss Davina flounced—I think you said—out of the study and went to her room. When did you hear all this conversation? It must have lasted more than a few seconds. Yet in that time you hear that Mr. Glentyre is going to cut her out of his will and her saying that she did not care."

"Well, that's what I heard."

"I suggest that you heard voices and as time passed you imagined you heard those words spoken."

"No, I did not."

Ninian smiled and said: "That will be all."

Mrs. Kirkwell, flushed and indignant, left the witness box.

Hamish was next. He looked slightly less jaunty than usual.

"I am Hamish Vosper," he said, "coachman to the late Mr. Glentyre. At the beginning of this year I saw a rat in the stables. I bought sixpennyworth of arsenic at Henniker's drugstore and managed to get rid of three of them in a week."

"Did you mention this in the kitchen to the servants?"

"Yes, I did."

"To Mrs. Kirkwell and the maids? Was anyone else there when you talked of the efficiency of arsenic?"

He looked across at me and hesitated.

"Was Miss Davina Glentyre there?"

"Well, yes, she was."

"Did she express interest?"

"I . . . I don't remember."

"Did the maid Ellen Farley tell you she had seen a rat near the kitchen . . . in the dustbin?"

"No."

"Did Miss Farley ever speak to you about rats?"

"I don't think so. She didn't speak much to me. She wasn't the talking sort."

"Are you sure that she did not tell you she had seen a rat jump out of the dustbin?"

"If she did I can't recall it."

"That will do."

Ninian rose.

"Mr. Glentyre was pleased with your services as a coachman, was he not?"

Hamish preened himself. "Oh yes, he reckoned I was very good."

"So good that you took the place of your father?"

"Well . . . yes."

"Excellent," said Ninian. "And you were naturally proud of your skills?"

Hamish looked pleased. I could see he was enjoying this.

"You like to go out with your friends . . . in the evenings?" went on Ninian.

"What's wrong with that?"

"I ask the questions, remember, please. There is nothing wrong with it unless you decide to use the family carriage for these excursions . . . without your employer's permission."

Hamish flushed.

"Did you do this on several occasions?" persisted Ninian.

"I . . . I don't remember."

"You don't remember? Then I will assure you that you did and I can produce evidence to prove this. But your memory is not good. You forgot. Might it not be that you could also have forgotten that Ellen Farley mentioned to you that she had seen a rat in the dustbin and you recommended her to try the arsenic which had proved effective?"

"I . . . I . . ."

"No more questions."

I saw how successfully Ninian had planted doubts in the minds of the jury as to the reliability of Hamish's evidence; and he was, after all, a key witness.

Zillah made a good impression on the court, but I felt it was not the Zillah I knew who stood in the witness box.

She even looked different. She was all in black; her face was pale, her hair simply dressed under the small black hat with the veil. She gave the impression of being a young, beautiful and lonely widow, suddenly bereft of a loving husband, looking out in bewilderment on a cruel world which, with one stroke, had taken her husband and put her stepdaughter in the dock.

She was a superb actress and like all her kind enjoyed having an audience to perform to. On the other hand, so well did she play the part that she did not appear to be acting.

She had I supposed cared for my father. She had always behaved to him most lovingly; she had seemed genuinely concerned about his illness. She had made the last months of his life happy. Yet I wondered.

The Lord Justice Clerk was clearly impressed by her—as I think was the whole court. Her beauty seemed the more outstanding because of the simplicity of her dress and her quietly tragic manner.

"Mrs. Glentyre." The questioner spoke in a gentle voice. "Could you tell us what happened on that tragic night?"

She told them that her husband had not been well on the previous day and she had insisted on his remaining at home.

"Was he very ill?"

"Oh no. I just thought he should have a restful day."

"That night at dinner he took a glass of port wine?"

"Yes."

"The wine was in a decanter on the sideboard?"

"Yes."

"Your stepdaughter, Miss Davina Glentyre, offered to pour it out?"

"Yes. There was nothing unusual about that. Kirkwell, the butler, was not present."

"He was usually present, was he?"

"Er . . . yes, mostly. But he had been bringing up another decanter."

"You did not take a glass of wine on that occasion?"

"No."

"Nor your stepdaughter?"

"Neither of us did. We rarely did."

"So it was just Mr. Glentyre who had his glass from the decanter which was poured out by Miss Glentyre?"

"Yes."

"Did you know that there had been trouble between your husband and his daughter about her determination to marry a young man?"

"Yes . . . but I didn't think it was very serious."

"But he had threatened to cut her out of his will."

"I just thought it was one of those little upsets that would blow over."

"Did he talk to you about it?"

She shrugged her shoulders. "He may have mentioned it."

"Did he want her to marry someone else?"

"Parents do have plans for their children. I think it was all rather vague."

"And did your stepdaughter speak to you of this matter?"

"Oh yes. We were good friends. I tried to be a mother to her." She made a little gesture.

"More like a sister, I imagine," said the Justice Clerk smiling and allowing his admiration for her to show a little.

"And you talked to her about this matter? Did she mention how bitterly she felt against her father?"

"No. Not at all. I convinced her that it would come all right in the end. Parents often disapprove of their children's marriages."

It was Ninian's turn.

"You and your stepdaughter quickly became good friends?"

"Oh yes."

"You came as governess originally, I believe."

"That is so."

"And within a short time you married the master of the house."

I could see that the court was with her. It was charmingly romantic and the most natural thing in the world that the master of the house should be overcome by her charms. A happy ending for the governess—but, oh, how tragically her happiness had been cut short!

"We have heard that traces of arsenic were found in your husband's body. Can you give us any idea how they came to be there?"

"I can only say that he must have taken it himself."

"You have heard that it is a practise among some people to take arsenic for certain purposes. Do you think there is a possibility that your husband may have been one of these people?"

"Well . . . there is a possibility."

"Why do you say that?"

"He once told me that some time ago he had taken small doses of arsenic."

There was tenseness in the court. Everyone was watching her. I felt myself caught up in it. My father . . . taking arsenic!

"What effect did he say this had on him?"

"It made him better, he said. Someone told him that it was dangerous . . . and he stopped taking it."

"Did he tell you where he got this arsenic?"

"I did not ask him and he did not say. He travelled sometimes abroad. He could have got it somewhere on the Continent. He was there on business some years ago. It may have been then."

"Did he say so?"

"No. I did not think to ask. I was just surprised that he had taken it."

"This could be important evidence. Why did you not mention it before?"

"I only remembered it when you asked."

"Did it not occur to you on your husband's death that the arsenic found in his body might have been taken voluntarily by himself?"

"No . . . only just now."

"And now you think that is a possibility?"

"Oh yes, I do."

There was a hushed silence over the court. I had the feeling that she was lying. I could not believe that my father would take arsenic. It was true that some years ago he had gone to the Continent on business. Could it possibly be that he had acquired the arsenic then? After all, what did I know of his secret life? Much had recently been revealed to me, but there must be so much of which I was ignorant.

I could sense Ninian's excitement.

The Prosecution wanted to question Zillah further.

"If your husband had a secret store of arsenic in the house, where would he keep it?"

"I don't know. He had a cabinet in which he kept certain medicines."

"Did you ever see arsenic there?"

"I hardly looked at it. I had no reason to go there. I don't think it would have been labelled 'arsenic' if it had been there."

"Was not the bedroom searched at the time of Mr. Glentyre's death?"

"I think so."

"No arsenic was found then. If he were taking it, would it not be strange that there was no trace of it in the room?"

"I do not know."

The Prosecution was shaken; but I could see the dawning triumph in Ninian's attitude.

I should have been elated, for there was a possibility that my father had killed himself. But was this true? Was Zillah inventing this story in an attempt to save me?

The first day was over. I had an idea that there would be many more to come.

NINIAN CAME TO SEE ME that evening. He was elated.

"It's a breakthrough," he said. "This must be our line. If we can prove he has taken the stuff himself, we've got the answer. It's plausible. A man who is no longer young married to a beautiful young wife. Naturally he wants to improve his health. He wants to be young again . . . so he resorts to this."

"I cannot believe that my father would ever have taken arsenic."

"You cannot be sure what people will do. If only we could find this Ellen Farley who would confirm that she asked you to buy the arsenic . . . we should be in the clear. We could romp home. I can't think what's happened to the woman. It's not easy to find people in London . . . particularly on such little information. If it had only been some country town . . . or village . . . we should have had her by now. They are still searching, of course. But I did think something would have come to light by now. Your stepmother was a wonderful witness. I have the idea that she desperately wants to help you."

"Yes, I think she does."

He took my hands and gripped them hard. "Bear up," he said. "We are going to get there."

I was thinking: Zillah is my friend, but I never feel I know what is in her mind. As for Jamie, I knew too well what was in his, and it meant that his love was not strong enough to bear this trial.

THE NEXT DAY Jamie went into the witness box.

"You and Miss Glentyre met by chance in the street?" he was asked.

"Yes. She was lost."

"I see, and she called on you for help?"

"Well . . . I saw that she was lost."

"You took her home and arranged to meet again?"

"Yes."

"And you became engaged to be married?"

"It was not official."

"Because you, as a student, were unable to support a wife?"

"Yes."

"What did Miss Glentyre tell you about her father?"

"That he had forbidden her to see me."

"Yet she continued to do so?"

"Yes."

"Do you think that was becoming conduct?"

"I was upset by it."

"You hated deceiving Mr. Glentyre?"

"Yes, I did."

"But Miss Glentyre insisted?"

Ninian was on his feet. "I protest at the question," he said.

"Miss Glentyre could not force the witness to the tryst. He must have gone willingly."

"A forceful young lady," said the Justice Clerk. "But this was a man in love. The court will realise he went to the meeting willingly as Mr. Grainger insists."

The questions were resumed. "What did you propose to do about the matter?"

"We were to wait until I had finished my training."

"That would be in two years' time at least?"

"Yes. Miss Glentyre suggested . . ."

"What did she suggest?"

"That we elope."

I paused. I could see the picture the Prosecution was trying to build up of a forceful woman who knew exactly what she wanted and was determined to get it even if it meant eloping with her lover against her father's wishes . . . or alternatively murdering her father.

"And you did not fall in with this suggestion?"

"I knew we could not do it."

"Because you had no money of your own. All you had came from your family and if Miss Glentyre were cut off as her father had threatened she would have nothing either."

I felt sick, praying for him to stop. I knew that Jamie was regretting that we had ever met; and that was the most cruel realisation of all.

It was Ninian's turn.

"Had you discussed marriage with Miss Glentyre before you were aware of her father's disapproval of the match?"

"Yes."

"Do you think that because she was indifferent as to whether you would be poor or rich she wanted to show her loyalty by being prepared to endure a few years of hardship before you could become established in your profession?"

"Yes, I suppose so."

It was the best he could do with Jamie, and I wondered if we had lost the advantage won by Zillah's evidence.

• • • •

Two MORE DAYS dragged on. The coming and going of witnesses continued. There were more doctors and a great deal of scientific terms which I could not understand, but I knew that it was not going well for me.

There was no news of Ellen's whereabouts. I thought: there is only one consolation. It will soon be over.

Then something happened. Ninian visited me and I saw at once that he was excited.

He sat down opposite me and smiled.

"If this works out, we've done it," he said. "Thank God for the divine Zillah."

"What's happened?"

"You remember she told the court that her husband had once confessed to taking arsenic?"

"Yes."

"She has discovered a piece of paper, screwed up, she says, at the back of a drawer in which your father kept things like socks and handkerchiefs. A piece of white paper with the remains of a seal on it. She opened this paper. There was nothing on it . . . no writing to show what it might have contained, but she thought she detected a few grains of powder on it."

"Powder?" I echoed.

He grinned at me, nodding. "In her husband's drawer! She immediately thought . . . you know what she thought. Wise woman. She took it to the police. It is now being analysed."

"What does this mean?"

"That if the paper contained what we hope it did, there is a possibility . . . a great possibility . . . that the dose that killed your father could have been self-administered."

"When shall we know?"

"Very soon. Oh, Davina . . . Miss Glentyre . . . don't you see?"

I had rarely seen anyone as overjoyed as he was at that moment; and in the midst of all my muddled thoughts I wondered whether he brought such feeling to all his cases.

•   •   •   •

EVENTS MOVED QUICKLY from there.

Dr. Camrose was recalled. There was no doubt that the piece of paper had contained arsenic.

The court was astounded. Zillah was recalled.

"Can you explain why this piece of paper was not brought to light before?"

"It was right at the back of the drawer."

"Can you explain why it was not seen when the room was searched?"

"I suppose because the searchers were not careful enough."

There was a ripple of mirth throughout the court.

Zillah went on: "You know how things get caught up in chests of drawers? It was not actually lying in the drawer. It had got caught up and really was midway between the upper and lower drawers, if you know what I mean."

She smiled beguilingly at her questioner who grunted. But there was nothing he could do to spoil the impression she had made on the court.

Ninian said he had no questions to ask.

From that time the atmosphere changed and it was time for the speeches from the Prosecution and the Defense.

The Prosecution was first. The Lord Advocate spoke for a long time. He set out all the facts against me. First there was the disappearance of the elusive Ellen Farley which seemed highly suspicious. Then there was the fact that I wished to marry and my father had threatened to disinherit me if I did. There was motive for murder.

As I listened I thought how strange it was that so much that was innocent could be misconstrued.

When the day ended with this speech I felt that everything had turned against me.

Ninian came to see me.

"You look troubled," he said.

"Aren't you?"

"No. I am certain that you will soon be free."

"How can you be so certain?"

He leaned towards me. "Experience," he said.

"Tomorrow . . ." I began fearfully.

"Tomorrow is our turn. You shall see."

He took my hand and put it to his lips and we looked steadily at each other for a few moments.

"This means more to me than anything," he said.

"I know. There has been a great deal of notice given to the case. If you win you will have that partnership surely."

"Perhaps. But I wasn't meaning that."

Then he released my hand.

"Now you must have a good night's sleep," he said. "I've asked them to give you a mild sedative. Please take it. It's necessary. You have been through a trying ordeal and now we are nearing the end. But remember this: we are going to win."

"You are so certain."

"I am absolutely sure. We can't fail. Things looked black at the start, I admit. But it's working out now in our favour. A good night's rest . . . and I'll see you in court tomorrow. I promise you you won't be there much longer."

I fell asleep thinking of him.

He was magnificent. His eloquence carried the jury along with him. He was so confident.

"Members of the jury, can you convict this young woman who is so clearly innocent?" He went through it all. I had met a young man. Most young women meet young men at some time in their lives. I was carried along on the stream of young love. I had been prepared to elope and lose all chance of my inheritance. Was that the attitude of one who could plan cold-blooded murder?

He went on at length about my father. A man who had fallen violently in love with the beautiful woman who had come to the house as a governess. She was many years younger than he was. What would a man do in such circumstances? Who could blame him for trying to recapture his youth? And when he thought he had a chance of doing so, rather naturally he took it. He had admitted taking arsenic. It seems likely he obtained it when he was abroad. He had tried it and knew it was a dangerous practise so he stopped. But then he married a young woman. Let us say that he had a little of the poison stowed away somewhere. He found it and once more experimented.

He had one or two bouts of illness which were obviously due to what he had been taking. This did not deter him, however, and on that fatal night he took the remains of that packet. It was more than he realised. In fact it was a very large dose. He screwed up the paper and put it in the drawer where it became caught up with the drawer above and was missed when the place was searched.

"You, members of the jury, will agree with me that that is a logical explanation of what happened that night.

"Members of the jury, you see before you a young girl. How many of you have daughters of your own? Those of you who have will understand. Think of your own daughter . . . or the daughter of a friend whom you love well. Think of her caught up in a chain of circumstances over which she has no control . . . and suddenly finding herself—as this young girl did—in a court of law facing a charge of murder.

"You have heard the evidence. If you have the shadow of a doubt you cannot find this young girl guilty. She is not the perpetrator of crimes but a victim of peculiar circumstances.

"You are observant. You are shrewd and when you think over the evidence, when you consider all we have heard in this court, you will say to yourselves and each other: 'There is only one verdict we can give. That is Not Guilty.' "

There followed the summing up by the Justice Clerk. He went through the evidence very carefully.

I was young and that must influence them. But this was an indictment of murder. There was the mysterious Ellen Farley who, according to me, had asked me to buy the arsenic for her and this I had done. The signed book at Henniker's drug shop was evidence of that. But no one had heard Miss Farley ask me to buy arsenic; no one had seen the rat in the dustbin except— it might be—Ellen Farley. And Ellen Farley was unavailable. So that was a piece of evidence about which the jury would have to come to some conclusion. Did the mysterious Ellen Farley ask the accused to buy arsenic for the rats? Or did the accused buy the arsenic for the purpose of killing her father? She had reason. He was going to disinherit her if she married her lover.

On the other hand, the deceased had confessed to his wife that he had taken arsenic at some time and this he may have procured outside this country, which meant that it was impossible to trace the purchase. Did he find what was left in the packet, misjudge the amount, and so kill himself?

"That is what you have to decide, and only if you are convinced that this is not so and the arsenic was administered from the almost empty decanter by the accused who put it there— only then can you find the accused guilty."

It was a fair summing up and the Lord Justice Clerk had made the jury's duty clear to them.

They went out to consider their verdict.

I WAS TAKEN BELOW. How the time seemed to drag. An hour passed and there was no verdict.

What would happen to me? I wondered. Could this be the end? Would they condemn me to death? That was the penalty for murder. I wondered how many innocent people had been sent to their deaths.

I should be taken back to the courtroom. I should see Ninian . . . tense and waiting. And yet he had seemed so sure.

The Kirkwells would be there . . . Bess . . . Jenny . . . the whole household. Zillah would be waiting. If I were found Not Guilty I should owe my life to her. Jamie had shown me quite clearly that what he had felt for me was not true and lasting love.

I kept remembering incidents from my life, as they say people do when they are drowning. Well, I was—metaphorically— drowning.

I tried to look ahead. Suppose Ninian was right and I came through this? What would it be like? Nothing would be the same. Everywhere I went people would say: "That is Davina Glentyre. Do you really think she did it?"

No . . . nothing would ever be the same. Even if I walked free out of the courtroom, the memories of it would be with me forever . . . with others, too.

The jury was out for two hours. It had seemed like days.

As soon as I went up I was aware of a breathless tension in that room.

The jury had filed in. The Lord Justice Clerk asked them if they had reached a verdict and would they let the court know what it was.

I held my breath. There was a long pause. Then I heard a clear voice say: "Not Proven."

There was a hush in the court. I saw Ninian's face. For a moment an expression of anger touched it; then he turned to me, smiling.

The Lord Justice Clerk was talking to me, telling me I was dismissed from the bar.

I was free—free to carry with me as long as I lived the stigma of Not Proven.

Lakemere

At the Vicarage

I LAY IN MY OWN BED. The house seemed wrapped in an obtrusive silence—a silence broken only by whispering voices.

"They have let her go? But is she guilty? Her innocence was not proven."

Those words seemed to go on and on in my mind. I could hear the foreman of the jury. I had so desperately wanted him to say "Not Guilty" and he had said "Not Proven."

"The case is over. You are free." That was Zillah, exultant.

But I knew I should never be free. Not Proven. Those words would come back again and again over the years. People would remember.

"Davina Glentyre," they would say. "Haven't I heard that name somewhere? Oh yes . . . she was the girl who murdered her father. Or did she? It was Not Proven."

What a cruel verdict! A stigma to carry through one's life.

Zillah had said: "I am going to put you straight to bed and you are going to stay there for a while. You've been through a terrible ordeal. It's been a great shock. More than you realise. But you are going to be all right. I'm going to look after you."

I was not really listening. I was still in the courtroom. I could not escape from those pictures which kept crowding into my mind. I could hear Ninian Grainger's voice—vehement, tender, angry, sentimental, pleading to the jury's good sense and humanity. He had been magnificent and I believed I owed my life to him . . . to him and Zillah, of course. When it was over he had held my hand briefly while the triumph shone in his eyes.

Of course, I represented success to him, for if he had not gained the verdict he wanted, he was halfway there. The case had been black against me and at one stage a conviction of murder seemed almost certain, but he had averted that—with Zillah's help, and we must think ourselves fortunate that the verdict was Not Proven. I was a feather in his cap, a big step towards promotion; a case which had seemed hopeless and if it had not exactly been won, had been as successful as it possibly could have been in the circumstances.

I was glad to be alone. I did not want to have to face the rest of the household. They would be tactful, but I should read their thoughts.

"Did she do it?" they would be asking. "Who could be sure? But they let her go because it was Not Proven."

Not Proven! Not Proven! It was like the tolling of a funeral bell.

ZILLAH HAD BROUGHT ME HOME. She had had the carriage, with Hamish Vosper, waiting for us.

"I knew it was going to be all right," she said. "And I wanted to hustle you away from that place as soon as I could."

We sat side by side, close. She held my hand, every now and then pressing it reassuringly and murmuring soothing words. "It'll be all right. I'm here to look after you, dear."

Everything seemed strange and unreal. Even the street seemed different.

"Don't take the carriage to the front, Hamish," I heard Zillah say. "Go straight to the mews. There might be people hanging about in the street."

Yes, I thought. Come to see the peep show, to take a look at the young woman who might have been condemned to a murderer's death. Who was to say whether she deserved it? Her innocence was not proved; it was a murder which was Not Proven.

There would be people like that always. They would be there to stare at me. They would remember. It was not proved against me but . . .

"Right you are," said Hamish jauntily. "Mews it is."

Then I was getting out of the carriage and entering the house by the back door. Mr. and Mrs. Kirkwell were embarrassed. How do people greet a member of the household who has just been on trial for murder and has come home because the case was Not Proven?

Mrs. Kirkwell managed: "Nice to see you back, Miss Davina."

Mr. Kirkwell nodded and Jenny and Bess just stared at me. I was a different person to them all.

Zillah took charge.

"Now, dear, we're going to get you to your room right away. I'll get something sent up. You need to eat a bit . . . and you need rest. You've got to get your strength back. I'm going to see you're all right."

In my room she shut the door and faced me.

"It's hard at first," she said and repeated once more: "but it will be all right."

"They don't know what to say to me. They think I did it, Zillah."

"Of course they don't. They just don't know how to express their feelings. They're as pleased as dogs with two tails, because you're back and the miserable business is over."

How long those days seemed! I did not want to emerge from my room. I could not face the ordeal of seeing people and reading their thoughts. Zillah was often with me. She brought my food and sat and chatted while I ate it.

"Talk about it if you like," she said. "It might help. I always knew you were innocent. I wish they'd given the proper verdict. Ought to have been clear to that pompous old judge and the stupid jury that you couldn't have hurt a fly."

Zillah had changed subtly. I fancied she was not keeping such a curb on herself. Her conversation was a little more racy, the red of her lips was brighter, her cheeks more coral-tinted. There was an air of something like triumph about her.

Occasionally she spoke of my father and when she did a mask of melancholy would slip over her face.

"He was such an old darling . . . always so good to me. He used to say he had never been so happy in his life as he was with me."

I could not help myself saying rather sharply: "He was very happy with my mother. He loved her."

"Of course he did, dear. That was different. And she'd gone and he was just reaching for a bit of comfort. He found me . . . and at his time of life. Oh well, I know men. It's just that he never expected to find all that again . . . and that something extra . . . if you know what I mean. It's a consolation to me that I was able to do so much for him. Not that he didn't do a lot for me."

"He seemed to change so much. He was quite different from what he had ever been before."

"He used to say I'd made him young again. That was nice. But it was wanting to be young that made him take that horrible stuff."

I shivered.

"We won't talk of it, dear," she said. "But when I think of how I found that bit of screwed-up paper, I can't help saying 'What luck!' That did the trick. Got you off. Put you in the clear."

"Not Proven," I murmured.

"Never mind that. You're here. You're free. The case is over. They can't bring it up again."

But I thought: I shall never be free because the verdict was Not Proven.

• • • •

I WENT SHOPPING with Zillah. Hamish Vosper drove us. I found him looking at me almost conspiratorially. He was jaunty and I fancied a little more familiar. I preferred the embarrassment of the other servants.

I wrote to Lilias. I could tell her more easily than anyone else how I was feeling. She had suffered a similar tragedy—not so serious, of course; but it had been momentous to her, and the case against her had been hastily judged and she had been branded Guilty.

I was comforted by a letter in reply to mine.

My dear, dear Davina,

I feel so much for you. I have read about the case in the papers, of course, and have been with you in spirit all through the trial. How I wish I could have been there in fact. When I heard the verdict I was overcome by relief. I wish it could have been more certain, but at least you are free now.

I have tried to picture what it must have been like in the house with your father's second wife. The papers imply that her evidence changed the course of the case. She seemed to be a kind person and very attractive—according to the press.

It is so long since we met. I can guess what a turmoil you must be in, and it has occurred to me that you might like to get away. You could come to stay here for a while . . . if that appealed to you. We should be able to talk and be together. The vicarage is roomy, so there would be no trouble on that score. But don't expect the same degree of comfort that you get at home. What I can offer you is the comfort of my love and sympathy . . . and belief in your innocence. Think about it. There's no hurry. Just when you are ready, write and tell me you will be coming.

You are always in my thoughts.

My love to you,

LILIAS

What a lovely letter! I wept a little over it and read it again and again.

I did think about her suggestion. To get away from this

house where it had happened would be good for me. In the secluded atmosphere of the vicarage I could talk to Lilias of the future, for I was realising that I could not go on in this state forever. I had to go forward. I needed to talk with someone who knew me well. I wanted advice, and who better than Lilias to give me that?

I mentioned the invitation to Zillah.

"I think it is a good idea," she said. "You like Lilias, don't you? You get on well with her. Typical governess, your father said she was . . . until she was overcome by temptation."

"She never was tempted," I cried indignantly. "It was all a terrible mistake. She was innocent."

"I was just telling you what your father said. Poor girl. She might have been worried about money. They have a hard time of it, governesses. I can understand the temptation. After all, I've been a governess myself."

"Zillah, Lilias did not steal. She had nothing to do with the wretched pearls. I'm sure of it."

"Oh well, you'd know. You were here with her. But your father seemed to think . . ."

I felt exasperated and was about to make a further protestation, but Zillah held up her hand.

"All right. I'm sure you'd know best. After all, she was special for you, wasn't she? You're sweet and I love you—honest I do. There are some stepmothers who'd say you oughtn't to go to someone who's under suspicion . . ."

"I'm under suspicion, Zillah."

"Well then, there you are. I think it would be good for you to go." She put her arm round me. "I can see you really want to . . . and therefore I think you should. That's settled then. You write to her and tell her you'll go. I agree it would do you a world of good to get away from here for a bit."

"Zillah, I do assure you that Lilias is quite incapable of stealing anything."

"Of course. I don't doubt it for a moment. You go. It'll be nice for you and that's what concerns me. By the way, there's something I've got to tell you. I've been trying to say it for some days. It's about your father and . . . er . . . money. He

was most anxious to provide for me and . . . he's left me everything . . . almost. This house . . . bonds . . . and things
like that. Poor darling, he said he was so grateful to me. He was
going to cut you right out. He said if you'd married Alastair
McCrae you would have been well taken care of, and if you
went to Jamie, well then . . . he would certainly have cut you
right out. I told him that wasn't right. I said if he didn't leave
something to you I couldn't take it. I worked on him and, well,
I made him see my point. He has left you something. The solicitor reckons it would bring you in about four hundred pounds
a year. I feel awful about it. All the rest comes to me."

"I . . . I see."

She pressed my hand. "This is your home, dear. Always will
be as long as you want it. I told him it would be like that. He
said I was too good. I said I was not. I said, 'I just love the girl. I
look on her as my daughter.' He was ever so pleased really. Of
course, I never thought he'd go off like that. How was I to
know he was taking that stuff?"

I was silent and she went on: "Four hundred a year! It's quite
nice. It's not as though you will be penniless. And I'm always
here. I want to share it all with you."

I don't think I was surprised. Of course, he had left everything to her. He had doted on her. I was not concerned with
money just now and I had a little of my own that would suffice.

My thoughts were with the possibility of a visit to Lilias.
There was one thing which made me hesitate. They would
naturally have heard of the case in Lakemere. What would
Lilias' father's parishioners think of their vicar's harbouring
someone who might be a murderess? I knew he was a good man
for he had taken Kitty in and found a post for her, but I must
not allow him and his family to be made uncomfortable because of me.

"What is it?" asked Zillah anxiously.

"I can't go," I said. "People will have heard of me in
Lakemere. It will be most uncomfortable for my hosts."

"Well," said Zillah, "why not change your name?"

"What?"

"You can't very well do that here where people know you. But you could when you went away."

"I . . . I suppose I could."

"No suppose about it. Why shouldn't you? Choose a name they won't connect with the case. It's simple." She warmed to the subject, her eyes glistening. "It's advisable to keep to your initials. You never know when they might turn up on something . . . and then there would be a bit of explaining to do. D.G. That's what we've got to look for."

"What a good idea!"

"It's being on the boards, dear. Lots of people there change their names. Have to sometimes for show business . . . if not for anything else. Now let's think. Davina. Well, that is the sort of name people would remember. What about Diana?"

"Oh yes. That starts with a *D*."

"Diana. Now we want a *G*."

"What about Grey? Diana Grey?"

"You're taking my name. I was Miss Grey before I became Mrs. Glentyre."

"It's short and it begins with a *G*."

"I think it goes well. Diana Grey. Well, that's what you're going to be while you're with the parson's family. It's better for them and you."

"I'll write to Lilias at once."

I went straight to my room to begin the letter.

My very dear Lilias,

I want so much to come to you, but it would be unfair to come as I am. I hope your father won't think this deceitful, but I want to escape from myself. I want to be a different person . . . and I do not want to bring gossip to you. I am sure people in your neighbourhood would know of the case, so I have decided I shall come as Diana Grey. I'll keep my own initials, which Zillah says is very wise. I will come if you agree to this deception. I don't think I could face coming if there was a danger of people's suddenly remembering.

I just want you to write and tell me that you approve of this, and then I shall pack my bag and come right away.

I hope to hear from you soon.
With my love,

DIANA

I sealed the letter and was surprised to find my spirits had lifted considerably.

I would take it down to the hall and put it on the silver salver where letters which were to be posted were laid until, at a certain time, Kirkwell would collect them and take them to the post.

I laid it on the salver and as I stood in the hall I was suddenly startled by the sound of a door being loudly shut. It was followed by an immediate clatter of footsteps. I was not anxious to come face-to-face with any of the servants, so I slipped into the sitting room and half closed the door.

The footsteps were coming down the stairs. I looked out and to my amazement saw Hamish Vosper. His face was scarlet and distorted with rage. He rushed through the hall and out by the back door.

What had he been doing in the upper part of the house? I wondered. Had Zillah sent for him because she wanted the carriage? Surely not at this time.

It was very strange.

My thoughts however were centered on Lilias. I wondered what she would have to say about my changing my name.

It would only be for the visit, of course; but the idea had occurred to me that I should get right away . . . start a new life with a different name. It would mean leaving Edinburgh. Where could I go? It was a wild dream really. But it would be something to discuss with Lilias.

I WAS IMPATIENTLY WAITING for a reply, but had started to pack for I was sure she would tell me to come soon. Then I had a caller.

Bess came to my room. "There's a gentleman to see you, Miss Davina."

"A gentleman!"

"Yes, Miss. I've put him in the drawing room."

Who was it? I asked myself. Jamie . . . come to tell me he loved me after all; he was ready to face anything with me? Alastair McCrae?

"Who is it?" I asked.

"A Mr. Grainger, Miss."

I felt a tremor of excitement. Could it really be? What could he want? The case was over as far as he was concerned.

Hastily I went down to the drawing room. He rose to greet me and took my hand, looking searchingly into my face as he did so.

"Miss Glentyre, how are you?"

"I'm all right, thank you. And you?"

"Well, thanks. It's . . . just a little difficult, is it?"

"Yes, but I'm thinking of going away for a while."

"Ah, that would be the best thing."

"I'm going to stay with my governess."

He looked surprised.

"Oh," I said. "I mean the governess I had years ago before . . ."

"I see there have been several governesses in your life."

"Only two."

"And both important to you. Tell me, where?"

"In England. Devonshire actually. A place called Lakemere."

"Devonshire is, I believe, a very attractive county."

"I'm going to stay at a vicarage. Miss Milne was a vicar's daughter."

"That sounds ideal."

The habit of confiding in him was still with me. When we had been fighting for my life he had let me know that I must hold nothing back, that every seemingly trivial detail might prove to be of the utmost importance. So now I found myself saying: "I'm . . . thinking of changing my name because it might be uncomfortable for my hosts."

"It's often done in such circumstances."

"So you think it's a good idea?"

"I do really. You see, there was a great deal of press coverage. It could be uncomfortable, as you say."

"Yes, I was thinking mainly of my hosts."

"Well, they apparently invited you."

"I know, but I imagine Lilias' father is a little unworldly."

"Oh?"

"He's such a good man . . . a saint almost."

"Do you think the saintly are unworldly?"

"Not exactly, but if he thought someone needed help he would give it without considering whether it would be inconvenient to him."

"He sounds like a most unusual person."

"He is. Lilias—that's Miss Milne—says he is a true Christian. So many talk like them and are not. He was wonderful about Kitty whereas others . . ."

I paused.

"Kitty?" he prompted.

"She was one of the maids. She was caught in a compromising situation with one of the grooms. She was promptly dismissed whereas the man . . . because he was a good coachman . . . was allowed to stay."

"That was in this household?"

"Yes. What I was saying was that Lilias' father took Kitty in when she had nowhere to go and he found a job for her. And, of course, he was wonderfully understanding when Lilias went."

"What happened about Lilias?"

I felt I was going too far. I was forgetting that he was no longer my legal adviser who had to learn everything about me. His profession made it second nature for him to extract information. Nonetheless I found myself telling him the story of Lilias and the necklace, to which he listened earnestly.

"So she was dismissed," he mused. "The parson's daughter."

"Yes, it was terrible. I can't think how it could have happened. There is only one thing I am certain about and that is that Lilias could not have stolen the necklace."

"It seems hardly likely. Did anyone have access to the house from outside?"

"No. There were only the servants. Why should any of them take and put it in her room? If they had taken it surely they would have wanted it for themselves? It's worth a considerable amount of money."

"It looks as though someone might have had a grudge against her."

"I can't think who. They did not have much to do with her, but none of them disliked her."

"Someone wanted her dismissed."

"Why should they?"

"That's the mystery."

"Well, it happened long ago and I don't suppose we shall ever know."

"And meanwhile poor Lilias has been unable to prove her innocence."

"Like . . ."

He touched my hand gently. "It seems clear that your father took the arsenic himself. The jury thought that."

"Then why?"

"Because there was a shadow of a doubt."

"And for the rest of my life, I . . ."

"You must not let it hurt you more than you can help. You must grow away from it. Go to this parsonage. Try it for a while. Your new name will help you to forget. Leave me your address. Perhaps we could keep in touch."

"But the case is over for you."

"A case such as this would never be over for me. I don't like the verdict. In my heart I know it should have been Not Guilty. I shall always hope that someday the truth will come to light."

"You do not think my father really killed himself?"

"It's the most likely possibility, but there remains that shadow of a doubt." He lifted his shoulders. "However, let me have that address."

I gave it to him and he put it into his wallet.

"So the governess was dismissed," he went on, "and the new one came: the beautiful Miss Zillah Grey whose surname you are going to use."

"Yes."

"And in a very short time she was married to your father. That's very interesting."

"I suppose it is. I believe governesses occasionally do marry the widowed fathers of their charges."

"It comes about in . . . a natural kind of way," he said slowly.

Then Zillah came into the room.

He rose and I said: "You remember my stepmother."

"But of course." He had taken her hand and was smiling warmly at her. "We met in court."

She returned the smile dazzlingly, and in spite of the fact that I was accustomed to her beauty it struck me forcibly. She seemed to blossom in the society of men—like a flower in the rain.

"You were wonderful," she said. "I can't thank you enough for what you did for . . ."

"I was grateful to you. Your evidence was vital to our case."

She sat opposite him, rather carefully, I thought, placing her back to the light as though she did not want to be seen too clearly. She was deferential, as though displaying admiration for him. He liked it obviously and did not appear to question the fact that it might be a little false.

She immediately engaged him in conversation.

"Has my stepdaughter been telling you her plans to go away for a while? Do tell me. Do *you* think it's a good idea?"

"I think it's an excellent idea. I was just saying so to Miss Glentyre."

"And did she tell you . . . ?" she began anxiously.

"About changing her name? Yes. I think that might be a good idea, too."

"I am so glad. It was my suggestion. I was a little worried. I do so want . . ."

"To do the best for Miss Glentyre, of course. Yes, I am sure it is a good idea, both to get away and to ensure a little anonymity."

"Then I shall feel happier about it now. Davina, my dear, did you offer our guest refreshment?"

"No, we were talking and . . ."

She looked at me with indulgent reproof.

"It's very kind of you," said Ninian quickly. "But I must be on my way. I just called in to see how Miss Glentyre was faring."

"How very good of you! So sympathetic and understanding. I often think how lucky Davina was to have you to defend her."

"I don't really deserve so much praise."

"You do!" She added almost archly: "And I shall insist on giving it to you."

I smiled. I felt he was very pleased that she had joined us. There was a little more chat—mostly between him and Zillah—then he rose to go.

I felt disappointed in him. He had been so obviously impressed by Zillah's charms. Of course, I had always known they were considerable, but I would not have thought that he would succumb to them so easily.

Zillah's mood changed abruptly when he had gone.

"Why on earth did he want to come here like that?" she demanded.

"He said he just wanted to know how I was getting on."

"Does he go round visiting all his ex-clients?"

"I think he regards this as a rather special case."

"*I* think he is rather inquisitive. He got you off . . . and that is where the case ends for him."

"He very much wanted a verdict of Not Guilty."

"Didn't we all?"

"Well, he seemed to get on well with you."

She allowed a self-satisfied smile to cross her face.

"Oh well, it's all over now, and what we have to do, dear, is forget about it."

As if I ever could!

LILIAS' ANSWER had arrived.

I am expecting you. We understand about the name. So from the moment you arrive you will be Diana Grey. Don't worry. No one will know except my father, my sister Jane and myself. We all want to do what we can to help. Dear

Davina—but I suppose I must start thinking of you as Diana —rest assured that I have convinced my family that you have been as wrongly suspected as I had. We are a closely knit family and trust one another absolutely.

It has occurred to me that it is a rather strange coincidence that we have both been wrongly accused. It is almost as though there is some malignant spirit in the house. That's nonsense, of course, but it does seem odd. Oh, what a lot we shall have to talk about! I am so looking forward to seeing you.

It's going to be a long journey for you. You'll have to come to London first and then take the train to the west country. We're about three miles from Tinton Crawley, but I'll be at the station with a dogcart to meet you.

I can't wait. With love,

LILIAS

P.S. I am enclosing instructions about the journey, together with the address of the London hotel where I spent the night. It's small, quiet and near the station.

I started at once to make my preparations.

IT WAS WITH GREAT RELIEF that I set out and even as the train steamed out of the Edinburgh station I felt as though a great burden had dropped from me. I believed that I had, to some extent, made a gap between the present and the nightmarish past.

As we speeded to the Border I looked anxiously at my fellow passengers, for I had the sudden fear that one of them at least might know me. My picture had been in the papers; and there had been one in particular, an "artist's impression," which had horrified me. The sketch had been sufficiently like me to be recognisable, but the artist had managed to twist my features into a mask of cunning. At that time the world had made up its mind that I had murdered my father and the artist was fitting the face to what he believed were the facts.

There was a young couple opposite me, perhaps going on

their honeymoon; they seemed entirely absorbed in each other and gave me no qualms; nor did the man intent on his newspaper. But there was a rather garrulous woman in the far corner who was determined to talk to someone, and as the others were obviously engrossed, she turned to me. She was going south to visit her married daughter and was longing for the reunion with her grandchildren. She asked me a few questions about my destination, but rather perfunctorily, I realised. Her thoughts were clearly for her coming visit, and I breathed more freely.

I need not have worried. My confidence returned. I was just nervous. I must stop imagining that people would recognise me. I was escaping to Lilias, that refuge to which she had returned, confident of love and understanding.

I spent a night in the London hotel near the station, just as Lilias had explained. It was not a very restful night, but I did not mind. I was on my way.

The following morning when I caught the train from Paddington Station the sense of relief was growing with every minute. Settling in a corner of the railway carriage, I looked out on the green countryside, noticing that the plants and trees were a little more advanced here than they were in the harsher north. My fellow passengers were agreeable, and there was a little general conversation. I knew that none of them had the faintest idea who I was, and that I had been oversensitive on that score.

The train steamed westwards; the country had grown even more verdantly lush. I caught a glimpse of the sea. I had seen little villages clustering round churches such as Lilias had often described to me in the old days; I saw the rich red soil of which she had talked, and I knew that we were in the county of Devonshire.

At last I had arrived. As we came into the station I saw Lilias on the platform and I was happier than I had ever been since the nightmare began.

We ran together and clung for some seconds. Then she held me at arm's length. "It's wonderful to see you. And you are looking better than I expected to see you. Oh, my dear, what a time! But it is over now. Come on. The dogcart is waiting. We'll get the luggage out."

The stationmaster was standing by, smiling at us.

"Oh, Jack," she said. "Could you get Jim to put the luggage into the dogcart?"

"Right you be, Miss Lilias. Jim, Jim! Hi, Jim! Luggage for Miss Lilias." He smiled at me. "And you be come to Lakemere, Miss. You be staying long?"

"I . . . er . . ."

"We're hoping Miss Grey will stay for a long time. There it is, Jim."

She took my arm.

"They are waiting impatiently at home," she said. "Longing to meet you."

Then we were gambolling along lanes so narrow that the hedges almost brushed against us as we passed.

"I'm so glad you came," she said.

"I feel so much better since I left Edinburgh."

"Of course. You wanted to get away. It's the right thing. It's the only thing. And we can talk. It will be just like the old days."

I was overwhelmed by emotion as I sat beside her. She talked animatedly, stressing every now and then how delighted she was that I had decided to come. It was a wonderful welcome.

"We shall soon be there," she said. "Oh, look down there! You can see the church tower. Our church is just about one of the oldest in the west country. More than seven hundred years old—a perfect example of Norman architecture, as it says in the guide books. Oh yes, we get visitors. There's some lovely stained glass, too. My father is very proud of it. I must make sure he doesn't bore you about it. Jane and I tell him he gets obsessions, and one of them is his dear old church."

As we drew nearer I saw the grey stone walls of the church, the graveyard with the old stones leaning a little askew in some places among the yews and the cypresses.

"Some of those trees have been here for centuries," Lilias told me. "They have seen many vicars come and go. Aren't the cypresses lovely? Someone told me they represent eternity and that is why they are so often planted in graveyards. Country lore! I'm preparing you. You'll get plenty of that from my father. And here we are . . . the vicarage."

It was a largish house, grey stone like the church; before it was a well-kept lawn with flower beds surrounding it. And there at the door was a man whom I knew at once was Lilias' father—and with him a woman, clearly sister Jane.

They came towards us as Lilias brought the dogcart to a halt.

"Here we are," cried Lilias. "The train was on time, for once. This is . . . Diana."

My hands were clasped in a firm grip and I was looking into the smiling, benign face of the Reverend George Milne.

"Welcome, welcome, my dear," he said. "We are so pleased that you have come. Lilias has been so happy since you said you would."

"And this is Jane," said Lilias.

Jane was rather like Lilias and I knew I was going to like her for that reason alone.

Her greeting was as warm as that of her father had been. I said how glad I was to meet them and what a peaceful spot it was. The flowers were lovely.

"You've won Jane's heart," said Lilias. "She has an obsession with the garden."

"It's a good thing that I have," retorted Jane. "Someone has to do it. It would be like a wilderness left to you. Come along in. I expect you're hungry. Dinner's almost ready. We hoped the train wasn't going to be late and took a chance on that. So . . . in half an hour? Lilias can show you to your room and Daisy will bring up some hot water."

"Thank you. That would be lovely," I said. "One gets grimy travelling."

I felt at home immediately. I had slipped into a new role. I must get accustomed to my new name, and when I had I should be able to believe I really had stepped away from the past.

We went into a hall. I noticed the highly polished furniture; on a hall table was a large bowl of flowers, colours exquisitely blended and beautifully arranged.

Lilias noticed my glance. "That's Jane," she said. "She fills the house with flowers."

"They are so lovely," I said. "Oh, Lilias . . . I am going to be happy here."

"We are going to do our best to make you," replied Lilias.

I followed her up the staircase to a landing.

"We've put you on the first floor," said Lilias. "You have to mind your head when you enter some of these rooms. I think people must have been smaller at the time places like this were built." She opened the door of a room and I followed her in. It was large but rather dark and there was only one window and that was leaded. There was a bed in one corner, and a dressing table and a mirror and a wash hand stand. A large cupboard almost filled one wall.

"There you are," she said. "I'm afraid it's not like your home in Edinburgh, but . . ."

"It's lovely," I said, "and I can't tell you how happy I am to be here with you . . . and your family."

I went to the window. I was looking over the graveyard. I had a view of the tottering gravestones, the ancient yews and cypress trees. It was fascinating.

Lilias came and stood beside me. "I hope you don't think it's a little morbid? I chose this room for you because it is a little bigger than the other spares and the graveyard has a kind of friendly feeling when you get to know it. At least, that's what my sister Emma used to say. She's married now, you know. I have a niece and nephew through her and two nephews through Grace who married a clergyman. Emma used to say that if there were ghosts they were nice ones."

At that point the door was opened by a middle-aged woman who came in carrying a can of hot water. Lilias introduced her as Daisy.

"It's nice to see 'ee, Miss," she said to me. "I hope you'll enjoy your stay."

"We're going to make sure of that, Daisy," Lilias told her.

"That we be," said Daisy.

"Thank you," I murmured.

When she had gone Lilias said: "Daisy has been with us all

our lives. She came when my father and mother were married and this is her home as it is ours. We just have a girl coming in some mornings to help with the cleaning. Jane is an excellent housekeeper though. Otherwise I don't know how we'd manage. I'm rather a poor replacement for Alice."

I remembered that Alice was the sister who had left the household to become a governess when Lilias had been forced to return home.

"No," went on Lilias, "I'm not much of a help in the house. My father calls Jane and me his Mary and Martha."

"I daresay you have your uses."

"I shop and help with the local good works . . . bazaars and so on . . . everything that goes with the routine of a country vicarage."

"Which is very important, I've no doubt."

"Well, I suppose I could say I am of some use."

"What strikes me so forcibly about the place is the peace of it."

"I'm glad you find it so. It's what you need."

"Oh, how I wish that I had come in different circumstances! But it's no use wishing you can change what's gone before."

"No good at all. But it is going to get better. We're going to put the past behind us. We both have to do that. We're just going to forget it all happened. It's the only way."

"But can we?"

"We can try. Now, I am going to leave you to wash and change if you want to. Can you find your way down?"

"I'm sure I can."

She was gone and I was alone. I washed and changed. I felt elated. I knew I had been right to come here.

As the days passed I became more sure of this. I had slipped into a new identity and was no longer startled when I heard myself addressed as Diana. I was caught up in a new way of life. I was becoming very friendly with Jane who was quite different from Lilias. Jane was no dreamer; she was practical in the extreme which was very necessary in running the vicarage household on what I imagined was by no means a large stipend.

I wanted to contribute to the household expenses, but my hints that I should do so were so firmly brushed aside that it was difficult to pursue the matter. Jane and Daisy put their heads together so skillfully that there was no sign of any deprivation. Meals were simple but wholesome. Daisy had taught Jane to cook long ago and she had taken to it, as Daisy said, like a fish to water.

Lilias lacked an interest in domestic affairs. She and Alice had been "the clever ones." Alice was now making use of her skills while alas Lilias, because of that unfortunate incident, was unable to do so.

The vicar was very much as I had expected him to be, due to Lilias' description. He was one of the most contented people I had ever met. He was completely unselfish and his life seemed to have been given over to the service of others. He was a little absent-minded, but between his daughters and Daisy he was taken good care of. He was greatly loved by all with whom he came into contact and his little foibles were looked upon with the greatest indulgence. He was indeed a very happy man. I thought how lucky Lilias was to be his daughter, which sent my thoughts back to my own father; I recalled his anger over my friendship with Jamie and his outraged dismissal of Kitty and how Zillah had crept into his bedroom at night.

But I must not think of my father—nor of Jamie. Jamie had failed me. His love had not been strong enough to stand up to trouble and at the first sign of it he had crept away.

That had hurt me deeply. But I supposed it was the terrible nature of what had followed which had helped to subdue the bitterness of that particular blow.

On my first day I heard that Major Jennings, who ran the riding stables, was a great friend of the vicarage family. He knew that Lilias liked to ride and could not afford to, so he had asked her if, as a favour to him, she would help with the exercising of his horses. Lilias had accepted the offer with the greatest alacrity. Therefore she rode a good deal.

"I go over to help with the grooming and clean out the stables," she said. "I enjoy being with horses. Sometimes, if they

are hard-pressed I give people lessons. It's a wonderful opportunity. How would you like to ride?"

"I'm not a rider, but I did have a few lessons in Scotland, so
I'm not exactly a novice."

"Well, here's your opportunity."

"What a good idea! I could pay for my lessons and you,
Lilias, could teach me."

Lilias looked disturbed, so I explained hastily: "It's all right.
My father left me some money. I have a small income so I am
not exactly poor. The house and the bulk of his fortune went to
Zillah."

Lilias was thoughtful: "It all happened so quickly. It seems
odd. It's not so very long since I was there. She came . . . and
almost immediately she married your father. It's almost as
though it were arranged." She hesitated, staring into space.
"I'm talking nonsense," she went on. "Let's go to the Jennings'
this morning and see what can be arranged about the riding.
You'll like them. Besides the major there are Mrs. Jennings and
Florence, their daughter. They all work with the horses."

"Tell me about the other neighbours."

"Well, there's the manor."

"I remember your telling me about that. It's where the
squire lives . . . and the young man you were going to
marry."

"Yes. Charles . . . Charles Merrimen."

"Is he still there?"

"Oh yes, he's there. I go and see him quite often. He's in a
wheelchair most of the time. He's such a fine man."

"Shall I meet him?"

"Of course. And then there are the Ellingtons at Lakemere
House. They are the important family here. They are the rich
ones, the benefactors of the village. It was to them that Kitty
went. Oh! I'd forgotten Kitty. Just in case you meet her she'll
have to be prepared, won't she? We don't want her blurting
out . . ."

It was as though a cloud had settled about us. The euphoria
was slipping away. Was it always going to be like that? Should I

constantly be wondering whether someone was going to recognise me?

Nanny Grant's voice came back to me over the years:

Oh, what a tangled web we weave
When first we practise to deceive.

NEVERTHELESS the harmony of the vicarage was bringing back to me a sense of security. I would wake with a feeling of anticipation, wondering what the day would bring.

I would stand by the window looking out over the graveyard. Those ancient tombstones might have looked eerie in moonlight, but somehow they conveyed a sense of peace; the troubles of those who lay beneath them were over. Friendly ghosts indeed.

Lilias' company had a further healing effect. I could open my heart to her; and how good it was to share my troubled thoughts! I could tell her how hurt I had been by Jamie's desertion.

"It was just as well," was her verdict. "If he failed you when you most needed him, he would not have been the partner with whom you could have gone happily through life. He might have cared for you . . . a little; but he cared more for himself. Better not to marry than marry the wrong one. You were young, inexperienced and lonely; you had lost your mother; you and I had parted; your father had remarried and you were not sure of your stepmother. I believe you were ready to fall in love. In love with love, as they say. And that's not so hard to get over as the real thing."

Yes, she was indeed comforting.

Then there was the riding. Major Jennings was a hearty middle-aged man, bronzed through service in India; when he came home he had settled down to run his stables with the help of his wife and daughter. Both Mrs. and Miss Jennings were brisk and jolly people; they were surrounded by dogs—four at least, but they were large and intrusive and made their presence felt.

The first time I met the family we were taken into a comfortable but rather shabby room, on the walls of which hung several pictures of horses, and given tea by Mrs. Jennings. Miss Florence Jennings came in while we were having it. She was a tall young woman of about thirty, I imagine, with abundant reddish hair and a crop of freckles. She was in a riding habit. I was to discover that she spent most of her days garbed thus.

"This is Florence, my daughter," said Mrs. Jennings. "Horses are a passion with us, and Florence, if anything, is more besotted than the rest of us over the four-legged darlings, aren't you, Flo?"

Florence admitted that she was.

There were a great many brass and carved wooden ornaments in the room as well as two Benares tables—all obviously from India. They seemed to have brought a flavour of that country into their home.

The dogs came in to inspect us, one fawning, one curious and the other two inclined to be suspicious.

"That's enough, Tiffin. You, too, Rajah. These are good friends."

The dogs immediately drew back at the sound of the voice of authority.

Both Mrs. Jennings and Florence were interested to hear that I intended to ride and so far had only had a few lessons.

"You'll soon be a rider," Florence assured me. "I sense it. Long practise, you know. Don't let your mount know you're nervous. That's when they play up. Let them know you're in charge . . . right from the start. Pet them a little, and they are yours."

Lilias said she thought it would be a good idea if she gave the lessons, at which Mrs. Jennings slapped her thigh and said that would be just the ticket.

The outcome was that I was instructed by Lilias and after three or four days of discomfort, I was well on the way to becoming a horsewoman.

Lilias took me to the manor and there I met Charles Merrimen. I liked him from the beginning. There was something almost saintly in his acceptance of his disability and there was clearly a bond of deep affection between him and Lilias. His father, the squire, was a rather taciturn and dignified man and the family had lived in the manor for centuries. There were Charles' elder brother David, his wife and two sons, but it was Charles who was of special interest to me for he might so easily have married Lilias and then she and I would never have met. That made me ponder on the strangeness of chance.

I accompanied her on one or two occasions when she visited him, but I quickly began to feel that those meetings should be for the two of them alone. She told me that she was reading Gibbon's *Decline and Fall of the Roman Empire* aloud to him and he enjoyed it so much. So I excused myself and, as Lilias and I had always understood each other, she accepted my decision not to go with her.

Then came the invitation from Lakemere House.

"Mrs. Ellington regards herself as lady of the manor," Lilias explained. "I think she feels that the Merrimens are rather lax in carrying out their duties. Well, the squire is getting on, David is quite absorbed in his family and Charles, of course, can do nothing. Mrs. Ellington is very efficient, of course. She is one of those women who thinks she knows what is good for people better than they do themselves. The maddening thing is that she often does. We are invited to tea. If she approves of you you will be invited again. By the way, we shall have to do something about Kitty before we go there . . . just in case we run into her. I wonder if I could get her over here for some reason? Let's see. I'll ask Jane. She might have some ideas."

Jane did.

"I heard Father say that she has never been confirmed. She wants to be and, of course, Mrs. Ellington is all for it. Get her over here on the pretext of discussing that."

The message was sent and on the day before we were due to visit Lakemere House Kitty arrived. We arranged that I should keep out of sight until Lilias had talked to her.

I had a glimpse of her from my window as she arrived. She looked plumper and more contented. I thought: the life here suits her.

She had not been in the house long when Daisy came to my room and told me that Lilias thought I should now go down to the drawing room.

When I arrived Kitty ran to me and threw her arms about me. Then she withdrew—a little shocked, I think, at her temerity.

I kissed her cheek and said: "It's good to see you, Kitty."

"Oh, Miss D . . . er, Miss er . . . It was terrible . . . the things they said . . ."

"It's over," I said. "We try to forget it."

She nodded. "But I'll never forget what you done for me, Miss . . . you and Miss Milne. I just don't know what I would have done without you."

"So you're happy at Lakemere House?"

"Oh yes. It's nice. I really like it there."

"I hope it will stay like that."

"You mustn't forget that it is Miss Diana now," said Lilias. "Miss Diana Grey. It is important, Kitty, that you should not forget."

"Oh, I won't, Miss."

She told us how different from Edinburgh it was living in Lakemere House. She had made friends and Mrs. Ellington took an interest. She knew she had done wrong, but she couldn't think what had come over her. It was just that . . . She blushed and we changed the subject.

Lilias hustled her off to the vicar that the subject of her confirmation might be broached. Lilias was a stickler for the truth and she wanted to adhere to it as much as possible.

I could not help feeling a little apprehensive when we drove over to Lakemere House in the dogcart, even though I tried to repress my fear and assure myself that I must not feel so nervous every time I was going to meet someone new.

Lilias was saying: "As she regards herself as the guardian of the village, Mrs. Ellington likes to know everything that is going on. She is especially interested in the church. I think she believes it is her duty to watch over my father. She respects his goodness, but deplores his unpractical way of going about life. She regards him with a mixture of affection and exasperation. She admires his Christian virtues and despairs of his unworldliness. I daresay she will try to get you to give a hand in village affairs while you are here."

"I shan't mind that. Is there a Mr. Ellington?"

"Oh yes. He's very rich. He goes back and forth to Exeter and is often in London. He never interferes with Mrs. Ellington's affairs—he just supplies the comforts which enable her to continue with her good works. He is said to be a lion in business and a lamb in the domestic circle."

"So Mrs. Ellington is the resident lioness."

"That's about it. Then, of course, there is Miss Myra Ellington—the fruit of the marriage. She must be approaching thirty. She is unmarried."

"I'm surprised at that. I should have thought Mrs. Ellington would have found a suitable match for her daughter."

"There are some who say that Miss Myra is not the marrying kind. She is pleasant . . . but rather quiet, self-effacing almost, which seems strange in Mrs. Ellington's daughter. I believe that she is rather well off in her own right. Rumour says her grandfather left her money . . . the bulk of his fortune, they say. That would give her a certain independence, I suppose."

"I see. I suppose a great many people marry for security."

"A great many, I fear. Well, Miss Ellington doesn't have to think of that. Though I did hear through Kitty that she seems to be rather interested in a man who is visiting the house."

"I suppose in a village it is difficult to keep secrets, however much one tries . . ."

Lilias was looking at me severely. "You've got to stop thinking that everyone is obsessed by your case. It was just a nine days' wonder. People quickly forget what doesn't affect them."

She was right. But so many conversations seemed to lead back to the subject.

Lakemere House was an impressive building of eighteenth century elegance. Marble steps led up to a portico. On the lawn, which was bordered by flower beds, was a large pond, in the centre of which was a statue which could have been Aphrodite.

A maid took us up to the drawing room where Mrs. and Miss Ellington were waiting to receive us.

Mrs. Ellington, seated in an armchair which resembled a throne, held out a hand. "Oh, Lilias . . . how nice to see you."

Miss Ellington had risen and hovered beside her mother.

"This is Miss Diana Grey," said Lilias.

The hand was extended. I took it, feeling I should curtsy, for there was something decisively regal about Mrs. Ellington.

"So nice. Welcome to Lakemere, Miss Grey. This is my daughter."

We shook hands.

"So pleased you could come," murmured Miss Ellington to which I replied that it was kind of Mrs. Ellington to invite me.

I studied the rich Miss Ellington. She was tallish and rather angular. There was an awkwardness about her and she had no real claim to beauty whereas her mother must have been a very pretty woman in her youth. But there was something appealing about Miss Ellington. It was due to a certain gentleness in her big brown rather spaniel-like eyes.

"I hear you have come to stay at the vicarage, Miss Grey," said Mrs. Ellington. "What do you think of our little village?"

"I haven't seen a great deal of it yet, but what I have seen I find charming."

"We're rather fond of it. So much is going on. It keeps us busy."

A maid came in, wheeling a trolly on which everything needed for tea was laid out, including thinly cut sandwiches and a fruitcake.

"Thank you, Emma," said Mrs. Ellington. "You may go. We'll manage. Miss Grey, cream? Sugar?"

Miss Ellington took the cup and brought it to me.

A few minutes later the door opened and a man looked in. He stood in the doorway conveying surprise and penitence.

"Oh, I am so sorry. I had no idea you had guests. I'm interrupting."

"Come along in, Roger," said Mrs. Ellington warmly. "And indeed you are not interrupting. Mr. Lestrange is staying with us," she said to me. "Come in and meet our guests."

He was tall and powerfully built. I imagined he was in his late thirties. He was a very striking looking man—probably because of his physique. But it was something more than that. His complexion suggested he had been in a country with a warmer climate than ours; and he had intensely blue eyes which contrasted vividly with his almost black hair.

He advanced into the room, looking at me with interest.

"We have met," said Lilias.

"Of course, but . . . er . . ." He was smiling at me.

Miss Ellington said: "This is Miss Grey who is staying at the vicarage."

"How interesting!"

"Do sit down, Roger," said Mrs. Ellington. "Myra, my dear, take Roger his tea."

While the tea was being served Mrs. Ellington said to me: "Mr. Lestrange comes from South Africa. He is in England for only a short while, and he is spending a little time with us. He and my husband have business interests in common."

"I've been riding," he said, smiling at us all. "I find the countryside fascinating."

"A little different from where you've come from, I daresay," said Mrs. Ellington.

"Delightfully so. You are visiting, too, Miss Grey? From what part do you come?"

"From Scotland."

"A beautiful country. What part?"

"From . . . er . . . Edinburgh." I felt myself flush a little. I must control my fears. Since my ordeal I had felt so uneasy when anyone asked questions about myself.

"And what part of South Africa do you come from, Mr. Lestrange?" I asked quickly.

"A place called Kimberley. You may have heard of it."

"Who has not heard of Kimberley?" said Mrs. Ellington. "Your diamonds have made you famous."

"Perhaps notorious," he replied, smiling at her. "Oh yes. There is no doubt that diamonds have put us in the news."

"Mr. Lestrange is attached to one of the biggest diamond companies in the world," said Mrs. Ellington proudly.

"Oh come," he said with a laugh. "There are others."

"You are a very modest man, Roger," said Mrs. Ellington almost fondly.

"It must be very exciting when diamonds are discovered," I said.

"Yes, and it can create chaos. Diamonds . . . gold . . . we've had our share of both. People begin to think they are lying in the ground just waiting to be picked up."

"Once they are found there is a great deal of work to be done on them, I suppose," said Lilias. "When people talk of diamond discoveries I do believe they think of bracelets and rings just waiting to be worn."

"That's true. And for every find there are hundreds of disappointments. I'm glad to say I have been one of the lucky ones."

"Do you actually live *in* the town of Kimberley?" I asked.

"Yes. I have quite a large house . . . well, it's adequate. I must say that since my wife died I have thought of moving. But . . . well . . . I have had to travel a great deal and have just not got round to it."

There was a brief silence of respect for the death of his wife which he had spoken of with some feeling. He bit his lips and smiled brightly at us, and Miss Ellington said quickly: "It must be very interesting to be in a *new* country. Here, everything is so ancient."

"Well, I would hardly call Africa new," said Mr. Lestrange. "But here you have so much to remind you of a not-so-distant past. For instance your Norman churches and some of the houses."

"The climate must be very different from here," said Lilias.

"It is. But ours in Kimberley is healthy . . . so we are told."

"One only has to look at you to see that," said Mrs. Ellington.

"Are you staying long in England?" I asked.

"Until my business is completed. I am tempted to make it last a long time. You've no idea how they spoil me here."

"We enjoy having you," said Mrs. Ellington, "don't we, Myra?"

Miss Ellington agreed, with real feeling, I thought.

"It makes a change in our simple life," went on Mrs. Ellington. "My husband's friends stay from time to time." She raised her eyes to the ceiling. "But on this occasion Myra and I are finding it most enjoyable and we shall do our best to make you extend your visit, Roger."

I could not help noticing Myra Ellington. She had changed since he came in. Her spaniel's eyes strayed often to him. She is attracted by him, I thought.

As for him, he was different from anyone I had ever known. I wondered about him. He came from South Africa. Had he been born there or was he one of the men who had gone out from home in search of diamonds? He was not what I would imagine an Afrikaner . . . which would mean that he was of Dutch origin. His name suggested he might be French. I believed that when the Dutch agriculturists who were Boers settled in South Africa, they were joined by some Huguenots who were in flight from France. But he did not look French either.

However, since his arrival the tea party was turning out to be more interesting than I had thought it would be. Instead of the expected conversation of village affairs we were given an interesting insight into a world of which hitherto I had known nothing.

Mrs. Ellington allowed Roger Lestrange to dominate the conversation, which surprised me; but she, like her daughter, was clearly very attracted by him.

He was a vivid talker and obviously enjoyed his attentive audience. He touched briefly on the beauty of the scenery, often rugged, majestic, awe-inspiring; he talked of the animals —lions, leopards, panthers, giraffes, buffalo, rhinoceros and hyenas; and as I listened I felt I was there in a new world, far away from all the fears and nightmares which seemed to be constantly with me.

"It sounds like paradise," said Myra Ellington.

"There is another side to it," he said ruefully. "You can see a lion descending on a beautiful deer—the poor creature's terror when it realises its fate. That is nature. Every animal must fend for itself. They go in fear of their lives. One moment they are running along, exulting in the joys of being alive and free. They do not see the powerful enemy waiting for the moment to spring. Suddenly they are powerless. Death is facing them."

"It sounds awful," said Myra, shivering.

"It's nature."

"Thank goodness we are not like the animals in the jungle," said Lilias.

"People find themselves facing dangers sometimes," I could not help saying.

Roger Lestrange was looking intently at me. "How right you are, Miss Grey. We are all in a jungle of sorts. Ours is different, of course . . . but the dangers are there."

"What a morbid conversation!" cried Mrs. Ellington. "Mr. Ellington will be returning home tomorrow. I am sure you will be pleased, Roger. Then you won't have to see so much of us tiresome females."

"They are far from tiresome! I promise I shall try to see more and more of their delightful company."

It was not long before the conversation turned back to Africa and I learned more about that country during that tea party than I had known before.

Roger Lestrange said he could see trouble coming. The Boers resented British rule in South Africa. There had been discontent since the British came in as far back as 1814. They were far too eager to give privileges to the black races since they had brought in emancipation of slavery. This had crippled the farmers for it deprived them of free labour.

He talked of Cecil Rhodes who had founded the state of Rhodesia and had wanted British rule all over Africa; of how he had shared that dream with a man called Leander Starr Jameson who, two years before, had been engaged in the famous raid which had ended in disaster for him.

We all remembered hearing of the Jameson Raid, but had either forgotten or never really known what it was all about.

"Jameson was a hothead," said Roger Lestrange. "That was surprising because he was a doctor. He was born in your city. You did say you came from Edinburgh? He studied medicine there and came out to practise in Kimberley where he became friendly with Cecil Rhodes. There was a good deal of trouble between the Uitlander party (those are the people settled there who are not Boers—mostly English) and the Boer government.

The President was Stephanus Johannes Paulus Kruger, usually known as Paul Kruger. You must have heard of him."

"We have heard of him most certainly," said Mrs. Ellington grimly. "There was all that trouble about the letter sent by the German Kaiser congratulating him."

"Ah, yes, that was about the Jameson Raid. Rhodes and Jameson had planned together to surprise the Boers west of Johannesburg. Rhodes then decided that the plan could not succeed and called the whole thing off. But, as I said, Jameson was a hothead; he thought he could act alone and win—so he decided to carry on. When he arrived at Krugersdorp just west of Johannesburg he was surprised by a strong force of Boers, was overwhelmed and taken captive. The Jameson Raid was therefore a failure and responsibility for it was disowned by Rhodes and the British government. It was a complete disaster."

"And nearly resulted in war between us and Germany," said Mrs. Ellington. "Mr. Ellington was horrified at the prospect. It was a near thing. We felt we had to put that horrid Kaiser in his place."

"However," went on Roger Lestrange, "the British government decided that what was happening in South Africa was not worth a war with Germany and so allowed the trouble to blow over."

"I should have liked to teach those arrogant Germans a lesson," said Mrs. Ellington.

"The situation is explosive," went on Roger Lestrange. "Rhodes and Kruger are very watchful of each other. The Jameson Raid may not have succeeded in what it was meant to do, but it is not forgotten."

"I should like to see South Africa," said Myra Ellington.

Roger Lestrange smiled at her. "Perhaps one day you will."

Mrs. Ellington evidently felt that for too long the conversation had been out of her control and I could see she was determined to change it.

She talked about the village and the fête which was some weeks off but needed a lot of planning.

"I wonder if you will be with us then, Miss Grey," she said.

"Diana's plans are a little uncertain just now," Lilias told her.

"But of course. Well, if you are . . . I wondered if you would take over one of the stalls?"

"I am sure I should like that," I told her.

"And you will help, too, Roger?"

"I don't think I should make a very good stall holder."

"Oh, we'd find something for you to do."

"Is there a possibility of your being here?" asked Myra.

"I am not sure how long my business will take. But I must not continue to encroach on the hospitality I have received in this house."

"Oh, nonsense," cried Mrs. Ellington. "It's a pleasure to have you."

"So kind . . . but I am afraid sometimes that I am imposing."

"Nonsense. I would not hear of your leaving and going to some hotel. My husband would be most displeased . . . and so would I."

He smiled at Lilias and me. "You see what a wonderful hostess I have. I consider myself most fortunate to be here." He included us all in his smile.

Lilias was glancing at her watch. It was five-thirty, I saw from my own. I knew that visits with Mrs. Ellington were usually on village business and given a limited time.

And now it was clearly the time for us to depart.

We thanked Mrs. Ellington and said goodbye.

Mr. Lestrange, with Myra Ellington, accompanied us out to the dogcart.

As we turned out of the drive, Lilias said to me: "Well, what did you think of that?"

"Very interesting. I enjoyed hearing about South Africa. I think Myra Ellington is quite fond of him."

"Exactly my impression. It would be nice for her if he married her. I think she would like a husband."

"I wonder how she would feel about leaving home?"

"She was very eager to hear about Africa."

"Well, we shall see."

• • • •

THE NEXT DAY I had a letter from Zillah. She had written once before. She really seemed to care and to understand my feelings.

My dear, dear Davina,

I hesitated whether I should call you Diana, but somehow it seemed going a bit too far. But perhaps I should have, in case this falls into someone else's hands. You will have to destroy it as soon as you have read it—which sounds rather dramatic.

How are you getting on? I think a great deal about you. But I'm sure you did right to go and become Diana. You're going to feel better . . . calmer and all that.

It seems very strange here without you. People are different. Well, I fancied those round here never much approved of me—so I don't miss them. I keep saying "I must tell Davina that" and then . . . you're not there.

Do let me know how things are.

By the way, your Ninian Grainger has called twice. Really, it is most extraordinary! And, I think, a little indiscreet!

I hinted this but he shrugged it off. He gets me to talk about myself. He's very inquisitive. I suppose he gets so used to asking questions that it's a habit with him. He's attentive. Perhaps I ought to ask him what his intentions are! Pretty obvious, I suppose. But I am rather surprised.

Well, it makes a diversion.

He took me out to dinner one evening. I am sure he thought I was going to ask him in when he brought me home. There's men for you! I suppose I ought to send him about his business. Then I remember that he did get you off and I'm tremendously grateful to him for that.

I thought I might go to London for a little spell. I feel I want to get away.

Do write. I am thinking such a lot about you.

Lots and lots of love,

ZILLAH

I sat back, the letter in my hand. I was thinking of Ninian Grainger, and I was disappointed in him. I had thought he had some regard for me, but from the moment he had seen Zillah he had become bemused by her. I thought of those sessions together when we had talked so earnestly and the most important thing in the world to him seemed to be to prove me Not Guilty. I remembered that when the verdict had been given, he had held my hands and I had seen with emotion the joy in his face; and, smarting as I was from Jamie's desertion, I had felt uplifted by it. At that moment I had seen so clearly what Jamie's affection for me had really been. It had simply grown out of the meeting between two lonely people in the streets of Edinburgh; and so we had believed ourselves to be in love—but it was a love which had wafted away on the first harsh wind.

I had seen it then for what it was and I had allowed myself to believe that Ninian's care for me—I might say his dedication—was of a very different calibre.

I must remember, of course, that I had been in a hysterical state of mind. I had just stood on trial for my life. I should have realised that my relationship with Ninian was that between an advocate and his client in a case which, if he won, could greatly enhance his reputation.

He had not had a clear win, but still he had triumphed to some extent.

That was all it was; and I had seen in it the beginnings of a deep friendship which might lead to something deeper. That was because I was naïve, completely unworldly. As soon as my attractive stepmother had appeared he had lost interest in me.

And now he was actually pursuing her! I felt dismayed and bitterly disappointed.

I could not get the thought of him and Zillah out of my mind. It had affected me more deeply than I had thought possible.

Lilias was aware of my depression and tried hard to interest me in village affairs. I could now ride reasonably well and that provided a diversion. We went out often and I began to know some of the villagers quite well.

As the daughter of the vicarage, Lilias was expected to call on the inhabitants from time to time—especially those who were infirm. She explained to me that Jane was well occupied in the house and this task naturally fell to her, Lilias. She had developed quite an aptitude for it and took the burden off her father's shoulders.

"They're all interested to see you. Some of them are confined to their houses and a new face in the village creates a lot of interest."

That was how I came to be with her when she paid her periodical call on Mrs. Dalton.

She always explained to me a little about these people on the way to them so that I had some idea of what I was going to find.

As we rode along she said: "Mrs. Dalton is an interesting old lady. She must be all of eighty and has lived in this village all her life. She had six children—four girls and two boys. Two of them went abroad—one to America, one to New Zealand—and it is a sore point with her that she doesn't see those grandchildren as well as their parents. They keep in touch and it's a great day when she hears from them. The whole village soon learns the contents of the letter. She's an inveterate gossip and a purveyor of scandal. It's all she has to do. She can only just move about and she's in her chair most of the day . . . just sitting . . . looking out of the window. Two of the daughters and a daughter-in-law live nearby, and take it in turns to come in and look after her—so there is no worrying on that score. But she loves to have visitors and there is usually a stream of them going in and out. One of the grandchildren goes in to read the paper to her every day; then she relates what she has heard to her visitors. She's bright and uncomplaining as long as she can get plenty of people to talk to her."

"I'll be interested to see her. I like meeting them all. It's a different way of life here from what I have ever known before."

"Oh, you'll be amused by Eliza Dalton."

We walked across the green to the cottage. The door was on the latch, so Lilias knocked then opened it and walked in.

"Good morning, Mrs. Dalton. Is it all right if we come in?"

"Oh, it's you, Miss Lilias? Yes . . . yes . . . come in. I'm all alone."

"I've brought Miss Grey to see you. Remember, she is staying with us."

"So you're Miss Grey." She peered at me intently. "Nice to meet you. A friend of Miss Lilias. I've heard all about you."

I felt that uneasy qualm and immediately suppressed it.

"Bring up your chair close, so that I can see you."

"And how are you, Mrs. Dalton?" asked Lilias.

"Well, it's my rheumatics . . . come and go, they do. Some days worse than others. The weather don't help, I can tell you."

"No. I suppose not. Tell me about the family."

"Charley's doing well. Got his own bit of land. He had to go all the way to New Zealand to get it. He says he's got on quicker out there than he could here. And his daughter's getting married. My granddaughter and me not there to see her wed. What do 'ee think of that?"

"A great pity," said Lilias. "Still, you've got plenty of your family close and that's a good thing."

"I think of them that's far away."

"Well, you've got good daughters and a daughter-in-law to see to your comforts."

"I've nothing to complain of in them. Only Olive . . ." She turned to me. "That's my daughter-in-law . . . she's in and out like a flash. A good cleaner. But do you know what she says? 'There b'aint time to sit and chat, Ma. I've got things to see to at home.'"

"One can understand that," said Lilias soothingly. "But you do have lots of visitors."

"Oh yes . . . yes . . . they come and see me." She turned to me, her eyes in her wrinkled old face alight with curiosity. "It's nice of you to come and see me. Tell me, what do you think of our village, eh?"

"I'm finding it most interesting."

"Seen many of us?"

"Quite a number."

"And what part of the world do you come from? I can see you're not a Devon girl."

"No. I come from Scotland."

"Oh." She looked at me with some suspicion. "That's a long way."

"Well, it is not really so far by train."

"I've never been in one of them newfangled things."

Lilias laughed. "Oh, they have been going for a good many years, Mrs. Dalton."

"All these years . . . it's been the chair for me. You can't go about when the rheumatics strike. And before that there was the family to bring up."

"Well, you see the world . . . the world of Lakemere . . . from your cottage window."

"There was that murder case up in Edinburgh. Edinburgh, wasn't it?"

"Edinburgh . . . yes, that's the capital," said Lilias. "How is young Clare doing at school?"

"She's all right. There was a lot about it in the papers."

My heart had begun to beat so loudly that I thought they might hear. Lilias was looking at me anxiously. She said: "It was a good year for fruit, Mrs. Dalton."

"Do ye say? There was this terrible murder in Scotland. Edinburgh . . . that's where it was. The place you come from. They let her off."

"Has the doctor been today?" asked Lilias.

"Oh, he says there's not much he can do for me. Just got to live with it, he says. People of my age is bound to get something. He calls in when he feels like it . . . takes a look at me and says, 'Just rest. Do what you can.' It was as plain as the nose on your face. She had her reasons, didn't she? Going off buying that stuff. And her own father! That woman . . . beautiful, wasn't she? I reckon she was making it all up. Him taking arsenic to make himself more of a man! I never heard the like. What's the world coming to?"

"Well," said Lilias who was becoming quite agitated. "I really think we should be going. We have some more calls to make."

"You've not been here much more than five minutes. I wanted to tell you about Mrs. Mellish's lodger and that daughter of hers. Oh, and I'm forgetting the great news. It's not out yet. It will soon be all over the village. What do you think?"

"I've no idea," said Lilias coolly.

"It's them at the House. He's a very upstanding sort, don't 'ee think? It's all very nice and proper and I reckon Mrs. Ellington be pleased. As for Miss Myra, well, it's about time, I must say. She's getting a bit long in the tooth. Must have been thinking she was right and truly on the shelf. Then he comes . . . this rich and good-looking widower. Well, no wonder they're pleased up at the House. 'Tis going to be announced tonight."

"How do you know about this?" asked Lilias.

"Mrs. Eddy told me and her being housekeeper up there, she'd know. We're mates. I went to school with her oldest sister so if she couldn't give me a bit of news, who could? She popped in this morning. Hadn't gone more than a minute or two when you arrived. There's a dinner party tonight . . . so it's all cut and dried. It won't be long before there's a wedding up there. That Mr. Lestrange will be wanting to go back to Africa and taking his bride with him."

"I see," said Lilias.

"So, Miss Myra will be off to Africa." Mrs. Dalton grimaced. "Rather her than me. Wild horses wouldn't drag me to an outlandish place like that."

"Let us be thankful that those wild horses will not be needed," said Lilias. She had been deeply put out by Mrs. Dalton's references to my father's death and wishing, I knew, that we had not paid this call.

As we untied our horses, Lilias said: "That old gossip!"

"It's always going to be like that, Lilias," I reminded her. "I've got to face it. At least she didn't know who I was."

"No. What a good idea it was to change your name."

We did not speak much as we rode back. I thought it was just another incident . . . another warning that I should never be able to escape from the past.

Overseas Assignment

WHEN I RETURNED HOME there was a letter awaiting me. It was addressed to Miss Diana Grey. Eagerly I took it to my room and impatiently opened it. It was from Ninian Grainger.

Dear D,

Forgive me for addressing you thus, but you will know the reason. I have been thinking a great deal about you and wondering how you are getting on. I think you were very wise to get away and I do hope you are recovering from your ordeal. I have seen your stepmother on one or two occasions. She seems to have put all behind her remarkably well.

Do write to me and tell me how you are feeling. I assure you I am most concerned.

Sincerely,

NINIAN GRAINGER

It was a letter an advocate might send to a client whose case had been of especial interest to him. How foolish I had been to imagine that, because he had meant so much to me during that trying time, he held deeper feelings for me.

I was still so shocked by the encounter with Mrs. Dalton when I sat down to write to him.

Dear Mr. Grainger,

Thank you for your letter. It is kind of you to be concerned. I have heard from my stepmother that you have been meeting.

Everyone here is very kind to me and they are all trying to make me comfortable. But it would not be true to say that all is well.

I have to face the fact that taking a new name is not enough. I am uneasy every time anything leads to some disclosure from my past life, however trivial. When people ask me where I live and I tell them Edinburgh I am afraid they may connect me with the case. Miss Milne and I have just visited one of her father's parishioners who actually talked about it when she learned that I came from Edinburgh.

Do forgive my writing thus. It happened only today and I feel rather shaken.

The terrible truth is that it is always going to be so.

Thank you for your kind concern, but it is something I have to live with and it fills me with dread.

However, you did what you could for me and I shall always be grateful for that.

Sincerely,

D.G.

When I had posted the letter I wished that I had not. What would he think of such an hysterical outburst? I should not have been so outspoken. Nor should I if I had not so recently been shaken by Mrs. Dalton's comments.

I WAS SURPRISED by the promptness of his reply. It came within a few days.

Dear D,

I was distressed to read your letter. I do so understand your dilemma. It is no use telling you this sort of thing will not happen again, though, of course, it will become less likely as the years pass.

My father remembers a case in his youth. There was a young lady in a similar position. She went abroad. She married there and has had a very good life ever since. She has been able to put the past right behind her.

That is a way you might decide to take. Let us face the fact that the case did attract a great deal of attention; there was a wide coverage, but it is hardly likely that there would have been much interest outside the British Isles.

You might want to consider this—I mean to make a new life somewhere outside this country . . . as my father's client did, most successfully.

A friend of the family, a Mrs. Crown, works with a society which was formed some twenty-odd years ago. It is called the Female Middle Class Emigration Society. The object of the Society is to find posts abroad for those who are seeking them. This would be mainly in the Colonies . . . Australia, New Zealand, South Africa . . . and even in America. This is for ladies who, for some reason, wish to leave the country. It may be that they cannot find employment at home, or they wish to leave for some other reason.

This client of my father's went to America through this Society. My father still has the occasional letter from her. She said it was a great opportunity and gave her new interest in life. She took a post as a governess, which is the usual practise, although other occupations are dealt with.

The Society will lend money to an applicant who will pay it back by degrees when she is working, thus paying travel and living expenses until the applicant is settled in.

I am just sending you this idea for you to ponder on. It is not something you would be able to decide in a hurry.

If, however, you feel it would be a way out of your difficulties, and that it could release you from the perpetual fear that someone might know what happened, I could arrange for an interview with Mrs. Crown. The offices of the Society are in London and if you think there is something in this suggestion, just let me know.

In the meantime, my very best wishes to you.

Sincerely,

NINIAN GRAINGER

I read that letter several times. I was not sure what I thought about it. Leaving the country was something which had not occurred to me. It was running away, of course. And to a foreign country. Many women became governesses. It was a fate which had befallen Lilias and Zillah. True, they had stayed in their own country . . . or near enough. They had both come from England, not Scotland, but that was not like going overseas.

Lilias saw how preoccupied I was and asked if something had happened.

I told her I had had a letter from Ninian Grainger.

She looked at me steadily and I guessed I had betrayed something of my resentment because he was so taken with Zillah.

"And it has given you food for thought," she said.

"He suggests I must go abroad."

"What?"

"I wrote to him. I was probably rather hysterical. I felt so awful after what Mrs. Dalton had said. I knew it was what people were saying everywhere and that it was going to happen again . . . perhaps as long as I live. I hate hearing people talk about it . . . and they are saying it all over the country, that I should not have been freed . . . I shall have to be on guard against it all my life."

"Oh no . . . it won't go on. People forget. After all, it is really rather recent as yet. What is all this about going abroad?"

"Apparently there is some society he knows of which arranges it. He could put me in touch with it . . . if I thought about leaving."

She was speechless.

"I . . . I have never thought of that," she said slowly.

"To go right away, Lilias . . . just think of it. One might never come back."

She said nothing for a few seconds. Then: "It would take a lot of thinking about."

"That's what Ninian Grainger says."

Lilias was silent, obviously deep in thought.

LOOKING BACK afterwards, I felt that Fate was leading me to make my decision, and that all around me events were falling into place to make me go the way I did. It was like a jigsaw puzzle when all the pieces fit into place and the picture is complete.

The main topic of conversation was the coming wedding of Myra Ellington and Roger Lestrange. It would be a grand affair—none the less so because preparations would have to be hurried, in view of the bridegroom's need to return to South Africa.

Mrs. Ellington could be trusted to overcome difficulties.

Tradespeople were arriving at Lakemere House every day. Excitement prevailed. It was a nine days' wonder. Most people had decided that Miss Myra would never make her journey to the altar, and now that she was about to achieve it, it was a matter of wonder and perhaps hope to those who felt themselves to be in a similar position to that of the bride-to-be.

Moreover the bridegroom was eminently suitable. He was good-looking and rich; and if he were a widower, which might just tarnish the romance a little, there was the fact that Miss Ellington was not so young herself and a mature man was just what she needed, even though it was rumoured that he had a child in South Africa. Well, Miss Myra could be a mother to him.

It was all very agreeable.

Kitty came over to see me one morning. She was as excited as everyone else about the wedding. She thought Mr. Lestrange was ever so nice. "There is no side about him, Miss, if you know what I mean. He's nice to us servants . . . just as though we were of importance. The family like him . . . from the mistress to the stable boys. I reckon Miss Myra's lucky."

Lilias and I often talked about Ninian Grainger's suggestion. There were times when I thought it would suit me to follow the example of those young governesses; and there were others when I would swerve away from the notion. A terrible uncertainty would sweep over me. As Lilias had said, it was a step that should not be taken lightly.

While we were at breakfast one morning a message came from Lakemere House. Mrs. Ellington wished to see Lilias and me at eleven-thirty that morning. She could only spare a short time, but it was important and could we please be as punctual as possible?

Lilias grimaced at me. "The royal command. It's a nuisance. I promised old Mrs. Edge that I'd take her some of the wine that Jane makes. She says it puts new life into her."

"Couldn't we take it another day?"

"Well, she's so lonely. She'll be watching for us. There's time to take it and we can go straight from her to Lakemere."

That was agreed.

We delivered the wine and chattered for a while, Lilias keeping her eye on her watch.

Mrs. Edge was disappointed, but Lilias explained that Mrs. Ellington wished to see her and me as well—and we all knew how busy Mrs. Ellington was at this time.

Mrs. Edge wanted to talk about the wedding so we indulged her for another five minutes, telling her all we knew, and then we departed.

We put our horses in the Ellington stables and were taken to Mrs. Ellington's private sitting room. She was seated at her bureau with papers before her.

"Oh, Lilias," she said, "and you, Miss Grey. So good of you to come. I'm so frightfully busy . . . guests and so on. Some will have to stay in the house. I shall see you both at the reception, of course. But you've no idea. It's all so sudden. If only we had more time. But needs must."

"I am sure you are very happy about it, Mrs. Ellington," said Lilias.

"I should be if I could be sure everything will go well on the day."

"You couldn't fail to make it so," said Lilias perfunctorily.

"No, of course not. I did want to speak to you both about the stalls at the fête. That's why I asked you both to come. My big concern is the village drama meeting. As you know, they usually have it here, but I simply cannot have them. It's tomorrow . . . short notice, I know, but could you possibly have it at the vicarage? You've plenty of room there and . . ."

"But, of course, we can," said Lilias.

Mrs. Ellington beamed on her. "I knew you would, but I wanted you to call personally because there is the list of the cast for the Nativity play. It's early yet, but they need lots of rehearsal . . . and they'll be discussing it tomorrow. I wanted them to see my suggestions. They do need guidance; otherwise they select the most incongruous people . . . and then once it's done . . . it's awkward to change."

"I'll see that everyone knows it will be at the vicarage and I'll give Miss Crew the list. She's in charge of all that, isn't she?"

"Thank you so much. I hope I have not dragged you away from something, Miss Grey."

"Oh no, not at all."

"We'll talk about the fête later. Thank you so much for coming. Now . . . I have to get on."

"We should be going anyway," said Lilias.

"Thank you. Thank you for coming."

We were graciously ushered out and made our way to the stables.

"There was no need to summon us to the presence," said Lilias. "She could have sent a note with her cast of players."

"I think she enjoys being frantically busy."

Kitty was standing outside the stables chatting with one of the men. I was reminded of Hamish then and how she had fallen victim to his lust. I supposed some people never changed. Kitty had also reminded me of Zillah. They both seemed to sparkle in the admiration of men.

The man went into the stables when he saw us and brought out the horses. Just at that moment Roger Lestrange rode up.

"Oh, good morning, Miss Milne, Miss Grey. How nice to see you! Are you just coming to the house?"

"No," said Lilias. "We are just leaving. We've been to see Mrs. Ellington."

"Oh . . . what a pity!" He smiled at us warmly. He was a very attractive man. I could understand why people thought Myra lucky. Soon she would be going to a new country with this charming husband. I might be going away. But how different my departure would be.

"We must be getting on," said Lilias, mounting her horse.

I was not sure what happened next. I had my foot in the stirrup and was about to mount when suddenly my horse turned abruptly. The next thing I knew was that I was on the ground, my foot caught in the stirrup. The horse began to move away, fortunately at only a slow pace. Nevertheless I was dragged along the ground.

"Miss Davina!" It was Kitty's voice—shrill, loud, audible to all.

The incident was over in a few seconds. Roger Lestrange had seized my horse and brought it to a standstill. My foot was released and I stood up, unhurt.

He put an arm around me and looked at me steadily. "All right?"

I could not answer. All I could hear was that shattering cry of "Miss Davina!"

Lilias looked shaken. She was standing beside me and she took my arm.

"How are you feeling?" she asked. "What a nasty shock! What happened?"

"He just moved in the wrong direction, that's all," said Roger Lestrange. "You shouldn't have let him do that, you know."

"Miss Grey has only just learned to ride," said Lilias.

Roger Lestrange was looking at me intently, his eyes more blue than I remembered them. "You'll have to look on it as an experience, Miss Grey. It's lucky we were here and the horse didn't gallop off. That could have been . . . well . . . let's not think of it. You're not hurt . . . that's the important thing. It was just a bit of mischief on the part of the horse. He knew you weren't up to all the tricks he could play . . . so he tried one. They're like that sometimes, aren't they, John?"

"Aye, sir, they be that," said John. "You make sure when you mount him, Miss. Look, like this. He couldn't have done it then."

"All's well that ends well," said Roger Lestrange. "Do you feel like mounting again, Miss Grey?"

"I must."

"That's the spirit. Never give up. At least you won't do that again. Just give him a pat to show he's forgiven and he'll be friends again. That's so, isn't it, John?"

"Aye, sir, that be it."

Rather shakily I mounted the horse; but I was not thinking of the danger I might have been in but of the shrill penetrating cry of "Miss Davina!"

Lilias and I rode back to the vicarage in silence. We had no need for speech. Each of us knew what was in the other's mind.

I went straight to my room, and sat staring out at the graveyard.

"Davina," Ninian Grainger had said. "It's an unusual name." What if Roger Lestrange had noticed? What if he remembered that I came from Edinburgh?

There was a knock on the door and I knew it was Lilias. She came in and stood for a few seconds looking at me.

"He must have heard," I said.

"He probably didn't notice."

"It was so loud and clear."

"Only to us because we understood. I am sure Kitty was very upset about it. It came out involuntarily. It's understandable. She was worried about you. She looked so . . . penitent. She didn't mean any harm. That's the last thing. But she thought you were going to be hurt and it slipped out naturally. I don't think anyone noticed. We were too concerned about you."

I said suddenly: "I'm going to write to Ninian Grainger to ask him to put me in touch with Mrs. Crown."

"Well . . . I suppose you might go and hear what she has to say. There's no commitment in that."

"I think I have made up my mind. It's what I'm going to do.

I can't stay here . . . on edge, as it were . . . just waiting for something to come up . . . like this morning."

"I think you have been more upset by that than by the accident. If that horse had started to gallop you could have been very seriously hurt."

"I know. But it's showed me that when Kitty called out my name like that, it's the sort of thing that could happen at any time. I am going to explore this possibility."

Lilias said slowly: "I see."

She left me and I sat down and wrote a letter to Ninian Grainger.

Dear Mr. Grainger,

It has taken me some time to make up my mind, and I cannot be sure that I have done that yet, for this is such a big step I have to take. There was another incident today and this has decided me that at least I must see Mrs. Crown and discuss a few details with her.

It is so kind of you to take so much trouble to help me. I do appreciate that.

With grateful thanks,

Sincerely, D.

The letter was posted. I had taken the first step.

I was preparing for bed that night when there was a knock on my door. Lilias came in wearing a dressing gown and carrying a candle.

"I thought you might have been asleep," she said.

"I shan't sleep. I have too many things to think about."

"This is only the first step."

"Yes, but it's an important one."

"I've been thinking . . ."

"Yes?"

She paused for a moment and then she said quietly: "I might come with you."

Joy swept over me. This would change everything. That which I had contemplated with fearful apprehension could be planned with excitement. Two people together could face difficulties so much more easily than one alone; and if that person was the best friend one ever had . . .

"Lilias!" I cried. "Do you really mean that?"

"I have been considering it ever since I heard of it. The Society . . . it sounds interesting to me. You see, I feel this isn't what I want to do . . . visiting people like Mrs. Dalton, being directed by Mrs. Ellington. I suppose I get through . . . as anybody would, but it's not what I want. I want to be teaching. I really feel I have a vocation for that. I want to get back to it."

"Lilias . . . this is so unexpected. You didn't tell me . . ."

"No. Like you, I couldn't make up my mind . . . but I have been thinking more and more of it."

"If we went together . . . it would be so exciting. If I could believe you were coming with me, it would be so different."

"We both have something we don't want revealed."

"Oh, yours wasn't like . . ."

"No. My ordeal was not so horrific. Yours was carried out in the light of publicity. But I have a slur on my character. I'm in a quandary. I don't know whether it's the right thing or not . . . but if you go, I want to go with you."

"Oh, Lilias, I can't tell you how much I want that, too. Have you really thought about it . . . deeply?"

"From every angle. Alice could come back. She is much more useful at what I am trying to do. She doesn't like teaching in any case, though she pretends all is well. I know her, and I sense this is not entirely the case. If I went, she could come back."

"There's Charles Merrimen," I reminded her. "Have you thought of him?"

"I've thought a great deal about him. It's over really. It seems we were just trying to keep something alive . . . something which isn't really there. I go and read to him. Several people could do that for him. We talk about the books I read to him. We could go on like that till one of us dies. I am beginning to realise that if there had been deep love between us we should have married. It's rather like you and Jamie. There is something for a time . . . but it's a fragile plant."

"You were away from him all those years when you were with me."

"And when I come to think of it, those were the most rewarding years of my life so far. One has to be realistic. We have our lives to lead. I want to teach. I think I have a vocation for it. I do believe I want that more than anything. Also I want to get away from the past . . . just as you do. Yes, if you go, I am coming with you."

"Oh, Lilias, I feel so much better. I know I can face whatever there is to come if you are there."

We talked far into the night. We both knew that sleep was impossible; and for the next few days impatiently we awaited Ninian's reply.

At length it came. Mrs. Crown was writing to me and I should be hearing from her very soon.

And in due course the letter arrived. The heading was The Female Middle Class Emigration Society with an address in the City of London. Mrs. Crown would be pleased to see me round about three o'clock in the afternoon of the fifth of June.

This gave us a week to make our plans to go to London and this we did without delay.

WE HAD BOOKED into a small hotel recommended by Ninian which was not very far from the Society's premises; and at the appointed time were mounting the stairs to Mrs. Crown's office.

She came to the door to greet us—a fresh-faced middle-aged woman with a kindly smile.

"Miss Grey . . . Miss Milne . . . Mr. Grainger has written to me about you. Do sit down."

When we were seated she went on: "You want to emigrate and take posts as governesses, I understand. This is the usual profession ladies such as yourselves undertake. Our Society deals with all kinds of employment, but governesses are the most usual because so many of our people are ladies of education and small means. Let me tell you something about the Society. It was founded by a lady who believed that women should be given more chances of employment. The lower classes have been engaged in domestic service for centuries, but she felt that the educated woman should be brought more into public life. She discovered that such ladies were badly needed in the Colonies and she believed that women of strong character and high moral sense should take charge of the young. So she formed this Society to help people like yourselves who want to go abroad for some reason. So many people in these circumstances cannot afford the fare and they need something to enable them to support themselves until they get settled. The object of the Society is to help them over this difficult time. It is, you might say, a philanthropic association, kept going by voluntary subscriptions, and the object of our members is to be of assistance in helping the right people to start a new life in another country."

She then asked us for our qualifications. I could see she was impressed by Lilias' experience, but, as she said, I was a young lady of obvious education and she thought we should have no difficulty in finding employment.

"So many of our colonists deplore the fact that they cannot get a good education for their children. The Society does what it can to find that employment, but it is difficult being so far away, and many of our people go out and find employment for themselves. The most popular countries are Australia, America and New Zealand. South Africa, too."

"Mr. Grainger has given me some idea of the Society's methods," I said.

"Ah yes. Mr. Grainger, Senior, has a very high opinion of us; and has indeed been very benevolent towards us. I understand, Miss Grey, that you have a small private income."

"That is true."

"And you would not be needing financial help from us for your passage?"

"That is so. Does that mean . . . ?"

"It means that we will help in arranging your passage just the same. Now, Miss Milne . . ."

"I'm afraid I cannot afford to pay my passage," said Lilias.

"I want to help Miss Milne," I said. "But I fear I am not rich enough to pay for her passage as well as my own."

"That's perfectly easy. We will advance what is needed, Miss Milne, and you can pay us back gradually, when you are in employment."

"I don't care to be in debt," said Lilias.

"I know how you feel. But you will pay back when you can. We have always found that most of our clients in time meet their obligations. We have no fears . . . nor need you have. You have to decide to which country you wish to go."

"We heard that Australia is more like England," I ventured.

"In the towns maybe. It depends where you are employed. However, would you like to think about it? If you know someone who is connected with Australia . . . then that would be good. But of course there is the difficulty of finding employment when you arrive."

"That could be a little daunting," said Lilias.

"It is an undertaking, of course," agreed Mrs. Crown. "I will show you some of the letters we have received from people that will give you some idea of the difficulties and the rewards."

She took us into a small room, the walls of which were lined with files, and she gave us letters to read from people whom they had helped. The letters were from Australia, South Africa, New Zealand and the United States of America.

They were very revealing. The majority of the writers had found posts fairly easily, but some had not been so fortunate. There were very few who regretted their decision to leave England.

We spent more than half an hour reading those letters before Mrs. Crown came back to us.

"It gives you an idea of what you may find," she said. "How do you feel now?"

Lilias was more practical than I and therefore perhaps less certain. But perhaps she did not feel the same urgent need to escape as I did. I could not stop myself going over Mrs. Dalton's words and hearing that sudden cry of horror from Kitty when she used my real name. I was sure I had to get away.

There was another point. Lilias was not very happy about borrowing the money, even though it was lent by philanthropists. I wished that I could have afforded to pay her passage; but she would not hear of that. I consoled myself with the fact that my money would be a bulwark against absolute destitution.

It was Lilias who said: "May we have a little longer to think about this?"

"But of course. It is your decision."

"We shall have to think where we should go. It is very difficult to make up one's mind when one knows nothing, or very little, about such places."

"You are right to make absolutely sure that you want to go," said Mrs. Crown.

"We could make up our minds in say a week," said Lilias, appealing to me.

I said I thought we could do that and it was a good idea.

So we left the Society's offices and after another night in our hotel we went back to the vicarage.

WE HAD, of course, made no secret of our intentions. Lilias' father and sister had been informed right from the first. Jane understood absolutely why Lilias wanted to get away. She knew she had felt frustrated. I believed that Jane thought it was rather a reckless step to leave one's country, but she understood the need for it. So did the vicar. They were saddened at the thought of Lilias' departure but made no efforts to persuade her to stay. It was not quite the case with Daisy. She laboured under the assumption that heathens lived in foreign parts and the idea of Lilias' travelling to such places appalled her. She expressed her disapproval and, as she was something of a gossip, very soon the whole village was aware of our plans.

So there was great excitement in Lakemere that summer with two major events about to take place: the marriage of Myra Ellington to Roger Lestrange and the possible departure to foreign parts of the vicar's daughter.

The annual fête always took place in June and, since the Manor House was lax in its duties, the gardens of Lakemere House were thrown open for the occasion. This was posing some questions this year as the wedding was to take place about a week later.

Mrs. Ellington, however, was not one to shirk her duties and, awkward as it might be, she decided that the fête must go ahead.

We were all summoned to work for it. I was not sorry, because my thoughts were dominated—not so much as to whether we should go abroad as to where to. Lilias and I talked endlessly when we were alone; but it did seem to me that we covered the same ground again and again. Lilias' doubts centred on the fact that we should have to find posts when we arrived at whatever place we decided on. She feared we might not do so immediately and she would already be in debt—a state of affairs which she deplored.

In vain did I point out that I had a little money of my own which I would share with her. It was no use. I was afraid that she might decide she had been rash to agree to come with me and would change her mind.

They were uneasy days and that was why it was a help to be caught up with the fête.

I was in charge of what was called bric-a-brac, which mainly consisted of articles which had been given as presents, put away in a drawer and never used, to be brought out and presumably passed on to others who would do the same with them as their previous owners. However, it was all in a good cause; Norman churches needed constant bolstering up.

It was a warm sunny day which was a blessing, for the stalls could be set up on the lawns. Lilias had said it could be a nightmare if the weather was uncertain. At least if it were definitely raining they could be set up in the hall which was quite spacious.

I was presiding over my stall, attending to the occasional customer, when Roger Lestrange strolled up.

"Good afternoon, Miss Grey," he said. "How is business?"

He was smiling at me with that intent expression which made me feel a little uncomfortable. But that was only because I harboured secrets. It was something I had to live with while I stayed here.

"Hardly brisk."

"What do you suggest I should buy?"

"Here's a delightful little pig."

"Not my favourite animal."

"Look. There's a little slit in his back where you can save your pennies."

"How useful!"

"Here's a pillbox. Such a pretty picture on the lid."

"Enchanting," he said, looking at me.

"Here's a figurine. The *Venus de Milo.*"

"Certainly more attractive than the pig and I have not much use for pillboxes. Let me have Venus."

I handed it to him and our hands touched. He was smiling. "I have been hearing news of you. You're leaving this country."

"Oh yes."

"What a decision for a young lady to make!" Again that quizzical look. I was afraid I was going to blush. I took a firm grip of myself. I must overcome this terrible suspicion that everyone knew who I really was. It would be different when I was away, I consoled myself.

"It's rather an exciting project," I said.

"Indeed it must be. Miss Milne is going with you, I gather. I don't remember hearing where."

"We haven't decided yet."

"Oh?" He looked surprised.

"We have been making enquiries. There are several possibilities. Australia . . . America . . . somewhere like that."

"And what did you propose to do when you get there?"

"There is only one thing women in our position can do. Take a post."

"The ubiquitous governess?" he said. "Well, if that's the case, why not here?"

"We like the idea of travel."

He nodded. "It has its appeal . . . to the adventurous. But you say you haven't decided. Does that mean you have no posts in view?"

"It's something we have to arrange when we get there."

He raised his eyebrows. "Yes," he said slowly. "I would say

you are adventurous. Why don't you try South Africa? It's a beautiful country. And I'm sure there is a shortage of the right sort of governesses—which you and Miss Milne would undoubtedly be. As a matter of fact there is a school in Kimberley. Not exactly the sort of thing you had in mind perhaps . . . but something on the lines."

Someone had come up to the stall and had picked up a case containing needles and cottons.

"How much is this?"

I turned reluctantly from Roger Lestrange who lifted his eyebrows and smiled. I was afraid he would go away, and I wanted to ask him more about the school. That we might go into a school was a prospect which had not entered our minds.

While I took the money from my customer I was thinking: but wouldn't they want qualified teachers for a school?

The woman had gone.

"Yes," went on Roger Lestrange. "This school in Kimberley had to close down. There was no one to run it. I wonder . . . ?"

"It sounds interesting."

Someone else had come up to the stall.

"Business is getting brisk now," said Roger Lestrange.

He lingered. The newcomer fingered a few things, bought a glass ashtray and departed.

"We ought to have a talk," said Roger Lestrange.

"With Miss Milne," I replied. "Could you come to the vicarage? It's impossible here."

"Tomorrow morning, yes. Ten o'clock?"

"That would be kind of you. Oh dear, someone else is coming. I'll see you tomorrow morning."

I hardly noticed what I was selling. I could not wait to see Lilias and tell her the news.

And when she heard it she shared my excitement.

He arrived at the vicarage precisely on the stroke of ten next morning. We were both eagerly waiting for him and took him into the sitting room which the vicar used for listening to the trials of his parishioners, and we settled down to talk.

"The more I think of it the more suitable it seems," he said.

"We need a school, but we had to close this one down. The lady who had run it for some years was getting old. She gave up, and up to the time I left they had not found anyone to replace her. One or two did come but did not stay . . . and then there was no one, so they had to close it. I've written to a man I know who is in charge of these things in the town and I posted the letter last night. I hope you don't think I was precipitous, but I thought there was no harm in finding out what the position was. My opinion is that they'll be delighted at the prospect of finding someone who'll open up the school and run it successfully, as I am sure you two will."

"We'd be working together," said Lilias, her eyes shining.

"That's the idea. The head—I presume that would be you, Miss Milne, your being the senior and the experienced one . . ."

He looked at me apologetically and I said quickly: "But naturally."

"Of course, if you don't like the idea you can always try something else, I suppose, but after I had heard . . . and then our little conversation at the stall yesterday . . . well, it did occur to me that it was a better proposition than going out there and not knowing what you were going to find."

"It is so very good of you, Mr. Lestrange," said Lilias earnestly; and I echoed her words, for it was wonderful to see the anxieties dropping from her and to experience the pleasant feeling that the way was being made easy for us.

"There'll only be a small salary, I believe . . . at the moment, that is. There are not all that many young people seeking education. Some of the inhabitants don't see the need for it alas. So much would depend on how many pupils you could muster. There might be only a few at first, but if you could build it up. There are living quarters, I know, in the schoolhouse, and they would go with the job."

"It sounds like an . . . opportunity," said Lilias.

"Someone will probably be writing to you. I've told them to get in touch."

"We don't know how to thank you," we said in unison.

His eyes held mine for a moment and he smiled.

"I only hope it works out well and I deserve your thanks," he said.

LILIAS was growing enthusiastic. She had naturally been fearful that we might arrive in some foreign place without any hope of employment—and now that fear was gone. And the prospect of a school where we could work together was wonderful.

"It's ideal!" said Lilias, and I began to believe her.

All the same, to leave one's country meant a great upheaval in one's life and now that the time for our departure was growing near I could not contemplate it without some misgivings. I found that I wanted to be alone now and then; I had to practise stopping myself going over that dreadful ordeal; I was trying to instil a peace into my mind, trying to look forward instead of back.

I found a certain peace in sitting in the graveyard which I could see from my bedroom window. It seemed so quiet there.

I was sitting there one day when Roger Lestrange came along.

"Why hello, Miss Grey," he said. "I was just coming to the vicarage to see you and Miss Milne, and I find you sitting here contemplating the scenery. I thought you should have the address of the schoolhouse. I expect to hear before long how delighted they will be to receive you."

"It is kind of you to take so much trouble."

I took the paper he gave me, glanced at the address and put it into my pocket.

"It's peaceful here," he said. "Here, among the dead. Do you often come and sit here?"

"Quite often. I can see it from my bedroom window in the vicarage. I thought it might be morbid, but it is far from that. The quietness and peace is . . . appealing."

"I hope you will like South Africa."

"We have to get used to the idea. We had almost settled on Australia and had been reading quite a bit about it."

"And now you have switched to South Africa. I don't think you'll be disappointed. How soon do you plan to leave . . . when you hear from the school, I mean?"

"As soon as possible."

"Myra and I will be sailing in the not-too-distant future. After the wedding and the honeymoon and I've settled a little business. It may be that we shall sail together."

"I suppose that is a possibility."

"Then I can keep an eye on you."

"That sounds comforting."

"When you sit here, do you wonder about the dead?"

"Yes. I suppose one would, wouldn't one?"

"You read the names on the stones . . . when you can. Many of them are half-obliterated. Just think, some of these people have been lying there for a hundred years!"

"More than that, some of them."

"Do you wonder what their lives were like . . . all their troubles . . . all their joys . . . how they lived and how they died?"

"Yes, I do."

"And think of the people you have known and who are gone . . ."

I was silent. In spite of the fact that he had taken such pains to help us, I was wary of him. I had the feeling that there was an ulterior motive in what he said and did. He knew I came from Edinburgh; he had been present when Kitty had called out my name.

"We have all known people who have died," he went on. "Died . . . before their time."

My heart was beating fast, and I drew away from him, for I had suddenly realised that he was sitting very close to me.

"I suppose it is natural that we should think such thoughts in a place like this," I said briskly.

"I lost someone . . . my wife. She was very young to die."

"I'm sorry."

"It was tragic . . . unexpected. That makes it harder to bear."

"Yes," I said quietly. "Was it long ago?"

"Two years."

I suppressed my astonishment that it was so recent and said: "It must have been very sad for you."

He nodded. "I thought I should never marry again."

"Well, I hope you will be happy now. I am sure Miss Ellington will make you so."

"Thank you," he said. "You see, I have a child . . ."

"Yes, I did hear that."

"Paul. He is named after a very distinguished man whom his mother greatly admired. Of course, she couldn't give the child the name exactly . . . rather too ponderous, one might say. Stephanus Johannes Paulus . . . so she was contented with simply Paul. After Kruger . . . the great man over there. If the child had been a girl I've no doubt it would have been Paula. People do that sometimes . . . turn the male into the female and vice versa."

Why did he say this? I was Davina; my father had been David. It was almost as though he were hinting at something. He was a disturbing man; I was sorry that he was the one from whom we had to take help.

I said quickly: "How old is the boy?"

"Nine, coming up to ten."

"You will be pleased to be home with him."

"I shall be pleased to be back, yes. I shall be starting a new life. It is no use living in the past, is it? We have to realise that."

He gazed at me intently and I rose.

"I must be going," I said. "Lilias . . . Miss Milne . . . will be so glad to have the address. I can't tell you how grateful we are. This has made such a difference."

"It has been my pleasure," he said. "Don't forget, either of you: I shall be there . . . if you need me."

He took my hand and pressed it.

"Well," he said. "You've saved me a journey to the vicarage, and it was so pleasant to have a little chat with you in the graveyard, Miss Grey."

I went back to the vicarage, trying hard to shake off that feeling of uneasiness which he aroused in me.

I THOUGHT I OWED a letter of thanks to Ninian Grainger, after all the trouble he had taken, to tell him of the progress we had made. I wrote:

Dear Mr. Grainger,

Miss Milne and I are so grateful for your help. As I told you, we went to see Mrs. Crown and shall be calling on her again shortly, we hope.

It is our great good fortune that a Mr. Roger Lestrange, who is here on business and staying at the big house in the neighbourhood, comes from South Africa and he is helping us considerably. He knows of a school and it seems that Miss Milne and I may be able to work together there. This is a wonderful piece of luck because, as you can imagine, we were somewhat apprehensive as to how long it would be before we were able to find posts in a foreign country. We feel much happier now and are awaiting confirmation from South Africa. When this comes we shall be very relieved.

I hope all goes well with you and thank you once more for all the help you have given us.

D.

I had, of course, written to Zillah.

She wrote back and said how sorry she would be when I had gone, but she quite understood why I wanted to go.

Your Mr. Lestrange sounds an absolute darling and I should love to meet him. Your Mr. Grainger continues to call. I wonder why! South Africa seems a very long way away. I shall come down to see you off. I must do that. I suppose you haven't any dates yet? Still . . . let me know when you have.

I'm going to hate it when you've gone. True, you've been away for some time, but I know you are not far-off.

Keep in touch.

Your loving ZILLAH

The wedding day had arrived. I went to the church and heard Lilias' father pronounce Myra Ellington and Roger Lestrange man and wife.

Afterwards we went to the reception to which Mrs. Ellington had graciously invited us and in due course the couple left for their honeymoon.

Myra looked very happy and I remarked—with fervour—to Lilias that I hoped she would remain so.

"You sound doubtful," said Lilias.

"Do I? Well, they do say that marriage is something of a lottery. You have to draw the right number or whatever it is."

"You've become a cynic."

She was full of hope now, and I understood how frustrating those months at home must have been for her.

The honeymoon was still in progress when we received a letter from South Africa. It was signed by a Jan Van Der Groot. He said he was pleased to hear from Mr. Roger Lestrange that we contemplated coming out to South Africa to teach. There had been only one teacher in the school in the past, for it was very small. But if we liked to come and share the salary, there would be room for us both, for the living quarters which were part of the school would certainly be big enough. The place had been shut up for some months, but it would be made ready for our arrival.

We read it together.

"One salary," said Lilias.

"It's yours. I have my own money. I shall be all right."

"It's a little disappointing . . ."

"It's not, Lilias. We'll be together. It's a chance to make a fresh start."

"But the money . . . and I have to pay back . . ."

"There's nothing to worry about. I don't need to work. I'll be all right. We'll make that school grow, Lilias. It's a challenge . . . a way out."

Her spirits revived. It was not all that we had hoped for, but it was more than we could expect.

Everything moved quickly after that.

We went to see Mrs. Crown once more. We had decided. We were going to South Africa. We already had employment waiting for us.

"Congratulations!" said Mrs. Crown. "You've been lucky. We'll get you a passage as soon as possible."

And this is what she did.

We were to sail on the *Queen of the South* to Cape Town and from there make the journey across the country to Kimberley.

Kimberley

Outward Bound

THE TIME for our departure was approaching. In less than a week we were to sail. Acting on the advice of Mrs. Crown, we had sent the bulk of our luggage to the docks; and after the harassed preparations of the last few days we had come to a lull when there seemed to be nothing to do.

Lilias and I were sitting in the garden going over, for at least the hundredth time, all the things we had to do before we left, asking ourselves if we had packed all we needed in the little luggage we were taking with us. We were to leave the vicarage the day before we sailed, spending a night in a hotel near the docks which Mrs. Crown had arranged for us. Zillah had been helpful and had sent those possessions which I had wanted to take with me straight to the docks; this was a great help and it had meant that I had not had to return to Edinburgh which would have been very painful for me.

Now everything was settled and there was nothing to do but wait.

As we sat there Jane came out.

"There's a young man who has called to see you, Diana," she said. "His name is Mr. Grainger."

I felt myself flush. I was tingling with pleasure. All I could say was: "Oh . . . so he's come . . ."

Lilias, to whom I had talked of him and confessed something of my feelings for him, and who, perhaps, guessed a little more, said: "He'll want to talk to you. I'll go in." Then: "Bring him out, Jane. They can talk in the garden. It's pleasant out here."

Ninian came to me and, taking both my hands in his, held them firmly.

"I felt I had to come and see you before you left," he said.

"That is very good of you."

"It's a big step you are taking."

"Let's sit down. A big step? Yes. But we have thought a good deal about it and in the circumstances it seems a good thing."

"I'm so glad Miss Milne is going with you."

"Yes, that is a great piece of luck for me."

"Tell me about this Mr. Lestrange."

"He's a friend of the Ellingtons who live in the big house here. He's engaged in big business and I think Mr. Ellington has some connections in it. I don't really know much about it. But I expect it has something to do with diamonds. He lives in Kimberley, you see, and when he came over Myra Ellington and he fell in love and married."

"It sounds like a whirlwind romance."

"It was. He was a widower. I gathered his wife died . . . not long ago. He probably came to England to get away from it all . . . and he met Myra Ellington."

"So it all turned out well for him."

"The fact of the matter is that they are going back to Kimberley. I believe they will actually be sailing on the same ship."

"I'd like to meet Mr. and Mrs. Lestrange."

"I don't suppose you will. Are you going back tomorrow?"

"I thought I'd come and see you off."

"Oh!" I was amazed but inordinately pleased. I kept thinking how strange it was that he should continue to show such interest. I had told myself many times that it was because I was still

smarting from Jamie's rejection . . . but it was something beyond that. I hated to confess it, but one of the reasons why I
regretted leaving England was because I should never see him
again. That was quite foolish, I knew; I constantly reminded
myself that all I meant to him was an interesting case which
had brought him quite useful success.

"I've booked in at the Royal Oak," he said. "I thought I could
travel down to Tilbury with you and be of some help."

"What a lovely idea! But can you spare the time?"

"Just about," he said.

"Are you comfortable at the Royal Oak?"

"Very comfortable."

"That's good, because it is the only hotel around here."

"I'm glad it's so near. Tell me about the school."

"I don't know much except what I have told you already. I
am sure we shall be able to manage all right. Lilias is a wonderful teacher, and I shall try to follow in her footsteps."

"And this has all come about through Mr. Lestrange. What
do you know of him?"

"Only what I've told you. He's engaged in the diamond business; he's apparently wealthy; he's a widower with a son named
Paul; he is considered to be very attractive and is a good match
for Myra Ellington."

"What about Myra herself?"

"I don't know much about her either. She is very pleasant
and quiet . . . not like her mother. She's very good at . . .
doing what she is told. I could never understand why she has
not married long ago. I should not have thought Mrs. Ellington
would have been the sort of woman to allow her daughter to
remain unmarried. But I suppose most of them want to ensure
their daughters' financial security . . . and with Myra, Mrs.
Ellington does not have to consider this. It seems that she is
quite well off in her own right."

"Perhaps I shall meet them."

"Perhaps. But everyone's very busy. Mrs. Crown has been
very good. She has arranged everything for us. We are spending our last night in England in a hotel called Harbour View,

which speaks for itself, and we shall be right on the spot for the day we sail."

"I'll book in there."

I must have shown my surprise, for he said: "I feel responsible for you! After all, I introduced you to Mrs. Crown."

"It was the best thing you could have done."

"I do hope so," he said fervently.

Daisy came out with some coffee.

"Miss Jane thought you could do with this," she said.

There was a small table under a tree and she set the tray on this; and we drew up our chairs.

"This is delightful," said Ninian.

I was happier than I had been for a long time—just for a moment; then the thought hit me: I am going right away . . . out of the old life . . . out of his life.

He watched me as I poured out the coffee. I wondered what he was thinking and what had really prompted him to come so far to see me before I left.

He said suddenly: "If this should not work out . . . if you should want to come home for any reason . . . let me know. I'll do what I can to arrange it."

"You are so good. And all because you defended me. There must be so many . . ."

He shook his head. "It was unfair, that verdict. It rankles."

"I see."

"One day perhaps . . ."

I waited and he shrugged his shoulders. "It has happened, you know. The truth comes out, even after years."

Then we talked of those young women who, as Lilias and I were doing, had left their homes to go away and work in foreign countries. I told him about the letters we had read in the Society's offices. He was very interested, but he kept bringing the conversation back to Roger Lestrange.

He stayed to dinner. It was clear to me that he had made a good impression on the vicarage family.

Lilias said, after he had left for the Royal Oak: "What a charming man! It is so kind of him to care about what happens to you."

I was very happy that night. I dreamed that I was sailing away from England, and Ninian Grainger was standing on the dock watching. Then suddenly he lifted his arms and cried loudly: "Don't go! Don't go!"

I knew that I must not go, that it was wrong for me to go. I tried to leap overboard, but someone was restraining me, saying: "You can't go back. None of us can go back. It's too late . . . once you've started."

And that was Roger Lestrange.

THE NEXT DAY my pleasure in Ninian Grainger's care was dampened.

It was in the morning. Daisy came to my room and said: "There's a visitor for you, Miss Grey. In the sitting room."

I went down, expecting to see Ninian. It was Zillah.

She looked even more beautiful than I remembered. She was dressed in a black silk dress with a big green bow at the neck and a black hat with a green feather which tipped down to her eyes, calling attention to their colour.

"My dear!" she cried, embracing me. "How wonderful to see you! I had to come. I'm going to see you off. I'm staying at the Royal Oak."

"Oh," I said blankly.

She laughed almost coyly. "Who do you think is staying there? Your Mr. Grainger. Well, it's the only one, isn't it? And I couldn't expect to be put up at the vicarage. I hope you're pleased to see me. I'm not really very happy about all this, you know. You'll be so far away. I had hoped we could be together. Oh, I do hope this is going to be the right thing for you."

"I had to get away," I said. "And this seems as good a method as any."

"It's so sad. But I mustn't go on about it. We've got to make the best of things, haven't we? How have you been getting on in this place? I'm longing to meet your friend, Lilias. I wonder what she'll feel about me. I took her place, didn't I . . . in the house, I mean."

"You'll like her. She's a wonderful person."

"Oh, I do hope this is going to be all right."

She meant well, and it was good of her to take the trouble to come. But she had shattered an illusion.

I did not realise until then how deeply I had been affected by Ninian's coming here.

I had been very foolish. I had been so stimulated, so happy because I had thought he had been so apprehensive on my account that he had come down to see for himself what was happening. I had had a ridiculous feeling that he was regretting having introduced me to Mrs. Crown and that he was going to beg me to relinquish the project and go back with him to Edinburgh so that we could fight together to prove I had played no part in my father's murder.

I was naïve. I was reaching out for someone to care for me . . . someone to fill that bitter void left by Jamie.

Face facts, I admonished myself. You are going away . . . right away from the old life, from everyone you ever knew—except Lilias.

He came because *she* was coming. You were misled by Jamie once. Be on your guard that it does not happen again.

I saw a good deal of Ninian during the next day. We talked a good deal. I felt that he knew as much about the place to which I was going as I did. Zillah was there, too.

On the morning before the day we were due to leave for Tilbury, I went down to the village to buy a few oddments which I had found I needed and Ninian had said he would accompany me.

Zillah, who happened to arrive at that moment, said she would join us.

It was on our way back from the village that we met Roger Lestrange. He was riding a big grey horse from the Ellington stables and he lifted his hat as we approached.

"Miss Grey. Ah, the last-minute shopping. All ready to sail?"

I introduced them. I could sense Ninian's interest. He had always wanted to hear all he could about Roger Lestrange.

I noticed that the latter was surveying Zillah with appreciation while she put on that especially seductive air she used for attractive men.

"We are going to see the dear child off on her travels," said Zillah. "It is going to be very sad for me."

"I am sure it will be." He spoke soothingly.

Ninian said: "I understand you are from South Africa."

"Yes, it's my home now. I shall be returning to it on the *Queen of the South.*"

"Oh yes. I understood you would be sailing on her."

"Shall you be glad to go home?" asked Zillah.

He looked at her almost slyly. "Well, there are temptations to stay, but alas . . ."

"And you sail . . . the day after tomorrow, is it? So it is hail and farewell. How sad."

"I agree . . . wholeheartedly. Well . . ." He shrugged his shoulders. "I'll see you on board, Miss Grey."

"So that is Roger Lestrange," said Ninian when he had ridden off.

"He seemed to be a most interesting man," added Zillah.

Then we rode back to the vicarage and the next day we left for London, Tilbury and the *Queen of the South.*

As soon as I stepped on board I felt a sense of irreparable loss. Melancholy took hold of me and I was sure that no exciting new experience could dispel it. This was largely due to having said goodbye to Ninian. I had taken this step and there was no going back.

Ninian and Zillah had travelled to the ship with us. So, Zillah had said, that she could spend every possible moment with me. She constantly expressed her sorrow at my departure, but I could not get rid of the notion that she was rather relieved. Perhaps she was thinking what was best for me and was fully aware that while I remained in England I should be constantly on the alert for someone to recognise me. That was no way to live and a sacrifice was worthwhile to change it.

I had to keep remembering that and then I could be reconciled to leaving everything that was familiar to me and going off into the unknown.

I did have a short time alone with Ninian. I think Lilias helped to arrange this by making sure that she kept Zillah away. My spirits were lifted because I sensed that this was what Ninian wanted, too.

He talked seriously about my future.

"You don't need to look on it as permanent," he stressed. "You will come back. But for a time I believe this is the best thing to do. I want you to promise me something."

"What is that?"

"That you will write to me and tell me everything . . . however seemingly trivial. I want to know."

"But surely . . . ?"

"Please," he said. "It may be important."

"Do you still regard me as 'a case?'"

"A very special case. Please, I am serious. Give me your word. I know you will keep it."

"I will write," I said.

"I shall want to know about the school . . . and the Lestranges . . . and how everything works out."

I nodded. "And you will let me know what happens at home?"

"I will."

"You sound so serious."

"It is very important to me. And there is one thing more. If you want to come home, let me know. I will arrange it."

"You . . . ?"

"I shall see that you get a passage home at the earliest possible moment. Please remember that."

"It is comforting to know that you are so concerned about me."

"Of course I'm concerned about you . . . Davina."

I looked at him in alarm.

"I can't get used to that other name," he said. "I always think of you as Davina."

"Well, no one can hear now."

"One day you will come back."

"I wonder."

"You will," he insisted. "You must."

I remembered that conversation for days to come and it brought me comfort.

We were on deck as the ship sailed out. The hooters were sounding all round us; the quay was crowded with the friends of passengers come to see the last of them. It was a moving scene. Some people were weeping, others laughing, as slowly the ship glided out of her berth and sailed away.

Lilias and I stood there waving until we could no longer see Ninian and Zillah.

I SHALL NEVER FORGET those first days on the *Queen of the South*. I had not dreamed of such discomfort. In the first place we had to share a cabin with two others. The cabin was little more than a large cupboard and there were four berths, two lower and two upper. There was one small cupboard for the use of the four occupants and there were no portholes. We were shut in with many other similar cabins and the noises around us never seemed to cease. We were at the after end of the ship and there were barriers to prevent our leaving that section.

Meals were taken at long tables. I suppose the food was adequate, but eating in such conditions was far from pleasant and neither Lilias nor I had much appetite for it.

Our section of the ship was overcrowded. Washing was not easy. There were communal quarters for this and little privacy.

I said to Lilias: "Can you endure this till Cape Town?"

"We must," she answered.

When the weather turned rough, as it did very soon, this was an added trial.

The two women who shared our cabin were prostrate in their bunks. Lilias felt queasy, too. She could not decide whether to venture out on deck or withdraw to her bunk.

She decided on the latter and I went on deck. I staggered along as far as the segregating barrier and sat down. I looked at the grey heaving waves and wondered what I had let myself into. The future seemed bleak. What should I find in this country to which we were going? I had been a coward. I should have stayed at home and faced whatever I had to. People would say that if I were innocent I should have nothing to fear. I should have held my head high, faced whatever was coming and not hidden behind an assumed name.

And now here I was, in a condition of acute discomfort, being carried over this turbulent sea to . . . I could not know what.

I was aware of someone on the other side of the barrier.

"Hello," said Roger Lestrange. He was looking down on me over the top of the fencing which separated us. "Facing the elements?"

"Yes . . . and you, too?"

"You find this uncomfortable, do you?"

"Yes, don't you?"

"Mildly. Nothing to what it can do, I assure you."

"Well, I hope it doesn't attempt to show me."

"I didn't see you when you boarded. You had friends to see you off, I believe."

"Yes."

"That was nice. How are you liking the trip . . . apart from the weather?"

I was silent for a while and he said quickly: "Not good, is it?"

"It's hardly luxury."

"I had no idea you would travel in such a way."

"Nor had we. But we did want to do so as cheaply as possible. Miss Milne has a horror of debt. How is Mrs. Lestrange?"

"Laid low. She does not like the weather."

"Who does? I am sorry for her."

"We'll soon be out of this and then we'll all forget about it."

I had been standing up while I was talking to him, and a gust of wind threw me against the deck rail.

"All right?" he asked.

"Yes, thanks."

"I think you should go below," he continued. "The wind can be treacherous and one really shouldn't face the decks when it is like this." He smiled wryly. "I'm sorry I can't conduct you to your quarters."

"You're right," I said. "I'll go down. Goodbye."

"Au revoir," he said.

And I staggered down to the cabin.

• • • •

LATER THAT DAY the wind abated. Lilias and I were alone in the cabin. The other occupants, feeling better, had gone out, as they said, for a breath of fresh air.

One of the stewards came to our cabin.

He said: "I've got orders to move you."

"Move us?" we cried simultaneously.

"Some mistake, I expect. You shouldn't be in this one. Get your things together."

Bewildered we obeyed. He took our cases and told us to follow him. We did so and he led us through the ship, opening one of the dividing doors. He took us to a cabin which seemed magnificent after the one we had just left. There were two bunks which served as sofas by day, a fair-sized wardrobe, a washbasin and a porthole.

We stared at it in amazement.

"That's it," he said, and left us. We could not believe it. It was such a contrast. Lilias sat down on one of the beds and looked as though she were going to burst into tears, which was extraordinary for her.

"What does it mean?" she demanded.

"It means that they made a mistake. They should never have put us in with the emigrants."

"But we are emigrants."

"Yes . . . but here we are. Isn't it wonderful? I feel dignified. I don't think I could have borne much more of that."

"Yes, you would . . . if you had to."

"Well, don't let's worry about that. Let's rejoice."

"I wonder how it happened," said Lilias.

"Doubtless we shall hear."

We did ask the purser, who told us there had been some mistake and we were so relieved we did not take the matter farther than that. All we knew was that we could now continue the rest of the voyage, weather permitting, in a comfort we had not dared hope for.

EVERYTHING CHANGED after that. We were often in the company of the Lestranges; and it was during that voyage that I began to know Myra.

She was a self-effacing person, rather timid, in contrast to her mother. I often wondered whether having spent so much of her life in close contact with such a woman had made her as she was, for in such a presence even the most confident people must be aware of their shortcomings. I grew to like her. She was rather withdrawn in the presence of her husband, and rarely spoke unless addressed. I noticed that he often finished a sentence with "Is that not so, my dear?" as though trying to draw her into the conversation. "Yes, yes, Roger, indeed it is," she would invariably reply.

"She's completely subservient," said Lilias.

"I think she wants to please him. After all, he is always kind and courteous to her."

"Well, if he likes absolute obedience, she must suit him very well," was Lilias' rather terse rejoinder.

Practical Lilias might dismiss her as a woman of no spirit, content to be dominated by her husband, but I saw some character beneath that attitude, and perhaps because she sensed my feelings she revealed a little more of herself to me than she did to most people.

Our first port of call was Tenerife and as it was not easy for two women to go out alone, Roger Lestrange suggested that we accompany him and his wife. We accepted willingly.

We had a pleasant day, and under the guidance of Roger Lestrange went for a ride through the town and some miles out into the country. We revelled in the balmy air and marvelled at the brilliant flowers and shrubs, the poinsettia trees growing wild by the roadside, the banana plantations and the mountains.

Roger Lestrange was an amusing and knowledgeable companion and when we returned to the ship Lilias said how fortunate we were to be travelling with them; and I agreed.

Myra said: "It is a great pleasure to have you with us." I was glad she felt that as the thought had crossed my mind during the day that we might be intruding. After all, it was not long since their honeymoon, and that was a time when newly wed people liked to be alone together.

As we came down the west coast of Africa the weather was

warm, the sea smooth, and life on board was very pleasant indeed. Neither Lilias nor I wanted the days to pass too quickly. After our change of cabin, which had brought us to another part of the ship, we had found the life very congenial. We were meeting people who interested us.

Roger Lestrange was quite sought after. He was an asset to social gatherings; he was on good terms with the captain whom he had met on a previous voyage; and, as his friends, we were drawn into his circle.

It was delightful to sit on deck, to look over the water which scarcely moved, to watch the dolphins sporting in the distance and the flying fish skimming over the surface of that pellucid sea. It was conducive to confidences.

Myra was reluctant to talk, but eventually she began to give me a glimpse into her childhood.

"It would have been different if I had been brilliant," she said to me one day. "But I wasn't. I was slow . . . slow to walk . . . slow to talk. Right from the beginning I was a disappointment. My mother wanted me to be outstanding . . . not so much clever as beautiful . . . a success socially. You know the sort of thing . . . something she could arrange and then . . . grandchildren whom she could plan for."

"People have to manage their own lives."

"My mother would never accept that. She was so good at managing everything, so naturally she wanted to manage me. I was lucky in one way because there were the grandparents . . . my father's parents. I spent a great deal of my childhood with them. I was happy there. They did not care whether I was clever or beautiful. They liked me just as I was. My mother said they spoiled me. She did not want me to be so much with them, but they were important. They were very rich and she respected that."

"I can well believe it."

"My grandmother died." Her voice trembled a little. "I was fourteen then. After that there was just Grandpa. I was often with him. He wanted me to live with him. My mother could not allow that. My place was at home with her, she said; but I was with him a great deal. We used to read together; we would sit in the garden and play guessing games. Then he was in a wheelchair and I used to wheel him about the garden. My mother said it was no life for a girl, but I loved to be with him. I had to have a season in London. My mother insisted and my father agreed with her. The season was a failure. Nobody asked me to marry him. Soon after that my mother gave up. I went to stay with Grandpa. He said, 'Don't let them push you. You do what you want. And never marry a man because they tell you you ought to. That's the biggest mistake a girl can make . . . or a man for that matter.' He was wonderful. I was twenty-four when he died."

"How sad for you."

"I was heartbroken. I was very rich. He had left everything to me. It made a difference. My mother changed towards me. I knew she thought I should get a husband now, but when she started managing I said to her, 'Grandpa told me I was never to marry anyone just because people told me to. I was to marry only if I, myself, wanted to.' "

"I think your grandfather was very wise," I said.

"Oh, he was. But I'm talking all about myself. What about you?"

That freezing sensation came over me. I heard myself say: "Oh, there's nothing much to tell. I just had a governess . . . and then . . . I went to stay at the vicarage."

"And your father?"

"He . . . he died."

"And now you have to take this post in South Africa?"

"I don't exactly have to. I just wanted to do something. I have a little income . . . not a great deal . . . but adequate, I suppose."

"Did you ever think of marrying?"

"Well, once. But it didn't work out."

"I'm sorry."

"Don't be. I'm sure now that it was all for the best."

"Are you sure? I think you seem a little sad sometimes."

"Oh no . . . no. It's all in the past. Our families didn't approve and . . ."

"Oh dear."

"It would hardly have been right for us. If it had been we should have married, shouldn't we?"

"I rather liked that lawyer . . . the one who came down to see you. It seemed that he was really concerned about you. And your stepmother. She's very beautiful, isn't she? When I look at her . . ." She laughed a little mirthlessly. "Well, I think she is all that I am not."

"You are very nice as you are, Myra. You must not denigrate yourself so much."

"And *you* are nice to say so. But tell me about this lawyer. You knew him in Edinburgh, did you?"

"Yes."

"He was a friend of your family, I suppose."

"You could say that."

I had to stop the trend of this conversation.

I said quickly: "And it all turned out well for you."

She said: "Yes. My grandfather was right. I might have married someone my mother found for me. But I didn't and if I had there wouldn't have been Roger."

"So you are completely happy now?"

"Well . . ."

"You are, aren't you?"

She hesitated, looked at me thoughtfully and then, I believed, decided to confide in me. "Sometimes . . . I'm afraid."

"Afraid of what?"

"He is so distinguished, isn't he? Sometimes I wonder . . ."

"Tell me what you wonder."

"Whether I'm good enough. What does he see in me? If he hadn't been rich himself I should have thought it was the money . . ."

I laughed at her. "Myra, you must stop thinking like that. He married you, didn't he? He loves *you*, not your money."

"It's so hard to believe. He is so wonderful. Of course, if he had needed the money . . ."

"Stop it, Myra!" I laughed again and she laughed with me. I was so relieved. I had thought she was afraid of *him* and all she feared was that she was not attractive enough for him.

I must overcome this ridiculous feeling that there was something rather sinister about Roger Lestrange.

IT WAS NO USE trying to hold back the days. They were passing with alarming rapidity.

Very soon we should arrive at our destination and reality would take the place of this dreamlike idyllic existence which we had been enjoying for the last few weeks.

We should have to face whatever we found—our school. Where should we find the pupils? Lilias had said it was no use planning anything until we saw what we were coming to.

We were due in Cape Town in two days' time.

Roger Lestrange had said we must accompany him and Myra to Kimberley. It was a longish journey, but he had done it more than once and he could help us and take us to our new home.

We accepted his offer with alacrity.

"It really was good fortune for us to be travelling in the same ship," said Lilias. "They have made it all so much more interesting for us than it would otherwise have been."

She did not realise how much we owed to Roger Lestrange, but I was soon to discover.

That night I went out onto the deck as I often did. I loved to sit there underneath the velvety sky with the stars more brilliant than they seemed at home. The air was warm and there was hardly anyone about. It was perfect peace.

It will soon be over, I thought, and what shall we find? Myra and Roger Lestrange would not be far away. It was good to have them as friends—particularly in a foreign country.

And as I sat there I heard a light footstep on the deck and before I looked up I guessed who it was.

He said: "Hello. Revelling in the starry night? May I?" He drew up a chair and sat beside me.

"It is pleasant, isn't it?" I said.

"It's more than pleasant. It's delightful."

"I agree."

"I wonder more people don't take advantage of it. Never mind. It gives us an opportunity to talk in peace. How are you feeling? Nearly there, you know."

"I was just thinking of that when you came up."

"It's a bit of a gamble, isn't it?"

"Rather more than that."

"You'll be all right. We shall not be far away."

"You must be looking forward to getting to your home."

"I've enjoyed the trip."

"Of course. You met Myra."

"Yes, and you . . . and Miss Milne. It has been very illuminating."

"Illuminating?"

"It is always interesting meeting people, don't you think?"

"Oh yes, of course."

"You and Myra seem to get along very well."

"I think we do. I've grown fond of her."

"That's good. She's rather retiring. I like to see you two friendly. I couldn't bear to think of you down there in that steerage . . . or whatever it is."

"Oh . . . yes, at first it really was rather dreadful."

"I'm glad I rescued you from that. Glad for myself as well as you."

"Rescued us?"

"Well, I couldn't leave you down there, could I?"

"You mean . . . you . . ."

"Look, it was nothing. Forget it."

"But . . . they said there was a mistake. We thought . . ."

"I insisted that you were not told."

"Please tell me exactly what happened."

"It's quite clear. You paid for a cabin and you got what you paid for."

"I . . . I see. Lilias wanted to have the cheapest. That Society was lending the money and she could not bear to be in debt."

"Very worthy sentiments."

"So it was you who . . ."

"I had you moved. I paid the extra so that you could enjoy the voyage in comfort."

I felt myself flushing. "But . . . we must pay you back."

"Certainly not."

"Lilias . . ."

"Lilias need know nothing of the transaction. Just imagine her feelings. Besides, she would feel she had to pay me. That would be as bad as paying the Society. And you know how she hates to be in debt."

I was silent for a moment. Then I said: "I can pay you."

"I shall refuse to take it."

"But you must."

"Why? It was a little gift. It was nothing. And think what a pleasure it has been for me . . . and for Myra . . . to have your company, which we could not have had, you know, if we had had to be separated on different sides of the barriers."

"It was very good of you, but you must allow me to refund the money, my share at least."

"I will not allow it."

"I cannot accept."

"My dear . . . D–Diana, you already have."

"But . . ."

"No buts please. Think of proud Lilias. She must go on be-lieving that there was a misunderstanding in allotting the cab-ins and when it was realised it was put right."

"Why should you do this?"

"Because I could not bear to think of you two ladies in such conditions. I should not have told you."

"But you have."

"It slipped out. Perhaps I wanted to let you know that I wanted to help you. After all, it is a big step you're taking and I suggested you should come to South Africa. I very much want it to be a success."

"You are very good and I am grateful to you. But I would rather . . ."

"Will you please me in this matter? Say no more about it. I have been delighted to have your company . . . so has Myra. In fact, we have all had a pleasant voyage." He laid his hand on mine. "Please see it this way . . . and not another word about the matter."

I should have guessed. We had paid so little for the voyage.

We had been so inexperienced in these matters. It was good of him to be concerned. That was how I must try to see it.

But the discovery did make me feel a little uneasy.

IN TWO MORE DAYS we should reach our destination. One could sense the tension throughout the ship. For myself—and I knew that Lilias felt the same—there was an immense excitement which at times would almost be overcome by a fearful apprehension. There were times when it was brought home forcibly to us that, somewhat blithely, we had decided to leave all that was familiar to start an entirely new life.

We now began to ask ourselves how well equipped we were to do this and we were very preoccupied. We would sit in silence staring out over the sea, each aware that our thoughts were running on similar lines.

Roger Lestrange, I was sure, was fully aware of our feelings; he continually sought to allay our fears. All was going to be well. He would be at hand. We must remember that we had friends.

I remember vividly that sunny day, sitting there on the deck, looking out over an aquamarine sea with scarcely a ripple to disturb its tranquility. Lilias and I had been joined by Roger and Myra. Poor Myra; I guessed her apprehensions about her new life were as deep as mine and Lilias'.

The captain, who was on his daily round of the ship, came into sight.

"Good afternoon," he said. "Lovely day."

We agreed that it was.

"Soon be there," he added.

"On a day like this it seems too soon," said Roger.

"Yes . . . and the weather is set fair for the next few days, it seems. Though the Cape can be tricky."

"Indeed," said Roger. "I've had experience of that."

The captain smiled and his eyes rested on Lilias, Myra and me.

"You young ladies will be visiting South Africa for the first time."

"Yes," said Lilias.

"You could have chosen a better time, wouldn't you say, Mr. Lestrange?"

"It will probably blow over," said Roger.

"This time it seems to be a little more serious."

"Oh, there's been trouble before?" said Lilias.

"Oh yes . . . brewing for years, but I'd say that now it seems to be coming to the boil."

"The captain is referring to Kruger. He's getting rather truculent just now."

"It's been seething for some time, I know," said the captain. "But after the Jameson Raid . . . well, things have gone from bad to worse."

"Why is this?" I asked.

"What would you say?" asked the captain, looking at Roger.

"It's simple. Cecil Rhodes wants a British South Africa. Kruger wants it for the Afrikaners. It will be all right. Kruger wouldn't dare go too far."

"We'll wait and see," said the captain. "Well, I must be getting along. I'll see you later."

After he had gone I turned to Roger. "I should like to know more about these matters."

"Of course. You're going to live there. Naturally enough you want to know."

"The captain seemed quite concerned," said Lilias.

"Well, to put it briefly," said Roger, "this jostling for power has been going on for some time, but when diamonds and gold were found in the country, it meant that people came and settled from elsewhere. They were mostly British subjects. Consequently the population changed and the newcomers, whom the Afrikaners called Uitlanders—Outlanders, of course—wanted to play a dominating role in the administration of the country. Paul Kruger was President of the Transvaal and he could see what was coming."

"He's a very strong leader, I believe," said Lilias.

"Indeed he is. He realised at once that if the Uitlanders were given a vote the Afrikaners would be outnumbered, with disastrous consequences to them. They were suspicious of the British who, right from the first, had maintained a different attitude towards the black population. When the emancipation of slavery had taken place in Britain the British wanted to extend it to South Africa. This was something which the Boers could not tolerate because it robbed them of the labour on their farms. It is a long story of conflict."

"And now the captain seems to think it is 'coming to the boil.'"

"We've been thinking that for some time. The reason that there is a scare now is because Kruger has ordained that no Uitlander may have a vote in the presidential elections, and only those who have lived fourteen years in the country and are forty years old can vote in the Volksraad elections. That is for the parliament, of course."

"It seems hardly fair if these Uitlanders had settled in the country."

"Exactly. Besides, many of them have become wealthy and are contributing considerably to the finances of the country and yet are denied a vote. You could not expect men like Cecil Rhodes and Jameson to stand aside and let such a state of affairs go on."

"Then, of course, there was the Jameson Raid," said Lilias.

"That delayed matters for some time. Especially when the Emperor of Germany sent a telegram congratulating Kruger on his success in the affair; on the other hand, there is no doubt that the British government is more determined than ever to show its strength."

"So it does seem as though there is some danger of big trouble?" said Lilias anxiously.

"As I say, the trouble is not new. It will be sorted out, no doubt. Negotiations are going on now, I believe, between Joseph Chamberlain, who is Secretary of State for the Colonies, and Jan Smuts, Kruger's young State Attorney. Being away all this time, I have only heard what is happening through the British press."

"We did not take very much notice of it," said Lilias. "Since we decided to come to South Africa there has been so much to do."

"I should forget it."

"But if there is this conflict between the Afrikaners and the Uitlanders, of whom we should be regarded as members, might they not be a little hostile towards us?"

"My dear lady, nobody would be hostile to you, I am sure. No, no. They will be delighted to have you come to give your skills to their children. I am sure you will find a warm welcome awaiting you. Moreover, I shall be nearby. Riebeeck House is not far from the schoolhouse. So I shall be at hand if needed."

I felt he was expecting us to say that we were greatly comforted, but I—and I am sure Lilias felt the same—could not truthfully say that. We were beginning to wonder with a certain trepidation what lay ahead of us.

CAPE TOWN WAS BEAUTIFUL. I wished that we could have stayed to explore. The sun was welcoming; the people seemed friendly. From what I had heard from Roger and the captain, I had been prepared for a hostile reception from some members of the community. We were Uitlanders; and there was a controversy in progress among the people here. But there was no sign of this.

I marvelled at the grandeur of the Table Mountain and Table Bay.

"What a beautiful country!" I cried; and Lilias agreed with me.

We smiled at each other. We both felt that it was going to be all right.

The long train journey through the veldt was of absorbing interest, if somewhat exhausting. It was five hundred and forty miles from Cape Town to Kimberley and Roger had warned us that it would take thirty hours.

"It's fortunate that you do not have to trek," he added.

We had to be grateful to him. Throughout the journey, his air of authority brought him the best and immediate attention; and we shared in that.

"How different it would have been without his help," I said to Lilias, and she agreed.

At last we arrived in Kimberley.

Roger Lestrange insisted on taking us to the schoolhouse before going on with Myra to Riebeeck House.

As we drove through the town, Lilias and I gazed intently from the windows of the carriage.

"It's a prosperous town," Roger told us. "It's growing fast. That is what diamonds have done for it. Besides, it's on the direct route from Cape Town to the Transvaal." With pride he pointed out some of the fine buildings—the Town Hall, the High Court and the botanical gardens.

Lilias and I exchanged gratified glances. We had said when we heard of the troubles of this country that we should have been better in Australia or New Zealand. But this was very agreeable.

The carriage had drawn up before a small white building set back from the road in a kind of courtyard.

"The schoolhouse," announced Roger.

The door opened even as he spoke and a man emerged. He was in his early thirties, I imagined, fresh-complexioned and smiling.

"Mr. John Dale," said Roger. "Let me introduce you to the new schoolmistresses, John."

"This is Miss Milne and Miss Grey?" said the young man, looking from one of us to the other.

"This is Miss Grey," said Lilias. "I am Miss Milne."

He shook her hand and then mine.

"And this," said Roger Lestrange, "is my wife."

John Dale held out his hand and shook Myra's.

"Welcome to Kimberley," he said. "I hope you will be very happy here, Mrs. Lestrange."

Roger stood smiling benignly and said: "Well, we have had a long journey and my wife and I will be off. Can I leave the ladies in your care, John?"

"Certainly." He turned to us. "Do please come in. Let me take your baggage."

"There is much more to come," said Lilias.

"Of course. But now, let's get in."

"So," said Roger, "we'll leave you."

We thanked him sincerely for all he had done.

"We shall be seeing you soon. We shall want to hear what you think of it and how you are settling in, shall we not, Myra?"

"Oh yes . . . yes. Please come and see us soon," said Myra.

"Of course they will, my dear," put in Roger. "We're so close. You're not going to lose them. Well, we shall be getting on. You're safe in John's hands. Au revoir."

We had stepped into a hall and John Dale brought in our bags and set them down.

"Now," he said. "Let me explain who I am. I'm a member of the council which looks after the town. We have been very concerned about the education of our young people. It's a very small school, as you will see. We've never had more than about twenty pupils. The difficulty has been to get teachers who stay. Originally we had a Miss Groot who was here for twenty years. Then she became too old and we had a young woman who stayed for two years, married and went away. Since then we have found it difficult to find someone who would come and feel a real interest in the school. When Mr. Lestrange told us about you, we were delighted. I hope you will like it here."

"And I hope you will find us satisfactory," said Lilias.

"There are two of you . . ."

He hesitated, and Lilias said quickly: "Yes, we know that you only needed one teacher."

"The fact is that we should like to have two teachers . . . but the funds won't run to it. If we had more pupils, well then, we should need more teachers. But the fees we charge are not large and the school is really supported by the town . . . and sometimes it seems that not everyone gives education the respect it deserves."

"We do understand," said Lilias. "That is quite satisfactory. We wanted to be together and we are prepared to come and work here."

He still looked worried. Then he said: "I am forgetting. You must be tired and hungry. I have brought with me a bottle of wine and some food. Would you like to eat now or would you prefer that I show you the place?"

"Let us see the place and perhaps we could wash some of the

grime from the journey from us. Then we could eat and talk in comfort, if that is agreeable to you."

"That's an excellent idea. There is an oil stove on which we can heat water. I'll put that on and while it is heating I can show you round."

We were quite pleased with what we saw. There was a large room with a long table and chairs in it together with a large cupboard. We opened this and found books and slates inside.

"The schoolroom," said Lilias with approval.

In addition to the schoolroom there were two small rooms on the ground floor, and a kitchen with a back door which opened onto a small garden. Shrubs grew in profusion and Lilias gave a cry of pleasure.

John Dale was smiling, evidently delighted by our appreciation.

Lilias said: "We had no idea what we were coming to."

"And feared the worst?" he asked.

"Well, we did not imagine anything so good as this, did we, Diana?"

Upstairs there were four small rooms, simple but quite comfortably furnished.

"Bedrooms and a study and still one room left," said Lilias. She went to the window and looked out on the street. Then she turned to me with shining eyes.

"I want to make this into a flourishing school," she said.

"You will," replied John Dale. "And now that water will be hot and I'll bring it up for you."

"We'll help," said Lilias. I had rarely seen her so excited.

In the room downstairs John Dale had set out the meal. There was cold chicken, crusty bread, a bottle of wine and some luscious pears.

"This is a lovely welcome to our new life," said Lilias.

"I want you to know how glad we are that you have come," John Dale told us. "Let me tell you something about the town and the people."

"We are longing to hear."

"I think you will like the climate, although you may find it a little too hot in summer."

"We are prepared for that," I said.

"Kimberley, as you probably know, owes its prosperity to diamonds. Before '71 it was more or less a village. Then, of course, there were the discoveries . . . and everything changed. Kimberley *is* diamonds. Most of us here are engaged in the business in some form or other . . . if not finding them, preparing them for the market and actually marketing them."

"You, too?" asked Lilias.

"Yes, I work in the offices of one of the biggest companies."

"Would that be Mr. Lestrange's company?"

"Oh no . . . not ours. When he came to Kimberley some years ago, he bought a share in one of the other companies. Shortly afterwards he married and acquired Riebeeck House. It is one of the finest residences in the town. Tell me, when did you propose to open the school?"

"There is no reason for delay," said Lilias. "Let us have a day or so to settle in and find out what pupils we have and what materials there are . . ."

"Of course. What about starting on Monday? That would give you the rest of this week and the weekend."

"And the pupils?"

"There are about ten of them so far. There will be more."

"What ages?"

"Varying." He looked at her anxiously. "Will that make it difficult?"

"It is what one expects and as there are two of us, we can divide into two classes perhaps. However, we shall have to see."

"I'll circulate the news that school will start on Monday."

"How very kind you are."

"Not at all. I am delighted that we are getting the school started again. Education is so necessary. I wish everyone here agreed with me."

"These pears are delicious," I said.

"We grow the finest fruit in the world here."

"What a beautiful country it is!" said Lilias. "To us it is like the Promised Land."

He laughed. "I'll remember that. I am going to drink a toast. May it live up to that."

When he had left and we were alone in our schoolhouse, Lilias and I agreed that it had been a wonderful welcome.

The Kimberley Treasure

THE NEXT WEEK was a busy one and most enjoyable. I had never seen Lilias so excited.

"If I had tried to imagine something I wanted to do, it would have been exactly this," she announced. "It's like starting a new school . . . my school."

She went through the books that were there and made lists of what she would like to have. John Dale, who was quite a frequent visitor, joined in the enthusiasm. He would see the council and discover whether she could have what she wanted.

"He's a great ally," said Lilias. "How lucky we are to have him here!"

On the appointed day the children arrived. There were fourteen of them—not a great number but more than we had dared hope for. Their ages ranged from five to fourteen and Lilias decided that I should take the fives to sevens, of whom there were six, and she would teach the elder ones; I with my pupils would be at one end of the largish room and she at the other.

It was a strange feeling to be confronted by the young children. They stared at me with interest and I felt it was going to be a trying ordeal and I only hoped that I should be able to deal with it satisfactorily. I managed to struggle through and began by teaching the alphabet and nursery rhymes.

When the children had gone to their homes Lilias and I cooked simple meals for ourselves in the little kitchen and discussed what had happened during the day. Lilias was in her element; I was less sure of myself. This was Lilias' vocation, I reminded her. My abilities in the teaching field were yet to be tested.

"You'll come to it," she assured me. "You must remember that you mustn't lose your patience. Never let them see that you are ruffled in any way. You've lost the battle if you do; and there is a certain battle on. They're watching you as closely as you are watching them. You have to show the right amount of authority. Be kind. Be patient. But make them aware all the time that you are in charge."

"I'll try to remember that. I'll stick to the rules . . . if I can."

For the first week I thought of little but doing the job. The days started to pass quickly. The routine had to be followed rigorously. Lessons all morning. The children came at nine and left at twelve. Then we would cook something light and eat a meal to be ready for when they returned at two o'clock; they stayed till four.

We were becoming known in the town and the shopkeepers were very pleasant to us. We had the impression that the townsfolk were pleased that the school was open again.

Of all the children in my class there was one girl who interested me particularly. I was haunted by her rather sad little face. Her name was Anna Schreiner and she was about five years old. Her mother brought her to school each morning and called to pick her up at the appointed times with most of the parents of the younger children. She was a quiet child and, if addressed, usually replied in monosyllables; she hardly ever smiled. Her mother was young and pretty, fair-haired, blue-eyed and rather plump. It struck me that Anna was brooding on something which she could not get out of her mind.

One day the children were copying the letters I had put on the blackboard; so deep in concentration were they that there was hardly a sound except that of pencils scratching on slates. I wandered round, looking at what they were doing, commenting now and then. "Is that an *O* or a *Q*? A *Q*? It hasn't got its little tail on, has it?" "The loop on that *P* comes down too far. See?" Then I came to Anna. She was working laboriously and all her letters seemed perfect.

I sat down beside her. "That's very good," I said.

She did not smile. She just went on with the letters.

"Is everything all right, Anna?"

She nodded.

"Do you like school?"

She nodded again.

"You are happy here?"

Again the nod. I was getting nowhere.

She continued to bother me. I thought she was an unnatural child, aloof from the others.

I watched her with her mother. Her face did not brighten when she saw her. She just ran up to her and took her hand; and they went off together.

I told Lilias of my interest in the child.

"Children vary," she said. "She's just a solemn child."

"She has that pretty mother. I wonder if she is an only child?"

"John Dale would probably know. Ask him next time you see him."

That time would not be far off, I guessed. He was a frequent visitor to the schoolhouse. He often brought food and wine as he had on the first day and we would share what he called a "picnic."

When I asked him about Anna Schreiner he said: "Oh yes. Poor child. I understand her living in perpetual fear. She probably imagines Hell's Gates are open wide to receive her if she's five minutes late for school."

"Her mother looks as though she is quite a jolly person."

"Greta, yes. Well, she was . . . once. I don't understand why she married old Schreiner. Although there were rumours . . ."

"Rumours?" I cried.

"It's probably a lot of scandal."

"Mr. Dale," said Lilias. "It helps us to teach our children if we know something of their background."

"Well, I'll tell you what I know. Piet Schreiner is rather a formidable character. Calvinistic . . . puritanical. There are a few like him in this town . . . and all over the country, it seems. There is a strong feeling of puritanism among the Boers. He is even more fanatical than most. One could imagine his going off on the Great Trek. Hard-working . . . strictly honest and . . . godly—so he would say. It seems sad that someone with his virtues should put such an interpretation on his religion as to make life miserable for everyone around him. For such as he is, everything people do seems to have its roots in sin. I suppose he himself is always on guard against it."

"And that's little Anna's father?" I said.

"Well . . . on the surface. There are some who say that is not the case."

"What do you mean?" asked Lilias.

"Schreiner is all of twenty years older than Greta . . . she's the child's mother. A pretty girl who was inclined to be flighty . . . once. Her family were strict with her . . . and I suppose that may have added to the incentive to stray . . . or to do something that shocks. The fact of the matter is that her family were very friendly with Schreiner. He's a lay preacher in the chapel which they attend. Whether or not Greta married him because she was in trouble, I am not sure, but I cannot imagine she could have had any other reason for doing so."

"So Schreiner is not Anna's father . . ."

"He calls himself her father. It's all on the records. The girl is Anna Schreiner all right. The fact is that Schreiner married Greta in a bit of a hurry. No one had thought he would ever marry anyone—let alone a young girl like that. There was a lot of talk about it. However, there it was. They married—that frivolous young girl and the hellfire preacher so much older than herself. It was a nine days' wonder. There was as much talk about it as when Ben Curry found the Blue Diamond and made a millionaire of himself. But that happened more than five years ago. People forget. They only remember now and then."

"So that poor child lives with her flighty mother and this fanatically religious man who may or may not be her father."

"Poor little thing. I don't suppose she has too good a time."

"I must try to help her in some way," I said.

"Don't get into conflict with old Schreiner," warned John. "Holy men can be fiendish when they are fighting the enemies of the righteous . . . which means anyone who doesn't agree with them."

"That's not likely," said Lilias. "But I know Diana will be gentle with the poor little thing."

After that I took an even greater interest in Anna Schreiner, but no matter how I tried, it was impossible to get her to talk. She just worked more diligently than the others and quietly walked away with her pretty mother.

What sort of life did they have with each other? I wondered.

ON OUR SECOND SUNDAY in Kimberley Lilias and I were invited to lunch at Riebeeck House.

Myra had called on us on the previous Wednesday about four-thirty, after school had closed.

She said: "I guessed that I should be interrupting school if I came at any other time. Do tell me how everything is going."

"Very well indeed," Lilias told her enthusiastically. "We have been agreeably surprised."

"That's wonderful. I hear that the school is a great success."

"That's a bit premature," cautioned Lilias, but she was well pleased. "Where did you hear that?"

"From Mrs. Prost, our housekeeper. She is one of those women who know what is going on everywhere."

"Useful to have around," I commented. "And how is everything with you?"

"Oh . . ." There was a brief hesitation. "Everything is very well."

"And you like the house?"

"It's . . . very large and one is apt to get lost. The servants are nearly all Africans. It makes it difficult to . . . be understood."

"But this Mrs. Prost, she looks after everything, I suppose."

"Oh yes. I came to ask you over to lunch on Sunday. It has to be a Sunday for you, doesn't it?"

"Yes," said Lilias. "That is the best day."

"Roger wants to hear all about the school. He says you will have settled in and formed an opinion by now."

"People have been so good to us," said Lilias. "It was lucky for us that we met you on the ship . . . and since that mistake about our cabin, we were able to be with you. And now that we are here, well, Mr. Dale has been quite invaluable to us, hasn't he, Diana?"

I said that he had, for from the moment we had arrived he had taken us under his wing.

"They're so glad to get the school going again," said Myra. "You will come, won't you?"

"But of course," I said. "We shall be delighted, shall we not, Lilias?"

So it was arranged.

When she had gone, I said to Lilias: "I can't help feeling that all is not quite right with that marriage."

Lilias laughed at me. "You and your fancies! First it's little Anna Schreiner, and now it is the Lestranges. The trouble with you is that you have too much imagination and you let it run wild. You like something dramatic to happen and when it doesn't you set about creating it."

"Perhaps you're right," I said. "But all the same . . ."

Practical Lilias. She could only smile at me.

And as I liked to see her happy I smiled with her.

RIEBEECK HOUSE was something of a mansion. Although it was situated in the town, once one had passed through the gates and entered the grounds which surrounded the house, one might have been miles away from any other dwelling.

The drive in was about a quarter of a mile in length, but the foliage was so lush and abundant that one felt one was in the heart of the country. Flowering shrubs of colourful blossoms were huddled together. Flame trees and poinsettias added a further dash of colour. I shall never forget my first sight of the place as we came through this mass of vegetation to the white house.

It was an imposing place, built in the Dutch style. There were steps leading up to a stoop in front of the house and on this were urns which were almost hidden by the prolific plants.

It was large and there seemed to be many windows. It was one of those houses which had a personality of its own. Lilias laughed at this when, later, I mentioned it to her. Practical Lilias saw everything with absolute clarity for what it was.

Very soon I felt there was something a little repellant about the house. Perhaps it was because I could never feel absolutely at ease in the company of Roger Lestrange. I also had an idea that Myra was not as happy as she should be and that she shared with me that vague lack of ease.

Mrs. Prost came down to greet us.

"You must be Miss Milne and Miss Grey," she said. She had small light eyes which darted everywhere. Her light brown hair was plaited and wound round her head. I had the impression that there was little she would miss. "Do come in," she went on. "I'll tell Mrs. Lestrange that you are here."

"We're glad to meet you, Mrs. Prost," said Lilias.

"Welcome to Kimberley. I hear the school is doing well."

"It's early days yet," said Lilias cautiously. "But all is well . . . at the moment."

"Very pleased to hear it, and so is everyone."

Myra appeared.

"I thought I heard your arrival."

Mrs. Prost stood watching while Myra greeted us.

"Luncheon will be served at one o'clock, Mrs. Lestrange," she said.

"Thank you, Mrs. Prost." Myra turned to us. "Do come up. Roger is in the drawing room. He is so looking forward to hearing your news."

She took my hand and held it lingeringly.

"Are you well?" I asked.

"Oh yes . . . thanks. I am so glad you came. I wanted to call at the school, but I thought you would be so busy just at first."

"We're teaching in the mornings . . . and then again from two till four," said Lilias. "Any time after that we love to receive visitors."

"Roger says that John Dale has been looking after you."

"He is," said Lilias warmly. "We are so grateful to him. He has made everything so easy for us."

We were taken through a large hall with white walls and vivid red curtains, up a staircase to a room on the first floor.

Myra opened a door and said: "They're here."

It was a spacious room with tall windows. My first impression was that of an interior painting by one of the Dutch masters. The floor was of delicately tinted tiles which gave an impression of coolness. Later I noticed the heavy furniture—baroque style—the table with the scrolls and the inlaid ebony, the cabinet on stands, impressive with pilasters and decorative carving.

But there was no time to look round then for Roger Lestrange had risen and was coming towards us, hands outstretched.

"Miss Milne . . . Miss Grey . . . what a pleasure!"

He took our hands and smiled warmly. "How good of you to come. I have been hearing of your success. It is especially gratifying as I shall receive the thanks of the grateful townsfolk for bringing you here."

"We have been here only a short time," began Lilias tentatively.

"And," I added, "we have fourteen pupils, so there has hardly been a stampede to our gate."

Lilias smiled at me. "We are really very pleased," she said. "We were warned that there would only be a few pupils and Mr. Dale did not really expect so many as there are."

Roger looked at Myra expectantly and she said hastily: "Come and sit down. Luncheon will be served at one."

"What do you think of our house?" asked Roger.

"We are very impressed by what we have seen," said Lilias.

"After luncheon you shall see it all and then you will be able to pass judgement."

"You seem to be isolated, though, of course, you are not really," I said.

"I'm glad you get that impression. And you are right, of course. No one can really be isolated in a town. But it is good to be here for business reasons and I like to create an impression of detachment, even if it is not strictly true. That was one of the reasons why I bought the house."

"Oh? I had the impression that it was a sort of house which had been in your family for years."

"Oh no. I bought the place . . . lock, stock and barrel . . . furniture and everything. It belonged to an old Dutch family who had been here for a hundred years. They decided they did not like the way things were going and they sold up and went back to Holland. It was very convenient for me. We . . . my first wife and I . . . wanted a place and this seemed to suit. So there it was, waiting for us. We just walked in and took on everything that was here . . . furniture, Mrs. Prost, most of the servants, I believe. Mrs. Prost would know how many."

"You didn't mind just walking in and taking over someone else's possessions?"

"We didn't mind in the least. We found it convenient . . . That was Margarete . . . my first wife."

I glanced at Myra. I saw her flinch slightly. I wondered what that meant. Or did it mean anything? Was I imagining again?

We went into luncheon . . . to a similar room. I noticed the tiled floor, the heavy table and chairs.

Roger Lestrange sat at one end of the table, Myra at the other, Lilias and I facing each other.

As we ate Roger said: "There is one thing I wanted to ask you. It's about my son, Paul. He is at present without a tutor. I was wondering whether it would be a good thing to send him away to school in England? It's a big undertaking for him and I am not sure that he is ready. I thought that . . . for a while . . . if you would have him, I might send him along to your school."

Lilias cried: "Of course, we should be delighted."

"You must meet him before you go."

While silent-footed Africans served the food, Roger Lestrange made a few comments about the weather and I could see that Lilias was impatient to hear more about Paul.

"Isn't he rather young to be sent overseas?" asked Lilias.

"Oh no. He's nine years old. Isn't that the time boys go away to school? I should imagine many boys in England would be in boarding schools at that age."

"Yes, but this is sending him overseas . . . right away from his home."

"I don't think he would mind that, do you, my dear?"

Myra agreed that he would not mind.

"He's a strange boy," went on Roger. "He keeps out of our way since we've been back." He was looking at Myra, who seemed embarrassed, as though it were her fault that the boy kept away. Perhaps he resented his stepmother. Very likely. In any case, it appeared that Myra might be accepting the blame.

"Oh well, you'll see for yourselves." He wrinkled his brows and looked at us rather anxiously. "Do you know," he went on, "I'm seriously beginning to wonder whether you were wise to come here."

"Why?" I asked sharply; Lilias was looking at him questioningly.

"I don't much like the way things are going. I haven't liked it for some time . . . but now that I'm back, I see what's happening more clearly."

"What is happening?"

"Kruger is getting very stubborn. Trouble is blowing up fast between him and Chamberlain."

"Chamberlain?"

"Joseph Chamberlain, Secretary of State for the Colonies. The trouble goes back a long way . . . you might say, right to the beginning of the century . . . ever since the British captured the Cape from Napoleon's Dutch allies. I believe I have mentioned the trouble about the slaves when the British tried to reform conditions for the Khoi servants and made laws to protect them against cruelty. There has been antagonism between the Boers and the English ever since."

"They don't seem to be antagonistic towards us . . . individually."

"Oh no. It's the leaders who are at each other's throats. They don't blame us for what they call the arrogance of our leaders."

"We have become quite friendly with a number of them now," I said. "They have all been . . . well . . . rather especially nice to us."

"It's a quarrel between states. All the same, it can blow up. There would not be another Great Trek. This time they would stand firm and fight for their land."

"What Great Trek was this?" asked Lilias.

"It happened about fifty years ago, but it's still remembered. The conditions imposed by the British had robbed them of their slave labour, and they were unable to exist on the land, so they gathered their families and their goods together and set out across country in their ox-drawn wagons. Life was difficult. They were hard-working people, sternly religious, self-righteous, as such people often are, and they firmly believed that all who were not of their way of thinking were on the road to hell. All they wanted was to be left in peace with their slaves and their dogma, to work and make a living. So, harried by African tribes . . . the Zulus, the Ndebele and the Matabele . . . prevented from making a living by the British laws against slavery, what could they do? Only escape from their rulers to another land. Hence the Great Trek across country. They went as far as Natal and settled in the Transvaal."

"They had a great deal of courage," said Lilias.

"That's something no one could accuse them of lacking. Then, of course, diamonds were discovered . . . and gold. That was to have a marked effect on the country. People came pouring in and Rhodes and Jameson dreamed of a British Africa. They managed to persuade Lobengula, King of the Matabele, to let them have mining concessions, and you know these lands are now Rhodesia . . . a British colony. But the trouble is between Kruger and Chamberlain."

"That," said Lilias, "means trouble between the British and the Boers."

"There was a possibility at one time that Germany might

come to the aid of the Boers and it seemed unlikely that the British would want to risk a war with Germany. It was a different matter with South Africa alone. That is what people are afraid of."

"Wouldn't it be better to come to some compromise?" asked Lilias.

"The Boers are not people to accept a compromise . . . unless it were forced on them."

"And would it not be forced upon them by the power of Britain?" I asked.

"That might be, but I believe they are prepared to put it to the test. That is the crux of the matter: the franchise which Kruger is imposing in the Transvaal. The Uitlanders outnumber the Boers, so Kruger can't give them the vote. Oh dear, I am spoiling this luncheon which I wanted to be so pleasant. It makes us very happy to have you here, does it not, Myra?"

"It does indeed," she said fervently.

"Forgive me for bringing up a subject which would have been better left alone."

"If it's happening we would rather know about it," said Lilias.

"Well, don't let's worry about it. There is peace so far. No one wants war. It is devastating to a country and almost always profits no one."

"Yet there are constantly wars," said Lilias.

He sighed. "That is the nature of man. Now . . . you must see more of this country. You will find it impressive, beautiful . . . often awe-inspiring."

It came out during the course of the conversation that he had only been in South Africa some six or seven years. When I had first met him I had decided that he could not be of Dutch origin as so many of the people in South Africa were; but I had read somewhere that a certain number of French settlers in Africa were Huguenots who had left their own country to escape persecution, and I had assumed from his name that he was one of those. When I told him this, he said that he was indeed of French origin and his family had come to England at the time of the Edict of Nantes. So I was right in thinking that he came from a Huguenot family. He had, though, lived in England most of his life.

"You are very knowledgeable about your adopted country," I said.

"I always believe in finding out all I can." He looked at me steadily. "About everything," he added.

I felt myself flushing and felt annoyed. Must I always suspect someone was probing my secret?

It was when the meal was over that a messenger arrived at the house asking that Mr. Lestrange go and meet a business colleague without delay as something important had turned up and needed his immediate attention.

"I am desolate," he said. "At such a time as this! It is too bad I have to leave you."

"Perhaps we should be going," I said.

"Oh no!" cried Myra. "You have to meet Paul, and I want to show you the house."

"Please do not run away because I have to go," said Roger. "We will do this again . . . very soon. We must, to make up for my early departure. So . . . au revoir."

It struck me that Myra was rather relieved when he was gone and with his absence she seemed to acquire a certain dignity. She's afraid of him, I thought.

I was looking forward to meeting Paul Lestrange and I knew that Lilias was. We were different, Lilias and I. She would assess him as a pupil; to me he was an actor in what I felt might be some mysterious drama. I could not get rid of the idea that there was something strange about this household and that Myra was aware of it and that was why she appeared to be nervous.

Paul was tall for his age and bore no resemblance whatsoever to Roger. His hair was flaxen, his eyes blue-grey; and there was a cautious air about him.

"Paul," said Myra, "these are the ladies who have opened the school, Miss Milne and Miss Grey."

He came forward rather awkwardly and shook hands with us both.

Lilias said: "We have just heard that you may be joining us."

He said: "I am going away to school."

"Yes, we were told that, too. But it isn't certain yet, is it?"

"Oh, no."

"Do you think you would like to join us while you are wait-ing for things to be settled?"

"Oh yes, I should, thank you."

"It is such a small school," went on Lilias. "And there are pupils of all ages."

"I know."

"But, of course, we shall be expanding . . ."

"When shall you start?" I asked.

"I don't know."

"Why not tomorrow?" said Lilias. "The beginning of the week."

"I don't mind."

He was noncommittal . . . cautious still. But at least he did not appear to dislike us.

Myra said: "I am going to show Miss Milne and Miss Grey the house and after that the garden. Would you like to come with us?"

To my surprise he said he would.

I wondered if Lilias was thinking the same about him as I was. Rather shut in on himself. Difficult to know. A little suspi-cious of us. Lots of children were like that.

The tour of the house began. There were several rooms on the first floor, all similar to the ones we had already seen. The rather ornate spiral staircase descended from the top to the bottom of the house. The heavy furniture was everywhere and I could not help feeling that it had been lovingly collected over the years.

"You haven't lived here all your life, have you?"

"Oh no. We came here . . . just after they were married."

I was puzzled. "Who . . . were married?"

"My mother . . . and him."

"But . . . ?"

Myra said: "Do you like these drapes? Look at the embroi-dery on them."

Lilias took the material in her hands, but I turned to Paul. He was looking at me as though he wanted to talk.

"You thought he was my father," he said. "He's not. He lets people think it, but he's not. He's not."

Myra said: "It came from Amsterdam, I think. You can tell by the style of the embroidery."

I said to Paul: "You mean Mr. Lestrange is not your father?"

He shook his head vigorously. "My father died. He died in a diamond mine. That was before . . ."

I moved away from Myra and Lilias . . . with him.

"I didn't know," I said. "Mr. Lestrange always speaks of you as though he is your father."

"No, my father died and then my mother married him. I'm not his son. I have a real father. Only he's dead."

"I'm sorry about that."

He pressed his lips together and held his head high.

I was thinking: I knew there were secrets in this house.

Myra was saying: "Paul is very interested in the house, aren't you, Paul?"

"Yes," said Paul. "Let's show them the staircase."

"We'll come to it in time."

"And the Model House?"

"Of course."

"The staircase is very fine," I said.

"Oh, not that one," said Paul. "The other."

"Oh, there are two, are there?"

"Yes," he said, and I noticed his lips tightened again.

In due course we came to the staircase. It led from the hall to the second floor. It was obviously a back staircase, used by the servants, I supposed; it was covered in a green carpet held in place by brass stair rods.

"That's it," said Paul.

I could see nothing unusual about it. It was certainly not comparable with the spiral one by which we had ascended. It was natural, I supposed, to have two staircases in such a house.

"Interesting," I said perfunctorily; but Paul was looking at it with gleaming eyes and Myra looked decidedly uncomfortable.

I had a strange and uncanny feeling that they were seeing something which was not visible to Lilias and me.

A short while later I was inspecting the Model House. It was quite extraordinary. It was like a large dolls' house. It was in a smallish room, the whole of which was needed to accommodate it, and it reached from floor to ceiling.

I suddenly realised that it was an exact replica of the house. The rooms were all there, the two staircases, the heavy furniture, all in miniature.

I couldn't resist saying: "It's like a huge dolls' house—the biggest I have ever seen."

"It's not a dolls' house," said Paul. "It's not for children."

"No," said Myra. "Roger explained it to me. It's an old custom. It started in Germany and was adopted by the Dutch. Their homes mean so much to them so they have models made of them . . . exact copies. When furniture is taken away it is removed from the model house and when new comes in a small copy is made."

"What an extraordinary idea!" said Lilias. "I have never heard of it."

"Yes," said Myra. "They don't follow it now. But the people who lived here before did. They probably thought it was unlucky to dispense with an old custom. People do, don't they? It's a bit of an oddity and amuses people, Roger says."

Paul was apparently very proud of it. He said: "You've seen it with the doors open. It's like taking away the front of a house. It's the only way to see inside, isn't it? You can see it all in this one. In ordinary houses you can't see what's inside. This house hasn't got doors. It's all open. So it doesn't have the inscription which is on the door of this house. You didn't see it when you came in because it was all covered up with creeper. I think some people are glad about that. It says: 'God's Eyes See All.' It's in Dutch. Most people here know what it means. But it's covered with the creeper. But that wouldn't stop God's seeing all, would it?"

He gave me a rare smile.

I said: "No, it wouldn't."

"You liked it, didn't you?" he said. "I mean the Model House?"

"I thought it was fascinating. I have never seen anything like it."

That seemed to please him.

After that we went into the garden. It was extensive and that section near the house was laid out in lawns and flower beds and little paths; but there was a large area which had been allowed to grow wild and I could see that was what would appeal to a boy of Paul's age.

He grew excited as we approached it.

"I think we ought to get back to the house," said Myra. "You can get lost here. It's like the jungle."

"Just as far as the Falls," said Paul. "I won't let you get lost."

"The Falls?" I said.

"Well," Myra explained. "It's a kind of miniature waterfall. There's a stream . . . well, it's more than a stream. It's supposed to be a tributary of some river miles away, I think. It flows down from higher ground and makes this little waterfall. It's quite attractive."

It was, as she had said, although it was little more than a stream. It was about six feet wide and there was a rickety wooden bridge over it. But it was indeed attractive with the water cascading from a higher level making, as Myra said, a little waterfall.

Paul was pleased when we admired it.

"And now," said Myra, "we must go back to the house."

"Oh, let's go just as far as the rondavels," begged Paul.

He seemed to have attached himself to me, and I said: "What are the rondavels?"

"That's where the servants live," he explained.

"Sort of native huts," said Myra. "They are circular and have thatched roofs."

We had come to a clearing and I saw them. There must have been about twenty of them. It was like a native village. There were some very small children playing on the grass and at the door of one sat an old woman.

Myra had paused and we all stopped with her.

"It's like a little colony," said Myra. "They couldn't all live in the house. There are too many and they wouldn't like it. They like their own way of life."

A young boy of about Paul's age came running towards us. He stood before Paul smiling. Paul put his hand on the boy's shoulder and patted it.

Myra said: "That's Umgala, isn't it?"

"Yes," said Paul.

The boy had put his hand over Paul's. It was a greeting, I guessed. Paul nodded at the boy and the boy nodded back. This was some sort of ritual. Neither of them spoke.

"Come along, Paul," said Myra. And to us: "They don't like us to intrude, I'm sure."

Obediently Paul turned away.

"Poor Umgala," said Myra. "He's a deaf-mute. Both his parents work about the place."

We had started walking back to the house.

"How can you communicate with that little boy?" I asked Paul.

"Like this," said Paul, waving his hands.

"It must be difficult."

He nodded.

"His parents are good workers," said Myra. "Luban, his mother, works in the house, and his father, Njuba, in the garden. That's right, isn't it, Paul?"

"Yes."

"It must be terrible to be born like that," said Lilias.

"Yes, but he seems happy. He was pleased to see Paul."

"Yes, Paul has established quite a friendship with him, haven't you, Paul?"

"Yes," said Paul.

"This has all been so interesting," murmured Lilias.

We walked slowly back to the house and very soon afterwards we left.

Back at the schoolhouse Lilias talked a great deal about what we had seen. She was delighted that we were to have a new pupil.

"I had no idea that Mr. Lestrange was not the boy's father," she said. "I heard what the boy was saying."

"He has always referred to him as his son."

"Well, he's his stepson, of course."

"But he did give the impression that he was the boy's father. He couldn't have been married very long to his first wife. Did you get the impression that Myra was afraid of something?"

"Well, Myra was always afraid of her own shadow."

"I just thought she was especially afraid."

"She seemed afraid of the boy, too. She's just a nervous person."

"I shall be interested to see more of Paul."

"So shall I. I'm sure he'll be an interesting pupil."

"I think he might be difficult to get to know. He seems to have some morbid obsession."

"About what?"

"I'm not sure."

"I am sure of one thing. You'll do your best to find out."

That night I wrote to Ninian Grainger. I told him that Roger Lestrange had paid for a better cabin for us and that I had kept this from Lilias because she would have been so worried about the debt which would have been a great strain on her; so I had let it pass and accepted.

"It was good of him," I wrote, "and he did not let me know about it until right at the end of the voyage."

I also told him about the school and our high hopes for it. We liked Kimberley and were getting on well with our pupils' parents; and the friendship of the Lestranges made us feel we were not so far from home.

"I was surprised to discover that Roger Lestrange was not a native of this place. He apparently came out from England some years ago. He married out here and acquired this really rather fascinating house . . . and then his wife died. She must have been quite young. The son who I thought was his is his stepson. The boy's mother must have died soon after the marriage.

"Well, there have been lots of surprises and I expect there are more to come. Mr. Lestrange, with whom we lunched today, told us that there is a certain unrest in the country, but there is no sign of it here . . ."

What a lot I was telling him! But I had promised I would tell him the details and I think the visit to Riebeeck House had excited me.

I sealed my letter. I would post it tomorrow.

PAUL JOINED THE SCHOOL and Lilias was very pleased. Like all good teachers she was delighted at the prospect of a responsive pupil.

"I wish I had more like him," she said. "I'd like to give more attention to him. But, of course, before long I daresay he will be going away to school."

Lilias was very efficient and my position was more or less a sinecure and I was afraid I contributed very little.

The school really resembled one of those village schools of which there were many at home. In isolated villages where there were too few pupils to make a large school possible, they were run by one schoolmistress. Everything depended on her. If she were good then so was the school.

Lilias said that in her early days she had attended such a school and she had found that when she went away to a boarding school she was in advance of the other girls who had been brought up by governesses.

"How I should love to have a big school with several teachers working for me and a hundred pupils! But, for the time being, this will suffice."

She had wanted to share the salary, but I impressed on her that this was absurd. She did far more work than I did. I was prepared to take nothing at all. My income sufficed. She would not hear of that, so all I could do was insist that she take the larger share of the money. The truth was that she could have run the place very easily by herself.

She was happy and I was delighted to see her so. She dreamed of enlarging the school. But, of course, that was for the future. I realised more than ever that teaching was her vocation and how frustrated she must have been, confined to the domestic affairs of the vicarage. John Dale shared her interest in the school. He was a very frequent visitor. He used to call after school with a bottle of wine and some delicacies and we would talk far into the evening.

One afternoon when Greta Schreiner brought Anna to school she lingered behind to have a word with one of us. I saw her and she asked if we would keep Anna for an extra half an hour when school was over as she would be delayed coming to pick her up. This happened now and then with some of the children, for we would not consider letting any of the little ones go off without their parents. I told Greta that that would be all right.

When school was over Lilias went off to see a parent in the town who was thinking of sending her two children to the school, so I stayed behind with Anna.

We sat at the window watching for Greta to arrive. I tried to interest the child in a game in order to pass the time, but I received little response, and I was rather pleased when I saw Greta hurrying towards the schoolhouse.

Anna went quietly to her mother and I led the way to the door.

"Thank you, Miss Grey," said Greta. "It was kind of you. I hope I wasn't too long."

"Oh no. You're earlier than I had expected. Well, goodbye, Anna. Goodbye, Mrs. Schreiner."

I went back into the schoolhouse and as I did so I heard the sound of horse's hoofs. I went to the window. Roger Lestrange was riding into the courtyard. He pulled up, leaped from his horse and approached Greta Schreiner. They seemed to know each other well by the manner in which he was talking and laughing and she was responding. My thoughts flashed back to the house in Edinburgh and Kitty laughing in the kitchen with Hamish Vosper . . . and then Kitty in the stables at Lakemere chatting with the grooms. Some people were like that. They blossomed in masculine society. Zillah was another.

I watched them for what must have been five minutes. Roger had turned his attention to Anna. Suddenly he picked her up and held her in the air above him. He was laughing at her. I wondered what solemn little Anna thought of this familiar behaviour. It was not the sort of treatment she would be accustomed to from her puritanical father.

Roger set her down. He put his hand in his pocket and brought out what must have been a coin which he pressed into the child's hand.

Then a strange thing happened. Piet Schreiner came striding across the courtyard. He must have been lurking close, watching, for he took the coin from Anna's hand and threw it on the ground at Roger's feet.

For a moment it seemed as though Greta, Roger and the child were turned to stone. No one spoke; no one moved; then Piet Schreiner seized Greta's arm and dragged her away, Anna clutching at her hand.

Roger looked at the coin on the ground, shrugged his shoulders and came walking towards the schoolhouse, leading his horse which he tethered to the post there.

He was coming to see us.

When I opened the door he was smiling urbanely and showed no sign that he was in the least ruffled by the little scene in which he had taken part.

I said: "Hello, so you have come to see us?"

"To see *you*, Miss Grey."

"Is everything all right? Paul . . ."

"I think Paul is enjoying his new school."

"I couldn't help seeing what happened just now."

"Oh, that pious old fool! It was because I gave the child money."

"It was so extraordinary."

"He's a little mad, I suppose. Religious maniac. He thinks everyone is destined for Hell Fire—except himself."

"It seemed so amazing . . . when you have merely been generous to the child."

He shrugged his shoulders. "I feel sorry for his poor wife."

"I suppose everyone must be. I thought she seemed very pleased that you were friendly towards her."

"I'm a friendly person. I can't tell you how pleased I am about the way things are working out here. Miss Milne is out, isn't she?"

"How did you know?"

"Ha! I'll tell you. Mrs. Garton, whom I happen to know, was visiting us yesterday and she was talking about sending her girls to England to school. I pointed out that that was something of an undertaking—particularly as things are now—and while she was waiting why didn't she send the girls to the school which was really an excellent one since the new ladies had taken it over. I could vouch for that as I was sending Paul there. I said, 'Why don't you consult Miss Milne, who is the senior teacher?' She said, 'I'll do that tomorrow.' I said, 'I daresay Miss Milne would come and see you when school is over.' So there you are. That is why I knew I should find you alone."

I felt a twinge of uneasiness. In spite of his urbanity and obvious desire to help, I felt vaguely suspicious of his motives.

"I expect you are wondering how Paul is getting on with his studies," I said. "I can tell you that Miss Milne thinks he is very bright. She knows a good deal about children, of course."

"And you, too."

"The fact is I am not really needed here. It's a post for one . . . at the moment."

"And you came out because you wanted to get away from England."

"It seemed an exciting adventure."

"And you were not very excited by life at home?"

He was looking at me quizzically. What does he know? I was asking myself. I could not quite understand the expression in his eyes. I fancied they were a little mocking. I did not understand this man. In spite of his flattering words and his attitude of gallantry, I felt he was taunting me, and that he knew it had been imperative for me to get away.

I had to turn the conversation away from myself.

"I was surprised to hear that Paul is not your son."

"Oh . . . did you not realise that?"

"But . . . I think you said he was your son. Or that was how I understood it. You spoke of him as though . . ."

"He is my stepson, but I wanted him to regard me as his father. When I married his mother I felt I had a duty to him."

"He remembers his father too well to accept someone else, I imagine. Children are faithful, you know."

"I realise that now." He smiled at me deprecatingly. "But I shall go on trying."

"If he had been a little younger," I said, "it would have been easier. He might have forgotten his father and have been ready to accept you."

"I know."

"How old was he when his father died?"

"About five, I think."

"He's nine now, isn't he? It was only four years ago."

"Yes, it happened rather quickly."

"You must have married his mother soon after."

"Well, it was more than a year . . . eighteen months perhaps."

"I should imagine the speed of it all was too much for him. At seven his mother dies . . . and at nine he has not only a stepfather but a stepmother. Oh, I understand how difficult he must find it to adjust to all the changes."

"I hadn't thought of it like that. It seems that Margarete has been dead for a long time. Margarete . . . oh, she was such a sweet and simple girl! She could not deal with everything that had to be done when her first husband died. I helped her with her affairs. She was lonely and I was sorry for her. We slipped into marriage. And then . . . she died."

"Was she ill?"

"When she lost her husband she was quite, quite bewildered. She felt she couldn't cope with life. She was the sort of woman who needs someone to look after her. I did that as best I could. But it had all been a terrible shock for her. She began . . . well . . . please don't mention this to anyone . . . but she began to drink a little . . . at first. I suppose she found some solace in that. I did not realise what a hold it was getting on her. She did it secretly, you see. But it was undermining her health, and one morning she was found . . ."

"Found?"

He turned away, as though to hide his emotion. He reached

for my hand and gripped it hard. Then he said: "Found, at the bottom of the staircase."

I knew which staircase. I understood now Paul's obsession with it.

"She had fallen," he went on. "It was an accident. I was greatly relieved when nothing came out about the secret drinking. They thought she had tripped over the carpet. One of the stair rods was loose. However, she fell from top to bottom. Her neck was broken."

"What an awful thing to happen! And you had only been married for such a short time. Poor Paul."

"He was dreadfully upset. It's changed him. Made him moody. He misses his mother."

"I understand that. And then you married Myra . . . quite soon after."

"Myra is a sweet and gentle person. I think she reminded me of Margarete." He was silent for a while and then he said: "I'm rather worried about Myra. I think she may be a little homesick. Do you think she is happy here?"

I hesitated and he went on: "Please tell me the truth."

"Well . . . I don't think she is entirely happy. I think she is afraid of disappointing you."

"Disappointing me! Why should she be?"

"She is quiet and a little nervous, and you . . ."

"I am the opposite."

"Well, you are, aren't you?"

"I thought she would enjoy a little freedom. Her mother was a bit of a gorgon . . . and in that village . . . well, it was hardly riotously merry!"

"Perhaps she does not want to be riotously merry."

"I thought I could get her away from it . . . make her happy, Diana . . . May I call you Diana? Miss Grey is so formal and we are good friends and we shall see more and more of each other here. I wanted to talk to you about her. I want you to help her."

"In what way can I help?"

"I want you to see more of her. Come to the house. Go out with her . . . shopping . . . and all the things you ladies like to do. Be a friend to her. Come and stay at the house. Miss Milne is so efficient. She can manage without you now and then. I'd be so grateful if you could . . . get closer to Myra. You're someone from home . . . you're already friends. Try to find out what will make her happy."

I could not understand him. He had always given me the impression that he believed himself capable of dealing with any situation. And here he was, almost humbly pleading for help.

I was intrigued. I had always been interested in people and their motives, the reasons why they acted as they did, the manner in which they often covered up their true intentions with subterfuge. Lilias was so different, so realistic, so practical. I really wanted to know what went on in that house. It fascinated me; Paul, the staircase, the hasty marriages, the strange death of Margarete. I could find life in the schoolhouse a little dull. What suited Lilias did not necessarily suit me, and I was not going to be as dedicated to the school as she was.

"Will you do this for me . . . for Myra?" he asked.

"I should very much like to help if I can."

"Oh, you can. I know you can. Myra needs a friend. She needs you."

I said: "It takes two to make a friendship. It may be that Myra will like to make her own."

"But she is already your friend. She brightens at the thought of your visits. Please . . . Diana . . . come and see us often."

"Of course I will."

"Get her to confide in you. You can help her."

It was then that Lilias returned.

"Two more pupils!" she cried out, then: "Oh . . . Mr. Lestrange."

"And I know who they are," he said, rising and shaking her hand. "It was I who suggested to Mrs. Garton that she should see you."

"Thank you. How kind . . ."

"I am so pleased it has turned out to your satisfaction," he said. "As a matter of fact I was just on the point of leaving. I hope you will both come and see us very soon. What about luncheon next Sunday? It has to be a Sunday, does it not?"

"Oh yes, that's the best day because of school," said Lilias. "I should enjoy it . . . and you, Diana?"

"Yes, thank you very much. It will be a great pleasure."

When he had gone, Lilias said: "Why did he call? Surely not just to ask us to lunch?"

"He's worried about his wife."

"Oh?"

"He thinks she's lonely . . . homesick. He wants us to be friends. He really seems concerned about her."

"Well, he married her, didn't he?"

"I've promised I'll go and see her more often."

Lilias nodded and said it was time we thought about getting supper.

It was after school. Lilias was marking essays which she had set for the older children.

She said: "The subject was 'The Most Important Thing That Ever Happened to Me.' I thought that would stretch their imaginations a little. 'The Day My Mother Gave Me Thomas, My Terrier.' 'A Picnic with the Wagons' and such like. But here's one that's different. Paul's. He's got a real touch of the dramatic, that boy. It's interesting. Here, read it."

I took the exercise book from her and studied Paul's clear, round handwriting.

"The Kimberley Treasure," I read.

"The most important thing that ever happened to me was when my father found the Kimberley Treasure. The Kimberley Treasure is a diamond. It weighs eight hundred and fifty carats and that is a lot—almost more than any other diamond has weighed before. We were ever so excited when he found it because we would be rich when he sold it.

"I saw it. It looked like a lump of stone, but my father told me it was a diamond all right. I'd see when they got to polishing and working on it. My mother said, 'Now we're all right.'

"The others were jealous of us because they all wanted to find some big diamond that would make them rich for the rest of their lives. Then somebody said it was unlucky. Big diamonds can bring bad luck, they said. But we didn't believe them. We thought they were just jealous because they had not found the Kimberley Treasure.

"My mother said we should sell it and give up mining. But my father said that there must be more where that came from. He wanted to be not just rich but very rich. He was sure he knew where to find another diamond like the Kimberley Treasure. He went to look for it and he was killed in the mine. So it was right about the Kimberley Treasure. It was unlucky.

"My mother cried a lot. She didn't care about the old diamond. What was the use of it if he was dead? But she would not sell the diamond. She said he wanted to keep it so she would too.

"Then she married my stepfather and he said what was the good of keeping a diamond like that just to look at it? Diamonds were comfort and riches. So he sold the diamond and we came to Riebeeck House. He missed the bad luck because the diamond had never really been his. But my mother had owned it, so she had the bad luck. My stepfather turned the diamond into Riebeeck House, but my mother had the bad luck and so she fell down the staircase and died.

"That is why the day my father found the Kimberley Treasure was the most important in my life."

I dropped the book and stared at Lilias.

"What an extraordinary essay!"

"I thought so. The boy has imagination and a rather powerful way of expressing it."

"I don't think he's imagining that. That is just how it happened."

"Do you think it's true?"

"I know that his mother married Roger Lestrange soon after her husband's death and that she died by falling down a staircase."

"And soon after he married Myra?"

"Yes. What do you think of it?"

"That that boy has a certain talent for expressing himself."

• • • •

I said: "That was an interesting essay you wrote, Paul."

His eyes lit up. "Did you like it?"

"Very much. That diamond. It must have been exciting when your father found it. You were very young then. Do you remember very much about it?"

"Oh yes. When things like that happen, it's so important. Everybody . . . however young . . . gets to know. Everything was different."

"Different from what?"

"From what it was before."

"What was it like then?"

"It was nice . . . nicer really. We were all together . . . my Daddy, my Mummy and me. We were there . . . the three of us . . . and neither of them are there anymore."

"It sometimes happens like that, Paul."

"Did you have a mother?"

"Yes. She died."

"How did she die?"

"She was ill for a long time . . . and then she died as we knew she would."

"And your father?"

I felt myself shrink. "He . . . he died also."

He said nothing for a while. Nor did I. Too many unpleasant reminders were chasing themselves round in my mind.

"They said it was unlucky," he said at length.

"What?"

"The diamond. Diamonds can be unlucky if they're big. I suppose it is because everybody wants them. They were all right before they found that. My father ought to have sold it. We ought to have gone away. But he had to go on looking for more just because he'd found that one. He wouldn't have died if he hadn't gone looking for more. He left it to my mother. So it was there and she took the bad luck with it."

"That's pure fancy, you know, Paul. Things like diamonds are not unlucky in themselves."

He looked stubborn. "She had it and she kept it and a lot of people wanted it. There was another man who wanted to marry her. It was all because of the diamond."

"How can you be sure of that?"

"I just know. And then she married him. He had the diamond then. But he sold it. And he bought Riebeeck House. But the diamond had *been* hers . . . so . . . she died."

"Perhaps she was not well before she died."

"She *was* well."

"Tell me, Paul, what it is you have on your mind."

"She died because she fell down the stairs. She was all right. Why did you think she was not well?"

I could not mention to him that she had been drinking.

He went on: "If she hadn't had the diamond, he wouldn't have married her. There wouldn't have been that house. She wouldn't have fallen down the stairs. It was all because of the diamond." I thought he was going to burst into tears. "That's why the most important thing in my life is the Kimberley Treasure."

"Oh, Paul," I said. "You mustn't think like that. Diamonds can't hurt anybody."

"Not by themselves . . . but what they mean."

"How could a diamond have made your mother fall down the stairs?"

"I don't mean that the diamond did it. But because of it, someone might have . . ."

"What?"

"I don't know. I only wish my father had never found it. I wish we could have gone on . . . finding little ones . . . little ones that were enough to keep us happy."

"Paul," I said firmly. "You have to stop brooding on this. It's over. It isn't going to help to go on thinking about it . . . making up what might have been. Try to grow away from the past. There's so much that's good for you. Miss Milne thinks you are going to do well at school."

He looked at me sadly, frustration in his eyes which I knew meant: nobody understands.

I felt I had failed him. It was cowardly, but had I been afraid that he might have said too much?

Figures on a Staircase

I WENT TO SEE MYRA as Roger had suggested.

"Go in the afternoon," Lilias had advised. "I can manage for two hours on my own. I'll set the older ones an essay or arithmetic problems which keep them occupied and I can easily look after the others. I'll enjoy it. It will be a challenge."

Myra was delighted to see me and I spent a pleasant afternoon with her. She was a little reticent and I did not probe; we talked lightly, mentioning Lakemere and village affairs. I remembered some amusing incidents and was able to make her smile. When I left she begged me to come again.

When I returned to the schoolhouse Lilias said: "I don't see why you shouldn't go now and then. I managed very well. It's not really difficult."

"The fact is, you could do very well without me here."

"Oh no. I should be desperately lonely. It's wonderful to have you to talk things over with. In any case, I shouldn't have come out here without you and I think it is one of the best things I ever did. John is such a good friend and so interested in the school. I'm happier than I have been for a long time. I felt so frustrated at home after that terrible affair of the necklace. But I do believe I'm getting over it now. How do you feel?"

"Oh . . . I don't think I shall ever forget."

"Yours was such a terrible ordeal, but you will get over it . . . in time. It's nice that you meet people. How lucky we are that John is here to help us."

"Yes, we are."

"And your seeing Myra will be good for her and you. You must go again soon."

I did and it was on my third visit that Myra began to talk a little more freely, and I felt I could ask her if she were worried about anything.

She hesitated for a while and then she said: "It's this house. There's something about it. Do you feel it?"

"What do you mean?"

"It's as though it has two parts. One just an ordinary, normal sort of house . . . and the other that's . . . haunted. Sometimes, Diana, I feel that she is still here."

"Who?"

"Margarete . . . Roger's first wife."

"She's dead, Myra."

"But some people think the dead can return. Sometimes I feel . . . that she can't rest. She was his wife . . . just as I am. I think she must have been rather like me. Quiet . . . not very attractive."

"That's being foolish. Roger must have found you attractive. He married you."

"I feel she and I are like one person."

"Really, Myra, you're getting fancies. He married her and she died soon after. It was a tragic accident. These things happen."

"I know. That's what I tell myself. I am beginning to believe she can't rest. When people die violent deaths, it is said that they can't rest. They sometimes come back. Just imagine it! You are alive one moment and then . . . without warning

. . . you're dead. You've left everything unfinished." She looked at me fearfully. "I should hate to go like that."

"Why do you think of such things? You're here. You're healthy. And you're by no means old. Your whole life is before you."

"Sometimes I wonder."

I looked at her intently. "What do you mean?"

"Oh . . . nothing. I suppose I'm just nervous. My mother was always telling me to pull myself together." She laughed. "You're reasonable, Diana."

"Am I? Lilias thinks I am very unpractical. I've got a wild imagination, she says. I don't know what she would think of you and your fancies."

"Even my mother admired Lilias. I can't tell you how much better I feel now you are here. And it is lovely to have our afternoons together. I look forward to them. I expect I'm like this because I haven't been very well. Roger got a tonic for me from the doctor."

"So the doctor has been to see you?"

"He came to dinner . . . he and his wife. Roger told him that I wasn't as well as he would like me to be. I was listless and homesick. It was all natural, of course, but he wondered if the doctor could give me something to 'buck me up.' Well, the result was he sent round this stuff. It's something mixed with wine . . . and something else, I suppose. It's not very pleasant to take."

"Is it doing you any good?"

"I haven't felt much different. Your visits do me more good than the doctor's tonic, I think."

"Then we must continue with that medicine."

"I'm so pleased Roger asked you to come."

"Yes, he was really concerned about you."

"He's always so good to me." She hesitated and I waited for her to go on. She bit her lips slightly and said: "He wants me to settle down, I know. I try to. You like it here, don't you?"

"Yes. Lilias is delighted with it. It's such a change from the village. She always wanted to teach."

"We wondered why she gave it up."

I thought then how difficult it was to throw off a part of your life which you wanted to forget. It kept coming back to hurt you.

"Perhaps she needed a rest," she went on. "She had just come to the end of one post and maybe did not like the prospect of facing another—though I should have thought Lilias would always be ready to face what she had to. Oh well, I'm glad it is turning out so well for her." She paused and went on: "What were we saying about the house? Do you know I avoid going to the part where it happened?"

"You mean . . . ?"

"The staircase. I always feel there is something . . . haunted . . . about it."

"That's your imagination."

"Maybe, but I want you to come there with me. I want to make you understand what I feel."

"Now, you mean?"

"Why not?"

She rose and led the way, looking over her shoulder, as though to reassure herself that I was with her.

We reached that part of the house and stood at the top of the staircase. I could see what she meant. In the first place it was dark and shadowy. There was only one small window which gave little light, even in the afternoon. It might have been due to that that one felt it was gloomy, plus the knowledge that someone, not so very long ago, had plunged to her death down that staircase.

"There," said Myra. "I see you can feel it."

"I was just thinking that there was so little light here."

"It's more than that."

"It's because you are thinking of what happened here."

She moved away and said: "Come and look at the Model House. I always do when I'm in this part of the house. I find it fascinating to see the house . . . just as it is . . . though on this small scale."

As we came up to the house she stopped short and gave a gasp of dismay. "Oh . . . look!" she said.

I looked. A small carved figure, which was clearly meant to represent a woman, was lying at the foot of the staircase. I thought she was going to faint . . . and I caught her.

"It's only a piece of wood," I said.

"Who put it there?"

I said: "Would you like to go to your room? You really look shaken."

She allowed me to take her there. She was trembling visibly. I suggested she lie down and when she did so I sat beside her. She held my hand and I was sure there was something she wanted to say to me but could not bring herself to do so.

"Stay with me," she said. "Don't go back to the schoolhouse tonight. There's plenty of room here. Stay."

I was astonished. "But . . ." I began.

"Please . . . *please*. I want you to. It's important to me."

"Myra . . . why?"

"I just feel . . ." She looked so earnest, her eyes pleading more than her words. I thought: she is afraid of something. I have to help her. If I did not and something happened . . .

I was romancing again. What was it about this house . . . the staircase . . . the Model House? She was making me feel, as she probably did, that there were evil forces at work.

I could not leave her.

I said: "I'll send a note to Lilias. I'll tell her I'm staying the night."

"Oh, thank you. Will you really? Ring the bell . . . please ring the bell."

I did so and a woman arrived.

"Luban," she said. "Will you prepare a room? On this floor please. Miss Grey is staying the night."

Luban was a lithe youngish woman; her skin was black as ebony and her large dark eyes seemed to hold some tragedy. I remembered that she was the mother of the deaf-mute I had seen on my previous visit, and I guessed that her air of sadness might have something to do with that poor boy.

"I must send a note to Lilias at once," I said.

Myra found a pen and paper and I sat down and wrote:

Dear Lilias,

Myra wants me to stay the night. She is not very well and I think it is rather important to her. I hope that will be all right.

DIANA

Luban took the note and said it would be sent at once.

I was still in a state of amazement that I had fallen into this situation. It was only when I received Lilias' note that I realised that it was not so extraordinary, after all.

Of course, it is all right, [she had written]. I'm sorry Myra is not well. Give her my best wishes.

LILIAS

As usual she brought calm common sense into the matter.

Nevertheless that night I spent at Riebeeck House was an uneasy one. I had dinner in Myra's room as she said she did not feel well enough to leave it. Roger joined us. He seemed very pleased to see me there.

"This is delightful," he said. "It was so good of you to stay with Myra. I am sure you are very grateful to . . . er . . . Diana, Myra."

Why did he stumble over my name? I wondered. It was almost as though he knew it was not my true one.

Myra said that she was grateful and it was delightful to have me there.

"And this faintness?" he went on in deep concern.

"It was nothing. Just the heat, I suppose. I'm not accustomed to it yet."

"Do you think we ought to consult the doctor?"

"Oh no . . . no."

"Have you been taking your tonic?"

"Yes."

"Well, we shall see. If you have any more attacks like this I am going to insist on your seeing the doctor." He smiled at me. "You and I will take care of her, won't we, Diana?"

"She will soon be well, I am sure."

When I was alone in my room that night I found myself

going over what had been said that evening. Roger Lestrange did seem to be a devoted husband, but, as always, I could not be sure of him. I wondered why he hesitated over my name. It really did seem as though he knew it were not mine.

I must talk to Lilias. She would soon drive away my misgivings. But Lilias was not here, and I was in a strange bed in a house which Myra thought was haunted.

There were times during that restless night when I had an idea that I was being caught up in something mysterious, perhaps sinister, which I could not understand.

WHEN I AWOKE next morning I could not for the moment recall where I was. I sat up in bed startled: and then when I looked at the unfamiliar Dutch-style furniture I realised I was in Riebeeck House and I recalled the events of last night.

After a while Luban came in with hot water.

"Mrs. Lestrange was ill in the night," she told me, in her melancholy sounding singsongy voice. "She very sick. Mr. Lestrange . . . he very worried."

"Oh dear! She is better now?"

"Yes. Yes . . . better now."

After she had gone I washed and dressed. Poor Myra! She was rather delicate, I supposed. It was not easy to uproot oneself and live in another country; and she had been terribly upset by that little figure in the Model House. I wondered who had put it there and why. Was it meant to represent Margarete? I supposed so, as it was lying at the foot of the staircase. It was a mischievous thing to do. I wondered if Paul had had a hand in it.

I went downstairs. The breakfast things were set out on the table, but there was no one there. I stepped out onto the stoop and walked down the steps to the garden. I was struck afresh by the lush beauty of the place. It seemed particularly delightful in the early morning. The sun was not yet too hot; everything seemed fresh; the scent of the flowers was almost overpowering and there was a murmur of insects in the air.

As I stood there Roger Lestrange came out.

"Good morning," he said. "It was good of you to stay last night."

"I felt a little guilty about leaving Lilias."

"Lilias is quite capable of looking after herself."

"I know. How is Myra? I heard from one of the servants that she was not well during the night."

"She is better this morning, thanks. Who told you she had been ill?"

"It was the one who brought my hot water. Luban, I think."

"She must have heard from Mrs. Prost. Luban doesn't live in the house. She is with her husband and family in one of the rondavels."

"Yes, I know. I did go out there and saw them once."

"Yes, I had to call Mrs. Prost in the night. I was worried about Myra."

"So it was as bad as that?"

"I wasn't sure. I don't know much about illness. I'm worried about her . . . Myra, I mean. What do you think?"

"I think she's taking a little time to adjust to this new life. After all, she lived so long in that village and this is all very different. In time she will settle down."

"Do you think so?" He sounded relieved. "She has never been ill like that before. She's had her headaches, but she was sick . . . really ill. I was really alarmed. I thought of sending for a doctor . . . but she begged me not to. And then she began to recover a little. She probably ate something which did not agree with her."

"Oh, maybe that was it. I know the heat can be very trying to people who are not used to it. I daresay she will soon be all right."

"I was just wondering if I should get the doctor to have a look at her."

"I should see how she feels."

"You are a comfort, D–Diana."

"I'm glad. I think she was rather upset by that figure in the Model House."

"Figure? What figure?"

"A carved figure. It was supposed to be a woman, I think."

"In the Model House?"

"Yes. I was with her. She was showing me one or two things about the house and there it was . . ."

"What was it like?"

"Oh, rather crudely carved."

"Native work?"

"I suppose it could be. It was there at the foot of the staircase . . . not the spiral one, the other."

His face had darkened. He muttered: "Who, in God's name, could have put it there?"

"Myra had no idea. It was . . . just there."

"Show me," he said rather fiercely. "Show me exactly where it is."

He went hurriedly into the house and I followed him. Swiftly we passed through to the other end of the house.

The figure was no longer in the Model House.

"Where is it?" he cried. "Show me."

"It's gone. It was lying there . . . just there, at the bottom of the staircase."

For a few moments he did not speak. I had never before seen him at a loss for words. Then he said slowly: "It was that spot where we found her. Someone . . . is playing some silly joke. We must find out who."

"Well," I said, "it upset her. I thought she was going to faint. That was when I took her back to her room."

He had recovered, but the colour had faded from his face and he looked rather pale.

"Thank you, Diana," he said; and I noticed he used my name without the usual hesitation. "Thank you for looking after her."

We walked to the other side of the house and descended the spiral staircase. "Don't mention the figure to anyone. It might upset people."

I said I wouldn't.

Myra joined us for breakfast. She told us she was feeling considerably better.

"I thought I was going to die in the night," she said.

"Oh come, my dear," replied Roger. "You know I wouldn't allow that."

She laughed. She seemed quite happy.

"Thank you so much for staying, Diana. I did feel comforted to have you there. You will come and . . . and . . . stay again, won't you?"

"*I* am going to insist that she does," added Roger.

WHEN I RETURNED to the schoolhouse it was to find that two letters had arrived. One of them was from Ninian, the other from Zillah.

Ninian began by saying that we should come home without delay.

Things are getting worse and I can see no solution to the problem but war. Chamberlain and Milner are going to reject this five years' franchise suggested by Kruger and Smuts. It is only to be expected. Those who contribute so largely to the wealth of the country cannot be denied a say in its affairs. The British foray into South Africa some years ago was something of a humiliation for us. We cannot allow that to happen again. There is a rumour that Chamberlain is sending ten thousand troops to augment the army already there. You must realise what a dangerous situation is brewing. There is time. You cannot have settled in very firmly yet. You and Miss Milne should get the next ship back to England while there is time.

He had clearly not received my letter as he had made no mention of it.

I reread his letter. It contained little else but the need for us to come home.

I turned to Zillah's. Hers was more lighthearted.

I hope you are getting on all right. Ninian Grainger goes on and on about the trouble out there. He is certain you ought to come home. He asks me to write and add my persuasion to his. So I will. I miss you. Life is rather dull here. I think I shall travel a bit. I've been to London several times, but I mean go abroad. I think that would be fun. Wouldn't it be nice if you were here? We could go together. I hope you will soon be home. We could have fun.

I showed Lilias Ninian's letter. She read it and frowned.

"Go home!" she said. "Of course we won't. Just as the school is beginning to expand. It's doing us so much good here. The people are nice to us. They don't want to make war on *us*. This insistence of his is almost hysterical."

"People in Kimberley are mainly British."

"But the Boers and the natives . . . they are all very friendly."

"Well, it wouldn't be our war . . . yours and mine, Lilias."

"You're not hankering after going back, are you?"

I hesitated. I was thinking how kind and thoughtful Ninian was. I liked what Lilias called his hysterical insistence. It surprised and comforted me that after all this time I was still more than an ordinary case to him. I should love to talk to him and it saddened me that we were so far apart. So perhaps the answer was yes, I was hankering after going home.

I believe that if I had not suffered such bitter disillusionment over Jamie, if Ninian had not shown such an interest in Zillah, I might have faced my true feelings towards him. But having been so deceived, how could I be judge . . . even of myself? Perhaps I had been in a bewildered state since the trial.

"Are you?" Lilias was demanding.

"Well . . . we do seem to be settling in here, I suppose."

"And you are so much better. I know you are. You don't jump every time someone mentions something from the past."

"No, I suppose I don't."

"What are you going to do? Write to him?"

"I suppose so . . . in due course."

She nodded. "Tell him that these matters are exaggerated. Everything is just the same out here as when we came."

"Yes, I will." Lilias was right. We could not pack up and go home at a moment's notice just because Ninian . . . miles away . . . had heard rumours of war.

•   •   •   •

I WAS BECOMING a frequent visitor to Riebeeck House. Sometimes I stayed the night. Lilias did not mind that; I felt she rather enjoyed dealing with all the pupils; and I was realising more and more that my presence in the school could be easily dispensed with. Lilias was delighted to have paid off the first instalment to the Emigration Society. I said that as I was taking more and more time off to be with Myra I did not deserve what I was paid and it should be hers. But she was adamant. "That matter is closed," she said.

Meanwhile I was becoming well acquainted with the Lestrange household. Paul and I were good friends. He liked school and was doing very well; and although I sensed that he still bore a grudge against his stepfather for marrying his mother, he seemed to be accepting it. Roger was always charming to me, as he was with everyone. The servants all liked him; and I gathered that the house was a more pleasant place than it had been under the Riebeecks.

Mrs. Prost, the housekeeper, appeared to take quite an interest in me. She was a woman who liked to gossip; and I must confess, so did I.

A strong friendship was growing between Myra and me and I fancied that she was less nervous. Mrs. Prost said my visits did her a power of good. I stayed a night or two occasionally. We played chess together. Lilias had taught me and I taught Myra. She was becoming quite an enthusiast.

There was one day when Roger went to Johannesburg on business and he asked me if I would spend the night at the house to keep Myra company. I said I would and we spent a pleasant evening chatting and playing chess.

In the night Mrs. Prost came to my room to tell me that Mrs. Lestrange was ill and she needed my help with her. I went with her to Myra who was very sick.

After a while she recovered and I said I would stay with her, which I did. I was very relieved when, in the morning, she was considerably better.

She took great pains to make light of her disorder.

"Don't tell Roger," she said. "I'm glad it happened when he

was away. He doesn't like illness . . . and he worries about it too much."

"Perhaps he ought to know," I said. "Perhaps we ought to call the doctor."

"Oh no . . . no. That's the last thing. I tell you I'm perfectly all right. It was just something I ate . . . something that didn't agree with me. I'm going to be all right now."

She did admit to feeling a little tired and said she would spend the morning in bed.

While she was resting I went down to Mrs. Prost's sitting room.

"Do you think it was something she had eaten?" I asked the housekeeper.

Mrs. Prost was a little shocked.

"Cook wouldn't be very pleased to hear that, Miss Grey."

"Well, certain things upset some people. It may be something that she just can't take."

"I don't know, I'm sure. But I reckon we ought to be watchful. She was really bad. She frightened me. I was glad you were here . . . Mr. Lestrange being away."

She told me it was a different household from what it used to be. "When the Riebeecks were here . . . my goodness. You had to be all right and proper then, I can tell you."

"You must know this house very well, Mrs. Prost."

"I was here before I was married. Then my husband and I . . . we were both here together. He was a butler and I was a housemaid when we met . . . and I stayed on when we were married. It worked well, the pair of us . . . and then he died . . . a heart attack. Very sudden. And I stayed on."

"That all happened when the Riebeecks were here, of course."

"We never thought there'd be change. The house had been in the Riebeeck family for years . . . about two hundred, I think. Very strict they are . . . Boers . . . I know because Mr. Prost was one of them. My family came out when I was a little girl. And once you're English, you're always English, and though I married Mr. Prost I was never one of them . . . if you know what I mean."

"It must have been a great shock when the Riebeecks decided to sell the house."

"You can say that again! It was all this trouble that's been going on for ten years or more. The British and the Boers. It went badly for the British, but old Mr. Riebeeck said it wouldn't end there. There'd be more trouble and he didn't like the look of things. The British would never let things stay as they were, so he thought he'd get out while the going was good. He'd always been back and forth to Holland . . . something to do with business. He was more Dutch than anything else . . . and I suppose, getting old, he had this hankering for going home. So he just sold Riebeeck House, lock, stock and barrel."

"All the furniture and everything . . . and the Model House."

"Yes, that and all. The lot. So it's all just as it used to be as far as that goes. Well, Mr. Lestrange, he'd just got married to Margarete Van Der Vroon."

"So you were here when all that happened!"

"Of course I was. I can tell you there was quite a stir in the town when Jacob Van Der Vroon found that diamond. They reckoned it was one of the biggest finds, not only in Kimberley but in the whole of South Africa."

"Did you know the Van Der Vroons?"

"No . . . not really. I didn't know any of the miners. They lived in one of those places near the mine . . . more like huts than houses. No, I can't say I knew them. What a find, though! The whole town was buzzing with it. They were nothing and then overnight . . ."

"Paul was quite a child then. I was surprised to hear he was not Mr. Lestrange's son."

"Oh, Mr. Lestrange is such a *good* man. He tries to be a father to that boy. He's put up with quite a lot from him. When I think of all he's done for that boy . . ."

"Poor Paul. He remembers his father and a child can't be expected to switch fathers just when he is told to."

"All the same, I think young Paul ought to be a little more grateful. But Mr. Lestrange makes the best of it. It was a bit of luck for Margarete Van Der Vroon that she got such a man."

"I didn't think she was very lucky. Didn't she die soon after?"

"Oh, a tragic accident, that was. Poor Mr. Lestrange. He was heartbroken. They'd only been married a year. I used to think how lucky she was. To come to a lovely house like this with a man like Mr. Lestrange as her husband. She'd never had much before, I can tell you. They bought this house soon after they married. It fitted in nicely. The Riebeecks leaving everything like . . . the house and all the furniture that went with it. A ready-made home for them, all waiting."

"I heard that."

"And Mr. Lestrange was here with his bride. It must have been an eye-opener for her . . . after living in one of those little places . . . and Paul a little boy who'd lost his father, now to have another who'd look after him. There she was . . . a frightened little thing when she found herself left a widow . . . but a widow with something worthwhile . . . this Kimberley Treasure as they call it. There were one or two after her . . . or shall I say after the diamond. Mr. Lestrange was different. He had money of his own. He just fell in love with her. I think it was because she was a poor helpless little thing. It touched him somehow . . . and that sort of thing can lead to love. The present Mrs. Lestrange is rather like that. He's a tender-hearted man, is Mr. Lestrange."

"You admire him very much."

"Anyone would who'd worked for the Riebeecks. They are as different as chalk from cheese."

"The marriage didn't last long. There was that dreadful accident."

Her voice sank to a whisper. "I think she drank . . . too much."

"Oh?"

"Mr. Lestrange was upset about that. He didn't want a slur on her memory. But I think what happened that night was that she had been drinking too much . . . she didn't see the top step . . . and down she went and killed herself."

She paused, clearly upset at the memory.

I said: "Who found her?"

"I did. I was the one. It was early morning. I just went down to see her. I'd just gone to see that everything was all right, as I did most mornings, and there she was . . . lying on the floor. All twisted up. It was a terrible shock."

"It must have been. How long had she been there?"

"Since the early hours of the morning, they said."

"And Mr. Lestrange?"

"When he woke she wasn't there. He thought she'd got up early as she sometimes did. She'd get up without him being aware. She'd go down to the garden. She loved the garden . . . then they'd meet for breakfast."

"What did you do?"

"I ran up to their room and knocked on the door. Mr. Lestrange was asleep. I went in. I couldn't stop myself. I cried out, 'It's Mrs. Lestrange. She's lying at the foot of the stairs and she looks . . . she looks . . .' He stumbled out in his dressing gown and we went together. It was just terrible. We knew she was dead. He was so shocked. All he could say was 'Margarete . . . Margarete' just like that. I've never seen a man so shocked. He was very upset he was . . . heartbroken."

"He soon married again."

"Well, there's some men who have to have a wife . . . lost without one. And the present Mrs. Lestrange . . . well, she reminds me of the first. She's gentle. Not very sure of herself . . . and very much in love with her husband. Of course, Mrs. Myra has been brought up as a lady. You couldn't really say that of the other . . . dead though she is. She wasn't exactly a lady . . . but there's something similar about them . . ."

"I think I understand what you mean."

I came away from that conversation feeling that Roger Lestrange must be a very good master to arouse such admiration and loyalty in his servants.

THERE WAS A CERTAIN TENSION in the streets. Trouble was coming. Everyone was talking of it and speculating what the outcome would be. Negotiations were ensuing between Paul Kruger and Jan Smuts on one side and Joseph Chamberlain and the

High Commissioner Sir Alfred Milner on the other. There was deadlock while we all waited for the result.

There were changes in the town. The garrison was being strengthened and one saw more and more soldiers in the streets. There were other new faces. The Afrikaners were coming into the town. I heard their voices, saw their faces . . . stern, weather-beaten, determined.

I had discovered during my brief spell in South Africa that most of the Boers were farmers, whereas the Uitlanders had settled in the towns. The latter were the people who had come to find diamonds and gold and had set up the banks and official buildings, changing the entire aspect of the place.

"It is small wonder," said Lilias, "that they will not tolerate being deprived of taking part in government."

It was in October of that year 1899—the last of the century—when the storm broke and South Africa was at war with Britain.

When school was over John Dale came to see us.

He was very concerned. "I don't know what this is going to mean," he said.

"Surely these people will not be able to stand out," replied Lilias. "They will be subdued in a week."

John was not so sure. "It's difficult terrain and the Boers are familiar with it. Moreover it is not easy to fight so far away from home."

"We shall have the men."

"There are not so many British forces here now."

"More will surely be sent. Why, ten thousand came not so long ago."

"We shall have superior arms, of course, and well trained men. The Boers are only farmers . . . part-time soldiers, but remember they are fighting on territory they know, and which they regard as theirs. I have an uneasy feeling that it is not going to be as easy as some seem to think." He looked from Lilias to me, the anxiety in his eyes obvious. "It was all going so well," he said ruefully. "But perhaps you should not have come."

Lilias smiled at him. "I don't regret it," she said. "I never shall."

He returned her smile rather sadly, I thought. Then he said: "The town is already different. It's full of strangers. They are getting ready to take it over when the time comes."

"It would not be for long," said Lilias.

"What difference will it make to us?" I asked.

"I don't know. We shall be regarded as the enemy, perhaps."

"Most of the people in the town are what they call Uitlanders."

John lifted his shoulders. "We shall have to see," he said.

We attempted to go on with our lives as we normally did. But we were all so uncertain and when news began to filter through of the Boers' triumphs over the British our hopes for an early end of the war deserted us.

Roger Lestrange, John Dale and most able-bodied men joined the garrison, for it looked as though it might be necessary to defend the town. The Boers might be farmers, unaccustomed to urban life, but they were shrewd and would recognise the importance of a prosperous town such as Kimberley. They would surely attempt to capture it.

It was early November, approaching the height of summer in South Africa, and the weather was almost unbearably hot.

Myra seemed to be growing weaker. She admitted to me that she had periodic bouts of illness.

"I feel quite weak," she said. "I don't feel any·desire to eat. Of course, if there is a siege we shall all have to go short of things, I suppose."

"I expect so," I replied. "But in the meantime we are trying to keep everything normal. The children are coming to school and life goes on."

One afternoon I went to Riebeeck House and I found Myra in a state verging on hysteria.

I went to her bedroom. She and Roger had separate rooms now. She had told me that she preferred it because she was worried about being restless in the night.

"What is it, Myra? Would you rather tell me . . . or . . ."

"I want to tell you," she said. "I'm being foolish, I think. But it really frightened me. It's uncanny."

"Yes?" I prompted.

"It was in the Model House. I know I shouldn't go there. It upsets me after I saw that other figure. But this . . . it was there. It looked so real . . . I just stared at it. What does it mean?"

"But tell me what you saw."

"It was those carved figures. It was so like . . . something that happened. You could imagine it."

"But what actually did you see?"

"It was the figure of a man cut out of wood . . . and in his hands he was holding . . ." She shivered and buried her face in her hands.

"What was he carrying, Myra? You must tell me."

"He was carrying a woman. Holding her up. Just as though he were going to throw her down the stairs."

"Oh no," I murmured.

She looked at me fearfully. "It was awful. Because she . . . Margarete had fallen down the stairs . . . I just ran away . . . screaming. I couldn't help it. It was because . . . it seemed to mean something. Roger was there. He tried to comfort me. It was some time before I could tell him what I had seen. He went there then . . . I followed him. I was afraid that the figures might not be there and it would seem that I had imagined the whole thing."

"And were they there?"

"Yes . . . he saw them."

"What . . . did he do?"

"He picked it up and broke it. He was so angry because it had upset me so much. He held it in his hand, just looking at it for a moment. Then he put it back, but it wouldn't stand up. He laid it on the top of the staircase; then he put his arm round me and took me back to my bedroom. He said some person was playing silly tricks and he was going to find out who . . . and whoever it was would no longer be a member of his household."

"And he did not find out?"

She shook her head. "Oh, he is so kind to me, Diana. He made me lie down. He said it was all nonsense . . . nothing to worry about. It was just silly and the only reason why he was so angry was because it had upset me."

"Who, do you think, would do such a thing?"

"We don't know. Roger tried to find out. He summoned all the servants to the library and he asked the one who had done it to own up. Who was it who had thought it was amusing to put figures in the Model House? That house was not to be touched by any of them . . . except those who were to dust it under the supervision of Mrs. Prost."

"Did anyone own up?"

"No one. But Roger is going to find out. He is determined to."

"Myra, why should anyone do such a thing?"

"I don't know."

"They would have to go to the trouble of carving the figures in the first place and getting up there . . ."

"I think it was someone trying to frighten me."

"With little figures like that?"

"I don't understand."

"Tell me what's in your mind, Myra. Why are you so frightened?"

"It's because of that staircase. I think someone is saying that Margarete did not fall down the stairs because she had been drinking too much . . . I think they are saying it was not an accident."

"And you wonder whether . . ."

"I sometimes feel the figures in the Model House are meant to be a warning . . ."

"Oh, Myra!"

"I'm afraid to go near that staircase. But there is a sort of compulsion to go there. It is as though someone . . . is luring me there."

"Someone?"

"It sounds silly, but strange things do happen. Roger is a very attractive man, isn't he, and I . . . well, I'm rather insignificant. It is rather miraculous that a man such as he is should want to marry me."

"He did marry you, Myra. He must have wanted to."

"I thought that Margarete might be a little . . . jealous."

"But she's dead!"

"They say that sometimes the dead return. And we are in the same house. Just imagine! She was happy here with him. She had never been happy like that before."

"Paul says they were a very happy family when his father was alive."

"But he wouldn't understand the sort of love she had for Roger. In this house I can believe the past lives on, and I think that she is there waiting to separate us . . . to lure me to my death . . ."

"Really, Myra, that's nonsense."

"I know. But I am just telling you my feelings."

"Well, she couldn't make carvings and put them in the Model House to frighten you, could she? And how is that going to lure you to fall down the stairs?"

"I go there sometimes. I stand at the top and think of her plunging down."

"Look here, Myra, you're not yourself. These attacks have been weakening you. They've given you odd dreams and fancies . . . hallucinations perhaps. You've got to get back to normal. No ghost can make you do what you don't want to, nor can it put figures in certain places. Promise me you won't go wandering round this part of the house alone."

"I promise," she said.

I was very worried about her. I talked of it to Lilias. It was a change from the perpetual topic of the war, but, to me, it was almost as alarming.

"She must be losing her mind," said Lilias in her practical way. "They used to say in the village that Myra was a little simple."

"She's not simple . . . just nervous. She has never been confident in herself. That's quite different."

"You don't think she is secretly drinking, do you?"

"I did wonder that. It could give her fancies."

"It might well. It looks to me as though that's the answer."

"But there is no doubt that the figures were there. Roger saw them."

"I must admit this is an odd business."

"You see, first there was a figure lying at the bottom of the staircase, and now these more intricate ones of a man holding a woman and preparing to throw her down."

"I can only suggest one thing."

I nodded.

"That he pushed her down the stairs."

"Or someone did."

"Well, she did have that diamond which was worth a fortune. And he had married her rather promptly. Someone may have a grudge against him."

"I wonder who?"

"Well, there are more important things to occupy us at the moment. I was wondering how long we can go on like this. They are all around us. Oh yes, we certainly have other things to think about than little carved figures."

THE NEWS which filtered in to us continued to be disquieting. The quick and easy victory expected by the British was not forthcoming.

There was an old music hall song which I remembered from my youth and at the start of the conflict it had been revived again. I had heard people singing it in Kimberley when there was talk of war.

> *We don't want to fight*
> *But by Jingo if we do*
> *We've got the men, we've got the ships*
> *We've got the money, too.*

Somehow now it had a hollow ring. The stark realities of war were different from the dreams of glory.

Depression was descending upon us. The war had started in October and December had come; so far there had been no news of any success. Rather it had been the other way.

I sensed an air of triumph among the Boers in Kimberley.

We did not communicate with them; there was suspicion between us, for how did we know who among us were not spies?

Those were difficult weeks. Several people were leaving the towns—young men who wanted to go and fight.

One day when I went to Riebeeck House I saw Njuba in the gardens.

I said to him: "Is anything wrong?" for there was a look of abject misery on his face.

"My boy . . . he gone," he said.

"Umgala!" I cried. "Where has he gone?"

"I do not know, Missee. He just gone. He not home all night."

"He can't have gone far. What could a boy like Umgala want to leave home for?"

"He good boy. No speak . . . no hear . . . but good boy."

"I know," I said. "How long has he been gone?"

"Only one night . . . one day."

"Has anyone tried to find him?"

"I ask Massa. He say we try find. But many go now . . . say Massa. Perhaps Umgala, too."

"I am sure he will come back, Njuba."

"I know . . ." He tapped his chest. "I feel here, Missee. He gone. He no come back."

I left the poor man shaking his head.

When I saw Paul he was very upset. He said: "Umgala's run away."

"His father told me he'd gone."

"Where could he go to? He can't speak. Besides, who would he fight for? Whose side would he be on?"

"He's a strange boy, Paul. He may have had some reason for going."

"I know him. He didn't want to run away."

"Well, it seems he has. There are lots of people slipping out of this town, Paul. We live in strange times."

"I wish they'd stop this silly old war."

"I am sure most people feel the same," I said.

It was the next day when Roger talked to me. I was coming to the house to see Myra when he intercepted me in the garden.

"I wanted to talk to you, D–Diana," he said. "Things're coming to a climax. The Boers are doing well. They'll be taking over the town soon."

"Surely it can't go on? There must be change soon."

"In time perhaps . . . but not yet. I wanted to tell you that I am leaving tonight."

"Leaving? For where?"

"I can't tell you that."

"You mean . . . some secret mission . . . ?"

"We need more reinforcements. The Boer commandos are getting close. We've got to get help. I'm going to see what can be done."

"So . . . you leave tonight?"

He nodded. "I want you to look after Myra. I'm so worried about her. She is really in a nervous state."

"I know."

"I wonder if you would mind staying with her some nights. You know . . . when she is not so well. With things as they are . . ."

"Of course, I will do what I can."

"I've spoken to the doctor. He thinks it's largely in the mind. She's finding it difficult to adjust. He's given her that tonic."

"It doesn't seem to be doing her much good."

"Dr. Middleburg said it would take time. This . . . er . . . upheaval has been too much for her."

"You mean . . . marriage?"

He smiled at me. "Oh no. I didn't mean that. God knows, I've done my best to make her happy. It's the strange country . . . leaving home . . . and just as we were settling down, all this blows up. Will you persuade her to go on with the tonic? I think she hasn't been taking it regularly and that is why it hasn't been as effective as we hoped. Would you see that she takes it as prescribed?"

"I'll do what I can."

"Good. I am sure this will soon be over, and we can get back to normal."

"Do you really think so?"

"Before long we shall have them on their knees. It's inevita-

ble. It's just at first that there are difficulties to overcome. The
Boers are a stubborn race; and they think they have God on
their side."

"Don't they all think that?"

"I suppose so, but there is a fervency about these commandos."

"Perhaps that is because it is their home and this is where
they live. They don't want anyone to take it from them."

"As they took it from others?"

"Oh yes, of course. Well, that was a long time ago and the
place where people have lived for generations means something special to them. To us it is a gold mine . . . a country
worthy of development . . . another jewel in the Crown of
Empire."

"You are very eloquent, but we all agree on one thing: we
want this war over so that we can return to our normal way of
life. Please . . . look after Myra for me."

"I will do everything in my power."

"Thank you. Now I can feel more at peace."

He left Kimberley that night, and two days later we were a
town under siege.

Siege

CHAOS REIGNED for the next few days. Rumours flew round the town. The Boer commandos were a mile away and advancing on us. They had decided not to take Kimberley and were surrounding the place. We did not know what to believe.

People came out into the streets and stood in little groups huddled together . . . watchful, fearful. They went into their houses . . . gathering their families together. Then the streets were deserted. It changed from hour to hour, and nobody knew what was really happening.

Then the refugees from the outlying districts came straggling into the town . . . exhausted . . . some needing medical attention as they stumbled in with more tales to tell. Soldiers from the garrison patrolled the streets. Everyone was alert for the approach of the Boers.

The town was well defended, said some.

It would never stand up to an onslaught, said others.

Under the cover of darkness several men who had managed to break through the commando forces arrived. Some of them were wounded and the hospitals were full and all the doctors of the town were working there.

Life had changed completely.

It was during those first days that, in spite of what was happening in the town, my mind was completely diverted from the uncertainty which hung over us all by the events at Riebeeck House.

A messenger came from Mrs. Prost. She was sorry to bother me at such a time when we were all so worried, but Mrs. Lestrange was very ill and she was asking for me. Could I come to the house?

I went at once.

Mrs. Prost greeted me eagerly. "She's in a terrible way," she said. "I've sent for the doctor, but he's not there. I expect he's at the hospital. I thought I'd better wait a bit . . . things being as they are. I don't know . . . she seems to me to have lost her senses."

"Take me up to her."

"Yes . . . of course. I thought I'd better warn you."

In spite of the warning I was deeply shocked. I hardly recognised Myra. Her eyes were wild, her pupils dilated. She stared up when she saw me.

"Who are you?" she said. And then: "Oh yes . . . yes. It's Diana. Diana, send her away . . . send her away."

I looked at Mrs. Prost who nodded her head towards the window. Myra was staring straight at it.

"She sees something there," whispered Mrs. Prost.

I said: "It's all right, Myra. There is no one here except Mrs. Prost and me."

"Stay," she begged. "Don't go. Or . . . she'll come back."

I went to the bed and put my arm round her.

"You'll stay with me?" she pleaded.

"I will. Of course I'll stay."

She lay back against me and closed her eyes. She was murmuring something which I could not hear.

Mrs. Prost looked at me. "I'll leave you with her. I'll send for the doctor again. Let me know if you want me."

She went out.

Myra lay still, her eyes closed. She was breathing heavily.

She opened her eyes suddenly. "Diana," she said.

"I'm here. I'm going to stay, Myra. As long as you want me, I'll stay."

That seemed to please her. She took my hand and gripped it.

"She was there," she murmured. "She kept looking at me. She beckoned."

"Who was there?"

"Margarete," she said.

"She's dead."

"I know. She came back."

"It must have been someone else you saw."

"No. It was Margarete. She was jealous, you see. She had lost him. He was mine now. She couldn't bear it. She wanted me to die."

"Margarete is dead, Myra. And you are here."

"But I am going to die."

"Of course you are not."

"Who'll stop me?"

"I shall," I said. "I'm going to look after you."

"Roger looked after me. He was so good . . . so kind. I wasn't good enough for him, but he never showed it. I was always afraid . . ."

I said: "I know."

"He wanted me to be well. He said: 'Take your tonic. Make sure you take it. It'll do you good.' And I did. I didn't miss . . ."

Her eyes went to the little table at the side of the bed. The bottle was there. It was about half full.

"So you have been taking it regularly?"

"I promised him I would."

"He asked me to impress on you the need to take it regularly while he was away."

"He cares for me. He really does. It shows . . ."

"Well then, Myra, you are a lucky woman. And you must get better."

"I try. I do take my tonic . . . just the same as though he were here."

"I'm sure you do. Myra, suppose you try to sleep a little."

"If I sleep you'll go away . . . and if you go away she'll come back."

"I shall not go away and she will not come back. Myra, she isn't here. She's something you've dreamed about and she doesn't exist except in your imagination."

She shook her head and I saw a tear seep out of her closed eyes.

"Try to sleep," I said.

"Promise to stay."

"I will. I shall be here when you wake."

She smiled and I was surprised that she was soon asleep.

I studied her face. It was pale and drawn. She was very different from the young woman I had first seen in Lakemere. True, she had been reserved, uncertain, overawed by her authoritative mother, but how different from the poor haunted creature in this bed.

She was gripping my hand and I was getting a pins and needles sensation in it; I managed to release it without waking her.

I went to the window and looked out. How peaceful it seemed. It looked just as it had when I had first seen it. It was hard to believe there was so much change all around us.

What would happen to us within the next few months? I wondered. I thought of the great sieges of the past which I had heard of. The Siege of Orleans, when Joan of Arc had taken the city and brought it back to the French, putting new heart into them; the Siege of Paris which was not so very long ago. What was it like living under siege? Food grew short, of course. There would be no means of getting new supplies. People died of hunger. I had heard that some of them had been reduced to eating dogs and rats. The thought was nauseating. This was different. We were being besieged by a handful of commandos . . . guerrilla troops, not trained for fighting . . . farmers, most of them. They could not last long against the trained British Army. We should be relieved very soon.

And Myra. Poor Myra. She had been happy. She had married a most attractive man; she had come to a new country; and now she was in this state. She had not believed that such happiness as she envisaged with Roger Lestrange could ever have been hers. She had not thought herself worthy of him. Her mother had made her feel her inferiority. Poor Myra, who was accepted because she was an Ellington . . . and because she had a fortune of her own.

I went back to the bed and looked down on her sleeping face.

A light tap on the door startled me. I moved too quickly and in doing so overturned the small bedside table. I tried to grasp the bottle, but it was too late. Myra's tonic was running over the carpet surrounded by specks of glass.

Mrs. Prost came into the room.

"Look what's happened," I said.

"Oh dear. I'll send someone to clear it up. It's Mrs. Lestrange's tonic, isn't it?"

"Yes, I'm afraid so. We shall have to get some more. I thought perhaps you'd brought the doctor."

"There's no hope of getting him just yet. The doctors are so busy at the hospital. A little party of men managed to get through last night and some of them are badly wounded. We'll try again later. How is she?"

"She's sleeping."

"Poor lady." Mrs. Prost shook her head.

"I'm terribly sorry about the mess," I said. "It was careless of me. And then there's the tonic . . ."

"Never mind. It's just the tonic. The doctor will give her some more though . . . when we get hold of him."

"I hope she'll be all right without it for a little while."

"Oh, it won't be for long. I daresay we'll be able to get that. Even if he can't come . . . he can give her that. These are terrible times. You'll be staying here for a while, I expect, Miss Grey."

"I promised I would. Could you send someone over to the

schoolhouse to explain to Miss Milne that I may be here for a few days?"

"I'll certainly do that and I'll send someone up to clear that mess. I don't like broken glass lying about."

"I do hope she'll be able to get some more soon."

"That'll be all right, I'm sure. We'll do our best anyway. Can't do more than that."

I stayed with Myra all through the day. She slept a great deal of the time, and as soon as she opened her eyes she looked for me. I saw the relief when she was assured that I was still there.

"I feel safe," she said. "She can't do anything when you're there . . . because you can't see her and you don't believe she's there, do you? She's only there in my mind. That's it, isn't it?"

"Yes," I said. "That's it."

"Then please stay."

"I have promised I will."

"All night?"

"Yes. I shall be here. I have sent a note to Lilias."

That comforted her.

I spent the night in her room, sitting in a chair by the bed, dozing fitfully. Her looks had alarmed me so much that I wondered whether she would live through the night.

I was relieved when the dawn came and I looked at her in the clear morning light.

She was breathing more easily and she seemed more peaceful.

Mrs. Prost brought me coffee and bread and butter.

"Not very much," she apologised. "But we have to go carefully. I don't know what things are coming to. How is she?"

"She's had a quiet night."

"She's better when you're here. I'll send something up for her if she wants it. She's been turning away from food. A nice bit of porridge would be good for her. There are some oats left. Goodness knows when we'll get the next."

"I'll let you know when she wakes and we'll see if we can get her to eat something."

"And I'll send someone to see if we can get hold of that doctor. She'll need her medicine."

"Oh yes. It was careless of me."

"Accidents will happen. Well, let me know when she wakes."

She left me. The coffee and food tasted good. I thought: we are beginning to appreciate food now that we realise we may not have it for much longer.

It was about ten o'clock when Myra awoke. I had determined to be there when she did and I was glad, for her eyes alighted on me immediately, and she said: "Oh, Diana. I'm so glad you are here."

"How are you? You've had a good night's sleep."

"Is it morning then?"

"Yes, ten o'clock."

"I've slept all through the night!"

"That's rare, is it?"

"I usually wake and see things . . ."

"Well, you didn't last night. I've been here all the time."

"What? Sitting there?"

"It was nothing. The armchair is very comfortable. I dozed for hours. I just wanted to be here if you awakened."

"Oh, Diana, I am lucky to have such a friend."

"I have a confession to make. I knocked over your tonic. I'm afraid I've spilt the lot. It made such a mess on the floor. Be careful where you tread. They've taken it up, but little splinters of glass can be dangerous."

"The tonic!" she said. "I was supposed to take it last night."

"I hope we shall be able to get hold of the doctor today. We have tried already, but apparently the doctors are all in the hospital. I hope you aren't going to miss the tonic too much."

"Roger made me promise to take it."

"I know. He had great faith in it. But don't worry. I daresay the doctor will be here today and then we shall get some more."

During the day she seemed a little better. She was talking quite reasonably and there were no more hallucinations.

I stayed with her all during the day and the doctor did not come. Mrs. Prost suggested that on the following night I should use the room immediately next to hers so that if she needed me in the night all she had to do was knock.

"You can't have two nights sitting in a chair," she added.

To my surprise Myra agreed with this.

The room I slept in, I realised, was the one Roger used. It was not quite so large as the one he had shared with Myra and which she now occupied alone. The bed was comfortable and there was a bureau by the window. I did not sleep very well. I was waiting for a tap on the wall.

I was glad when the morning came. I went immediately to Myra's room. She was sleeping peacefully; the stick with which she was going to tap on the wall was in the same position as I had left it last night.

During the morning she seemed almost like her old self; I was delighted. And in the afternoon the doctor called. Mrs. Prost and I were with Myra while he examined her.

Afterwards he sat in the drawing room and talked to us both.

He was full of apologies for not having come earlier.

"There is chaos in the hospital," he said. "People are still creeping through the enemy's lines . . . if you can call them lines. It can't be much longer, I'm sure. Now, for the time being, there is nothing to worry about with Mrs. Lestrange. I don't know what happened to her. But she is going to be all right. She's weak . . . but her heart's all right and so are her lungs. Well, everything is. Might have been poisoned by some insect or other. There are some venomous ones here, as you know, Mrs. Prost . . . and they like a bit of new blood. They go for the newcomer. And I think some of the old-timers become immune. She needs building up."

"She has had hallucinations," I said.

"That could well be. I haven't been out here all that time myself. I am sure newcomers react more rapidly to these poisonous things. She needs some good red meat. It's a pity things are as they are."

"By the way, Dr. Middleburg, I had an accident and knocked over the tonic you gave her. She needs more."

"She shall have it."

"We were worried about her missing it."

"Oh no. It was only a mild pick-me-up. I think she might go on with it. If you could send someone round, I'll give you some more."

I felt very relieved when he left us, and so did Mrs. Prost.

That afternoon one of the servants collected the tonic and I said we should not leave it on the side table again. There was a little cupboard in the room and I put it in that.

I spent another night at Riebeeck House and in the morning was delighted to see that Myra's improvement had continued.

I went back to the schoolhouse and promised I would call the following day.

That was a grim time. No food could be brought in and stores had to be guarded. Military law prevailed and we did not know what our fate would be from one day to the next.

Lilias made an effort to carry on as normal at the school, but not all the pupils came. John Dale continued to be a frequent visitor.

"He's a wonderful friend to us," said Lilias more than once. He was very eager to protect and often smuggled special items of food into the schoolhouse.

Soldiers now and then broke through the commandos who were surrounding the town. That usually happened after dark. They brought us news and we learned that we were not the only town under siege. Ladysmith and Mafeking were in a similar plight.

The situation was growing more and more alarming. The easy victory expected by the British was even longer delayed. They were learning something of the difficulties of fighting in a strange land far away from home in a terrain unknown to them, while the enemy were fully aware of all its hazards.

"Ninian was right," I said. "We should have gone home."

"I shouldn't have wanted that," replied Lilias, and John Dale, who happened to be there at the time, smiled at her; it occurred to me that the feeling between them was strong and growing stronger, as such feelings will in a situation such as we were in.

Of course *she* wanted to be here. But what of myself? I wished I had gone home, no matter what I should have to face there, because then I could have seen Ninian. When one is close to death—and how could we know at that time what would happen to us?—one faces up to the truth. I had been halfway to falling in love with Ninian. It was only my affair with Jamie which had made me cautious.

Yes, I should have liked to be home with Ninian.

And here I was in a besieged city, only half aware of what was going on around me, never knowing from one moment to another when violent conflict was going to break out.

It was no use denying it. I did wish I had gone home. It was not because I was afraid of this war, but simply because I should be near Ninian.

I WAS GLAD that the schoolhouse was close to Riebeeck House. One could not walk short distances without being stopped by soldiers. They were everywhere. A watchful eye was kept on the commandos who encircled the town and every now and then one heard the sound of gunfire. Soldiers patrolled the town and no one ventured out after dark.

Christmas was with us. How nostalgic I felt, and so, I am sure, did countless others, for the Christmasses at home: the Yule logs in the grate, perhaps the snow falling outside . . . the security. How different was this!

And here we were in a strange land, so different from our own, in a city besieged by an enemy who could at any time come in and force our garrison to surrender.

Lilias and I would sit on the little stoop and talk. Dragonflies and insects whose names we did not know flew around us. Even the evenings, when the sun had dropped out of sight, were hot. I was homesick for the rain and Ninian. I dreamed of a life wherein I had met Ninian at some other time and place than at my trial; I dreamed that everything was as it had been when my mother was alive. I imagined Ninian had been brought to the house by one of our Edinburgh friends and love had grown between us. Zillah was not in that dream, of course. She belonged to the nightmare life which I was trying to pretend had never existed.

Foolish dreams! But Ninian had cared about me. His last

letter had been urgent. "Come home." Would he have written so if he had not cared a little?

Then reality would creep in. I remembered how he had turned his attention to Zillah.

"We ought to try to do something for Christmas," Lilias said.

"Such as?" I asked.

"Give the children some sort of party. Say on Christmas Eve."

"Give them a feast? Goose? Turkey? Delicate chestnut stuffing? Plum pudding to follow? I do not think, Lilias, that those items are on the rations this week."

"I wish we could give them a party, though. Play games . . . that sort of thing."

"We could play the games, I suppose. And that is about all. We're in the wrong place for feasting."

"Nevertheless, I think we should try something. Perhaps they could all bring their own food."

"Surely not! Where would they get it?"

"From their allowance."

"I don't think it would amount to much. Has it occurred to you, Lilias, that food is getting more and more scarce?"

"Well, I suppose that is the way with sieges."

Lilias was determined. A few children still came to school, though the numbers were dwindling. Paul was one of those who came. Lilias was determined to act as though there was nothing to worry about. She told the children we should soon be relieved. The Queen and her soldiers would never allow us to remain in this state. One of the glories of being under the protection of the British flag was that it flew over almost the whole of the world. She pointed out the red sections on the map. "It is the Empire on which the sun never sets," she told them, "for when it is nighttime in England it is daytime in some part of the world which belongs to our great Empire."

She spoke with such fervour and passion that every child believed that we should be rescued before long, and some, I am sure, expected the Queen herself to appear at the head of her soldiers.

Paul was very enthusiastic about the Christmas party. He

suggested some games we might play. Lilias told all the children who still came to school that they must let the others know there was to be a party on Christmas Eve and they must all come if they could.

On the twenty-third of December, Paul came to school in a state of great excitement. He was carrying a large can and when he took off the lid he revealed four fair-sized fish.

"It's for the party," he said. "We can give them a feast after all."

"Where did you get them?" asked Lilias.

"In the Falls," he said. "In our grounds."

"I didn't know there were fish there," said Lilias.

"I was walking past and I saw the fish leap over the Falls and I thought, that would be good to eat. So I went back and got a rod and things . . . and I caught these."

"What a find!" cried Lilias. "It's Providence. Paul, you are going to make our Christmas feast possible!"

"We can make some bread. We have a little flour," I suggested.

"The loaves and fishes," said Lilias. "This is truly a miracle."

The party was a great success. Most of the children came. Anna Schreiner was absent. Her father said that Christmas was not a time for feasting and making merry but for prayer. Poor little Anna! I did not think she would have much to rejoice about this Christmas.

However, we cooked the fish. There was not a great deal of it. But it was different. We were able to make lemonade and, if the children were not overfed, at least they were able to play games.

The story of the fishes spread through the town. Food! And discovered in the stream which ran through the grounds of Riebeeck House! People took their rods and went down to the stream.

I do not think there were any great catches, but even a little was welcome.

• • • •

WE HAD MOVED INTO JANUARY. Little had changed except that
food had become more scarce and there were no means of getting fresh supplies. Hopes for early relief were fading.

Myra had made a surprise recovery. She was still weak and
nervous, but there were no more hallucinations. She was even
surprised that she could ever have believed in them.

I made a point of being there when the doctor visited her
again, because I was anxious to hear what he had to say.

I sensed that he thought she was a rather hysterical woman
who had found it difficult to adjust to a new country, especially
in the prevailing circumstances. He was growing more and
more certain that she had been poisoned by some insect. Her
symptoms could have been due to a form of poisoning; and she
had reacted badly in view of her state of health. However, the
trouble was over now and she was getting better every day. All
she needed was to eat good food—not very easy in the circumstances—but the main thing was to stop worrying about herself. Then all would be well.

"You must make sure that your mosquito net is secure at
night. Avoid those places where you know there are insects. I
really don't think there will be any need for me to visit you
again."

It was good news.

It must have been about a week after the doctor's visit. I was
on my way to her and, as I approached the house, I knew that
something disastrous had happened. There was a great deal of
shouting from the servants who seemed everywhere. They
were gabbling together. I could not understand their language,
although I had picked up a word or two.

When I discovered what had happened I felt sick with shock.

Mrs. Prost, who was in the garden, saw me and came up. She
told me what had happened. It seemed that one of the boys,
fishing near the Falls that afternoon, had discovered the body
of the little deaf-mute in the water. The boy had immediately
gone to tell Njuba.

"He's been there ever since . . . just kneeling, staring into
the water. It's terrible. That poor child."

"How could it have happened?" I asked.

"We wondered at the time," said Mrs. Prost. "You remember how he disappeared. We thought he'd run away . . . and to think all that time he was lying there . . . dead."

That afternoon stands out clearly in my mind. Whenever I smell the frangipani blossom I remember it vividly. I can see Njuba kneeling there on the bank. I have never witnessed such abject misery. When the men came to take the body away he was still there. Then he stood up, his hands clenched. He cried out: "This my boy. Someone kill him I will not forget."

Luban took his hand and led him back to their rondavel and we heard lamentations all through that day.

It was true that the boy had been murdered. There was sufficient evidence to prove that he had been strangled even though he had been so long in the water.

"Who could have done this to a little boy?" demanded Myra.

"And why?" I asked.

"What terrible times we live in. Do you think it has anything to do with the war?"

"I don't know. What harm could he do to either side?"

It was a mystery and for a few days people talked of little else. It was all, who did it? and why? That was a question no one could answer.

But when there was so much about which to be concerned, the mysterious death of a little native boy did not seem so very significant.

LIFE MUST NECESSARILY become more difficult as time passed. We knew we were all in acute danger. With the arrival of each day we wondered whether this would be the one when the Boers attacked the town. But the garrison had been strengthened just before the siege began; there were soldiers everywhere; it would be no light task and the battle would be fierce.

Lilias was as strong and practical as ever; and because of her growing friendship with John Dale, I did not feel that I was deserting her because I was so frequently at Riebeeck House. Myra needed my company more than she did.

I was getting to know Paul better. He was a pleasant boy and I sensed he rather enjoyed the dangers of living in a besieged town. Danger to him meant excitement, which was preferable to dull ordinary living. He was learning to shoot, as many boys of his age were, but, of course, they lacked live ammunition, which was hoarded in case it should be needed for real battle.

I seemed to have become part of the household at Riebeeck House because I was so often there.

Mrs. Prost's attitude towards me puzzled me a little. I was never quite certain of how she regarded me. There were times when I thought I was welcome and she was quite fond of me. At others she seemed to be regarding me with something like suspicion. This surprised me a little, for I should have said she was a predictable woman, with fixed ideas from which she would find it difficult to swerve.

She had an affectionate contempt for Myra. Nobody could dislike Myra. She was always thoughtful to the servants and never behaved with the slightest arrogance. She was as different from her mother as one person could be from another. She was gentle, inoffensive and likable.

I understood Mrs. Prost's feelings towards her, but in my case her attitude seemed to sway between confiding friendship and a strange aloofness.

I discovered the reason for this one day and it was a great shock to me.

Myra was lying down, as she did most days, for she still tired easily, and Mrs. Prost asked me if I would go along to her sitting room.

I did so and when I was seated there I thought her manner decidedly strange. It was almost as though she were forcing herself to perform some unpleasant duty.

At length it came.

"I've been meaning to talk to you for some time, Miss Grey," she said. "It's been on my mind and I couldn't decide what to do for the best."

"Is it about Mrs. Lestrange?"

She pursed her lips and frowned.

"Well, it's not really . . . although I suppose you could say she might be concerned."

"Please tell me."

She rose and went to a little chest in the corner of the room. She opened a drawer and took a handkerchief which she handed to me.

To my amazement I recognised it as one of mine. It had been given to me by my mother with six others. They all had my initials embroidered in a corner. I looked down at the *D* and *G* attractively entwined. Davina Glentyre. I flushed slightly, for into my mind had flashed a picture of Zillah. "It's safe to use the same initials." How right she was.

"It's yours, isn't it, Miss Grey?"

"Oh yes, it is. Where did you find it?"

"Well, that's what upset me a bit. I've been meaning to talk to you for some time. You see, you've been so good to Mrs. Lestrange and I know she's really fond of you. But when I found that . . ."

"I don't know what you mean?"

"I think you do, Miss Grey. Cast your mind back. It was the day . . . right back, you know. It was one of the times when you spent the night in this house. I found the handkerchief under the master's bed."

"What? How did it get there?"

I was flushing hotly while she looked at me, gently shaking her head.

"Now," she went on, "I'm not one of these people who thinks everybody ought to live like monks and nuns when they're not. I know these things can happen . . . men being men. But it's different somehow with a woman."

I stood up indignantly. "What are you implying, Mrs. Prost?"

"Now sit down, Miss Grey. I'm not exactly blaming you. The master is a very attractive man. He's a kind man, but even kind men find their fancy straying, and it's not in men's nature to control that sort of thing. It's different with a woman. She's got to be a bit more careful."

"What you are saying is absurd."

She nodded her head. "I know, I know. The temptation comes and I must say he is a very good-looking man and he's got all the charm you could wish for. And I know things are

not . . . well, what they might be with him and Mrs. Lestrange. Separate rooms and all that. But I just thought you
ought to be careful. I just happened to glance under the bed to
see if it had been swept. It hadn't . . . and there was this
handkerchief."

"I have no idea how it came to be there."

"Well, I thought I'd better warn you. When he comes back
. . . and you being in and out of the house . . . and all that
. . . just like family."

"You have no need to worry about that, Mrs. Prost. There
has never been anything of an intimate nature between Mr.
Lestrange and me."

"I guessed you'd take it like this. That's why I didn't say
anything before. I'm not what you might call a prude. I
thought it might have been just a slipup. These things happen.
I'm not saying it's very nice . . . but there it is."

"I must insist . . ." I began.

"Well, I've said my say. It's not my affair, but I think it could
lead to trouble."

"I keep telling you there's nothing . . . nothing . . ."

"Oh, I suppose it got in there somehow. You never know, do
you? But there it was . . . and I wouldn't have liked anyone
else to have found it."

I stood up, still clutching the handkerchief. "Mrs. Prost," I
said, "I assure you that I had never been in that room until the
night I slept there when Mrs. Lestrange was so ill and Mr.
Lestrange had gone away."

"Then if you say so, dear, that's all right with me. I just
thought I ought to mention it . . . because when he comes
back . . . well, it wouldn't be very nice, would it, for you or
him or Mrs. Lestrange?"

"I see," I said, "that you do not believe me."

"Look. We're good friends. That's why I told you . . . warning you like. These things can cause a lot of trouble."

"But I keep telling you . . ."

"All right," she said. "I've said my say and that's an end of
the matter."

But was it an end of the matter? Mrs. Prost believed that I

visited Roger Lestrange in his bedroom. I felt as though I
wanted to run out of that house and never come back again.

As soon as I entered the schoolroom Lilias knew that something had happened.

"What's wrong?" she said.

I was silent for a few seconds, then I burst out: "I never want
to go to that house again."

"Riebeeck? What's happened?"

"Mrs. Prost . . . she believes I have had a . . . relationship
. . . with Roger Lestrange."

"A relationship?"

"She found a handkerchief under his bed. It was the morning
after I had stayed in the house when he was there, too. She
drew conclusions."

Lilias stared at me.

I said: "You don't think . . . ?"

"Of course not."

"It's horrible, Lilias. She seems to think he is irresistible. It
was awful. She kept saying she understood. I think that was the
worst thing. And I think when she showed me the handkerchief I looked . . . guilty. It was one my mother had given me.
It had my initials on it. And for the moment it took me right
back. I had thought it best not to change my initials . . .
whereas if I had changed them, she wouldn't have known the
handkerchief was mine."

"Wait a minute," said Lilias calmly. "There's not much tea
left, but this is the occasion to use it."

Sitting talking to Lilias was a comfort.

"Do you think," she said, "that someone put the handkerchief there?"

"Who? and why?"

"Someone who wanted to suggest that you had spent a night
there."

"Not Mrs. Prost."

"No. There doesn't seem much point in that. But suppose
someone put it there for her to find."

"It might have been someone else who found it."

"Perhaps that wouldn't have mattered."

"What are you thinking, Lilias?"

"I don't quite know. But someone in that house might have wanted to suggest that you and Roger Lestrange were lovers."

"But why?"

"That's all part of the mystery. How could your handkerchief have got into a room in which you had never been at that time, unless someone had taken it there?"

She was frowning and I said: "What are you thinking, Lilias?"

"I am not sure. Myra was there . . ."

"She was not well. That was the reason why I stayed."

"She was a little strange, wasn't she? Imagining things? Perhaps she wanted to prove something against her husband and you."

"She is devoted to him and I think he is to her."

"But she was seeing visions. Or did that come later? I'm just letting my thoughts run on. The fact remains that the handkerchief was there. It had to be put there. Then who . . . and more to the point . . . why?"

"I feel I never want to go into that house again."

"If you don't it might look as though you are guilty."

"How could I tell Myra?"

"Stay away for a while and see how you feel. Something may occur to you. A handkerchief! It's strange what trouble such insignificant objects can cause. Think of Desdemona. But try not to brood too much on it. I think there's enough for another cup in the pot. We mustn't waste the precious stuff."

We had come to no conclusion, but it was, as always, a comfort talking to Lilias.

THERE WAS A FEELING of desperation in the town. We knew that something had to happen soon. There was no actual talk of surrender, but the thought was in the air. No matter how strong the spirit, people could not live without food.

Nothing was coming in now. All through that stiflingly hot January we waited for news. We would hear the sound of sporadic gunfire which seemed to be getting closer. Occasionally a shell hit the town and there were casualties. We lived with the thought that at any time we could be among them. All through those hot days death hovered over us. Familiarity made it easier to live with. I suppose we accepted it and it ceased to be uppermost in our minds.

All the same it seemed almost incongruous at such a time to be upset because a suggestion had been made about me; but it was constantly in my mind. Images suggested by Mrs. Prost's conclusions kept recurring and there was always the mystery as to who could have put my handkerchief in such a place. It could only be that someone wanted to prove something against me.

Lilias, with whom I talked again of the matter, said I was making too much of it.

"You've suffered a great shock," she said, "and you must be on guard against allowing yourself to imagine some evil fate is working against you."

I knew that she was right when she said I was haunted by the past. I had hoped to escape it by leaving England. I knew as well as she did that there was no hope of a peaceful life for me until I had cut myself away from what had happened.

"Innocence should be your shield against all that," said Lilias. "You know you were innocent. I knew I was innocent when I was accused. It helps. I've told John about the affair of the necklace and he agrees with me."

She was right, of course. I had to be reasonable. The handkerchief must have been caught up in something and got carried into that room. It seemed implausible, but strange things did happen.

After a few days I began to feel a little better about the affair, but I had no desire to go back to Riebeeck House.

Myra came to the schoolhouse. She was looking much better now. Her cure had been quite miraculous and she had lost most of her nervousness.

She looked at me in some consternation.

"You haven't been to see me."

"Well . . . there's been a lot to do here."

She looked surprised, but did not ask what.

"We missed you," she went on. "Mrs. Prost was quite upset."

And so she should be, I thought. It is because of her that I've stayed away. All the same I was glad she had mentioned what was in her mind. I would rather know than have her continue with her speculations.

"She thought you might have been offended about something. I told her that was nonsense. But I thought I'd come to see you. Is everything all right?"

"Hardly all right, Myra. Things are getting worse. We shall all be starving soon."

"Yes, I know. And someone was killed last night . . . near the church."

"It's unsafe to be in the streets."

"It's unsafe to be anywhere, so one might as well be in one place as another. I wonder when it is all going to end. Oh, Diana, I wonder about Roger. Where can he be?"

"He didn't say, did he? Well, he couldn't, of course. It was some mission from the garrison . . . to let people know what was happening in the town, I suppose, and get help if possible."

"I pray he is all right. It's awful that he's not here now that I am so much better. He couldn't understand what was wrong with me. He used to worry so much. And to think it was that wretched insect. Who would have thought little things like that could do so much harm? We've had rather an upset at Riebeeck. It's poor old Njuba."

"It was so terrible about the boy."

"If it had been an accident it would have been different . . . though that would have been terrible enough. But to think he was strangled and someone had deliberately killed him . . ."

"Who could have done that, Myra, to a helpless little boy?"

"It's a mystery. If it wasn't for the siege there would have been an enquiry, I suppose. But now nobody thinks of anything but how long we can hold out."

"That is understandable."

"What I was going to tell you was that poor Njuba is acting strangely. He just wanders about, muttering to himself. He got into the house and was found going in and out of the rooms

. . . as though he were looking for something. Mrs. Prost found him turning out cupboards. She asked what he wanted and he wouldn't tell her. She didn't know what to do. She sent for Luban to take him home. It's very sad. Poor Luban. She's lost her son and her husband seems as though he is losing his wits. What terrible things happen, Diana!"

"Yes," I replied. "That's true."

"Please come and see me."

"It is just as easy for you to come here."

"Yes, but there is more room at the house and the gardens are nice."

"All right. I'll come."

Lilias was pleased when I told her. "It's the best thing. Mrs. Prost would think she had been right if you stayed away. You can convince her how wrong she was, I'm sure."

"But *I* am not sure about that," I replied. "I think she has made up her mind that her beloved master is irresistible, and she exonerates him absolutely; and she doesn't take too stern a view of me because he is the man in the case."

FEBRUARY HAD COME. We were living on small rations. When we awoke in the mornings we wondered what the day would bring. This state of affairs could not continue. Something had to happen soon.

There were constant outbreaks of gunfire; it had ceased to be sporadic and was normal now. One night a party of three men arrived in the town, having broken through the forces surrounding us; one of them was wounded.

There was jubilation in the streets next morning. People stood about talking with an animation which I had not seen for some time. We should not give up hope yet. The British were advancing. They had suffered a major defeat at Spion Kop, but after that things had changed. Ammunition had been pouring into the country. Two names were mentioned with awe: Major General Horatio Herbert Kitchener and Field Marshal Sir Frederick Sleigh Roberts. They were marching on and were coming to our relief.

New hope was springing up everywhere. People were saying

that it was not possible for the great British Empire to be beaten by a handful of farmers. The British now had the measure of the land. "We've got the men, we've got the ships and we've got the money, too."

Hope was a great reviver. People were smiling in the streets. "It won't be long. Kitchener and Roberts are on the way."

I went to Riebeeck House. Lilias was right. To stay away could imply that Mrs. Prost's suspicions were correct. All the same I did not like staying in the house. I often suggested to Myra that we sit in the gardens. In any case, they were beautiful. The scent of the flowers, the murmur of insects suggested peace . . . even in these troubled times. Sometimes we walked.

We went along past the waterfall where poor Umgala's body had been found and on as far as the rondavels.

I do not know what impulse led me to that particular rondavel. It was a little apart from the others and it looked as though it were falling into decay. The grass grew tall about it. There was a hole in the thatched roof.

"That would have been repaired, I daresay, if all this hadn't happened," said Myra.

"Who is supposed to keep them in order?"

"The natives. They are their homes. They look after them themselves."

Something urged me to go forward and as I did so a small boy darted up to us. He smiled, his teeth dazzlingly white against his dark skin.

"Whose home is this?" Myra asked him.

His smile disappeared. He looked furtively over his shoulder. "No one live here, Missee. Devil man there."

"Devil man?" I said.

"Bad place. Missee no go."

"It's only one of the rondavels that has been left to decay. That's what's wrong with it."

"Old man live there. He die. No one want place. It bad. Umgala . . . he not know. He go . . . he like. He always there. He die . . ."

The mention of Umgala startled me. I wanted to go into the rondavel.

"Let's just take a look," I said, and started forward.

"No . . . no, Missee." The boy was really alarmed. "Bad place. Big snakes in grass. Devil's snakes. They wait . . . to catch . . ."

"We'll be careful," I said, and I went forward.

Myra said: "Perhaps we'd better not . . ."

But I was already making my cautious way through the long grass.

I reached the door, lifted the latch and went in. There was a buzzing noise and a huge insect, which looked like an enormous dragonfly, cruised across the rondavel and settled on a small bench.

"Let's go!" said Myra. "We don't want to get stung."

But something held me there. Under the bench was a rough drawer and below it on the earth floor I noticed wood shavings and splinters of wood.

I went across the room. The insect was still perched on the bench. Keeping my eyes on it I opened the drawer. I had to shake it to get it open and when I did so I saw several carved figures, among them that one which I had seen lying at the bottom of the staircase in the Model House.

I turned to Myra who was standing in the doorway.

"Come away!" she cried. "I don't like this."

I said slowly: "That boy . . . he said Umgala came here . . . no one else did. He was often here . . . before he was murdered."

Myra said: "I'm going. It's horrible here . . ."

I followed her. She was already pushing her way through the long grass.

"Myra," I said. "Myra, it was Umgala . . ."

At that moment we saw the snake. It had risen and was close to us. It hissed ominously. It had been lurking in the grass.

Evading it, I ran after Myra. I think we were lucky in seeing it in time.

We had reached the clearing. We stopped, panting. I turned to look behind us. There was no sign of the snake.

Myra was trembling. I put an arm round her. "It's all right now," I said. "It's back there in the grass." And all I could think of was: Umgala made the figures . . . and Umgala was murdered. This was a momentous discovery. I was bemused, bewildered. Ideas were jostling each other in my mind. I felt I must not mention my discovery to Myra. I wanted to talk it over with Lilias first.

Myra was clinging to me.

"It was awful . . . that horrible thing in the grass. It was waiting there for us . . . while we were in that place . . . it was there in the grass . . . waiting for us. I didn't want to go there. I knew there was something dreadful about it. I hate these places. Diana, I want to go home."

I knew that by "home" she did not mean Riebeeck. She wanted to be in Lakemere.

"You'll feel better after a rest," I said, calming her and myself at the same time. But I was not really thinking of her but of that boy who was the carver of the figures and who had died because of them.

Mrs. Prost was coming across the lawn.

"Oh, good afternoon, Miss Grey. Mrs. Lestrange, you look as if you've seen a ghost."

"We've seen a snake," I said.

"Nasty beggars."

"It was close to us," said Myra. "It was lurking in the grass. It hissed at us."

"What sort of snake?"

"I don't know. It was big. We just thought of getting away."

"Quite right, too."

She came with us into the house.

"A nice cup of tea's what's wanted now," she said. "There's none left. It's come to a pretty pass when you can't have a cup of tea when you want one."

I wanted to get away. I desperately wanted to talk to Lilias.

"You ought to have a lie down, Mrs. Lestrange," said Mrs. Prost. "You look all shaken up."

"I think that's a good idea, Myra."

She agreed. So I said goodbye to her and prepared to leave. But as I came out of her room Mrs. Prost was waiting for me.

"There is something I ought to say to you, Miss Grey," she said.

I hesitated. Was she going to apologise for what she had suggested on our last meeting?

"Come into my room," she said.

So I went.

Mrs. Prost looked embarrassed and I began to feel uneasy, suddenly fearful of what she would reveal next.

She said: "I ought to have told you before. I couldn't bring myself to. But I've got fond of you . . . and I couldn't believe it and yet there it was."

"Yes?" I said faintly.

"I . . . er . . . know who you really are."

"What . . . do you mean?"

"You're Miss Davina Glentyre."

I gripped the sides of my chair. I felt sick and dizzy. That which I had never ceased to dread had come to pass.

She was looking at me steadily.

"How . . . did you know?" I asked.

She rose and went to a drawer—the same one from which, on that other occasion, she had taken the handkerchief. She brought out two newspaper cuttings and gave them to me. The headlines stared back at me.

"Guilty or Not Guilty? Miss Davina Glentyre in Court. Dean of Faculty Addresses Jury."

I could not read the print. It danced before my eyes. All I could see was those damning headlines.

"How long have you known?" I asked, and I thought at once: what does it matter how long? She knows now.

"Oh . . . for some time."

"How?"

"Well, it came about in a funny way. I was dusting Mr. Lestrange's room and he came in. He was one to have a little chat . . . always the gentleman . . . never making you feel small like. I said, 'I won't be a minute, sir. I always like to do your room myself, to make sure everything's all right.' He said,

'You're very good, Mrs. Prost. I've just come in to get some papers. Don't let me stop you.' He went to his desk there and took out some papers, and as he did so these fluttered to the floor. I picked them up. I couldn't help seeing them."

"He had them in his drawer? Then . . ."

She nodded, and went on: "He said, 'You've seen these cuttings now, Mrs. Prost. So I think you and I should have a little chat. Sit down.' So I sat and he said: 'You recognise the young lady?' I said, 'Yes, it's her that calls herself Miss Grey.' He said, 'She was most unfortunate. I believe in her innocence. She was definitely not guilty of killing her father. You couldn't believe that of her, could you, Mrs. Prost? Not a nice charming young lady like Miss Grey.' I said: 'No, I couldn't, sir, but . . .' Then he said: 'She's come out here to start a new life. I want to help her, Mrs. Prost. Will you, too?' I said, 'Well, I'm ready to do what you say, sir.' 'Take these papers,' he said. 'Put them away somewhere. Just hide them. I shouldn't leave them about. The servants . . . you know . . . one of them might find them. Just take them and make sure no one sees them. I want you to help me rehabilitate Miss Grey. I like her. I like her very much. She is a young lady who deserves another chance.' Then he gave me these cuttings."

"Why did he give them to you? Why did he want you to keep them?"

"He didn't say. And I thought I'd better, since he'd said."

She took them from me and put them back in the drawer.

"Nobody comes in here," she said, "unless I invite them. I do my own room. He's quite right. They're safer here with me than they are with him."

"But why should you want to keep them?"

"I don't know. I just feel I ought to . . . as he said. He might want them back. But what I wanted to say to you was that I knew. I suppose Mrs. Lestrange doesn't?"

I shook my head.

"Well, it's only the master and me."

I was feeling ill. I just wanted to get away. First the shock of what I had discovered in the rondavel and now, immediately afterwards, this which had temporarily driven all else from my mind.

I said: "What are you going to do?"

"I'm not going to do anything. But I thought you'd understand me better if I told you I knew. I could see Mr. Lestrange was very fond of you. After all, he's gone out of his way to help you, hasn't he? Didn't he let you know about the school? That's why you're here. Your secret's safe with me. It's some time since I knew. It was just before Mr. Lestrange left, of course. When he comes back I shall tell him I've told you. I shall say it was only right and proper that I should. Now look, don't you worry. Mr. Lestrange doesn't believe you did that terrible thing . . . and nor do I. Nice girls don't go round murdering people . . . especially their own fathers. He took it himself. Men are like that . . . and him with a young wife. It's easy to see . . . and that's what they thought it was, didn't they, because they let you off. So don't you worry. I'll go on calling you Miss Grey though you're not. But you couldn't very well use the other, could you?"

I wished that she would stop. I stood up.

I said: "I'm going now, Mrs. Prost."

"All right. But don't worry. I just thought that you ought to know that I know and I didn't hold it against you. You just have to be careful, that's all. I understand. I'm the sort of person who can put myself in other people's place. I was young myself once. But you don't want trouble."

"If you don't mind, I'll go."

"Get a nice rest. I know this has been a bit of a shock . . . but it's safe with me. So don't you fret."

I hurried back to the schoolhouse. At the sight of me Lilias knew something was wrong.

"What news?" she said. "There's been a lot of activity out there. Something's going to break soon."

"Lilias, I've had a terrible shock. Mrs. Prost . . ."

"Oh, not on again about that handkerchief!"

"No. She knows who I am. She has cuttings . . . newspaper cuttings of the case. She knows what happened in Edinburgh."

"No! How?"

"Roger Lestrange had them. He gave them to her. So he knew . . . and now she knows. You see, there was no escape. You can't run away from a thing like that."

"Let's get this straight. She told you, did she, that *he* gave her these cuttings?"

"She was dusting the room. He went to get something out of a drawer and they fell out. She picked them up for him . . . and saw."

"Rather fortuitous, wasn't it?"

"It sounded accidental, the way she told it. She rushed to pick them up. She couldn't help seeing. There was a picture of me. He realised that she had seen. He said he believed in my innocence and wanted to help me."

"So he kept the cuttings and dropped them at her feet?"

"He gave her the cuttings, he said, because he thought they might fall into the hands of one of the servants."

"What's wrong with a nice bit of fire?"

"I don't know why they had to be kept. But she has them. She *knows*, Lilias. She says she believes in my innocence and wants to help me as he does. Oh, Lilias, I wish I had never seen Roger Lestrange. I wish I'd never come here."

"I am wondering what this means. Why should he have let her see those cuttings? Why should he have given them to her . . . to keep? What does it mean?"

"I don't know."

"I don't like it."

"Oh . . . and something else has happened. I'd forgotten in all this. I've found out who did those carvings and put them in the Model House. It was Umgala . . . the little deaf-mute who was murdered."

"What?"

"There is one of the rondavels which is empty. Someone died there, and you know how superstitious these people can be? It's a little apart from the others and quite dilapidated. One of the boys warned us about going there and told us that Umgala used to go there often . . . and he was unlucky. He was murdered. The boy seemed to think it was because he had gone to that place. I went in and saw the wood shavings on the floor. I opened a drawer and there was one of the figures. The one I'd seen in the Model House."

She was looking at me incredulously.

"And you think he was murdered because he did those figures and put them in that place?"

"Oh, Lilias, I'm beginning to think all sorts of things."

"The figures were significant."

"Oh yes. There was one lying at the bottom of the stairs. I didn't see the others . . . the ones which upset Myra so much. It was a man holding a woman and it was set at the top of the staircase. Myra said it was placed so that it looked as though the male figure was throwing the female down."

"It would seem that Umgala saw this happen. He couldn't speak . . . so he tried to explain in some other way."

"Yes, he was trying to convey something . . . that it was no accident. Margarete Lestrange had not fallen down the stairs accidentally. She had been deliberately pushed . . . murdered, in fact."

"And that was why the boy died. Someone did not like those figures."

"Roger Lestrange did not like them. He was furious when he found them. Though he gave the impression that it was because it had upset Myra."

"And soon after that the boy disappeared."

"Do you think that he . . . murdered his first wife . . . and would have murdered Myra? She has been so much better since he has gone. She is almost recovered. She began to get better after I broke the bottle by her bedside. Was she being poisoned . . . not by an unspecified insect . . . but by her husband through the tonic? It's a terrible situation. Did he murder his first wife and was he trying to remove his second?"

"That's a theory," said Lilias slowly. "He had reasons, didn't he?"

"His first wife had the big diamond . . . the Kimberley Treasure. He bought Riebeeck with her money . . . and then she died. He came to England looking for a wife . . . one with money . . . one who was docile and unassuming. You see, Myra fitted exactly what he wanted."

"Are we running on too fast? Was it as simple as that? And following on those lines, I see another aspect of the case. Why was he interested in you?"

"Was he?"

"Certainly he was. That was obvious."

"True, he paid for the cabin."

"What?"

"I never told you. I knew you'd hate it. The cabin we had at first was the one we had paid for. There was no mistake. He paid the difference. That was why we went to a better one."

"What a fool I was!" said Lilias. "I might have known. Why didn't you tell me?"

"I didn't know until we were almost at Cape Town, and then it was too late. We couldn't have gone back. I thought you would be upset about the money . . . so I decided to accept graciously."

"I shall pay him back," said Lilias. "But that is not the point now. That's for later. I am trying to make sense of this. That handkerchief story. Found under his bed the day after the night you spent in the house. What if he put it there? And the newspaper cuttings . . . fluttering onto the floor. A likely story! He *wanted* her to see them. And why should he give them to her? She was to keep them. Why? Oh, Davina, I don't like this. I think you could be in danger."

"How?"

"Don't you see? His first wife died in mysterious circumstances."

"Did she? She fell down the stairs . . . after she had been drinking."

"There may have been suspicions. She had inherited this diamond and she had died soon after their marriage. Then he married again—an acquiescent woman, rather like the first; she also has money. She is being slowly poisoned. Now he may be clever and get away with the second, as he did with the first . . . but suppose he doesn't? He'd want an escape route. And there is a woman who has been accused of poisoning her own father who was threatening to cut her out of his will. She is tried for his murder and suspicion still hangs over her as the verdict is Not Proven. She comes to the house; the housekeeper finds her handkerchief under the bed. A little indiscretion perhaps . . . but indiscretion is not murder. She is interested in the handsome master of the house, but he has a wife already. Once she was on trial for the murder of someone who stood in her way. Suppose she were really guilty? Might she not try the same method again? I know this is a wild supposition. He could hope to succeed and then you would not be necessary. But if he did not . . . well then, he has his scapegoat. Oh, Davina, I may be romancing . . . but this could just be the truth!"

"How can you think of such terrible things!"

"Because I'm being practical. I'm being hard-headed. I'm trying to get a clear picture. I am asking myself why this, why that? And I'm putting the worst construction on every thing just to see whether it fits . . . and it could, Davina. It could."

"I'm frightened, Lilias. I couldn't go through all that again. So much of it fits. He has always made me feel a little uneasy. And now . . . now I feel he was there right from the first . . . like that snake in the grass . . . waiting for the moment to strike . . . lurking there . . . laying the snare . . . because of what had happened to me. Thank God he went away. I can even thank God for the siege. If he had stayed . . . oh, I can't bear to think of it! Lilias, if this is true, when he comes back he will expect to find Myra dead."

"Perhaps he won't come back . . . perhaps we shall never know. How do we know what is happening all over the country? People die in wars. Where did he go? We do not know. He was on some secret business, he implied, did he not? How could one know with a man like that? But if he comes back . . . perhaps we shall know more."

"He can hardly come back while we are in siege."

"Then we shall never know the truth."

"What shall we do, Lilias?"

"We can only wait and see. But I tell you one thing. When he comes . . . if he comes . . . we shall be prepared."

We sat up late that night, talking, for we knew neither of us would sleep. We went over and over everything that seemed significant.

I could not really believe that he had helped to bring me out here because he planned to murder his wife and wanted a scapegoat, should the need arise.

Lilias said: "It might not have been deliberately planned. Such things often are not. Perhaps in the first place he really wanted to help you. He must have discovered early on that you were Davina Glentyre."

"I remember there was an occasion . . . you were there. We had been visiting Mrs. Ellington and I fell while mounting my horse. Kitty was there. She called out my name."

"I remember. That would have been enough."

"It's an unusual name. It might have started a train of thought in him. He has certainly been very friendly. He was so anxious that I should go to the house to be with Myra. Then there are the handkerchief and the cuttings . . ."

"We can go over and over it, Davina, and still we shall not be sure. Let's wait and see what happens when he returns. Perhaps we shall learn more."

And so we talked.

WE DID NOT HAVE TO WAIT very long. We knew the Army was closing in. Between it and the town were the Boer commandos, and what hope had a group of wartime fighters, fresh from their farms, in conflict with trained soldiers?

How could Kruger and Smuts stand up to Kitchener and Roberts . . . and the British Army? The breakthrough was inevitable. It would be any day now. We were waiting for them. And at last they came.

It seemed that every man, woman and child was in the streets. We were out there to greet them as they came in and their welcome was tumultuous. People were embracing and kissing each other.

"It's over. They're here. We always knew they'd come . . ."

It seemed as though it was worth living through a siege because it was so wonderful when it was over.

Mafeking. Ladysmith. They were now free.

"Good old Bobs. Good old Kitchener," cried the people.

We were all carried along on the wings of victory during those days.

THE RELIEF OF KIMBERLEY was such an exhilarating experience that, in spite of all that had so recently happened to me, I was caught up in the rejoicing. But the terrible realisation of what evil might have been hovering over me was never far from my mind.

After the first days had passed, after we had grown accustomed to having the Army in town, to food arriving, to feasting, to singing "God Save the Queen," I became haunted by the thought that now Roger Lestrange would come back. And then . . . what? What could I say to him? I could not accuse him of attempting to poison his wife and devising a devious plot to implicate me. I could not say to him, "Myra started to recover as soon as she stopped taking the tonic which you insisted on her having." What could I say of the handkerchief and the cuttings? It was, as Lilias had pointed out, nothing but theory even though it did seem a plausible one.

But I did not have to speak to Roger Lestrange again.

Four days after the relief of the town he returned.

I never knew what he said or thought when he came back and saw Myra alive and well, for on the night of his return he was shot dead by someone who was waiting for him in the gardens of Riebeeck House.

The news travelled quickly and John Dale came to the schoolhouse to tell us about it.

"Who killed him?" I asked.

"Nobody knows as yet. They suspect one of the servants who has been acting strangely for a long time."

Lilias and I were certain that Njuba had shot him because he had discovered that Roger Lestrange was the murderer of his son.

I said: "Poor Myra. She will be distraught. I must go to see her."

"I'll come with you," said Lilias.

There was chaos at Riebeeck House. Roger Lestrange's body had been laid in one of the rooms. Myra was weeping bitterly.

Mrs. Prost was present. When she saw me she looked relieved.

"I'm glad you're here," she said. "There's no comforting her. To think he came home for this."

They found Njuba in the gardens. He seemed bewildered and his eyes were wild.

"He's mad," said Lilias. "Poor man. It's turned his brain."

"What will happen to him?" I whispered.

"It's murder," said Lilias, "whichever way you look at it. It may be rough justice, but it's murder."

Njuba kept murmuring: "He killed my son." He held up a button. "This . . . in my son's hand. It from his coat. I find. He killed my son. Held fast . . . in my son's hand. Still there . . . when I find him."

They took him away.

So there was proof that Roger Lestrange had killed the poor little deaf-mute. It could only have been because he knew the secret of Margarete's death and, because he could not explain in words, was doing so by using the figures he carved. If Roger Lestrange could kill his wife . . . if he could kill a small boy . . . the theory of his idea of shifting the blame to me did not seem so implausible, particularly as we were now certain that he had paved the way with the handkerchief and the cuttings. He had meant to snare me . . . so that I should be there if the need arose. Serpent-like he had waited for the moment to strike.

Poor Luban was half crazy with grief. We all tried to comfort her. Myra helped with this. Luban had lost a son and was about to lose her husband; but Myra had also lost a husband. It seemed ironical that she had so loved a man who was callously plotting to kill her while at the same time he set out to enchant her. But I think that by helping Luban she found some solace for her own grief.

The sequel to the story amazed everyone when, the following day, Piet Schreiner made an announcement in the chapel.

He stood in the pulpit facing the congregation. The chapel was full of those who were there to give thanks to God for the relief of the town.

"This is the justice of the Lord," cried Piet Schreiner. "I killed Roger Lestrange. He deserved to die. He was a sinner. He seduced the woman I married and deserted her. I married her to save her family from shame and to give the child a name. God directed me to do such and I will always obey the Lord. Now He has directed me to destroy this despoiler of virgins, this fornicator, this evil liver, who now stands before his Maker. He will be judged for what he is, and the fires of Hell await him. The man Njuba has been wrongly accused. He had murder in his heart. He had his reasons. I and I alone destroyed this wicked sinner. I am the messenger of the Lord, and now that my work is done, I take my leave of this world and go to that place of glory which awaits me."

The congregation listened spellbound to this peroration. And when it was over, Piet Schreiner took up a gun and shot himself.

THE RELIEF OF KIMBERLEY did not mean that the war was over, and the euphoria began to evaporate fairly soon. The comfort of being able to walk about the streets without fear of sudden death and the fact that food was not growing more and more scarce had ceased to be such a great delight to us. The country was still in the throes of war, and a victory here and there was not going to deter the Boers. They were a persistent people. Not unaccustomed to hardship, they believed they were fighting for their homeland and were determined to hold out.

They were fully aware that their army was inferior to that of the British, but that did not prevent their forming into guerrilla bands which attacked the British Army quarters and the lines of communication which were essential to bringing the war to a conclusion.

So the expected peace was delayed.

However, our siege was over; we tried to return to normal life as far as possible and the pupils came back to school.

I went to Riebeeck House frequently, in spite of the fact that I had to meet Mrs. Prost which was an embarrassment to me. She had been deeply distressed by the death of Roger Lestrange. The revelation that the dead boy had been clutching a button from one of his coats had shocked everyone profoundly. Njuba had taken the coat and it was unmistakable evidence. Then there was the accusation that he was the father of Greta Schreiner's child. Roger Lestrange had been a hero in Mrs. Prost's eyes and no doubt she would want to think that another man had been the father of Greta's child. But she could hardly condone the murder of a helpless child.

As for Myra, she was prostrate for some days after the death of her husband, but gradually she began to rouse herself. She took Njuba and Luban under her care. Njuba was very ill and in danger of losing his mind. I was amazed at the manner in which she and Luban helped each other at that time. Paul was with her a great deal. He had been fond of Umgala. He told me afterwards that the boy had been trying to tell him something, but he could not discover what, and Umgala must have tried to do so through the figures. If he had been quicker to comprehend there would not have been any need for Umgala to make the figures and, presumably, be caught putting them in the Model House, and so meet his death.

Both he and Myra had need of each other at that time.

I used to lie in bed at night going over the dramatic events of the last months, and I would brood on our conjecture that Roger Lestrange had planned to use me. There was little doubt in my mind that he had planned to murder Myra and he would have succeeded but for the turn of events, for if the town had not been besieged he would have been able to come back and complete his work.

I would let my mind run on and imagine Mrs. Prost perhaps going into Myra's room and finding her dead . . . poisoned by some insect. But would there have been an enquiry? Would they have discovered that the tonic was poisoned? And if her husband was suspected . . . he would produce his trump card . . . all ready to play. Diana Grey was in fact Davina Glentyre. She had been with the deceased a great deal during that time when she was taking the tonic. She had stayed in the house. A handkerchief was found under Mr. Lestrange's bed which suggested that she was a visitor to his room. Mr. Lestrange had helped her a great deal. Did she have hopes of marriage? In which case there was a motive and Davina Glentyre had stood trial for the murder of her father who had once stood in her way.

I would sweat with fear . . . imagining the courtroom. The only difference would be that this one would be in Kimberley instead of Edinburgh. But it did not happen, I kept telling myself. You were saved from that . . . by the war. But I could not stop thinking of what might have been.

I said to myself, you were in danger . . . because of what happened before. There is no escape from the past. It has followed you here. He brought you here because of it. He planned to murder her and if necessary shift the blame to you, but now he cannot harm you. But people know of the past. There is no escape from it.

We had news now of what was going on. Johannesburg and Pretoria were now in the hands of the British, but de Wet and de la Rey, with their bands of commandos, were harrying the Army everywhere. Kitchener was growing impatient with the Boers who would not accept defeat. He was following a scorched earth policy, setting fire to those farms which he believed harboured guerrillas; he was setting up concentration camps in which he imprisoned any suspects. But resistance continued; the Boers were as determined as ever; and the war went on.

It was afternoon. The children were leaving after their lessons and Lilias and I were putting the books away when there was a knock on the door.

I went to open it. A man was standing there. I stared at him. I thought I must be dreaming.

He said: "This must be something of a surprise."

"Ninian!" I cried.

Lilias had come out. She was as dumbfounded as I was.

"Is it really . . . ?" she stammered.

As he stepped into the hall, I felt an overwhelming joy take possession of me.

HE SAT IN THE LITTLE ROOM near the schoolroom and told us how difficult it had been to get here.

"All the formalities . . . all the ships carrying troops. I managed, though . . . pleading an important case for a very special client."

"A client? Then . . ."

"*You* are the client," he said.

Lilias made us a meal. She would not allow me to help.

She guessed, as I did, that Ninian wanted to be alone with me. But I was still bewildered, marvelling at the fact that he was here.

I sensed that he had important things to say to me but was waiting for the appropriate moment, and Lilias announced the food was ready. She apologised for its simplicity.

"We are no longer in siege, but things are still a little difficult."

We talked about the siege and the news of the war. Ninian thought it could not last much longer. The Boers were outnumbered. If it had not been for the difficulties of the terrain they would not have had a chance in the first place . . . and so on.

I was aware of his impatience . . . which I shared. I wanted to know what it was which had made him undertake such a journey in wartime.

Lilias was very perceptive and as soon as the meal was over she said she had to go and see John Dale. Would we forgive her if she went?

As soon as she had gone, Ninian said: "I know she is in your confidence and that you are great friends, but I did feel that what I have to say is for you alone."

"I want so much to hear," I told him.

"You know I was very uneasy about your coming out here, and when I heard that Lestrange had paid for the cabin and befriended you . . . and that you were seeing a great deal of his wife who was very ill . . . I began to get more and more disturbed."

"You know that he is dead?"

"Dead?" He looked at me blankly and I explained.

He put his hand to his head. "Then you are safe," he said.

"That explains so much. I was right. Oh, what a lucky escape you have had!"

"Tell me what you know."

"It's damning against him. I thought I recognised his face, but it didn't come to me until after you'd sailed. I just could not remember where I had seen that face before. The fact of the matter is that the man was a murderer . . . the worst sort. Not the man who kills in the heat of passion . . . or from sense of injustice . . . but in cold blood . . . for the lust for money. He killed two women whom he married for their money, and was planning this third crime . . . Myra Ellington. How is she?"

"She is well now. She has been very ill. But Roger Lestrange went away before the siege and was unable to get back." I explained about the tonic.

He breathed deeply. "Thank God that you broke the bottle, or it might have been too late. Let me tell you more of this man. The reason I was suspicious about him was that there was a case in Australia. It came to my notice because there was a lawsuit about money. It brought out one of the finer points of law, and as you know, we keep records of that sort of thing. A man named George Manton went out to Australia from England. There he married a wealthy young heiress and within nine months of the marriage she was dead through drowning. Her fortune passed to her husband of a few months: George Manton. It appeared that some years after his wife's death, the heiress's father had travelled to England. His daughter was then four years old. While he was in England he married again; the marriage was unsuccessful and the couple agreed to part— the husband returning to Australia, the wife remaining in England. But there was a son of that marriage and this son in due course claimed his share of his father's fortune. The case was tried out in both the English and Australian courts; and during it a picture of George Manton was published. That is when I saw it. But it was not until after you had left that I remembered the case and looked up the relevant papers. When I heard that Myra was ill I was very alarmed. You remember, I wrote to you, telling you you must come home."

"I thought that was because war was imminent."

"It was . . . but there was this as well . . . and there was another reason."

"What was that?"

"A personal one. I will talk to you about that later. I had a strong feeling that you might be in acute danger."

"Lilias and I have thought that I might have been. But tell me first about this wife in Australia."

"In your letter you mentioned that he had had a wife who died through falling down stairs. It was too much of a coincidence. One wife drowned in Australia shortly after marriage, another falling down the stairs, and the third . . . very ill . . . doubtless being poisoned. He was varying in his methods. And then . . . he had taken great pains to get you out here."

I told him about the handkerchief and Mrs. Prost.

He was shocked. "I don't think there can be any doubt," he said. "What an escape!"

"I believe he killed a little native boy who must have seen him push his wife down the stairs. The child was both deaf and dumb. He was often in the house. Nobody took much notice of him. His mother worked there. He made carved figures which he put in the Model House. I must tell you about that. I discovered it in one of the dilapidated rondavels where I saw wood chippings. Roger Lestrange must have found out the boy did them. Perhaps he caught him in the house . . . putting that figure there. Then he would have guessed that the boy knew something. It is all falling into place and it is horrible."

"You should never have come here, Davina."

"I know now."

"I cannot forgive myself for introducing you to that Society."

"It seemed a good idea at the time and we might have gone to Australia or America which was what we planned in the beginning."

"As soon as I had suggested it I was furious with myself. But you wanted to get away."

"I thought it was the answer. I now know that there is no safe escape. As you see . . ."

He nodded.

"I tried to get out here before."

"You have come all this way . . . ?"

He smiled at me. "Yes, I have come all this way. It is miraculous that everything turned out as it did. It could have been so different."

"I am sure he was going to suggest that I hoped to marry him and therefore removed his wife."

"He was probably hoping that he would get away with it, as he had on two other occasions. Perhaps he thought that the second time in the same house might have aroused suspicions . . . even though he had used different methods. It seems reasonable to suppose it was a good idea to have you standing by, as an escape route for him, if anything went wrong. He would, of course, have hoped that it would not have been necessary to use you in that way, as the less fuss the better. But he wanted you at hand just in case you should be necessary."

"It is so cold-bloodedly calculated."

"He *was* calculating . . . cold-bloodedly so. How thankful I am that he was not able to carry out his diabolical schemes. He lived violently. It was rough justice that he should die so."

"Two people had marked him down for death: the father of the murdered boy was so upset because someone killed him before he could."

"But we should be rejoicing, Davina. I could have come too late to save you."

"I don't think I could have gone through all that again. The court . . . the dock. It is the terrible stigma that I find so hard to bear."

He stood up and came to me. He drew me to my feet and put his arms about me. On impulse I clung to him.

"Thank you, Ninian," I said. "Thank you for coming."

"I could not forget you," he told me. "You haunted me. That verdict. Not Proven. They should have known you could not have done it."

"The evidence was there against me."

"That woman, Ellen Farley. They never found her, you know. She just disappeared. Why should she have disappeared?

She could have come forward. Heaven knows, we tried hard enough to find her. Her evidence would have been so important."

"I can't forget that you came all this way."

"I felt a letter was not enough. I asked you to come home before. I knew it would be difficult to come, because of the war. But here I am."

"And that personal reason you were going to tell me?"

"I realised after you'd gone what it meant for me not to see you again. I knew then that I was in love with you."

"You . . . in love with me?"

"Couldn't you guess?"

"I knew you had taken a special interest in my case . . . but advocates have to be interested in their cases. I thought you were rather taken with my stepmother."

He smiled. "The enchanting Zillah!" he murmured. "I had a feeling that she knew more than she let us know. It was due to her that we got the verdict we did. She was a vital witness. But I still felt there was more. I wanted to find out what. That was why I cultivated her acquaintance. What I wanted more than anything was to get to the truth. I know what it feels like to come out of the courts Not Proven."

"Well, thank you, Ninian. You have been wonderful to me. You have helped me so much."

He shook his head.

"I have not done enough," he said. "I should have shown my devotion to you. I want you to know exactly how I feel. I love you and want you to come back to Scotland with me."

I stared at him in amazement.

"I want you to marry me," he added.

I thought I must have misunderstood.

"I have been hoping that you might care for me," he went on.

I was silent. I was too deeply moved for speech. I had longed to be with him. I remembered how his interest in Zillah had hurt me. When I had seen him standing at the door I could not believe my eyes. I could not get used to the idea that he had come all this way to see me.

Did I care for him? I had always cared for him. He it was who had drawn me from the slough of despond, who had sustained me with his determination to defend me. When I had left England, as I thought never to see him again, my desolation had been so deep that I had forced myself not to admit it. I had insisted to myself that my depression was due to the fact that I was leaving my native land. But it was not that so much as leaving Ninian.

I said: "I have never forgotten you."

He took my hands and kissed them. "In time," he said, "you could care for me."

"I don't need time," I told him. "I care for you now. The moment when I opened the door and saw you there was the happiest in my life."

He looked suddenly radiant. "Then you will come back . . . now. You will marry me . . . ?"

"Go back with you . . . to Edinburgh? You can't mean that!"

"But I do. It is the reason why I came here . . . to take you back with me. I intend that we shall never be parted again."

"You haven't thought of this seriously."

"Davina, for weeks I have thought of little else."

"But have you considered what this would mean?"

"I have considered it."

"You, a rising figure in law, married to someone who has been tried for murder . . . the case Not Proven . . ."

"Believe me, I have considered all that."

"It would be very bad for your career."

"To be with you will be the best thing that ever happened to me."

"I should have expected you to show more calm common sense."

"I am doing so. I know what I want and I am doing my best to get it."

"Oh, Ninian, how foolish you are, and how I love you for your folly! But it could not be. I should go back to Edinburgh . . . the place where it all happened. How could I? Everyone knows me there. It is bad enough here to be aware that Mrs.

Prost knows who I am. But back there . . . they would all know. And if you married me . . . it would all be brought back. They would suspect me, Ninian. We have to face the truth. There will always be those who believe that I killed my father. It would ruin your career."

"If I couldn't stand up to that I don't deserve much of a career."

"I should prevent your rising. I could not do it, Ninian. But I shall never forget that you asked me."

He took me by the shoulders and shook me gently.

"Stop talking nonsense. We're going to do it. We're going to defy them all. I know that you love me . . . and I love you. That is at the root of the matter. The rest . . . well, we'll deal with that when the time comes."

"I couldn't let you. It's wonderful . . . it's quixotic . . . it's noble . . ."

He laughed. "It indulges my own wishes. I want to marry you. I shall never be happy again if you refuse me. Listen, Davina, there will be difficulties. I know that. There may be unpleasantness now and then. But we shall be together. We'll face it together . . . whatever it is. I want that, Davina, more than anything in the world. I cannot explain to you what these last months have been like for me. All the time I have been thinking of you in this place . . . here . . . under siege. It was more than I could endure. And then I learned about Roger Lestrange . . . I thought of his efforts to get you here. I could not imagine what his motives were. I had to come out here . . . I had to see you . . . I had to explain my feelings . . . and now I am not letting you go again. I am going to be with you for the rest of my life."

"It is wonderful to contemplate," I said sadly. "But it cannot be . . . I know . . ."

"You do not know. Whatever there is to face, it is better for us to face it together."

"But there is no need for you to face it at all. You should go back to Edinburgh . . . carry on your successful career . . . become Lord Justice . . ."

"Without you? Certainly not. I am going to sweep away all your excuses."

"But you know they are . . . sensible."

"Maybe, in some respects. But we are talking about love. Now, Davina, will you marry me?"

"I want to say yes . . . more than anything I want to."

"Then that is enough."

So I gave myself up to dreaming.

Lilias returned with John Dale. There had to be introductions and explanations. There was a great deal of talk about the war and the feeling about it home in Britain.

Ninian said there were some enthusiastic and some dissenting voices. But there was always great rejoicing at the victories; and Kitchener and Roberts were the heroes of the day. He explained the difficulties of travel in wartime and how he had been trying some time to get a passage.

The men left together—John Dale to his home and Ninian to his hotel. He said he would see me tomorrow morning. There was a great deal to discuss.

When they had gone Lilias looked at me questioningly.

"That was a surprise," she said. "He's come out here to see a client. What does that mean? He's come out here to see you, hasn't he?"

"Yes," I said. "He has confirmed a great deal of what we thought about Roger Lestrange. He had another wife in Australia who died by drowning."

Lilias stared at me.

"And," I went on, "I think our theory about what my role was to be in his scheme was the correct one."

She closed her eyes and clenched her hands together.

"What an escape!" she murmured. "So Ninian found this out."

"Yes, there was some court case over his first wife's money and Ninian had some records."

"So he thought you might be in danger. It was a long way to come. I suppose he thought he'd defend you . . . if necessary."

"He has asked me to marry him."

"I see. And . . . ?"

"How could I accept? How could I go back to Edinburgh
. . . his wife? It would ruin his career."

"Well?"

"Lilias, how could I accept?"

"He's asked you. My goodness, he's come right here to tell
you this. That gives you some idea of the depth of his feelings,
doesn't it?"

"Yes," I said happily. "It does. But all the same, I can't accept."

"Yes, you can," she said. "And you will."

How COULD I HELP this feeling of intense happiness which had
gripped me? I could not suppress my true feelings. I was
happy. Ninian loved me. He had come all this way at this most
difficult time because he feared I was in danger.

What could I do? I could never escape from my past . . .
nor would Ninian, if he shared it. He knew this. None could
know it better. And yet he chose it . . . it was what he
wanted.

So I was going home.

Ninian was making plans. We were to be married in Kimberley. Then we would travel home together as husband and wife.

There was no point in delay. The journey home might be
long and difficult. We should have to get to Cape Town and
wait for a ship. But we knew where we were going and it did
not matter as long as we were together.

I had wondered about leaving Lilias, but everything seemed
to be working out neatly. With one wedding in view it seemed
only natural that there should be another. I had known for a
long time that there had been a special relationship between
Lilias and John Dale. He asked her to marry him—and how
delighted I was when I heard the news.

There would be two marriages on the same day which would
be appropriate as we had come out together.

Myra was sad at the prospect of my going. She did not know
everything about her husband. We did not speak of him. The
murder of the deaf-mute was revealing, for there was the indis-
putable evidence of the button from one of Roger Lestrange's

coats to prove the case against him. Umgala had obviously witnessed the crime and was attempting to reveal what he knew—
so he had had to die. And now Roger himself was dead and
Myra was no longer a wife. She had been fascinated completely
by her husband—but at the same time she had been fearful of
him. She could not be aware that she had come close to death
herself.

But we did not speak of it. She had been bemused and bewildered, but gradually she seemed to realise that she must start a
new life. Strangely enough she turned to Paul. Together they
made Njuba their concern. They looked after him and Luban
and it brought them close together.

I had thought she might want to come back with me and for
a time I think she considered doing so. But as her new relationship with Paul began to ripen they both decided that he would
be better if he stayed in his native land; and she decided to stay
with him.

So Ninian and I were married, and in due course we were
able to set sail for England.

Edinburgh

Proven

I HAD NEVER BEEN SO HAPPY in my life as I was during those first months after I became Davina Grainger. There was a tacit agreement between us that we should not think beyond the immediate future.

Ninian knew as well as I did that when we reached Edinburgh there would be certain difficulties to be faced; but for the time being we must forget about them.

This we did very successfully. We were close companions by day and passionate lovers by night. It was an idyllic existence, if one did not look ahead.

But, of course, it was impossible not to and there were moments when I thought with apprehension of what it would be like when we returned home. People would remember and, even if they had the good manners not to speak of it, it would be in their minds. We must be prepared for the little moments of unpleasantness . . . the moments of distress.

All the difficulties of travel at such a time became amusing to us because we were together. We laughed at them.

We managed to get down to Cape Town where we spent a week waiting for a ship; and when it did come, we had a wonderful voyage home. The storms at sea were fun to us; and we revelled in the long hot days when we sat on deck and talked of our good fortune in being together. But as we came nearer to home, I felt I wanted to hold back the days to make them last longer. I knew that Ninian felt the same. But there was no holding back time, but I kept reminding myself that I was going back with Ninian and that made all the difference.

We arrived in due course at Southampton, said goodbye to the friends we had made on board and spent a night in London before making the long journey to Edinburgh.

The city looked cold and unwelcoming. Ninian had lived with his parents, but now that we were married he would buy our own house. It would be near the courts for convenience. But at first we must go to his home where we should stay until we found our house.

I felt uneasy about meeting his parents, and as soon as I did I realised they did not approve of the marriage.

Mrs. Grainger was a gentle lady with greying hair and bright dark eyes. His father was not unlike Ninian himself, tall, of rather commanding appearance, with an aquiline nose and bright shrewd blue eyes.

"Ninian, how wonderful that you are back," said Mrs. Grainger. "And this is Davina . . ."

She had taken my hands and was kissing me on the cheek, then looking at me, trying to hide the fact that she was assessing me. But of course she would, I told myself. I was her new daughter-in-law. Naturally she would sum me up. I must stop thinking that when people met me they immediately asked themselves: did she or did she not kill her father?

Mr. Grainger was less inclined, or less able, to hide his feelings. His attitude towards me was cool. It was clear to me that he thought his son was foolish in marrying me.

I tried to be reasonable. Their reaction was natural. Of course, they were disappointed. Mr. Grainger, Senior, had risen high in his profession and he would wish his son to do the same; and none could realise more than I that I should be a hindrance rather than a help in his career.

Ninian assured me again and again that his parents would grow accustomed to the marriage. People always regarded their offspring as children throughout their lives. The fact was they objected to his marriage . . . not to me.

I could not expect them to be pleased that their son had married a woman who had been on trial for murder and was only free because the case had not been proved against her. What parents would? I understood them thoroughly, and I knew that the halcyon days were over.

Ninian said: "We'll soon find our house."

And I thought, we must.

Ninian's parents entertained frequently and most of their guests were connected with the law. They were all extremely well-bred and, although they would have been well acquainted with my case, they took pains not to mention anything that might lead to it. Indeed, there were times when they seemed to make studied efforts to avoid it, for they often discussed cases which were of particular interest to their profession.

But there was one occasion when an old friend and his wife, whose daughter and her husband had recently come home from India, came to dine and brought the daughter and her husband with them.

The conversation was mainly about some new statute which had recently come into force and the company was expressing views for and against it.

The young woman said: "All these laws about stuffy old cases which no one is interested in . . ."

"My dear," interrupted her father. "This matter has engendered tremendous interest throughout the profession."

She replied: "Well, *I* think it's boring. You ought to tell us about some of your more interesting cases. Murder, for instance. You must have had some of those."

Silence across the table. I found myself staring at my plate.

"I was very interested in what the Lord Chief Justice was saying," began Ninian's father.

"Like Madeleine Smith," went on the young woman. "Do you remember that case? Oh, it was ages ago. She got off . . . though I'm sure she did it. Not Proven, they said. Is it true that they have that verdict only in the Scottish courts? They say she went to the United States of America to start a new life. It's the only thing she could have done really . . ."

I felt the embarrassment round the table. The girl who had spoken was, I supposed, the only one who did not know who I was.

The subject was immediately changed. She looked bewildered. It must have been clear to her that she had said something indiscreet. I was sure that afterwards she would be told who was present.

I felt very upset about that. When we were alone, Ninian tried to comfort me. But it was not easy.

"You should never have married me," I said. "This sort of thing should never have happened to you. You have been drawn into it. And it will go on for ever. It will be there all our lives."

"No . . . no . . . people will forget."

"She didn't forget Madeleine Smith and that must be nearly fifty years ago."

"That was a notorious case."

"So was mine, Ninian."

"We'll get our own house."

"People will still talk."

"If only we were not here . . . in the city."

"It would be the same wherever I was. I couldn't escape in Kimberley."

Ninian tried to shrug it off, but I could see that he was as upset as I was.

I suppose that was why he decided on the house the very next day.

It was a pleasant house in one of the squares of grey stone houses. We were close to Princes Street and, in spite of everything there to remind me, I could still find pleasure in it. I passed the garden and thought of Jamie, and Zillah who had found us there.

When we told Ninian's parents that we had found a house which would suit us, they could not hide their relief; and I felt that the shadow which was overhanging my life was spoiling Ninian's, too.

The house was not very far from my father's, where I had spent my childhood, where the terrible tragedy had happened. I could not bring myself to call on Zillah, which would have meant going back there. I wondered if the Kirkwells and the Vospers were still there; and I asked myself if Zillah would have heard that I was in Edinburgh.

We moved into the house and I felt a little better. Shortly afterwards I discovered that I was pregnant.

That made a great deal of difference. I stopped brooding and ceased to think that everyone was remembering. My joy was intense; so was Ninian's. Even his parents softened towards me. They were delighted at the prospect of a grandchild.

One day I received a note. It came by hand. It looked like Zillah's handwriting, but it was slightly less bold than it used to be; and when I opened it I found that it was from her.

My dear Davina,

I believe that you have reverted to your true name now, and I hear that you are in Edinburgh. My dear child, why did you not come to see me?

Things have not gone very well with me. I am wretchedly ill. It smote me suddenly and here I am . . . more or less an invalid. I don't know how these things happen. I was hale and hearty one day and ill the next. It is very annoying. I just had a horrid cough at first, which I could not shake off. It's consumption, they tell me. It's a bore. I sometimes feel quite ill and at others my jaunty self. I make plans and then can't act on them.

Do come if you can bear with a poor invalid.

My love as always,

ZILLAH

After receiving such a note there was nothing I could do but call immediately, though I had to steel myself to do it.

Mrs. Kirkwell opened the door. I guessed she had been warned that I was coming.

"Oh, good afternoon, Mrs. Grainger," she said. "It's nice to see you again."

"Good afternoon, Mrs. Kirkwell. How are you?"

"As well as can be expected, thank you."

"And Mr. Kirkwell?"

"He's all right. And you look just the same. My word, you did get caught up in that awful place. Siege, don't they call it? You should have seen the people in the streets when we heard it was relieved. Mafeking and Ladysmith, too. Mr. Kirkwell knows all about it. He was watching for news all the time and telling us what was going on. And of course . . . you being there . . . well, we wanted to know. I couldn't get it out of my mind, our Miss Davina out there with all them savages."

"They weren't savages, Mrs. Kirkwell."

"Well, near enough . . . foreigners. And you shut up in that place . . . And I remember you when you was a little thing no higher than my knee . . . and then to be stuck in that place. Mrs. Glentyre is waiting for you."

"Is she very ill, Mrs. Kirkwell?"

"Up and down. She's right as a trivet one day. You'd never guess. Of course, she passes it off. Last person you'd have thought would get caught like that. She's that pleased you're coming to see her. I'll take you right up. That was her orders."

I went up the familiar stairs to the familiar room.

She was sitting in a chair by the window. I was amazed at the sight of her. She was so much thinner, but her hair was as bright as ever, but somehow it did not match her rather gaunt face.

I went to her and took her hands in mine.

"Oh, Davina . . . my sweet Davina. It was wonderful of you to come."

"I'd have come before if I had known."

"Just because I'm a poor old thing?"

I said: "It was difficult for me to come back here. I'm afraid I put it off."

She nodded. "So you married your Mr. Grainger. How is that going?"

"Very well."

"He was always asking questions. And then he went out and brought you home. News travels in a town like this. My word! That was something! Shows how keen he was to get you. And at one time I thought he was interested in me! But I realised it was just because he wanted to probe. He's a real old prober. I soon got his measure. But it *is* good to see you. Tell me about the awful time you must have had. Shut in like that . . . not much to eat, I suppose . . . living on what you could get." She shivered. "We heard a lot about it here, you know. I'll not forget Mafeking night in a hurry. The noise in the streets! It went on all night. And I thought of you out there. It is good to see you."

"Tell me about yourself, Zillah."

"Oh, things didn't turn out as I thought they would. I had plans. I was going to have a house in London. I was going abroad. I was going to enjoy life. All planned, it was, and then, suddenly, I got this cough. Just a nuisance at first. Then I couldn't get rid of it. The doctor shook his head and wanted examinations. So I had them and they found this. I reckon I picked it up in those draughty old digs when I was with the Jolly Red Heads."

"I'm so sorry, Zillah. It is the last thing I would have expected of you. So you have to stay quiet, do you?"

"Don't only have to, want to sometimes. I have my down days and my up days. Sometimes I feel . . . almost well. I make the most of that."

"Everything else seems more or less the same here. Mrs. Kirkwell is just as ever."

"She's like an old monument . . . she and her old man. I never forget them when I first came here. What a long time ago that seems, Davina!"

"I remember it well. I thought I had never seen anyone less like a governess than you."

"You always paid nice compliments, dear. And to think that

you once thought of becoming one! What happened about that old school?"

I told her and that Lilias was now married.

"You both found husbands. It can't be such a boring old profession, after all."

"So did you," I said.

For a moment we were both sober.

"And the servants here?" I asked.

"The girls left. There are new ones now. Only the Kirkwells stayed."

"And the Vospers?"

"They're not here. I've got Baines now. Baines and Mrs. In the mews, of course. She helps in the house; he's a good steady man. Not that I use the carriage so much nowadays."

"What happened to the Vospers?"

"Oh, they shot up in the world. Hamish did anyway. He's in the horse racing business . . . or something like that. Making money, so I hear."

"He always had such a good opinion of himself!"

"Apparently he has made other people have one, too."

"Do you ever see him?"

"Now and then. He comes to see the Kirkwells. I think he likes to show off his affluence to them and remember the old days."

"Did you ever hear any more of Ellen Farley?"

"Ellen Farley? Oh . . ."

"You remember, she used to work here. She was the one they tried to find at the time . . . of the trial."

"That's right. Ellen Farley, the one who disappeared into the blue."

"Ninian used to say that if we could have found her she could have corroborated my story . . . you know . . . that she asked me to buy that stuff."

She leaned forward and laid a thin white hand over mine.

"Don't think about it, dear," she said. "It's all over and done with. That's what I tell myself. Doesn't do any good to go over it."

"It's not all over for me, Zillah. It never will be. All through my life, I shall be waiting for someone to remind me and to wonder whether I was really guilty."

"Oh no. It's all done with. People forget."

"I wish they did."

"What a morbid subject! Your Ninian is charming, isn't he? I thought so. He truly loves you, doesn't he? Be thankful for that, and you wouldn't have known him if . . . that hadn't happened. That's a consolation, isn't it? He must love you a lot, mustn't he, or he wouldn't have gone all the way out to South Africa to find you, would he?"

"No, he would not."

"Well, that's nice. Think of that and not the other."

"I try. And there is something I want to tell you, Zillah. I'm going to have a baby."

"Really? Isn't that the most wonderful news! You must bring the baby to see me."

"It's not due just yet."

"I can't wait. I'm going to live long enough to see it."

"What do you mean?"

"Nothing. Just talking nonsense. It's this old cough. It gets at me sometimes. I'm ever so pleased to see you happy, and I'm pleased you're going to have this baby. Won't Ninian be pleased!"

"He's very pleased."

"And so am I. I'm glad it all turned out right for you."

Being with her was exhilarating, and talking to her I forgot, temporarily, that physically at least she was just a shadow of what she had once been.

I RECEIVED A LETTER from Lilias' sister Jane. She hoped that I would come and stay with them for a few days. She was longing to hear firsthand news of Lilias and to see me, of course. Perhaps I could come with my husband? We should be very welcome.

I could understand their anxiety to get news of Lilias from someone who had been with her during the siege, and I decided that I must go before I was too advanced in pregnancy.

An opportunity came. Ninian had to go to London on business. He would have taken me with him, but I thought it would be a good idea if I spent a few days at the vicarage while he was in London. We could travel down together and I could go on to Devon.

I had to tell Jane every detail I could remember, beginning with the voyage out and right through to the siege and our marriages. She and her father listened intently, now and then asking a question.

They were very interested in John Dale naturally, and I told them what an admirable young man he was and how he and Lilias were devoted to each other. The vicar's eyes were bright with unshed tears and Jane unashamedly allowed one or two of hers to escape.

"When things have quietened down," I said, "she will want you to go and pay her a visit. Perhaps she will come to see you."

"We will manage to go and see her," said Jane firmly to her father.

I had to tell them more of the siege, more of our first impressions. The talk flowed on until it was time to retire for the night.

The next day there was a message from Mrs. Ellington. She had heard that I was at the vicarage and begged me to come and see her before I left. She wanted to hear news of Myra.

So I went.

"She was so distressed," she said, "at the death of dear Roger. Shot by some madman." I guessed she did not know all the full story and it was not my place to enlighten her.

Poor Myra. She wondered she did not come home.

I said: "Myra is making a home for herself over there. She seemed to be settling. You see, there is Paul."

"Dear Roger's son. He did tell us of him."

Still I did not explain. There was no need for her to have even a glimmer of the truth.

"He's not very old," I said. "He needs someone to care for him."

"I understand. But it would be better for Myra to bring him

back. I would look after Roger's son. He could be brought up here . . . so much better for him."

"You see, that is his home. He was born there."

"But it would be so much better for him to be here."

It was not much use contesting Mrs. Ellington's opinions, but I persevered.

"It is quite a large house to run and Myra enjoys doing that. She has adjusted herself to it and her main concern at this time is the boy. He is helping her to grow away from her tragedy. She has had a terrible shock."

"And all those people daring to rebel . . . and her being in the middle of it."

"You mean the Boers."

"I should have thought that war should be over by now. People are saying it cannot be long now."

She asked a great many questions and I was able to satisfy her curiosity to some extent, and I think when I left she was a little reconciled to Myra's absence.

She thanked me for coming and hoped I would find time to do so again before I left. She added that she would insist on Myra's coming home for a visit and they would go on from there.

As I went out I saw Kitty. I fancied she had been waiting for me.

"Hello, Kitty," I said. "How are you?"

"Married now, Miss. I married Charlie who works in the stables. We live over the stables. I've got a little baby."

"Oh, Kitty, that's wonderful."

"Miss Davina . . . there's something I ought to tell you. It's been on my mind ever since."

"What is it, Kitty?"

She bit her lips and looked over her shoulder.

I said: "Could you come over to the vicarage and see me? I shall be there for another two days."

"Yes, Miss. When?"

"Tomorrow afternoon?"

"Oh yes, Miss. I could come then."

"It's very nice to see you, Kitty. I'm glad about the baby. That must be wonderful."

"She's a lovely little girl."

"I must see her before I go."

The next afternoon, she came to the vicarage. I told Jane that she was coming and wished to tell me something, so Jane left us to ourselves in the little room where the vicar saw his parishioners.

Kitty began by saying: "It's been on my mind because Miss Lilias did say not to mention it . . . and I promised I wouldn't . . ."

"What?"

She bit her lips and continued to hesitate. Then she said: "It was when you fell off your horse that time . . ."

"I remember. You called out my name."

"That was it. 'Miss Davina,' I said. I could have killed myself as soon as I said it, but it sort of slipped out. I thought that horse was going to drag you along. That would have been terrible."

"I understand how it happened."

"Well, Mr. Lestrange was there . . . and he heard."

"Yes. I had thought he might have done."

"He was a lovely gentleman . . . ever so kind, he was. Always a word and a smile. Mind you, since Charlie I've never . . . you know what I mean. I wouldn't want anything to go wrong between Charlie and me. I've never looked at nobody since."

"But you . . . looked at Mr. Lestrange?"

My mind switched back to the courtyard before the schoolhouse and Greta Schreiner smiling up at him. I had been reminded then of Kitty. I thought: so he had beguiled Kitty, too . . . beguiled her so that he might get information from her about me. Kitty was physically attractive, with that attraction, as Lilias had once remarked, of a girl who can't say no. What was it? A sort of promise, an assurance of a speedy seduction?

"He asked a lot of questions about you and it just sort of slipped out . . . all about how your father died and they'd accused you."

"I see."

"I did tell him that I'd seen your picture in the paper . . . twice, I did. I cut it out and got one of the men who could read to read it to me. I kept the papers . . . and . . . well, him being so interested . . . I showed them to him. He took them and said he'd like to read them sometime. He never gave them back to me. I'm ever so sorry. As soon as I'd done it I knew I shouldn't have. But he was such a nice gentleman, I knew it wouldn't do no harm with him knowing . . . It didn't, did it? He was always ever so nice to you."

I said nothing. I just sat there listening.

"I knew it was all right, but you see I'd said I wouldn't say anything and I just did. He was the sort who could get anything from a girl if he wanted to. And you and Miss Lilias had been so good to me . . ."

I said: "It's all right, Kitty. It's over now. He's dead."

"Yes, I heard. I was ever so shocked. A lovely man like that."

"You don't want to think of lovely men anymore, Kitty . . . except, of course, Charlie."

She hunched her shoulders like a child and smiled.

"Oh, I'm glad it's all right," she said. "I've had it on my mind ever since."

I asked about the baby and Charlie and I walked back with her to the stable quarters to see the child. I told her I was expecting one. Her eyes lit up with pleasure. Kitty was a good girl at heart, and I knew it was as though a great burden had dropped from her shoulders.

She had really been very upset because she had betrayed a confidence. But now she had confessed and had been forgiven.

I RETURNED to Edinburgh and was happy during the months that followed. I could think of little but the coming of the baby. While I was able, I visited Zillah frequently. I was surprised at her interest in the coming child.

Once, when I was coming away from the house, I met Hamish Vosper. He was flashily dressed in a brown check suit and wore a carnation in his buttonhole. With an exaggerated gesture he swept off his hat to greet me and I noticed his black hair glistening with pomade.

"Why, if it isn't Miss Davina! My word, you look in the pink of health!" His eyes assessed me with something like amusement, I thought.

"Thank you," I said.

"All going well?" he went on.

"Very well."

"That makes two of us." He winked.

"I see you are very prosperous."

He slapped his thigh with an exaggerated gesture. "Can't deny it. Can't deny it."

"Well, good day."

I was glad to escape. I found him as repulsive as when he had sat in the kitchen watching the maids slyly while he pulled at the long black hair on his arms.

My son was born in the May of that year 1902—in the same month that the war with South Africa was finally over and the Peace of Vereeniging was signed, depriving the Boers of their independence.

I wondered how Lilias was getting on. There would be tremendous relief out there, I was sure.

My days were taken up with my son. We called him Stephen after Ninian's father who, with his wife, was so delighted with this grandson that I was sure they almost forgave me for being who I was.

As for myself, I could forget, at this time, all that had gone before.

I took the child to see Zillah. She was delighted. It had never occurred to me that she would have much time to spare for children. Her illness had changed her. In the past she had seemed to be straining for excitement, looking for adventure; now she seemed almost reconciled at times.

I was happier than I had thought possible, for I could not regret anything which had brought me to this state. I remembered Zillah's saying that if that nightmare had not come to pass, I should not have met Ninian. Stephen would not have existed.

I wrote to Lilias telling her about the wonder child and, now that the war was over, I heard from her. She was expecting a child. The bond between us seemed stronger than ever. We had both come through tragic times together and both found happiness.

Happiness was sometimes fragile; but now I had Ninian and my baby, I felt secure.

The months passed. Stephen was beginning to smile, then to crawl, and then to take notice. He liked Zillah. He would sit on her lap and gaze at her. He was quite fascinated by her red hair. She still took a great deal of pains with her appearance. Her skin was delicately tinted, her eyes bright under her darkened brows. Sometimes I thought she could not be so very ill—except that she was thin.

One day there was news which startled us. Hamish Vosper had been killed in a fight by a rival. There was a hint of something called the Edinburgh Mafia.

It was revealed that for some time there had been trouble between two rival gangs, both engaged in nefarious practices, and that Hamish Vosper, who was the leader of one, had been killed by the other. Such men, said the press, were a disgrace to the fair city of Edinburgh.

They were suspected not only of deciding which horses were allowed to win races, by the use of drugs so that they could back the outsider winners, but many other crimes.

"We want no such gang rule in Edinburgh," wrote one commentator. "The death of Hamish Vosper is rough justice on one of our ignoble citizens."

I went to see Zillah when I heard the news. Mrs. Kirkwell received me in a mood of subdued triumph.

"I always knew that Hamish Vosper would come to a bad end," she said. "I don't want to speak ill of the dead, but the master ought to have got rid of him years ago when he was caught with that maid. Well, I've seen something like this coming. I said to Kirkwell, 'He's up to no good, mark my words. There he was in his fancy clothes, throwing his weight about.

Ah,' I said to Kirkwell. 'He's up to no good, mark my words.' It's terrible to think that he was here . . . one of us, you might say . . . though never really that. And then after you'd gone . . . he used to come here . . . even going up to see Mrs. Glentyre. I never could understand why she allowed it."

I went up to Zillah. She was looking better. I thought, something has happened.

She said: "I feel fine today. Just like my old self."

"You certainly look it. Have you read the newspapers to-day?"

"Why yes. You're thinking about Hamish."

"It's rather shocking . . . particularly as he was here and we knew him."

"Yes."

"I never liked him . . . but to think of him . . . dead . . ."

"These things happen. It seemed he was living dangerously, and when you do that you can't be surprised if you come to a bad end."

"Had you any idea . . . ?"

"Well . . . yes . . . I guessed he was up to no good. He was that sort. He was dabbling in all sorts of things . . . playing with fire, you might say. Well, he got burned."

"You must have seen him quite recently. I met him here not long ago."

"He used to come to the house. He wanted the Kirkwells to see how he'd got on. Foolish man. A lesson to us all, Davina."

I was surprised at her attitude. But then Zillah had always surprised me.

Ninian's comment was: "Gang warfare. This sort of thing has been going on in some places for years. It's not what one would expect in Edinburgh. But it is an indication that it can happen anywhere. Let's hope that will be the end of it . . . here at least."

ZILLAH CONTINUED TO IMPROVE. She was quite lighthearted. I was seeing more of her, for she so enjoyed having Stephen with her.

I vividly remember one conversation I had with her at that

time. Stephen was playing in a corner and we were both watching him.

Zillah said suddenly: "He's the most adorable child. I never thought I should want children. But, do you know, when I see him I think of what I have missed."

"Perhaps you'll marry again."

She smiled at me ironically. "It's a bit late in the day to think about that."

"One never knows. You are so much better. You could be cured. You're not old and you are very beautiful."

She laughed quite lightheartedly.

Then I said: "I worry about Stephen sometimes."

"Worry? There's nothing wrong with him, is there?"

"Oh no. He's in perfect health. I just think that someone might say something."

"Say what?"

"Someone might remember. It might come out that his mother stood trial for murder . . . and what the verdict was."

"That's all over and done with."

"Not as far as I am concerned, Zillah. It will always be there. How would one feel to learn that one's mother might have been a murderess?"

"Stephen would never think that."

"How could he help it? The question is there and always will be."

"It's a morbid thought."

"But it is the truth, Zillah."

"People are going to forget . . . by the time he grows up."

"There could be some to remember. Not long ago someone referred to Madeleine Smith, and that happened fifty years ago."

"It was a very famous case."

"Mine was very well-known."

"You must stop worrying about it. Stephen is going to be all right."

She spoke with conviction, but I could see that my words had made her very thoughtful. She knew that what I had said was true.

I told her the truth about Roger Lestrange then; how, through Kitty, he had discovered who I was; how he had the newspaper cuttings of my trial; how he was going to use me, if need be, to indicate that I was an unconvicted murderess who might be ready to try the same methods again.

She was deeply shocked. "It's hard to believe . . ." she whispered.

"Nevertheless it's true. Now you see what I mean? It will be there as long as I live."

She was silent for a few moments, staring blankly before her. Then she reached for my hand and pressed it firmly.

She said slowly: "You must stop worrying about it. You're going to be all right. Stephen is going to be all right."

I CALLED ON ZILLAH and, to my surprise, Mrs. Kirkwell said she had gone out.

Mrs. Kirkwell's lips were pursed disapprovingly.

"She's not fit," she went on. "I told her so. 'You must be mad to think of going out, Mrs. Glentyre,' I said. She was well wrapped up, but she looked far from well . . . and she's so thin. You notice it in her outdoor clothes."

"Why should she go out? She hasn't been out for some weeks, has she?"

"Only when she gets this letter. That's the only time she goes out."

"She had a letter then?"

"Yes. It comes now and then. And then she always insists on going out."

"I hope she'll be all right. Of course, she's seemed better these last days."

"That's true. But I'm worried about her. I wished you'd come earlier, Mrs. Grainger, then you might have gone with her."

"You've no idea where she's gone?"

"Well, as a matter of fact I have. I happened to hear her give orders to the cabby. That's another thing. I said, 'Why shouldn't Baines take you?' and she said she wouldn't bother him. And there he is, hardly ever taking the carriage out."

"That's strange. Perhaps she wasn't going far."

"It's to a place called the Coven."

"The Coven? Isn't that the little tea shop in Walter Street?"

"That's it. Little place not been open long. I'm really worried about her. She seemed a bit shaky."

"I see," I said.

I came out of the house and walked to Princes Street.

She must be going to have tea, since the Coven was a tea shop. I thought, she wants to get out, that's what it is. It must be boring for her to be always indoors. That would be a real trial for someone who had always liked gaiety. I pictured her taking a cab to the tea shop, having tea and cakes . . . and then going home. It was just a little outing.

She was really very frail. Suppose I went to the Coven, just to see if she was all right. I might have a cup of tea with her. I would suggest that we make these little excursions now and then when she was feeling well enough. That would get her out of the house.

I came to the Coven. It was small. In the window were home-made cakes and a sign which said "Lunches. Teas."

I looked through the window between the cakes and I saw her at once. She was not alone. There was a woman with her.

I stared—first at her and then at her companion. There was something familiar about the latter. Then she turned and I saw her face clearly.

It was Ellen Farley.

I could not take my eyes from her, and just at that moment Zillah turned her head and gazed towards the window. We were looking straight at each other.

Her eyes dilated slightly and I saw the colour rush into her cheeks.

I turned and walked away.

I went straight home and up to my room.

Zillah going out to meet Ellen Farley—the key witness who could not be found!

What did it mean? What could it mean?

•   •   •   •

I COULD NOT REST. I wanted to tell Ninian. I thought of the pains he had taken to find Ellen Farley without success. It would have meant so much if she could have told the court that she had asked me to buy arsenic. It would have explained that entry in the book which was so damning against me.

I could hear Ninian's voice: "If only we could find that woman!"

It so happened that he was working late that night on a specially demanding case. He had brought some books home with him on the previous night in the hope of finding a similar example which could be of use to him. It was a point of law which he wanted to verify.

I must tell him that I had seen her! Could I have been mistaken? It might have been someone who looked like her. I should have confronted them. Why had I been so foolish as to go away? I had been so shocked . . . so shaken . . . so bewildered.

But Zillah had seen me. She had looked horrified. It must have been Ellen Farley. But even now doubts kept coming into my mind. Could I trust myself?

I was in bed when Ninian came home. He looked very tired. He would be in court the next day. I thought, I will speak to him tomorrow evening . . . after I have seen Zillah.

The next morning I went to see Zillah. Mrs. Kirkwell met me in the hall.

"She's very bad," she said. "I've sent for the doctor. He should be here at any minute. It was going out yesterday. She came back in a state."

"Was she alone?"

"Oh yes. The cabby knocked at the door and helped me in with her. He said he didn't think she was well. I got her to bed right away and said I'd get the doctor. But she said no, she'd be better in the morning."

"And she wasn't?"

Mrs. Kirkwell shook her head. "So I sent for him without asking her. I thought I'd better."

"I'm sure you're right. I'll go up and see her."

She was lying propped up with pillows and seemed to be finding difficulty in getting her breath.

"Hello, Davina," she said. "Can't talk very much. It's my breathing."

I went to the bed and sat close.

"Zillah," I said. "Tell me . . ."

She pointed to the table on which lay a large, rather bulky envelope.

"For you," she said. "There's another, too."

I saw that beside the large envelope was a smaller one. They both had my name on them.

"You . . . can read them when I've gone."

"Gone? Gone where?"

She smiled at me. "The big one, I mean. The little one you can read when you get home."

"This is mysterious."

She lifted her hand in a feeble gesture. "You'll understand. You'll see . . ."

"Something's happened," I said. "You shouldn't have gone out yesterday."

"Had to," she said. "You saw . . ."

"Was it really? I couldn't believe it."

"You'll understand. I had to. You'll see."

I heard someone coming up the stairs. There was a tap on the door and Mrs. Kirkwell came in with the doctor.

"Ah, Mrs. Glentyre . . . not so well today, I hear," he said.

Mrs. Kirkwell looked at me meaningfully. I was to leave, she was implying.

I went downstairs, wondering what had happened. I had not been mistaken. She had been with Ellen Farley. What could it mean?

I was clutching both envelopes. The large one and the small one. She had said she wanted me to open the small one when I arrived home. I went into the drawing room to wait for the doctor's visit to be over, and I opened the small envelope.

I read:

Dear Davina,

I have been thinking so much about you, particularly since

you have come back. There is so much you ought to know and you shall. I have been on the point of confiding in you many times but I could not. I just hadn't the courage. But you shall know and it won't be long now.

I know I haven't much time left. The doctor has more or less told me so. I begged him to tell me the truth. I didn't want to be kept in the dark. There's no cure for what I have. It may be a day . . . a week . . . or a month. But it is not far-off. Who should know that better than I?

I want you to read what I have written. It's taken me a long time to get it all down. I did it some time ago as soon as I knew how ill I was. But I can't tell you yet. You'll have to wait. And when you do know, you'll understand.

I didn't think I was going to get so fond of you. I am so happy you married your Ninian. He's a good man and he truly loves you. He's proved his devotion and any woman would be grateful for that.

So be happy. There isn't going to be anything to stop you and Ninian and little Stephen having a wonderful life. That's what I want for you. But please . . . please don't open the other until I am dead. I know you ought to, but I'm selfish . . . and I want you to wait.

One who loves you,

ZILLAH

I reread the letter. I had a burning desire to open the other, but I restrained myself.

I had not been able to ask her the question I had come to ask. Why had Ellen Farley been at the tea shop with Zillah? She had been upset when she received the letter which must have come from Ellen. She always went out when she received such notes. Why should she be seeing Ellen Farley?

The door opened and Mrs. Kirkwell came in with the doctor.

I stood up uncertainly. He was looking very grave.

"She's very ill," he said. "It's a turn for the worse, I fear. She's resting now. She'll rest all day. Her breathing's bad. I'll send a nurse tomorrow. She'll be all right today because she'll be sleeping most of the time. I think you should be prepared."

Mrs. Kirkwell said: "We've known, of course, doctor, that she was getting worse."

He nodded. "I'll look in tomorrow. Let her sleep. It's the best thing for her."

Mrs. Kirkwell took him to the door and when she came back she said: "It was silly of her to go out like that. If I've told her once I've told her twenty times."

"Well, there's no point in my staying, Mrs. Kirkwell. I'll just take a look at her before I go."

"Just peep in. Don't wake her."

I went up the stairs . . . very much aware of the envelope I carried. I looked in at her. She was still propped up by pillows. I supposed that made it easier for her to breathe. She was very still and her white hands lay inert on the bed coverlet.

She was in a deep sleep.

I was not able to talk to her again.

Three days later she died.

I was very sad indeed to realise I should never see her again . . . never be able to talk to her.

I had called at the house as I did every morning.

I had looked in on her on those occasions, but she was very tired and always half asleep.

I was not really surprised when I approached the house and saw that the blinds had been drawn at the windows.

It was a house of death.

I OPENED THE ENVELOPE and read:

My dear Davina,

I am going to tell you all that happened. I am going to, as they say, tell you the truth, the whole truth and nothing but the truth. And I am going to tell it my way, because it is important to me that you should understand how it all came about, and I hope you won't judge me too harshly.

I want you to imagine a girl who hadn't had very much. I won't go into details about my origins, but they were sordid. I was a sad bewildered child. I had my mother, it was true. I was an only child. My father seemed to be always drunk. I can hardly remember him anything else. Every penny he earned went into the local ginshop. It was a struggle. There was not always enough to eat. I was fourteen years old when my mother died. Then I ran away.

I won't bore you with all that happened but I did finally work in a rather sleazy boarding house near the Tottenham Court Road. All I had was my red hair and the sort of appearance that made people notice me. I had long before learned that this was something I could use to my advantage, and I did.

In the hotel I caught the attention of a minor theatrical agent and it was through him that I got one or two little parts. I wasn't much good. All I had was my looks.

All the little things that happened to me at that time don't really come into this, so I'll skip them. Finally I joined the Jolly Red Heads and we toured the music halls when we could get engagements.

And then we came to Edinburgh. That's where it all began. Men used to come to the theatre to look out for the girls. They'd be at the stage door. You know the sort of thing. And one night Hamish Vosper was there.

I know how you dislike him. You always did. But there was something about him which appealed to some women. He was arrogant and selfish, but he was virile . . . he was a man. He thought he was irresistible to women and somehow he made them feel he was—and for a time, I was one of those who did. He used to come to the theatre every night we were there and after the show we'd be together.

He told me about his employer—a gentleman who was strict and the glory-be-to-God type, but underneath all that he liked to indulge in a little fun now and then. Hamish said he had a hold over him because he'd discovered what he was up to. He had this invalid wife, said Hamish, and of course there had not been much between them for some years, which was more than the old fellow could take. So he had his little jaunts. He knew that Hamish knew and Hamish only had to give him what he called "the eye" and the old fellow would turn a blind one to whatever Hamish wanted to do.

It was an intriguing situation . . . and one night Hamish brought me to the notice of your father.

He took me to supper and we liked each other from the start. He was a courtly gentleman and I hadn't seen many of that sort. And I can say he was very taken with me, which made me like him all the more. It wasn't long before we were going to hotels together. It was all very discreet because of his position. I thought it wouldn't last but he got more and more fond of me in a sentimental sort of way.

Hamish was tickled to death and he had an idea. "You ought to come to the house," he said. "I know . . . you could be a governess. There is a girl." That made me laugh. Me . . . a governess? Well, the Red Heads were on the way out. We had the occasional boo when we came on. We'd known for a long time that we simply weren't good enough for the West End. That was why we were touring the provinces. I thought it would be nice to have a comfortable home and not have to do all this travelling, so I said I was interested in this governessing business.

I swear I did not know how Hamish arranged it. I had no idea that there was already a governess and she had to be got rid of. I wouldn't have agreed to that . . . or I don't think I would. I want to be absolutely honest, you see. And I was rather desperate at that time.

Well, your Lilias went and Hamish suggested to your father that he brought me in. It shows how besotted your father was about me . . . for he agreed.

I took to you from the start. I knew, of course, I couldn't teach you anything. You were far better educated already than I ever could be, but I thought it was a bit of fun . . . and much better than doing the Jolly Red Heads to audiences who were growing more and more critical.

Then your father asked me to marry him. I couldn't believe my luck. I would leave the old life behind me. It was the chance of a lifetime. I could be comfortable for the rest of my days, the darling of a doting old man. It seemed too good to be true.

I was more contented than I ever hoped to be. I had

forgotten Hamish. I would have a secure home and a promise of comfort for the rest of my life. I would be the mistress of the house. But Hamish was still the coachman.

He was dissatisfied. Whose idea had it been? And who was getting everything out of it while he was getting nothing? Then he had a plan. He wanted to marry me . . . and be master of the house. I was horrified at what this implied. I was fond of my new life, fond of my husband, fond of my new stepdaughter. I liked it all. But Hamish wouldn't have it. He had started it and he was going to see it carried through as he wanted it.

You can guess the rest. I was weak. Hamish still had some power over me. I knew what was in his mind. I should have exposed him. I should have confessed to my relationship with him. Oh, there were lots of things I should have done!

Davina, you don't know what the comfort of that house meant to me . . . the easy way of life and all that. No one could understand unless they had been through what I had. I am not making excuses. There are no excuses. It just seemed that I had started on this and I had no choice but to go on.

Hamish had planned it. We would get rid of the old man. I would mourn for a year. Hamish would comfort me. I would, after a respectable period, marry him. I would, of course, have to make sure that the old man's fortune was left to me. We wouldn't want to stay in Edinburgh. People would raise their eyebrows when the ex-governess married the coachman. We'd sell the house and go abroad. He had it all worked out.

Ellen Farley—that's not her real name, of course—was a friend of Hamish. He recommended her to your father and he brought her into the house. He thought it would be a good idea to have one of the servants working with us.

Well, he bought the arsenic for the rats. There were some near the mews so he made sure others had seen them and it was the fact that they were there which gave him the idea to do it that way. Hamish said he knew something about arsenic. Hamish said he knew something about everything.

His idea was to poison your father slowly. He thought through the port wine.

Then there was all that fuss about you and Jamie and the whole house knew that your father had threatened to disinherit you. We knew too that he had chosen Alastair McCrae for you. If you had married Alastair McCrae you wouldn't have come into Hamish's plan, but you didn't and Hamish wanted to have a way out, as he called it, if things shouldn't turn out as he planned. Just like Roger Lestrange, he thought it would be a good idea to have a scapegoat . . . if anything should go wrong. I suppose these calculating murderers think alike. And like Roger Lestrange, he laid the snare to entrap you . . . to have someone at hand in case he should need to shift the blame to someone else. He set you up to be that scapegoat because Fate had given him a reason —your father's objection to the young man you wanted to marry.

Hamish arranged for you to buy the poison. Ellen was to ask you to. Please believe me when I say I did not know of this at the time. Hamish did not tell me. He thought me squeamish—soft and sentimental—and he knew I was getting fond of you. Do you remember the night I was late back? I was with Hamish. We went to a place outside Edinburgh. It's true we were lovers then. I know how dreadful it must sound . . . and it is no use my offering excuses because there really aren't any. Hamish was anxious not to be caught because that would have spoilt the whole plan . . . so we always went some little way out of the town.

Do you remember that inquisitive old woman who came to the house? It was when we were late back and made that excuse about the carriage breaking down. She was going to tell your father that she had seen the carriage outside that rather disreputable hotel. She had even waited and seen us come out together. She was going to tell your father. That was when Hamish decided it would have to be done that night.

Ellen took fright at her part in it and made her excuses to get away.

Then it happened. Your father died.

It hadn't worked out as Hamish planned. First I want to tell you that I did not know that Ellen had asked you to buy the arsenic. Hamish had not told me that. I suppose I must not make excuses for myself. I was in the plot. I played my part in it. I am guilty of murder. But I would not have used you. And when you were on trial I suffered . . . I really did. You might ask why did I not then confess to everything? I hadn't the courage for that. I want to say that I was dominated by Hamish . . . but I am not sure of that either. I felt I was caught up in it and there was no way out for me but to do exactly what I did. You see, Hamish really thought we should get away with it. He did not plan that you should be accused. You were only there in case things turned against us. He didn't want to take chances. He really thought we'd get away with it. Your father had already had one or two attacks. The doctor had seen him and not suspected. At the back of Hamish's mind was the thought that he was so clever that everything must go as he had planned.

Well, you know what happened. You were arrested and charged with murder. It was terrible for you. But please believe me when I tell you it was terrible for me, too. I wanted to tell everything . . . confess. Hamish threatened me. He was in a rare panic. All his swagger deserted him then. We were all in a state of terror.

What hurt me most was what they were doing to you. I really thought your father's death would be accepted as natural. I couldn't sleep. I had to do something.

In the shed near the stables I found a little of the arsenic which Hamish had bought. Just a few grains still on the paper it had been wrapped in. Hamish hadn't bothered to get rid of it because he had a perfect alibi about the rats. I had this idea then. I knew arsenic had certain powers. I remembered a man I had known in my Jolly Red Heads days who had taken it. He had told me he took it to make him feel younger.

I took the paper. I put the grains into another piece and I said I had found it in the drawer and that your father had confessed to me that he had once taken arsenic acquired on the Continent.

I provided the doubt. I knew I should never have had another moment's peace as long as I lived if you had been condemned as a murderess.

When I heard that verdict I was furious. I had wanted you free of all doubt. I've wanted to make up to you ever since. I wanted to put it all behind us and start again. And those idiots had made it Not Proven.

But you were free. I could rejoice in that. I wanted you free but I did not realise that you would have to go through life under that shadow of doubt.

I was wicked. I agreed to the plan. It is no use my saying I was under Hamish's spell, that I suffered from an unhappy youth. I am guilty and I shall never forgive myself.

I don't enjoy what I have gained. There is not a great deal left of your father's fortune which seemed such riches to me in the beginning. Hamish had a large part of it . . . and kept wanting more. It set him up in the business which finally brought him to his end . . . I was blackmailed all the time. I would not marry him. I think he realised that that might have been dangerous. The murder of your father was Not Proven; there might be some who wanted to discover the truth. He ceased to press for that but he wanted the lion's share of the spoils.

Then there was Ellen. She used to come back regularly claiming her dues. Ellen is not a bad sort, though. She, too, has found life hard. She is planning to go abroad. I told her of that place which helped you and Lilias Milne. But she wanted a little behind her before she went. She made her regular demands and I think she may well be on her way to Australia or New Zealand. I think she learned a lesson. She was a frightened woman . . . always afraid that someone would find her. Hamish should never have brought her into it. She was almost as upset as I was every time she came to make her claim. She wasn't a *natural* criminal . . . no more than I think I am. Impulsive we both were . . . trying hard to get a place in the sun . . . not realising how much we should have to pay for it.

Well, Hamish will not be able to do more mischief . . . and I am on my way.

You will find enclosed an account of what happened. I do not want the sordid details of my life made public. That is for you alone. The letter enclosed you will give to your Ninian. He will know what to do with it. It is my confession. It explains everything that is necessary. It is all people need to know and you will be completely exonerated from all guilt. No more Not Proven.

God bless you, Davina. In spite of my wickedness I did love you. You became like a daughter to me. I love little Stephen and I want everything to be perfect for you. I want to rub out that stigma forever.

No one can say now that the case against you was Not Proven.

Be happy. You have a chance now.

Goodbye, Davina,

ZILLAH

I could scarcely read the note she had prepared because of the tears in my eyes.

And later I showed it to Ninian.

He read it through and when he lifted his face to mine I saw the joy there.

He stood up and took my hands in his. Then he held me tightly against him.

"She's right," he said. "We're free. It's over, Davina. I knew we were right to come back and face it. It happened here and here was the solution."

"It is strange," I said. "She did that . . . and I really loved her. She was truly . . . lovable . . . and yet . . . she could do that."

"Life is strange. People are strange. And she is right when she says we can be happy now. The case is proven, Davina, my dearest, proven without a doubt."

He was radiant with joy; I suppose we both were. Life was good and seemed the brighter because of the darkness. I could now look ahead without fear. I had my husband; I had my child; and Zillah had cleared for me the way to contentment.